REDTAILS HOCKEY

OMNIBUS 1

REDTAILS HOCKEY

STEPHANIE JULIAN

MOONLIT NIGHT PUBLISHING

PRAISE FOR REDTAILS HOCKEY

"Stephanie Julian has given us another new series to fall in love with."

"This one had everything, great story, great characters and hot sex. Can't wait to read more."

"Great characters and excellent storytelling. Hockey romance done well."

Includes the first four books
in the REDTAILS HOCKEY series

THE BRICK WALL
THE GRINDER
THE ENFORCER
THE INSTIGATOR

Join Stephanie in her private Reader Salon on Facebook. And be sure to sign up for all the news and information on her website at www.stephaniejulian.com.

Don't miss any of the books in the Redtails Hockey series:

The Brick Wall

The Grinder

The Enforcer

The Instigator

The Playboy

The D-Man

The Machine

The Comeback Kid

The Ghost

Merry Hockey Holiday (includes The Playboy and The Comeback Kid)

THE BRICK WALL

He needs to keep his head in the game...

Redtails Hockey goaltender Shane Conrad had been having a great year...until recently. His slump couldn't happen at the worst time. He needs to get his head in the game, not find a woman to screw with it.

Bliss Vescovi isn't looking for a commitment, especially not from an intense, driven man used to control. But a one-night stand with a hot hockey player who won't be around forever? Totally doable.

When Shane gets called up, Bliss breaks off their relationship. But Shane's nickname isn't Brick Wall for nothing. He won't go down without a fight because he knows, no matter where he is, Bliss belongs at his side.

ONE

"Son-of-a-motherfucking bitch."

Stalking into the empty locker room of the Reading Civic Arena, Shane Conrad tossed his helmet, swearing even more when it smashed into the wall. Something cracked, either the wall or his goalie helmet, and he didn't much care either way.

One more nick in the cinderblock meant shit. One more ding in his helmet... Well, his game was fucked at the moment and he probably wouldn't need the goddamn helmet much longer anyway.

Not the way he was playing.

"Fuck."

The rest of the team was still on the ice for practice, though they'd be making their way back here in a few minutes. Tonight, they'd play their last game before the three-day Christmas holiday.

And it looked like Shane would be riding the bench.

Christ, he felt like he was back in high school—the fat, awkward kid at the school dance, sitting alone on the bleachers while his friends danced with the hot chicks. The ones who only gave him the time of day because he had a wicked sense of humor and he'd led his high school hockey team to three straight victories.

Throwing himself onto the bench, he ripped open the laces on his skates then threw them on the ground for good measure.

Fucking hell, this sucked.

Get your damn head out of your ass.

Good advice. Wished he knew how to do it.

Frustration burning through him like lit gasoline, he started stripping off the rest of his gear, careful not to rip his practice jersey and shorts. Didn't give a shit about the rest. He hung his pads in his locker out of habit before he grabbed a towel and stalked naked to the showers.

He stood there for at least five minutes, let the scalding hot water pour over his head and back, trying to get the frustration and the anger to roll away with it.

So far, not working.

And didn't that just make him want to suck down a gallon of Jack Daniels?

"Shane."

He stiffened as his teammate Cary Lenville's voice penetrated the fog in his head. He considered ignoring him but no one ignored Cary.

The assistant captain of the Reading Redtails Hockey Club, Cary was the glue that held the team together. At thirty-six, he was the oldest player and, even if he wasn't the most skilled player, he was the one everyone went to when they had problems. Cary always had an answer, didn't matter what the question was. And even if it wasn't the completely right answer, it was better than anything you'd come up with on your own.

But Shane knew Cary couldn't help with this problem. Not when Shane was pretty damn sure it was all in his messed-up head.

Shutting off the water, he grabbed his towel. "What's up?"

He didn't meet Cary's gaze and he tried to keep the edge out of his tone but couldn't manage it. Not when frustrated embarrassment threatened to choke him.

Goddammit, he was supposed to be the team's number one

goalie. They'd nicknamed him the Brick Wall, for fuck's sake. So why the fuck wasn't he playing like it?

The guys were depending on him to help them get to the Calder Cup championships this year. They'd been playing well enough to consider it a real possibility. But Shane had to pull his head out of his ass...like, now.

"Coach said you're not going home for the break."

Huh?

He turned to give Cary a look before heading back to his locker. Luckily, no one else was off the ice yet so he had time to pull himself together.

"Yeah, that's right."

He didn't add that he couldn't bear to go home to Minnesota, where his mom would fuss over him like he was still in high school and his pop would lecture him like he was still his coach.

He loved his parents, but if he had to deal with them for an extended period of time, it would totally fuck with his head.

And that just made him feel worse.

Could he be *any* more screwed up? If he continued like this, Coach would trade his ass to Alaska or send him down to the ECHL.

"Then what're you doing tomorrow night?" Cary asked.

Shane snorted with disgust and shook his head. "Besides drinking myself into a coma? Not one goddamn thing. Why?"

"Come to my place. Lori and I are having some people over."

Shane automatically shook his head. "Nah, man. I don't think I'd be good company. Thanks anyway."

Cary went silent but he didn't move. And that was never a good thing. The six-foot-two, two-hundred-plus defenseman not only was built like a brick shithouse but was pretty much as immoveable as one.

As the silence stretched on, Shane sighed and turned, forcing himself to look directly into Cary's eyes.

"What?"

Cary had crossed his arms over his chest, emphasizing just how broad the fucker really was. "You're strung tighter than a drum and you need to decompress or you're gonna explode. And that won't be good for you or the team. Won't be anybody there you know and we won't talk hockey all night, unless Lori goes on a bender. Besides, I could use the backup." He grimaced. "Lori's always collecting strays. I swear I won't know half the people there. And her cousins are crazy."

Hearing Cary talk about the love of his life coaxed a smirk out of Shane. The guy was married to an abso-fucking-lutely gorgeous woman who seemed to think Cary hung the moon and stars. Cary apparently thought the same of her.

It'd be sickening if they weren't so perfect for each other.

But... *Christ.* Cary wanted him to spend a few hours making small talk with a bunch of people he didn't know? He opened his mouth to say no again but Cary just stared at him.

Shit. Shane's resolve crumbled.

With a sigh, he began to pull on his clothes. "How crazy?"

Cary's shit-eating grin made Shane want to smile back, but he squashed the impulse. Didn't want to give the guy the impression he'd won. Even if he had.

"Let's just say they have some holiday traditions that'd put the Addams family to shame."

Shane tried not to sigh but couldn't help it. "As long as there's alcohol, I guess you can count me in."

Cary nodded, his grin disappearing. "You find it helps?"

Shane didn't bother to misunderstand him and shook his head. "Not really. And no, I don't have a problem. At least, not with alcohol."

Cary took him at his word. Another thing that made every single one of the guys worship him like he was the goddamn King of Hockey.

"Good to hear it. And yeah, I know you've been having a few bad weeks. It happens. The break'll be good for you. Get your head on straight. If you want, we can run some drills tomorrow, just the two of us."

And *this* was why Cary was rumored to be the front runner for the next Redtails coach. The gossip mill outside the locker room had been working overtime lately. Their current coach, according to the gossip, had a lock on an NHL job. Everyone expected Cary to step into the vacated position.

The players loved him. The front office loved him. The fans thought he walked on water.

Shane found himself nodding. "Yeah. That'd be... That'd be helpful." He hoped.

Cary grinned then punched him on the shoulder and practically knocked Shane off the bench.

"Good. And come to the party. You'll have a good time."

———

"SO I TOLD HIM, he needed to pick one pattern or the other. Honestly, how hard is it? I mean, it's not like I'm the only one getting married. It's his wedding, too. Shouldn't he at least be a little interested in the china we're going to be using for the rest of our lives?"

Bliss Vescovi sat on a loveseat in a corner of Lori Lenville's comfortable great room, sipping champagne and nodding sympathetically at the two women sitting across from her on the couch.

She'd only just met them but they seemed nice. And when they'd discovered Bliss worked at the With This Ring Bridal Boutique... Well, you would've thought they'd found a long-lost soulmate at Lori's pre-holiday party.

At any other time, Bliss would've been thrilled to talk weddings. She actually enjoyed them, even when she had to handle the occasional bridezilla, momzilla, bitchy sister-in-law-to-be, drunken sorority-sister bridesmaid, and snotty three-year-old flower girl. She knew how to deal with them all.

Her boss, Aunt Rosie, called her a godsend. Bliss actually thought her aunt was the godsend for giving her a career when she'd had no idea what the hell she was going to do with a degree in business.

And even after her own wedding had fallen apart two years ago, she still got teary when she helped a bride-to-be find that perfect dress for her walk down the aisle to the man she'd decided to spend her life with, even if Bliss had no time or inclination for a life partner.

But a one-night stand? Absolutely. Bring it on. And, oh please, could he be good in the sack? Hell, she wouldn't even wish for great. Just good enough with his hands to get her off at least once.

She'd had no such luck lately. And it didn't look like tonight would be any better. Not one of the guys here tonight made her want to go to the trouble of giving up a few hours of sleep.

Jeez, what's wrong with you? You're only twenty-six, not eighty.

But between working with her aunt, whose business was steadily growing, and the fact that her friends were either married or hooked up with Mr. Right Now... Well, she didn't get out much.

And when she did, she had to wonder if there were any decent guys left in the world. Most were dicks with attitude problems or nerdy man-children who lived in their parents' basements, played video games until three in the morning and spent their weekends drinking with their buddies who were lucky or mature enough to have an apartment.

And... *Oh my god.* Was she really this much of a bitch? No wonder she couldn't find anyone to screw. Honestly, she wouldn't want her either.

"Lori's been *amazing*," one of the women gushed, drawing Bliss back into the conversation. "She helped us smooth over the problem with the zoning and made sure we had all the right permits. She'd been our guardian angel..."

Bliss nodded, in complete agreement with her new friends on this.

She'd met Lori at a local Chamber of Commerce mixer. Aunt Rosie hadn't been able to attend but she'd begged Bliss to go in her place. She couldn't even remember why her aunt had sent her. She only knew she hadn't wanted to go. But then she'd met Lori and they'd bonded over a few drinks and a mutual admiration of hockey.

Lori's husband played for the local professional hockey team, and though Bliss had only been to a few games, she'd gained an appreciation of the sport from her dad. It'd been the one thing the two of them enjoyed watching together. If it hadn't been for hockey, she and her great, hulking bear of a father might never have held a conversation that didn't begin and end with "How was school?"

Her dad loved her and he tried, but she'd always been a girly girl and that had been her mom's domain.

"So I told him if he didn't at least attempt to get along with my cousin, we might as well call off the wedding. I mean, my family is so important to me and…"

Yep, she totally got that. Family was important. She'd seen more than one wedding disintegrate into factions more fierce than anything in the Hunger Games during the planning stages.

And anyone who said words would never hurt you had never dealt with a bridezilla whose mother-in-law dared to have an opinion on what color napkin should be used on the cake table.

Bliss swallowed a sigh.

What the hell are you doing here anyway?

She should be mingling, flirting, having a good time. It wasn't like there weren't any good-looking guys here. A few of them had even made eye contact, and two had tried to start conversations.

Until five minutes later and she realized they only wanted to talk about what they did and how much that should impress her. Sure, they had decent jobs and wore decent clothes and were attractive but—

What's wrong with you?

"And who tells your mother her dress makes her look fat? You know what I mean? I just wanted to punch…"

Bliss knew exactly how the bride-to-be felt. She wanted to punch someone, too.

Except Bliss didn't do physical violence. She was no tough

cookie. More like a cupcake with fluffy frosting. And who didn't love cupcakes, right?

Sighing again, she took another sip of her drink and tried to wipe the pissy look off her face.

She knew she was no great beauty but she certainly didn't look like an ogre. Sure, her nose was a little too big and her body a little too curvy. But she still managed to attract guys who liked big tits and a decent ass. She knew that because most guys she talked to couldn't stop checking out either one long enough to hold a rational conversation.

Then again, she hadn't exactly allowed any guys close enough to get to know her better. A vicious cycle, one she didn't know how to break.

So, here she sat. Smiling and nodding through a conversation with two women she barely knew.

This had been a mistake. She should just take her pitiful self home and—

The front door opened, catching her attention simply because it was directly in her line of sight.

But then *he* walked through.

And she actually felt her mouth drop open. Like, literally, her jaw dropped. Then her lips parted and she sucked in a sharp breath that she immediately tried to cover with a slight cough.

She assured her new friends, who interrupted their conversation about guest lists to make sure she wasn't choking, that she was fine and managed to come up with a question to get them back on their conversational track.

So she could go back to checking out the newcomer.

The really *big* newcomer.

And she didn't mean fat. She meant *built*. Big as in broad. Wide. He looked like a—

Hockey player.

Like Lori's husband, Cary, who greeted the newcomer with a big smile and a firm handshake as he pulled him farther into the house.

Cary led the new guy right into the great room, where she sat against the far wall, and walked him straight to the bar.

Bliss tried not to stare. Really, she did. But how could she *not* when this guy ticked off every box on her Yummy Meter, including a few she hadn't know she had?

Like his dark, wavy hair. Everyone in her huge Italian family had dark hair so every boyfriend she'd ever had had been blond, pretty, and clean-cut, like he'd just walked off a magazine shoot.

Like her ex-fiancé, the prick.

Nope, not thinking about him.

This guy looked like he hadn't cut his hair in months or seen a razor in days, if the dark stubble on his strong, square jaw was anything to go by. He looked scruffy but not like he was trying to be trendy.

Now, the bright blue eyes... Yeah, she absolutely had a thing for those. And his were a perfect ocean blue she could see from across the room. Combined with that nose that looked as if it'd been broken a few times...

Damn. Her mouth watered.

And when her gaze slipped south... Hell, she was pretty sure her thighs just clenched.

The guy had to be at least a few inches over six feet, which means he'd tower over her. And his clothes couldn't hide the fact that he had muscles in places all men should have muscles. Like in their thighs. And their abs. And their arms—

When he took off his coat to let Cary hang it in the closet, she had to swallow because... *Oh my god.* The man's arms bulged beneath his blue dress shirt.

With black dress pants and that blue shirt, he looked good enough to eat.

Wouldn't you love to get your mouth on him?

Yes, please. Anywhere he had skin.

And when he turned to walk with Cary to the makeshift bar on the other side of the room, she thought she might have actually squeaked at the wonder of his ass.

Ho-lee shit.

"Bliss, are you okay?"

Blinking, she turned her attention back to the two women, now staring at her with identical expressions of knowing amusement.

Damn. Had she been that obvious?

She forced a smile. "Yes, I'm fine. Sorry, I, uh..."

"Got a glimpse of Shane Conrad." The bride-to-be, whose name was Crista, smiled with commiseration. "He certainly is nice-looking. Kind of shy, though. Lori's tried to set him up with a few girls before but nothing's stuck. He's apparently a really nice guy but doesn't talk much. Or he doesn't like girls." Crista shrugged. "No one's been able to figure out which yet. Would you like to meet him? I'm sure Lori would be thrilled to introduce you. He's kind of become her pet project."

Is that why Lori had invited Bliss tonight? To introduce her to Shane? Not that that would be a bad thing but...

But what?

"I think I need a drink. Anyone need another?"

Both Crista and her friend shook their heads, their grins widening.

Bliss didn't care. For the first time in months, she wanted to jump a guy's bones. She'd be damned if she didn't follow up on it.

And maybe later, she'd get to strip off his pants and shirt and rub against his naked body like a cat in heat.

Just as long as she didn't stick her foot in her mouth first.

TWO

Why the hell are you here? You're a goddamn glutton for punishment. Should've stayed the hell home.

Shane knew his strengths and his weaknesses. He could be the life of the party, but only if he felt comfortable with his audience.

He didn't know a single person here, except Cary and Lori, and he had the almost overwhelming urge to slink back to the door and make his getaway.

Dork. Get a grip.

He glanced around for Cary, but the guy had disappeared not long after introducing him to Damien and Lynton.

Shane would make him pay for that. Somehow.

"...must be amazing to get paid to be an athlete. You have like... what? Two games a week? Better than working in an office ten hours a day, six days a week. My fucking boss..."

Shane nodded and agreed, letting the guys continue to tell him how amazing his life must be.

Of course, they didn't have a fucking clue what they were talking about.

If they did, they wouldn't be giving him those sly smiles when they talked about all the "fun" he must have on the road.

Oh, yeah, he was just swimming in pussy all the fucking time. Between daily practice and working out and three or four games a week and travel and—

Yeah, he loved playing hockey. Couldn't think of anything he'd rather do. But like everything else, it had a downside.

Playing in the AHL meant he didn't move around as much as when he'd been in the ECHL, but it wasn't the easiest way to make a living.

Hockey was tough on the body. Plus, he had a shelf life. Goalies especially had knee problems. He might last until thirty-three. If he was lucky, his knees would hold out until he was forty. But eventually he'd have to leave the ice and find something else to do to make money. Especially if he continued playing the way he was and never made it to the NHL.

Damn, what he wouldn't give to be home binge-watching *Daredevil* and drinking beer.

"So I told him I could work that weekend just so I wouldn't have to be home when her parents showed up. I know I was being kind of a dick but if I had to listen her dad..."

Shane nodded like he knew what Lynton—what the fuck kind of name was Lynton anyway?—was talking about but he really had no clue. He hadn't been in a serious relationship...well, ever.

He'd had no time and no opportunity.

Shit, where the hell had Cary disappeared to? Maybe Shane could slip away and no one would notice.

Out of the corner of his eye, he saw Cary coming toward him. *Oh, thank Christ.* This had been a mistake. He'd make his excuses and—

"Hey, Shane." Cary turned and smiled down at the smallish redhead by his side. "This is Bliss Vescovi. Bliss, this is Shane Conrad. He's the goalie for the Redtails. And—" Another knock at the door and Cary grimaced. "Sorry, I gotta get the door again. Hang tight, I'll be back."

Shane barely noticed Cary's departure as Bliss smiled and held out her hand, "Hi. Nice to meet you."

Her voice made the hair on Shane's arms stand straight up. And sent a shock straight to his cock.

Holy shit. Pure fucking sex.

If Shane believed in heaven, he figured he'd just died and gone there because, Jesus Christ, this woman was a fucking angel.

Red hair so deep it had to be fake and hazel eyes that were a swirl of green, blue, and brown. A face that belonged on a billboard and a body slapped together like a porn star.

And damn, if he wasn't standing there with his mouth hanging open.

He shut his trap and took her hand. "Shane Conrad. Nice to meet you."

Then he glanced down and watched as her fingers wrapped around his.

Warm. And soft. Damn, she's soft.

His cock sprang to attention before he could rein in his response. He'd be sporting one hell of a boner in a few seconds. He couldn't remember ever getting hard just by shaking a woman's hand, not even as a horny teenager who hadn't had a chance in hell of getting laid by even the sweetest cheerleader in his high school.

He couldn't believe he hadn't noticed her when he'd come in a few minutes ago. Then again, he hadn't really been interested in anything other than grabbing a beer and something to eat. Since he'd been in this slump, he'd fallen into old habits of using food for comfort. If he wasn't careful, he'd be putting on pounds that'd slow him down. And he definitely didn't need that.

But, damn, wouldn't it be great to work them off in bed with her?

When she didn't say anything else, just stood there staring at him with a smile that made his balls tighten, he forced himself to release her and think of something to say. Anything at all, just to keep her here. But she beat him to it.

"Nice to meet you, too."

"So Cary said you're a hockey player? You play for the Redtails?"

"Yeah, I do. So how do you know Cary?"

Her head tilted to the side, silky red hair sliding along her shoulder. "I don't really. I know his wife, Lori. We met at a chamber mixer a few months ago and we've kept in touch."

Oh hell, that voice. It made him want to beg her to take pity on him and allow him to strip her naked so he could get a look at her beautiful body. To let him put his mouth all over her until she melted into a puddle of lust on the ground.

On the ice, Shane was known for his flexibility and his ability to work well with both hands. He'd show her how well that translated in the bed.

"Lori's really sweet and Cary's a great guy."

Her smile regained a little of its former brightness. "He must be. Lori can't say enough good things about him. And Lori's amazing. I swear she knows everyone in the county. Unlike me. I have to confess," she leaned closer and he bent his head. "I really don't know anyone here except Lori."

"Then we're pretty much in the same boat." Shane couldn't stop staring into those gorgeous eyes. "I don't know anyone except Cary and Lori. And right now, I don't care if I don't meet another person in the room."

Shit, probably shouldn't have said that. But Bliss—damn but he loved her name—smiled again, brighter this time. Then she laughed. Holy fucking hell, did he love her laugh. Low and husky, it sank straight into his gut and made his blood heat like lava.

And when she leaned closer, he caught a whiff of sexy perfume that made his mouth water. Christ, if he wasn't careful, he'd throw this woman over his shoulder and make a break for the nearest bedroom.

He was pretty sure she'd be pissed about that, but he didn't have much experience with a woman who looked like she'd stepped off the pages of some fashion magazine, in her slim black skirt and some sexy-as-hell shirt that showed off enough cleavage to make him drool.

His fingers twitched and he stuffed them in his pockets to keep them from flexing. Or from reaching out to lace his fingers through her hair.

Fuck.

But then she stepped closer and he sucked in another breath, laced with her scent.

Damn, maybe he'd hit his head at practice today and was passed out on the ice, hallucinating.

And wouldn't that fucking suck?

Then again, if he was having a hallucination, maybe he needed to hit his head more often because, holy hell, she was only inches away and his heart revved like a muscle car.

And when she put her fingertips on his chest and tapped twice, his heart actually answered by pounding against his ribs.

Strangely enough, he knew what she wanted him to do, even though his teammates accused him of being the most clueless guy around when it came to women.

He bent down, turning his head so she could whisper in his ear.

"I know exactly what you mean. I'm really glad we met."

His abs clenched, and when he straightened so he could look into her eyes again, her expression made his lungs seize up.

Her lips curved in a smile he wanted to taste.

Christ almighty, he hoped he was reading her right. She was flirting with him, wasn't she?

He'd been making all the wrong moves on the ice lately. Maybe he couldn't trust his instincts.

Even so, he couldn't stop himself from blurting out the words on the tip of his tongue. "Maybe you and I could slip out of here and get to know each other better."

She blinked, her eyes widening as her smile froze.

Jesus, you are a fucking idiot. Why the hell—

"I would love that." Her smile nearly took him to his knees. "But maybe we could wait until after dinner? I have a feeling I'm going to need fuel for later."

. . .

BLISS WATCHED Shane's mouth drop open, and her grin widened as anticipation made her body tingle like she'd downed shots of grain alcohol.

It'd been a long time since she'd tingled over anything. And that had sucked.

But so far, tonight didn't suck at all. Not while there was the possibility that she would take this man home with her, strip him down to his skin then run her hands all over every hard muscle in his body.

While she contemplated that scenario, Shane continued to stare at her until finally he shook his head.

"Damn, I didn't... I mean, yeah. Sure. After dinner." Then he shook his head again and his lips curved in a kind of rueful smile. "So can I get you a drink?"

Was he actually embarrassed? Yeah, he'd shocked her by being blunt, but the way he'd said it hadn't made her feel like a piece of meat. No, she'd felt desired.

Adorable. The guy was freaking adorable.

"I'd love one, thanks."

The relief on his face made her smile widen. "Anything you don't like?"

"Not much." Totally the truth. She had three older brothers with a healthy admiration for alcohol in any form. They'd given her a wide breadth of knowledge to pull from.

Shane started to shake his head again but stopped when a bemused smile twisted his lips.

Oh, please tell her this man wasn't one of those closet cretins who thought women shouldn't enjoy sex and alcohol. Chauvinists who believed simply because they had a dick, they were entitled to pass judgment on women.

She'd leave him with a serious case of blue balls—

"So you want it sweet or hard?"

Oh my.

Heat lit through her at the deep, suggestive tone of his voice, and she had to take a quick breath before she could answer.

"Can't I have both?"

The curve of his lips made her thighs clench, and when he spoke, she went wet between her thighs.

"Honey, you can have whatever the hell you want."

Her answering smile made her face hurt, it was so wide. "Then I'll have a shot of tequila and a beer."

"Coming right up." He took a step away but looked back over his shoulder, those blue eyes shining as if lit from within. "Don't go anywhere."

She raised an eyebrow and made an X over the exposed flesh above her breasts, drawing his gaze down before he snapped it back up. "I'll be right here when you get back."

"I'm gonna hold you to that."

"I hope that's not the only thing you're going to hold me to."

His gaze darkened with sexual intent. "Wherever and whenever."

Then he turned and headed for the makeshift bar on the other side of the room.

Bliss sucked air into her starved lungs. Damn, she felt light-headed.

It'd been so damn long since a guy had had this response to her. Or that she'd had a response like this to a guy.

And boy, did she like it.

Across the room, she watched Shane handle two tall bottles and two shot glasses as he made his way back to her. He didn't stop to talk to anyone and he didn't seem to notice the looks the women in the room were giving him. Looks she sincerely hoped he'd never see because she wanted him all to herself.

When he stood in front of her again, she took a glass and a shot off his hands and immediately downed the shot. *Nice.*

Setting the shot glass on the table beside her, she took a sip of beer, aware that Shane watched her every move. When she lowered the bottle, his gaze slipped to her mouth then down to her breasts, which she'd displayed to their full potential tonight. What good was having a decent body if you couldn't dress to please yourself? The lace bra and panty set she'd decided on tonight would be worth the expense, especially if Shane got to see them.

"So you're a goalie. How's the team this year?"

He blinked and his gaze popped back up to hers. She actually thought he blushed at being caught staring at her chest.

"Good. We're doing good." Then he grimaced. "Mostly."

He looked like he wanted to say something else but stayed silent.

Since she pretty much couldn't, she asked, "And you play with Cary?"

Shane nodded and kept his gaze glued to hers. "He's a great guy. He'll make a great coach."

The reverence in Shane's voice made her smile again. He obviously looked up to Cary.

"Are you from the area?"

He shook his head. "Minnesota. Didn't feel like going home for Christmas this year." Something crossed his expression but passed quickly. "We have a game the day after Christmas and I didn't want to do all that traveling. What about you? You're local?"

Apparently, he didn't want to talk about his family. No problem. Everybody had family issues. "Yep. Born and raised. My whole family's still here, including all four older brothers. We're disgustingly close."

Just how close... Yeah, she typically didn't go into that, especially not when she first met someone.

His eyebrows raised at the mention of her four brothers, and she almost expected him to back away slowly. Some guys did. And when she mentioned that one was a cop... Well, that thinned the herd even more.

Then he smiled...and stole her breath. "Sounds like my family.

Even though I'm not home anymore, my parents and my sister and brother still need to know every little thing about my life."

"Is it hard being away from them at the holidays?"

Nodding, his smile slid toward a grimace. "Yeah. But I've been traveling for hockey since I was twelve so I'm used to it."

"Wow. That seems really young."

He shrugged. "Not really. At least not where I come from."

"I have to admit...I've only been to two Redtails games and mostly I sat in a box and talked to my friends. It's not that I don't like the game. I do. I just always have something else going on."

Now his grin widened. "I can take care of that problem. Let me get you a ticket to our next home game."

HOLY HELL, when this woman smiled, which she did a lot, Shane had the almost overwhelming instinct to fall to his knees at her feet and repeat, "I'm not worthy."

And he knew exactly what he'd do when he was down there. He'd shove that skirt down around her ankles, put his hands on her naked thighs, and pull her closer. Then he'd put his mouth—

Holy shit. He needed to stop before he had no hope at all of hiding his boner.

"Sure." Her smile brightened. "I'd like that. Will I get to see you play?"

Grimacing, he shrugged. A few weeks ago, he would've told her yes because he'd been starting most games. The past few weeks, though...

Damn it, he'd sucked. And he needed to get her off the topic of hockey.

"You might, yeah. So what do you do?"

"I help my aunt run her bridal shop in West Reading. She has three boys and none of them wanted to work in the shop. I've been helping her since I was fifteen. Now it's a full-time job. My uncle retired last year and they like to travel, so I'm alone there a lot of the time."

"You run it all by yourself?"

Her eyebrows raised and he wondered if he'd stuck his foot in his mouth.

"It's not that big so, yeah. On the weekends another one of my cousins helps out. My dad was one of ten so I've got a lot of cousins. I actually love helping brides pick out their dresses. We also do bridesmaids and mothers' dresses and prom and special occasions. It's actually really fun." She leaned in and he bent closer. "Don't tell my aunt but I'd work for free if I didn't need to pay my rent."

"Where do you live?"

"I have an apartment in West Reading."

"Me too. I live with one of the guys on my team. But he's home for the holiday."

Something sparked in her eyes. "So I guess, if we wanted to go back to your place for drinks later..."

He tried not to let his mouth drop open but... Damn, this girl made him feel like he'd won the fucking lottery. He needed to thank Cary for twisting his arm to come tonight.

"There'd be no problem with that."

Damn, he hoped they ate soon. Her smile made him want to skip dinner but that'd be rude. Totally worth it but rude.

Besides, she hadn't exactly said she wanted to go home with him. She could just be flirting. He honestly didn't have enough experience with girls to know.

Maybe he should just resign himself to a few hours of foreplay and eventual blue balls. At least he wouldn't be disappointed.

Luckily, Lori announced that dinner was ready and everyone headed into the kitchen for food.

Small talk got a little easier then, mainly because there were other people around to carry the load. He wasn't good at making conversation unless they were talking about golf, working out, video games, or, of course, hockey.

Which made the fan meet-and-greets torture. He'd learned to cover his awkwardness to some extent, but most people still found it hard to draw him out.

But Bliss didn't seem to be put off. He didn't think she had trouble talking to anyone.

As everyone came together to fill their plates then retreated back to the great room or the dining room to find somewhere to sit and eat, she chatted up several people but never left his side.

By unspoken agreement, he and Bliss found space in the great room, where another woman sat next to Bliss and began to run at the mouth about her upcoming wedding.

Bliss didn't seem to mind. Probably because they were talking about wedding stuff. A subject Shane had absolutely no interest in. At least, not at this point in his life.

No way did he have time for a wife or even a steady girlfriend. He had to concentrate on his game. Or he'd be ending his career sooner than he expected.

But he could listen to Bliss talk for hours. And then he wanted to spend a few hours with Bliss *not* talking.

"So, Shane, how's it going?"

Shane turned with a smile for Lori, who'd sat on the arm of his chair.

"I'm pretty sure you know the answer to that already." He grimaced. "I pretty much suck right now."

"I know that's not true." Lori smiled that cool, mysterious smile that had reeled in Cary like a trout with a hook in its mouth. "I've seen you play. You're just having a rough patch. It'll pass. You need to get out of your own head for a while. Enjoy life a little and not always be so focused on work."

If only it was that easy.

Nodding, he forced a smile for her. "You're right. Cary's always telling me to keep my head up. But when you play, your moves have to be instinctive. The game's too fast to stop and think. I need to be able to see the move before it happens and react before I think about it."

"Very true." Then she leaned closer and her voice dropped to a whisper. "But the advice wasn't only for hockey."

Ah.

He might not be the sharpest blade on the ice but he was no fool.

Lori squeezed his shoulder but Bliss's laughter grabbed his attention. She was still talking to the other girl, but now it was about veils and lace and some other shit Shane had no clue about.

Didn't much matter, though, so long as he could listen to Bliss talk. The sound of her voice made him hard. Maybe he *had* been concentrating a little too hard on hockey lately, especially if he got a boner just listening to a girl talk.

As if Bliss had heard him thinking about her, she turned and smiled at him.

He nearly swallowed his tongue.

When the hell could they leave without looking suspicious?

Now. Ask her back to your place for a drink.

Yeah, all he had to do was open his mouth and get the words out.

But he kept getting distracted by the sight of all that red hair falling down her back in perfect waves and a pretty face that put some actresses to shame.

And her body... Christ, he was salivating. He wanted to put his hands on her breasts then slide them down her body to her gorgeous ass. Then he'd lift her so she could wrap her legs around his waist.

Naked. He wanted her naked and under him. Or over him. He wasn't picky.

Lori made a soft sound, almost like a muffled laugh, and his gaze shot back to hers.

Shit. She knows exactly what you're thinking.

"Have a good time tonight, Shane." Lori stood, smiling down at him. "Tomorrow will take care of itself."

Then she left, but not before ruffling his hair with her fingers.

Like his mom would've done. Made him feel like a kid but not in a bad way.

Smiling, he turned back to Bliss and found her watching him.

"Are you enjoying yourself?"

Her question barely registered because her expression made every muscle in his body tense in anticipation and a strange hum sounded in his ears.

Then her adorable nose crinkled. "I know I've been monopolizing your time and—"

"Please." His smile disappeared, replaced with deadly serious intent. "Monopolize me. All night. I'm begging you."

Her smile faded but he saw the heat in her gaze increase.

Leaning closer, she put her hand on the cushion between them, almost touching his thigh but not quite. "I'm going to take you at your word."

"I really fu—hope you do."

Her smile returned, slowly, and with enough sexual heat to make his heart pound against his ribs.

"Um, I think my fiancé needs me." The woman who'd been talking to Bliss also had a smile on her face as she rose to her feet. "Nice talking to you."

Bliss's nose wrinkled as the other woman walked away but did nothing to stop her.

And when she turned back to him, her lips had curved in a tiny smile that made his heart race.

Okay, maybe he really had gotten banged around at practice and this was a hallucination. And wouldn't that totally suck.

Then Bliss put her hand on his knee and a jolt of electricity poured through him. Nope, definitely not a hallucination.

"So how many are on your team?"

Amazingly, he could still talk. "We've got twenty-two guys on the roster."

"Does everyone get along? I can't imagine that many guys spending that much time together and getting along all of the time.

My brothers were always fighting over something and there were only four of them."

"For the most part, yeah. We've got a good group of guys."

And that was no bullshit. He really enjoyed the hell out of his teammates. At least, the ones who'd been around for most of the season. There'd been a few guys who'd been traded or moved up or down but mostly, they'd hung together. And were a stronger team because of it.

"Sounds like you enjoy what you do."

"Can't imagine doing anything else. Even when—" Shit. Probably better not to finish that sentence, especially to a girl he'd just met. She didn't want to hear about all the gross shit guys did to one another in the locker room. "Even after we've lost three straight on the road and the coach is chewing our asses and we've got a seven-hour bus ride home."

She laughed, low and soft. "You're right. That sounds like hell."

"Yeah. You don't want to be in a locker room full of hockey players after a losing game. We're barely human."

Bliss laughed and Shane swore every guy in the room turned to look. He knew if he weren't sitting here with her, he would have looked because, damn, her laugh made his gut clench with lust.

Shane was pretty sure he could fight off anyone who attempted to poach her. He was one of the biggest goalies in the league. He looked like a brawler and he wasn't afraid to take a hit if he needed to.

And if he had to move someone out of his crease...

"I'm sure that's an exaggeration. Some men look great sweaty." Bliss leaned closer, her voice dropping into bedroom territory. "Makes a girl want to lick him. All over."

Shane had to fight hard to swallow his groan, but he couldn't do anything about his rock-hard erection. That bastard refused to stand down.

Staring into Bliss's beautiful hazel eyes, he said the first thing that came to mind. "You can lick me anywhere you want."

Jesus Christ, he hoped like hell no one else had heard that. Not exactly dinner party conversation.

Good thing Bliss didn't seem to mind. In fact, he thought her gaze actually got hotter.

"Don't be surprised if I take you up on that."

Her voice had dropped to a husky whisper and her breath brushed against his cheek.

Oh fuck.

With one last, hot look in his direction, Bliss turned her attention back to her meal.

Since he couldn't take his eyes off her, he watched as she slid her fork from between her lips. Moaning, she closed her eyes. The look of utter...well, bliss on her face made his lungs feel like they'd been gripped in a vise.

"Oh my gosh." Her eyes snapped open. "This is amazing. Have you tried this?"

He had no idea what she was talking about because he had no idea what she'd put in her mouth.

"I can't wait to see what's for dessert."

Shane seriously hoped he was on the menu.

THREE

Half an hour later, Shane was ready to climb the walls to get to the door.

He'd spent the last half hour talking to Cary, who'd been true to his word. They hadn't mentioned hockey once. Instead, they'd been tasting and discussing the new beers Lori was considering adding to the taps in the bar she ran.

Well, Cary was talking. Shane was pretending to listen but was really obsessing over Bliss, who was talking to Lori.

Until a few seconds ago when she turned to him with a smile as Lori walked in the opposite direction.

Now he fucking ached.

And beside him, Cary laughed under his breath, like he knew exactly what Shane was thinking. Bastard probably did.

"Have a good night, Shane." Cary clapped him on the shoulder and gave him a little shove in Bliss's direction. "Call me tomorrow and let me know you survived. I'll let you know about the ice time."

Shane held onto his manners long enough to say thanks to Cary before he walked to Bliss's side.

When she looked up at him and her lips curved in a smile, he swore everyone else in the room vanished.

"Do you want to come back to my place for a drink?"

He wanted to smack himself on the forehead for just blurting that out but at least he hadn't been stupid enough to add "and hot monkey sex" to the end of that question.

Yeah, it's exactly what he hoped would happen but still. Three hours of foreplay had given him a massive case of perma-erection and he knew exactly how he wanted to lose it. Buried deep inside Bliss.

His hands itched to touch her and he practically had to bite his tongue so he wouldn't lean down and kiss her. Like he'd been fantasizing about for the past hour.

And then he'd strip her down to her skin and—

"Would you like to leave now?"

Bliss's quiet question and her slight smile hit him low in the gut and nearly made him groan.

Holy fuck. He wasn't sure he'd make it all the way back to his place without embarrassing the hell out of himself.

This girl brought out something in him he wasn't sure he could control. And he was all about control. It's what made him a good goalie.

But he'd loosen the reins a little if it meant she came home with him.

"Or," she continued, "we can wait—"

"I'm ready to leave whenever you are." Damn but her smile slayed him. "Do you want to follow me?"

"Sure. That'd be great."

He wanted to pump his fist in the air. "Great. Just let me say goodbye to Lori."

She put her hand on his arm and his pulse thumped through his veins. "We can do that together. Let me get my coat and purse. Be right back."

Ten minutes later, she followed behind his truck in her little red Jeep Renegade and he had to keep from speeding the entire way. The drive wasn't long but he kept looking in the rearview mirror to make sure she was still there.

By the time they parked in the lot behind his building, Shane had clenched his jaw so tight, he was afraid it'd crack.

With his roommate home in Ottawa for the holidays, they'd have the place to themselves. Luckily, CJ was anal about everything and Shane had learned to be a little less of a mess while they'd been living together this season. So the apartment wasn't in bad shape.

And he'd actually changed the sheets on his bed yesterday. How was that for blind dumb luck?

Stepping out of her car, Bliss shivered a little, tucking her hand around his arm as they walked to the building's entrance.

"My car didn't even have time to warm up on the drive," she said. "You're probably used to the cold, aren't you?"

"Pretty much. When you spend as much time on the ice as we do, this is nothing."

"When did you start playing hockey?"

He opened the door to the building and waved her in ahead of him. "Honestly, I don't remember a time when I wasn't on skates. My mom says I was born with them strapped to my feet. Where I grew up, you either skated or you spent a hell of a lot of time cooped up inside from November 'til April."

"So you've played all your life?"

A short walk down the hall to his apartment and he had the door open as he answered.

"Never wanted to do anything else. I love the game."

She slipped by him as he reached inside to turn on the light. "I don't know much about the game."

"I'll teach you whatever you want to know."

She stopped just inside the door as he continued into the living room, shrugging out of his coat so he could put it in the small closet next to the kitchen.

"My own personal player. Hmm, I think I'd like that."

The husky tone in her voice made his head snap around to her and the amused light in her eyes made his muscles clench.

"What do you want to know? Ask me anything."

"Well, now." Her eyes widened. "That's almost too good to pass up."

The teasing note in her voice, combined with that private little grin, made another shiver run up his spine.

"What do you want to know?"

Her head tipped to the side, as if she were thinking. "Do you enjoy what you do?"

Too easy. "Love it. It's all I've ever wanted to do."

"That's amazing. So many people have jobs they hate just so they can eat. But you get to do what you love."

Something in her voice made him ask, "Don't you enjoy what you do?"

She shook her head as she unbuttoned her coat. "Oh, don't get me wrong. I love working for my aunt. And I love what I do. It's just..."

He walked back to take her coat, trying not to salivate as she stripped it off. "What?"

She shrugged, drawing his gaze down to her chest. Then he gave himself a figurative slap upside the head and dragged his gaze back up.

"It's kind of isolating." She shrugged. "It must be nice knowing you've got an entire team at your back."

He laughed. Couldn't help himself. "Well, it's kind of like having this huge family of brothers. You spend so much time together that you get to know everybody really well. That also means you get to know them *too* well. We've got a good group of guys this season but there's always a few, you know? The ones you want to strangle when they tell the same damn joke for the thousandth time. Or is always borrowing something and never returning it. And they all know just what to do to get under your skin."

Her smile made his cock twitch. "*That* I totally understand. I have a big family and there are days I want to strangle them all and days I wouldn't know what to do without them. It's tough growing up with four older brothers."

She seemed to want to say something else but never finished.

"Were you ever able to date? I figure with that many brothers, they'd scare off anyone who tried."

He waved her toward the couch. She took the hint and sat, toeing off her shoes before curling her feet under her legs.

"My two older brothers were away at college when I started dating and my younger brothers... well, they had their own stuff to deal with. But my dad... He used to be a cop. Want to get rid of a guy fast? Have your dad tell your date he'll throw his ass in jail if he dared lay a hand on me. Of course, when I told my mom, she read him the riot act. After that, he just glared at every guy I brought home and then my mom would do something to distract him. They're pretty much the perfect couple. Always have been."

Shane laughed. "Yeah, my parents were pretty freaking perfect, too. My mom worked at home so she was always there. Dinner on the table every night, homemade cookies after practice. My dad worked days at the paper plant so he coached all of my teams from the time I was five until I went to high school."

"Sounds like the American dream."

He grimaced at how perfect it'd been. "Yeah. I can look back on it now and know that, but back then... Man, it felt like I never had a minute to myself."

She propped her arm on the back of the couch and rested her head on her hand. "Do you have siblings?"

"Younger brother and sister. Twins."

But he'd been the focus of his parents' lives for seven years before his mom had gotten pregnant again. And when it'd become evident that he had enough talent to actually make a career out of hockey, his parents had done everything they could to get him where he needed to be.

"My brother plays too but my sister spent most of her childhoods in hockey rinks and doesn't play. She's actually a damn good ice skater but..."

"But what?"

She sounded genuinely interested and he couldn't not answer.

"Sometimes I think my parents invested a little too much time into me and my sister got the short end of the stick."

"Has she ever said that?"

Bliss's voice held a sweet concern that made him want to kiss her.

"No. But I still wonder."

"Does she still skate?"

He shrugged. "Not a lot. She's in college. Going for her veterinarian's degree."

He and his brother teased Giselle relentlessly about the fact that she was the only one of them to go to college. But he was damn proud of her.

"Sounds like a smart girl."

"She is."

"So if she'd wanted to skate, she would've found a way. Right?"

A grin caught him off guard. Giselle wasn't the only smart woman he knew, apparently.

"Probably, yeah. She's always known how to get what she wants. Guess she had to with two brothers."

"What about you, Shane? Do you get what you want?"

He thought about how shitty he'd been playing lately, about how he was letting down his team. About the fact that she'd agreed to come home with him.

"Not always, no. But I hope I will tonight."

And there was her smile again. "I don't think you have to worry about that."

Grinning, he shook his head. "I love that you're not afraid to say what's in your head."

She shrugged. "No one should be."

"You're absolutely right. I'd much rather hear you speak your mind than not say anything at all."

He swore he felt the heat of her smile as she leaned closer and laid her hand on his arm, muscles bunching at her touch.

"Then let me tell you how much I look forward to kissing you." Her head tilted to the side. "And touching you. And...anything else that might come up along the way."

BLISS PULLED BACK FAR ENOUGH that she could see Shane's face in the room's low light. Saw the deep breath he sucked in and the way his throat convulsed as he swallowed. Then he ran one hand through his dark, shaggy waves and she wanted to do the same. She knew it'd feel like silk against her skin.

"Great. That's great." He paused, frowned, then shook his head like he was trying to get something to fall back into place. "I just don't want you to think I'm trying to take advantage of you."

Wow, was he for real? He seemed too damn sweet. Not at all what she'd been expecting. Not that that was a bad thing. But it made her wonder if she was starting to come off a little too strong.

Then she looked into his eyes and saw lust. A blazing heat that stole her breath. And she realized Shane was the real deal. An actual, genuinely nice guy.

She'd begun to believe they were pure myth.

Her thighs clenched and she sucked in air, suddenly finding it hard to breathe.

Holy hell, when had the temperature risen to the point that she wanted to start shedding clothes? Okay, maybe she just wanted him to start shedding clothes.

But first she needed to ask him a very important question. "What if I want you to take advantage?"

That heat in his eyes burned even brighter, and the wry grin that curved his beautiful mouth made her thighs clench.

"Maybe I'd rather you take advantage of me."

Oh yes, please. She could *so* work with that.

As his bright blue eyes narrowed to slits and his mouth flattened into a straight line, Bliss swore she felt sexual intensity coming off him like heat.

Then he moved closer and, as she had to crane her head to look up at him, she realized just how much bigger he was. Broader and heavier and more muscled.

Amazing, she felt no fear. She knew instinctively this man wouldn't harm her. Of course, if she asked him to slap his hand across her ass...

Oh hell, just thinking about it made heat flush across her cheeks.

What would he say if she asked him? Maybe he didn't do kinky? Not that spanking was really kinky but—

Fuck it.

Reaching for him, she wrapped her hands around his neck and pulled him forward, meeting him halfway and pressing her lips against his.

She needed him to have no doubt about what she wanted. That she wanted whatever he had to give.

And when he kissed her back, she realized not only was he a really good kisser, but what she'd thought was shyness was really reserve. And she had just given him permission to release his restraints.

His hands wrapped around her shoulders, tight but not threatening. And it definitely didn't hurt. But he wasn't going to release her unless she asked.

Be still my heart.

Her heart beat just a little faster.

So strong. So...demanding.

With a soft moan, she shifted closer as his mouth opened over hers and his tongue slid between her lips.

She might've been the one to initiate the kiss, but she realized she wouldn't be the one who controlled it. She was okay with that. Totally okay.

With a sigh, she tilted her head so he could kiss her more deeply. He didn't need any more encouragement than that.

His kiss became more intense, threatened to burn. Heat flashed through her, making her nipples tighten and her thighs clench.

His tongue slid against hers, tangling with hers. No teasing, no hinting. Just flat-out demand.

Shane had gone straight from zero to a hundred in record time.

And though she didn't have a problem with that, it took a few seconds for her body to catch up. To allow him to take control.

And when she did…

Her lungs froze as his lips moved over hers with a skill she hadn't expected. A skill that made her brain fuzzy when he stroked his tongue along hers then sucked with a sexy demand that made her want to agree to anything he asked.

How had that happened? How had he gone from slightly awkward and adorable to hot and demanding?

And honestly…who cared? Especially when lust thrummed through her body, making her sex slick with desire and… Holy hell, when had he flattened those huge hands across her back to urge her closer?

She felt each finger through her shirt as he pressed them into her skin. He wasn't hurting her but she certainly wasn't going anywhere unless he allowed it.

Oh my god, did she love that.

Wrapping her arms around his neck, she arched her back, mashing her chest against his, trying to ease the ache in her breasts. She wanted him to put his hands on them and squeeze, not to hurt, just…

God, she *hurt*.

With a little moan, she rose to her knees, cursing her tight skirt. She couldn't spread her legs without rutching up her skirt, and she couldn't do that without actually reaching down and pulling it up.

Maybe he'd just tear the damn thing off her.

Her heart began to beat double-time and it got harder to breathe.

Stroking down her back with heavy hands, he cupped her ass in his palms and pulled.

She had a second to wonder if her skirt was going to split at the seams before he leaned back and took them horizontal. Without releasing her mouth.

The man certainly was talented. He stole her breath and never gave her time to regain it. His hands never stopped touching her, cupping her, molding her.

Not a shy bone in his body now. Which just meant she couldn't think straight.

Especially not when lying flat-out on top of him and feeling his impressive erection pressed against her stomach.

Wow.

She wanted to slip her hands in his pants and wrap her fingers around him, but she'd have to maneuver to get a hand between them and she didn't want to distract him from...whatever spell he was weaving over her body.

His hands seemed to be everywhere. Stroking down her back, petting her ass, sinking into her hair to twist her head a certain way so he could kiss her harder, hotter. A lot harder.

She wanted to move. She didn't want to move. She wished they could get rid of their clothes and skip to the good part.

Although there definitely wasn't anything wrong with this part.

He kissed her like he was starved for her. Like he couldn't get enough and she was the only person in the world who could give it to him.

His intensity threatened to overpower her. Stole her breath and sapped her will to move. It'd be so easy to give him the control he wanted.

But it wasn't in her nature.

She began to battle her way back to the surface. Not fighting him but slowly giving more than she was getting.

When his tongue retreated the next time, she followed him, flicking against his teeth and teasing him until she heard him groan.

His hands smoothed over her ass then cupped her and held her to him so he could thrust against her. Hard. As if he could penetrate her through their clothes.

A split second later, he released her and pulled away.

"Shit, I didn't— Sorry. I mean— *Fuck*."

The heated look on his face made her pelvis rock against his.

She slid her hands up his body to cup his jaw, the scruff rough and enticing beneath her palms. "Don't be. Please don't be sorry. Trust me, I'm right here with you."

She watched him swallow hard, his eyes narrowing slightly. Had she come on too strong?

Then his mouth curved in that little grin again and she swore her bones went liquid. Or at least, she did between her thighs.

In the next second, he twisted their bodies in a move she couldn't quite follow, his body so incredibly agile.

She found herself on her back looking up at him, slightly stunned. Not frightened. Too turned on to be frightened.

But damn, the guy was big. He blocked out everything. The light. The surroundings. Made her feel as if she was the only thing in his world right now.

Sweet heaven.

And when his head descended to kiss her again, she met him halfway, his mouth crushing against her lips in a clash of teeth and tongues.

Shoving one hand into his hair and winding her fingers around the almost-shoulder-length strands, she held him close, sucking in air through her nose as their tongues dueled.

God, she could do this for hours. Just let him kiss her until she honestly thought she might pass out from lack of oxygen. She'd never been with a guy who could kiss this well.

Where the hell had he learned to do this? And was he just as talented in other areas?

The thought hit her like a punch to the gut as he began to gentle the kiss, withdrawing his tongue until finally he pulled away.

Propped on his elbows, he stared down at her. Those bright blue eyes, so intent and focused on her, made her want to pet him. All over. While he was naked.

"If I'm moving too fast, just smack me, okay?"

No way. "If you were moving too fast, my knee would be in your groin. I told you I grew up with four older brothers, right?"

His gaze narrowed. "Yeah, you did." He paused and he got a look in his eye that made her want to lick his throat. Or anywhere she could reach. "So if I ask if I can take your clothes off, am I gonna find your knee somewhere I don't want it?"

Letting her hands stroke from his shoulders to his waist, she began to pull his shirt out of his waistband as she smiled up at him.

"No. I don't want to...damage you. In any way."

There was that blush again, the one that made her grin. Then he wove one of his hands through her hair and tugged. Not enough to hurt. Just enough to make her sex clench.

"I'm pretty tough. I can take a lot of damage."

Heat flashed through her as she thought about just what he could do with that body. "I have no doubt."

With his shirt separated from his pants, she slid her hands under the fabric to press against his sides, just above the waistband of his pants.

The definition of his muscles made her fingers itch to bare him completely.

While he held himself above her on stiff arms, she reached for the buttons of his dress shirt.

Before she started, though, she glanced up and had to swallow at the lust defining the sharp angles of his face.

Oh my.

She'd never been the recipient of that much pure desire from anyone. Ever. It was intoxicating. It made her want to strip naked and give him free rein.

Dangerous. Way too dangerous.

Why? It wasn't like she was going to marry the guy. They were going to have hot sex for one night.

"I think you need to take your clothes off now."

His only outward response to her husky demand was the ripple of his throat as he swallowed. Then he pushed up onto his knees above her and went to work on his shirt buttons.

Her fingers actually twitched to help him but she kept them curled into the couch cushions. She'd never seen anything as sexy as this man methodically pushing buttons through their holes to reveal the amazing body beneath.

Wide shoulders, broad chest bulky with muscle. Freaking washboard abs that would've made an underwear model salivate.

But this man was no model. His collarbone showed the long scar of an incision and he had a bruise on his left arm that covered most of his bicep and another huge purple splotch just above his right hip.

"Do those hurt?"

His gaze never left hers. "Does what hurt?"

She reached out to trail her fingers just above the bruise on his hip. He looked down, watching with narrowed eyes as she barely touched him.

"No." His voice held a deep note of control that made her want to whimper. "But I'll show you what does."

She swallowed convulsively as his hands dropped to the waistband on his pants then flashed him a grin when he stopped after popping the button.

"Do you need some help?"

His eyes narrowed and she had to suck in a quick breath before she started to pant.

"I'd say yes but it might derail my plans."

Oh wow, where had all the air gone? "And what plans are those?"

"Making you come at least twice before I get inside you."

Holy shit. Adrenaline drop-loaded into her bloodstream and her lips parted but nothing emerged. She was at a loss for words and that didn't happen often. If he knew her better, he'd know just how amazing her silence was.

That thought was obliterated a second later when he pulled down the zipper and shoved his pants off his hips.

She had a quick glimpse of his thick, rock-hard erection before he reached for her shirt and began to pull it up her body.

As she wiggled beneath him to help get the shirt over her head, she had a quick second to think, *Damn, I'm glad I wore the green satin bra and panty set this morning.*

And if the look on Shane's face was anything to go by, he liked it too.

Then he bent and put his mouth on the exposed curve of her upper left breast, pressing kisses along the lace-edged cup before opening his mouth over the thin satin covering her nipple and sucking it into his mouth.

Her back arched as she gasped, the sensation so sharp, all of her muscles tensed. She reached for his head, sliding her fingers into his hair to hold him to her. The soft strands felt like silk against her palms and she wanted to rub her cheek against the crown of his head. Or better yet, have him brush the longer strands against her breasts, her stomach. The inside of her thighs.

Sucking in much needed air, she pressed his head closer. Shane took direction well. He bit at her, laved her nipple though the material then blew a cool breath across it to make it pucker.

He moved to do the exact same thing to her other nipple and, for the next several minutes, proceeded to drive her more than a little crazy.

With her other lovers—at least the two after she'd broken up with her ex—she'd been the one in control. Maybe she'd unconsciously chosen men who allowed her to be in control.

Maybe it wasn't that unconscious.

But not Shane. He had his own plan, apparently, and she was more than happy to go along with it.

His tongue flicked at her nipples, which she'd never considered all that sensitive. Tonight...they ached with sensation, almost painfully. She squirmed so much, she realized he'd moved his hands to her ribs to hold her down.

She liked that. Oh, hell, she liked that a lot.

And when he began to kiss his way down her body, her hands dropped to his shoulders. Just to make sure he didn't stray.

But Shane had a definite purpose in mind.

His fingers didn't fumble at all with her skirt, just slid down the zipper with a move so smooth she had a second to wonder if he got a lot of practice.

Then he tugged on the skirt and had it down around her ankles in seconds. Now all she wore were a pair of barely there panties and her bra. And a smile.

A really big smile as he pulled a condom out of the wallet he grabbed out of his pants, still hanging around his hips.

"I'm gonna take these off now." He stuck the fingers of his right hand in the string holding the two sides of her panties together and tugged. She had to lift her bottom to help him get them off, her feet braced on his thighs until he had them down around her ankles.

As soon as he'd dropped them, she reached for him. Wrapped her hand around his cock and stroked him.

His eyes closed as she pumped him from root to tip. Damn, he was thick. Not stubby, though. Just long enough. Mouthwatering. Perfect.

A smile curved her lips and she watched his gaze narrow as he leaned forward, planting his hands on the cushions just above her shoulders.

His lips were close enough that she could lift her head and kiss him. And she could tell that's what he expected.

Instead, she leaned back...and lifted her hips to brush the tip of his cock against her labia.

His jaw clenched, eyes narrowing until she could barely see any blue at all. She loved the feel of his hot flesh against hers, could have teased him for the next hour at least.

Or not. Because when he deliberately slipped the tip between labia, her brain short-circuited. She arched her back and sought to get him deeper.

Instead, he pulled away and pushed back up onto his knees.

Moaning, she reached for his hips but he leaned back, out of her grasp. And made sure she watched as he rolled the condom down his length. His intense focus made her lungs struggle for air. She'd never had another man affect her like this. It was almost too much to take.

She wanted to close her eyes, take back a little bit of control, but she didn't want to break the connection between them.

So she saw the way his expression tightened when he leaned forward again and rubbed the tip of his cock against her clit. Biting back a moan, she reached for his forearms, fingers digging into taut muscles as the ache between her legs built.

Her hips rose to meet his and his lips covered hers again for a kiss that fuzzed her brain.

She needed him inside, to fill the aching void and make her come.

But the damn man wouldn't move.

Not that his kisses weren't amazing. They were. She just needed more. Sliding her hands up his arms as he worked his mouth over hers, she stopped for a few seconds to pet his shoulders before gliding down his back.

His skin heated beneath her palms, so smooth. And then she had her hands on his ass. Jesus, the man had muscles everywhere.

As her hands smoothed down to his thighs then back up again, teasing closer to the seam splitting his cheeks, she felt his groan rumble in his chest as his hips rocked forward.

Yes, that's what I want.

Hands on his hips, she tugged him closer. Or tried to. The man was immoveable.

With a moan, she pulled away from his lips, one hand rising to sink into his hair. She tugged, not hard enough to hurt but enough to get his attention.

Or so she thought.

Apparently when Shane was set on a course, he didn't falter.

Instead of pulling back, he bent to put his mouth on her neck. He laid a string of kisses down her neck to her collarbone then followed that to her shoulder. And then he bit her.

The sting made her gasp and lit her entire body on fire, a blazing hot lust eating her up from the inside. And then she felt his fingers rubbing between her thighs, testing her readiness.

If she was any more ready, she'd be really freaking embarrassed.

"Oh my god. Shane."

"I like hearing you say my name. Do it again."

"Shane, please."

"I think I want to hear you scream it."

Which she did when he pulled his hand away. But he immediately replaced it with his cock and slid inside, fast and hard and all the way.

Her scream wasn't exactly his name but he must've been satisfied because he gave her exactly what she wanted. What she needed.

His hips thrust with a controlled speed that teased the possibility of more, even if she didn't think she was capable of taking any more.

She already felt wound too tightly but unable to get off.

Because Shane kept her on the edge. Every time she thought she might come, he adjusted his pace or the angle to keep her on the brink.

He'd lowered his body until they were pressed together but his height meant her face was pressed against his shoulder so he had to hold himself up on one elbow so she didn't suffocate.

Not that she would've noticed. And she was too far gone to care.

She came with a shudder and a moan, her teeth sinking in his pec as he rode her through it.

Only when she'd gone limp beneath him did he thrust one last time before holding still and letting his cock pump inside her.

Several minutes later, still panting, he wrapped his arms around her.

"Next time, you're on top."

Next time? Oh god, please let that be soon.

He kept his word.

FOUR

Shane woke the next morning—

No, wait.

He peeled open his eyes and looked at the clock. Almost one in the afternoon.

Damn, how the hell had he slept so late?

Duh, asshole. A few drinks and about five hours of the best sex of your whole frickin' life, that's how.

Luckily, he didn't have a hangover, which was kind of amazing, because he was a lightweight when it came to alcohol.

But, holy hell, he was wiped. If he could, he'd go back to sleep but now that he was awake, he knew that wouldn't happen.

Why hadn't she stayed?

With a groan, he sat up, glancing over at the empty space beside him. The pillow she'd used still had an indent from her head. She'd left sometime after that last round when she'd climbed on top of him and made his eyes roll back in his head. Which had been after the two times he'd made her scream.

So why the hell hadn't she stayed for breakfast?

Sliding his legs off the side of the bed, he ran a hand through his hair, adjusted his morning wood out of habit so it wasn't poking through his shorts, and headed for the bathroom across the hall before making his way down to the kitchen to forage for food. He was fucking starving.

And he wished like hell he was eating something other than bagels and peanut butter, two pears and a half gallon of chocolate milk. What he wouldn't give to be sliding down her body and putting his mouth over her—

His cock throbbed.

Fuck.

With a sigh, he lifted the chocolate milk container to his lips, practically able to feel his mom's hand smacking him on the back of his head.

Why the hell had she snuck out?

She hadn't seemed like the kind to fuck and run. Then again, he didn't know her. Like...at all.

Hey, dude. He could practically hear CJ's voice in his head. *You got laid. She saved you the hassle of getting rid of her this morning.*

The problem was, he wasn't a dick who would've smacked her on the ass, said thanks for the great night, and called her a taxi.

No, he would've made her breakfast or at least taken her out to eat before saying, "Can I get your number? I'd like to see you again."

Because, yeah, he really wanted to see her again.

Who wouldn't want to see her again? She'd rocked his fucking world last night. Of course, he wanted to do it again. And again.

Maybe she doesn't want to see you again.

A very real possibility.

Bliss had her shit together, had a life and a career.

Maybe she didn't want to get involved with a guy who moved every six months or so to whatever team needed a goalie that particular day. This stint with the Redtails had been the longest in his career but before that he'd played with teams in Ohio, California and Massachusetts. He'd actually allowed himself to think maybe he'd finally found a niche where he could prove himself. And he had been. Until he'd hit this slump—

His cell phone rang and he grabbed for it, hoping...

Nope.

Shit.

"Hey, Cary." He forced himself to sound normal. And probably failed miserably. "What's up?"

A slight pause. "Just wondering if you're up for a few drills today."

He wanted to groan. Wanted to crawl back to bed and spend a few more hours wallowing. Which was stupid.

"Yeah, sure. That'd be great."

Cary laughed. "I can tell you're really into it. Long night?"

"Uh..." What the hell did he say to that?

Now Cary really started to laugh. "How 'bout we forget I asked that question and you meet me in an hour on the ice. Then you can tell me all about it."

A grin pulled at Shane's lips. "What are you, now? My priest?"

Cary snorted. "Worse. I'm your fucking captain. Get your ass to the arena."

Forty-five minutes and a fifteen-minute shower later, Shane parked beside Cary's truck in the side lot and walked to the door where Cary waited for him.

The guy had a shit-eating grin on his face that made Shane want to punch him.

"Well, you look like you can walk okay, but can you skate?"

Shane gave Cary the finger as he walked by him into the lower level of the arena, headed for the locker room. There was enough light to see where he was going, but he spent enough time here that he could do this walk blindfolded.

"Still faster than you, old man. And who gave you a key to the arena? I can't believe management's letting just the two of us use the ice."

"Called in a favor. Besides, it's not that big a deal. That ice show's coming in tomorrow and they're gonna be using the ice to practice. So no big deal."

"Sweet."

They walked the last few yards to the locker room in silence. Shane had been expecting Cary to cross-examine him about last night, but surprisingly, he didn't say a word. And when he stepped out on the ice to warm up while Cary was still in the locker room gearing up, Shane felt his muscles relax as he made a few circuits around the boards.

Yes.

He sucked in a deep breath, drawing in the cold air rising off the ice. Just the feel of the smooth surface under his blades and the sound they made as he circled the rink was enough to drop his blood pressure. Always had been. He stepped onto the ice and it felt like home.

Having the ice to himself, even for these few seconds, was like being in his own private paradise.

His mom had always complained that hell wasn't hot. Hell was cold.

Shane didn't have an opinion on that, but he did know the cold helped him feel things more intensely and see things more clearly.

"So, you have a good time last night? At dinner."

Cary matched his pace to Shane's but Shane kept his gaze forward.

"Yeah, the food was great. Thanks again for inviting me. Really appreciate the home-cooked meal."

"You left with Bliss."

"Yeah."

No way was he adding more. Cary was a friend but Bliss was friends with Lori. Shane wasn't about to diss Bliss. No fucking way. And he couldn't bring himself to drill Cary for information.

Besides, he didn't fuck and tell like some of the team. A few of the guys were worse than high school kids the morning after a date, spouting off about shit Shane never wanted to know. At least, not and be able to look the girl in the eyes the next day.

"Everything...okay?"

Shane shot his teammate a look. Cary sounded worried about something.

"Yeah." He frowned. "Wait, why? Did Bliss—"

"Nope." Cary help up his free hand. "Not why I'm asking. Lori hasn't heard from her. I'm just...kinda worried about you."

Okay, this conversation was heading off the rails fast. "What the hell?"

Cary shrugged. "Never mind. So, you ready to do some work?"

Because he didn't want to talk about what'd happened, at least not yet, Shane grabbed his helmet and stick from the bench and headed for the goal.

For the next half hour, he and Cary ran through a series of drills meant to increase his acuity.

Cary was one hell of an offensive defenseman so he was no stranger to scoring goals and he got a few by Shane early, which just frustrated the hell out of him.

Cary skated in from the left circle, where he'd scored his last one. "You're leaving that top corner open every time. You gotta get that glove up."

Shane swung his stick from side to side, clearing the ice out of the crease. "I know." Frustration made his tone sharp. "It's always been one of my weaknesses."

"Then we'll work on it until it's not. But you gotta retrain your brain so you're not constantly thinking about that as a weakness."

For another twenty minutes, that's all they worked on until Shane knew he was gonna have to ice his right shoulder for the rest of the fucking week.

But by the time they headed for the showers, Shane thought he might actually have a little better handle on that corner.

"Hey, thanks, man. I really appreciate you taking the time for this."

Shane was already dressed while Cary pulled on his jeans. He was ready to leave but couldn't force himself to get off the bench and head for the door.

He'd been able to keep Bliss out of his head for the past hour while he and Cary had been on the ice but now...

Fuck, now he had to bite his tongue to keep from asking about her.

"All right, Shane." Cary finally lifted his head, a wry grin on his lips. "Spit it out. You should know by now that nothing you tell me goes anywhere."

He knew it. It was part of the reason Cary had the trust of every guy on the team.

But damn, he hated the fact that he was gonna come out of this looking like a dick. He must've done something wrong for her to sneak out in the middle of the night.

But since he didn't even know how to get in touch with her and he didn't want to put her on the spot by walking into the shop where she worked...

"Can you give me Bliss's number? I didn't get it last night and I want to call her."

Okay, that didn't sound too creepy stalkerish. He hoped.

"I thought you left with her."

He forced himself to hold Cary's steady gaze.

"I did. But she left before I could ask for it."

Cary's brows lifted slightly. "Any reason for that?"

His back straightened. "No. I thought... No."

Now Cary nodded. "I knew that, Shane. Just had to ask. Yeah, I can get her number for you. Let me text Lori."

He almost bit his tongue through, trying not to ask the next question. But finally, he couldn't help himself. "So is she seeing someone?"

"Do you think she would've left with you if she were?"

Fuck. "No. Shit. It's just..." Jesus, what could he say that wouldn't make him seem even more like an ass? He sighed. "You know what?

Never mind. She left while I was sleeping, didn't leave me a number. If she wants to see me, I guess she knows how to find me."

Now Cary started to laugh. "Damn, kid. How the hell do you manage to be so damn clueless?" He whipped out his phone and started to text. "Hang tight. I'll get you the number. Then you need to call her. And Shane?"

"Yeah?"

Now Cary looked serious as all hell. "We're heading into the stretch. Don't let anything fuck with your focus."

Shit. "You don't think I should call her?"

Cary's shit-eating grin made a return. "I think you'd be an idiot not to. And you're no idiot."

———

"I CAN'T BELIEVE you didn't leave him your phone number! What the hell were you thinking?"

Bliss groaned between sips of her too-hot coffee, which she needed to mainline if she was going to be any good today.

"I wasn't thinking. Remember? Too much mind-blowing sex. My brain was stuck somewhere between 'Oh my god, I'm never going to get any sleep tonight and be worthless tomorrow' and 'Oh god, I want to stay all night and lick his pecs.' I mean, come on, my brain wasn't exactly functioning correctly. Not after he—"

"Nope." Faith Donovan took one hand off the arm of her wheelchair and held it in the air. "Don't wanna hear it again. The first time was more than enough."

Grimacing, Bliss fluffed the skirt of Faith's wedding dress hanging on the stand, waiting for its big day, which happened to be tomorrow.

A Christmas Eve wedding. Just thinking about it made Bliss teary.

Too bad the groom—

Nope, not going there.

"Sorry, sorry. But now I don't know what to do. Should I ask Lori for his number? I mean, I snuck out of his apartment like I was embarrassed to be there. He probably thinks I'm a bitch. Or worse, he doesn't care and was happy I left and didn't have to deal with the morning-after bullshit."

"From what you were telling me about him, that doesn't sound like something he'd do. But I never met him so..." Faith shrugged and sipped her own coffee.

"I know. *Ugh.* Maybe I just have to let this one go. I mean, last night was amazing but I know from talking to Lori that these guys are always on the move. The good ones barely ever stay in one place more than a few months. And from what I've heard, Shane's good enough for an NHL slot. He won't be here long."

Faith's eyebrows rose. "Sounds like you've been doing some online creeping."

Sighing, Bliss picked up Faith's veil from the chair and hung it on the rack with her dress. "Maybe a little. Just to depress myself even more." With a huff, Bliss sank into the seat across from Faith. "All right, no more. So, is everything ready for tomorrow night?"

Faith laughed, though Bliss swore she heard a little strain that hadn't been there before.

"You've met my mom so you know the answer to that."

Bliss had met Faith's mom, Shelly, at the same time she'd met Faith. A year ago, just after Faith had gotten her chair. Bliss's shop had been the third one Faith and Shelly had visited. Faith had been near tears but unwilling to give up in pursuit of the perfect dress. Shelly had been ready to strangle the next person who treated Faith like an invalid.

Bliss had shaken their hands, asked Faith her size, and started to pull out dresses, never once mentioning that they could be altered to take her "condition" into consideration.

Faith had smiled and Shelly had burst into tears. And Bliss had gained a new friend who didn't let her disability define her. Something Bliss had a little experience with.

"So then everything's been checked at least five times."

"You know it." And there was that look on Faith's face again. "I just..."

Bliss set her coffee cup on the table and leaned forward, concerned. "Just what?"

With a shake of her head, Faith smiled. "Jitters. They suck. You know what, I think I do want to hear more about this amazing guy you met last night."

Since Faith was getting married tomorrow, Bliss decided not to push. Every bride had jitters before her wedding. They came with the territory.

"There's really nothing else to tell. Except I think I made a really stupid mistake by not leaving my number."

"It's not like you don't know how to get his."

Bliss rolled her eyes. "Then I look pathetic, and if he really doesn't want to hear from me, then I'm being clingy."

Faith's nose scrunched. "Yeah, I get it. But still, if you want to see the guy again, and I think you do, then get his number. You never know, he could be the one."

And there was that tone in Faith's voice again, and she couldn't ignore it this time.

"Hey." She reached over and grabbed Faith's hand. "Is something going on? I mean, other than the fact that you're getting married tomorrow?"

Faith didn't answer right away, wouldn't meet Bliss's gaze for several seconds. When she finally did, Bliss knew her friend was having more than jitters.

"I'm afraid Jimmy doesn't want to get married."

Bliss didn't say anything...mainly because she wasn't sure Faith's fiancé deserved her.

She'd only met Jimmy Collins a few times but hadn't been impressed. Yes, he'd stuck by Faith after the accident that had put her in the chair. Faith's spine had been badly damaged, to the point that the doctors had told her she'd never walk again.

But between Faith's will and Shelly's determination, Faith had been working her ass off at physical therapy with the goal of being able to walk down the aisle at her wedding.

Bliss had no doubt Faith would manage it. But she wasn't sure Jimmy was worth that effort from her. Faith needed to walk again for herself. Not because she thought her fiancé would feel better about himself because she could.

And maybe Bliss was being a total bitch to a man she really didn't know. Then again—

No. Bliss was damn good at reading people. And Jimmy Collins didn't deserve this woman. Not one bit. But no way would Bliss ever say that to Faith.

"Why do you think that?"

Faith made a wry grimace. "I'm probably being stupid."

Faith sounded as if she wanted Bliss to agree, but Bliss couldn't bring herself to lie, not even to set her friend's mind at rest the night before her wedding. There was still time for Faith to call it off. But it had to be her decision and not something Bliss advocated in any way.

"You're one of the smartest people I know." Actually, Faith was *the* smartest person Bliss knew. She designed rockets for a living, for chrissake.

"Well, I don't feel smart at the moment. I think I've been really, really stupid. Or maybe just blind. He's been so distant lately and I think..." She took a deep breath. "I think he wants to tell me he doesn't want to get married but doesn't know how to say it. And I'm afraid..."

Faith's expression made Bliss want to punch Jimmy right in his perfect nose. The guy had walked away from the accident with barely a scratch. He'd been going too fast for conditions and had sailed off the road around a sharp curve. And then there'd been the matter of a few drinks at dinner...

Yes, he'd stuck with Faith through her long recovery. But there was just something about the guy that made Bliss want to scratch at him every time he came toward her.

"What are you afraid of?"

Faith's fingers tightened around hers. "That I'm making a horrible mistake."

Bliss practically bit her tongue in half not to speak her mind.

"Why do you think that?"

"He's been...quiet." She paused. "Dismissive."

Bastard. Bliss would cheerfully cut Jimmy's balls off with a dull spoon.

"Have you talked to him about it?"

Faith nodded slowly. "He says everything's fine. And it is. For a little while. And then it's not again. I just...don't know what to think."

Bliss knew exactly what to think. She just couldn't bring herself to say it to her friend's face. Maybe her personal dislike of Jimmy was coloring her judgment. Maybe he really was just having cold feet and everything would be fine.

Maybe...not.

Bliss had made more than one mistake in the past few hours, including sneaking out of Shane's apartment this morning. She didn't want to make a completely horrendous one now.

"I think you need to talk to him again. Tell him exactly what you just told me and see what he says."

Maybe the bastard would actually man up and make things right for this incredible person.

And maybe, just maybe he'd completely screw Faith over. And then Bliss would cheerfully find that spoon.

Faith's lips lifted in a completely fake smile that broke Bliss's heart, and she tightened her grip on Faith's hand.

"I'm sure I'm just being paranoid. And I guess I should try on my dress one last time."

Which was the reason for Faith's visit today. Her final fitting. Tomorrow, Bliss would help her dress at the church then attend the wedding and reception as a friend.

"And speaking of tomorrow, did you decide to bring anyone to the wedding?"

Bliss knew Faith had closed the door on their other conversation. And really, what more was there to say?

"I told you not to hold that spot open. I just don't have anyone in my life right now."

Immediately, images from last night popped into her head. Shane, naked and braced over her body on strong arms, his hips pounding against hers, his mouth on her breasts.

Damn. If she wasn't careful, she'd have a hot flash and need to change her panties.

"Uh huh." Faith's tone definitely held a hint of laughter so at least Bliss had been able to lighten her friend's mood. Even if it was at Bliss's expense. "I'm thinking maybe you wish there was."

Nope, not touching that. "All right, lady. Let's see—"

Her cell rang and her heart gave a little extra thump.

Stupid.

She picked it up, checked the number, and didn't recognize it. But that didn't mean anything. She used this as her work number and she got calls all the time from vendors.

Swiping it into voice mail, she refocused all of her attention on Faith. Where it should be. And not on a random hookup that would never go anywhere.

———

HIS CALL WENT STRAIGHT to voice mail and Shane was all set to end it when he heard her voice.

"Hi there. You've reached With This Ring Bridal Salon. We can't get to the phone right now but we want to help you find that perfect dress. Please leave us a message and we'll call you back."

And damn if he didn't get hard.

So, yeah, he waited through the recorded message, trying to figure out what the hell he should say.

"Uh, hey, Bliss. This is Shane...from last night." Christ, he sounded like a fucking teenager. "I'd like to see you again. I'm free tonight or tomorrow night. Oh wait, tomorrow's Christmas Eve. You're probably busy. We have a game the day after Christmas but then I'll be gone for a few days after that. Road trip." Which she probably didn't care about. "Anyway, give me a call. If you want. I had a great time last night."

He cut off before he sounded like even more of an idiot.

So now what?

Blowing out a frustrated breath, he pushed away from the dining room table and tried to think of something else to do today that didn't involve sitting in front of a screen alone.

Only a couple of guys from his team were still in the area, including the Russians. Actually, only Vladislav Marchenko was Russian. Jakub Mozik was Czech and got super pissed if you called him Russian. So, of course, they all did.

They held the first-line defensive positions and were pretty much inseparable. Had been since being drafted by the Redtails' NHL affiliate, the Philadelphia Colonials, when they were eighteen and sent to the Colonials' ECHL affiliate before being called up to the Redtails last season.

Those two would probably play video games all day, order in pizza, and sleep off a couple bottles of vodka. They had the ability to drink men twice their age and size under the table.

Not exactly how Shane wanted to spend the day.

No, he wanted to spend the day with Bliss.

With a sigh, he figured he could at least do something worthwhile. Like the wash piling up in his bedroom. He hadn't been near a washing machine for a couple weeks. Might as well get that out of the way.

So he was in the basement, where he got totally shitty reception, when his phone rang.

He didn't recognize the number at first glance but then his brain kicked in and he started to grin.

"Hey, Bliss. I'm glad you called me back."

"Hi, Sha...How are you do...I was hop...I know it's...but—"

Shit. The reception down here sucked. He ran for the stairs.

He got to the first floor in time to hear her say, "Shane? Are you—"

"I'm here." He had to take a quick breath because he'd taken the stairs two at a time. At least that's what he told himself. "Sorry. Bad reception in the basement."

She laughed and his cock jerked.

"Is that where you keep the bodies?"

"Only the ones I can't fit in the walls."

She paused and he wanted to smack his head. Jesus, could he be any more of an idiot—

Then she laughed even harder and...

Holy shit, she got his sarcastic sense of humor and didn't think he was a serial killer.

Even more amazing? He didn't feel like a complete ass.

"So," she drew the word out for several seconds, making his heart beat faster in anticipation. "I was wondering what you're doing tomorrow night?"

"Nothing at all." Please, god, let that be what she wanted to hear. Or was that pitiful? Oh wait. It was Christmas Eve. He'd forgotten.

A light huff of laughter came through the line and he hoped like hell she wasn't laughing at his pathetic lack of a life.

"Well, I actually do have something and...I was wondering if you didn't have anything to do, you'd want to go with me."

The question in her voice should've rung a warning bell, but he knew he'd do anything she asked, just to spend time with her. Did that make him creepy or pathetic? Or both?

Then she continued. "A friend is getting married tomorrow night and I was thought maybe you could be my date?"

His brain short-circuited for a second. "Did you say wedding?"

Her laugh was softer and sweeter this time and made his muscles tighten.

"Yeah. I told you I work in a bridal salon, right? Well, one of my clients is getting married and she invited me to the wedding."

She wanted him to go with her to a wedding? As her date?

His brain kicked into gear, tossing out danger signals.

Take a girl to a wedding and she'll get ideas.

Which was total bullshit.

Dude, you're not that great a catch. Seriously, get over yourself.

"Uh, sure."

Somewhere in Nova Scotia, his roommate CJ was shaking his head and he had no idea why.

"I mean," she quickly started to talk, "if you have something else, I'd totally understand—"

"No, no. I've got nothing to do. I'd like—love to go with you."

Another pause and then, "Okay, great. That's...good."

He swore he heard a smile in her voice now and that made him smile, too. "So this is a formal thing, right? Suit and tie?"

"Yeah. Oh, is that a problem?"

"Nah. We're required to dress for games. Unless I need a tux. Then you're out of luck."

"Nope, no tux needed."

"Then we're good. So what time should I pick you up?"

"I have to be there early to help the bride with her dress."

"No problem. I've got nothing to do and nowhere to be."

"Okay then, can you pick me up at four-thirty? I'll text you the address. The wedding's at six. I told her I'd be at the church by five but I want to be there early."

"Great. I'll see you tomorrow."

"Thanks, Shane. I'm looking forward to it."

When the call disconnected, he took a deep breath and couldn't stop grinning.

———

BLISS HUNG UP WITH A SMILE.

That was either the stupidest thing she'd ever done or the bravest. Guess she'd find out which tomorrow night.

Aren't you the one who said you didn't want to get involved with anyone? That you were just looking for a one-night stand.

That had definitely been her. But...there was something about Shane. Something about how quiet he could be and not seem withdrawn. Or how his humor was a little goofy, a little sarcastic and sometimes just plain weird.

How she knew all of that just from spending one night with him was weird. And a little scary. And a little exciting.

So she wasn't surprised by the flutter in her stomach. Or the pulse between her thighs because, holy hell, the man had been amazing in bed.

The kind of guy a girl could fall for and who could break her heart.

With a sigh, she tried to shake some sense into her head.

"Completely getting ahead of yourself. It's just sex."

Really great sex. And a seemingly great guy.

Too good to be true.

Weren't they all?

She'd found that out the hard way when she'd found the man she'd thought was her happily-ever-after in bed with another woman.

Oh, Rich had sworn up and down that nothing had happened between him and the ex-girlfriend passed out on his bed. Sworn he'd only allowed her to sleep there because he hadn't wanted her to drive home in her condition.

Bliss had wanted to believe him. She couldn't. Couldn't bring herself to trust him. Couldn't help feeling like a fool. Apparently she'd been right because when she'd gotten rid of him, he'd immediately started dating his ex.

So much for trust.

No, Shane would be a great diversion until it ended. And it would end. And when he moved on... No harm, no foul. But in the meantime, she'd enjoy the smoking-hot sex.

"Liss! Hey, Liss. Guess what?"

She jumped as her door slammed open but smiled when she saw her older brother, Mike, in her living room.

"Hey, Mike. We've talked about knocking before, remember? You're supposed to knock before you come into my apartment. Or anyone else's."

Mike's sweet face screwed up into a frown, and Bliss had to bite her tongue against the words that wanted to escape.

But she knew if she said, "Never mind, it's okay," it wouldn't help Mike. The therapist had been crystal clear about that. He'd stressed, when she and her parents had first talked to him about Mike moving into his own apartment, that they had to hold him to the same standards as they would a person who didn't have his disabilities.

Mike had to be held accountable, Dr. Farouk had said.

"Damn. I'm sorry, Liss." He hung his head, ginger hair shades lighter than her own, hanging over his forehead. "I'll remember for next time. I promise."

Now she smiled. "I know you will, bud. Now what's so important you forgot your manners?"

And that fast, his grin returned. Her parents swore Mike had taken one look at her after she'd been born and hadn't stopped smiling since. And she'd hadn't known a time when her brother wasn't a fixture in her life.

"My boss told me I'm getting a raise!"

Her brother's infectious joy made everything in life just a little brighter.

Throwing her arms open, she hugged Mike tight and said a silent "fuck you" to the few so-called friends who'd told her she was crazy to agree to have her "disabled" brother move in next to her. Mike wasn't disabled. He was differently abled. In her mind, the distinction was huge.

"That's great! I'm so happy for you."

Mike pulled back, but not before putting a smacking kiss on her cheek.

As he told her about his day at the grocery store where he

worked, she let herself get caught up in his joy. Since they'd moved into their side-by-side apartments, she'd watched him gain so much more confidence.

Her parents had never tried to hold him back but even they'd been worried about his plan to move out on his own. But when her former neighbor had told her he needed to sublet his apartment immediately because he'd gotten a new job out of state, she'd gone straight to her parents and Mike.

She'd known Mike would be fine. Her parents had taken some convincing but, in the end, Mike had moved in next to her and she'd never regretted the decision.

Her ex had never understood why she'd want to "chain" herself to her brother, "with all his problems."

With an internal sigh, she knew that should've been a question she'd asked herself about Rich at the time.

She'd learned her lesson. Wouldn't make the same mistake twice. You never knew who was going to turn out to be a dick.

She really hoped Shane proved to be the decent guy he seemed to be.

FIVE

"Seriously? You're going to a wedding with a girl you just met? Are you insane or just stupid?"

Shane showed off his dexterity by giving Lad the finger without losing his grip on the game controller or getting his character killed.

"Leave the guy alone." Jake knocked his controller against Shane's in a show of solidarity as they sat on the floor, backs against the couch. "He has obviously taken too many shots to the head. Addled his brain."

With the press of a button, Shane killed off Jake's character. "Yeah, fuck you, too, Jake."

With a burst of Czech that probably called Shane's parentage into question, Jake tossed his controller over his shoulder to Lad. Jake had no doubt Lad would catch it. The guys were more in sync than an old married couple. It made them a great defensive team on the ice.

"So I take it the sex was amazing." Joey Constantino sat on the couch beside Lad. "Why else would you subject yourself to a wedding, especially when you won't know anybody there?"

Shane elbowed Joey's thigh, hard enough for the guy to flinch. "I didn't say anything about sex. And...what the fuck, man? I thought you were on my side."

Joey smirked as he got his character up and running. The wiry forward skated with a blinding speed that totally contradicted his laid-back personality.

"I *am* on your side. But not if you're gonna be a total dickhead. You haven't stopped talking about her since you got here. You only met her last night. You got laid. The sex was obviously great or you wouldn't have agreed to go to a wedding with her because, yeah, who goes to a wedding with a girl they just met unless they're expecting more awesome sex?"

Okay, Joey might have a point but still... "Fuck that. I haven't talked about her that much."

Had he?

When the other three guys exchanged a look then started laughing, Shane wanted to grab the nearest stick and slash the hell out of all of them.

"Yeah, fuck you, assholes. Just because you aren't getting any—"

"Who says we are not getting laid?" Lad punched him on the arm.

Shane snorted. "You spend most of the time we're not on the ice here playing video games like twelve-year-olds."

Jake stuck his elbow in Shane's side. "And aren't you sitting here, right now?"

"Visual acuity exercise."

Joey burst out laughing. "You're so full of shit. You don't have anything better to do than sit around with us. Why didn't you go home anyway?"

Shane shrugged. Didn't want to admit that he was avoiding his Hallmark parents.

Lad and Jake wouldn't understand. They would've been on the first plane out if they'd had enough time to fly home and get back in time for the next game.

Joey... Well, Joey's parents were a living nightmare so he didn't go home. Ever. He wouldn't understand why Shane wanted to avoid his perfect family.

"I needed to work on some things and Cary said he'd help. So I stayed. I need the practice."

"Don't sweat the past few games, man." Jake shrugged. "This shit will work itself out."

Jesus, he hoped so. Otherwise... "I just want to stay focused on the game and not get caught up in all the family stuff."

Jake snorted. "And nothing says focus like screwing around with some girl you don't know."

"It's not like that. She's..." Amazing. Sexy. Smart. "Nice."

Silence.

Shane looked over his shoulder to see Joey staring at him with wide eyes. When he looked at the other guys, they had identical expressions of what-the-fuck.

"What?"

"Nice?" Jake said. "This girl is so *nice*, you told her you would go to a wedding with her?"

Jake's accent got thicker with each word and his blond eyebrows rose until they were hidden by the fringe of pale hair that fell over his forehead.

Shane shrugged, feeling a little WTF himself over the guys' reaction. "Yeah, she's nice. So what?"

Jake and Lad exchanged a glance then they both looked at Joey, who started to shake his dark head.

"Nice girls are the ones you really have to watch out for, "Joey said. "They'll screw with your head and you'll never know what hit you. Seriously. You should run now. Before you're totally fucked."

———

SHANE ADJUSTED HIS TIE, grabbed his coat, and headed out the door.

For some stupid reason, he was having trouble breathing. It wasn't like he hadn't been on a first date before but it'd been a while. At least six months, maybe more.

Damn, he couldn't even remember. Had to have been after last season, when he'd been home. Couldn't even remember the girl's name. Did that make him a dick? Probably.

Pitiful. Fucking pitiful.

Sliding into his truck, he double-checked the address Bliss had texted him, took a look at the map to make sure he knew where he was going, then headed out of the parking lot.

His phone rang seconds later and he answered through the truck's Bluetooth system when he recognized the number.

"Hey, what's up?"

"Yo, Brick. We are checking up on you before your date tonight. Jakub and I are planning to get shitfaced and watch...that show. What is that show?"

The last of that sentence had faded, probably because Lad had turned away from the phone to talk to Jake.

"I have no idea what the hell you're talking about." That was Jake, hard to make out because he must have been farther. "Shane, please come save this asshole's ass before I fucking kill him out of boredom."

Lad responded in Russian, some of which Shane understood, but only the swear words, and then Czech, which Shane didn't understand at all. And then he heard what sounded like a scuffle.

Shane started to laugh but the other two guys didn't hear him until at least a minute had passed.

"Bastard laughs at us." Jake's voice, closer to the phone now. "But we are not the ones going to a wedding tonight."

Still laughing, Shane shook his head. "At least I'll be drinking for free."

"It is not the drinking you go for." Lad's voice got sly.

Very true. "Fuck you, Drac. It's a date. You remember those, don't you? Or are you and Jake still playing with each other on and off the ice?"

Despite the language barrier they'd faced when they'd first arrived in the states three years ago, Lad and Jake had picked up English quick. But they still fell back on their native languages when they wanted to insult you.

So when Jake spouted off something in Czech and Lad started to laugh, Shane figured he didn't want to know what Jake had said.

"Well, then, fuck you," Jake finally said in English, disgust in his tone. "Ignore your buddies for a slice of ass cake."

"If I had the chance to get some of that," Lad added, "I'd leave you at home, too."

Shane laughed so hard, his chest started to hurt.

"You two are fucking assholes, you know that, right? You deserve each other."

"Dude, you definitely need to get laid more often." Lad sounded serious now, such an abrupt switch that Shane had to shake his head. "This will help you get your head out of your own ass. You need some...what's the word?"

"Ass!" Jake yelled from the background again.

"No, not— He is an asshole. Do not listen to him. No. Distraction! You need distraction. So go be distracted. We call you tomorrow. Or maybe you call us if you're not busy, yes?"

Shaking his head and trying not to laugh, Shane agreed then hung up to the sounds of Jake singing Marvin Gaye's "Let's Get It On." Bastard had a decent voice.

He still had a smile on his face when he pulled up to Bliss's apartment building, which turned out to be a renovated school building on a side street not far from his place.

Since she'd also texted her apartment number, he parked on the street and buzzed her from the lobby to let her know he was there.

"Bliss, hey—"

"Oh wow. You're here. Come on up. I just need a minute."

She sounded distracted and maybe a little out of breath and he didn't even get a chance to respond when the intercom cut off and the door buzzed.

He found her apartment on the second floor and knocked, hearing the faintest trace of heels clicking against wood before the door flew open.

His mouth dropped open and his brain literally froze for a second. Then he practically swallowed his tongue.

Holy shit.

"Hi, sorry, I'm running just a minute behind." She took a step back and waved him in, but not before her gaze dropped and she checked him out from head to toe. "Um. You look...great."

He could've sworn her cheeks flushed but she turned away before he could be sure.

One thing he did know...she looked fucking spectacular. If he'd thought she looked edible at the party two nights ago...

Now, he wished like hell they could skip the wedding so he could strip off her dress, throw her over his shoulder, and toss her on her bed...wherever that might be.

"I hope you don't mind if we take my car tonight," she called over her shoulder as she hurried toward the back of the apartment. Her legs looked amazingly long in high heels.

The open floorplan allowed him to watch her as she headed for an alcove where a long, white bag hung from the top of an open door.

"I have an SUV so I can lay the dress out in the back, and my sewing kit's in there already."

"No problem."

As long as he got to spend time with her, he didn't care how they got where they were going.

With the dress bag now in her hand, she walked back to him with a wry grin. "You're awfully agreeable. Are you always going to tell me yes?"

"I guess it depends on the question." He thought about letting her respond to that but wasn't sure his cock would behave if she started to tease him. "You want me to get the door?"

She blinked and nodded. "Yes. Please. The keys are on the table."

Grabbing the key ring, he opened the door, waited until she walked through, then followed her and locked the door.

Walking behind her down the hall, he marveled at the view.

Jesus, her ass looked perfect, outlined in that tight dress.

"You look amazing."

Looking over her shoulder, she smiled, sweet and hot. Christ, he nearly tripped over his own feet.

How the fuck did she do that? How did she make him feel like a fucking teenager, tongue-tied and horny and clumsy?

"Thank you. You clean up pretty well, too. But then I knew that at the party."

He would've continued to simply stare at her gorgeous ass as they walked through the building to her car but that'd be a dick move so he looked up—and found his gaze caught on her breasts as she stopped next to her SUV.

He knew how soft those breasts were because he'd had his hands and mouth all over them two nights ago.

Fuck.

He was going to spend the entire night with a hard-on in front of a couple hundred people he didn't know.

Fuck.

And...crap. He'd totally missed what she'd said. Something about how he cleaned up...

"Uh, thanks. We dress for games so...yeah, you get used to wearing suits pretty fast."

"Doesn't hurt that you look good in it."

His turn to smile. He really liked that she wasn't afraid to flirt but didn't come off too abrasive. Basically, he liked everything about her.

A lot of women he'd met after becoming a professional threw themselves at him. He'd felt more like a conquest than someone they really wanted to get to know.

"I'd say the same about you," he spoke slowly so she heard every word, "but it wouldn't do you justice."

As he clicked the remote to open the car, she threw another smile his way as she hung the dress on a bar she had rigged above the back seat just below the car ceiling. Then she moved to the back, opened the gate and arranged the bag so it looked like a white waterfall.

"Looks like you've done this a few times."

She huffed out a laugh as she closed the door then took the keys he held out to her. "Just a few. You learn the tricks. My aunt's been in the business for thirty years."

As she walked back to the driver's side, he walked with her then offered her a hand getting into the car. She looked surprised at first but let him help her in. He'd seen his dad do this a hundred times for his mom, who only stood five-three.

In those heels and that tight dress, Bliss would've had to do some fancy maneuvering to get into that seat. Besides, he got to put his hands on her.

Win-win.

And the smile she gave him—part heat, part sweet—made his gut clench.

"Thank you."

Her tone had dialed down a notch, low and a little husky. And damn, if that didn't make his balls tighten and his cock throb.

Only another six hours of foreplay.

He nodded but before he moved away, she reached out, stroking her fingers along his jaw. He froze, his lungs catching at the sizzle along his nerve endings.

When she let them play across his lips, he couldn't help himself. He opened and bit lightly on the tip of her index finger.

And watched her eyes narrow and darken and her smile turn a little more wicked.

He flicked the tip with his tongue, heard her suck in a sharp breath, then let her slide her finger away.

"I can see you're going to be a handful."

Damn, but her voice made him want to shove her skirt around her hips and put his face between her legs so he could lick her until she came. He hadn't gotten around to that the other night. Tonight, it'd be first on his to-do list.

"I know how to behave in public." Then he shrugged. "But all bets are off later."

MAYBE BLISS SHOULD'VE PACKED an extra pair of panties because, oh my god, the man made her wet.

If she hadn't needed to be at the church with the dress, she might've said fuck it and taken him back to her bed. Or maybe they would've gotten as far as the door. She could've pulled up her dress and dropped her panties and he could've undone his belt—

Oh wow.

Sucking in a breath, she pulled her hand away from his mouth, and the tempting scruff on his jaw, and dropped her gaze on the pretense of putting the key in the ignition.

Because she couldn't think of one sane thing to say, she said, "We should get going."

Shane didn't miss a beat. Stepping back, he made sure her dress was safely out of the way of the door before he closed it. Her heart gave a serious flutter.

Then he walked around to get in the passenger side, his knees nearly hitting his chin before he adjusted the seat back.

When he buckled himself in, she put the car in gear and headed for the church, trying to ignore the way he took up so much space in her car.

Damn, he was *big*.

Yes, she'd known from being in bed with him two nights ago. But here, now, enclosed in the car together... He took up so much space, it almost felt like there wasn't enough air.

Of course, that could just be from the way she couldn't catch her breath when he was around.

"So is the bride a friend or a client?"

Ridiculously relieved that he'd asked a question she didn't have to think about, she said, "Both, really. I mean, she started out as a client but became a really good friend. She has mobility issues and," *I have a brother with mental disabilities that I'm not going to mention because you could still turn out to be a dick,* "I told her I'd help her get dressed."

"What kind of mobility issues?"

The kind caused by a fiancé who got careless and flipped the car he was driving and crushed Faith's spine.

"She was injured in a car accident and needs a wheelchair."

"Damn, that sucks."

The true emotion in his voice hit her somewhere in the middle of her chest.

"It does. But Faith's amazing. They told her she'd probably never walk again but she's not giving up. I have no doubt she'll be able to get rid of that chair. But for now, she knows she needs it and doesn't take shit or pity from anyone."

"She sounds amazing. Can't wait to meet her. Gotta say I noticed you haven't said anything about the guy she's marrying."

She tried not to grimace and barely managed it.

"He's...fine."

Shane laughed. "Damned by faint praise."

Grimacing, she shot a quick glance at Shane as she stopped for a red light. "Is it that obvious?"

"That you don't like the guy? Yeah, kinda."

She huffed. "Well, the feeling's probably mutual. I just don't think he's good enough for her. Honestly, I'm not sure anyone's good enough for Faith. She's just one of those people, you know? She's almost too good to be true. But she's absolutely the nicest person you'll ever meet. I just think..."

"He's not worthy."

She slid him another look and found him watching her. God, she really hoped she wasn't coming off as a self-righteous bitch. "Yeah. And please, just tell me to shut up. I can't believe I'm bad-mouthing a groom on his wedding day."

"I don't want you to shut up. You can talk all night. I love the sound of your voice."

Oh my god, was he really for real? Every word out of his mouth made her want to pull over, put her car in park, and crawl all over him.

He looked amazing tonight. That suit fit him like a glove, an extra-large glove. Suit-porn was *so* a real thing.

Shaking her head, she huffed out a laugh. "You're dangerous."

Luckily, she couldn't see his smile but she heard it in his quick laugh. If she'd glanced over at him, she might've driven off the road.

"Glad you think so." A pause. "Be nice if the other teams thought so, too."

She slid him a quick glance. "Why do you say that?"

His shoulders barely moved in a shrug. "Just...having a little trouble lately. I've been—" Another pause. "In a slump."

"What does that mean?"

She heard him suck in a breath and, when she glanced his way again, saw him shake his head, his beautiful mouth a flat line.

"It means I'm letting my team down."

She heard his anger and frustration so clearly, she wanted to soothe him in some way but didn't know him well enough to know how. But she couldn't stop herself from trying.

"Is that why you didn't go home?"

Everything about this man intrigued her and she wanted to know every little thing about him.

Which was foolish. He wouldn't be around long enough for her to get to know him that well. This...whatever they were doing, was just for fun. He wouldn't be in Reading forever.

And she certainly wasn't in the market for an emotional attachment to a guy who could pick up and move across the country at the flick of a coach's fingers.

That didn't mean she didn't want him to talk to her.

After a few, long seconds, he finally said, "A little, yeah. I just need some time to think. Get my head straight."

She almost said, "I'm sure you'll be fine," but knew that was bull-shit. Sometimes things weren't fine and you needed to work through your issues before they got better. And sometimes they never got better and you just learned to handle them.

So she reached for his hand, resting on his knee, and laced her fingers through his.

"So you thought a Christmas Eve wedding was just the thing to take your mind off your game."

She glanced his way again, made sure he saw her smile.

But he didn't return it. Instead, he stared at her, even after she returned her attention to the road. She felt his gaze on her.

"Actually, you're the one taking my mind off my game. You're a distraction. A good one."

Heat shot through her and she had to suck in air. "Then I'm glad I asked."

"Yeah, me too."

They fell silent then but they were only a few minutes from the church so it didn't have a chance to get awkward.

By the time they reached the church, they were a few minutes early but Faith's mom's car was on the street so she parked behind it.

Shane was waiting for her at the back of her car.

"You want some help?"

She smiled again. Her ex would've watched her struggle with her purse and the dress and her kit before asking her if she'd needed help.

What the hell had she ever seen in Rich? And why the hell was she even thinking about him now?

Shoving those thoughts aside, she nodded. "If you don't mind, could you grab my kit? And..."

The ultimate test. She held out her clutch with an apologetic grin.

He didn't even blink. Just took it and shoved it under his arm before grabbing her kit.

"Jesus, my gear bag's heavy but it's huge. This thing's half its size and weighs more. What do you have in here? A sewing machine and a weight bench?"

His wry smile made her laugh, but she hoped he didn't hear the breathiness in it. Damn him. Every time he smiled at her, her lungs reacted like she'd just finished a marathon.

She wanted to fan her face with her hand. Instead, she reached for the dress.

"I never know what I'm going to need so I make sure I have everything."

"Gotta love a girl who's prepared."

Her mouth twisted in a grimace that she quickly wiped away. The last man who'd said something similar hadn't been complimenting her.

Shane's not Rich.

Maybe she should just keep chanting that little mantra for the next few hours.

Especially when she was pretty sure this man had meant it as a tease. A sexy tease.

"I try my best. Besides, I think you can handle it."

She wanted to say something else, something that would make him as hot for her as she was for him, but couldn't think of one damn thing. And that wasn't like her. She wasn't usually at a loss for words.

"Nice to know you have faith in me."

That almost stopped her cold because she realized she did. After spending only a few hours talking and a few hours rolling around in bed together, she *did* trust him.

Bad idea.

Telling herself to shut up, she smiled over her shoulder at him and continued into the church.

Since she'd been here before, she knew she'd find Faith in the basement. Faith had decided to get ready in the church instead of arrive dressed. With her chair, there was always the possibility that the dress could get caught in the wheels and that would be a disaster.

Kinda like this wedding.

She really needed to stop with the negativity. It wouldn't do Faith any good and it would only make Bliss feel bad when Jimmy turned out to be a decent guy.

Ha.

"Watch your head," she said as she headed down the stairs.

"Holy— Uh, yeah. You gotta be a hobbit to work here."

Stifling a laugh, she shook her head instead and stopped at the bottom of the stairs to make sure he didn't hurt himself.

When he'd made it out of the stairs in one piece and stood beside her, towering over her in the narrow hall, she met his gaze.

"Thank you."

He shook his head, his mouth curved in a confused grin. "Why?"

"Because you're here."

SHANE WASN'T EXACTLY sure what Bliss meant, but he couldn't miss the sincerity in her voice.

He could've blown her off and told her he had nothing better to do tonight. Which would've been true. He had absolutely nothing better to do tonight than spend it with her. And he didn't mean that this was better than doing nothing.

No, he honestly meant he couldn't think of anything he'd rather be doing than spending the night with her. Even if it meant going to the wedding of two people he didn't know.

But that wasn't something you blurted out to a girl you'd just met. It went against the guy code...whatever the hell that meant.

"Well, I'm here for whatever you need. Just point me in the right direction."

And there was her smile again. The one that made him remember exactly how she'd looked in his bed two nights ago before—

Fuck, he needed to think about something other than her naked body.

"I'm going to take you up on that offer." Then she scrunched up her nose and shook her head. "But not now. Right now, I have to get Faith ready. Let me introduce you and then I'm going to abandon you for about half an hour. Sorry."

"No problem. I know how to amuse myself and not get into too much trouble."

She laughed and his gut tensed. Hell, he might embarrass himself standing here listening to her.

Then she did something he wasn't expecting. She crooked her index finger at him, her lips curved and a playful gleam in her eyes.

He bent because he didn't want to deny her.

When their noses were almost touching, she closed the last few centimeters separating them and brushed a kiss across his lips.

His lungs fucking froze in his chest and he was pretty sure he had an erection no one would be able to miss.

All because she'd barely kissed him.

The only good thing... When she pulled back, she looked like he felt.

Like he'd taken a wicked slap shot off his helmet and gotten his bell rung.

Damn, he liked this girl. A lot.

"I'm just gonna go find a place to hang until you're finished. I can meet your friend later. You probably have a lot to do."

She nodded, still looking shell-shocked.

"Sure. That's..." She took a breath. "That sounds like a plan."

Then she smiled and he couldn't think of one damn thing to say. So he nodded and turned to walk back down the hallway. But before he walked away, he turned again, leaned forward and kissed her way harder than she'd kissed him.

———

"SHELLY, I need to talk to you."

Bliss knew something was wrong the second Faith's dad stuck his head through the door and stared at his wife. Frank's expression made Bliss's stomach clench.

Luckily, Faith was facing way from the door and couldn't see her dad. Her mom's eyes narrowed for a quick second before she smiled in Faith's general direction and hurried out of the room.

"If my brother's kids are causing problems, I'm gonna strangle them myself. Those little demons are adorable but they're spoiled rotten." Faith paused, her expression solemn. "I can't thank you enough for everything you've done."

"It's been my pleasure. I just—"

"Faith, honey." Her parents walked back into the room together and Bliss knew something had just hit the fan.

Because they looked pissed. Not angry. Not upset.

They looked pissed off and holding it together by a thread.

Shit.

Sheer terror flashed through Faith's expression before she wiped it away and turned to face her parents.

"What's wrong?"

Her parents paused and Bliss squeezed her hand before making a break for the door. Whatever was going down, she figured Faith's parents would want to break it to her alone.

As soon as the door closed behind her, she headed back down the hall, figuring she'd find Shane upstairs. He surprised her by straightening away from the wall at the base of the stairs.

"So I guess you heard." He shook his head, disgust plain on his face. "What a douche."

She shook her head. "Actually, I don't have a clue what's going on. But you do, obviously."

"Shit. Yeah." He grimaced. "I wasn't eavesdropping but they weren't trying to be quiet so..." He sighed. "I'm pretty sure the groom took a powder."

Bliss flashed cold then hot.

That bastard. That absolute bastard. I'm going to hunt him down and—

"Uh, Bliss? You gonna be okay? You look a little..."

"Furious? Yeah, you could say that."

Shaking her head, she sucked in a deep breath and tried to tamp down her anger. But...oh my god, if Jimmy ever dared to show his face—

"No, I mean you look like you took a puck to the balls."

She huffed out a laugh. She couldn't help herself. And then she shook her head because that's probably what it would feel like. If she, you know, had the right equipment.

Shaking her head, she looked up into his eyes and smiled, though a second ago, she wouldn't have thought she'd be able to smile at all tonight.

Dangerous man.

Her smile faded and she really hoped he couldn't read her mind.

"I'm not sure what's going to happen but if you want to go..." She shrugged. "I can call you a taxi?"

"Nah. I'll wait with you."

He waved at a bench along the wall, and when they sat, his thigh pressed against her, radiating heat into her body. If she leaned close, she'd be able to lay her head against his upper arm. Snuggle into his side.

It surprised her how much she wanted to do just that.

Instead, she distracted herself by asking, "When's your next game?"

"Day after Christmas." He paused. "Not sure I'll be playing. Coach had me on the bench last game."

Since that seemed like a touchy subject, she asked another question. "What are you doing for Christmas?"

He shrugged. "Sleep. Eat. Hang out with the guys who didn't go home. A couple of the booster club members invited us over for dinner so I'll probably do that. Then I need to get a good night's sleep so I'm ready to play. If Coach puts me in."

"I think...I'd like to come to the game."

She felt him shift beside her. "You want me to get you tickets?"

"I can do—"

"Nah, it's no problem. We get comps. How many do you need?"

She thought about her answer for several seconds. "Is two okay?"

"As long as you're not bringing a date, that's not a problem."

Smiling at his wry tone, she did rest her head against his arm for a few seconds. "I will be bringing a man. But he's related to me."

He tensed. "Your dad's a cop, right? Am I gonna need bail money?"

She laughed, just a quick huff of sound. "I'm not bringing my dad. I'd like to bring my nephew. He's sports crazy."

"Sure, no problem."

She'd given some thought to bringing her brother Mike but...

But what?

She knew, she just *knew*, that Shane was a good guy. An honest-to-god decent man.

SHE WAS SO USED to guys who lied to get what they wanted or told her what they thought she wanted to hear.

Shane seemed so genuine.

So why aren't you going to bring Mike?

Because it was habit to keep her brother separate from her dating life. Because you could just never be sure.

Down the hall, door hinges squealed and her head swiveled to see Faith's dad emerge. His chin almost rested on his chest, but she could see his hands clenched in fists at his sides.

The man was pissed. And heartbroken.

Touching Shane on the shoulder, she leaned in. "I'm just going to see if Faith needs me."

"No problem. Don't worry about me. I'll be waiting here when you're ready to go."

She flashed him a smile and got caught for a second in the sincerity of those blue eyes.

You are in so much trouble. This man is dangerous.

But it would be so much fun while it lasted.

———

"DO you want to come in for a drink?" Bliss looked over her shoulder at him as she opened the door to her apartment. "I'm afraid I might drink an entire bottle of rum by myself tonight and that wouldn't be a good idea. I don't want to be hungover at dinner at my parents' tomorrow."

Shane had been hoping she'd invite him in, but he hadn't wanted to count on it. And he really didn't want her to feel like she had to entertain him.

Bliss was upset. And yeah, he totally got why. He didn't even know Faith and he wanted to punch her douchebag former fiancé.

He also didn't want to make Bliss's night any tougher than it already had been.

But he didn't want to leave either.

"Sure."

Smiling, she opened the door and waved him inside.

He hadn't gotten a real look at her place before but now he let himself look as she headed toward the back of the apartment.

"I'm going to change. Give me a minute."

"No problem."

As he took off his jacket and loosened his tie, he glanced around. The open floor plan was pretty cool and the higher ceiling meant the bedroom area was a loft accessed by a short flight of stairs.

She'd hung fabric from the ceiling so he couldn't see her but he heard her rustling around. His brain supplied images of her naked body and his dick took the hint and got hard.

Shit.

"There's beer in the fridge if you want one," she called down. "Or wine. Help yourself."

Sounded like a plan.

"Do you want one?" he called back.

"I'll have wine. There's an open bottle in the door, and glasses are in the cabinet next to the fridge."

He'd poured her a glass and had just opened his beer when he felt her come up behind him.

Turning, he held her glass out...and nearly dropped the damn thing.

He'd thought she looked amazing all dressed up but... *Holy shit.*

She'd pulled her hair back in a ponytail that hung over her shoulder, washed off all her makeup, and wore a sweatshirt with the neck cut out over a tank top and a pair of yoga pants that clung to every curve.

His fucking dick was gonna have the imprint of a zipper.

Damn, he wanted to grab that hair and wrap it around his hand then he'd pull her close and kiss her until she melted against him. Then he'd lay her out on the bed and put his mouth between her legs.

He'd wanted to go down on her two nights ago but they just hadn't gotten around to it.

Tonight, if she let him into her bed...

As if she could read his mind, her cheeks turned pink and she swallowed hard.

Her gaze flicked away from his as she took the wineglass out of his hand. "Thanks. I need this. I can't believe—" She cut off with a grimace. "Sorry. I don't mean to keep talking about what happened."

"I guess it's better he called it off at the last second. Otherwise, she'd be stuck with the dick."

Her eyebrows rose as her lips curved. "You know, you're absolutely right." Then she started to laugh. "I'm really glad she didn't marry that asshole. I just hope someday he realizes what he lost when he decided not to show up tonight. And I hope he regrets it for the rest of his life."

"You're tough. I'd hate to get on your bad side."

Her nose wrinkled as she took a sip of her wine. "I'm really not. My family all think I'm a marshmallow."

Looking at her now, he could see why. Soft. She looked so damn soft, he wanted to curl his hand around her neck and pull her against him. Put his mouth over hers and let himself sink into the kiss.

Something niggled at the back of his brain, but he ignored whatever it was trying to tell him.

Especially because she was looking into his eyes with a heat he recognized from the last time they'd been alone together.

His hand had moved before he realized. And when he grabbed the end of her ponytail and began to wind it around his palm, he knew why his lungs suddenly felt like he'd done a half hour of sprints.

Because he was going to be inside her again.

"I happen to love marshmallows."

Her lips parted and he took that as all the encouragement he needed.

Setting his beer on the counter, he took the wineglass out of her hand and set it beside his beer.

They could drink it warm later.

Right now...

He cupped her face in his hands, tilted her face up, and kissed her.

He expected her to meet him halfway. He didn't expect her to come at him with such unbridled lust.

But damn, he appreciated it. Her enthusiasm released his own constraints.

Wrapping his arms around her, now that his mouth had engaged hers in a deep, wet kiss, he pulled her against him. Her pelvis flattened against his, rubbing against his hard-on in a way that let him know she was with him all the way.

His dick got even harder and jerked against her as she wriggled against him.

Fuck.

He tore away from her mouth so he could look into her eyes. "Fast and hard first time. I promise I'll make you come. Slower the second time."

Her cheeks went red but her eyes burned as she nodded.

"Absolutely."

Her hands were at his waistband in the next second while his grabbed the sides of her yoga pants and shoved them down her hips. He covered her mouth again, his tongue sinking into her mouth and rubbing against hers.

Then she pulled down his zipper and wrapped her hands around his dick.

Holy fuck.

She immediately started to stroke him as she wriggled her hips while he pushed her stretchy pants farther down her legs.

He had them to her knees when they finally started to fall on their own and he could use his hands for other things.

Like petting her between her thighs.

Her sex lips were silky soft and wet. So fucking wet. He let his fingers play there for several seconds and heard her moan deep in her chest.

Her fingers paused, her lungs working hard as he flicked her clit. Shuddering, her fingers clutched around his cock.

Fuck, yes.

He pulled away, grabbed her shoulders then spun her around before she realized what he was doing. He caught a quick glimpse of her slack mouth and surprised eyes before he plastered himself against her back and grabbed her wrists, stretching her arms out in front of her.

"Hands on the counter. Hold on."

He wanted to beat his chest in victory when she obeyed him. When she bent forward at just the right angle to let him know she was on board with his plans.

Whipping out his wallet, he grabbed the condom, dropped the wallet, and covered his dick in record time.

Then he put one hand on her hip, rubbed the head of his cock between those wet lips while he slipped two fingers inside her.

Tight. Hot and wet.

His.

Pushing back onto his fingers, Bliss moaned again. "Shane. No teasing."

He wasn't. Hell, he didn't think he couldn't. Not now.

Taking one step closer, he angled his cock, and thrust home in one motion.

Her back bowed as she took him in. And he nearly lost it at the feel of her wrapped around him.

Running his hand along her spine, he began to move. Short, jerky thrusts that made her gasp, her hands clenching at the edge of the counter, her ass tilting up to take him deeper.

Yes. That's it. Christ, not gonna take long.

He hadn't been kidding. This time was gonna be fast. But she hadn't come yet.

Keeping up the pace, he leaned forward until he could reach around and get one finger on her clit.

Rubbing in time with his thrusts, he found what she liked fast enough and worked her until she gasped out his name and her pussy milked him as hard as a fist.

He managed to hold out for a few more seconds but the temptation was too much.

His cock jerked and he came with a grunt, one arm wrapped around her waist, the other on her shoulder.

Damn, he wanted to stay inside her for hours. She felt so fucking good.

And he was still hard.

Without warning, he pulled out, her moan an aphrodisiac that lit his blood on fire.

Before she could speak, he spun her around again and lifted her onto the ladderback stool next to her.

"Wha—"

He was on his knees and had his mouth on her before she could finish.

"Oh my god. *Shane.*"

His tongue licked through her folds, slick and puffy. Her hand pushed into his hair, gripping the strands tight as he flicked the tip of his tongue against her clit. Moaning when he pushed inside her, tilting her hips up so he could reach more of her.

She tasted fucking amazing and he couldn't stop tasting her, especially as she wriggled and panted and let him know exactly what she liked. Which seemed to be everything he was doing.

It made him cocky, made him hot as hell. He wanted her again.

Luckily, he'd stuck two condoms in his wallet.

Pulling away, he looked up to find her staring down at him with dazed eyes. He wanted to beat his chest like Tarzan. Standing, he kept his gaze locked on hers as he reached for this wallet.

Her gaze dipped to his crotch, her eyes widened before her lips curled in a smile as he covered himself again.

But she said nothing until he finished with the condom and lifted her off the chair.

Then she swallowed hard. "Shane."

He didn't say anything, just let her slide down until his cock hit her mound. It only took a little adjustment for him to have her right where he needed her.

The tip split her sex lips and he let her sink onto his cock, filling her.

"Fuck, yes," he muttered. "So hot."

Her hands slid into his hair and her lips clung to his as he moved her up and down his cock. Her rounded ass against his palms made his heart pound harder, and every time he let her slide down his cock, she sighed into his mouth.

And he couldn't get enough.

He wanted to feel her pussy clinging to him all fucking night. Would stand here and hold her until his arms gave out but he wouldn't let her fall. He'd never let her fall.

Heaven. Absolute heaven.

———

"REMEMBER what we've been working on, Shane. Cut down on those corners. Lock up that five hole. Get out of your head and don't overthink. Eyes on the puck and keep your crease clear."

Shane nodded at each of his goalie coach's points, making sure Paul Collins knew he was listening even as he went through his pre-ice routine.

To his surprise, he was the starting goalie for tonight's game. Coach was giving him this shot to prove to himself and his team that he deserved it and he wasn't going to screw it up.

He'd already checked his stick and made sure his catcher and blocker were in good shape. Same with his helmet.

He had a system and god forbid anyone fucked with his system before a game.

Standing at the front of the line, where he'd been most of the season, Shane allowed himself five seconds to think about Bliss in the crowd. To let himself remember the scorching sex they'd had Christmas Eve.

Then he shoved it all back into that box where he kept everything that wasn't hockey.

He'd deliberately not asked where her seats were located when he'd requested them to be left at Will Call. He didn't want to know.

"And Shane?"

He turned his full attention back to the coach, blocking out everything else. It was almost time to head down the hall to the ice.

"Don't be so focused on the outcome. Handle each moment as it happens. Don't try to think too far ahead."

Yeah. He could do that.

Deep breath.

The music hit his cue and he started walking, vaguely hearing the other guys behind him.

But he knew they were there. Knew they had faith in him to see them through the night. And knew they had a damn good team.

His skates hit the ice to the cheers of the fans. He heard the cowbells from the crew directly behind him, heard the chant from the group to the right of his net.

As always, he took a lap around, tapped his blade on the blue line as he passed by then skated straight for his net.

This was his ice. His net. His game.

He'd show everyone he was worthy of it.

SIX

Two months later

"That was a great game, Lissy. Thanks for bringing me. Are we going to meet Shane now?"

Mike hadn't stopped talking all night, at least not since they'd taken their seats in the section just off center ice.

She'd been a little worried the other people sitting around them would get frustrated with the constant chatter. But she'd realized after about five minutes that their seats were in the middle of a large group of season ticket holders—who'd been just as talkative as her brother. And as friendly.

They'd set her at ease immediately and that had allowed her to enjoy the game.

And it had been a great game. The Redtails had scored four goals against the other team, which had only scored once.

Shane had played a great game.

For the past two months, she'd been at every home game. Sometimes she brought her nephew, Dillon. Sometimes she brought a girlfriend. Shane never asked but he made sure she had two tickets.

And at every game, she watched Shane improve.

Not that he won every game. He had a couple pretty brutal losses. But those were few and far between. And he was now on a five-game winning streak.

She didn't kid herself into believing she had anything to do with it, except allow Shane to use sex to get out of his head between games and blow off steam. And make her moan his name as she came, sometimes twice a night.

Just thinking about last night made her blush and breathe a little heavier. But not only because of the sex.

For these past eight weeks, they'd kept things casual. She didn't go downstairs to meet him after the games. They didn't spend every night together. They couldn't, simply because he'd been on the road for probably four of those weeks.

But when they did spend the night together, it was all night. And for the past two weeks, they'd spent more nights together than they had apart. Amazingly, no one but Shane's roommate CJ knew just how much time they spent together.

Then last night, Shane had asked, almost too casually, if she wanted to get something to eat after the game today.

She'd taken a few seconds to think through the buzzing in her head before answering. "Sure" she'd said in the most nonchalant way she could.

So today, for the first time, she'd brought Mike. Because

Shane had changed the unspoken rules of their affair without discussing them with her first.

So she'd brought Mike.

But not because introducing Shane to her brother was a test. One a lot of guys failed.

No, that definitely wasn't why she'd brought Mike.

Now, she turned to Mike with a smile. "Yep. Shane's going to meet us and then we're going to go to dinner." She looked around to make sure they had everything. Mike was notoriously forgetful, especially when he was excited. "We have to go downstairs now."

Mike kept up a steady flow of conversation as they made their way to the stairs Shane had told her about and gave their names to the guard. After checking them off his list, he nodded and waved them down.

Heading down the stairs felt like getting a peek behind the curtain, and she couldn't help but be a little excited.

When they reached the bottom of the stairs, she noticed pockets of people standing around.

Several other girls her age stood in a cluster, all of them checking their phones and talking without looking at each other. Players' girlfriends, she assumed. A girl closer to her age leaned against the wall, gently rocking a baby carriage, alternating her gaze between the baby and the hallway, where Bliss assumed the guys would appear.

A couple who looked like parents talked quietly at the mouth of the hall, and a trio of younger guys leaned against the opposite wall from the new mother, laughing at something and shaking their heads.

Mike's conversation had stalled as they'd descended but now he couldn't contain his excitement.

"Is the locker room down here? Are we gonna meet all the guys? Is this where they keep that machine that cleans the ice? I wonder if you can drive that on the street."

Usually she didn't mind Mike's constant stream of questions. She'd had her entire life to get used to it, but she knew it could drive other people a little crazy.

The player's mom smiled at Mike then flashed Bliss a smile she recognized. The commiseration smile. The father didn't even glance their way. She'd bet they had a disabled family member, if not their own child then a niece or nephew or a sibling.

A few of the girls glanced their way but only one of them made eye contact and smiled. The others dismissed them immediately.

Mike never noticed. She'd learned to shrug it off over the years. Mike wasn't the one with the problem.

"Look, Lissy, they're coming."

He'd spoken a little louder than normal and she winced at the volume.

"Yeah, but you don't need to shout, buddy. I can hear you."

Mike made a face. "Sorry." Then he pointed toward the hall. "Is that Shane?"

"Not yet. He's got a lot of equipment to take care of. He'll probably be one of the last guys out. Let's just wait over here out of the way."

The guys trickled out a few at a time. Several left together, a few paired off with the girls and headed out. Finally Shane and another player walked out together.

He caught sight of her right away and his grin made her body flush with heat.

What the hell do you think you're doing, introducing your brother to him?

Good question.

His gaze cut to her side, to Mike, and his grin faltered, but only for a second, then it actually seemed to widen.

"Hey." Shane stuck his hand out to her brother. "I'm Shane."

Mike lit up and his smile stretched until she thought his lips would crack.

"Hey, Shane. I'm Mike. I'm Lissy's brother. Great game. It was so much fun..."

As Mike continued to ramble on, Shane kept eye contact and managed to keep up with Mike's conversation. And she realized, right then, that she could be in really deep trouble.

Shane was the kind of guy a girl wanted to keep. But he'd leave Reading one day. And she couldn't.

No, not couldn't leave. She *wouldn't*. If she left...

Mike turned to her with a smile that made her heart ache. For all of Mike's developmental delays, the one thing he had no trouble with was sensing insincerity in others. He'd been the first to realize her ex hadn't been the decent guy he seemed to be.

No one had noticed Mike's reticence whenever Rich had been around. Probably because Rich hadn't been around Mike often. Looking back, she blamed herself for not seeing the warning signs.

But she'd been blinded by Rich's smile and by how much attention he'd paid to her. Luckily, she'd gotten out of the relationship before he'd managed to isolate her from her family and friends and hijack her life.

It'd taken her six months and, finally, the threat of a restraining order to get him to leave her alone.

She'd blamed herself for being gullible and letting that man into her life. And even though she knew, absolutely *knew* Shane was nothing like her ex, there was always the fear that she was missing something.

All because of one asshole.

Which Shane *definitely* was not.

Continuing his conversation with Mike, Shane got them moving toward the door.

Just before they left the building, Shane grabbed her hand, lacing their fingers together.

Tightening her own fingers around his, she returned the quick grin Shane gave her over his shoulder.

Her heart flip-flopped in her chest.

And she realized she might've made a huge error in judgment.

———

"SO, your brother. He's a nice guy."

Shane kept his eyes on Bliss as she walked through her apartment, setting her purse on the counter by the small kitchen then setting her coat on one of the chairs at the island.

"He is." She smiled over her shoulder at him. "One of the best I know."

"Was he in an accident or was he born disabled?"

She shook her head, her smile dimming a little as he walked closer. "He developed normally until he was around eighteen months old. And then my mom noticed certain things he wasn't doing. By that time, she was pregnant with me. All we know is, it's not genetic."

When he reached the counter he stopped a few inches away from where she stood, back straight and her eyes sharp on his.

He knew tonight had been a test. Knew instinctively that she didn't introduce Mike to most of the men she dated. And he knew that because Mike had told him when Bliss had gone to the restroom during dinner.

"He seems...pretty self-aware."

Nodding, her smile reappeared. "Sometimes I think he's the smartest person I know. There's no pretense with Mike. What you see is what you get. He's definitely the sweetest person I know. And he's a great judge of character."

Something about the way she said that pinged his radar.

Since the wedding that wasn't, he'd realized that despite her openness, she had a wall around her heart. A wall she only seemed to let her family behind.

He didn't know why the wall was there but he could guess. She'd been hurt before. Probably pretty badly.

And if he wanted to get closer to her, he'd have to break through that wall.

The question was, did he want to?

He'd thought he'd known the answer.

Yesterday, that answer had been no. This affair was supposed to be fun. Not a lifetime commitment. Hot while it lasted but over and done when it'd run its course.

And yet...

He'd asked her to go to dinner with him tonight. And she'd brought her brother.

"Shane?" She frowned up at him. "Is everything okay?"

It had been.

Until last night when he'd realized he wanted to take her out after the game. He'd wanted to see her waiting in the hall for him.

And he'd wondered what it would be like seeing her there every night. No matter what arena he was playing in, what city, what state. He wanted her face to be the first thing he saw after a game.

He shook his head.

Shit.

"Shane?" Her head cocked to the side. "What's wrong?"

He shook his head. "How long has Mike lived next door?"

Her smile popped out again. "Almost a year. He's done better than anyone expected him to. I mean, I knew he'd be fine but my parents...they were worried."

"You make sure he's okay, don't you?"

She shrugged like it was nothing. "Of course. That's what family's for. I can't imagine being so far away from them all the time. Do you miss your family?"

He nodded. "But I know they're just a phone call away if I need them."

Her chin lifted slightly. "I like knowing mine are twenty minutes away."

He leaned his hip against the counter and watched her take a deep breath, as if his nearness affected her.

Good to know.

"Don't you want to travel?" he asked. "Get out and see the world?"

"Sure. Some day."

"If I don't get called up next year, I've given some thought to playing overseas."

She blinked. "Really? I guess... I didn't realize that was an option. I mean, I'd love to travel but being away from my family that long... How long do you go for?"

"The seasons are shorter over there and you play fewer games but at least seven, eight months."

He saw her search for an appropriate response, saw how she forced a smile when she realized he was watching her.

"Sounds like a great opportunity, especially if you like to travel."

"And you don't?"

Her smile turned bittersweet. "Sure. Some day. But right now, I've got a job and an apartment and bills to pay."

Ties he wasn't sure she'd ever want to break.

Maybe that's a sign you're getting in over your head.

And maybe it was time he started facing his own problems instead of making new ones with a girl who was never meant to be anything more than a distraction.

He was getting his game back on track. The team was close to clinching a playoff spot. The parent club's goalie coach had been down to work with him and Nate a couple times in the past month and had seemed happy with what he saw.

Now was not the time to get hung up on a hometown girl.

And what if you're already hung up?

"Shane?"

He snapped back to attention. Damn it. He'd fucked this up. Like, seriously screwed their no-strings affair to the point that he didn't have a clue how to fix it.

But he knew one thing.

Reaching out, he curled his hand around her neck, brought her close, and kissed her until neither of them were thinking straight.

When he pulled away, finally needing to breathe, he made sure she was looking at him before he said, "I hope you got enough sleep last night, babe. Because I don't think you're going to get any tonight."

She didn't say anything but she got that look in her eyes, the one that said she'd just accepted his challenge.

Putting her hand over his hard-on, she made sure he maintained eye contact as she went to her knees in front of him.

And proceeded to show him exactly why she had him tied around her little finger.

———

"CONRAD. COACH WANTS YOU."

Shane's head snapped up as Assistant Coach Novak's voice punched through the noise in the locker room.

The guys were stoked. Jake had scored the only goal of tonight's game, and Shane had had his first AHL shut-out. His face hurt from grinning but he wasn't about to stop.

The Redtails were going to clinch a playoff spot. He could practically taste it.

The guys planned to go to Third and Spruce to celebrate and he would be there.

And he didn't want to go alone. He wanted Bliss with him.

The problem was he didn't know if he should ask her. He hadn't seen her since the last game, when they'd gone out to eat with her brother.

And where she'd blown his fucking mind when she'd gone down on him.

The team had been on a five-game road trip, so they'd been gone most of two weeks.

They'd texted and talked a couple of times but things had felt different. She'd seemed distant. Like she was pulling away.

Fuck.

"Be there in a minute," he shouted back and watched Novak nod before disappearing out the door.

He didn't know what Coach wanted, but the trade deadline had passed so he didn't figure he was going anywhere. Especially not after tonight's game. He'd been in the zone. Focused. Prepared. He'd lived up to his nickname, Brick Wall.

He'd already taken a shower so he only needed to pull on his clothes and shove his wet hair out of his face when he walked to the office.

And froze in the doorway when he saw Mark Arrons, the team's GM, in addition to the coach.

"Shane. Come in." Coach motioned him forward. "Close the door."

He followed orders without a word but his heart pounded against his ribs. "Hey. What's up?"

When Mark started to smile, Shane began to breathe again.

"Just got off the phone with Coach Angstadt. You need to be in

Philly tomorrow morning. Gragnani's hurt. You're backing up Stanton in tomorrow's game. Congratulations, Shane."

Two thoughts flashed through his head.

Holy shit was the first.

This was the call he'd been dreaming about since he'd been old enough to know what the NHL was.

The second... *Fuck, I don't want to leave my team.*

Snapping out of his thoughts, he took Mark's hand then shook Coach Scott's.

"Thank you. Do you know how long I'll be up?"

Coach started to grin. "Honestly, I don't. I only know Gragnani's injury is lower body. You could be up for one game, could be up for a few weeks. No way to know."

Weeks? Shit. "Yes, sir."

"You'll probably be riding the bench the entire time but take it all in. Listen. Learn. Watch. Even if you don't get to play, it's a chance to show your commitment. When you come back, I expect you to be that much better. Good luck."

"Thank you, sir."

Coach clapped him on the shoulder. "Now go out and celebrate. You played a damn good game tonight. Just don't be late for morning skate."

———

BLISS KNEW by the look on Shane's face. Something had changed.

She hadn't seen him for two weeks and she tried to tell herself it hadn't mattered.

Liar.

Swallowing hard, she sucked in a breath and forced a smile.

When he reached for her in the arena hall, she went into his arms immediately, hugging him tight before stepping away.

And if he didn't release her right away... Well, she had to be wrong.

"You were amazing tonight. Congratulations."

"Thanks. I felt...pretty damn good."

And he'd felt pretty damn good pressed against her. But something was up.

"Hey," he said. "Can we talk for a second?"

Her chest felt like someone had just stuck her in a vise and started to crank.

No, she refused to let herself get worked up over something she'd known was coming.

And this was it. She could sense it. He was going to tell her he didn't want to see her anymore. That the team had to come first and he needed to focus on the playoffs and that he didn't have room for her. Not now.

And she'd nod and smile and say she understood completely. Because she did. She'd known this relationship was going nowhere when they'd started. She hadn't let herself get involved so she wouldn't be devastated.

"Sure. Do you want to...?" She pointed to a quiet corner away from the other girlfriends.

"Yeah. That's good."

Putting his hand on her elbow, he drew her deeper into the hallway, until the only sound she could hear was the hum of the cooling units.

Then they stopped and she looked up.

And the smile on his face stole her breath.

"I got called up. I have to be in Philly for morning skate then I'm backing up Stanton for the game."

Time froze for one very short second while she thought about those simple words.

I got called up.

She blinked and sucked in a breath she hoped he'd interpret as surprise. Because it was. But it was a whole lot more.

And even as her smile came naturally, she couldn't help but feel as if she'd been kicked.

"Oh my god. Shane. That's wonderful."

And it was. It was amazing.

She wrapped her arms around his shoulders and hugged him tight. And when his arms came around her and clung, she knew why she felt like she was losing him.

Because this felt like goodbye.

Drawing back, she kept her smile pinned in place, though she didn't have to force it.

She was so damn happy for him. And so miserably sorry for herself.

Which totally sucked. She'd known this affair had an expiration date. She just hadn't expected it to be before the end of the season.

Stupid.

"So when do you leave?"

"I have to be in Philly tomorrow for the morning skate then I'll be on the bench for the game. I won't play unless something happens to Stanton. I probably won't see any ice time during the game but it's a chance for me to practice with the team, get to know the coaches a little better. I know it won't be permanent, at least not now. I mean, I really want to be back for the next game here. As it stands now, the Colonials aren't going to make the playoffs so I'd probably be back anyway but..."

"This is your team." She understood. At least, she understood him. How he thought. In the short time they'd been together, she'd learned to read him remarkably well.

Hell, a danger sign should've been flashing over his head.

Can't fall apart now.

That wasn't the deal she'd made herself. It'd been fun. That's all. They hadn't made promises, had never spoken about what happened after the season. For all she knew, he hadn't even considered it. Just figured they'd go their own separate ways.

He nodded. "Yeah. This is my team. I think we're gonna go all the way to the Calder Cup this year."

"Then you need to go celebrate with the team."

His gaze narrowed. "I want you there."

Her heart melted at his insistence. "Of course. Are you ready to go?"

"Yeah. I told the rest of the guys we'd meet them at the bar."

She brightened her smile. "Then let's go and have a good time."

He leaned in to kiss her, taking her a little off guard and taking her breath away.

"Always do with you."

Her heart stuttered but she refused to give in to the ache that wanted to bloom.

He'd never been hers to keep. She had to start letting him go.

Now.

———

SHANE STROKED inside her with that steady intoxication she was afraid she'd grown addicted to.

"Faster. Shane, please."

"No fucking way." If possible, he slowed even more. "You're gonna come again."

Considering he'd already made her come twice in the past fifteen minutes, she knew it wasn't an idle boast.

Sometimes, all it took for him to push her over the edge was a couple of words spoken in that deep, gruff way he had when he was inside her.

Digging her fingernails into his shoulders, she scraped them down his back, eliciting a groan but no increase in his rhythm.

The man's patience exhausted her. And his stamina... She might as well give in and admit defeat.

But not just yet.

Turning her head, she bit at his neck, a nip that made her hunger for more.

"*Fuck.*"

His hips pushed forward, pressing his cock deeper inside and making her thighs tighten against his side.

Moaning, she bit him again, this time on his chin. He took the hint and bent his head to kiss her.

His mouth sealed over hers, stealing her breath as his tongue slid against hers, coaxing her to play with him.

Overwhelmed by sensation, she broke apart on his next thrust as he pressed against her clit.

As she squeezed around him, she felt his cock flex and throb deep inside her.

With a groan, he bent until their foreheads touched and stayed there for several seconds, breathing heavily.

When he finally seemed to catch his breath, he rolled to the side, taking her with him until she lay on his chest. His softening cock remained inside her, as if her body was unwilling to give up any part of him.

Spread across him, she only wanted to stay there for the rest of the night.

"I should go," she said instead. "You need to be up early. You can't be late tomorrow."

He stayed silent for a few more seconds. "Stay."

How could he ask that?

Blinking away the hot tears that popped into her eyes, she pressed a kiss to his left pec and forced a smile, even though she wasn't sure he could see it. "I can't. You need to get a decent night's sleep. Tomorrow's a big day for you."

"It's not like I'm gonna be playing. The only time I'll see the ice'll be at morning skate and warm-ups. Then I'll be on the bench for the entire game."

"And you know it doesn't matter. You need to make a good impression and you won't if you'll be distracted by me all night."

Now she did look up, forcing herself to smile and hoping he didn't see the nerves behind it in the dark. Then, because she couldn't help herself, she rubbed her nose against his then pressed her lips to his for a quick kiss.

With a sigh she didn't have to feign, she rolled to the side and slid off the side of the bed, grabbing her underwear from the chair next to the door.

As she dressed, she felt his gaze on her.

"I should be back day after tomorrow," he said. "Thursday. We've got a game Friday. I'll leave tickets for you and Mike."

"Sounds good."

Even though she probably wouldn't claim them. Something would come up. She'd make sure of it.

"Bliss."

Shane was on his knees and leaning forward to catch her arm before she could get away.

"You'll watch the game tomorrow night?"

Because he sounded as if he didn't think she would, she turned, cupping his jaw in her hand and rubbing her thumb over the scruff he hadn't shaved in days. She had to admit she liked it.

"Of course I'll be watching. I wouldn't miss it for anything."

"And I'll see you when I get back."

She held her smile. "Yep."

Because she couldn't help herself, she leaned in to kiss him again.

"Good luck tomorrow, even though you don't need it. You wouldn't have gotten the call if they didn't already know how good you are."

In the dim light, she could just see the curve of his lips as she stepped away from the bed.

"Have fun, Shane. And don't forget to breathe."

———

SHANE WOKE the next morning with a knot in his gut and the most incredible urge to call Bliss and tell her he wanted her to come with him to Philly.

Which was stupid. She had to work and he needed no distractions.

He ate, checked his gear twice, loaded everything into his truck then went back inside to make sure he hadn't forgotten anything.

He knew he hadn't but he needed to be sure.

He was at the front door, ready to head out with a second water bottle in his hand when he heard CJ.

"Hey, man. Kick some ass today."

CJ stood in the doorway to his room, boxer shorts barely covering his junk, hair standing up all over the place on one side and flat on the other.

"Not gonna play, you know that. But thanks."

"Yeah, I know. But still. And man, don't take this the wrong, but I hope like hell they send you back for the weekend."

Nodding, he held out his hand and waited for CJ to walk over and bump his knuckles.

"Did you actually set your alarm to see me before I left?"

CJ grimaced and Shane thought he might've actually blushed.

"Fuck you."

"Dude. I'm touched."

"Uh huh. Have fun. I'll see you when you get back."

Shane turned back to the door but before he left, CJ said, "Wait."

"What's up?"

"Is Bliss in your room? I mean, I don't want her to, you know, catch a glimpse of me and throw you over."

Fuck. "Nah, you're safe. She went home last night. Before you stumbled in."

CJ's eyes narrowed but he didn't say anything.

"All right. Safe travels, man. And don't let shit fuck with your head."

Shane left with a smile on his face but it vanished minutes later.

His stomach ground in on itself as nerves started to hit him but he pulled on his years of training to steady himself.

By the time he reached the team's training facility in northeast Philly, he had himself under control.

This was what he'd been working for since he was five.

Since he'd been down for pre-season training camp, he knew where to park. After he'd checked in with the guard, he grabbed his gear from the back of the truck and headed for the locker room.

He wasn't the first one there.

"Conrad. Nice to see you. How's it going?"

Stanton turned away from his locker, where he'd been pulling up his compression pants, and came forward with a smile and his hand out.

Shane took it with a nod. "Not bad."

"The Reds are having a hell of a year and so are you. Congrats."

At six-three, Stanton was an inch shorter than Shane but the guy had almost twenty pounds on him, all of it muscle. He'd come by his nickname Tank for his methodical play.

"Thanks. The team's come together this year. We're looking forward to the playoffs."

Stanton's grin turned lopsided. "Gonna suck if you're stuck up here riding the bench. Between you and me, Gragnani's injury's not gonna keep him out longer than tonight so you'll be back. He's being a pussy about pulling a muscle in his leg." Stanton shook his head. "But you didn't hear that from me. Christ, the guy's nearly thirty-three. Guess I should cut him some slack."

Shane nodded, smiling. "Thanks for the heads-up."

"No problem." Stanton turned back to his locker and began pulling on his pads. "When you get back, tell Coach Scott I said hello."

That's right. Stanton had been the Redtails' top goalie before being called up to the Colonials two years ago.

"I will."

"Good." A voice came from the door. "You're here early. You and me are gonna spend a little time together this morning. I caught up on your tapes last night. Got a few things to go over. Get dressed and I'll see you on the ice."

Shane turned to see goalie coach Gary Ellis. The five-foot-eight bulldog had produced some of the best net minders in the league. A former goalie, he had a Stanley Cup ring and a reputation for being gruff, uncompromising, and arguably one of the best ever.

Then he disappeared back into the hall.

And Shane took a deep breath. And another.

Then he started to shed his clothes so he could get ready for his first practice in the NHL.

———

"LISSY, hurry up, the game's starting!"

"I'm coming, Mike. And my apartment's not that big. You don't have to yell. Besides, the game doesn't start for another half hour."

"Yeah, but they're talking about the players and they might say something about Shane."

Her heart fluttered at the thought. She was so damn excited for him.

And so damn sorry for herself. Something she would never admit to anyone else.

As she sat next to her brother on her couch in front of the TV, listening to Mike's almost breathless chatter about everything from how the Redtails' uniforms used the same colors as the Colonials to the way the announcers were dressed.

"And with Gragnani out, backing up Stanton tonight will be Shane Conrad, brought up this morning from the AHL Reading Redtails."

As Mike let out a whoop, Bliss turned up the volume to make sure they didn't miss anything.

"Conrad's been having a great year, but I doubt we'll get to see him at all tonight as Stanton will be in net..."

And that was all they heard about Shane. But she couldn't help the tears that pooled in her eyes hearing his name. She actually had to take a deep breath and hoped like hell that Mike wouldn't look over and see her trying to brush the tears away.

Damn it. She'd broken her own damn rule.

That whole not-getting-involved thing? Hadn't really worked, had it?

Now she had no one to blame but herself.

And what if he's the one?

She slid a glance at Mike. What happened if she and Shane actually did try to make a relationship work? His career might take him anywhere in North America. What happened to her when he got called up? If they traded him to Winnipeg or Los Angeles or Dallas?

Did she give up her apartment, her job, her life, and follow him?

And aren't you jumping ahead of yourself? The guy hasn't even asked you to move in with him, much less spend the rest of your life with him.

And was that part of the problem? Is that what she expected him to do? Is it what she wanted?

Maybe she needed to figure that out for herself first.

———

"HEY, Bliss. I'll be home tonight. I missed you. What are you doing for dinner? I'd really like to see you."

Bliss had missed Shane's call. She'd been with a customer and hadn't been able to get to her phone. That customer had been there until fifteen minutes after closing and Bliss had been late for her dinner date.

Which didn't explain why she hadn't texted him back last night. Oh, she'd congratulated him after the game. She'd called and left him a message right after the game. When she knew he'd still be in the locker room and unable to answer his phone.

Coward.

But she hadn't responded to the call he'd left around ten-thirty last night. She could easily explain. She'd been in bed early. And she had been. And if she'd also maybe been trying not to cry, well, no one needed to know that.

Tonight, she had the perfect excuse. She was "out with friends" and if he was smart, he wouldn't interrupt. That was part of the guy handbook, wasn't it? Rule No. 1: Don't interrupt a girl when she's out with friends.

"Whoa. I know why I get blamed for resting bitch face, but I can't say I've ever seen that look on your face."

Faith lifted an eyebrow at her across the table at the Greek tavern down the street from the bridal salon.

Bliss sighed and took a sip of her wine. "I know. But can we wait for Sophie so I don't have to repeat myself? She and her dad should be done arguing in a minute."

Bliss had helped Sophie Tsoukalos, the tavern owner's daughter, find a dress for the tavern's grand opening a few months ago, and since then, Bliss stopped in for a glass of wine whenever she could to talk to Sophie. The other girl's sunny personality drew people to her like bears to honey.

The only person Sophie ever fought with was her dad, Spiro. They were arguing in the kitchen in Greek, which they did at least twice a day. That might've been an exaggeration but Bliss didn't think it was. And when it blew over, as it did in a matter of minutes, life went back to normal.

Bliss could never live like that. Sophie seemed to thrive on it.

"That bad, huh?"

Bliss winced, knowing her problems were nothing compared to Faith's, who'd made it perfectly clear if she caught even a whiff of pity from Bliss, she was leaving.

So she sighed again. "It's just—"

"I swear that man is going to have a coronary and my sisters will all blame me." Sophie pushed through the swinging door from the kitchen then hurried over to lean on the bar in front of Bliss and

Faith. Her long, dark hair fell over one shoulder, dark eyes wide and inquisitive. "Now, what's going on? I can tell you're not happy. What'd the man do?"

Bliss's nose wrinkled. "How do you know it's a man?"

Sophie rolled her eyes. "Oh please. That's definitely not your 'had to deal with bridezilla' face. That's definitely a 'man did me wrong' face. Spill it."

Bliss's expression crumbled. "Honestly? I think I'm the one that did him wrong. I need to break it off with Shane and I don't know how."

Sophie and Faith went totally silent, their expressions shocked.

"What? Why are you both looking at me like that?"

The other women exchanged a glance then Sophie reached across the bar and patted her on the hand.

"What did he do? He must've done something if you want to break it off. I mean...seriously, I thought you liked him. I mean, really liked him. Why would you want to break it off?"

"Because the season's going to end and he's going to leave. Maybe he'll be back next year. Maybe he won't. And I just can't follow him around like a groupie. I mean, I've got a job and an apartment and what would happen with Mike if I moved away? My life is here."

She looked up to find her friends staring at her with raised eyebrows.

So she pushed on. "And it's not like he asked me to give up everything and follow him all the hell over the place. I mean, he's probably just in it for the sex and when the season's over he'll dump me anyway. So if I dump him now, I'm saving him the hassle."

Sophie and Faith exchanged another glance before Faith said, "Sounds like you've given this a lot of thought."

Shrugging, Bliss avoided their gaze by taking another sip...okay, a gulp of wine. "Maybe. Maybe more than I should have."

Sophie reached beneath the bar for the wine and topped off Bliss's glass. "I didn't realize you'd gotten that serious."

Bliss frowned. "We're not. I mean... I don't... Oh hell." She closed her eyes and dropped her head. "I don't have a clue. I just know it's better to end it now before either of us gets too involved."

Faith huffed, wry amusement in her expression. "Yeah. *Before* you get too involved. I think you're past that point, hon. But you're probably not wrong. If you know you're going to end it, better to do it before you really get hurt."

Sophie looked between Bliss and Faith, shaking her head. "Wow, you two are enough to make me swear off relationships forever. And I get it. I mean, I get Faith's reason. I totally think you should castrate that bastard if you ever see the prick again," Sophie's statement was all the more shocking for the smile she had while speaking, "but Bliss...damn, what made you so cynical?"

Resting her hand on her cheek, she grimaced at Sophie. "I may have dated a guy who might have turned into an emotionally abusive asshole."

At Sophie's gasp, Bliss held up her hand. "In all fairness, he didn't start out that way. He had everyone fooled. Except my brother. Mike figured him out right away. It took me a little longer to realize but when I did, I got out."

And she hadn't had a serious relationship since. But that didn't mean she wasn't right about ending her relationship with Shane. It wasn't because she was scared. It was because it was the right thing to do.

Bullshit.

She wanted to tell that sarcastic little voice in her brain to go fuck itself but that might prove she really was wrong in the head.

And wrong about giving up Shane.

Shit.

"Well, I haven't met the guy, so I don't have a clue what he's like." Sophie acknowledged the group who pushed through the front door with a wave. "But Bliss, the way you talk about the guy...maybe you need to think this through a little more."

Sophie moved to seat the new party, leaving her and Faith alone.

"And what do you think?"

"I think all men are pricks who will cut your heart out." Faith shrugged. "But that's just me."

After a few second, Bliss nodded. "No, I'm right about this. Better to break it off now before it goes any further."

And hope she didn't regret the hell out of her decision later.

SEVEN

"Hi, Shane, sorry I didn't get back to you sooner. I've had a million things to do."

And apparently he wasn't one of them.

Shane nodded though he knew she couldn't see him. He also knew something was up.

He'd gotten a bad feeling in his gut two nights ago when she hadn't called back after the game. Yeah, she'd texted but he'd wanted to hear her voice.

And then yesterday, she'd blown him off again with a text.

Now she'd finally called and he realized he didn't actually want to talk to her. Because he knew what she was doing.

He just didn't know why. He had a few ideas but...

Damn it. His jaw clenched.

"I thought maybe we could get some dinner after the game tonight."

Silence. Then, "I don't think I can make the game tonight."

Goddammit. Was she really going to do this now?

He sucked in a breath. "Something wrong?"

Another pause. "No, nothing's wrong. I just...I can't make it tonight. Aunt Rosie and I are getting ready for a bridal show on Sunday and there's so much we need to do before then. And the shop's open tomorrow and of course we've got three fittings and a consultation with a new client. And Sunday's going to be crazy. One of the models backed out and if we can't find anyone, I'll have to step in which means altering the dress and... well, it's just crazy right now. I'm sure you understand. I mean, you've only got two weeks left before the playoffs and I know you're going to clinch a spot so you're going to be busy too and..."

She finally stopped to take a breath but he felt like he couldn't catch his.

"Bliss. What—"

"I just don't know when I'm going to be free." She rushed to cut him off. "And I'm not sure—"

"Bliss. Don't."

He wouldn't beg. No fucking way would he beg for her not to do this.

But...

Hell, everything she said was right. He was going to be busy. Making it to the playoffs had to come first. He knew he needed to concentrate on winning the Calder Cup. Hell, he should be thanking her for making this easy on him.

Except this didn't feel easy. It felt the exact opposite.

"I've had a really great time with you these past few months," Bliss pushed on like he hadn't said anything. "But I know your life is going to get crazy and I don't want to feel like I'm getting in the way."

"Have I ever said that? Have I ever even mentioned that?"

Another pause and then a deep breath. "We both knew this wasn't going to last."

"And what if that's not what I want?"

FOR A MOMENT, Bliss's heart rose into her throat.

An old memory, one from her former relationship rose up.

She'd made the decision to break up with her ex and she'd asked him to meet her at a restaurant to talk. A public space, where there was no way he would do anything...physically to her.

But the look in his eyes when she told him she was leaving him and she never wanted to see him again? That look had made her want to run. It had made every muscle in her body tense, ready to flee.

And she'd felt like she was going to be sick.

Like she felt now.

But now it was the thought that she'd lumped Shane into the same mold as her ex that made her ill.

Shane was nothing like that bastard. He was a decent guy. A great guy, actually.

And you're just throwing him away.

No. It was better to end this now before either of them really got hurt.

"I know you're going to have a great run in the playoffs."

"Wait—"

"And you've made a superfan out of Mike. But I really have to go. Good luck. With everything. And...bye."

THE LINE WENT dead and Shane took a second to look at the screen to make sure she'd actually hung up on him.

She had.

What the fuck just happened?

He felt like he'd gotten taken out by Rager Bolden, the league's biggest linesman. Shaking his head, he reached for his keys but stopped when the front door opened and CJ, Jake, and Lad stormed in.

"Shane!" CJ rushed him, grabbing around the shoulders and hugging him. "You cocksucker. You're back. We are *so* fucking happy to see you!"

Lad and Jake smacked him on the back hard enough to make him wince.

"How was that NHL bench?" Jake headed for the fridge. "Feel different on your ass?"

It took him a second to switch gears, to shove the hurt down and concentrate on his friends.

"Felt the same to me and I was on it all night."

Lad grabbed his shoulder and squeezed. "Yeah, but you got the call."

For the next fifteen minutes, Shane answered a barrage of questions. Mostly from CJ. This was his first year playing in the AHL after spending two years in the ECHL. CJ might've been more excited than Shane about getting called up.

But even as he told the guys about his time in Philly, he couldn't stop thinking about Bliss.

Jake noticed his distraction first. His gaze narrowed as Shane talked about the strength of the shots.

When CJ would've asked another question, Jake held up his hand.

"What is wrong? Something is not right with you."

"Nothing." Shane shrugged. "Just tired. I took practice with the team this morning."

Jake wasn't buying it, and now Lad and CJ were looking more closely at him.

"No, that ain't it." CJ crossed his arms over his chest and leaned back against the kitchen counter. "What happened?"

Taking his beer, he headed for the sofa. Might as well be comfortable if they were going to cross-examine him.

"Nothing happened. Everything's fine. What'd I miss—"

"Why are you not going to see Bliss?"

Fucking Lad. The bastard could read other players like he had ESP.

"Because she doesn't want to see me. It's not a problem. With the playoffs coming up, I need to be focused. I don't need a woman fucking with my head."

The guys exchanged looks.

"Bullshit," said Lad and Jake in perfect unison.

CJ shook his head. "Damn. I don't get it. I thought she really liked you."

Shrugging, he sucked down more beer. "Guess not."

"That is bullshit." Lad cocked his head to the side. "What did you do?"

Shane frowned. "What the fuck? I didn't do anything."

"You must have done something." Lad exchanged a glance with Jake. "That girl had it bad for you."

Shrugging, Shane forced himself not to rub at the ache in his chest. "Obviously she didn't or she wouldn't have dumped me."

"This is not good." Lad looked at Jake. "We must do something."

"What? No." Shane shook his head. "Hell no. Just leave it."

"Oh, we definitely have to do something." Jake nodded. "We will help you with this."

Shane rolled his eyes. "Jesus...I don't need any fucking help. It's over."

Jake's gaze narrowed. "Can you honestly tell us you do not want her back?"

No. "Yes. I have more important things to focus on."

"Yes, I'm sure you do." Lad snorted. "Fine. So tell us more about the game."

Trying not to sigh in relief, Shane recounted everything he could remember.

And tried not to let Bliss totally dominate his thoughts.

———

THE TICKETS SHOWED up the next morning.

But not at her door.

No, they showed up at Mike's. And they didn't come from Shane.

"Lissy, look what Jake sent. Tickets for the game tonight. Can we go?"

Her heart pounding in her chest, she took the envelope, hating the fact that she'd almost wanted them to come from Shane. "How do you know they're from Jake?"

"He sent a note."

HEY, buddy. I hope you can make it. If you need a ride, just let me know. Jake.

DEFINITELY NOT SHANE'S HANDWRITING.

Damn it.

Not that she wanted it to be from Shane. She was glad he wasn't making this hard on her.

But she couldn't say no to Mike. Not when he looked at her with so much excitement.

"Sure. But Mike..."

She hadn't had a chance to tell him she'd broken up with Shane. She told herself it wasn't because she regretted her decision. She didn't. She'd done the right thing.

But...

Shit.

"Mike...Shane and I broke up."

The shock on her brother's face made her heart hurt. And her stomach clench.

He looked the way she still felt. And she'd been the one to break up.

Which had been for the best, damn it.

"Why? What happened?"

Yeah, what did happen?

She'd gotten scared, that's what'd happened.

But it was still for the best. Better to hurt a little now than be heartbroken later.

A little?

She wanted to tell herself to shut up but didn't want Mike to think she was talking to him.

Forcing a quick smile, she shook her head. "Nothing. It just wasn't going to work out between us."

Mike's head cocked to the side. "How do you know?"

She shrugged. "It's just wasn't. It's better this way."

Mike frowned hard. "Why?"

Because he would've left me anyway. "Sometimes relationships just don't work out."

"Was he..." Mike frowned even harder, "like your ex?"

"God, no! No, Mike. Shane is nothing like Rich."

"Then..." With a sigh, Mike shook his head. "I guess I just don't understand."

Christ, now she'd dragged her brother down into the dumps with her.

"There's really nothing to understand. It just wasn't going to work out."

After a few seconds, Mike finally nodded slowly. "Like me working at that restaurant. That's what the manager told me, that it wasn't going to work out. He didn't like working with me. So you didn't like Shane enough."

Blindsided, she went blank. The real reason the manager had fired Mike was because he was a prejudiced asshole and hadn't been comfortable around her brother.

"No, that's not it. I like Shane. It's just..."

"Complicated."

Looking into Mike's eyes, she saw an understanding she hadn't expected him to have. She shouldn't have been surprised, though. Her brother's brain functioned differently than most people but he was practically empathic when it came to reading people's feelings.

"Yeah. It's really complicated. Especially for me."

"Because of your ex."

She wanted to deny it but she wouldn't lie to Mike.

"Kind of. I just...don't want to be left behind when he moves on."

The truth rushed out but it finally felt good to admit it to someone who wouldn't judge her. It truly sucked that she knew it was her own screwed-up emotions that had pushed Shane away. It also sucked that she couldn't think of another way to handle it.

Because the truth still remained. He would eventually leave and she would stay. And nothing either of them could do would change that fact.

Mike reached for her hand and squeezed. "We don't have to go to the game."

"Of course we do. Jake wants you to come. And I know you want to go."

"But—"

"No buts. We'll have a good time."

Keep telling yourself that. Maybe you'll believe it in a year or so.

———

"HOLY SHIT, we fucking *destroyed* those fucking gerbils," CJ shouted as Shane walked into the locker room after taking a bow for being the first star of the game. "The Brick Wall lives!"

Shane smiled as teammates started to chant, "Brick! Brick! Brick!" and bumped gloves with Nate as he passed the other goalie on the way to his locker.

They'd clinched a playoff spot tonight with the win against the Maine Flying Foxes, whose mascot looked like the unfortunate mating of a chihuahua and a gerbil.

The game had been sweeter still because they'd played on home ice and the fans had gone crazy. The team had missed the playoffs the last couple of years so this was icing on the fucking cake.

"You played like a man possessed tonight, Conrad." Cary

smacked him on the back on his way to the showers. "Keep it up and we'll have that cup."

"Dude, you shut them *down*." Jake dropped onto the bench next to him and watched as Shane pulled off his gear. "Guess getting dumped was actually good for you, yes?"

Shaking off his blocker, Shane gave Jake the finger without bothering to look at him. He wasn't about to respond to that.

"You had a great game," Shane tossed over his shoulder. "Congrats."

"Ah, so we are still not discussing her. Okay. Yes, I did have a great game, thank you."

Shaking his head, Shane listened to the other guys on the team razz Jake about his almost nonexistent humility while managing to compliment him at the same time.

Thinking he was safe from any more of Jake's reminders of Bliss, he headed for the showers, where he stood under a scalding hot shower for at least five minutes.

It was part of his post-game ritual, which he'd let slide while he was with Bliss.

Should've been your first clue. Don't change the routine for a girl.

His dad had drilled that one into his head all through high school. Not that he'd been in danger of that, but it'd stuck with him through juniors and into his years in the ECHL.

But he'd done it for Bliss and not noticed any harm. In fact—

He shook his head. Didn't. Matter. Not one fucking bit because Bliss was gone.

And he was back to his routine and the team was winning and would continue to win.

"Hey, you heading straight home?" CJ stuck his head into the shower room, already showered and dressed. "I'm leaving now."

"Yeah, I'll be out in a few. Need a decent night's sleep before the game tomorrow."

They had another game against the Wolves tomorrow, and the other team would be out for payback.

"Okay. Oh, and just a heads-up. Bliss and Mike are in the hall. I'll make sure Jake gets them out before you come through."

His head shot up. "What the fuck?"

Justin Perry, the defenseman they'd just brought up from the ECHL after losing Joey Constantino to an injury last game, shot him a wary glance.

He knew he had a rep for being intense. Knew it was warranted. He also knew there was a fine line between intense and being an arrogant bastard. He'd always managed to walk it before. The tide could turn though.

Especially when he thought about Jake hitting on Bliss.

"No need to go psycho, dude. Jake sent the tickets to Mike. He didn't know Bliss would be here."

No fucking way did Jake not expect Mike to come without Bliss.

Bastard. Shane was gonna kill Jake. If he so much as laid a finger on her—

Shit. *Shit.*

Shane took a deep breath. That wasn't fair. He knew Jake and Mike had hit it off. Jake had a brother with Down syndrome, whom he missed more than he'd ever admit to anyone. Except to Shane, one drunken night a few months ago.

"Sorry." Shane shook his head. "Just...never mind. You don't have to do anything. I'm fine."

Shrugging, CJ waved. "Okay. See you at home."

CJ disappeared and Shane hung his head, letting the water pound against the suddenly tense muscles of his back.

It'd been three days since she'd told him she didn't want to see him again. Three days since he'd let her go without a fight.

Because she'd been right.

Their relationship had been going nowhere.

"Fuck."

"Uh, you okay?"

Justin shut off his shower and rubbed a towel over himself, carefully avoiding Shane's gaze.

Shane let out a big sigh. "Yeah. I'm fine. Good game tonight."

"Thanks. You too. It's good to be here."

Shane didn't want to be a dick but he had no interest in conversation. No, he was much more interested in what was going on in the hall.

"Glad to have you."

Luckily, the new guy didn't say anything else and walked away a second later. Leaving Shane alone in the showers.

He told himself he wasn't standing here just so he could avoid her. He was soaking his tight muscles.

Yeah, right.

With a muttered curse, he shut off the water, toweled off, and headed back to the locker room.

He glanced at the clock, figuring he'd give Jake another five minutes to say goodbye to Mike and Bliss.

And give himself another five minutes to tell himself he really didn't want to see her.

———

"DO YOU MIND, LISSY?"

Bliss smiled and shook her head. "Of course, I don't mind. Have fun."

Jake touched her on the shoulder. "We're just going to get something to eat at the West Reading Diner. We won't be out late. We have a game tomorrow. If you guys can make it, I'll make sure you've got tickets."

Mike's smile widened and she knew she couldn't say no. It was almost like they were ganging up on her. But she couldn't deny the friendship that had developed between Mike and Jake. She'd be suspicious of Jake's motives if she hadn't seen the way he treated Mike. There was no way she was going to throw up roadblocks to their friendship.

"I can get the bus in if you don't want to come tomorrow, Lis."

Because she was weak, she said, "No, I've got nothing going on. I can bring you."

Jake nodded, his expression serious, but she could've sworn he was hiding a smile.

And then her brain fuzzed over. Because Shane walked out of the locker room.

Damn it. She'd wanted to be gone before he got out. He was typically one of the last guys to leave.

And her heart hurt to look at him because... Oh my god, the man took her breath away.

Tall and broad, dressed in the gray suit that fit him like a glove and the blue shirt that matched his eyes. He hadn't bothered with his tie, which she was sure he had rolled up in his pocket.

His hair was still wet and he'd brushed it back from his face, which still bore the marks from his mask.

She had the opposing urges to run in the other direction and brush her fingers across those marks.

God, she'd been so stupid. She'd fallen for him. Hard. And she had no one to blame but herself.

As he came closer, she found herself sucking in a breath and holding it.

Which was so stupid because he barely nodded at her. He did stop to say hi to Mike and shake his hand but he left seconds later.

Her heart felt like he'd taken a knife and sliced right through it.

Still think giving him up was a good idea?

Absolutely. Because if it hurt this much after only a couple of months of dating, just think how much worse it would be after five or six months. Or a year.

Maybe...

She turned to watch him leave. Couldn't help herself. Just like she'd been unable to take her eyes off him throughout the entire game.

Why are you torturing yourself?

Because she was an idiot. But that didn't mean she wasn't right.

———

"JESUS, Shane, you're on fire. Dude, I don't know what the fuck you took but whatever it is, I want some."

Shane gave Nicky Thompson an acknowledging grin over his shoulder. The rookie forward from Ottawa had been a great addition to the team mid-season. The kid wouldn't turn twenty-one for another six months but he played like a ten-year pro.

"That's what happens when you don't have a life." Lad was already on his way to the showers after their final game of the season. "The Brick Wall eats, sleeps, and breathes hockey, son. Take notes."

Shane had a response on the tip of his tongue, one that would've made everyone laugh. But he just couldn't come up with the energy to care.

So he acknowledged the catcalls from the rest of the guys with a wave but stayed silent as he stripped off his gear.

The noise of the locker room faded in and out as the guys moved from here to the showers and back. Coach had already told him the local reporter and the AP stringer wanted to talk to him so he hustled. He knew the writers would wait however long it took, but he hated to keep them waiting. They had deadlines and he...would go home to a lonely bed and try to sleep without dreaming about Bliss.

Shit.

When he got out of the shower, only a few guys remained, including Jake.

"You should probably not go into the green room looking like you just ate puppies and kittens for dinner. You'll scare the pretty blonde with the tape recorder. New AP stringer. Much better-looking than the old dude they used to send."

Jake was already dressed as Shane hung the last of his equipment and wrapped a towel around his waist.

Shane spared him a glance, noting the bag he held in his hands. "You going out?"

"Yes. Mike and I are going to get some dinner and then I will meet the guys at that bar in West Reading. The one that's always empty. I can never remember its name."

Jake couldn't remember its name because it had some weird Native American spelling that no one but people from the area could pronounce properly.

"You want to meet us there?" Jake asked.

Shane automatically shook his head. "I'm tired. Need to get some sleep."

Jake didn't move but he didn't say anything either. Most of the other guys had already left.

"What?" Shane shot Jake a glance, frowning. "What's wrong?"

"You are." Jake crossed his arms over his chest, looking like he was digging in for a fight. "You need to snap out of this."

"Snap out of what? Christ, I'm playing the best I've played in years."

"I am not arguing with that. But Shane, you are miserable. Everyone can see it. No one wants to say anything because you are playing amazing. But man, there's more to life than hockey. Even during the playoffs. I mean, what good is winning if you sleep alone every night?"

"Jesus, Jake. Just leave it the hell alone."

Shane yanked his undershirt over his head...and ripped the damn neckline out.

The few guys left in the locker room gave him sidelong glances but quickly looked away again.

"Fuck."

Jake rocked back on his heels, his expression unchanged as Shane finished dressing...without the t-shirt.

"She misses you, too. And the way you're playing... Well, she's sure she made the right decision."

Frustration raged through him. "So what? I'm supposed to lose a few games so she'll come back to me? That's the stupidest fucking thing—"

"Damn, you are blind." Jake shook his head. "You only need to show her how much you love her. And play like you're playing now. Show her you can do both."

How much you love her.

Were his feelings that fucking obvious? They must be if Jake had picked up on them. But no way in hell was he about to admit it.

"Jake...Jesus."

"No, I am not. But I do know what I'm talking about. You have to make sure you show her you are worth it. And then you have to be."

EIGHT

The flowers showed up at the shop Monday. A bouquet of daisies.

No card. Just two tickets to the first playoff game. The Redtails opened at home this Saturday. Mike already had his ticket. Jake had hooked him up. Mike had asked if she wanted to go with him, that he would ask Jake for another ticket. She said no. She had to. It was just too hard to see Shane.

Mike didn't need her to get to the games. He was perfectly capable of getting there himself.

That didn't mean she didn't want to go.

"Ooh, Bliss, honey. Those are beautiful. Got a new beau I haven't heard about?"

Bliss gave her Aunt Rosie a distracted smile. "No. I'm pretty sure they're from Shane."

"Oh. Did you two get back together?"

"No. I haven't seen him since we...since I broke up with him."

"So why the flowers?"

"There're tickets to the first playoff game."

"Ah. The flowers are beautiful. And there's so many of them."

Rosie was right. There were fifteen total.

"That's an odd number." Rosie looked at her with a frown, her short dark hair swinging around her face. "Does the number mean anything?"

Bliss shook her head. "Not that I can think of."

"Huh. Well, obviously it means something to Shane."

Rosie was right. It did mean something to Shane. She just wasn't sure what and what it might have to do with her.

"So are you going to the game?" Rosie asked.

"I don't know."

With a sigh, Rosie finished hanging a dress for a first fitting later this morning before she turned to Bliss. "Honey, I know you said you don't want to talk about it but...you know you can tell me anything, right? It seemed like you really liked Shane. Did he do something? Was he—"

"No. No, it was nothing Shane did. It was me."

Rosie reached across the counter and patted Bliss on the hand. "Tell me, hon. You've been walking around here like a ghost for the past few weeks. What happened?"

She shook her head. "Nothing happened. I just realized I needed to break it off before..." She sighed. "Before he leaves. He's eventually going to move on. And I'll still be here."

"And why do you think you need to stay here?"

"My life's here. My job, my family."

Rosie made a face. "Oh, hon. You're smart enough to get a job anywhere. And your family will always be here for you. There's no reason you have to stay tied to this little corner of the world. I love working with you and you know you'll always have a job with me but I don't remember hearing you talk about wanting to run a bridal salon when you were young."

Nose wrinkling, Bliss shrugged. "I was always changing my mind about what I wanted to do when I was young. I went to college and got a business degree because..."

"Because what?"

Because she'd had no idea what she wanted to do with her life.

Except she'd known she needed to be able to support herself. Especially after she'd gotten herself untangled from her ex.

Had she been hiding here? Afraid to go out and do something else?

No, that wasn't it. She loved living here, in this town. Where her parents lived fifteen minutes away and her nieces and nephews ran to hug her when she babysat. Where she lived next door to her brother.

"Because I didn't know what else to do with myself."

Rosie humphed. "I don't believe that for a second. You're no little lost girl. Maybe you just haven't found what you want to do with your life yet but that doesn't mean you won't ever. And don't get me wrong. I'm not saying having a man will fix all your problems. I just don't want you to count them out of the equation totally. Especially one you really like."

"SO HAVE you figured out where she's sitting yet?"

Lad sat next to him on the bench, watching Shane lace his skates. His teammate had waited until Shane took out his earbuds before speaking. Everyone knew not to talk to him until he'd did.

The noise of the sold-out crowd reached them back in the locker room, stoking the players' excitement even higher.

The final series started tonight. They'd won the first series with a sweep. The second series had gone five games. The semifinals had gone six.

Shane was praying they broke the pattern and took this series in five games. That allowed for the other team to win one and for the Redtails to win at home. Of course, a sweep would be nice, too.

"No. I only know she's using the tickets." He shrugged. "Don't wanna know."

"You sure? Jake could ask Mike—"

"No. I know she's here. That's good enough."

"You really like her, don't you?"

Shane pulled his jersey over his head then gave Lad a look, which had Lad holding up his hands.

"Just an observation. Don't take my head off."

"Don't be fucking with his head before the game." CJ smacked his glove across Lad's shins. "He doesn't need to be thinking about *anything* but the game."

Actually, he'd been thinking about Bliss a lot lately and it hadn't affected his game at all. As a matter of fact, thinking about Bliss got him out of his head when he started getting too wrapped up in the game.

He didn't get to tell the guys that though, because the coach came in to give his last remarks .

Then he heard the crowd begin to roar and knew they only had a few seconds before he needed to lead the guys onto the ice.

Standing, he walked to the door, hearing the guys line up behind him. Nobody spoke but he heard Lad praying under his breath in Russian directly behind him. Shane had no idea what Lad was saying but he crossed himself when Lad muttered, "Amen."

And started down the hall.

———

"HOLY CRAP, I didn't think this place could get any louder but damn." Faith had to raise her voice to be heard. "I think my ears are going to bleed."

Bliss nodded and leaned in to speak closer to Faith's ear. "I know. It's amazing, isn't it?"

The sold-out crowd had been cheering since the start of the video showing highlights of the previous season and ending with solo shots of the team. Her heart stuttered every time Shane's picture appeared on the Jumbotron above the ice.

"I'm so glad you forced me to come to these games with you."

Faith's smile made Bliss put her arm around her friend's shoulders. "I'm glad you're enjoying it."

Bliss had had to exchange the tickets Shane had sent her for handicapped access seats but the ticket office rep had been more than happy to make that happen.

"Yeah, well, the guys aren't hard on the eyes," Faith continued, "and the game *moves*. I love that."

Yes, Faith would. Before her accident, she'd been a soccer player and a runner. And if Bliss thought about that much longer, her good mood would evaporate.

Instead, she shoved the thought out of her mind and watched Shane step onto the ice. In his gear with his mask on, he should've been indistinguishable from the other goalie. But she would've been able to pick him out of a lineup of men in the exact uniform. Something about the way he held himself captured her complete attention.

She didn't take her eyes off him as he went through his pre-face-off routine, roughing the ice in front of his net, taking a drink, then tapping the posts with his stick in a certain rhythm. Every goalie had their own routine. Or so she'd been told. She only ever had eyes for Shane.

Dangerous. He was so dangerous.

And yet, when the first tickets had arrived, she knew immediately she was going to use them.

He'd sent her tickets to every home game with a bouquet of flowers. The first bouquet had had fifteen daisies.

The second had had fourteen. They'd continued to get smaller. It had taken her until the start of the second series to realize that the flowers signified how many games they needed to win to capture the championship.

She couldn't help but feel like it was also a countdown and that made her heart ache.

He would still be leaving at the end of the season, going home to Minnesota or elsewhere to train until training camp started late this summer in Philadelphia.

Which isn't that far away.

She shook the thought out of her head. She couldn't go down that path. Not if she wanted to keep her distance.

And do you?

Snapped out of her thoughts by everyone around her standing, she shot to her feet as a group of schoolkids sang the anthem, but she couldn't take her eyes off Shane. He wasn't wearing his mask, of course, and she had the almost overwhelming urge to run her fingers along his jaw, covered by a thick beard. Not even his playoff beard could disguise the handsome lines of his face.

She wanted to feel his beard against her skin, preferably between her thighs—

Shit.

Luckily, the ref dropped the puck.

And she sucked in a breath and held it.

———

SECOND PERIOD.

The Redtails were up by one but they'd been losing at the end of the first period.

The defense had scrambled after a broken play in the other end and Pittsburgh Spikes' Greg Bruecker had skated off on a breakaway and scored the first goal of the game.

It'd been a beautiful shot and Shane would've been able to admire it—if it hadn't been against him.

As it was, he allowed himself to be pissed off for five seconds and then he shut it out and reset.

Between periods, the defensemen had apologized before the coach ripped their asses for getting dominated that first period.

And the Redtails had come out flying at the beginning of the second period.

CJ had scored the first goal, which had lit a fire under the crowd's ass. And then their top goal scorer, Tyler Richardson, had scored a short-hander after a questionable penalty on Lad.

And just that fast, the ice tilted back in the Redtails' favor.

Shane watched the play at the opposite end, never taking his eyes off the puck. So he saw Riley whiff on a one-timer from the top of the left circle and watched the Spikes' first line break away toward him with speed.

The Redtails defensemen scrambled to catch up and, as ten players raced toward him, Shane had a split second to set.

Skating out to meet the onrushing players, he kept his eyes on the puck as the right winger passed to the left winger setting up on Shane's right.

He lost sight of the right winger but saw the way his guys were moving and knew that winger now had to be behind him.

Which meant he was blindsided by the crash.

All he felt was the rush of bodies crashing into him at high speed.

He went down, his head hit the ice, and bodies fell on top of him.

Everything went black for a second and he had the terrifying thought that he'd blacked out.

Then he realized someone's arm had covered his mask. But his fight response had already kicked in and he was trying to toss players off him as his ears began to ring.

Fuck.

As he struggled to his knees, lungs working to replace the air that'd gotten knocked out of him, he saw his guys ripping opposing players away from him. Saw the linesmen jump in to separate bodies.

But it was all a little blurry.

Fuck. Fuck. Fuck.

Shaking his head, he tried to bring everything into focus. And that was when he heard Lad shout for the trainer.

He wanted to wave him off, wanted to get off his damn knees and get his skates under him.

But he wasn't sure he could do it without falling over.

So he stayed down and waited for the trainer.

And hoped like hell that he could finish the game.

———

BLISS SAW Shane go down under a pile of bodies and, around her, the crowd gasped and shouted.

She could do neither. She could barely breathe as her heart jumped into her throat.

She watched as his head hit the ice right before he disappeared from view as the teams swarmed around the net.

Several players paired up to fight but she only had eyes for Shane.

Rising slowly, too slowly, to his knees, he sat with his head down, unmoving.

Her lungs seized and she had to force air into her lungs.

"Oh my god," Faith muttered. "Is he okay?"

She couldn't answer. She could only watch as CJ leaned down to check on Shane then made a beeline for the bench, where the trainer took CJ's arm so he could race to Shane's side.

As the linesmen and refs got the fighting under control, everyone's attention turned to Shane. The crowd seemed to hold its breath waiting for him to get up.

The longer it took, the harder it was for Bliss to breathe.

She didn't realize she was on her feet until Faith took her hand.

And when it took two players to help him to his feet, she wanted to run for the stairs.

But she knew she wouldn't be allowed downstairs. She wasn't family. She wasn't even his girlfriend.

And still, she couldn't take her eyes off him. She watched as CJ and Lad helped him off the ice, watched him disappear down the hall to the locker room, the trainer on his heels.

She only returned to her seat when Nate came onto the ice to take Shane's position.

"Hey, hon, are you okay?" Faith had leaned in to speak into Bliss's ear because the crowd had erupted into boos as the announcer listed the penalties, including one for goaltender interference.

She had the totally insane urge to walk down the stairs to the penalty box and coldcock the player who'd taken out Shane.

Shaking her head, she turned to Faith. "I don't even know who to ask to make sure he's okay."

Faith's lips turned up in a bittersweet smile. "He'll be back. He's tough."

But he didn't return by the end of the second period.

And she honestly thought she might sit there and cry.

Until her phone vibrated.

She grabbed it before she considered the fact that it might not have anything to do with Shane. And slapped a hand over her mouth to stop her cry of joy when she realized it was from Jake.

HE IS FINE. Be back third period. Name on list to come down. Be there.

SHE WAS GOING to kiss Jake when she saw him.

After she hugged the hell out of Shane.

"So are you gonna tell me what you're smiling like a loon about or just leave me in the dark?"

Faith's wry voice drew Bliss's attention away from her phone.

"He's okay."

Faith smiled. "Glad to hear it. But are you?"

Bliss didn't even have to think about it. "No. I think I screwed up."

"Yeah." Faith nodded. "I'm pretty sure you did. But I don't think it's unfixable."

"We still have the same problem, though. He's eventually going to leave."

"And you'll go with him. And when he's done playing hockey in ten or fifteen years and you want to come back, then you do. But if you love the guy, and you must because you don't get this upset over someone you don't love, then you've got to make a choice."

Faith made it sound so easy. Bliss knew it wasn't.

She only knew she didn't want to be on the outside again.

————

AFTER SPENDING time in the dark room to assess for a concussion, Shane was pronounced fit to play by the doctor.

Damn right he was. He'd started this. He was finishing it.

"Guess you really are made of brick." Jake bumped his shoulder as they lined up for the start of the third period. "You okay?"

"I'm good. Ready to get this done."

Behind him, the rest of the team shuffled on their skates, sticks tapping.

"She's here." Jake leaned in to speak directly into Shane's ear. "In case you wanted to know."

The music queued up, the fans began to scream, and Shane's adrenaline began to pump. He could've said it wasn't because she was watching. He would've been lying.

So he turned to Jake and smiled.

"Yes, now that is the face we need." Jake nodded. "And so we go."

Shane shook his helmet into place and led his team out.

He'd win the game and then he'd get the girl.

Seemed like a plan.

————

BLISS GAVE her name to the guard at the stairs and practically held her breath. But he didn't even need to check his list. He just waved her through.

So she could have a momentary panic attack as she walked down the stairs.

What if Jake was wrong? What if Shane didn't want to see her?

Then why was he sending you the tickets?

Letting him go the first time had been heart-wrenching. If she was wrong about this now, her heart might just break.

Faith had assured her she'd be fine taking a taxi home. So here Bliss stood, smiling at the small talk between the wives and girlfriends but not saying much. She knew most of them by name now and, for the most part, they were sweethearts.

They didn't say anything about the fact that she hadn't been here for the past games. They just welcomed her back with smiles and continued on as if nothing had happened.

Which left her alone to gnaw over every little worry.

Her head popped up when she heard Chrissy squeak as her boyfriend, forward Colin Johnson, snuck up behind her and wrapped his arms around her.

Bliss looked down the hall, hoping to see Shane. A few other guys made their way out of the locker room but not hers.

He's not yours. You pushed him away.

And if he gave her another chance, she'd make it up to him.

"Hey, Liss, I didn't know you'd be down here."

She turned away from the locker room to smile at her brother. "Hey, Mike. You waiting for Jake?"

He nodded, his smile bright. "Yeah, we're gonna go eat." Then he looked over her shoulder for a second. "See you later, Lissy."

She figured Jake had appeared but a second later she heard her name in a familiar voice. A voice that made her thighs clench and her inside quiver.

"Bliss."

Sucking in a breath, she turned and had to bite her lips against the huge grin that wanted to escape.

Her gaze devoured him and she blinked back sudden tears. He looked amazing. Strong. Tall. *Hers.*

And the way he looked at her... Steady. With so much heat in his eyes.

She wanted to reach for him, throw her arms around his shoulders and beg him to forgive her for pushing him away.

"Hi."

"How'd you get down?"

And just that fast, she panicked again. "Jake put me on the list. I'm sorry. I should've warned you. I didn't mean to put you on the spot. I just wanted—"Curling his hands around her neck, he bent down and sealed his mouth over hers, kissing her until she could barely breathe.

When he pulled away, long seconds later, she vaguely heard the catcalls from a few of the other guys and laughter from the girls.

But nothing could take her attention from Shane.

"I'm glad you're here. And I'll thank Jake later—"

"You are welcome." Jake smacked Shane on the back as he walked past to bump his fist with Mike. "Just do not wear yourself out tonight. We have a game tomorrow. Be nice to him, Bliss. He might still not be right in the head. Considering he let you go way too easily the first time, he definitely is not thinking straight."

Shane's lips curved, making her heart beat faster. "I'm a fast learner. And I try not to make the same mistake twice."

Bliss shook her head, wrapping her arms around his waist. "I was the one who made the mistake. Can we—"

"Go? Absolutely."

Shane got her turned around and headed for the door in a split second, his arm around her shoulders. Bliss had to walk fast to keep up as he made for the door to the side lot where the players parked.

"My car—"

"We'll pick it up— Shit. I brought CJ." He stopped, turned, and tossed his keys at Jake, whose lightning-fast reflexes allowed him to catch them.

"Give those to CJ. Tell him not to ding my truck."

Jake's laughter followed them out of the building but Shane didn't slow and he didn't talk as they hurried to her car in the lot across the street from the arena. She figured that was because there were still fans heading the same way.

A few of them recognized him, called out congratulations and encouragement for the next game. He acknowledged every one with a smile and a wave but he didn't slow.

It wasn't until he folded himself into her front seat and she got them on the street that he spoke.

"We're going back to your place to work this out, right? Because I don't want there to be any misunderstandings."

She swallowed hard, sliding a quick glance at him, to find him staring at her. "Yes, we are."

"And we're going to work this out. Because I love you, Bliss. I don't want you to have any doubt about that."

Her hands clenched around the steering wheel at the absolute authority in his voice, and she nodded, not sure she could answer coherently and still drive.

"I missed you," he continued. "You know that, right? I never wanted to give you up but I didn't want you to think I was like your ex."

"I know. Shane—"

"You got the flowers."

"Yes. Shane—"

"When there were no more games, I would've shown up at your door and we would've talked. And I would've told you just what I'm telling you now."

Stopped at a red light, she turned so she could see him. Those blue eyes, always so intensely focused, made her burn from the inside.

And when she smiled, his expression lightened enough for her to see the heat in his eyes.

Then the light changed and she stepped on the gas. He didn't say anything else as she drove the last few miles back to her apartment.

He unfolded his big body from the front seat as soon as she put the car in park. Which meant he was at her door as soon as she opened it.

He took her hand to help her out and didn't release her as he hustled her toward her apartment building.

By the time they reached her door, she was laughing. She couldn't help it. She could barely keep up with him when he walked fast and, right now, he was practically running.

As she went to fit the key into the lock, he pressed himself against her back, short-circuiting her brain, and she dropped the keys.

"Let me get those," he grumbled, "because if you bend over…"

She went wet at the deep note in his voice and she might have whimpered as he scooped up the keys and opened her door.

With his hands on her hips, he hurried her through and, in the next second, he had her plastered against the door. His big body held hers against the door, so much hard muscle she wanted to bite him. Then his mouth sealed over hers. His full beard was a new sensation that only added to her sensory pleasure.

As the fury of his kiss infected her, she shoved her hands into his hair and held on tight. She'd already toed off her sneakers and locked her legs around his waist when he lifted her off her feet.

Tilting his head, he kissed her deeper, sank his tongue into her mouth, and made her moan as his hands worked at her jeans.

With a groan, he pulled away for a second. "I'm making it a rule that you always wear skirts."

She huffed out a short laugh but, at the moment, she couldn't agree with him more. "I may actually agree to that. But for now, just hurry."

His mouth slipped back over hers as his fingers worked at her jeans.

"Drop your legs."

She obeyed without thought, wrapping her arms around his shoulders so her legs could hang free and he could work her jeans down her legs.

It took a little maneuvering because that damn denim clung but finally she felt cooler air brush against her bare thighs and her mound.

Her moan sounded loud enough that she feared her brother might be able to hear her through the walls.

And then he slid his hand between her legs and flicked at her clit with two fingers and she didn't care who heard her.

She only wanted Shane to hurry.

Hips writhing against him, she felt him fumble with his pants.

"Fuck." He growled. "Condom."

"Good thing you're so good with your hands."

He sucked in a sharp breath then let out a sharp bark of laughter. "I fucking love you, Bliss."

He'd said it earlier in the car but here, now, she melted. Completely. Totally.

"I love you too."

He kissed her hard enough to press her head back against the door. Then he let her slide down until her feet hit the floor.

And handed her the condom.

Smiling, she looked down to see his cock pressing out of his open zipper. Hard, dark, and oh so enticing.

"Put the condom on, sweetheart. And then I'm going to fuck you against the door because I don't think I can make it to the damn couch."

She took the condom from his hand, hands shaking with need, and rolled it down his hard shaft.

Then she wrapped her arms around his shoulders again and would have climbed him like a pole if he hadn't put his hands on her hips and lifted her.

The next time they did this, she wanted them to both be naked and standing in front of a mirror so she could see his arms.

Then he lifted her like she weighed nothing, and the only thought her brain was able to process was *Now. Right freaking now.*

As if he'd read her thoughts, he settled her on the tip of his cock and let her slide down the shaft at an excruciatingly slow pace.

In this position, he felt huge and her arms tightened around his neck until she figured he might not be able to breathe. But she didn't let go.

And his hands tightened on her hips as his chest rose and fell with each gasping inhale.

When he was seated deep inside her, he held there until she couldn't take the anticipation any longer.

Turning her face into his neck, she bit him. And as he shuddered against her, his hips pulled back.

And he gave her exactly what she wanted.

All of him.

EPILOGUE

The crowd had begun the countdown at twenty seconds.

Shane heard them but kept his eye on the puck. The play was at the other end of the ice. The Redtails had scored the only goal of the game but the Arizona Rattlers weren't giving up yet.

The teams were battling in the corner for the puck, the Rattlers trying to make one last play to push the series to six games.

The Reds were doing everything they could to make sure this series ended here at home with the Calder Cup in their hands.

Ten... Nine... Eight...

The Rattlers left winger dug the puck out and made a break for center ice.

Shane set, catcher up, stick down. The massive roar of the crowd barely registered.

Five... Four... Three...

From the blue line, the winger took his shot.

And Shane cleared it just like he had every shot this game.

Shane roared along with the crowd as the horns blared, signaling the end of the game.

And the Redtails won the Calder Cup.

His team rushed toward him from the opposite end of the ice and poured off the bench, sticks forgotten, helmets torn off and tossed.

They met in a crush at the center of the ice, hugging, jumping, screaming.

And in the center, Shane grinned until he thought his face would break.

In the middle of crush, Shane hugged his guys and yelled along with them.

But after a minute, he looked into the seats and found Bliss.

She wore one of his jerseys and was hugging Faith and Mike and jumping up and down. And when she caught sight of him looking her way, her grin got impossibly wider.

Then she blew him a kiss.

Life was good. Life was really fucking good.

THE GRINDER

Game on...

Riley Hatch is a fast-talking minor-league hockey player with a reputation as a grinder. He goes in deep, hits hard and comes out with the puck. He's not known for giving up and, when he meets a cool blonde who trips all his switches, he's not about to take no for an answer.

Aly Martin's aversion to professional athletes falters when faced with the six-foot-four hockey god towering over her. He's everything she never wanted in a man...overtly sexy, rough around the edges and pushy. And absolutely irresistible.

Riley falls hard and fast but he knows he's going to need more than determination to break down Aly's reservations. But will his lifelong dream of making it to the NHL cost him the woman of his dreams?

The door to the billing office of the Reading Health Center squeaked open, causing Allison Martin to do two things.

First, she cringed because she was currently bent over at the waist trying to find the cord that'd fallen between two desks, and her ass would be the first thing anyone walking through the door would see.

And second, she hoped like hell whoever had just walked through that door was a coworker and not someone she'd actually have to talk to.

"Uh, hey. How's it going?"

Shit, shit, shit.

No such luck. The voice was male and unknown, deep, with just enough of a husky edge that her heart kicked up a beat.

And, of course, she'd been caught with her ass in the air.

With a sigh, she began to wiggle her way out from between the desks.

"I'll be with you in a second."

"Yeah, sure. No problem. Take your time."

Great, just great. He was a perv, too, which meant he was going to watch her ass the entire way.

And, since she was the only person in the office, she'd have to smile and pretend to be pleasant while he berated her for a bill he probably didn't understand.

Today, smiling would require a superhuman effort. The hospital's internet had been spotty all day, and the program the office used to bill patients had been glitchy since it'd been updated last week.

She'd just gotten off the phone with the tech guys, who'd told her to try the old unplug-replug method for fixing the connection. If that didn't work, she'd have to wait her turn because apparently every other department in the hospital had had the same problem today. Which meant she'd probably embarrassed herself for no reason.

Sucking in a deep breath, Aly finally freed herself and stood, pushing the hair that had escaped her pristine twist out of her face.

Then she forced a smile and hoped she didn't look like a rabid dog.

"Hello, can I help...you?"

Holy crap.

The man leaning his elbows on the counter had definitely been checking out her ass.

Quite frankly, she wasn't sure she minded.

Specimens like this didn't typically pass through her door, much less stare at any part of her. No, she usually only saw guys like this in memes about eye candy and fantasies.

He had to be at least six-two and probably weighed more than two hundred pounds. All of it muscle. Thick, bulging muscle that made his faded gray t-shirt stretch at its seams.

She felt small standing in front of him, which was a minor miracle because she wasn't. She stood five-seven and carried a few more pounds than she'd like. In heels, she could stare down most men she knew.

But not this one.

She had to look up, even as his gaze dropped to her feet then made its way up until he finally met her eyes.

And when they did...

Holy freaking crap.

She had to bite her bottom lip to make sure her mouth didn't hang open.

He was quite possibly the hottest guy she'd ever seen in real life. Seriously, he should be modeling underwear.

She had the urge to pick up the nearest stack of papers and fan herself. She couldn't remember ever meeting a guy who made her body flush with heat from her toes to her scalp. And everywhere in between.

Rugged features that reminded her a little of a young Brad Pitt but even more handsome. Damn, she never would've thought that possible.

His brown hair had a wave to it, and his eyes were a dark greenish-brown that made her want to lean over the counter and get really close so she could see them better. Like, maybe flat-on-his-back-lying-on-top-of-him close. With their noses almost touching and their lips only centimeters apart—

"Hey, yeah, I'm hoping you can."

Can what? flashed through her mind, but luckily she couldn't get her mouth to work right away. Oh yeah, she was at work.

When he reached behind his back to take something out of his back pocket, all the muscles in those arms shifted and bunched and generally made her feel like she was watching a porn movie. Which she never did.

"I got this bill..."

He grinned at her as he unfolded a piece of paper and set it on the counter.

And holy crap, she nearly swallowed her tongue.

Down, girl. He wants you to fix his bill, not lick him from head to toe.

"I'm not sure why I got it. It should've gone to my former team."

Swallowing hard, she smiled and reached across the counter for the paper. Tearing her gaze away from his, she focused instead on scanning the bill. After she'd taken a look at his hands. The man had huge hands, with long fingers covered in scars.

"Of course, Mister..." she looked down at the name, "Hatch. Let me take a look."

"It's Riley. And thanks, Miss...?"

"Martin. Aly Martin."

She happened to look up at that moment and found him smiling down at her. Not a full-out grin, but one of those half grins guys did so well.

"Nice to meet you, Miss Aly Martin."

She blinked and sucked in a breath. "Nice to meet you, too. I'll, ah, just take a look at your bill."

He leaned his forearms on the counter, getting even closer. "Got it a week or so ago but we've had practice every day and I haven't been able to get over here. I figured it was better to do this in person than try to explain over the phone."

And she was so grateful he had. "Practice?"

His smile widened and her ovaries practically exploded.

"I play for the Redtails."

"Redtails?"

She cringed as she parroted him for a second time, just as she realized that he must be a hockey player for the local Reading Redtails.

"Sorry. Stupid question." She shook her head and focused her attention on the paper in front of her. "Let me take a look at this."

"Are you a hockey fan?"

The bill was standard and nothing looked out of ordinary. The only thing that didn't make sense was that the bill was from this hospital for services at a hospital in another state that was in the same network. "You were treated for a shoulder injury last July?"

She looked up to find him watching her with a slight smile on his face, the kind of smile that invited her to smile back. Which she did.

"Yeah. Took a hit into the boards." He reached for his left shoulder and rubbed it with one of those big hands. She couldn't help but follow the movement before she blinked and snapped out of it.

"Does it still hurt?"

She wanted to take it back the second the words were out of her mouth and barely managed not to roll her eyes at her own words.

Damn it, she wasn't her younger sister, Vivi, who'd never met a guy she didn't want to sleep with. Although no one would blame her for wanting to see this man stripped down to nothing because, *holy crap,* he was hot.

His smile widened as he shook his head. "Not anymore, no. I just rub it out of habit. So what do you think?"

"That maybe you want to get another job? This one seems dangerous to your health."

He burst into laughter and, Jesus, if she'd thought he was hot before, now he was off-the-charts drool-worthy. His mouth alone made her want to grab him and kiss the hell out of him.

And since that was completely out of the question, she could only smile back when he stopped laughing.

"Yeah, it kinda is, but it's still fun and I love to play so I'm gonna until I physically can't."

He certainly looked physically able at the moment.

Her gaze dropped to his broad shoulders then to his muscular chest. She'd never been this up close and personal with a hockey player before. The only other professional athlete she'd ever been this close to before had been Vivi's ex, a football player. And he'd been a cocky asshole Aly had hated on sight.

This guy looked just as cocky. She'd reserve judgment on the asshole part.

Which doesn't matter because you'll never see him again.

She didn't go to hockey games, didn't think she'd like them. From what she'd seen on TV when her dad used to watch, the sport was rough and loud. Two things Aly tried to avoid as much as possible in her life.

She usually dated nice guys, nerds who spent hours in front of a computer every day and considered Hacky Sack a sport. The ones who took off the day the new Marvel movie released.

Nice, regular guys. Who left her completely cold.

Tearing her gaze away from his chest, she looked over his bill again.

Luckily, there was no one else here to see her make a fool out of herself. The five other women who worked in this office would have never let her live this down.

"So, what's the problem with your bill?"

"Well, it should've been paid by my previous team. The injury happened during a game so I figure it should've been covered under their policy. I don't know why it wouldn't."

"Which team?"

"The Colonials' ECHL team in Lancaster."

"How long have you played hockey?"

Okay, technically, that had nothing to do with his bill but, sue her, curiosity had taken hold.

Leaning his elbows on the counter, he cocked his head to the side. "For as long as I can remember. Have you been to a game?"

She shook her head. "No."

His eyebrows rose. "Would you like to? I could get you tickets. We have a game tomorrow night."

Yes and *No* popped onto her tongue at the exact same time.

Yes, because *hello*, hot guy. No, because, well, she didn't accept random offers of hockey tickets from unknown men. At least, she never had before.

She blinked, trying to reboot her brain. "I don't think I'm available."

Which was total bullshit. She didn't have a date. She and her last boyfriend had parted ways six months ago. He'd wanted more than a few dates a week and sex whenever they could squeeze it in. She'd been perfectly content with the arrangement.

It wasn't like she'd been planning to marry Paul.

And didn't that make you a stone-cold bitch?

Probably.

Still, she'd thought they'd been happy. Not in love but there'd been sparks. Well, more like a warm ember or two. But, really, wasn't all that chemistry stuff just a big lie to explain away the stupid stuff you wanted to do because you were in lust?

She wasn't some hopeless romantic who was waiting for "the thunderbolt," that lightning strike from out of the blue that was supposed to hit you when you met the man you were supposed to marry.

"Got a date?" Riley asked.

Was he teasing or fishing for information? And really, how badly was she deluding herself?

She wasn't some hideous troll but guys like this didn't ask out girls like her, with her reading glasses hanging around her neck and her skirt a safe two inches below her knees and her buttoned-up blouse.

She resisted the urge to look down at herself to see if she'd actually buttoned it all the way to her neck this morning.

Besides, professional athletes had bad reputations. Not that she'd ever dated one. But her sister had dated an NFL player she'd met at a party during training camp at a local college. And he'd been a huge asshole.

"No, I don't. But I—"

"Then I'll leave two tickets for you at the door." His smile widened. "Bring a friend."

"I'm not sure I can. I've—"

"Come on, you'll have a great time. We're playing the second-best team in the league. It'll be a good game."

He grinned and...oh wow. That smile should be illegal. It made her thighs...and other parts...clench.

And she couldn't resist asking, "So who's the best team in the league?"

"We are." His smile widened even more and she felt her insides tighten and heat. "Our team won the Calder Cup last year and we're looking to repeat this year."

She nodded like she knew what winning a Calder Cup meant.

Then she resisted the urge to bat her eyes at him and pet his chest.

"So, Miss Martin, wanna come to a game tomorrow night?"

RILEY WATCHED the woman in front of him think really hard about her answer to his question.

And he had to admit, his pride was taking a hit.

Usually, women jumped at the chance to accept whatever he was offering. Tickets, dinner, sex…

Then again, most of those women knew who he was and what he did. Most of them sought him out and, even if they didn't, he didn't have to do much chasing.

This girl was nothing like those others who went out of their way to catch his eye, except for one—she was *hot*. From the top of her blonde head to the tips of her toes in those little heels and everything in between, this girl flipped all of his switches.

But she didn't seem to want anything to do with him.

Well, damn. Wasn't that just par for his fucking course this year?

He hadn't really wanted to do this today, hadn't wanted to have to fight through the bullshit of medical bills and be reminded of the injury that'd nearly killed his career last season.

He'd figured he'd be up against some middle-aged battle-ax who'd question him for five minutes, make him feel like a criminal for daring to question the mighty hospital's bill, and make him fill out a shit-ton of forms.

But when he'd stepped into the office and seen that beautiful ass in that tight black skirt sticking up in the air, he'd been understand-ably turned on.

Then she'd stood and every naughty librarian fantasy he'd ever had flashed through his brain.

Hell, his mouth had gone dry.

"Um," she finally said, "I'm really not sure if I can get there tomorrow night."

Well, at least it wasn't a flat-out no. He could work with that.

Toning down his smile by a few watts, he leaned his arms on the counter separating them. "Well, how about this? I'll leave the tickets at will-call, and if you can come, you can pick them up there. Then maybe we can go out for a drink afterward."

Her pale-blue eyes widened and she didn't answer right away. Shit, maybe he should've waited to ask her out for that drink. But he wasn't known for keeping his mouth shut, on or off the ice.

"A bunch of us usually go out after the game."

"So... it'd be a group thing?"

He'd make it whatever she wanted. "Yeah, a group."

Her teeth sank into her bottom lip and he had to swallow a groan.

"I'd really hate to say yes and then not show up. The tickets will go to waste. I should really just—"

"The tickets won't go to waste," he assured her, knowing she'd been about to turn him down. "We never sell out. I'll leave two. Bring a friend."

Now her tongue came out to lick at her lips, and it was all he could do not to reach out and let his finger run over that plump bottom lip.

"Well, my sister loves sports."

There were more where she came from? Someone on the team was going to owe him big time. "Bring her along. The more, the merrier." Then his smile toned down even more. "Don't say no. I'll leave the tickets at the will-call window, and I'll give the guard your name so you and your sister can meet me downstairs after the game. I'll give you my number and you can text me for directions."

It took a second but finally she smiled. "Okay. I'll see if my sister can go."

Their gazes held for a few more seconds and, for the first time in his life, Riley found himself without a single thing to say.

If she hadn't looked down at the bill she still held in her hands, he wasn't sure how long they would've stood there, staring into each other's eyes. And he wouldn't have minded.

Then she sighed. "And I hate to say this but I think I'm going to have to get back to you about your bill. Our system is messed up and I can't get online at the moment."

"No problem." Just meant he'd have an excuse to talk to her again if he didn't see her tomorrow night. Grabbing a piece of paper and a pen from the counter, he wrote his name and number and slid it across the counter.

She took it, their fingertips brushing as the paper exchanged hands.

He didn't know how long they would've stood there, barely touching, him grinning like an idiot and her looking a little shell-shocked, if the door hadn't opened.

"Dude, you ready, yes? I need—oh, hello."

Controlling the urge to roll his eyes, Riley shook his head instead and turned to see Jake grinning at Aly.

The Czech player had a reputation as a manwhore, and with his looks it was easy to see why. Tall, blond and ripped, the guy smiled and women threw their panties at him.

Apparently, Aly wasn't immune. Her eyes widened as she stared at the Redtails' best defenseman.

Which made Riley want to kick the ever-loving shit out of Jake if the kid so much as hinted at making a move on her. Okay, Jake wasn't exactly a kid at twenty-three, but Riley was twenty-eight and had a few pounds on him, which Riley would use to kick Jake's ass if he didn't turn down that smile.

Luckily for Jake, Aly barely glanced at him and said "Hello" before staring at Riley again.

Take that, kid.

"I need a few seconds yet."

Sliding a glance over his shoulder, Riley saw Jake's mouth twist into a shit-eating grin. Oh, he would *so* make the kid pay for that at practice tomorrow.

"Yes, I see that. Fine. I will be in hall. You come get me when you are ready. Hopefully in the next hour."

If he had his way, Riley would spend at least another hour talking to this woman but she was obviously working and wouldn't be able to leave in the middle of the day.

Damn, he couldn't wait until tomorrow night.

"I guess you need to leave," she said, although she looked a little depressed at the thought.

"Unfortunately, yeah. I'm hosting the team dinner tonight. Twenty-two hockey players in one enclosed space. Always good for a few laughs."

Her lips curved in a flat-out smile that almost made him pant. "I don't know. Sounds like the setup for a sitcom."

"Not one they could show on TV."

The door to the office opened again and they both turned to look. This time, a short guy with a wrinkled dress shirt, black pants, and a mop of unruly black hair hustled through the door.

"Hey, Aly. Just gonna check out your terminal—"

"Wait! I haven't—damn it." She sighed. "I'm sorry. I really have to go."

"No problem. I'll see you tomorrow."

When she smiled, it gave him hope that he actually would. "I'll try. I just—"

"Hey, Aly," the guy in her office called out. "Can you come close out your programs?

With a little grimace, she turned and hustled toward the office in the back. Giving him another look at her great ass, which he watched until he couldn't see her anymore.

Then he turned and walked out of the office with a smile, which he knew would set off Jake.

Fuck it. He couldn't care less.

Sure enough, Jake fell into step beside him, still wearing that shit-eating grin.

"Dude, you look like the cat that ate that bird. I don't think I have ever seen you look this way. You know, like you are happy. You asked her out on a date, yes? I assume she said yes or you wouldn't be smiling. Good for you. I was worried about your skills with the women. I thought maybe you were still virgin."

With a sigh, Riley stuck his elbow in Jake's side, making him flinch.

"Hey, kid. We're in public. Tone it down a little."

But, of course, Jake couldn't contain himself. Or he just didn't care. Riley had never met anyone with less of a filter than Jake.

"What is to tone down? Since you are not virgin, you should not be ashamed. You did ask her out, right?"

Riley shook his head, knowing he wasn't going to be able to ignore Jake. They guy's focus was legendary on and off the ice. But Riley hadn't gotten where he was on skill alone. He'd been a sports management major in college and not far from the top of his class. If he hadn't been so damn determined to play professional hockey, he probably would've become an agent, which he still might do some day. He was good at talking.

"Yeah, I did. She'll be at the game tomorrow night."

Jake clapped him on the back. "And that is what we like to hear. Maybe you get laid now. Be good for you."

Riley couldn't contain his laughter. It rang through the parking garage as they reached his car.

"Dude, do you ever shut up?"

Jake just shrugged. "You talk on the ice. I talk off the ice. We make a good team, yes?"

Shaking his head, Riley had to agree.

"Yeah, we make a good team."

"Good. That is settled. Now, what are you going to make for dinner? Lad can't handle dairy and Tyler can't handle anything green..."

As Jake ran at the mouth again, Riley nodded at the appropriate spots, but his brain had latched on to something Jake had said and wouldn't let go.

It'd been a while since he'd gotten laid. Like, since before the beginning of the season.

Holy shit, how the hell had *that* happened?

For the past seven years of his professional career, he'd played hard, on and off the ice. He'd been through ten times as many women as he had teams. He didn't brag about it and he tried not to be a dick about it but it'd been a fact of his life.

But for the past five months, he'd been a monk.

He'd always been dedicated to the game, always showed up to win. But this year...well, this year, he was twenty-eight.

He was one of the oldest guys on the team. Still six years younger than Cary Lenville, who was probably playing his last season as he was groomed to become the Redtails' assistant coach, but a lot of the guys he'd come up with had either moved up to the NHL or had retired.

Retired. The word alone was enough to make Riley shudder. Hell, he wasn't ready to retire.

Which was why he was working so damn hard this season. This was his year to make it. He couldn't afford any distractions.

And yet...he hadn't been able to resist the blonde behind the counter.

Jake punched him on the shoulder hard enough to make Riley flinch. Luckily, they were stopped for a red light.

He shot Jake a glare. "What the fuck?"

"You have not listened to one word I said this entire time, have you?"

"How could I *not* be listening? You haven't shut up since we left the hospital."

Rolling his eyes, Jake sighed. "I supposed you are to be forgiven considering the hot girl you scored."

"That's not who I was thinking about."

Jake smirked. "So what are you thinking about? You don't look happy whatever it is. What is wrong? Tell me. I am good listener."

Then the guy fell totally silent. A minor miracle. No one on the team would believe it.

"Nothing's wrong. Just thinking about the season."

"Should be a good one. You are a good addition to the team since we lost our last grinder."

Riley shook his head, smiling. "Happy to be of service."

"And we are happy to have you. You and CJ make a good team."

"Yeah, well, I'm not on the first line." Which rankled, like a splinter in his heel. Damn it, he wanted to be on that first line but Coach had him on the second. Of course, it just made him work that much harder, which Coach knew would happen.

"Word is Knapper will not be here long. Duchene is having problems."

Dickie Duchene was the Philadelphia Colonials' third-line right-winger, notorious for playing as hard as he partied. Problem was, sometimes he didn't know where the line was and he crossed it more than he should.

"Yeah, I heard the same."

Sure, he'd briefly entertained the thought that maybe he'd be the one called up. Totally unrealistic considering he'd only been with the team since the beginning of this season and Sam Knapp had been a Colonials prospect since his draft four years ago.

"But this is an opportunity for you, yes? You will get Knapper's spot on the first line."

Riley just shook his head. "Life doesn't always work the way you want it."

Jake shrugged, the arrogance of youth written all over his face. "Then you just have to make it work for you. What is saying? When a door closes, you climb out the window. Sometimes you just have to make your own window by breaking down the wall."

When Jake looked at him with a smile, Riley laughed all the way to grocery store.

TWO

"So...I've got two tickets to the hockey game Friday night. Wanna go with me?"

Vivi looked up from her drawing table, shock written all over her sister's face.

"Did you just say *hockey*? As in ice hockey? As in, you're going to go to a Redtails game? With actual hockey fans all around you screaming and yelling and having a good time and possibly spilling their beer all over you?"

Aly rolled her eyes at her sister, unwilling to concede that Vivi had a good reason for her shock.

"Yes, I am. And I thought you could come with me since you don't work tomorrow night."

Sitting back in her drafting chair, Vivi narrowed her gaze at her and gave her a once-over, pushing rainbow-hued, waist-length hair over her shoulder. "You look like my sister but you're speaking in tongues. Who are you and what have you done with her?"

Flipping Vivi the bird, Aly spun her sister away from her desk, where she'd been drawing something that looked like erotic fan art

163

of... "Is that the Tenth Doctor and Ianto? Why is the Tenth Doctor kissing Ianto?"

Vivi shrugged. "Why shouldn't they kiss? I'd watch at least two episodes of them kissing, wouldn't you? And you're not getting out of this conversation that easily. Why do you have tickets for a hockey game tomorrow night? You hate hockey."

Aly wrinkled her nose. "I never said I hated hockey."

Vivi's stunning aquamarine eyes widened even more. "I distinctly remember having a conversation where you said something about hockey being a sport played by illiterate farm boys."

Wincing, Aly shook her head. "I did not."

Vivi nodded as she turned back to her drawing and picked up her pencil. "Yes, you did. I think you were dating that lawyer wannabe at the time. He was a total douche, by the way."

That much was totally true. He had been a douche.

"So what if I did. I'm a girl." Aly pulled the covers up on Vivi's unmade bed then sat on the edge. "I can change my mind. Come to the game with me Friday night."

"Why the sudden interest in hockey?"

Aly didn't answer the question right away. Instead, she let herself look around her sister's room.

The home they shared technically belonged to their parents, but Aly and Vivi now paid the second mortgage her parents had taken out so they could buy a home in Florida, which was where they now lived full time. Leaving Vivi and Aly with a very nice cottage home in a good neighborhood not far from the hospital where Aly worked. Aly's decent salary and Vivi's fluctuating salary as a freelance graphic artist, part-time tattoo artist and part-time waitress allowed them to pay that mortgage and all the bills with no problem.

And the fact that their parents lived a thousand miles away in Florida made it that much sweeter.

"Aly? What's going on?"

Vivi had abandoned her drawing again and now watched her with narrowed eyes.

"Nothing's going on."

Vivi snorted. "Yeah, right."

Aly finally looked at her sister. "So...I met this guy today."

A knowing expression now crossed her sister's face. "Ah. That's where you got the tickets. Let me guess. He works for the team. He's their...what? Their accountant? Their lawyer? Their marketing guy?"

Aly couldn't wait to wipe that smirk off her sister's face. "Second-line right wing."

Her sister's stunned expression made her smile.

"Holy fuck. Seriously?"

She shrugged, as if hockey players asked her out all the time. "He came into the office today with a problem with his bill."

"Well, damn." Scrambling up from her chair, Vivi grabbed her laptop off her desk and hopped onto the bed beside Aly.

Like two teenagers, they spread out on the bed with the laptop between them as they Googled Riley and clicked on the first listing for a site called hockeydb.com.

Vivi whistled as soon as the site came up. "Damn. He's *hot*."

She grinned at the breathless appreciation in her sister's voice.

"And he's even hotter in person."

Which he totally was. Tall. Dark. Handsome. Wicked grin and green eyes that made her want to kiss him...which made no sense at all.

She'd gone back and forth all day about accepting the tickets, had tried to tell herself she really shouldn't accept them.

She hadn't been kidding when she'd told him she'd never been to a game. And Vivi had every right to be shocked about her wanting to go. It definitely wasn't something she'd ever thought she'd do. And especially not as the guest of one of the players. Who wanted to take her out for a drink after the game.

She should've told him no and stuck to her answer. But there'd been something about him...

She'd already checked out his page on the Redtails site at work this afternoon, but now she read over his stats again.

Riley Hatch. Six-two. Two-ten. Just turned twenty-nine a month ago. He'd played for five different leagues, including Boston University. She hadn't expected that, which made her wrinkle her nose at her own arrogance.

"*This* is the guy who gave you tickets to the game? What did he want?"

"What do you mean?"

Vivi rolled her eyes. "I mean, what does he want from you?"

"He wants us to go out with the team after the game for drinks."

Vivi's eyes got even bigger. "No fucking way. Seriously?"

All right, now Vivi was starting to get on her nerves. She adored her younger sister but sometimes...

"Hey!" Aly smacked Vivi on the arm. "Why wouldn't he?"

Vivi knocked her shoulder against Aly's in retaliation. "You know that's not what I meant. I just mean, athletes have never been your thing. I can't believe you said yes."

"I didn't exactly say yes. Yet. I told him I might have plans."

Aly snorted. "Which, of course, you don't."

Her sister knew her too well. "I know, but...I'm not sure what he wants."

Vivi's eyebrows rose. "He wants what they all want. The question is, what do you want? If you want to go out with the guy, then do it. It's not like you have to sleep with him. I don't think he expects sex for a pair of tickets."

"I know that. He seems really nice. And when he smiles... No lie, I swear my ovaries exploded. Seriously hot."

Vivi raised her hand as if to testify. "No argument from me. The guy is totally fuckable. You should jump his bones, which I know you won't, but still."

Was she really that much of a puritan? No, she didn't sleep around. Never had. She had to have a connection with a guy before she fell into bed with him. Otherwise, there was no point.

Yes, she'd felt an immediate reaction to Riley, but that didn't mean she had to jump into bed with him right away.

Then again, Riley probably jumped in bed with every girl he asked out for drinks, and when she told him no, she'd never see him again.

"I'm not going to jump his bones tomorrow night."

Vivi rolled her eyes again. "Obviously. Just don't expect to hear from him again when you don't put out, you know?"

Aly heard the bitterness in her sister's voice and had the urge to go completely against her nature and beat the living shit out of Vivi's ex-asshole of a boyfriend who'd crushed her heart and her spirit. Jamie Dunbar might have a multimillion-deal with the NFL, but the prick had made her sister cry for weeks, and if Aly ever saw him again, she'd smack the shit out of him.

Yes, every girl had that one guy who broke her heart into a thousand pieces. Well, every girl except Aly. She'd never fallen that hard for a guy. And yes, she secretly worried that maybe there was something wrong with her.

BUT SHE NEVER WANTED TO BE LIKE Vivi, bitter and crushed because of a guy.. Or like her mother, stuck with a man she couldn't stand but wouldn't leave.

"So are you coming with me Friday night or not?"

Her sister rolled her eyes. "Of course. Gotta see this guy for myself. Besides, you won't go if I don't, and you need to get out and have some fun. You're starting to remind me a little of Mom and that's scary."

Aly's brows knit together. "What do you mean?"

Vivi rolled onto her side and propped her hand under her head. Aly mimicked her position.

"You know. You never have any fun and you're always worried about something."

"I'm not always worried."

Vivi's brows rose. "I notice you didn't say anything about having fun."

Now Aly rolled her eyes. "Work's been crazy lately and I haven't had a lot of time—"

"Excuses, excuses." Vivi waved her hand in front of her. "Just like Mom. She always has an explanation for why she doesn't do anything, and you're starting to act like that, too."

Aly opened her mouth to deny it...then closed it because she couldn't.

"That's a low blow."

"No, it's true. And you know it. But you have a *date*. With a real hottie." Vivi's smile widened. "Maybe you'll actually get to find out if he's good in bed."

"It's just a date. Don't get ahead of yourself."

"So you've never had sex on a first date?"

"Not since college. Older and wiser."

Vivi rolled her eyes. "Oh please. Live a little. Get what you can out of the guy before you dump him."

The flat tone of Vivi's voice worried Aly but she didn't say anything because, god forbid, she didn't want to sound like their mother, who she tried so hard not to be like.

"We haven't even gone out for a drink. Maybe he'll turn out to be a dick and I won't see him again."

"Oh, he'll turn into a dick sooner or later. Probably sooner."

She couldn't let that pass. "Viv, are you okay?"

Her sister's gaze dropped for a few seconds before she shrugged. "I'm fine."

"No, you're not. You haven't been for a while and I'm worried about you."

Vivi sighed heavily. "You don't need to worry about me. I'm fine. Honestly."

"But you haven't been yourself lately."

"Maybe I'm finally growing up."

"You're twenty-four and you're making ends meet working three freaking jobs. I think that's adult enough."

"But you're the one working fifty hours a week in an office where you have to wear grown-up clothes."

"And have no social life at all. Don't forget that."

"I guess that makes us both pitiful losers."

"Yeah, but I'm a pitiful loser with a date with a hot hockey player. And if you come along, I'm sure you'll meet lots of other hot hockey players."

Damn it, she shouldn't have said that. Vivi's expression hardened and her mouth pursed in a way that only happened when she thought about the former asshole boyfriend.

"Never gonna happen. But I will totally be there tomorrow to make sure he's not a complete dick."

"Gee, when you put it like that, maybe it's not even worth it."

"I'm not sure any guy's worth it."

Trying to lighten the mood, Aly grinned at Vivi. "I guess you really do want to live with me forever. We'll be known as the Spinster Sisters and have twenty cats."

Vivi rolled her eyes again and finally started to laugh. "All right, all right. I'll stop being such a downer. And no, I do *not* want to live with you for the rest of my life. We'd probably kill each other after twenty years or so. Doesn't mean there has to be a man involved. One of these days, I'm going to backpack across Europe and I'm going to hike Everest and..."

As her sister continued to rattle off all the things she wanted to do with her life, Aly considered the fact that she didn't really think about stuff like that.

Sure, she'd love to travel and see the world, but her sister wanted to escape.

And what's so bad about that?

She hated to admit it, and wouldn't never admit it to her sister, but she wanted to find a guy, someone to spend time with and do things with. Someone with mutual goals and—

Oh my god. She sounded like her mother.

"Hey, Aly?"

Her attention snapped back to her sister, who stared at her like she might have accidentally said all that out loud.

"Yeah?"

"I totally think you should do him."

With a laugh, Aly grabbed the pillow and smacked her sister across the head.

"I totally think that's *not* going to happen."

———

"WE HAVE a game tonight and you are taking a girl out on a first date? We have a streak going and you must fuck with it?"

Taking laps around the rink before the start of practice, Riley ignored Vladimir "Lad" Marchenko's taunt and kept skating.

He refused to allow any of the kids to get in his head. As the second-oldest player on the team, he sometimes was reminded that he'd actually grown up some since he'd been Lad's age.

"Seriously?" Defenseman Derek Flaherty flew by then turned to skate backward so he could get in Riley's face. "Chickie got someone to go out with him? How the hell'd that happen, old man?"

Restraining the urge to check the little shit into the boards for using that stupid-ass nickname and for commenting on his age, Riley once again took the high road and ignored the six-foot, hundred-and-eighty-pound redhead who couldn't keep his mouth shut, no matter how many times he took a fist to the face for opening it.

Okay, he and Derek had a lot in common but Riley would never admit it.

"Yes, unlike you." Lad pounced on Derek with the same droll wit he'd used on Riley. "Who cannot get a date because you open your mouth and speak."

Instead of taking offense, Derek grinned. According to his roommate, Adam Zappala, that grin got Derek laid more than a rabbit in mating season.

"Don't need to date if all you wanna do is get laid. Don't need a girlfriend, either. They just fuck with your head."

"Yeah, well, we all know he doesn't have a brain so they don't fuck with that."

Riley turned to smile at Cary, who'd skated up beside him.

"Hey. How goes it? So you got a date tonight?"

Riley let his head drop back. "Christ, not you, too? Seriously, you're all a bunch of teenage girls, I swear."

Cary laughed, a deep sound no one heard much. The guy had earned his reputation as a brawler almost twenty years ago when the game had been a lot different. Now, the skill players got most of the spotlight.

Kids like CJ Young, the twenty-one-year-old forward who'd started the first five games of the season with two points per game. And Robbie Lindback, the nineteen-year-old first-round draft pick from Sweden, who'd probably get called up the next time the Colonials needed a forward.

"At least they don't scream and giggle. Much. How's it going? Haven't had much time to talk since you got here. You need to come over and have dinner again with Lori and me. Does next Tuesday work?"

"Yeah, it should. Thanks."

"How's the roommate situation working out?"

Riley had to laugh. "Is this your way of trying to figure out if I'm pissed off at you for pointing me toward Pigpen?"

There was Cary's laugh again, this time even louder. "Yeah, maybe I shoulda warned you about that."

"A heads-up that the guy is basically a walking haz-mat spill would've been helpful."

Justin Perry, or "Pigpen," had been the only guy who'd needed a roommate when Riley had signed. He'd never talked to Justin except on the ice before so he hadn't known much about him personally.

The guy was really nice and skated like he'd been born on blades, but off the ice Justin was one big accident waiting to happen. Kind of like a twenty-four-year-old toddler. If he held it, he spilled it. If he ate it, he wore it, and if he was walking, sure as shit he knocked something over.

"So you really have a date tonight?"

Riley slashed Cary across the shins, not hard enough to hurt, of course. They had a game tonight. "Why is that such a shock?"

"Maybe because you haven't done it much since your divorce."

Ah, yes. He'd almost forgotten he'd known Cary that long.

"Been almost seven years since it was final. I've dated a few times since then."

"Yeah, no shit."

Okay, maybe more than a few times, but fuck it. He wasn't married. Not anymore. "Hey, just 'cause you're old and married doesn't mean the rest of us should be."

"Okay, if you're gonna insult me—"

Luckily, Coach blew his whistle, calling the team in to talk about the game tonight and what they needed to work on.

But Cary's remark about his divorce stuck in the back of his brain. He hadn't thought about Ann for months. At least, not since he'd left his parents' place in June. He'd gone home for a few weeks between the end of last season and the start of training camp. He hadn't seen his ex the entire time he'd been back, and his parents hadn't mentioned her at all. But he had seen her new husband, Thad, and their two kids.

He and Thad had graduated high school together. Ann had been a year behind them. They'd been close back then. Hell, Thad had been one of the groomsmen in Riley and Ann's wedding. Now, she and Thad were happily married with kids and a house and a mortgage.

And Riley still ping-ponged around North America playing a game he loved. A game Ann had come to hate because he'd loved it more than her.

But now...he had to admit he was getting a little sick of never really having anywhere to call his own.

Maybe he needed to think about hanging up the skates after this season.

The problem was...what the hell would he do if he didn't play hockey?

———

"SO THAT'S THE GUY. Damn, he's huge."

Aly could barely hear Vivi over the roar of the crowd and pumping music. They'd gotten to the arena only five minutes before the game had started and had barely gotten into their seats before the lights dimmed and the teams skated onto the ice.

She'd had to wait until the lights came up to see the program and find out what number Riley wore so she could find him on the ice.

But as soon as she spotted him, she knew she'd never mistake him for another man. There was something about Riley that made every single hormone in her body tingle and take notice.

"They're all huge. I think some of it's the gear."

"Maybe. But he's *really* big." Vivi looked over and grinned. "So not your type. I like."

Knocking her shoulder against Vivi's, she shook her head. "Don't even go there. Jesus, we haven't even gone out yet. And I talked to him for, like, ten minutes."

"Yeah, but you're going out with him tonight. Guess I shouldn't be surprised if you don't come home, huh?"

She felt a blush heat her cheeks. "Jeez. Tell the entire arena."

Vivi rolled her eyes. "Oh please. No one can hear us over this noise."

Probably true. The arena wasn't completely sold out but there had to be at least seven thousand people in the building, most of them standing and clapping for their team while they waited for the referee to drop the puck to start the game.

Since she'd never been to a game before, she wasn't really sure what to expect.

The speed was exhilarating but, oh my god, the game was *physical.* Players slammed each other into the boards so hard, the glass around the ice shook. They fell or were tripped and hit the ice so hard, she flinched, unable to believe they didn't break bones.

But milliseconds later, they were back on their feet and skating off after the puck.

After a particularly brutal-looking hit by an opposing player against one of the Redtails, the man sitting a few rows down yell, "Get off your knees, ref! You're blowing the game."

She and Vivi turned to each other and started to laugh.

As they continued to laugh, the buzzer sounded and the players exited the ice. Music started to play and everyone around them rose and stretched or headed toward the aisles.

She and Vivi stood but didn't leave.

"I think I might love hockey." Vivi grinned at her, no hint of sarcasm to be found. "I can't believe we haven't come to a game before."

Aly smiled back, happy to see her sister smiling. "I'm enjoying it but, oh my god, every time they get hit, I want to cringe. How do they take so much damage? It's brutal. They must be one big bruise afterward."

"Usually, yes, they are."

The friendly voice came from behind them and Aly turned to find a pretty redhead smiling at them.

"Sorry, couldn't help but overhear. Hi, I'm Bliss." She stuck out her hand, which Aly immediately shook. "You obviously haven't been to a game before and we are *so* loving your commentary."

Immediately on her guard, Aly's smile dimmed as she transferred it to the brunette standing next to Bliss.

"Hey, I'm Lori." She stuck out her hand, too. "And honestly, we're not being catty. My husband and Bliss's boyfriend are players. I've been living and breathing hockey for a few years so whenever I meet someone who doesn't, I love watching them fall in love with the game the way I did."

"I'm fairly new to the sport, too," Bliss said. "My boyfriend, Shane, is the goalie. Lori's husband, Cary, is a forward."

Then Lori and Bliss exchanged a glance before Lori's smile widened. "So I hope you don't mind me asking but...which one of you is dating Riley?"

Stunned, Aly's eyes widened.

What the hell?

Obviously, Lori read her expression because the other woman held up a hand. "Yes, I know we're being really intrusive but you're sitting in the wives and girlfriends section so we figured we'd say hi. And since hockey players are almost as bad as teenage girls about gossip, everyone knows Riley has a date after the game. We just wanted to say hi. If you have any questions, feel free to ask us. We've probably had the same ones."

Since they seemed nice, Aly decided to take them up on the offer. "Is the game always so...rough?"

Both women's smiles warmed and Aly felt her internal walls slipping even more.

"Sometimes, it's worse." Lori shook her head. "This game's actually been pretty tame."

"Since Shane's the goalie, he doesn't get hit a lot but Riley's a pretty physical player," Bliss continued. "He'll probably have more than a few cuts and bruises when he takes off his gear tonight. Just don't be shocked. The guys are used to it. You will be, too, when you're around the game long enough."

Aly had the almost overwhelming urge to reiterate the fact that she and Riley had just met and were having their first date tonight then decided against it when Lori continued.

"The first time I met Cary after a game, I thought he'd been in a fight in the locker room. He had a black eye from a fight in the second period and a huge bruise on his side. I was afraid to touch him." She exchanged a glance with Bliss. "He didn't have the same problem."

Bliss rolled her eyes while Lori laughed. She was a little older than the rest of them, probably mid-thirties, but her laughter was warm and inviting and Aly couldn't help but like her. Even Vivi, who didn't always warm up to people right away, smiled at Lori.

"Yeah, I'm not going there." Bliss shook her head. "But I will say they're usually a little...hyper after a game, especially if they win."

"Do they win a lot?"

"Well, we're two months into the season and they're twelve and three. Last year, they won the championship and this year, they're predicted to get to the finals again."

"So they're good?" Vivi asked.

Lori smiled. "Yeah, they're really good. Riley wasn't here last year but he's been a great addition to the team. Cary thinks this could be Riley's year to get called up."

Aly shook her head. "I don't—"

"Sorry, sorry." Lori made a face. "Forgot you don't speak hockey yet. Called up means he'd get to play in the NHL."

Okay, now that she understood. "And that's where he wants to be, right?"

"That's the ultimate goal, yes." Bliss nodded. "Not all of them make it, though."

Lori put her arm around Bliss's shoulders and hugged. "And some are destined. They don't call Shane 'Brick Wall' for nothing."

Aly was fascinated. "Does Riley have a nickname?"

Bliss grinned. "Well, some of the guys call him 'Chickie' because he chirps. It means he likes to talk shit to the other players, throw them off their game, draw a penalty. He's pretty well known for it."

"Cary swears Riley could get a saint to take a swing at him." Lori shook her head. "But he's mainly known as a grinder. He doesn't make a lot of goals but he makes sure his teammates have the puck so they can score."

Chirp. Grinder. The lingo was making her head spin.

Lori must have seen her brain misfiring because the other woman reached out and squeezed her shoulder. "Stick with us, ladies. By the end of the game, you'll be experts."

"SO YOUR WOMAN SHOWED UP. See, I told you. No need for worry."

Jake stopped beside Riley as he buckled his belt then grabbed his coat. They'd won the game so the noise level in the locker room approached deafening, but it barely registered.

Riley had played hard tonight. He' had one fight because one of the Lynx players had gotten in his face, and had three assists on four goals.

A good night. And hopefully about to get better.

"I wasn't worried," he told Jake as he headed for the hall where he'd told Aly he'd meet her after the game. He hadn't thought about her at all during the game. He never let anyone—not a girl, not another player, no one—mess with his head before or during a game.

But now... Yeah, maybe he had been a little worried she wouldn't show.

He'd purposely not looked into the stands to see if she was there tonight. He'd kept his mind on the game and it'd paid off. This season was off to a good start and he hoped to hell it continued.

"I know you do not worry during game. You are machine out there. Damn good game tonight."

"Thanks. I—"

Damn, there she was. And, holy shit, was she gorgeous.

Vaguely, he heard Jake laugh, but Riley dismissed him as the uncontrollable urge to grab her and kiss her nearly overtook him. The urge was so strong, his fingers clenched.

She didn't see him right away. She stood next to Cary's wife, Lori, and Shane's girlfriend, Bliss. They looked to be in deep conversation.

And then she smiled and, holy shit, he swore he was back in high school when a girl just had to look at him and he got hard.

Back then, his only desire had been to get laid. Until he'd met Ann and things had changed.

Damn, he'd have to stop thinking about his ex. That'd been a hell of a long time ago.He let himself stare at Aly instead.

Fuck, was she gorgeous. Sure, he'd noticed yesterday but now, in tight jeans and boots with heels, a tight white shirt and a blue cardigan, she looked so fucking hot, he thought he might break out in a sweat.

How the hell did she manage that looking like a kindergarten teacher?

Probably because the jeans fit her long legs like a second skin and the shirt had a v-neck that hinted at just enough cleavage to make him drool.

And her hair was down, nearly reaching the small of her back. Holy fuck. He wanted to wrap his hands in it and tug her head back so he could kiss her. And do other, less polite things to her.

Not that the way he wanted to kiss her was polite. No, what he wanted to do to her should be done in private. And naked.

He really wanted to do naked things with her.

A grin formed and she looked up at that moment, caught him staring at her.

Her smile softened a little as their gazes connected, but it was the look in her eyes that made his dick hard. Hot. Sweet. But definitely heat there.

He knew she wasn't like any other girl he'd dated in the past five years. And that meant he'd need to take this slow. It'd be a first for him but he'd do whatever it took to make sure Miss Aly hung around.

"You, my friend, should be very glad you saw her first." Jake bumped Riley's sore shoulder as he walked by but the shooting pain from the injury sustained in a late-third-period collision with the boards couldn't deflate his dick.

"There's no way a woman that gorgeous would give you a second look," Shane spoke from behind them. "Though why she thought Riley was a better option, I'll never know."

Shane gave Jake a shove as Shane came up behind the other guy. Jake barely moved and didn't even look at Shane. "Is too bad for her. I suppose Lad and I will go spread our joy to the women at West Reading. Have a good time, Chickie."

Riley let the hated nickname flow right past him.

"Oh I plan to, Jake. I definitely plan to."

———

"YOU DELIBERATELY BAITED a man who weighed fifty pounds more than you to take a swing at you? Are you crazy?"

Riley shrugged, the grin that had been driving Aly crazy all night reappearing on his lips.

"Some people say so, yeah. But he was killing us so we needed him off the ice. Took me until the third period but I finally got to him. While we were in the bin for five, my guys scored twice and tied up the game. We won in overtime."

"Is that where you got the nickname?"

"What nickname?"

The wince gave him away.

"Chickie."

He rolled his eyes as he turned onto the street where she lived. They'd spent the last three hours talking at the bar and he was a little amazed they hadn't run out of things to discuss.

Then again, everything seemed easy with this woman.

"Hockey players think they're funny."

"Aren't they?"

"Not most of them."

"Then I guess you're not like most of them."

He slid her a glance. "You think I'm funny?"

Her smile made his cock twitch in anticipation. "I think you're avoiding telling me how you got the nickname."

He laughed. "I got it in college. One of the guys on my team was a farm boy from Pennsylvania, and after a game he told me how I reminded him of this chicken he had that never shut up. The other players started calling me Chickie and it stuck."

"Did you play in high school, too?"

"My dad says I grabbed a stick when I was about four and never let go. It's been my life ever since."

"How long do you plan to play?"

He shrugged, not yet ready to admit his defeat aloud. "Not sure. When I'm done, I'll figure out what to do with the rest of my life. I have a degree in sports management. The plan is to work with kids when I get out, but beyond that, I don't really know. I've been too focused on playing for the past twenty years."

Her eyes widened. "Twenty years? You've been playing since you were eight?"

The shock in her voice kind of surprised him. "Well, more than that really, but yeah."

"Do you really love the game that much?"

"Yeah." Something his ex had accused him of more than once. That he'd loved the game more than he loved her. It'd stung at the time...mostly because she'd been right. He'd been selfish. "You have to or what's the point?"

After a short pause, she said, "You're absolutely right."

"Could you say that again so I can record it and play it for my mom? I swear, no matter what I do, she thinks it's wrong. So, did you and your sister have a good time tonight? She was welcome to come with us tonight, you know."

She laughed quietly and nodded. "I know but she, ah, had plans come up. But we did enjoy the game. I can't believe how physical it is. How are you still able to walk? I saw you get hit really hard a few times."

Shrugging, he automatically rolled his shoulder, happy there was no pain. "You get used to it. Besides, I knew I had a date to look forward to and I wasn't missing it because of a few bumps and bruises."

He slid her a glance and caught her smiling again.

"You're kind of a flirt, aren't you?"

"Just kind of?"

She laughed, as he'd hoped she would, and shook her head. "Okay, definitely a flirt."

"Thank you. Would hate to think I was half-assing something."

She was still laughing when he parked at the sidewalk in front of the address she'd given him.

"Is this yours?"

It looked so...suburban. He almost expected two-point-five kids to run out, screaming, "Mommy!"

"Mm-hmm. Technically, it belongs to my parents, but when they moved to Florida a few years ago, they asked my sister and me if we wanted to stay here. It was a no-brainer. My parents took out a second mortgage, bought a condo in Florida, and now my sister and I pay that mortgage and live here and my parents have their place in the sun and everyone's happy."

"You are *way* more adult than me."

She sighed. "So I've been told."

He looked back at her but couldn't figure out her expression. He wanted to ask her if he could come in but he didn't want to push her. They'd spent the past three hours talking, and even though he'd expected to carry the conversation, she'd held up her end. She was quietly funny, her laughter a husky rasp that bit him low in the gut.

And she seemed to think he was hilarious. She laughed at his jokes, which meant he'd had a constant hard-on. Still had one, as a matter of fact.

And when she bit her lip then said, "Do you want to come in?" he wanted nothing more than to say yes.

So why didn't he?

"Yeah, I do. But...we've got practice tomorrow. Well, this morning, actually. And if I come in with you, I won't want to leave."

She blinked and her lips parted and he had to bite back the urge to groan. So he did what he did best. He kept talking.

"But Coach gets pissy when we don't show up, especially the morning before a game. I might find myself riding the bench tomorrow night and that'd be a problem."

He was expecting a pout. A lot of other women would've been pissed off. This woman smiled, which made him want to kick himself in the ass for saying no, even though he knew it'd been the right decision.

Because for the first time, he didn't want to rush. Maybe he was growing up. Maybe he was learning some control. Whatever.

"And you would hate that, wouldn't you?"

"It would suck, yeah. I don't like riding the bench."

"You're too good to do it much."

"Now who's the flirt?"

And there was that smile again, the one that made him want to take a bite out of her. Her breast, her ass, the inside of her thigh... That smile wasn't shy. Aly was a little reserved, yeah, but not shy.

"Come to the game tonight. I'll leave tickets for you."

That smile made him want to rethink his decision.

"Okay, thanks. My sister has to work, but I'll be there."

"Good."

They sat there for a few more seconds, smiling at each other until she dropped his gaze and grabbed her purse.

Taking the hint, he got out and walked around to open her door. Without thinking about it, he wrapped an arm around her shoulders and drew her into his body. Her arms slipped around his waist, and when she put her hand on his hip, he tugged her even closer.

Walking her to the door, he stood by while she got her keys out of her purse and opened the lock. Then she turned and looked up at him with those blue eyes and no one could fault him for being unable to resist her.

He leaned in and kissed her. With his hand cupping the back of her head and the other on her hip, he pulled her in and didn't hold anything back.

He'd been so damn good all night and he wasn't going to follow her in that house. But he had to have a taste.

Her heat shocked him—in a good way. Her response nearly made him forget his resolution to take this slow.

And when her arms slid around his waist and she stood on her toes to kiss him, he might've groaned. Okay, he did groan. And then he opened his mouth over hers and inhaled her.

She opened to him immediately, her tongue meeting his without hesitation.

Holy Christ. Lust surged as their tongues tangled. Every nerve ending in his body lit up, and he pressed her mouth open even farther. Sucking in air through his nose, he sealed their lips together, his fingers spreading through her hair to hold her.

She didn't balk at his possessive hold. Instead, she went soft against him, and he got even harder.

If he hadn't been trying to be good, he would've lifted her against the door and pressed his aching cock into her soft mound.

It took every ounce of restraint he had not to grind against her or run his hands down her body. Her curves had taunted him all night. The woman had no sharp angles. She was made to be petted.

But not tonight.

He began to pull back but she followed him, going up on her toes to prolong the kiss until he was about to break his resolution to take this slow.

They were both breathing heavy when she took a step back.

Forcing himself to do the same, he fisted his hands so he wouldn't reach for her again.

She swallowed hard and licked her lips before tilting her head to the side and all that silky hair slid over her shoulder, making him want to groan. Christ, he wanted to feel that hair against his skin. Preferably against his chest and his thighs—

He sucked in air. "So...I'll see you tomorrow night."

She nodded. "Will I sit with Lori and Bliss again?"

"If you want, yeah, I can arrange that."

Her smile widened. "That'd be great. Since Vivi can't go, I'd rather not sit alone."

"No problem." He'd make sure to give a huge thank-you to Cary's wife and Shane's girlfriend the next time he saw them.

Another quick smile. "Good night."

He had to suck in air before he could answer. "Night."

Then he waited until she closed the door and he heard it lock.

He was still smiling when he got back in his truck. Hell, he was still smiling when he walked into his apartment.

"Dude. Didn't expect to see you back here tonight. Bad night? No luck, huh?"

Riley smacked Justin on the back of the head as he walked by on the way to his room.

"Fuck you. Great night. Going to bed."

"Damn, thought you were too old for quickies. Although at your advanced age, I guess if you can keep it up longer than a minute, that's pretty good."

Riley kept walking through he did shoot Justin the finger over his shoulder. No way was he getting drawn into a conversation now.

"It's past your bedtime, kid. You need to get your beauty sleep. St. John's is fast."

"Wait, are you really going to bed? You're not gonna share at all?"

"Night, Justin."

As he closed the door to his bedroom behind him, he smiled as he heard Justin bitch, "Dude, you suck."

THREE

"So." Vivi drew the word out to about fifteen syllables the second Aly stepped into the kitchen Saturday morning. "How'd it go?"

Aly didn't bother to answer right away. Yes, she was one of those disgustingly cheerful morning people though she did need coffee before she became fully functional for the day.

So she walked past her sister, got her mug and poured coffee that Vivi, amazingly, had already brewed. Since Aly was almost always the first one up in the morning, she usually made the first pot.

Bracing herself, she sipped...and managed to avoid a full-body shudder. Vivi made legendarily strong coffee. Aly was a little surprised she didn't immediately sprout hair on her chest.

"Holy. Shit." Aly managed to suck in a gasp of air before sliding into a seat at the little table by the window where Vivi sat. "How the hell do you drink this?"

"With my mouth." With a sarcastic grin, Vivi lifted her mug and saluted her before gulping down half of her mug. "And what'd you do with your mouth last night? Not much, I'm guessing, because he left without coming in."

Aly smiled, thinking about exactly what she had done with her mouth last night. And yes, all they'd done was kiss.

"But," Vivi continued, "I guess something happened or you wouldn't be smiling like a lunatic."

Aly wrinkled her nose. "I'm not smiling like a lunatic. I'm just smiling. It was a nice night."

"Nice?" Vivi hmphed. "How 'nice' could it've been if he didn't even come in the house? What's wrong with him?"

Aly took another sip of coffee and glared at her sister over the rim of her mug. "There's absolutely nothing wrong with him. He was a total gentleman."

"So he didn't touch you." Vivi shrugged. "Sorry."

With a huff and a roll of her eyes, Aly set her mug down. "Not every guy's just looking to get laid, you know. Sometimes, the foreplay's just as much fun as the actual sex."

Vivi's turn to roll her eyes. "And maybe the guy's got..." She held up her pinkie and wiggled it.

Aly laughed, shaking her head. "Yeah, no. I don't think Riley has to worry about that. From what I could feel, that's not even remotely a problem."

"So what happened?" Vivi leaned on the table. "Why'd he leave? Did you not invite him in?"

"I did but he had practice this morning and he needed to sleep. He has another game tonight and I'm going to that and meeting him afterward again. He's an actual nice guy, Viv."

"Did he even kiss you?"

She smiled and let Vivi figure out the answer to that on her own. "I'm starving. I think I'll make pancakes. You want some?"

"Sure, if you're making. But I gotta leave in an hour. Double shift at the studio today and I'm picking up a shift at the bar tonight. Hey, why don't you guys come over after the game? Chet won't be there tonight so you won't have to deal with his shit. And tell Riley to bring his team. The girls will love me if you do."

One of Vivi's three jobs was waitressing at The Bomb Shelter, one of the most popular bars in the area.

Aly didn't usually go there. The music sucked, it was always crowded on the weekends, and a lot of the guys who went there were douchebags who thought women existed for their personal pleasure.

"I'll check but I don't know what he'll want to do tonight."

On the other hand, she had some great ideas about what she wanted to do tonight. Last night, she hadn't been ready for anything really physical and somehow Riley had known that. She been a little worried, not that he'd force her, but that he'd push for something she wasn't ready to give.

They'd been so in tune and she'd almost convinced herself to give him whatever he wanted.

Or maybe she was kidding herself and he'd decided he didn't really want her and he'd text her today and tell her something had come up and—

Okay, she needed to stop.

Shaking her head, she ladled batter onto the skillet just as her phone rang.

She grabbed it off the counter, ignoring her sister's laughter, then sighed when she saw the screen.

"Oh, I know that look." Vivi shook her head. "You better answer it because if you don't, she'll call me and you know I'm not picking it up. Then she'll call the police because she'll think we were murdered in our sleep or some other horrible thing and I'm not dealing with it."

Because her sister was right, Aly took a deep breath and answered.

"Hey, Mom. How's it going?"

"Did I wake you? It's almost ten. I figured you'd be up by now. Were you out late last night? I know it's Saturday but I know you don't sleep in. Now, your sister..."

Aly rolled her eyes and sucked in a deep breath, hoping for patience as her mom continued to talk for the next thirty minutes.

She finished the pancakes while her mom relayed every ailment she and her dad had endured that week, in more detail than Aly ever wanted to know. Unfortunately, she was used to it because this was how almost every week's call went.

Mom would start with the health update. Sometime she'd stick to just her and Dad's health. If it was a slow week for them, Mom would throw in an update on the neighbors, all of whom were around the same age. The condo complex they lived in was mostly seniors but there were a few younger people. Younger being a relative term. Anyone younger than fifty was a kid to her mom.

After the health update, Mom would complain about the weather. Too hot, too windy, too rainy, or, oh my god, hurricane season. Aly would counter with the fact that, hey, it was Florida and they didn't have to deal with snow or cold.

Then Mom would ask what was going on at home, and if Aly didn't have enough to talk about, her mom would want to know what was wrong. Sometimes she'd ask specifics, like about work or she'd want to know what trouble Vivi was getting into.

If Vivi happened to be around, her sister would sigh, shake her head, and conveniently have somewhere else to be.

And sometimes, if Aly was *really* lucky, her mom would ask if she'd met anyone.

Yeah, that was fun. Especially when her mom decided she'd found the perfect guy for Aly. All she'd need to do was move down with them.

Apparently, it was Aly's lucky day.

"Oh, and I met finally met Susan's son. You remember Susan, right? She lives at the end of the first floor. Lost her husband to cancer a few years ago. Her son moved down here to be closer to her. He's got a job with some insurance outfit in Tampa. Seems like a nice guy. When you come down, you should meet him. I think you'll like him. He's only a few years older and he's handsome..."

Aly let her mom talk, replying when necessary. Her mom meant well but, oh my god, she was tired of this constant pushing. Her mom was convinced Aly would eventually move to Florida, marry some nice man—whom her mom would find for her, since Aly apparently couldn't meet nice guys on her own—and provide grandchildren.

Aly wasn't sure she even *wanted* to have kids. Especially not if she became just like her mom someday.

Sighing, she turned to Vivi, who was shaking her head and had her hand over her mouth so their mom wouldn't hear her laughing and want to talk to her.

Vivi never got the "I met this man you should meet" speech from their mom. Vivi was convinced their mom was afraid she would actually procreate and her children would be just like her.

Aly had always been the "good one." Good grades, never in trouble, college degree and job right out of college.

Vivi... Well, the local cops knew Vivi by name. And after the third or fourth time they'd shown up at the door asking to talk to their parents, Vivi had become the "difficult one."

It was a distinction that still pissed off Aly, even though Vivi had gotten past it years ago. Hell, she'd pretty much embraced it.

Which left Aly as the one her parents relied on. The one to visit her sick aunt in the hospital and help her cousin move into her dorm room and be sure she remembered everyone's birthday and went to every wedding and anniversary to represent "the family."

Everything she would've done anyway because that's what family meant to her. Hell, she didn't even know why being considered reliable pissed her off.

Maybe...maybe she secretly wanted to be a little less reliable and a little more wild. Like Vivi.

Maybe that's why she liked Riley. Because he wasn't a guy her mom would ever think she'd date.

"And I told him when you come down at Christmas—"

"Whoa, wait. Mom, I'm not sure I can come down at Christmas. I told you. Julie's probably getting married around the holidays so I can't make any plans."

"Oh." Her mom paused. "Well, I didn't honestly think that would last. Julie's always been so flighty."

Oh my god, her mom was going to drive her crazy.

Aly's friend, Julie, was marrying a smart, handsome guy who happened to be black. Aly's parents hadn't raised her and her sister to be prejudiced, but their own prejudices were deeply ingrained.

"Well, we still hope you and your sister will be able to get down for a few days around the holidays. It'd be so nice to have everyone together for Christmas."

"We'll have to wait and see how everything works out. You know Vivi's work schedule is a mess around the holidays and there's always something going on at the hospital."

Thankfully, her mom let that go and they chatted for another few minutes before finally saying good-bye.

And when her phone screen finally went black, she drew in a deep breath and released it on a heavy sigh. She felt like she'd run a marathon.

"And this is why I try not to talk to Mom more than a few minutes at a time." Vivi shook her head, waving her fork like a wand. "You look like you're about to heave. What'd she say about Julie?"

Aly grimaced. "That she didn't think 'that' would work. And I'm not sure but I think the only reason she called was to see when we were coming down so I could meet some guy, marry him, and move down there."

Vivi rolled her eyes. "Oh my god, I can't believe she still thinks she can get you to do it. Thank God they gave up on me. I don't know why you just don't tell them it's never gonna happen."

Because she wasn't sure she wouldn't. Which, of course, she couldn't tell her sister. Vivi would freak and tell her she'd be making a huge mistake. Which she probably would be.

But she also knew her parents weren't getting any younger and eventually would need help. But that would leave Vivi alone here.

"Aly?"

"Hmm?"

Vivi sighed and shook her head. "You need to stop thinking about everyone else and put yourself first for a change."

"I don't know what you're talking about."

"Bullshit." Vivi held her gaze. "Are you *seriously* thinking about moving to Florida with Mom and Dad? Because if you waffle even a little, Mom will put on the full-court press and you'll find yourself living in Florida married to some guy named Tad with two-point-five kids, a mortgage you can't afford, and Mom in your house every day 'just to help out.'"

Aly had to hold back a shudder at the thought. "I'm not. At least, not now." She rolled her eyes and huffed. "Okay, *maybe* I might've thought about it. Maybe I feel like I've been in a rut lately. I've had the same job for five years. I still live in the house I grew up in. Last night was the first time in months I've had a date because I'm so freaking boring. All my friends are married or getting married, and some of them have kids or they've moved away. So yeah, I'm thinking about it."

Vivi's eyes widened. "Wow. Aly, I didn't realize—"

"Sorry." Aly shook her head, grimacing. "Sorry, sorry, sorry. I don't mean to take out my frustration on you. I've just been...restless lately."

"Don't be sorry. You hide stuff so well. I had no idea you were so..."

"Bitchy?"

Vivi's mouth twisted in a rueful grin. "Conflicted."

Conflicted. Yeah, that was a good description.

Aly shook her head. "Don't mind me. PMS. I'll be fine."

Vivi's grin gained a wicked edge. "I think you might have found the cure for that. You can work out some of your frustrations with Riley tonight. Have some fun, sis. Try not to worry so much. And take the guy to bed tonight, for chrissake. Seriously. Get naked and get laid."

Was a night of sex with a hot guy the answer to everything?

Could it really be that easy?

———

"RILEY, sweetheart, how are you? Season going well so far?"

"Hey, Mom. So far, so good, yeah. What's doing at home?"

Kicking back into the recliner, Riley shoveled food. Practice hadn't been difficult but he needed to refuel before the game tonight.

"Oh, nothing much." She paused. "Well, not too much, anyway."

Riley put down the fork that was halfway to his mouth. "What's wrong?"

"Nothing's wrong." Another pause. "Nothing serious, anyway. Oh, your dad's been having some trouble with his leg again and I keep telling him he needs to go to the doctor, but you know your father. I thought you could talk to him, maybe convince him he needs to get it checked. You know you're the only one he listens to. When I talk to him, it goes in one ear and out the other. I don't think anything's seriously wrong but... Well, I was hoping you'd talk to him."

Riley closed his eyes for a second and took a deep breath. Being an only child had its perks but he'd been a late baby. His parents had been over forty when he'd been born.

Which made them almost seventy now. Not ancient but more prone to health problems, especially this past year when his dad had had pneumonia twice and his mom had had two biopsies on her breasts. Neither had been cancerous, but still. And of course, all of it had happened during the season.

"Have you gotten Julie over to see him?"

His parents' neighbor was an emergency room nurse who'd been their first stop for all things medical for as long as Riley could remember.

"I've tried. He says he doesn't need to talk to her because he's perfectly fine. Which makes me think he isn't. Can you talk to him, Rye? I know you probably have a game tonight but—"

"Mom, it's no problem. Where is he?"

"Thank you, honey." His mom sounded so relieved, he pressed his fingers against his temples, rubbing against the ache he felt starting there. "I'll take the phone to your dad."

His mom fell silent but he heard her footsteps as she made her way upstairs. He knew she couldn't navigate the stairs and continue to hold a conversation because her balance wasn't great. Another sign of her age.

Setting his plate on the table in front of him, he drew in a deep breath, trying not to let his deeply buried guilt rise any further.

Damn it, there was no reason for him to feel guilty. His parents wouldn't want him to feel guilty. They'd never played that card with him, had never made him feel like he owed them anything.

And yet...

"Harry." His mom's voice sounded muffled. "Your son's on the phone."

"Rye, everything okay?"

"Everything's fine, Dad. How're you doing?"

"I'm good, I'm good. How's the team? Saw you had three points last night."

Riley shook his head. The only way his dad could have known that was if he'd looked it up on the computer, which his dad hated but used so he could keep up with Riley.

Riley gave his dad a rundown of the past couple of games and gave him a preview of tonight's game. His dad had never played beyond the club level and didn't really understand Riley's consuming love of the game. But his dad had never told him to give up hockey and get a real job. Not even when Riley had taken that year off in college.

Finally, the conversation wound down and Riley took the opening.

"So, Dad, what's up with your leg?"

"There's nothing wrong with my leg. Your mother doesn't know what she's talking about. My leg's fine."

"No, your leg is *not* fine." Riley heard his mom in the background. "Tell him about the other day when you couldn't even stand."

"The damn thing just fell asleep. There's nothing wrong."

From almost two thousand miles away, Riley spent the next ten minutes refereeing his parents' argument while trying to figure out if his mom was overreacting or if his dad was downplaying.

By the time he ended the call, he'd convinced his dad to get his legs checked out and told his mom he'd call later this week to make sure his dad had gone.

Setting his phone on the table, he picked up his plate but his appetite was gone.

Fuck. What the hell was he supposed to do? He couldn't go home. He had a game tonight and he needed to have his head on straight. He already had Aly in there, fucking with his concentration. And now this stuff with his parents.

Shit.

"Dude, everything okay?"

Justin walked into the living room with a sandwich in one hand and a glass of chocolate milk in the other.

"Yeah. It's fine. It's just...my parents."

"They sick?" Justin sat in the chair opposite him, munching away, oblivious to the fact that he was already wearing some of the mayo from this sandwich.

"No. I don't know." He shrugged. "My dad's having trouble with his leg. My mom's worried. I'm not there."

"Hey, man. They were adults before you were born. I think they can take care of themselves."

The simplicity of Justin's statement made Riley blink. And then grin as he shook his head.

"So you going out with that girl again tonight?" Justin asked. "She was fucking hot, man."

Before Riley could answer, Justin continued. "You think Coach is gonna switch up the lines tonight? A few of the guys were talking about it— Why are you laughing?"

It took Riley almost a minute to rein in his laughter while Justin looked at him like he'd lost his mind.

"You gonna tell me what the hell you were laughing at?"

Riley shook his head. "Man, does your brain ever shut off?"

Justin shrugged, not offended at all. "Nope. So you seeing her again?"

"Yeah, I am."

And tonight, he wasn't stopping until she asked him to.

————

"HEY, fucknugget. I'm gonna fucking put you on your ass the next time."

"Fuck you, asswipe." Riley baited the opposing player as they came out of the corner. "Try not to play with yourself in the box, kid. Don't want everyone to see how small your dick is."

For a second Riley thought he'd managed to piss off the opposing player enough to take another swing at him, but the linesman had a good grip on the kid's arm and they skated toward the penalty box before Riley could say anything else.

Probably a good thing since the Redtails were going on the power play and Riley needed to get off the ice.

There were eleven minutes left in the third period and the Redtails were down by one. The St. John's team was fucking fast but they were young and a little undisciplined. They'd managed to get two goals in the first period but they'd taken five penalties, two of them drawn by Riley.

Now, the Redtails needed to capitalize on this one and tie the game. Then they needed to get their heads out of their asses and win this game.

They'd played like shit tonight, their first line sluggish and out of sync. The defense had broken down more times than he could count and they were lucky to only be losing the game by one goal.

"Good job, Hatch." Coach smacked him on the back as Riley sat on the bench then shifted down with the other guys to make room for the next line.

"Yes. Nice job, Chickie." Jake leaned over and bumped shoulders. "Now if only we make it count."

Their power play team hadn't been doing so well this year. They'd been working on their special teams hard the past week but they still hadn't gelled. Two minutes later, they hadn't scored and Riley skated back on the ice for his shift.

But the ice never tilted back in their favor and they lost the game two to one.

The mood in the locker room was subdued. Coming off last night's win, they'd been expecting another two points. Having their asses handed to them tonight sucked.

And now he needed to throw off the pissy attitude because he had a date.

For a split second, he considered texting Aly to call it off. Then he realized that was a shitty solution and took himself into the showers to soak his head.

By the time he came back out, he felt a hell of lot better because he hadn't been able to stop thinking about Aly.

Christ, he had half a chub now and he hadn't even seen her yet.

And when he walked out into the hall and caught sight of her, he had an instant hard-on and the rest of the night's disappointments faded.

All because she smiled at him.

Tonight, he had no intention of being good. Tonight, he planned to be as bad as he could convince her to be.

"Hi." He almost had to strain to hear her, even though the mood in the hall was pretty quiet as the guys left the locker room and headed for the parking lot.

He wanted to grab her and repeat that kiss from last night. Just thinking about it made his muscles tense in anticipation.

"Hey. You ready to get out of here?"

Her smile dimmed a little and he cursed himself for the pissed-off tone in his voice.

He was about to apologize when she reached for his hand and squeezed. "Sure. Tough game tonight."

"Yeah, you could say that."

Her teeth lodged into her bottom lip for a second before she spoke again. "Would you like to come back to my place for a drink instead of going somewhere? Vivi's working late and—"

"Yeah. I would. That'd be great."

Her smile warmed again. "Then let's go."

They walked in silence to her car in the lot across the street, her hand in his. He'd caught a ride in with Justin. If he needed to, he'd Uber it home tonight. He was hoping he wouldn't need to. Hoped like hell that her smile was an invitation he had no intention of turning down tonight.

"So do you have practice tomorrow morning?"

"Not in the morning, no. We've got an optional skate in the afternoon that I'll probably go to. We had our asses handed to us tonight. We're lucky the score wasn't ten to one."

"They seemed like a tough team."

"They're one of the worst in the league. A bunch of fucking kids with no— Shit. Sorry. Don't mean to take my frustration out on you."

She squeezed his hand as they reached her car, a sensible four-door gray sedan that would be a tight fit for him. He'd suffer through it for her.

The lot was mostly deserted now, the fans already on their way home. She'd parked her car in a dark corner and the next thing he knew, he had her backed up against her car with his mouth sealed over hers.

He hadn't wanted to wait another second to kiss her. Couldn't wait another second to kiss her.

And when she wrapped her arms around his waist and pressed against him, he wasn't sure they'd make it back to her place before he stuck his hand up her shirt so he could get his hands on her skin.

Christ, he felt like a teenager, all hormones and lust. But, holy fuck, she was hot and right there with him.

Her fingers bit into him, pulling him closer, showing him how much she wanted him. Damn good thing, too, because he had a burning ache deep in his gut that intensified with every passing second.

For the first time in months, maybe years, he felt wanted, not because of what he did but for who he was.

And how fucking awesome was that?

Her lips moved with his, opening for him to slide his tongue into her mouth. She tasted hot and sweet and made him want to suck all that sweetness into his own body.

Her natural reserve melted away under the heat of that kiss and she snuggled in closer, her stomach pressing even tighter against his cock.

Oh, fuck yes.

Sucking in air, he kissed her harder, more intensely, wanting her to be as crazy as he felt himself getting. He didn't want to be the only one out of control.

Sliding one hand into her hair, he tugged her head back even farther and spread his other hand across her back. She wasn't going anywhere unless he allowed it.

The thought made him want to growl, made him want to put his hands on her ass and lift her into him.

He wanted to strip off her clothes and—

Hell, that definitely wasn't happening here.

He stepped away, breathing hard, gratified to hear her gasp.

"I think we should probably get out of here."

She nodded, sucking in a deep breath. "I think you're right. Are you hungry? We could—"

"I'm not thinking about food."

And there was that smile again, the one that made every muscle in his body clench with anticipation.

"Then I guess we better go."

He didn't move for another few seconds, sifting his fingers through her hair before reluctantly releasing her.

But he didn't move away, his gaze locked with hers. Her eyes mesmerized, such a calm, tranquil blue.

"Riley?"

And her voice... Damn, he could listen to her for hours. Preferably while she screamed his name as he made her come.

After a few more seconds, he took a step back, just enough for her to slip out from between him and the car and head for the driver's door.

"I guess you don't want to talk about the game," she asked after he folded himself into her car.

He shrugged. "Bad night. Wasn't the first. Won't be the last."

She slid him a glance before putting the car in gear and putting them on the road. "You seem...like there's something else on your mind."

"The only thing on my mind right now is you."

Which was totally true. He'd worry about his game tomorrow. Tonight, he only wanted to think about her.

"Tell me what you did today." He honestly wanted to know. He wanted to know everything about her.

Her soft laughter did crazy things to his insides.

"Not a damn thing that isn't totally boring."

"Why don't you let me be the judge of that."

"Seriously, I cooked, I cleaned...I kept looking at the clock to see if it was time to leave for the game."

She looked at him and smiled, and he had to keep telling himself he couldn't touch her. Because if he did, they'd wind up in an accident.

"Glad to hear you're enjoying the games."

"I enjoy watching you."

Oh fuck. The things he wanted to say to her right now could get him arrested in some states and would definitely involve putting his hands on her. And then they'd be in real trouble.

"You can watch me whenever you want."

"I think I might like to watch you skate with a few less clothes on."

She startled a laugh out of him. "You're a little kinkier than you like to pretend, aren't you?"

"I never have been before. And I didn't say I wanted to see you skate *naked*. That might be...dangerous."

He shrugged. "Not as much as you might think. And you'd probably be surprised to find out it wouldn't be the first time."

She shook her head, her soft laughter raising goosebumps on his skin. "I don't think anything you could say would surprise me. I have a feeling you haven't exactly been a saint."

"Now why would you think that?"

Her smile grew at the teasing tone of his voice. "Let's just say you kiss like you've had lots of practice."

He wondered if she was put off by that. She didn't seem to be, but he still hadn't mastered the art of reading a woman's mind. Probably never would.

"Is that a problem?"

She slid him a quick glance as she drove away from the arena. "Only if you don't plan on continuing to kiss me."

"You only have to ask and I'll give you whatever you want."

"Better be careful. Keep giving me whatever I want and I won't want you to stop."

At the moment, that wasn't a problem. Actually, he wasn't sure that would ever be a problem, which was ridiculous because they'd been on exactly one date. Hell, they could be awful together in bed. She might love Brussels sprouts, which would be a total turnoff. She might grow to hate the game he loved. Been there, done that, had the divorce to prove it.

"Honey, I will give you as much as you want for as long as you want it."

He thought she'd laugh again. That's what he'd been going for. Instead, she gave him another one of those looks and another one of those smiles and he had to restrain himself from kissing her.

He knew from last night they'd be at her house in a few minutes and he'd be damned if he did anything to slow them down. But, holy hell, if she didn't drive faster, he was going to put his foot on the gas pedal himself.

Turns out, he didn't have to. She gave the car a little more gas, and soon enough she was pulling to a stop in front of her house.

Conversation had died but anticipation had risen with every second.

He held himself in check as she parked the car on the street but jumped out as soon as the car stopped moving and headed for the driver's door.

She smiled up at him as he reached for her hand to help her out of the car. And she didn't let go as they walked to the door. Lacing her fingers through his, she held on, moving close enough that he felt her breast brush against his arm.

And holy fuck, who would've thought that little bit of contact could make heat flush through his body like a flash fire?

If he wasn't careful, he'd embarrass the hell out of himself before he even got in the house.

He didn't want to give up her hand but she needed both to open the front door. He reluctantly released her but as soon as they were both inside, he took her by the shoulders, spun her around, and crowded her back against the door.

He heard her suck in a breath but he didn't hear any fear. And when he caught and held her gaze, he saw only desire.

She lifted her hands to his shoulders and settled them there, their warm weight setting a match to his already smoldering lust.

Her head dropped back against the door and she stared straight into his eyes.

"Do you want something to drink?"

He shook his head, his hands falling to her waist, caressing the flare of her hips.

Her dark blond eyebrows rose, a tease in the arch. "Not thirsty?"

"No."

"Something to eat?"

He let his mouth curve slightly and watched her cheeks redden slightly. "Not hungry...for food."

He felt her hips lift under his hands, felt the zipper of her jeans brush against his cock for a brief second before she moved away.

"Want to watch some TV?"

"Only if you're standing in front of it taking your clothes off."

She blinked and he thought maybe he'd just stuck his foot in his mouth. Then she laughed.

And hot sex against the door became a very real possibility.

She stepped into him, put her hands on his jaw and pulled him down so she could kiss him.

Surprise made him freeze for about a millisecond. Then he got with the program.

He tightened his hold on her hips and dragged her closer. She came without hesitation, plastering herself against him from chest to thighs and adding fuel to the fire already burning in his blood.

Kissing him hard, she wrapped her arms around his shoulders and opened her mouth to him.

The kiss went from blazing to inferno in the blink of an eye and his brain blanked out everything but her and his need to have her.

As his tongue slid along hers, he groaned when she returned the caress with her own.

Fuck.

His cock hardened into a painful, throbbing ache and he pulled her hips against his, pressing his erection against her mound, trying to get some relief. She moaned into his mouth and rubbed her hips against him.

Her lips soft and open beneath his, she arched her back, pressing her breasts against his chest as she rose on her toes. Her fingers slid into his hair and tugged on the strands. His scalp stung but, damn, he liked it.

Pressing harder into the kiss, he let his hands spread on her hips then slide around to her back so he could urge her even closer. But he didn't think he'd ever be able to get her close enough. At least not with her clothes on.

And since she seemed to be totally with the program, he didn't think she'd push him away if she slipped his hand under her shirt to get to her bare skin. Because, damn, all he wanted to do right now was touch her.

Putting one hand on her ass, he let the other slip under the hem and groaned as his fingers encountered warm flesh.

So damn soft.

God damn, this was gonna get out of hand fast.

He thought about slowing down but then she scraped her nails along his scalp, shooting lightning bolts through his body and nuking any thoughts of going slow.

Tangling his tongue with hers, he put one hand on her ass and took her off her feet. She gasped but quickly wrapped her legs around his waist, never breaking the kiss.

Fuck yes.

He let their tongues tangle for several more minutes, loving the taste of her and the feel of her body against his. She was soft in all the right places and the urge to have his hands touching every inch of her had become an overwhelming desire.

With her hands in his hair and her legs around his waist, she let him know she was right there with him.

All the frustration from tonight's game fed into his lust, made it burn hotter, until he couldn't stand to only have one hand and his mouth on her.

Pulling away, he wanted to say something but she followed him, her lips clinging and her hands pressing him back toward her. With a groan, he let her dictate terms since she seemed to be intent on kissing him and he had no trouble with that.

Her enthusiasm made his dick even harder, and he hoped like hell he didn't come in his pants. How fucking embarrassing would that be?

But damn, the woman knew exactly what to do to make him hot.

Her tongue slid along his with so much teasing eroticism, every muscle in his body clenched.

This girl might look sweet and innocent but her kisses could melt stone. Or make flesh hard as rock, which was what his cock felt like right now. A throbbing, stiff column of granite.

And now she was rolling her hips against his, pressing her mound against his erection and making him see stars behind his closed eyelids.

Turning his head so he could talk, he caught his breath as her lips pressed against his cheek and back until she sank her teeth into his earlobe.

"*Fuck.* Aly, hold up."

"Don't want to," she whispered in his ear. "Are you getting cold feet?"

"Honey, nothing on me's cold right now. I just need to hear you say yes."

Her soft laughter in his ear made him shudder.

"I guess the fact that I'm practically getting myself off rubbing against you right now isn't enough of a hint." As he practically swallowed his tongue, she licked his earlobe then put her lips right against his ear. "Yes."

His arms tightened around her and he had a quick second to say "Hang on" before he turned and headed for the first piece of furniture that looked sturdy. He'd broken a sofa arm once, practically ripped it off with some yoga instructor who'd been the bendiest person he'd ever met.

And there was the chair he and some puck bunny had busted in some hotel room in...oh hell, he didn't give a fuck where right now.

All he wanted was to get Aly to the couch.

Luckily, he had a clean shot straight to it, and when he finally had his ass planted on it, he had Aly right where he wanted her. With her knees spread on either side of his hips and his hands spread across her back, keeping her close.

Not that she seemed to want to go anywhere.

Her hands rose to cup his jaw and she brought their mouths back together for another one of those breath-stealing, heart-stopping kisses.

He had a brief second to wonder if he was the one being seduced instead of the other way around. Then he realized he'd be okay with that.

But only because it was Aly.

That didn't mean he was just going to sit there while she kissed her way down his jaw to his neck and made his hands tighten on her hips.

Fuck that.

Sliding his hands under her shirt, he spread his fingers across her bare skin and let the warmth of her body seep into his.

She let out a little moan as she rose onto her knees, her hands tugging on his hair until he complied and let his head fall back. She followed, her hands releasing his hair so she could slide her fingers into the back of his shirt.

He wore a dress shirt but hadn't bothered with his tie so the first few buttons were already undone. She took full advantage by sliding her hands around his neck to the buttons he had done up and started slipping them through their holes.

When she'd gotten almost to the top of his pants, she sat back and let their gazes connect.

The half-smile on her face made it hard for him to breathe.

"I didn't realize there'd be layers." She tilted her head, silky hair sliding over her shoulder. "Good thing I'm dedicated to finishing what I started."

The husky tone of her voice sliced straight through to his gut, making his muscles clench as she pushed the shirt off his shoulders then stared at him with raised eyebrows.

He knew what she wanted and leaned forward just enough for her to push it all the way down his arms so he could push it over his hands. He left it crumpled behind him, immediately forgotten.

His lips curved in a smile as she contemplated his plain white undershirt. He figured she'd say something about how unsexy it was when the corners of her mouth tilted up and she shot him a look that made his skin sizzle.

"I'll let you in on a little secret." She trailed her fingers over the neckline, barely brushing his skin. "Women think guys who wear undershirts are hot."

Smiling at the amusement in her voice, he figured she was teasing him. "Yeah? Why's that?"

"Well, you know how guys like women in sexy lingerie? Some women think guys look just as hot in t-shirts and tight boxers. The way they cling to your muscles." She ran her fingers over his pecs and barely brushed his nipples. "It makes me want to stroke my hands along the fabric and feel what's beneath."

His mouth dried with her every word until his lungs felt heavy and tight. He sucked in air, his gaze locked on hers. She could talk all night and he didn't think he'd ever get bored. Especially not if she kept talking like this.

And kept stroking her nails along the fabric over his nipples, making them hard and sensitive. Her nails were just long enough to catch on the fabric and on his nipples, the slight sting as she caught the little piece of flesh on each upward stroke making his cock throb even harder.

"Give me a guy in tight boxers and my panties get wet."

Holy fuck. This girl might actually give better sexy talk than he did.

How the hell had he gotten so damn lucky? Time to up his game.

"So I guess you wanna take my pants off now, too? 'Cause I gotta tell you, I think you're gonna like what you find."

Luckily for him, he was mainly a boxer-brief guy, though he did have a couple pairs of tighty-whiteys in his drawers.

Her smile widened as her fingers continued their way down his chest, over his stomach, stopping just short of his waistband, where his cock pressed against the zipper with ever-increasing force.

"I'm not sure I'm ready for the whole unveiling just yet."

Her fingers made that statement a lie as she moved her hand just enough that her nails brushed over the zipper of his pants.

"Then maybe you need to take a little time-out and let me help you out of a few of your clothes. Maybe I wanna see what you're hiding. Cotton? Silk? Bikinis? Granny panties?"

She laughed and the sound sparked fire along his nerve endings.

"You're out of luck if you're excited about the granny panties."

"Well, damn. Maybe next time."

Her fingers stuttered back up over his stomach. "Maybe we should concentrate on the first time for now."

"I'm a guy who likes to plan ahead."

"And what exactly are you planning now?"

"How I can get you to unzip my pants."

Her gaze flashed back up to his and, though her smile wasn't as wide, it was infinitely hotter and promised things he could only dream about.

"I think the magic word is 'please.'"

Lifting his hands to cup her face, he drew her closer. Their lips only a hair's breadth away, he whispered, "Please," and watched her lashes flutter before he sealed their lips together and kissed her like he needed her to breathe.

Her palms pressed to his chest as she opened her mouth and tangled her tongue with his, licking and sucking and giving him everything he wanted and more.

He almost missed the fact that her hands were moving down his body as she rose slightly onto her knees. But when her fingers danced along his waistband, he groaned and his hands dropped to her waist and tried to pull her closer.

She resisted, probably because her hands were working at his belt. So he eased up and gave her room to work. He'd be lying if he said he wasn't enjoying the way she was taking her time.

He'd always been a fast-gratification kind of guy. He loved hockey for its speed, got a rush out of the exhilaration.

He was getting the same thrill from Aly's breathtakingly slow unbuckling of his belt. Tensed from his shoulders through his calves, he tried to loosen his muscles. But when she finally separated the two ends and her fingers pressed into his abdomen to release the button, he jerked her closer.

Her lips curved against his and she pulled back just far enough to speak.

"I'm beginning to think you have no patience, Mr. Hatch."

"I'm beginning to think you like torturing me."

"This is torture?"

"Fuck, yeah, it's torture. The good kind."

She laughed. "Glad to hear you're enjoying it."

"I'd enjoy it a hell of a lot better if your hands found their way into my pants."

"I'm getting there. Are you always in such a rush?"

Because it's exactly what he'd been thinking about only seconds ago, he ran his hands from her hips up her sides to just under her arms, his thumbs barely brushing the sides of her breasts.

He heard her swift inhale and felt her shiver beneath his hands, making him that much hungrier for skin-on-skin contact.

"Sometimes fast is good. You can't catch your breath and your adrenaline's pumping and everything's hypersensitive."

"Are you talking about sex or hockey?"

She was definitely having trouble breathing now and his lips curved.

"Both. Hockey's much better when the pace is fast. Keeps your blood pumping and your attention focused. Fast sex can be mind-blowing. And I'm not just talking about the guy shooting off in five seconds and the girl left hanging."

Her fingers popped the button on his pants but she didn't reach for his zipper. "Glad to hear it."

"No, I'm talking about getting you so worked up in a couple of minutes that the second I get my cock inside you and start to pump, you come while I'm still getting off. You come so hard you can't breathe and your muscles don't work anymore and your brain's fuzzy."

He could barely control his own breathing right now, so fucking turned on by the woman in his arms and the images in his head. Images he planned to replace with the reality.

She sucked in a deep breath and he glanced down to find her fingers trembling over his zipper.

"Come on, baby." He leaned forward and sealed their lips together. "Let's blow our minds as fast as we can and I promise I'll take my own sweet time with you for the second round."

Her fingers hung in midair before she shook her head. "I don't know, Riley. Maybe I'm having fun tormenting you."

"Think about how much more fun you're gonna be having riding my cock."

He didn't know if it was the image he'd planted in her head or if she just took pity on him, but a second later she grabbed the tab of his zipper with deliberate fingers and began to pull it down.

Already pounding, his heart kicked into another gear as she released his cock. Her head bent, she reached into his pants and cupped his erection through his underwear.

Holy shit. Sensation shot through his erection to his balls and up his spine. If he wasn't careful, he'd come in her hands.

And that would be embarrassing as all hell.

But he didn't want her to stop as she traced her fingers around the tip of his cock, pushing at the band of his underwear

"Lift up."

He obeyed immediately, prepared to give her anything she wanted.

Her mouth curved in another one of those smiles that made his blood run lava-hot.

"You're so agreeable."

"Sweetheart, you keep stroking me like that and I'll do whatever you want. Go ahead, ask me to rob a bank for you."

Her laughter brushed against his skin, raising more goosebumps. "Why don't you just start by taking off your shirt?"

Shifting forward, he reached one hand over his shoulders and pulled the t-shirt over his head. After he tossed it to the side, he found her staring at him intently.

"What's wrong?"

She shook her head, her gaze wandering below his chin. "Not one damn thing."

Huffing out a laugh, he leaned back into the cushions. "Glad to know you approve."

Lifting her hand, she placed her right index finger on his shoulder, her nail digging gently into his skin. "Oh, I approve. Now, I need you to lose the pants."

"That means you're going to have to move."

"I'm sure you can figure something out. Come on, Riley. Show me how you maneuver in a tight spot."

Holy fuck. When she smiled at him like that, he almost expected to see flames sparking between them.

"Your wish is my command."

A flush burned her cheeks and it was his turn to grin as he moved his hands between them. He deliberately brushed his knuckles along the zipper of her jeans and had the satisfaction of hearing her suck in a sharp breath. Her hands rose to his shoulders and gripped him tight, fingertips digging into his skin hard enough to leave marks.

They'd blend in with all the other bruises on his body, but he was having so much more fun getting them.

Going as slowly as he could, he worked his hands between their bodies, making sure he made as much contact as he could.

As he reached for his waistband, he slid his hands between her legs, pressing the seam of her jeans against her mound. Her chest rose and fell in an ever-increasing rhythm, almost matching his own.

Hooking his thumbs in the sides, he tugged at his pants. Luckily for him, they weren't that tight. If he'd had to struggle at all, he might've put just enough pressure on his rock-hard cock to trigger his orgasm.

But because of her position directly over him, he did have to lift his hips to push them down over his ass, which meant his cock rubbed right between her legs, exactly where he was going to be soon.

Making sure to drag his underwear with his pants, he worked them down just far enough to expose his cock, which was so hard, it practically pressed against his stomach.

Aly's gaze had dropped to watch, and when the tip of her tongue came out to touch her top lip, he groaned.

Leaning forward, he cupped her cheeks and brought her forward so he could kiss her and let his tongue slide across those lips.

She caught him off guard when she drew the tip of his tongue into her mouth and sucked on it.

The sensation made him think of her sucking on his cock the exact same way.

Fuck, fuck, fuck. Concentrate, asshole, or you're gonna lose it.

He wanted to lose it inside her, not come on her stomach like a virgin.

But when she dropped one hand to wrap it around his erection, all bets were off.

Sinking his hands into her hair, he held her steady and opened his mouth over hers, eating at her with a hunger he almost couldn't control. It rose up in a rush, a tidal wave of heat, flooding his body and loosening the chains he'd been struggling not to break.

Aly appeared to have reached the same breaking point. She moaned low and deep, her hand tightening around his cock until he thought he'd have to tell her to stop. A second later, she loosened her grip. But that only made him want more.

He got to work on her jeans, getting the button undone and yanking down the zipper. But she was going to have to move if he was going to get those jeans off.

Grabbing her around the waist, he lifted her off his lap and twisted to the side, setting her on the cushion beside him.

Surprised at the sudden movement, she sprawled on her back, wide eyes blinking up at him as he shifted onto his knees to loom over her.

Her gaze locked with his, she came up onto her elbows as he grabbed her jeans and yanked them down her legs.

Unfortunately, they were a little tighter than he'd realized and she came with them. She started to laugh a split second later, her head falling back, sending all that blonde hair spilling across the cushions.

With a growl to cover his own laughter, he yanked again and was rewarded when she lifted her ass and the denim bared a few inches of flesh.

He looked into her eyes, bright with laughter. He loved her smile but in a few seconds, he was going to make her scream. "Sweetheart, if I have to strip them off with my teeth, they're coming down."

"How about you use your teeth somewhere else and I'll get rid of the pants?"

His turn to grin. "I like the way you think. But you get rid of the pants first. I know where I want to use my teeth."

She swallowed hard and leaned back, hands working at her jeans until she had them shoved to her ankles. He took over then, pulling them away and leaving her bare from the waist down.

"Shirt too, babe. I'm gonna work my way up."

"Why not work your way down?"

"Because if I get my cock anywhere near your pussy right now, I'll revert to a thirteen-year-old and come before I get inside you."

She blinked, sucking in a short sharp breath. Shit, he needed to watch his mouth—

Her grin appeared again and a wicked light shone in her eyes. Maybe that good-girl routine really was just a front.

Time to test that theory.

Twisting, he brought his knees up onto the cushion so he knelt between her legs. He put his hands on the arm of the couch, just above her head, then leaned down. Her gaze flicked to his arms for a few seconds before she swallowed hard and looked back up.

Her grin slid away but the heat in her eyes blazed hotter.

"Condom?" she asked.

"Wallet. Back pocket."

Lifting her back slightly, she reached behind him, her hand brushing across his bare ass, accidently or not, and sparking even more heat.

He growled as she took her own sweet time pulling out his wallet while her fingers danced over his skin. Those few seconds seemed like hours and passed way too quickly as she brought the wallet between their bodies.

His breathing started to sound like a freight engine, heavy and hard. His cock felt as rigid as steel and he had to clamp down on his response if he wanted to make this last more than a minute.

Something she seemed determined not to allow.

With the condom now in one hand, she used her free hand to stroke him, lightly, with just the tips of her nails.

Holy fuck, that felt amazing. His balls drew up tight, and his cock bobbed.

"Put it on then take your shirt off. I need to feel your skin against mine."

Another smile before she reached for him and rolled the condom down his length.

Gritting his teeth, he let her linger, let her take her time, but as soon as her hands moved away, he sat back on his heels and tugged her shirt up and over her head. Thank god her sweater was loose and didn't give him a hassle. Otherwise, he would've ripped it, no lie.

But now that he had her naked in front of him, he couldn't wait.

He put his hand over her mound, sliding his fingers between her slick lips to make sure she was ready before pressing inside with one and pressing the heel of his palm against her clit.

She moaned, her hands coming up to grip his forearms.

"You want me to stop?" he had to ask.

"God, no. Don't stop."

That was all he needed to hear. He added a second finger and began to fuck her with them, keeping up the pressure on her clit and watching her intently.

Every slight shift of her body, every sound, every time her fingers dug further into his arms, he became more intent on making her come at least once before he got inside her.

"Damn, you are so fucking gorgeous."

Her bare breasts were beautiful, the nipples pale pink, and before he knew what he was doing, he leaned forward and put his lips over one, sucking the tip into his mouth and sucking on her.

Her eyes closed and her head fell back on a moan, pushing herself harder against him.

With his fingers still occupied between her legs, he switched to her neglected breast, sucking even harder this time, as if he could make her come from just his mouth on her breasts.

Next time, he'd make that a goal. Right now, he couldn't wait any longer.

Kissing his way to the center of her chest, he grabbed her knees and spread her wide. Her fingernails dug even deeper into his biceps as he guided his cock to her opening and began to press forward.

Holy fuck. She was tight. And hot. And god damn, he wanted to sink as deep into her as he could before he pulled out and shoved in again.

"Put your legs around my waist, hon. Don't let go."

She responded immediately, her legs hooking over his hips, ankles locking behind his back. Her hands lifted to clasp around his neck and she tugged, bringing his mouth back down to hers.

With his cock buried deep inside her, his tongue shot into her mouth, sliding against hers and connecting them on another level.

Mine. She's mine. Only mine.

The thought didn't sound like him. He wasn't that guy, wasn't an asshole with a Tarzan complex. But this woman made him fucking crazy.

His hips pumped harder even as he tried to slow down, to use a little finesse, not be a rutting bull.

The problem was, she seemed to have no issue. In fact, she seemed to want him to go even faster.

She lifted her hips into his harder on each thrust, pressed her lips tighter to his, and scrambled every last working brain cell in his head.

Intense pleasure flooded his body and his hips swung faster, his cock stiff as iron and so damn sensitive he swore he'd stroke out from it.

Luckily, he didn't. He managed to hold on for another several minutes until he felt her tighten around him then moan as she came.

Mine.

Groaning, he came, wrapping his arms around her as tight as he could and holding on.

He didn't think he was letting go anytime soon.

———

HER BRAIN still fuzzy from the amazing orgasm Riley had just given her, Aly sucked in air, trying to calm her racing heart.

She wasn't having much luck.

Holy hell, what'd just happened?

Okay, stupid question. She knew exactly what had happened. She just wasn't sure she'd be able to process it for a week. Or a month.

What she knew right now was that she didn't want to move, didn't want to think. She only wanted to feel.

Riley was huge and heavy, and even though he'd shifted partly to the side, he still managed to cover most of her and take up more than half the couch as well.

She liked that, too. So much so that her brain kept throwing out warning signals but they weren't making sense because her body was still floating on a high of adrenaline and pleasure.

And every second Riley continued to breathe heavily into her ear, she grew more frantic.

This wasn't how this was supposed to work. She was supposed to be relaxed, boneless. Floating on a sea of bliss and contentment.

Instead, her brain wouldn't stop working.

She wanted him again, wanted him to kiss her like he had before, like he wanted to devour her. Wanted him to put his hands all over her, to cup her breasts and tweak her nipples then let his fingers trail down her body to between her legs and play with her clit, which still throbbed.

How could she want him again, so quickly? How—

He shifted against her and her arms automatically tightened around his shoulders, clinging. He didn't go far, just rearranged their bodies so she was lying more on top of him than beneath him and able to breathe more easily.

At least in theory. In reality, she still was having trouble catching her breath because each time she drew in air, all she smelled was him.

Clean, masculine male. The most potent aphrodisiac she'd ever encountered.

Careful now. This doesn't sound like you. You don't fall for guys like this.

It wasn't sensible. It wasn't anything like her.

But when Riley's big, rough hands began to pet her back, she could only think about the way those hands made her feel. Protected. Wanted. Desired.

Way too fast.

"Aly? You okay?"

And that voice. Oh my god, she wanted him to keep talking with that rough growl so close to her ear. Wanted to snuggle into him like he was her own personal full-size teddy bear and have him make love to her all night.

She wanted to go again in a few minutes. Wondered if he wanted the same.

God, please let him want the same.

"Aly, hon. What's—"

"I'm fine." Her hands clutched at him involuntarily, as if she was afraid he'd get up and leave. "Just...trying to recover."

He huffed out a laugh and drew her closer. "Yeah, I know. That was fu— ah, amazing. Let's do it again."

Yes. Oh god, please, yes.

She almost let one hand begin a downward slide to see if she could hurry him along then stopped when she realized what she was doing.

No. No, no, no. She shouldn't be trying to get him to stay. She should be hurrying his ass out the door. Even though she wanted him to stay.

And why would you ever want him to go home? Are you crazy? This is the guy you've been waiting for.

Holy crap, she was going crazy. He'd brainwashed her, put her under a spell that made her do whatever he wanted.

"Don't you have practice tomorrow?"

He sighed. "Yeah, but one sleepless night isn't going to pull me down. Of course, after a few like this, I might not be able to move. But it sure as hell would be worth it."

Putting his strong hands against her back and drawing her even closer, he pressed a kiss against her head, making her melt even more. And her panic response kicked in again.

She wanted to ask him to stay but she knew she wasn't ready for that. Didn't know how long it would take for her to be ready for that.

Except...she really wanted him to stay.

"Hey, hon. You sure you're okay? You seem a little...quiet."

She nodded but she couldn't force herself to meet his gaze and lie to his face. "I'm fine. I'm just tired."

She held her breath and hoped he'd take the hint. For a few seconds, she wasn't sure he would. She thought she was going to have to ask him to leave and that might've sent her into a spaz attack because she didn't really want him to leave.

Get a grip, you idiot. He needs to go before you beg him to stay.

So she waited, practically holding her breath. Finally, he seemed to get the hint.

"Well then, I guess I better get going and let you sleep."

She tried not to clutch at him as he shifted them around until he was on the edge of the couch. But he'd maneuvered them so they were face-to-face. She couldn't avoid looking into his eyes, and when she did, she was fairly certain she was going to beg him to stay.

She managed, barely, to keep her mouth shut but only until he leaned forward and kissed her. And when he slid his tongue against her lips, she immediately opened for him.

He made a deep sound in his throat, a sound that made her sex clench and beg for anything he wanted to use to fill it. Fingers, tongue, cock.

Shivering, she let her arms wind around his shoulders, pressing her naked flesh to his and feeling her resolution to send him on his way sink to the soles of her feet.

She was just about to move her hands from his shoulders down his back to his ass when he released her and swung his legs off the side of the couch and planted his feet on the floor.

"I really like spending time with you." He turned to look at her, shoving long fingers into his too-long dark hair to push it out of his hazel eyes and making her chest tighten. "So, tomorrow night. Are you free?"

Blinking as he stood and his perfect ass came into view, she had to take a few seconds to think about what he'd said before she could formulate an answer.

"Yes."

When he reached to pull his pants up, she nearly swallowed her tongue. She watched him tuck his cock into his jeans but not zip them.

He looked back at her. "Bathroom?"

She had to suck in air before she could answer.

"Oh, yeah." She pointed to a small door off to the side of the room. "Just in there."

She watched the play of muscle across his back and chest as he walked to the bathroom and sat there for several seconds waiting for him to return before she realized she was naked. She'd just pulled her shirt over her head when he walked out again and returned to pick up his t-shirt and dress shirt.

As he shrugged them on, he turned to smile at her. And her heart kicked into heart-attack pace.

Not fair. And oh, so very dangerous.

"You wanna get some dinner tomorrow night after the game?"

Yes, she did. Very much. She wanted to do anything he wanted.

Which made the words stick in her throat. She wasn't that girl, the one who tossed over her entire life for a guy she'd just met. Still, she wanted to see him again.

"Sure. That's sounds... great."

How did he manage to make her feel breathless and light-headed and heavy-limbed all at the same time?

Either he ignored her slight hesitation or he just didn't hear it. His smile widened. "I'll give you a call after practice."

Leaning down, he put his hands on the back of the couch on either side of her shoulders and bent close.

She braced for another one of his mind-numbing kisses but he put his mouth on her neck instead. He nipped at her skin, sending her into a full-body shiver. She reached for him, her hands landing on his hips, and she wasn't sure whether she wanted to pull him closer or push him away.

When he started to pull away, she almost didn't want to let him go. She actually had to force herself to release him so he could stand.

"See you after the game. Puck drops at five. Game should be over by eight."

"Okay."

Halfway to the door, he turned to look at her.

"I have a great time with you, Aly. I think..." He stopped, appeared to reconsider his words then smiled. And totally didn't say what was on his mind. "I'll see you soon."

Then he walked to the door and headed out, closing it quietly behind him.

She must have sat there for a full minute staring at the door, jeans in her hand, bare ass on the couch.

Holy shit.

She felt like she'd been run over by a steamroller.

That wasn't good, was it?

Could you actually fall in love this fast?

No. Absolutely not. That wasn't what this was.

She wasn't in love with Riley. In lust, yes. Hell, who wouldn't be? The man was worship-worthy.

But he wasn't a man you fell in love with. Not if you wanted two-point-five kids and a picket fence and a house in the suburbs.

Everything she'd always wanted.

When she was a kid, her parents had always been on the move because of her dad's job in quality control for a chemical company with plants all over North America. This house was the only one they'd lived in for more than four years and only then because her dad had exhausted himself and the company owners had insisted he take a desk job.

Aly had hated moving every couple of years. She didn't make friends as easily as Vivi and she'd loved everything about this house, which was why she'd jumped at the chance to continue to live here when her parents moved to Florida.

Riley had the kind of life Aly never wanted to live again. He could be on the move next month, next week. Hell, he could be called up to play in Philly tomorrow.

Definitely not a man she wanted to get too involved with.

FOUR

Riley eased open the door to his apartment.

The landlord still hadn't fixed the squeaky hinges and he didn't want to wake Justin. It was almost two a.m. and his roommate would probably be asleep—

"Guess the date went well."

Justin grinned at him from the couch, where he held a beer in one hand and a game controller in another.

Riley gave him the finger before heading into the kitchen for a beer.

"Still up playing with yourself, I see." Riley sank into the other end of the couch.

"Hey, now. No fair picking on those of us less fortunate. I'm guessing from the grin on your face, you had a good time."

Riley shoved his elbow into Justin's side. "What are you, my mother?"

"No, just the guy who hasn't gotten laid in three months."

"Ashley still mad at you, huh?"

Justin grimaced at the mention of his longtime girlfriend, who still lived in their hometown of Kanata, Ottawa.

"Yeah. She keeps harping on me about taking that offer in Toronto. And I keep telling her it's the worst damn team in the league. Why the fuck would I want to go there when I can play for the damn Cup defenders? You'd think she didn't know I played fucking hockey. Fuck that. Now...tell Daddy J all about your date tonight."

Justin smirked at him and Riley couldn't help but laugh.

"You're a sick motherfucker, you know that, right?"

"But I know you want to spill your guts."

Riley took a swig of his beer and shook his head, still grinning. "No, I really don't. It'll be all over the locker room tomorrow."

"Do you actually give a shit what the other guys think? Dude, your conquests are legendary."

The beer suddenly didn't taste as good as it had as he watched the on-screen battle rage.

Justin wasn't wrong. Riley did have a reputation. One he hadn't been concerned about for years. Different girl every other night. No repeats.

Until this season. This season, he'd sworn off hookups, had committed himself to his career with no distractions.

After tonight... He couldn't fucking wait to see Aly again. He'd wanted to go to bed with her and wake up in the morning to see her, hair messy, skin warm and soft from sleep. He would've stayed if she'd asked. She hadn't. And that just made him want it more.

She had no idea how much of a break from the norm that was for him. And he didn't want her to know.

"Yeah, well, maybe I'm turning over a new leaf this season."

Justin went silent and Riley shot him a glance.

"Dude, seriously? You just met this girl and now you're all ready to reform your manwhore ways?"

Riley shrugged. He didn't want to get into a discussion about his dating habits at two in the morning when he should be in bed.

"Maybe I'm starting to think about what I want to do after this season. What I want to do...after hockey."

"Seriously?"

Justin's shock rang clear in his voice. Riley slid him another glance and found his roommate staring at him with his mouth hanging open.

Shrugging, Riley took another swig of beer before answering. "I've been giving it some thought."

"You're not even thirty. What the *hell*, man? Is something wrong?"

He shook his head. "Nothing's wrong. Just been thinking maybe it's time to think about what's next. You know, figure out what I'm gonna do with the rest of my life."

Justin shook his head like he hadn't heard him right. "Why? I mean seriously, why? You're only twenty-fucking-eight years old. It's not like you're forty and you can't bend your knees and your shoulder's hanging on by a ligament."

All true. "Maybe I want to get out before that happens."

Justin continued to shake his head in shock. "Dude, what *happened* tonight?"

He'd had the best damn sex of his life, that's what'd happened. And he'd met a girl he might want to live with for the rest of his life.

Even his own brain went, *"Hey, now. That's kind of a huge leap."*

But Riley was used to making snap decisions and changing things on the fly. And he knew himself. He wasn't some teenager just out of the draft with mad skills and no polish.

"Nothing happened." Or maybe something really big had happened. But he wasn't sharing that with Justin. "It's just something that's been on my mind."

Justin gave a full-body shake, like a dog shaking off water. "Yeah, well, get it off your damn mind or you're gonna jinx yourself. And the team. Just don't go there."

He couldn't help it. He was already there. "Don't you ever think about what you're going to do after?"

"Why should I?" Justin shrugged. "I'm gonna play 'til I can't then I'll figure it out."

It was the mantra of a lot of players. Hell, Riley had lived by it for years.

"Rye." The tone in Justin's voice pulled Riley's gaze back to him. "Are you seriously thinking about giving up?"

Now there was an interesting way to put things.

Riley shifted on the couch to look Justin in the eyes. "Is it really giving up if you're going to find something else to do with your life?"

Justin's gaze was too damn sharp for almost two in the morning. "Is that what you want? To do something else?"

No. But he knew he wanted more. And he knew who he wanted more with.

"What I want is to get enough sleep before skate tomorrow afternoon."

"You mean this afternoon."

Shit, yeah. "Exactly. I'm going to bed. Night."

He got up and headed for his room.

"Hey, Rye."

Riley stopped and looked over his shoulder at Justin.

"This is your year, man."

He just shook his head and continued to his room.

"SOMEONE HAD A GOOD TIME LAST NIGHT."

Aly gave her sister the side-eye as she made her way to the coffeemaker Sunday morning. She'd slept until nine, which was as long as her body would naturally sleep before her eyes popped open.

"Don't worry," Vivi continued. "You don't have to say anything. I can tell by the smile on your face he must've been good."

A blush heated Aly's cheeks but she purposely ignored Vivi's sly remarks as she poured herself a mug of caffeine and headed for the cabinet for something to eat while the coffee kicked in.

"Obviously, the man knows how to move off the ice as well as on."

Yes, he certainly had. But she still wasn't giving her sister the satisfaction of responding.

Vivi sighed dramatically. "Guess I'll need to get earplugs if he's going to be sticking around. You two probably made enough noise to wake the neighbors. Maybe I should ask Tig if I can stay at her house tonight. I assume you're seeing him again tonight."

"I'm ignoring you."

Vivi huffed. "You're *trying* to ignore me. You're not doing a very good job of it. Come on, spill. You know you want to tell me all about it."

Aly grabbed the box of Lucky Charms out of the cabinet and poured a bowl. Every other day, she had something sensible, but on the weekends she needed her sugar. It was Sunday—and she'd probably burned enough calories last night to eat the entire box.

Which made her smile.

"Oh, now, that's just mean." Vivi threw her napkin at Aly as she sat across from her at the breakfast table. "If I had smoking-hot sex with a guy, I'd tell you all about it."

Aly gave her sister a raised eyebrow. "Whether I wanted to hear or not."

"At least admit you had a good time."

She shrugged, trying for nonchalant although she felt anything but. "I did."

"And that you want to see him again."

"I do. He's..." She struggled to find a word that wouldn't trigger all kinds of questions from her sister that she couldn't answer. "He's really nice."

Vivi's eyebrows rose again. "Nice? He's *nice*? Oh please. Any man who makes you look like you're still in shock from last night is not just *nice*."

"Please stop telling me how I look this morning. It's weird."

"Then maybe you should look in a mirror before you come to the table looking like you spent all night screwing your brains out."

Aly stuck her tongue out at her sister before she started eating, then proceeded to ignore her and read the paper.

For the first time since she'd played field hockey in high school, she looked at the sports pages. The article on the game took up about half a page but it mentioned Riley's name a few times, all favorably. The writer made special mention of Riley's work ethic, how he never gave up, even if he didn't get what he wanted the first time.

And yeah, she'd seen that part of him in action last night. Once he'd set his mind on something, he didn't stop.

When he'd said he wanted to hear her scream, he hadn't been kidding.

She swore she was still blushing when her phone rang a few minutes later.

She grabbed it...and sighed.

Not Riley.

"Hey, Mom." She exchanged a glance with Vivi, who shot out of her seat like her ass was on fire and disappeared. "What's wrong?"

"Nothing. I just forgot to remind you about the service contract yesterday. The one for the heater? You probably need to renew that this month. I remembered that when your dad complained about the heat yesterday. We've had the air running nonstop for the past six months, I swear. And we're supposed to be getting hit with that tropical storm next week..."

Stifling a sigh, Aly let her mom ramble, answering appropriately when required, feeling guilty when she looked at the clock and rolled her eyes when she realized her mom had just spent the last twenty minutes talking about her dad's refusal to go to the doctor for his constant intestinal issues and then ran down her own health issues. All of which she'd mentioned yesterday.

She loved her parents. She did. But sometimes...

Well, sometimes she wished she wasn't the one they relied on. The one everyone relied on. Sometimes she wished she could be a little more like Vivi, born with the ability to let everything roll off her back and not feel guilty about it.

She wanted to have fun and not worry about the consequences.

She wanted to have hot sex with Riley and not think about the fact that one day he'd move on to another team, another city. Another girl.

She wished she didn't feel like the two nights they'd spent together had been the start of something amazing.

———

"IF THAT KID skates by me again with that smirk on his face, I'm gonna lay him out on his ass." Riley glared at CJ. "I get it, he's young. But he's a twig and I'm gonna snap him."

"You can't hurt our best scorer." Justin laughed. "We need him. You know, you'd think you'd be in a better mood, considering you got laid last night."

Justin and Riley skated together Sunday afternoon. Almost the entire team was here, even though today's practice was optional. They'd had a good game last night and Coach had given them the morning off before the game this afternoon.

Riley hadn't considered skipping. Apparently most of the guys felt the same.

"Keep your damn mouth shut about that." Riley slashed his stick across Justin's shins, almost hard enough to hurt. "The whole damn team doesn't need to know."

"Umm, the whole damn team already knows."

Riley shot him a glare. "What the fuck?"

Justin grinned, completely unrepentant. "Come on, you know hockey players gossip worse than old ladies."

Yeah, unfortunately he did.

Shaking his head, he sighed and pivoted to skate backward. "Christ almighty. I don't want Aly to think I'm a douche who told my entire team we slept together."

"So you gonna see her again?"

"I'm gonna text her after practice to see if she's coming to the game tonight."

"Wow, three nights in a row. Must be true love."

Riley grimaced. "How fucking old are you? Seriously, like, twelve?"

Justin laughed maniacally and skated away, leaving Riley to skate by himself for a few blissfully quiet seconds, thinking about those two little, four-letter words.

True love.

Yes, he believed in love, enough to know he'd loved his ex but not in the way he'd needed to make their marriage work. He also knew what he felt for Aly, even after such a short time, might be something worth fighting for.

And he had the feeling he was going to have to fight for it, if her unwillingness to let him stay the night was anything to go by.

Their personalities were in direct opposition. She was quiet and calm, reserved. He wasn't. Maybe that was what drew him to her.

Out of the corner of his eye, he saw CJ coming up on him again.

Christ, this kid was gonna step on Riley's last nerve today.

Just keep skating, kid. You don't wanna mess with me today.

Apparently, CJ couldn't read minds. He slowed until they were skating together.

"Uh, hey. Hi."

Riley barely kept himself from rolling his eyes. "What's up, CJ?"

"Um, yeah, so I was wondering if I could work with you a little today?"

Riley took a longer look at the twenty-one-year-old, surprised and waiting for the punchline. When it didn't come, he said, "What's up?"

CJ shrugged. "Just wanna work on a few things. I know I need to get better in the corners and you're damn good at that. So maybe we could work together for a while."

"No problem."

The kid broke out in a huge smile. Midwestern farm boy from his gold hair to his broad shoulders and his powerful legs, CJ used those legs to propel him to blazing-fast speeds. He had one hell of a natural talent, but he was still young and still growing into that body. He also had a stutter that only appeared off the ice.

"Great. Thanks! So, how'd your date go last night? She was really pretty."

And the kid had no filter whatsoever around his teammates.

"Oh, for fuck's sake." Riley reached out and smacked the kid on the back of the helmet. "Do a couple more laps before I kick your ass."

CJ turned and back-skated, grinning all the way down the ice. "Only if you can catch me."

He didn't bother to chase CJ. The kid would come back to him, like a huge, gangly puppy, ready to play.

Riley had much prettier prey to pursue.

FIVE

"Hey, Aly. I had a great time last night and I really want to see you again tonight. Game's at five tonight if you want to come. I'll leave tickets at will-call. Then maybe we can get some food." He paused and, when he spoke again, his voice had dropped a few octaves and she had to listen closely to hear him. "Or maybe we can just find a bed and I can make you come a few times before we get to the really good stuff. Up to you. Let me know about the tickets."

Standing in her kitchen by herself, Aly blushed even though no one could hear the message Riley had left on her phone.

But that blush wasn't embarrassment. No, his words ignited a firestorm of heat in her body. Her thighs clenched, her nipples peaked, and her hand curled into fists.

It was her own fault. She'd told him last night she wanted everything he had to give her and to be as dirty as he wanted. He'd taken her at her word, which she loved.

Riley hadn't known her all her life. He didn't know that she was such a goody-two-shoes that most people who knew her were shocked when she said "damn."

They'd probably think she'd been possessed by the devil if they found out what she'd done with Riley last night. And what she planned to do with Riley tonight.

She wanted to be bad.

Shaking her head, she forced herself to put the groceries away instead of listening to that message again.

Vivi was at the tattoo studio, where she'd be most of the day before she and her friends headed out to the bars, where they'd be before hitting the after-hours clubs until four or five in the morning.

Aly had never understood the appeal of getting so drunk you couldn't remember what you did the night before, but Vivi seemed to enjoy the hell out of it. Mostly because their mom absolutely *hated* that she did it.

But tonight it meant that Vivi would probably crash on a friend's couch for the night and she and Riley could make as much noise as they wanted and she wouldn't have to hear about it from her sister tomorrow morning.

But it also meant she'd probably be going to the game by herself tonight. Hopefully she'd be able to sit with Lori and Bliss.

Finally, after every last can had been stowed, she pressed the call button on her phone and was a little disappointed when it went straight to voice mail.

"You've reached Riley. Leave me a message."

Holy crap. How amazing was it that just the sound of his voice made her want to pant?

"Hi. It's me. Aly." She rolled her eyes. "I'd love to come to the game tonight so thanks. And," she paused and sucked in a fortifying breath, "why don't we come back to my place for drinks afterward? See you soon."

She hung up, hoping she hadn't sounded like a rabid nympho whose only goal in life was to get laid. Or worse, like a pathetic twenty-eight-year-old who hadn't gotten laid for months before last night.

"Well, you got laid last night. And you can't complain about that."

With a smile, she looked at the clock and sighed, wondering if she'd be able to breathe by the time the puck dropped.

———

"YOU LOOK like the cat who ate the pussy. You obviously had a good time last night. She is very nice, yes, to put that smile on your face."

The noise level in the locker room was high as the team dressed for warm-ups, but Jake had made sure everyone could hear him.

Riley stifled a groan as the rest of the team threw things at Jake for his deliberate mangling of the English language. Everyone knew he'd done it deliberately. His English was perfect when it had to be.

Riley even managed to suppress his instinct to flip Jake off because that would just make him worse and draw attention Riley didn't want.

If the team didn't need the little prick so badly, Riley would lay Jake out on the ice. He'd ring his bell hard and then he'd do it once more for good measure. And the rest of the team would laugh because the guy fucking deserved it.

But the guy was too damn good on the ice.

"Dude, you fucking score more than Ovechkin." Winger Tyler Richardson shook his head, shit-eating grin on his face as he pulled up his shorts. "I wanna be you when I grow up."

On the other hand, Tyler would probably ride the bench most of the season. Riley could take him out with no hassle. Except then Riley would be riding the bench.

"Maybe you could give me some pointers," Tyler continued to needle him. "Like how you managed those twins last year. Your reputation precedes you, man. I bow down to your expertise."

And then the little shit actually got down on his knees and laid himself out.

"Dickardson, get your ass off the floor." Lad Marchenko put his foot on Tyler's ass and shoved him just hard enough for Tyler to feel it. And then roll over onto his back and act like he'd been shot.

Riley shook his head and gave Tyler the finger he'd been going to give Jake.

As the conversation thankfully moved on to something else as they got ready for warm-ups before the game, Riley shrugged off comments.

For fuck's sake, Tyler's reputation was almost as bad as his own, although he was five years younger. Then again, Riley hadn't gained his reputation overnight. He'd built it up over the past ten years. And it'd be a hard thing to live down in just a few short weeks.

He hoped like hell Aly never got wind of it.

"Just ignore him. He's being a dick." Shane sat on the bench across from Riley, strapping on his leg pads. "Bliss likes her. Said Aly's really smart. Like brainy smart. And maybe a little shy."

That made Riley's eyebrows rise. "Shy? Really?"

That certainly hadn't been Riley's impression.

"Yeah. She also said she was really nice." Now Shane looked up at him with raised eyebrows. "So you seeing her again tonight?"

Since it was Shane asking, and not one of the kids, he answered. "Yeah."

He didn't say anything else and Shane's eyebrows rose higher. "That's kind of unusual for you, isn't it?"

The words "fuck" and "you" were on the tip of his tongue, but Shane didn't have a shit-eating grin on his face and he wasn't looking to bust Riley's ass. He actually sounded curious.

"Actually, no, it's not." Riley tugged his sweater over his head and grabbed his helmet. "At least, not lately."

"Turning over a new leaf?"

"Don't you have a pre-game routine to go through?"

Like almost every goalie Riley had ever met, Shane had a specific ritual he performed before each game.

Shane grinned now. "Yes, I do. Talk to you later, Rye."

"Not if we're gonna talk about our feelings."

Now Shane laughed, drawing the interest of the rest of the team for the simple reason that the goalie was always so intensely focused before a game. This season, though, he'd been loosening up a little. And playing better than he'd ever played. Yes, they were only a couple months into the season, but everyone had noticed his playing had elevated to another level.

He wouldn't be in this league long.

Riley was thrilled for the guy. Shane worked hard and was talented as all hell.

And Riley should take that to heart and concentrate on the game tonight and not a certain woman who'd be waiting for him after the game.

"...OLDER than most of the guys...fuckable...gorgeous...a real manwhore...love to get in those pants...shouldn't have much trouble... Riley...never last..."

The two women holding the conversation behind Aly hadn't registered until she heard Riley's name. The noise level in the arena this afternoon was higher than it'd been last night. Bigger crowd, too.

Every seat around her was taken, a few by other girlfriends introduced to her by Bliss and Lori.

Most were friendly. But there'd been a couple who'd taken one look at her and immediately dismissed her, going back to their whispered conversation. Aly shrugged it off and dropped back into conversation with Bliss and Lori.

But now they were talking about Riley. *Her* Riley. She hadn't heard everything they'd said but she'd heard enough. Riley had a reputation, at least according to the girls behind her. He slept around. A lot.

Somewhere beyond the buzzing in her ears, she heard the horn announcing the end of the first period.

"Hey, Aly. You okay?"

She glanced up at Bliss's voice, forcing a smile she didn't feel.

"I'm fine." She stood to let Lori get by her. "It's really loud in here today. Hard to hold a conversation."

"Yeah, the team's been on a marketing push to get people in the seats. Seems to be working."

Bliss's gaze shot over her shoulder to the younger women who were still chatting away, although now it was harder to hear them, what with the throbbing music and the announcer talking about season tickets.

"There are definitely more people here today than last night." She raised her brows at Aly. "Some of them really don't need to be. Guess you heard the idiot twins spouting off?"

"No, not really. Sounds like they know Riley, though."

Bliss rolled her eyes. "They don't know shit. Ignore them."

Shrugging, Aly sighed. "I don't know him either. I only met the man two days ago. How can you get to know someone in such a short time?"

Especially when some of that time had been spent scrambling her brain cells with amazing sex.

Which just meant he'd had a lot of practice.

"Well, I'm glad you're here again today." Bliss smiled. "And that you're enjoying the game. I'd never really been to a Redtails game before I started dating Shane. Now I can't even think about summer and the off season. It's like being punished."

Aly laughed, shaking her head. "You've become a true convert."

"I have. It doesn't hurt that my guy is a damn good player."

Behind them, the younger girls who'd been talking about Riley exploded into laughter, though now they'd lowered their voices enough that Aly couldn't hear them.

Bliss rolled her eyes again and leaned over to whisper into Aly's ear. "The puck bunnies are just jealous because they haven't been able to snag a player yet this season. Most of the older guys are beyond screwing every girl who gives them a look. And a lot of this year's team seem a little more...grounded, if you know what I mean.

Don't get me wrong, there are still a few looking to get laid every night, but they're not all horndogs."

"But Riley has a reputation, doesn't he?"

Sighing, Bliss's nose wrinkled. "I'm really not trying to deflect and I'm not making excuses but...yeah, he has a reputation. Although I can honestly say, since he's been here, he hasn't dated anyone but you. I think, after his divorce, he—"

"His divorce?"

Bliss's eyes went wide. "Shit, he didn't tell you?" She groaned. "Me and my big mouth. Damn it, I thought you knew. I don't think it's a state secret or anything because he mentioned it in passing when we'd met. I think it's been years since it was finalized. She was his high school sweetheart but she couldn't deal with him being on the road all the time. Or something. I really don't know details. You need to ask him." She grimaced. "And then tell him I'm sorry for opening my big mouth."

Aly shook her head, feeling sorry for making Bliss feel bad. "No harm, no foul. I mean, we've all got a past."

"You're absolutely right. My past involved an emotionally abusive ex who almost made me give up Shane. Luckily I pulled my shit together and now I can't imagine my life without him. Stuff works out. And now I need a drink so I don't continue to run at the mouth."

Aly laughed and followed Bliss to the beer stand, but throughout the rest of the game, her mind continued to come back to the fact that Shane had been married.

She didn't know why it bothered her. Hell, they'd just met. It wasn't like they'd shared every aspect of their lives and he'd hidden that fact from her. It just hadn't come up yet.

And so what if he'd slept with a few girls, or maybe more than a few? She'd slept with other guys. Okay, maybe she could count on one hand the number of guys she'd slept with. That only made her picky. Nothing wrong with that.

Riley hadn't been picky. She couldn't exactly hold that against him. They didn't have an exclusive relationship. They'd had two dates and spent one absolutely amazing hour fucking each other's brains out.

It just meant there was no way she would get attached. Yes, the sex had been great. And she hoped there'd be more tonight. And if their affair continued for a week or a month...great. Eventually it would end. She'd keep her emotions out of the equation and enjoy the hell out of the orgasms.

As she waited for Riley, she saw Shane wrap his arms around Bliss and kiss her, smiling when Shane grabbed her tight and lifted her off her feet.

The expression on his face...no one could doubt how he felt about Bliss.

The guy loved her.

Aly wanted that kind of love. Where all you had to do was look at the person and you knew. And that didn't happen over a weekend. That took months. Sometimes it took years.

Riley emerged from the locker room at that moment. He spared a quick grin for Bliss and Shane then turned that grin on her. And that grin did weird and wonderful things to her body.

Easy, girl.

She smiled back, unable to do anything else.

And then he reached for her and pulled her against him. She had a quick second to appreciate how much bigger he was than her. And then he bent and kissed her and it was almost as intensely passionate as the kiss Shane had laid on Bliss.

"Get a room."

The taunt filtered through the open hall and Aly heard laughter. Maybe she should be embarrassed by the PDA, especially because Riley held nothing back. He kissed her like they'd been dating for years, not just since two nights ago.

But she couldn't be angry at him. She didn't want him to stop.

And he didn't, not for a good minute, while he fried her brain with his lips and his tongue. Hell, he only had to put his hand low on her back and she was ready to slide her hands down his pants and cup his ass.

Good thing she had some common sense left.

A second later, Riley pulled back, gave her another smile then hustled her toward the exit.

"Glad you could make it tonight. I'm starving. You mind if we get a drink somewhere that has decent food?"

"Of course not. You—"

"Hey, Riley. Good game tonight."

A woman Aly didn't recognize smiled at Riley as they made their way through the hall. He nodded at her but kept moving.

"Thanks a lot."

But she wasn't giving up that easy. "Will I see you at the Spruce?"

"Not tonight."

This time he didn't even bother to look at the woman, just gave a vague wave as he spoke over his shoulder. Dismissed her as if he hadn't even seen her. And maybe he hadn't.

Had he slept with her? Is that how he'd treat her one day?

Jesus, when did you become such a whiny, needy bitch?

"So where should we go?" Riley steered her around the maze of cars in the small parking lot next to the rink where the team parked. "I haven't been around long enough to figure out more than a few decent places."

"Are you sure you don't want to go out with the rest of the team? I wouldn't have a problem with that."

"I'd rather spend the time with you." His frank answer drew her gaze up to his, and she found him staring intently down at her. "If that's okay?"

She couldn't help but smile back at him. "I'm fine with that. What are you hungry for?"

"Red meat." His grin made a reappearance and he leaned a little closer. "And later, some a little more...pink."

She couldn't help it. She blushed. "Riley."

He looked so damn innocent. "What? What'd I say?"

Shaking her head, she kept walking. "Are you always like this?"

"Like what? Hey, where'd you park? Do we need to drop your car off at home before we head out?"

Another blush because her sister had insisted on driving her into the game tonight so Riley would have to take her home. "No, I don't have my car. I, ah, caught a ride with my sister. She works a few blocks away at a tattoo shop."

Riley's smile grew impossibly wider and hotter. "I like your sister."

He stopped at his truck, threw his bag in the back then opened the passenger door for her before getting in the other side.

"I'm sure you would. She's amazing."

"Then she's probably a lot like you."

She'd never dated a guy who was so comfortable dishing out compliments. It was a little unnerving. And completely endearing.

"Actually we're pretty different."

He just smiled. "So, where are we going?"

She thought about it for a few seconds as he started the truck. She wanted to have him to herself.

"There's a place in Exeter that does great burgers. The kitchen's open until midnight. It's kind of quiet—"

"Sounds perfect. Just point me in the right direction."

She thought about her response for a second. "You didn't seem to have trouble finding your way around last night."

His laughter filled the car, making her want to close the space between them and snuggle up to his side. "There you go, hon. You do have a little naughty in you."

Shaking her head, she rolled her eyes. "You're the only one who seems to bring it out in me."

His grin got impossibly hotter. "Glad to hear it. Now let's go eat so I can corrupt you a little more."

———

RILEY HAD HAD a great fucking game.

His line had actually had a better plus-minus than the first line tonight and he'd scored and had an assist.

Now, he had only one goal in mind: Get her in bed.

Before the game, he'd only been able to think about her. During the game, he'd compartmentalized that lust. But now it burned like lava in his veins.

It might have blinded him to the fact that he didn't realize Aly had something on her mind until they were on their way back to her place.

He hadn't noticed anything wrong during dinner. They'd talked and laughed and he'd flirted and she'd smiled. And his dick had gotten harder every time she looked at him and shook her head at something he told her.

But he'd noticed a hesitancy about her, like she had something on the tip of her tongue but every time she thought about speaking, she held back.

He'd thought maybe it was just because they didn't know each other that well and he was hyped from the game.

But now, sitting alone together in the quiet cab, he knew something was up.

He didn't want to get into it while they were driving, so he'd waited until he'd parked in front of her house.

As he watched, she glanced at her home then looked back at him. "Do you want to come in?"

"Yeah, I do, but... Are you sure you want me to? Is something wrong?"

She tried to hide her grimace but he caught it before she could.

He moved a little closer. "Did something happen at the game?"

"No, no. Nothing happened. I just..." Her nose wrinkled. "I heard about your divorce."

He blinked. "Oh. It's not recent. I mean, I've been divorced for almost five years. Sorry, I guess I should've said something but it never even occurred to me—"

"No, wait." She held up one hand. "I'm sorry. It doesn't matter to me that you're divorced. I just...you never said anything. And I know how stupid that sounds considering we only met Friday."

Grimacing, he shook his head. "How bad am I gonna sound if I say I barely ever think about being married anymore? It was years ago and I kinda...forget."

Damn, that sounded really lame or really self-absorbed. *Fuck.*

"Really, I don't mean to pry—"

"Whoa, no. You're not prying. Seriously. What do you want to know? Just ask. I'm an open book."

Her lips curved. "Okay but why don't we go inside where it's not so cold?"

He jumped out of the car and hustled around to take her hand and help her out. Then he put his arm around her shoulders and tucked her into his side. She didn't stiffen or try to pull away. If she had, he would've released her. Instead, her arm went around his waist and she pulled him even closer.

Now he wanted to run for the house and nail her against the front door.

He refrained, but just barely.

"Do you want something to drink?" She took off her coat and hung it on the hook by the door.

"Yeah, I'd love some water."

She smiled over her shoulder as she headed toward the back of the house. "I'll be right back."

Shedding his coat, he sat on the couch, grinning when he had a flashback to last night. He couldn't wait to repeat but first...

Aly returned with a bottle of water for both of them then sat next to him.

"I really didn't mean to pry," she said. "If you don't want to talk about your marriage, we don't have to. It just kind of took me off guard."

"It's not a big secret." He shrugged. "It's just been a while since I was married. Kind of seems like another life, if that makes sense."

Drawing her legs up underneath her, she propped her arm on the back of the couch and rested her head on her hand. "How long were you married?"

"Two years. The first year was good." He grimaced. "Mostly. We were high school sweethearts and the plan was to get married after I finished college. But...my second year of college didn't go so well." Total understatement. "I partied too much, didn't study enough. The only thing I had going for me was hockey but I... Well, I flunked out."

He could still remember the look on his dad's face when his parents had come to get him at the end of the semester. So damn disappointed.

"I'd planned to enter the draft that following summer, but my parents convinced me to take the year off, move back home and work, then go back to school for my degree and get drafted between junior and senior year."

"Sounds like you had it all planned out."

"What's the saying? Best laid plans?" He shook his head. "The only job I could find was working night shift in the local mill. And I fucking hated it. Then I got picked up by the Great Lakes Hockey league. It's a full-contact amateur league and it filled that hole."

That hole had been a gaping wound. He'd never told anyone, not even his parents, just how much *not* playing hockey had hurt.

"I think Ann figured since I was home, that's where I was gonna stay."

"Did you want to go back to college?"

Aly watched him with intent blue eyes. Those eyes mesmerized. He wanted the light to be on tonight when he made love to her so he could see those eyes.

"Yeah, I did. I wanted my degree. Even back then, I knew I couldn't play hockey all my life. I needed something for after. With a degree in sports management, I figure I can stay involved with the game even after I can't play anymore.

"I played amateur for a season and got married because I loved her and I figured there wasn't much difference between marrying her then and waiting a couple of years until I graduated. But Ann didn't count on me going back to school. We had a huge fight the night before I left to go back. That was pretty much the beginning of the end. I wanted her to come with me. She didn't want to leave our hometown. And I realized it was never going to work. I don't think she ever really believed I was going to make hockey my career."

"I'm sorry. That must've sucked."

It had. It'd sucked big time because it'd been his second failure. "I was divorced by the time I was twenty-one. Wow. Seven years ago. Seems like forever."

"But you finished college and you're playing professionally. That's a great achievement."

He nodded, her smile making him want to close the distance between them and kiss her. But he didn't want to push her. If she wanted to talk, he'd talk. He got almost as much satisfaction from that as he did from kissing her. Almost.

"Thanks."

Yes, it was an achievement but he still hadn't made the leap he wanted to make. The one to the NHL. And he was starting to realize it might be out of his reach.

"But?" she prompted.

He shook his head, amazed she'd read him so easily.

"But I still haven't made it to the NHL. A lot of the guys I started out with have been playing up for years. My parents have always been supportive but they're starting to ask when I'm going to come home and get a real job."

Her nose wrinkled. "Ouch."

He huffed out a laugh. "Yeah. They've always been my biggest supporters but my dad's a pragmatist. If I haven't reached my goal in ten years, it's time for a new goal."

"Is twenty-eight old for a player?"

"Not really, no. A lot of guys play until they're in their late thirties but," he sighed, "I guess I'm a lot like my dad. I told myself I'd play until I'd made it to the NHL or I turned twenty-eight. At the time, twenty-eight seemed like a lifetime away. Now…"

He shook his head.

"Now you're twenty-eight and you still enjoy playing." She tilted her head, blonde hair spilling over her shoulder and making him want to run his fingers through it. "So why are you even thinking about giving it up? Goals change all the time. Do your parents expect you to come home?"

"Probably, yeah. We've always been close and that's kind of what I figured I'd do. I'm their only and I think they're counting on me to be around when they get older."

She nodded. "My parents are the same. They keep telling me how much I'd love living in Florida and that I should come to visit more often and, oh yeah, Millie across the street, her son just moved down from Milwaukee and he's wonderful and they want to introduce me to him."

A surge of jealousy ripped through him and he had a moment to think "What the fuck?" before he got it under control. The feeling was still there but he reined in the urge to tell her to forget it.

This whole caveman act was not his deal but there was something about Aly that made him want to beat his chest and lock her in his cave.

"Do you *want* to move to Florida?"

She shrugged, her gaze sliding away. "I've thought about it. But… I'm settled here. I like my job. I like my house. We moved around a lot when I was a kid and I hated it. Every year or two, we'd end up in some new town where I didn't know anyone."

A pit opened Riley's stomach. There'd been seasons where he'd moved three or four times, sometimes across the country. Sounded like Aly would hate that.

"Guess you're used to it," she said. "Moving all the time?"

"Yeah. But I'm realizing there might be a good reason for me to stay in one place."

"And what would that be?"

Did he imagine the breathlessness in her voice? No, he didn't think so. Not combined with the look in her eyes.

Sitting here listening to her, he realized how much he'd miss her if he couldn't see her tomorrow. Or the next day. Or the day after that.

He also knew that if he blurted out exactly what he wanted to say, she would think he was crazy.

If there was one thing he'd learned about Aly, it was that she was nothing if not logical. And declaring his ever-lasting devotion after only three days wouldn't fit into her neat, logical life. And his life was anything but neat and logical.

So what the fuck should he say?

The truth, asshole. Anything else'll just get you in trouble.

He smiled, attempting to be both charming and disarming. Hopefully not failing at both.

"Well, you see, I met this woman..."

Her lips curved in a sweet smile, one he was fast becoming addicted to.

"And you're saying you'd stay for her? Even though you haven't known her that long?"

"Haven't you ever had that feeling that you know what you're doing is right? It's kind of like when you've got a good team. There's a feeling in the air in the locker room. An excitement you can almost touch."

Her smile dimmed a little. "And you'd stay just because you think she might be...important to you?"

He leaned forward, getting in her space now because he couldn't resist her anymore. "I'm saying I might be persuaded to give up every-thing for the right girl."

She opened her mouth to speak again but he'd waited too long to kiss her. He sealed his mouth over hers for a deep, intensely sensual taste of her.

Her hands had fallen to his shoulders as if to hold him off, but as soon as his tongue slid against hers, she gripped him and tugged him closer. He came willingly, breathing a sigh of relief that she'd initiated the kiss after he'd laid that bombshell on her.

And now that she had, all bets were off.

But tonight, he was taking his time. Last night had been frantic. Fantastic but over way too fucking fast. And she hadn't asked him to stay the night.

Tonight, he was hoping for an invitation into her bed.

But first, he was content to just kiss her. Because, holy fucking hell, he loved the way she kissed. Like she couldn't get enough of him.

He certainly couldn't get enough of her. And she definitely wasn't close enough. No way.

Reaching for her hips, he grabbed her and lifted her onto his lap, wrapping his arms around her and crushing her against him. She didn't seem to mind.

Her arms went around his shoulders, her hands sliding into his hair and fingers raking against his scalp.

Christ, that felt amazing. He really wanted to feel those nails elsewhere on his body. Like, lower. Along his thighs. On the inside of his thighs. On his cock.

Hell, he'd take her hands on his body anywhere he could get them.

He'd take her any way he could get her.

ALY'S HEART pounded against her ribs, lungs working overtime as her desire for Riley consumed her.

Yes, she'd felt out of control last night, but she was beginning to believe she'd never be in control when it came to Riley. Right now, that didn't bother her. Tomorrow morning, it was going to bother the hell out of her.

But it wasn't tomorrow yet.

It was tonight and tonight was going to be amazing.

Tilting her head to the side so he could deepen the kiss, she let herself sink into him, let him hold her tight against him like he couldn't bear to release her. Soaking in the heat of his body, she let herself disconnect from reality.

And Riley became her world. She could only see him, only smell him. Only taste him. Every muscle in her body relaxed and she gave herself over to him. She had no idea why or how. It just happened.

Apparently, Riley was so attuned to her, he noticed immediately, took the reins, and ran with it.

Dragging his mouth away from hers, he kissed his way down to her neck as his hands spread across her back and held her close to his chest.

He was so big, she almost felt small against him. But not lost. Riley held her too tightly for her to feel lost.

And his mouth... Oh my god, his tongue traced decadent patterns on her skin that made her shiver, her body moving against his until she'd begun to rub her mound against his erection, which she felt through his dress pants.

"Fuck, sweetheart. Keep that up. I'm loving that."

His voice fired her libido, her muscles tightening as his hands continued to pet her. Down her back then up again, several times, until her skin felt so sensitized, her clothing was a nuisance.

"I want your clothes off." She drew her hands down from his shoulders to his shirt, pushing buttons through their holes as fast as her hands would go. "You need to be naked."

She could feel his mouth curve in a smile against the sensitive skin where her neck met her shoulder.

"I agree. But you need to lose the clothes, too. You have the most amazingly soft skin I've ever felt. I want to rub my cock between your thighs then I'm going to flip you over and rub it between your ass cheeks. Do you know how soft you are there? Like silk, baby."

His hands landed on her ass and scooped her closer, making her shudder.

"And holy fuck, when I get my hands between your legs, it's like butter. So soft. I can't wait to put my mouth on you."

Her breath caught in her throat as he spoke, her brain unable to process the heat coursing through her body.

Her first instinct was to give him whatever he wanted. And since he wanted what she wanted, there was no decision to make.

She gave in.

Turning her face into his neck, she bit him, hard enough to make him flinch. And groan.

His hands clutched at her ass for a second before moving to her front, where he snapped the button on her black jeans and began to work them down her hips.

Her hands had already begun to work at his shirt but their actions kept getting in the way of each other.

Frustration began to make her fingers more frantic until finally she moaned.

And he grabbed her hands, forcing her to look up at him. "Aly. Hon. Wait."

She raised her eyebrows, barely able to breathe. "You want to wait?"

His smile made her thighs clench. It was playful and wicked and sweet all at the same time.

"No, I really don't. I want you naked and riding me right now, but I'd also like to do that on a bed. Because first, I'm gonna lay you out naked and put my face between your legs and make you come."

Her lips parted at the carnality in his tone and her lungs contracted. And, holy hell, she soaked her panties.

"That mouth of yours is dangerous."

That mouth curved into another one of his wicked grins.

"So I've been told. But usually only by people who want to punch it."

Scrambling to her feet, she held out her hand, which he grabbed as he stood.

"Well, I definitely don't want to punch it. I have much better uses for it."

"Lead the way, sweetheart. I'm all yours."

She continued to stare into his beautiful eyes for a few more seconds and the triumph she felt at his statement took the rest of her breath away.

With a grin of her own, she turned and pulled him along behind her. By the time they reached the stairs to the second floor, they were practically running.

And when he swung her into his arms and took the stairs two at a time, she very nearly lost her ability to function.

No man had ever made her feel like he couldn't wait to get her in a bed because he wanted to make *her* feel good.

Riley did.

"Which way?"

"Right then last door on the left."

"Damn, that's far away."

She laughed and he looked down, smiling like making her laugh was his main goal in life.

"Christ, you're gorgeous when you smile. You're fucking hot all the damn time but when you smile like that, I forget how to breathe."

"Riley, that's..."

She didn't know what to say to that but he'd reached the door to her room by then. In the next second, she was airborne for a split second before her ass hit the bed and she sprawled on top of her quilt.

A second later, Riley came down on top of her, covering her better than any quilt ever could. The heat of him seared through her clothing and the second his lips pressed against hers, all thoughts of taking this slow blew apart like fireworks exploding.

She had her hands on his shirt, ready to rip it open, when he rose to his knees over her, trapping her with his knees on either side of her thighs.

"I'll take mine off if you take yours off." He already had his hands on his belt buckle. "Don't wanna rip your clothes but I'm so hot for you, I might tear them off with my teeth."

The image that flashed through her head at what else he could do with his teeth made her gasp.

And he groaned. "God damn, hon. Look at me like that again and I'm not giving any guarantees."

She got to work.

"I'm going to need to get heavier clothes so I can wear less of them to the game."

His deep laughter did wild and wonderful things to her insides. "I'm all for less clothing. And skirts. I think you should wear skirts every damn day. They come off easy and your legs look fucking amazing in them."

She wanted to agree with him. She'd stripped off her top layers easily but her damn jeans were tight on her hips and a struggle to push down her legs. Especially with two-hundred-plus pounds of fucking hot man looming over her.

He'd stripped his pants and underwear down to his knees and his cock stood straight out from his body, ruddy and ready and tempting her to reach for it.

But she needed him to move if she was going to get her jeans off.

About to open her mouth and tell him to strip her, she let out a squeak when he backed off the bed and stood at the side, shoving his pants down then grabbing her jeans and yanking them off. It took him a few tugs but he finally got them down. She wanted to laugh because he had the same intense look on his face that she'd seen when he played. But she couldn't quite manage because she was way too excited.

And horny. Definitely horny.

When he put his hands on her knees and spread her legs then knelt between them, she was practically panting.

Even more so when he dragged his hands, palms down, up her thighs to rest right at the juncture of her hips. His thumbs brushed against her mound and she wanted to clench her thighs together but his knees held her open. Wet and aching, she held her hand out to him. But he just smiled and moved his thumbs closer to her clit.

Her stomach contracted and she sucked in a sharp breath.

"Something hurt, sweetheart?" His rough chuckle made her muscles tighten even more. "Do you need me to do something?"

"Yes, I need you to stop teasing me."

His grin widened. "Aw, that's half the fun." His thumbs moved infinitesimally closer to her clit, which was throbbing and tingling and dying for him to touch her. "I don't want to rush things this time. Last time, you made me lose my control. And it usually takes a hell of a long time to get me to break. So, this time, I'm determined."

"Determined to do what?"

"Well, how about I start with 'lick you until you scream'?"

Before she'd finished drawing in much needed air, he'd slid his hands between her thighs to spread her even more and bent to put his mouth over her sex.

She arched as his tongue flicked over her clit just before he sucked the little nub between his lips. Her eyes rolled back in her head before they closed completely and she sank her fingers into his hair so he wouldn't get away. At least not without a battle.

Because...*oh my god,* the man knew how to use his mouth. And not just to talk. His lips and tongue worked together to make her body do what he wanted. Which was to writhe in ecstasy, apparently.

Every flick of his tongue made her back arch off the bed. Every time he sucked on her clit, she pressed her mound even harder against his mouth.

She moved so much, he finally put his hands on her hips and held her down on the bed so he could make good on his promise to make her scream.

She resisted as long as she could. She wasn't a screamer. It just wasn't in her nature. But when he bared his teeth and nibbled at her, she couldn't help herself.

The sensation was too much for her to process and the sound that came out of her mouth was probably pretty close to a scream. Her body shuddered, sensation zipping through her, and she almost ripped his hair out by the roots before she relaxed her fingers.

She tried to catch her breath but he wouldn't let her. As his lips moved up her body, pressing open-mouth kisses along her belly, one hand slipped between her legs to play with her labia, already slick and full.

As he moved up her body, stopping to suck on each of her nipples before moving to nibble her neck, she got a quick chance to catch her breath before his fingers slipped into her channel and began to fuck her.

Her hands slipped from his hair and onto his shoulders, pulling him closer, that big body covering her like a heavy blanket, his heat searing her skin and driving her desire for him to a fever pitch.

But he still wasn't close enough. Her hands slid lower as his fingers spread her wide and stroked high inside her. If she lifted her hips, she might be able to rub her mound against his erection. And if she got her hands on his ass, she could pull him in even closer.

With her few remaining brain cells, she slid her hands to his ass and pulled him closer. He barely budged but it was enough to feel his cock brush against the trimmed curls on her mound.

She felt his groan rumble through his body, making her shiver.

"You want me closer, sweetheart? If I get any closer, I'm gonna be nailing you to the bed in a second and I'm not done playing yet."

Her fingers scraped over the sleek muscles of his ass and down to his thighs, her nails dragging along his skin. A shudder rippled through him and he bit her at the tender junction of her neck and shoulder.

"If you play any more," she gasped as he licked at his bite, "I'm going to come before you get inside."

"That's okay. I'll just make you come again." His fingers twisted inside her, making her arch as her hands clenched around his thighs. "And again. And again."

His fingers thrust in an ever-increasing rhythm that had her body moving along.

Kissing his way back to her mouth, he sealed their lips together and drew his hand from between her legs as he dropped over her.

He was so heavy, she almost couldn't breathe but she wrapped her arms around him so he couldn't get away. Her legs followed, draping over his hips as she arched into him, trapping his cock between them.

That made him groan again and he moved just enough so his cock was between her thighs, the tip nudging at her sensitive labia.

He rubbed there for a few long seconds, teasing her, before he punched his hands into the mattress on either side of her and pushed up so he could stare down at her.

Hazel eyes blazing, he leaned down to rub his nose against hers in a tender motion that made her heart melt.

Oh, wow. So not fair.

It made her want...so much more.

"Condom?"

She blinked and amazingly her brain figured out what he'd said. "Top drawer, bedside table."

"Can you reach it?" His lips curved. "I don't want to move."

Neither did she but she did want him to make love to her. Right now.

So she stretched her arm out and caught the drawer with her fingertips, grabbing the box and digging inside while he dipped his head and tugged on her left earlobe with his teeth.

She nearly dropped the condom when he flexed his hips and rubbed his cock head against her clit, making her moan at the sharp burst of pleasure. His tongue drew patterns along her throat, making her heart skip beats like a scratched CD. And making her frantic to have him fill the aching void inside her.

"What's wrong, hon?" Riley whispered directly into her ear before rubbing his bristly cheek against her temple...and rubbing the head of his erection against her labia in a motion guaranteed to make her crazy. "Something you need? Ask me for anything."

"I want you."

He pulled back until she could see his lips curved in a grin she'd seen him give opposing players. Usually just before those players attempted to take his head off.

"Really? I don't know about that. I think you're gonna have to be a little more convincing."

Her gaze narrowed as her thighs clenched at the teasing tone of his voice. "And how exactly do you think I should do that?"

His turn to groan. "Damn, I love when you talk like that, all prim and proper like we're not lying here naked and I've got my cock between your legs."

Jesus, if he kept talking, she might actually come without penetration. Her body tingled from head to toe.

Shoving the condom against his chest with one hand, she used the other to weave through his hair and tug, hard.

"Use the damn condom and fuck me, Riley."

His grin faded but the lust in his eyes tripled. "And then you talk like that and, holy shit, babe, I might just come now."

"Don't you dare."

"Then put it on me."

He rose back up on his knees and she realized the light in the hall was still lit and she could see every ripple of muscle in his abs as he breathed and the flex of his thighs as he moved his knees farther apart. Opening her legs even more.

Still holding the condom, she ripped it open with her teeth then reached for him, rolling it down his hard, thick shaft, barely able to breathe.

As soon as she was done, he dropped back over her, hands planted on either side of her shoulders. And still not where she needed him.

"Riley..."

"Guide me in. I fucking love having your hands on me."

Tilting her hips up, she reached for his cock with one hand and put her other hand on his jaw to guide him down to kiss her as he slid home.

Her eyes closed as their lips meshed and she groaned at the thickness of him. He stretched her tight, filled her completely and was almost too much to bear.

But she knew from the night before just how much pleasure it would bring her when he started to move. The man had a gift.

Moving her free hand to his ass, she gripped him hard and pulled.

And felt his lips curve against hers.

But he refused to move. Instead, he tilted his head to get a better angle and then slid his tongue into her mouth, doing exactly what she wanted him to be doing with his cock.

For at least a minute, he tormented her with his tongue, the rest of him perfectly still.

So she moved, arched her back to push him farther inside then sank down so he slipped out just the tiniest bit.

It was enough to give her some satisfaction but it was also enough to taunt Riley.

After a few moments, she heard Riley groan and his kiss became more frantic, his tongue sinking deeper and deeper until finally she felt him start to move.

Every time he pulled out, she followed him, tried to get him to come back. And every time, he pushed forward, she tried to take him deeper.

It almost seemed like they were working at odds but nothing could've been further from the truth.

Their bodies synced in seconds and then Riley loosened the chains.

Lowering himself, he wrapped one arm around her shoulders and the other behind the small of her back, lifting her hips into him so he rubbed against her clit every time he slammed into her.

She'd never been to bed with a guy as strong as Riley. Every thrust forced him deeper until she thought he couldn't go any further. And still she wanted more.

But he was so much bigger than her, he practically enveloped her. She didn't mind but he did, apparently.

Without warning, he rolled until she was on top. But he kept her wrapped so tightly against him, she could barely move. At least now she could breathe. Until he lifted his head and started to kiss her again.

She wanted to move with him, but his hand on her ass kept her where he wanted her. Not that it was a bad place to be.

It was an awesome place to be, actually.

With Riley's mouth on hers and his cock moving inside her and his hands spread on her back and her ass, she felt taken.

She loved it.

And when she felt all that tension inside her reach its breaking point, she moaned into his mouth as she came, feeling him freeze as she clenched around him before he pumped his own release into her with a groan.

SIX

An annoying beep woke Riley out of a deep sleep.

He frowned, ready to chew Justin's ass for not turning off his alarm, especially since this was their morning off.

Then he realized this wasn't his bed. And Justin was nowhere to be found.

Beside him, Aly was a sleek mass of warm, naked flesh and silky hair. He'd curled around her so her back was nestled against his chest and her ass snuggled against his groin. Of course, he had stiff morning wood pressed right between her cheeks and damn, if that didn't feel great.

Her head lay on his bicep and he was pretty sure his arm was asleep and would hurt like a bitch when she moved, but he could lie here all fucking day and never get up, if he got to keep her naked and warm beside him.

Turning his head, he rubbed his chin against her hair and curled his arm even more tightly around her waist.

He breathed in her scent, something warm and floral and sexy as hell.

Fuck.

She was going to have to get up soon, but he wondered if she'd have enough time for a quickie before she needed to get ready for work.

He was bending forward to nuzzle his nose into her neck before he bit her and slid his hand from her stomach to her mound when she sighed and shot straight up in bed.

"Oh *shit*."

Flopping onto his back, Riley laughed so hard his stomach hurt but it was worth it when she turned to glare at him.

Jesus, she was gorgeous. Her hair was all messy and it looked good on her, falling over those beautiful tits and making him want to get his mouth on them again.

Scrambling onto her knees, she put her hands on her naked hips and glared even harder. Which just made his cock stiffer. "How long have you been awake?"

"Long enough to want to get back inside you before you have to go to work."

She blinked at him a few times, her lips parted like she was going to say something, but she never did. Finally, she shook her head and huffed out a laugh.

"I really wish I had time for that. But I have to be there in an hour and I need a shower."

Crunching up, he grabbed her around the waist before she could move away, loving the little squeak she made when he lifted her into the air so he could move her over him. Her knees landed on either side of his hips and her hands slapped down on his shoulders.

"I could make that shower worth your while."

Laughing, she bent to kiss him, her hair hanging down around his face, a silky curtain he wanted to feel on his chest, his stomach. His thighs.

He wanted her to bend down and kiss him but she stayed where she was, staring in his eyes. "And then I would definitely be late for work. Don't you have practice this morning?"

"Not until eleven because of the back-to-back-to-back games."

Shaking her head, her lips were curved in a smile he wanted to taste. "Well, *I* can't be late. We have a staff meeting every Monday at ten."

"Then take the day off. I'll take you to breakfast and we can buy lunch and we can eat it in bed where we'll spend the rest of the day until I have to go to practice."

"Oh, so you go to practice but I can't go to work?" She lifted her eyebrows at him and his cock jerked in response.

She must have felt it move against her leg because she glanced down before looking back into his eyes. But she was still grinning.

"Okay, Plan B. Quickie now then you go to work and I go to practice. Then we'll meet up for dinner and we can get to bed a little earlier so we don't have this same problem tomorrow morning."

She sucked in her bottom lip and bit on it for a few seconds before she answered. "So you want to be here again tomorrow morning?"

"Of course." He shrugged like it was no big deal, but he could see by her expression that she was going to be a harder nut to crack than a pro with twenty years under his belt. "But we've got a road trip to Springfield Wednesday and we've got practice daily until then so maybe I should get some sleep, at least a few nights."

She smiled, but he could tell she still was trying to figure out what to do with him.

Besides the obvious.

And since it went against every fiber of his being to keep his mouth shut, he added, "But I'm willing to give up my beauty rest if you are. Not that you need much because, sweetheart, you're the most beautiful girl I've ever seen at seven in the morning."

The flush on her cheeks deepened but he knew it wasn't embarrassment. It was heat.

Just when he thought she might take him up on his offer, her lips twisted and she shook her head, silky strands catching in his scruff until he wove his fingers through her hair and pulled it back behind her neck. He fucking loved the feel of it in his hands.

She bent and pressed her lips against his, kissing him so sweetly, he panicked for a second. Fuck, what'd he say? Was she going to shove him out the door and he'd never see her again? He already knew he wouldn't let that happen. He knew this girl was something special and he wasn't about to let her go.

He was all ready to open his mouth and say whatever he could to get her to agree to see him again tonight when she said, "Can we take a rain check until tonight? I really need to get in the shower, and if I don't have at least two cups of coffee before work, I will rip someone's head off."

Her perfectly deadpan delivery amused the hell out of him, and he laughed before he lifted her off his body and to the side of the bed, where she put her feet on the floor.

But before she could get away, he shot up to his knees, grabbed her head in his hands, and kissed her hard, pressing her lips open and sliding his tongue into her mouth to tangle with hers. She responded immediately, her hands gripping his hips...but not pulling him closer. Which was where his cock wanted to be.

Down, boy.

Then again, he loved kissing her so he could deal. He'd see her again tonight and they'd figure out the rest of their lives when he got back from his road trip. Hopefully while they were naked in bed.

After several long seconds, she sighed and pulled away. He let her go, but not without one last, hard kiss. And a sweep of his hand down her sleek ass.

The look she gave him made him want to put both hands on her.

"You're dangerous." She stuck on finger in his chest when he made a move forward. "And I need to get in the shower."

"Want some company?"

She sighed and shook her head, but her expression was amused. "Like I said...you're dangerous. And I have to leave in less than an hour."

"Then I guess the least I can do is make you coffee."

Teeth in her lips again. Why the hell did he find that so sexy?

"Sure. But I really do have to go to work."

He held his hand up and tried to look like the Boy Scout he'd never had time to be. "Promise I won't distract you again."

Now her brows rose and she shook her head as she turned to the bathroom. "Like you can help it."

He barely heard her as she grabbed a robe from the hook on the back of her door then opened it as quietly as she could. But he couldn't help smiling as she turned to look at him just before disappearing down the hall and shaking her head, a grin flirting with her mouth.

Damn, he wanted this. Every morning. Wanted to wake up next to her and have her give him that smile before she left for work.

Wanted to crawl into bed next to her after a great game, after a shitty game... Hell, after any game. Wanted to come home to her after a two-week road trip and kiss the hell out of her before he tossed her into bed, tore off her clothes, and got inside her.

Tomorrow, the next day, most of the mornings after that.

But she wouldn't want to hear that. Not his Little Miss Cautious.

So how the hell was he supposed to let her know he was serious about her when he'd be gone for the next two weeks?

Usually he was good at talking. He could convince a rational man to drop his gloves by the end of the first period simply by talking shit. Hell, he was an expert at it. But he'd fucked up one relationship before. He didn't want to fuck this up.

But first...he'd promised her coffee.

Grabbing his clothes, he pulled them on then headed for the stairs, passing the bathroom, where he could hear the water running. Damn, he wanted to push the door open and join her but that wouldn't get her to trust him.

In the kitchen, he found the coffeemaker—a huge, twelve-pot monstrosity—on the counter, located the filters in the cabinet above it and the coffee in the freezer.

He'd finished his first cup by the time he heard the click of heels on the stairs.

He automatically looked toward the sound—and nearly swallowed his tongue.

Holy fuck, he was in so much goddamn trouble.

Her skirt was black and thin and reached her knees, her shirt was gray and tight and unbuttoned just enough that he could imagine he saw cleavage and her heels were black and red.

She'd pulled her hair into some twist on the back of her head that made his fingers itch to release it and she was wearing pearls. A double string that lay over her breasts and made him imagine how she'd look wearing only those damn pearls.

Jesus. He'd finally managed to will his erection away but now he was pretty sure he'd spend the rest of the day thinking about those pearls and getting a hard-on.

"You know, I never understood the whole librarian fixation." He grinned as she gave him a bemused look and headed for the coffee. "I totally get it now."

She rolled her eyes at him but he caught her smiling before she put the mug to her mouth.

And groaned.

"Oh. My. God. Where did you learn to make coffee this good?" Her eyes widened as she took another sip. "My sister's always tastes like sludge and is so damn strong, I feel like I'm on speed all day. Mine never tastes this good. I think I'm going to keep you locked in my house as my personal coffee slave."

"Not your sex slave, huh? Well, damn, I guess I'll have to up my game in bed."

Her eyebrows rose. "What time is practice?"

"Eleven. We go until one then refuel and hit the gym for a few hours. Refuel again." A thought occurred to him. "Shit. Forgot I've got a thing this afternoon. An after-school program. Don't know how long that'll go but I should be done by six. Let's get some dinner after that. Or we could cook. Which I can do, by the way. If you don't mind someone in your kitchen. I'd have you over to the apartment but my roommate's kind of a slob so..."

She didn't say anything right away, just watched him with those steady blue eyes. He couldn't tell what she was thinking and he was about to open his mouth and keep going when she nodded.

"Sure, we can cook here, if you don't mind having my sister around."

He shrugged. "Course not. Her house, too, right?"

"Should I—"

"I'll pick up everything after the event and be here around seven. That work for you?"

"That's fine."

"Anything you don't like?"

Her lips quirked. "I'm assuming you mean food?"

"I did but if you wanna talk about something else, I'm all ears."

Her head tilted to the side, as if she were thinking about it, but then she shook her head. "I really do need to get to work. And you're dangerous to my concentration."

He didn't bother to hide his smile and she shook her head and walked to the sink to dump her mug.

Standing, he did the same then wrapped an arm around her waist to bring her in against him for a quick kiss.

"I'll see you tonight, hon."

Then he walked out before she changed her mind.

———

"DUDE, you look like you had a good night's sleep, which is weird because I could swear you didn't make it home last night." Justin's shit-eating grin spread. "Whose couch did you sleep on? Must've been comfortable."

Riley had been the last one into the locker room by only a minute. But it was late enough for Justin to jump on his ass about it.

In response, Riley gave him the finger, which made Justin laugh maniacally.

"And where did you sleep last night, jackass?" Jake smacked

Justin on the back of the head as Riley started to strip. "All by your-self in your own bed. I think maybe you are a little jealous."

Stripping as fast as he could, Riley pulled on his base layers then began strapping on his pads. For the first time in god knew how long, he had no desire to talk shit with his teammates. Especially not about Aly.

"And when was the last time a girl let you in her bed? I think it was never, yes?"

Lad directed the dig at Jake. The two defensemen were tight as brothers and trash-talked each other like mortal enemies. It worked for them.

They were the best defensive line in the league and they came to play every day. And if they occasionally acted like douchebag teenagers... Well, nobody was perfect.

"Says the man who still does not know what a rim shot is."

"Rim *job*," shouted CJ as the rest of the team either groaned or laughed hysterically. "It's rim *job*."

Lad and Jake exchanged a look, said a few words in Russian then Jake focused his famed Russian glare at CJ. "This from the child who still hordes his cherries."

Now the entire team busted into laughter and CJ turned the same color as the fruit Jake had just mentioned.

Riley shook his head, his brain working on a smart-ass response, but when CJ sat next to him on the bench, his mouth snapped shut.

CJ's downbent head and bright red neck brought out Riley's protective instincts. Same as if they'd been on the ice and someone went after the kid, Riley jumped to CJ's defense.

"Considering you two need each other to get laid, I figure you have a few cherries you haven't popped yet."

With an almost imperceptible glance at CJ, Lad took the hint. "I have no cherries. Jake, however, has entire bush."

Holding his gut, he was laughing so hard, Derek turned to Jake. "Son, if you have a bush instead of a tree, maybe that's the problem you been having hooking up."

"Hey, something up?" Riley asked CJ as he pulled his sweater over his head, just as Coach walked in the room.

Before CJ could answer, Coach said, "Listen up," and launched into his game plan for the week. Twenty minutes later, right before the team was ready to hit the ice, Coach looked at him and inclined his chin.

"Hatch. Young. Stick here. Everyone else, on the ice."

Not expecting anything other than Coach Scott wanting him and CJ to work together on technique or drills, Riley nearly fell off the bench when Coach started to talk.

"The big club had a couple of injuries last night and you two are headed to the Colonials. They get back from a road trip today and Coach Angstadt wants you two at the practice barn for morning skate tomorrow. Today, you skate with us but they want you down to talk to the assistant coach tonight."

Coach turned to grab a piece of paper from his desk, detailing where they needed to be and when and the hotel they'd be staying at. He and CJ would be bunking together for the duration, could be an extended stay, but they would probably see ice time.

Beside him, CJ vibrated like a fucking puppy, running at the mouth with questions Coach answered with a grin. Riley just sat there.

Holy shit. Finally. Fucking finally.

And on the heels of that...

I can't fucking wait to tell Aly.

Yeah, he couldn't wait to tell his parents. But Aly was different. He wanted to share everything with her. Wanted her to be happy for him. Wanted her to come to the game and be waiting for him afterward.

Philly wasn't that far away. If he stayed with the Colonials for any length of time, he and Aly would make it work—

"Riley, you have any questions?"

Coach's question knocked him out of his thoughts and he smiled, shaking his head. "Nah. I think I'm good."

"All right then. Get out on the ice. You can text your parents after practice."

CJ bounced up, grinning from ear to ear, and headed out. Riley got up slower, watching the kid disappear down the hall to the ice.

He took a few seconds to make sure his laces were tight and found Coach watching him, arms crossed over his chest.

"Sure you don't have any questions?"

"Honestly," Riley shook his head, "I've got a shit-ton of them but I don't think you can answer any of them."

Coach grinned and slapped him on the shoulder. "Keep your head in the game. Just like you've been doing for the past eight years. You made it this far. Just keep pushing. You've got the skills, Riley. You've proved it. I have no doubt you can make this happen. Don't let anything get in your way."

Riley had no intention of letting anything get in his way. But he had no intention of giving anything up either.

———

ALY HAD GONE to work with a smile on her face that faded about fifteen minutes after she walked in the door.

The billing system had gone down and the techs weren't sure why. Which meant her department was hamstrung. Which meant the people who called in to get their bills straightened out had something else to complain about.

And they did. All morning.

It left her very little time to daydream about Riley and last night, but when she did, holy crap, she couldn't stop.

So when his number popped up on her phone after lunch, she shut herself in her office and sank into her chair.

"Hey," she said. "I was hoping you'd call."

"And I've been dying to talk to you. I got called up. I'll probably be on the ice tomorrow night with the Colonials in Philly."

It took her a second to process what he'd said then she started to smile. "Riley! That's amazing! Oh my god, that's so wonderful. We can celebrate tonight at dinner."

"Yeah, about dinner. I need to cancel. I hate to do it but CJ and I have to be in Philly tonight. They're putting us up in a hotel for the night so we're ready for morning skate tomorrow. I'm really sorry—"

"Are you kidding? Don't you dare apologize for getting what you've been working for for so long. I'm so happy for you."

"Happy enough to want to drive to Philly tomorrow night? Game starts at seven and I know it's short notice but I can get you a ticket."

He wanted her at the game? Her heart began to pound and she wanted to say yes.

But she also had to be practical. She worked until five-thirty and then had an evaluation with her boss that she couldn't miss. Even if she didn't go home to change and left straight from the office, she wouldn't be on the road until six-thirty and it'd take her at least two hours to navigate the Schuylkill Expressway at that time of night.

"Aly?"

But he wanted her there. Just the thought made her heart pound against her ribs and her thighs clench like he'd told her he wanted to strip her naked and do her against a wall.

It made no sense whatsoever because they'd met four days ago. *Four days.* People didn't become this invested in another person's life that fast.

And if they did, it wouldn't last.

"I would really love to go," she said. "I just...I'm afraid I wouldn't make it in time."

He paused and her throat dried. Anxiety made her stomach ache.

But realistically, she'd probably get stuck in traffic and would probably miss the entire game.

And maybe he was only asking to be nice. Maybe he felt obligated to ask her because they'd slept together.

Maybe—

"Yeah, okay, no problem. Seriously, I get it. I'll give you a call after the game, okay?"

And maybe he really hadn't wanted her there to begin with. "Of course."

"Great. Okay, I really gotta get moving. CJ and I need to be on the road in a few. We have to check in with the assistant coach…"

"Oh, that's—"

"…before six. And yeah, traffic's gonna be a bitch."

Feeling sick to her stomach and fighting the urge to hyperventilate, Aly sucked in a deep breath. "Riley…you're going to be amazing tomorrow."

"Thanks, hon." He huffed out a little laugh. "I hope like hell you're right. You can probably catch the game on TV. Let me know how I look."

A lump formed in her throat.

"Of course. Riley…I'm really happy for you."

"Thanks. Appreciate it. Look, I hate to cut this short—"

"No, I totally understand. You have to go. Just…have a great game. I have no doubt you'll be wonderful."

"Let's hope. I'll talk to you tomorrow night."

"That's great. Good luck, Riley."

"Thanks, hon."

He didn't say good-bye, just disconnected.

And by the time Aly put her phone down on her desk, she had to suck in air because it was getting tougher and tougher to breathe.

Her eyes burned and she blinked fast, willing back the tears that had popped up for no reason.

It wasn't like she'd never see him again. And if she didn't, well…

It would suck. Go ahead, at least you can admit it to yourself.

Her desk phone rang, startling her so badly, she flinched and gasped, her hand flattening over her heart.

After another three rings, she grabbed it and tried to go back to work.

Knowing she'd made the totally wrong decision and still unable to do anything to change it.

———

CJ RAN at the mouth the entire drive to Philly.

Riley was driving, partly because he was worried the kid would be overly excited and run them into a wall. And partly because it would keep his mind off his conversation with Aly.

While CJ catalogued every player on the Colonials—their strengths, their weaknesses, their freaking PIMs, for chrissakes—Riley answered when he needed to and kept his eyes on the road because, holy fuck, was there a shit-ton of traffic.

Logically, he knew Aly had been right. She never would've made the game for puck drop.

So why the hell are you so fucking frustrated?

Because he'd wanted her there. He wanted to share this with her, wanted her to be there after the game to celebrate. Hell, he didn't care if he got five minutes of ice time or twenty.

He'd finally fucking made it.

And he found the girl he wanted to share this milestone with.

But the girl had turned him down.

Yeah, he knew it wasn't that simple. She had a job, a demanding job. She couldn't just take off at a moment's notice and follow him wherever.

Except...

"Oh, and hey, I got a heads-up from Ian MacDonald that Duchene isn't really hurt. Mac says Duchene and the coach got into it over something and that the team wants to trade him. I heard some of the stories about Duchene. Do you think it's true?"

Hell, everyone had heard the stories about the Colonials' third-line right winger. He partied hard, played a physical game, and led the team in penalty minutes. A loose cannon who'd been a scoring machine. But he was thirty-five now and didn't score as much as he used to.

Riley had heard the talk that the team had considered not picking up his contract last year and he'd been a late addition on a one-year contract.

Sucked for Duchene, but it opened up a spot if they actually decided to get rid of the guy. Still, Riley knew he was a long shot for the position. More likely the club would go with CJ. He'd been a first-round draft pick and the kid improved every day. And even though Riley had better numbers this season, the Philly coach would probably go with the rookie if he kept one of them up.

And for a split second, Riley thought that would be okay.

Are you fucking crazy?

He must be. Because he was seriously thinking that if he got sent back to Reading, he'd be closer to Aly.

How fucked was that? He should be doing everything he could to grab a spot with the Colonials, not hope to be sent back to the Redtails.

"Riley?"

"Yeah, sorry. Got a lot on my mind. Do I think it's true? Probably. Does it mean they'll trade him? Hell if I know. They've got some money invested in him so they'll wanna make that back, and with his record, I don't know that anyone'll want to take a chance on him."

Same could've been said about Riley last year. But Coach Scott had taken a chance on him and he thought he'd proven himself this year.

"So how long do you think we'll be up? I heard Vanderske's injury won't have him out long...and I'm bugging the shit out of you, aren't I?"

Riley glanced over to see CJ shaking his head and grimacing.

"Sorry, man. I don't know how to shut up sometimes. I'm—"

"CJ, you're not bugging me. Everything's good. Just got stuff on my mind."

"Like the girl you're seeing?"

Riley shot the kid another glance and now the little shit wore a smart-ass grin. "Why the fuck do you think that?"

"Everybody knows you didn't go home last night and Justin said you can't stop talking about her and—"

"All right, all right. Forget I asked. And..." he sighed. "Yeah. She's part of it. But I'm not sure she's as...invested as I am."

"What do you mean?"

Damn, was he really going to do this? Spill his guts to this kid?

Well, he had no one else to talk to for the next two hours, did he?

"I mean I don't think she likes me as much as I like her."

CJ shrugged. "Did you ask her if she likes you?"

He laughed. The kid really was young.

"I'm pretty sure she likes me. I'm just not sure she likes me enough to keep me."

"Why? What'd you do?"

"Good question."

"Did you piss her off?"

"Not exactly. I asked her to come to the game tonight. She said she had to work."

"Well, she's got a job, right? My parents can't get to the game tonight either." CJ shrugged. "It sucks but I know they'll be watching. There'll be another game. I know I just need to focus tonight. Probably better if they're not here."

He huffed out a laugh then shook his head. "Damn, kid. Maybe you're smarter than you look."

"Hey, what do you mean maybe? I'm way smarter than I look."

And maybe Riley needed to take a page out of the kid's book and just focus on tomorrow.

And when he'd made his mark in Philly, he'd be back to make his mark on Aly.

SEVEN

Aly had too much work to do Tuesday to let herself be distracted.

That didn't mean Riley didn't creep into her thoughts at all.

He did. More than she would've liked. Or would admit to. Especially to her sister.

"He's gone already." Vivi snorted at the dinner table Monday night. "That didn't take long."

Taking a bite of the corn bread Vivi had made to go with her homemade chili gave Aly a few seconds to formulate a response. The sharp edge in Vivi's voice made Aly want to jump to Riley's defense. Which was ridiculous. He didn't need to be defended.

"I'm really happy for him." Aly nodded, deciding to ignore Vivi's snark. "It's what he's been working toward for so many years. I hope they keep him. I can't wait to watch the game tomorrow night. It'll be amazing to see him on TV. I really hope he gets to play."

Vivi gave her a sidelong glance. "Huh. Guess he wasn't that good in bed. You don't sound all that broken up over him leaving."

Aly shrugged and spooned up chili, trying for nonchalant and probably ending up somewhere around pained wince. "We've known each other for four days. No one falls in love in four days."

Vivi went quiet and they ate in silence for at least a minute. Aly thought her sister would let it go. She should've known better.

"No, *you* don't. You're too smart for that."

Aly put her spoon down. "What does that mean?"

Vivi grimaced. "Sorry. I didn't mean that to sound...so bitchy. It's just...I did. Fall in love in four days. Actually, it only took me one. And we both know how much disaster *that* ended in."

Yeah, that had been a disaster. "But none of that was your fault, Viv. He was the asshole. Riley's not an asshole."

Vivi shrugged, her mouth twisting. "Maybe not. But athletes have this special power. They blind you to everything except what they want you to see. They draw you in and make you think you're the most important thing in their world, when, really, it's just all about how important they are to you. They see you as a reflection of themselves. And when they don't see themselves being reflected back enough, they're not interested anymore."

Aly heard so much bitterness in her sister's voice, she had to blink away the tears that popped into her eyes.

"Viv..."

Damn, Aly didn't know what to say to that, wasn't sure she could say anything to make her sister feel better.

If Aly ever saw Jamie Dunbar again, he better have his running shoes on because Aly would beat him to a pulp for making her sister hurt like this.

But of course that would never happen because the guy was now the star running back of the Dallas NFL franchise, who would probably sue her to hell and back if she dared lay a finger on the man. Which didn't mean she hadn't considered multiple ways to exact revenge.

Vivi rolled her eyes and shrugged, as if it didn't matter anymore.

"At least the guy didn't publicly humiliate you in front of his team when he dumped you. He gets points for that."

No, Riley hadn't dumped her at the first sign of stardom.

"He wanted me to be there."

Vivi frowned. "What?"

"He offered to get me tickets for the game. But Wednesday's my busy day. Meetings all day and I've got an evaluation after work and…"

"And?" Vivi looked at her with raised eyebrows.

"And I can't imagine that he'd want some girl he just met there for the biggest night of his life."

Vivi sat and blinked at her for several long seconds. "He actually said he wanted you there?"

She nodded. "I think he was disappointed when I said I couldn't go."

"Do you *want* to go?"

Yes. "I'm not sure."

Vivi's eyebrows rose again. "What was your first response?"

Aly bit her tongue because she'd wanted to say yes. Then she shook her head and dropped her spoon back into her bowl. "Of course I want to be at the game. But I have a job that I need. I can't just drop everything and drive to Philly because some hot guy wants me to go to his game."

Vivi's lips curved in a surprisingly bittersweet smile. "You've always been so much more grown-up than everyone else. Even our parents. When Mom and Dad used to have their shouting matches and they'd throw things at each other and slam doors, you'd be the one to go talk to them and get them to calm down. Some days, I still think you're the only adult in the family."

Aly's back stiffened. "That's not a bad thing."

Shaking her head, Vivi sighed. "No, it's not. I didn't mean to sound like it was. I'm just saying…you don't always have to be the grown-up. You don't always have to be rational and sane and fair. Sometimes you need to cut loose."

"I did." *And see where it's gotten you.* "I slept with him. I didn't even wait for the third date. Or until I had a background check done." At her sister's startled face, she rolled her eyes. "I'm kidding. Jeez, do you really think I'm that anal?"

Vivi shrugged. "Sometimes, yeah, because you are. And that's not always bad. You and I wouldn't be able to live here if you weren't because you're the one that makes sure we have enough money to pay the bills."

"And that makes me the most boring person on earth."

"Oh please." It was Vivi's turn to roll her eyes. "Obviously you're not or Riley wouldn't want you at his game. And...I think you should go."

"No." Aly shook her head. "I already told him I couldn't."

Besides, she'd checked for tickets. The game was sold out and resales were way beyond her means.

"Anyway, it's better this way. He needs to concentrate and I don't want to be a distraction. And I don't even know if I could see him after the game. He'll probably want to go out with the team and I don't want to get in the way of that."

Vivi stared at her with a bemused expression. "You have it all figured out, don't you?"

"I have to. I'm an adult."

"And what if you're wrong?"

"What do you mean?"

Vivi leaned forward, her expression intent. "I mean...what if he's the one?"

Her breath caught in her throat and she had to swallow before she could speak. "Then I guess if it doesn't work out, I'll have to be rational and move on."

"Or maybe it's your time to do something just for you."

"No—"

"Aly. Go to the game."

Smiling, she shook her head. "I wish it was that simple."

"Are you sure it's not?"

Yeah, she was. Because nothing in life was.

———

"GOOD PRACTICE, boys. Hit the showers, get some food then rest up for the game. New York's a tough defensive team, but I've got confidence in our offense. Doesn't mean I don't want our defense to slack. I'm expecting you all to play hard and smart. Special teams are going to be crucial tonight and we're down two of our regular penalty killers so everyone's expected to pick up the slack. See you tonight."

As Coach Angstadt left the room, the team stood and most began to file out. A few hung back and two headed toward Riley.

"Hey, man. Haven't seen you for...what? Like a year?" Holding out his hand to Riley, center Colin Williams grinned. "It's great to see you. Congrats on the call-up."

Riley smiled back as they shook. The blond Canadian stood an inch or so shorter but was built like a bulldog. Powerful body and a face that looked like it'd taken a few too many beatings, the scar from a horrific skate-to-the-face injury from years ago fading but still visible.

"Been at least a year," Riley said. "Heard the Crush traded you after I left. Glad to know it's working out."

"Aw, yeah, it's been great. Suki loves the area and at least we're on the same coast as her parents now. With the new baby, that's been a real help."

"I heard. That's great, man. Congrats."

Colin's grin grew even wider. "Thanks. You wanna see her picture?"

The man beside Colin groaned, but the smile on his face was amused. "At least tell me you got new ones. The last ones I saw were at least two days old."

Colin flipped Travis Walker the finger as he dug out his phone, which made Travis bray like a donkey.

Riley took Travis's hand when he stuck it out.

"Welcome up, bud." Travis shook his hand with a punishing grip but Riley had been ready for it. "Good to see you again."

"Good to see you, too." Riley and the defenseman had been team-mates years ago in Grand Rapids, where they'd played in the ECHL right after Riley had graduated from college. Travis had been a hotshot with a huge talent until he'd taken a devastating hit to the boards that'd nearly ended his career. But the guy had bounced back to become one of the league's steadiest defensemen.

For a few weeks three seasons ago, the three of them had played for the same AHL team before being traded to different franchises.

They caught up for a few minutes while Colin swiped through his phone for pictures of his adorable baby girl. Riley smiled at pictures of the hulking Colin holding a tiny human with his arm around his college sweetheart-now-wife.

Riley had met Suki several times when they'd been on the same team and he'd liked her. She had that no-nonsense Canadian humor he'd grown accustomed to playing hockey. And she could swear like a man. Better than her husband, actually.

It wasn't until a few minutes later that Riley saw Travis glance over his shoulder and grimace.

"Hey, man. Looks like your kid's gonna need a watchdog. He's... what? Twenty-one, right? He does not want to get messed up with the Strakas. Looks a little green to be messing in their shit."

Looking over his shoulder, Riley saw CJ nodding at something Hubert Straka had said. CJ didn't look like he was in trouble but he didn't exactly look comfortable either.

Hubert and Christian Straka, Russian machines straight out of central casting, were tall, blond, and almost identical, from their intimidating faces to their wicked right-hand slapshots. They were great defensive wingers and racked up serious points every season, but they had a reputation for partying hard and had occasionally dragged some of the younger players down with them.

Riley stuck his fingers in his mouth and whistled, catching CJ's and the Strakas' attention. "Kid, let's haul."

Relief crossed CJ's face but he covered it by turning his head to check his locker then grabbing his bag and nodding at the brothers before hustling over to Riley's side.

After he introduced CJ to Travis and Colin, they all walked out together. While Colin went home, Travis offered to take Riley and CJ to lunch before they went back to the hotel before the game.

The hostess at the restaurant knew Travis by name, and the smile they exchanged made it clear she knew a lot more than that.

Riley shook his head. Some things never changed. He and Travis had slept their way through half the population of women under thirty in Rapid City during their time there.

When they were seated and had ordered, Travis motioned with his head toward the hostess.

"She's got a sister." Travis smiled at Riley. "Dude, we could relive Wilkes-Barre."

CJ's eyes rounded and he glanced between Travis and Riley but kept his mouth shut, shoveling bread like they wouldn't bring more.

With a soft huff, Riley shook his head. "Nah, man. I'm turning over a new leaf."

Travis looked stunned before he started to smile.

"Yeah, right," Travis scoffed. "You're too young to be tied down. And when you lock down your slot on the team, you're gonna want your freedom. Dude, women will be crawling all over you. And I'm not just talking small-town sweethearts. I'm talking Victoria's Secret models and fucking porn stars. You will think you've died and gone to heaven. The sheer amount of ass and the quality available for the taking will be overwhelming at first but you'll learn to weed out the ones who want to land a husband fast."

Actually, that sounded...like hell.

He shook his head. "Maybe I'm actually looking for a wife."

Travis blinked, like his brain was trying to process input and couldn't. Riley started to laugh, which actually made CJ pause with a piece of bread halfway to his mouth.

"Just keep eating, kid." Riley grinned at CJ. "You're gonna need the calories for tonight. And Travis, more power to you but if I stay, I think you're gonna be chasing women without me."

With a bemused smile, Travis started on the second basket of bread the server had brought. Apparently, Travis was a regular here.

"Well, damn, I can't wait to meet the woman who brought you to heel. Is she coming to the game tonight?"

Riley shook his head, the subject still tender. And one he'd have to shelve until later. "No, she has to work. Besides, I need all my concentration focused on the game tonight."

"You're absolutely right. Try not to overthink it. This is your time. You're gonna nail it."

Travis looked so damn confident, Riley had to smile even as he shook his head. "Let's hope I'm not the one getting nailed to the boards."

"Nah, that's your specialty, man. You're a grinder. Go out there and fucking grind them into submission. And if that doesn't work, you do some of your best work with your mouth. Mind-fuck 'em. New York won't know what hit them. And if you really want the girl, same thing applies. Talk until she agrees just to shut you up." Travis shrugged. "Or punches you in the mouth. With you, it can go either way."

———

ALY GLANCED AT THE CLOCK, her heart pounding a mile a minute.

Six-fifty. If she left now, she'd still get to see the start of the game.

But as her boss droned on about performance issues to one of the men in Aly's office, she knew she wasn't going to make it home for puck drop.

Yes, she was recording the game and the pre-game show but she'd wanted to be home to see if Riley made the lineup.

She hadn't heard from him overnight but he had texted her earlier today. He must have sent it before he left for the arena this afternoon.

Getting ready for the game. Hoping like hell I don't forget anything. Hope you get to watch the game. Let me know. Talk to you soon.

Since then...nothing.

So why do you feel slighted?

Because she was a bitch who couldn't be bothered to drive two hours to his first NHL game.

Grr.

Hell, even she knew that wasn't fair. This, her job, was important to her and so were the people she worked with. Which was why she was in this evaluation. Because her job mattered.

But when her boss finally wrapped up the meeting after they'd managed to resolve at least a few of her coworker's concerns, she excused herself and took off as fast as her heels would let her.

She was tempted to take off her pumps and run but figured that'd be a little too out of character.

Grabbing her stuff from her office, she swapped out her pumps for sneakers and now she took off at a restrained run. Okay, more like a hurried shuffle because her damn skirt was so tight, but she cleared the building in two minutes and was home in ten.

"Vivi! Do you have—"

"Don't worry." Her sister called back from the TV room. "The game's on. You didn't miss anything."

"Is he on the bench?"

Breathless from her sprint from the car to the house, Aly fell onto the couch next to Vivi and started to scan the players on the ice. The game was in motion so she couldn't tell who any of the players were. She could barely see their numbers much less their names on their jerseys.

"Did you watch the pre-game show? Did they mention him? Did they—"

"I just got home, too. So, no, I didn't see any of it. And I already ordered pizza so we don't have to worry about dinner."

Without taking her eyes off the TV, Aly hugged her sister. "Keep your eyes peeled. I know he's going to play tonight. I just know it."

"You know if he plays well, he might not come back, right?"

"I know that."

"And you're okay with that?"

No, she wasn't. She just didn't know how to fix it. Couldn't fix it. "Maybe I'd be willing to find a way to make it work."

Vivi didn't say anything right away and Aly snuck a glance away from the TV.

"What?"

Her sister smiled. "It's kind of nice to see you want something enough to mess with your schedule."

Aly held Vivi's gaze. "Am I really that rigid?"

Vivi grimaced. Then she nodded. "Yeah. Sometimes. You know I love you, sis, but sometimes I think you're never going to bust out of your shell and have a real life. And you're gonna miss so much."

"And now Hatch takes the puck for the Colonials. The twenty-eight-year-old is making his NHL debut tonight..."

The rest was lost as she and Vivi squealed and locked hands, bouncing up and down on the couch.

Tears actually popped into her eyes as she watched Riley race down the ice with the puck before passing to another player and getting checked into the boards.

For the next two hours, as they watched the game and ate dinner between periods, Aly watched Riley's every move. She held her breath every time he was on the ice and only breathed when he headed for the bench.

Even with her extremely limited knowledge of the game, she could tell he was doing well. He seemed to be on the ice often, CJ always with him. They played well together, and by the end of the night, although neither of them had scored, the announcers had mentioned Riley as a good addition to the third line.

She had no idea what that meant other than that he'd done well. He'd had an assist on one of the team's goals, which helped because it'd been a tie game until then.

The Colonials had gone on to score again and won the game.

She and her sister had high-fived then Vivi had said she was heading out to meet up with friends.

And left Aly alone.

She reached for her phone without thinking, even though she knew there was no way he'd call or text now.

But she still sat there with her phone in her hand until she went to bed an hour later.

————

"WE WANT you to take practice with the team tomorrow and Thursday, and we'll make a determination about Friday then. You had a great game tonight, Riley. We're all pleased with your play and looking forward to seeing what else you can do. See you tomorrow."

"Thanks, Coach. I appreciate this opportunity."

Coach Angstadt smiled and clapped him on the shoulder in his office. He'd called Riley in as soon as he'd been showered and dressed after the game.

Because of the cellphone-blackout in the locker room, Riley had been counting down the minutes until he could call Aly. And his parents, of course.

But first, he wanted to hear her voice. Couldn't fucking wait to hear her voice.

"Just keep doing what you're doing and I think you'll be pleased with the results."

Riley left with a nod and headed out of the office, not surprised to see CJ waiting in the hall, looking nervous as hell.

Riley grabbed his shoulder and gave him a little shake. "Breathe, CJ. You played a great game."

That made the kid smile. "You, too, man. All right. You gonna wait for me?"

"Won't leave without you."

Another smile and the kid headed into the office and Riley headed back to the locker room.

He wanted to grab his coat and his bag and head out so he could call Aly, but Travis met him at his locker.

"You ready to get out of here?" Travis smacked him on the back as he pulled on his jacket. "Time to celebrate."

Riley grinned at him and nodded. "Sounds good. I just need to make a call. Told CJ I'd wait for him, too."

He had to raise his voice to be heard over the rest of the team. They'd been on a three-game losing streak before tonight and were psyched about the win.

"Well, hurry up. There's alcohol to drink and women to hit on."

Colin joined them, nudging Riley with his shoulder. "What'd Coach say? You staying?"

"At least until Thursday. I'm gonna take practice with the team then I guess he'll make a decision."

Riley was cautiously optimistic but wasn't getting his hopes up

"You don't have anything to worry about." Travis clapped him on the back again. "Come on. Let's get the hell out of here."

"Sure. CJ should be out in a— wait, there he is."

Colin twisted to look over his shoulder. "You two had a great night."

CJ was grinning like a loon as he practically ran over to them. Apparently, he was staying, too. Good. The kid had played an amazing game.

"Coach said you're staying, too. That's awesome."

Laughing, Riley put his arm around CJ's shoulders and steered him toward the door.

"Yeah, it is. Come on, kid. Let's go celebrate. I just gotta make a call first."

CJ's grin turned sly. "Gonna call Aly?"

Now he smacked the kid on the back of the head. "You're just jealous. You gonna call your parents?"

"Shit." CJ shook his head. "We better leave now."

Riley was still laughing when he finally found a quiet spot in the hall to make his call.

She answered on the second ring.

"Riley?"

"Hey."

"Hi. We saw the game. You looked great!"

Damn, it was good to hear her voice. "Thanks. We had a great game."

"I'm so happy for you. Are you going out to celebrate?'

"CJ and I and a couple of the guys are heading to a bar."

She paused for a second. Or maybe he just imagined it. "I'm really happy for you, Riley. So...are you staying in Philly?"

"Yeah, at least until Thursday. Coach said they'd decide whether or not to keep me or send me down."

"I have no doubt they're going to keep you."

Well, hell. She didn't have to sound so damn happy about it. Which was stupid to even think about.

"Thanks. I'm happy with the way I played."

"You should be."

"If I'm still here Friday, do you want to come to the game?"

Another quick pause. "I... Can I let you know that morning? I'd really love to come but—"

"Yeah, no problem. I guess I'll wait to hear from you."

"Oh, wait. Do you—oh, I forgot. You're going out."

"Yeah. And I still need to give my parents a call."

Another pause.

"I'm so glad you called, Riley. I don't want to keep you from your parents. I just... I'll talk to you soon."

"Sure. Night."

He hung up before she could respond and the second the call disconnected, he wanted to throw his phone against the wall.

Goddammit.

That was not how he'd wanted that conversation to go.

He felt like he'd just blown playoff game seven with a turnover in the defensive end. His heart pounding, he took a couple of deep breaths. Getting pissed wasn't going to help. Besides, if he stayed in Philly, he might never see her again.

Which would totally suck.

Shit.

And there wasn't a damn thing he could do about it now. Now, it was time to celebrate finally achieving his goal.

Tomorrow, he needed to make sure he held on to his spot on this team.

And maybe to start getting over this damn crush he had on a girl who obviously didn't care enough about him.

———

"YOU LOOK LIKE SHIT."

Aly gave her sister a death glare as she headed for the coffeepot. "Gee, thanks. And what are you doing up this early, anyway?"

Vivi shrugged. "Haven't been to bed yet. And I wanted to know if he called last night."

Pouring herself coffee, Aly didn't answer until she'd taken her first sip.

"Yes, he called."

And she'd been an ass.

"That's it? He called." Vivi sighed. "What'd he *say?*"

"That he'll be staying in Philly at least until Friday."

"Ah."

Yeah, ah. That kind of summed up her feelings this morning.

She'd told herself last night that she was happy for him. And she was. She really was. But she was also practical and she knew that if he stayed with the Colonials, their relationship was doomed.

What relationship? You spent two nights together. What the hell did you expect? A proposal?

Of course not.

"Aly? You're thinking way too hard this early. You're making *my* brain hurt."

"You're right. It's too early for this."

Vivi tipped her head to look at her. "Why do I get the feeling we're not talking about the same thing?"

Because they weren't and her sister was no fool. "I need to break it off. Tell him it was nice while it lasted and cut ties."

"Uh-huh."

Aly shot her sister another glare. "And what does that mean?"

"Doesn't mean a thing." Vivi shrugged, pissing off Aly even more. "I think you're totally right."

Of course, she was right.

Then why is it so hard to breathe?

"It would never work out." Aly took another sip of coffee and watched her sister nod.

"Uh-huh."

"I just need to let this go."

Her sister nodded sagely. "Yep."

"You're totally mocking me, aren't you?"

Vivi shrugged but her lips twitched. "Maybe a little." Then she rolled her eyes. "Jesus, Aly. A blind person could see how much you like the guy. So you won't be able to jump his bones every night. If he likes you as much as he seems to, he won't be a prick and cheat on you. He'll wait for you and you can send disgustingly sweet texts every day, and when he's on a road trip, you can send him tit pics."

About to open her mouth and protest, she snapped it shut when Vivi started to laugh.

"Okay, maybe no titty pictures. But, Aly...live a little. Life doesn't only happen in this little bubble of our house and the hospital. Hell, even Mom and Dad figured that out. And now, I'm going to bed. I have used up all my brain power and need to recharge."

With a wry grin, Vivi headed out of the kitchen.

And Aly sipped her coffee, wondering how to break a two-decade habit of being a stick in the mud.

———

"HATCH, come in and close the door and take a seat."

Stone-faced, Riley followed Coach's orders Thursday morning

and slipped into the chair in front of the desk. Still angry with himself for a shitty practice this morning, he figured he was headed back to Reading and the Redtails.

The guys would probably be glad to see him. At least he had that to look forward to.

"Tough morning. You struggled to hit the net, had some trouble making passes."

"Yes, sir." His jaw locked against the need to make excuses. He didn't have any. He'd sucked. Maybe self-sabotage. Maybe nothing more than a bad morning. He only knew one thing. He—

"Well, hopefully you'll play better tonight." Coach smiled. "We're adding you and CJ to the third line. We like what you add to the team. Your grit and determination and his speed, combined with your ability to work together, are exactly what we need right now."

Coach went on to say more and Riley heard and responded to everything, but half of his brain was doing somersaults in victory.

He'd made it. He'd fucking made it.

"Get yourself fed and rested and back here ready to play tonight. And send CJ in if he's out there."

As Coach stood, he held out his hand. Riley jumped to his feet and shook, his face actually hurt from smiling.

"Yes, sir. And thank you."

He walked out into the hall, still grinning, and caught sight of CJ, slumped against the wall waiting. The kid shoved away from the wall, eyes wide like a deer in the headlights.

Riley nodded toward the coach's office. "You're up." He reached for CJ's shoulder. "Breathe. Seriously. Try not to pass out."

"What'd he say?"

"We'll talk when you get out, okay? I'll wait for you."

CJ looked ridiculously relieved. "Okay, yeah. Sounds good."

Then he disappeared behind the door and Riley started to grin again. He needed to call his parents. His dad had mentioned flying in for a game. He didn't think they'd be able to get in by tonight, but they had another game Saturday night and one Tuesday. Maybe they'd be able to get here for one of those.

And what about Aly?

Should he call? Text? Hell, did she even want to hear from him? Or had she already written him off? They'd exchanged a few texts over the past two days but he'd been busy so there hadn't been many.

Fuck, maybe he needed to face facts. She just wasn't that into him. Maybe she never had been. Or maybe she'd only wanted him when it'd been convenient.

Either way, she fucked with his head, and he didn't need that right now.

So he pulled out his phone and called his parents.

And tried not to think about a certain blonde.

EIGHT

Aly paused Friday afternoon, teeth lodged in her upper lip, thumbs poised over her phone.

Bliss's text enticed like the promise of a strong margarita at Third and Spruce after work.

Come over to our place tonight to watch the Colonials game. Lori and Cary will be here and a few other guys from the team. We can't wait to watch Riley and CJ again!!!

She *so* wanted to go. The desire was a gnawing ache in her gut.

She'd been moping most of the afternoon, figuring she'd be home watching the game by herself tonight because Vivi had to work.

For the past day, she'd thought about contacting Bliss but had talked herself out of it. The Redtails probably had a game or, if they didn't, why would they even think to invite her along with them? She really didn't know anyone on the team.

But Bliss hadn't forgotten her. And she wanted to go.

But...Riley hadn't called or texted.

Not since yesterday morning. And even though she'd picked up the phone a thousand times to contact him, she hadn't. She hadn't known what to say. That wasn't right either.

She'd known exactly what she should've said.

"I miss you. I'm so happy for you. I can't wait to see you."

But she also knew this was the biggest break of his career and she wanted him to succeed so she didn't want to distract him.

If you'd even be a distraction.

Maybe he'd moved on. Maybe he'd spent the last two nights picking up women.

But she knew that wasn't right, either. She knew there was no way Riley would screw up this chance.

Fuck it.

I would love to! Thanks for asking. What can I bring?

Glancing at the clock, she sighed when she realized she still had two hours before she could leave. And another two before the game started.

Damn, how much did that suck?

About as much as waking up this morning and wishing he was lying next to her, smiling that grin of his. The one she'd seen Monday morning. The one that made her toes curl. And the one that usually made opposing players want to punch him.

God, she was so stupid. She wanted Riley any way she could get him.

And you probably lost him for good.

No. Just...no.

She'd figure something out, even if she had to go to Philly and bang on the glass at the next home game to get his attention.

But for that, she was gonna need help.

Good thing she knew a few guys who would know exactly what to do.

———

"RILEY, MY FRIEND. HOW ARE YOU?"

"Jake." Riley grinned, his mood immediately lifted as he held his phone to his ear. "Hey, man. How's it going?"

"That is a question I will be asking you. You looked good last night. You and CJ. Tonight you will be even better."

Last night's game had been a hard-fought battle for sixty long minutes. The Colonials had been on top of the game the entire night until the final minutes when the Hawks had scored twice, winning the game.

"Thanks, man. So you got to watch?"

"Yes, most of the team was at Shane's place last night to watch. Some people who weren't with the team, too."

If he'd been a dog, Riley's ears would've pointed. "Oh yeah? Like who?"

"Like Allison. Very pretty. Confused as to what she saw in you but seems like a smart lady otherwise."

Sitting in his car in the arena's underground parking lot, Riley shook his head, ignoring the sharp pain in his chest at the mention of her name. He'd arrived early for tonight's game, but once he entered the arena, he'd have to turn his phone off. The team banned cell phone use once the guys got to the arena before a game and until they were on their way home afterward.

"And fuck you twice, my Russian friend. Don't you have a game tonight that you need to be getting ready for?"

Jake laughed. "That is all you have to say? I am disappointed. What happened to Chickie? Seems your new team might need a guy like you tonight. Get people fired up. And your geography skills remain sadly lacking. Okay, I only want to call and give you hard time. And tell you good luck tonight."

By the time Jake had shut up, Riley was grinning.

"Hey, Jake. Thanks. I appreciate the love."

"I have much love to spread today so is no problem. Just remember the little people you came up with, yes? Talk to you soon."

Riley nodded though he knew Jake couldn't see him. "Keep in touch. Seriously."

"You too. Kick ass tonight, Hatch."

Jake didn't say good-bye. The call simply disconnected, leaving Riley with one burning question.

Why had Aly watched the game with his team?

Only because she and Bliss had become friends? Or was he right to think maybe—

Fuck. He shook his head. Now wasn't the time to think about this. He didn't want it to fuck with his head before the game. Last night had sucked, to be ahead for all of the game and to lose it in the last seconds. Coach hadn't been happy last night and a few of the guys, Riley included, had gone out to drown their sorrows.

Probably not something he'd do again. He'd gone only because he had nothing else to do. No one to go home to, no one he wanted to call to talk to.

No Aly.

But she'd been at Shane's last night.

So what? That only proved she liked Bliss.

She hadn't called or texted him the entire day.

And there's your answer, asshole.

Time to move on.

He got out of his car and headed into the arena.

———

"SO? ARE YOU READY?"

Aly rolled her eyes and sighed. "I don't know. Maybe this wasn't such a great idea, Viv. What if he doesn't want to see me? What if he's already dating someone else? What if he just doesn't care that I'm here? I don't want to make him uncomfortable. This is his job."

"He'll feel the same way you would if he showed up at the hospital with a sign proclaiming his feelings for you. You'd melt into a little puddle of goo and promise him sexual favors when you get him alone."

Sitting in her seat in the Colonials offensive end of the arena, Aly pulled a face at her sister and reached inside her purse to tap the sign she'd made in a moment of sheer stupidity.

It'd seemed like a good idea last night after a couple of beers and a profane discussion with Riley's friends, who'd been more than eager to help her figure out what her sign should say.

But now that she was actually here, common sense was trying to kick in. Or maybe it was fear.

Hell, maybe he wouldn't remember what the sign meant.

"Oh, I know that look. Don't wimp out now, Aly. Come on, we braved the Schuylkill Expressway. Don't let a little performance anxiety get in your way."

Yes, the Schuylkill had been a mess today. They'd passed two accidents, had crawled at five miles an hour for long stretches, and got lost twice in Center City on the way to the arena.

Now here she was, waiting to get her first live glimpse of Riley in his uniform during the pre-game warm-up. Trying to work up the courage to walk over to the other side of the arena, walk down the stairs to the glass at the ice, and wait for Riley to notice her standing there with her little sign that was meant only for him.

Could she do it?

Hell, yes, she could.

She checked the clock. Only three minutes until the teams made it out to the ice for warm-ups.

Standing, she took a deep breath. "If this doesn't work, we're leaving. Immediately."

Vivi grinned and settled deeper into her seat. "You forget. I drove. Besides, I figure I'm driving home alone tonight."

Aly could only hope.

———

"OKAY, boys. Work out the kinks, get loose, and get ready to play."

Assistant Coach Domenic Mann slapped each man on the back

as they passed through the hall for warm-ups and Riley nodded before hitting the ice.

The music was nothing more than a throbbing beat in his ears, the crowd noise barely a consideration at this point. It'd get louder when the game started but he'd learned how to put it aside and concentrate on the game.

Tonight, it was merely noise.

Just like the people gathered at the glass, banging and cheering. None of them were there for him. No one knew him yet. Hopefully that would change and soon. But for now, he was okay with anonymity.

It wasn't until he and CJ and a few other guys were flipping the last pucks into the ice before the buzzer rang that CJ skated up next to him.

"Uh, Riley."

"Yeah, what's up?"

"Uh—"

"Dude." Travis flanked him. "There's some girl here with your jersey on. Don't know how the fuck you got puck bunnies already but if you throw this one back, put in a good word for me. I got a thing for blondes."

Riley nearly tripped himself as his head shot up.

"Seriously? Where?"

Travis laughed and shook his head. "Right corner. She's a few rows up and she looks way too civilized for you. She needs a guy like me."

His head shot around to the direction Travis pointed and he sucked in air.

Christ, how the hell had he missed her?

Aly stood perfectly still, five rows back from the ice. She was wearing a Colonials sweater and damn if Travis wasn't right. She was wearing his number. He could just make out the seven on her arm when she lifted her hand to wave. Her wary expression made him smile.

He was so fucking happy to see her, his heart literally felt like it could pound out of his chest.

She was here. Holy *fuck*, she was *actually* here.

All the bullshit he'd told himself about how he was over her and how it didn't matter if she didn't like him... Yeah, that was all shit. He knew that now.

The only thing that mattered was that she was here. She'd taken that huge first step and showed up.

And he wasn't about to let her hang.

Skating over to the ice, ignoring the catcalls from the few guys still there, he put his hand on the glass and waited.

The fans on the other side high-fived him but soon realized that he wasn't looking at them.

He only had eyes for Aly.

He watched her make her way down the stairs, trying to wade through the sea of blue-and-white-clad fans to the glass, where the usher, a guy wearing a huge, shit-eating grin, made a space for her.

She didn't say anything. He wasn't sure he would've heard her anyway. But the smile on her face was all he needed to see.

And then she looked down and pulled something out of her purse.

A piece of paper that she held up on the glass next to his hand.

She'd only written one word in perfect block letters.

Please

Then she put her hand on the glass to mirror his and he smiled until his face hurt.

"Stay."

He wasn't sure she'd heard him, but she nodded and her smile widened.

And Riley knew, no matter how the game ended, he'd already won.

———

THE GUYS WERE PUMPED after tonight's win and the locker room sounded like a frat house on homecoming weekend.

"So, Riley. Guess you're not coming out to celebrate tonight, huh?"

Ignoring Travis's sly dig was easy, considering Riley had somewhere infinitely more interesting to be tonight.

He'd been able to keep his attention focused squarely on the game, but the second the final buzzer rang, he'd started to grin. And not because his team had won. Well, not only that.

"Hell, I wouldn't be going out with you tonight if I had someone who looked like that waiting for me tonight," Colin responded. "Damn, Riley, how'd you snag her, anyway? Seriously, man, she looks way too smart for you."

Riley didn't bother to look up as he shoved his legs into his pants then shrugged into his shirt. He was on a mission and wasn't about to be deterred. But he did manage to shoot Colin and Travis the finger over his shoulder.

While the two of them laughed, Riley rolled his tie and stuffed it in the pocket of his jacket. He didn't want to take the time to knot it. Coach had already done his post-game talk, which meant Riley was free to go as soon as he was ready.

And he was pretty much ready to go now…when he remembered he'd driven in with CJ. Because he was sharing a hotel room with him.

Shit.

He stopped, totally stymied.

"Uh, Riley?" Sitting next to him on the bench, CJ looked up, frowning. "You okay?"

"Yeah, but I need you to find somewhere to crash tonight. I'll make it up to you, I swe—"

CJ's laughter cut Riley off.

"Dude, I'm not stupid. As soon as I saw Aly at the game, I checked around. I'm gonna crash at Malone's place tonight. He's got an extra bed since O'Neill's still in the hospital—"

Riley grabbed CJ by the nape and yanked him forward to kiss his head. "I love you, kid."

CJ pushed him away with a laugh. "Yeah, yeah. You owe me, Rye. Just don't fuck it up."

"Don't plan to."

Seconds later, Riley was out of the locker room and into the hall. Pulling out his phone, he breathed a sigh of relief to see a text from Aly.

Not sure where I should meet you so I'll wait outside until I hear from you. If something changes, I'll go home with Vivi and you can text me.

Hell, nothing was going to change his mind. She'd made the next step and he was going to make sure the only way they kept moving was forward.

I'm done. Where are you?

Already on his way out of the building, Riley stopped and looked around. There were still a crowd of fans milling around, waiting for the crush at the train station to ease. He didn't think he'd be recognized. He wore a beanie that hid his hair but had forgotten to factor in the suit. Dead giveaway.

"Riley! Will you sign my program?"

A little girl in pigtails and a Colonials sweater asked him to sign her souvenir stick, the smile on her face adorable. Of course, he said yes. Five seconds later, he had a crowd of people around him.

And the vague remembrance of a conversation with the team PR woman to be polite at all times and not to open his mouth too much.

Which was a virtual impossibility for him.

He spoke to everyone who stuck something in his hands. Mostly they were kids who wanted him to sign their sweaters or their programs. He'd done it thousands of times before but never on an NHL sweater.

His face hurt by the time he'd signed every piece, he'd smiled and talked and took photos.

And when he looked up after the last person walked away, he

found Aly, smiling at him from a bench lining the walk to the entrance.

She had her hands stuffed in the pockets of her coat and she looked cold. Standing when she saw he'd noticed her, she walked toward him. He met her halfway, trying to find the perfect thing to say.

She looked like she was doing the same thing, her smile a little strained, like she didn't have a clue what he was going to say.

When she stood right in front of him, he realized he didn't need to say anything.

Wrapping his arms around her, he pressed his lips against hers and kissed the hell out of her.

He kissed her like a parched man gulped water after three days in the desert.

Her lips softened under his and her arms went around his waist to hold him almost as tightly as he held her. He lost himself in her taste and her touch. Not even the catcalls from the security guards and the few lingering fans made him want to stop.

Hell, if he could continue to kiss her and still get to his hotel room, he would've considered it.

He didn't know how long they stood there, kissing each other like they hadn't seen each other in weeks. He couldn't get enough of her, probably would never get enough of her. This... She was exactly what he wanted to come home to every night.

But when Aly pulled away, he let her go. Reluctantly. And not far. He kept his arms around her shoulders and her body tucked against his.

"I fucking missed you." He spoke before she could say anything and probably should've taken time to think of something better. But the truth was, he meant every word. "I don't want to miss you again. I want you to be the first person I see when I get back from a road trip. I want to be the first person you want to talk to in the morning and the last person you want to talk to before you go to sleep. And I want to be inside you as often as I can. Starting in the next half hour."

Laughing, she slipped one hand under his beanie, into his still-wet hair, and tugged him down for another kiss that made every part of his body hot and ready. Some more than others. "I missed you too, Riley."

His cock hardened even more than it already was. The walk to the car would be interesting. "You have no idea how damn glad I am to hear that."

Her smiled softened a little. "I'm not sure how we're going to figure out the distance, but," she pressed her fingers to his lips when he opened his mouth to respond, "I want to make this work. I will try my damnedest to make it work. I would rather have you some of the time than not at all."

His heart practically hurt at the sweet tone of her voice and the look in her eyes. "And I will take you any way I can get you. Every way. All ways." He waggled his eyebrows at her. "Some ways we haven't tried yet."

She laughed again and settled her hands on his shoulders, staring up into his eyes and making him wish for a dark corner. "Then take me to your hotel and let me do bad things to you."

"Honey, you can do anything you want to me. As long as I get to return the favor. I will make it my mission in life to please you in ways you never imagined."

Pulling his head down, she rubbed her cold nose against his. "I think I'll be the one owing you favors. And I'll love every minute of it."

His grin grew even wider. "Then let me show you some of my moves, hon."

"I'm all yours, Riley."

He wrapped his arm around her shoulders and pointed them in the direction of the parking garage. "Damn right, babe. Damn right."

———

DON'T MISS Will and Jess's story in The Enforcer.

THE ENFORCER

He's ready to fight for love...

Coming into a team in the middle of the season is never easy but veteran hockey player Will MacDonald is a tough guy. He's not afraid to drop his gloves in defense of his teammates and he's never met a woman who made his heart pound as hard as a good fight. Until he has a chance collision with a curvy brunette.

Jess Gardiner has been around hockey all her life. Her dad, an NHL scout, taught her everything he knows about the game and she believes Will is exactly what the young Redtails team needs. He's just not what she needs in her life, even if he is huge, hot and hard-bodied.

Will is used to fighting for what he wants but winning Jess's heart might be the toughest battle of his life.

ONE

Head down as she glanced over the contracts for the new promotional opportunities, Jessica Gardiner grinned at her own handiwork as she hurried through the hall.

She had no doubt she'd get approval from the Redtails' front office to go after sponsors. She knew exactly who she'd approach first—

"Oh!"

A huge, immoveable object suddenly appeared in front of her, and in the next second, her ass hit the floor and the papers in her hands went flying.

"Holy shit. Damn, I'm sorry. Here, give me your hand. Let me help you up."

As pain started to radiate up her back, a large hand appeared in front of her face. Stunned, she stared at it for several seconds.

"Hey, hon. You okay?"

Hon?

She looked up...and up...into eyes so dark, she wasn't sure if they were black or brown. Or possibly navy.

A face she didn't know but that looked familiar.

Scowling up at him, she shook her head. "Who are you?"

His lips quirked into a grin that made his eyes narrow down to slits. "Will MacDonald. And you're still on the floor. Come on, take my hand. You're gonna get that skirt all dirty."

Her lips parted in surprise. Well, damn. That's why he looked familiar. Coach had taken her recommendation seriously.

She started to grin and noticed MacDonald's eyes widen.

"Uh, you sure you're okay, miss? How hard did you hit?"

For a split second, she wondered what the hell he was talking about. And then she remembered she was sprawled on the floor.

Looking down at herself, she realized her skirt had ridden up almost to her hips and was damn close to revealing what color underwear she'd picked out this morning. Her legs were spread wide, and the few strands of hair falling in her eyes meant she'd lost a few of the pins holding it up in an already messy bun.

Grimacing, she reached for his outstretched hand, knowing it'd be easier to accept his help than try to scramble up on her own.

"Well, my skirt wouldn't be dirty if you hadn't body-checked me—"

She gave a totally girly squeal as he ignored her hand, grabbed her under her arms, and lifted her off the floor.

Holy crap. The guy had some serious muscle to have deadlifted her off the floor like she was a kid and not a full-grown woman.

Duh, you work for a hockey team.

And this was definitely a hockey player.

Unkempt dark brown hair, curly and way too long to be civilized. At least a week's worth of stubble on his chin. Broad shoulders and chest that filled her vision when she stared straight ahead. Even in four-inch heels, she knew the top of her head didn't reach his chin.

He wore a suit but no tie, but she could tell, even in dress pants, he had powerful legs. Again, not surprising considering what he did for a living.

"Sorry, but I'm pretty sure you walked straight into my back. And since I don't have eyes in the back of my head..."

Okay, maybe she hadn't been looking where she was going, but she was the one who'd ended up on her ass on the floor. He could be a little more sympathetic.

Then again, he was a hockey player. As much as she loved the game, she'd been around the sport all her life. Most players were interested in only two things—hockey and sex.

If it didn't directly affect their game or getting laid, it didn't register.

And since she didn't mix business with pleasure... Probably best to just keep walking.

With a sigh, she decided to ignore him and turned to pick up the papers still scattered all over the floor.

"Let me give you a hand with that."

Amazingly, he brushed by her to gather up her contracts scattered all over the floor.

Okay, maybe he wasn't a total prick.

Bending over to reach the papers at her feet, she winced as pain shot up her hip.

Sucking in a sharp breath, she rubbed one hand on her abused hip and shook her head. Yeah, that was gonna hurt. Maybe she'd go down to see the trainer about an ice pack.

"You sure you're okay? You must've gone down a little harder than I thought. Do you need a hand getting wherever you're going? Where *are* you going anyway?"

"I'm fine. Really." *Just need to get away from you before you accidentally put me in a full body cast.* "I'll take those."

She held out her hand and refrained from rolling her eyes when he didn't immediately hand over her papers.

Great. One of those.

With a barely repressed sigh, she reached for calm and took another look at the man standing in front of her.

If anyone asked, she might admit that she found him attractive. Okay, hot. The guy was totally hot.

But she'd been around professional athletes all her life. She was used to handsome faces and ripped bodies. And huge egos.

She had to admit that even the less...attractive players still had that certain something that made them irresistible to most women.

Most women being *other* women. Jess had made the mistake of dating a few hockey players in her time. But she'd learned her lesson by the time she was twenty, when the last one had packed up his bags and moved to a team in Europe without so much as a good-bye.

That had been eight years ago.

This one...

Going through the files of hockey stats in her brain, she searched for Will's. She knew he was older than most of the guys on the Redtails. Close to mid-thirties. Somewhat unusual for the AHL, but he still had several good years in him. At least that's what she'd told Coach at the staff meeting last month.

Coach Scott always listened when she spoke up about players. She didn't do it often, but when Coach had been talking about possible replacement players at the monthly staff meeting a few weeks ago, she'd piped in with her two cents on MacDonald.

The guy's stats spoke for themselves, but for some reason, the Colonials talent scout had put MacDonald low on the list of potentials, far below players she wouldn't have given a second glance.

Okay, yeah, the NHL scout had a few decades of experience on her, but she knew her team.

And MacDonald was the perfect fit.

But she didn't have to personally like the guy.

"Do you think I can have my contracts back now?"

He blinked and looked down at his hands, as if he hadn't realized he still held them.

"Oh, yeah. Sorry about that. And about knocking you on your ass."

Then his gaze slid down her body and her eyes rolled again.

What did you expect? Hockey player.

The voice in her head was her mom's and she had to grit her teeth against the urge to growl. Like, seriously, she wanted to growl.

Then again, her mom wasn't wrong. Which just pissed her off even more.

Forcing a smile, she held her hand out. "Not a problem. I just need those."

"Sure." He held them out with another smile.

Okay, maybe he had a nice smile. Maybe better than nice. He didn't look so...arrogant when he grinned like that. It also made him look younger than he was.

No. Nope. Not a chance in hell.

Taking the papers, she nodded and started to walk past him.

And damn if the man didn't start to walk along with her.

"So, any chance you're heading to the main office? Just got here and not exactly sure where I need to be."

Looking up, she found him grinning down at her, that smile getting more attractive by the moment.

And, oh, that was *so* not good.

She stifled a sigh. "Sure. I'm headed there anyway."

"Great. Thanks, Miss..."

"Gardiner. Jess Gardiner."

Out of the corner of her eye, she saw him shoot her another glance, and when she looked up, his eyes were narrowed, as if he was thinking really hard.

"Any relation to Doug Gardiner? The NHL scout?"

So he did know her dad. "Yep, that's my dad."

"Ah."

She snuck another glance his way and noticed his easy grin had been replaced with a bit of a scowl.

Okay, *not* a fan of her dad's. Well, he wasn't the only one.

"So, what do you do for the Redtails?"

Small talk. *Lovely.* Luckily, the office was just down the hall.

"I'm the marketing and promotions manager."

"Nice. I guess."

Now an awkward silence fell and Jess almost wished he'd continue to talk. He had a nice voice, deep and rough, like he had gravel in his throat.

And what the hell does that matter?

Shit.

"So, Jess the marketing and promotions manager, do you like working here?"

Because answering was easier than an awkward silence, she said, "I do." It just wasn't where she wanted to spend the rest of her career, but he didn't need to know that. "The organization's great, we're drawing well, and the team's playing well. You're coming in at a good time."

"So I've been told."

Something in his tone caught her ear and she looked up again to find him grimacing, though his expression quickly cleared.

Curiosity made her ask, "I haven't heard of any trades lately so how did you get here?"

She wanted to take the words back when he looked at her with another one of those smiles. That smile said, *Hey, I know you want me.*

Though it took some effort on her part, she refrained from rolling her eyes.

"Picked up off waivers yesterday from the Roadies." He shrugged. "Been riding the bench for a month there so hopefully I'll see some ice time here. Heard good things about Coach Scott. Looking forward to playing for him."

Her smile was genuine now. "Coach is wonderful. The team's having a great year, even though we recently lost two of our best players to call-ups."

"Not a bad way to lose them."

"It's great for them. CJ will probably be back at some point, but I don't think Riley will. CJ's offensive game is tight but his defense needs some work to play at the NHL level. Riley's a damn good grinder and the Colonials need a player like him to get them going."

"Sounds like your dad rubbed off."

Now why didn't that sound like a compliment?

Slowing to a stop outside the door to the front office, Jess turned to look up at Will. He'd stopped beside her, watching her with raised eyebrows. Kind of seemed to Jess that he was daring her to say something.

Or maybe she was totally reading something into his expression that wasn't there.

Either way, she didn't have time for this. She had several businesses to contact about future events, needed to get started on the design for next season's Ugly Christmas sweaters and giveaways, and had several phone calls to return about an upcoming affiliation night program. They had two well-known Colonial alumni coming to sign autographs at next Friday's game and she needed to smooth some ruffled feathers over billing.

Ugh.

She loved the game of hockey. Always had, always would. It was in her DNA. And growing up, she'd idolized the players. They'd been her heroes, her idols. Her first crushes.

But she'd learned quickly that those heroes didn't always measure up to the public image.

"Here we are. Welcome to the Redtails, Will."

He nodded, watching her with sharp eyes. "Thanks. Nice to meet you, Jess. I guess I'll see you around."

She nodded. "I guess you will."

———

WILL OPENED the door for Jess and watched her walk through.

And yes, his gaze might have fallen to her ass. The girl had some curves, even though she couldn't weigh more than a hundred pounds soaking wet and she probably only stood about five-two, more than a foot shorter than him.

Not his typical type. He usually liked them tall, stacked, and exotic. Blonde, brunette, redhead, didn't matter. What did matter was that they were beautiful.

He'd never been attracted to the girl next door. Not even in high school. College had been a blur of hockey, classes, and parties. And a whole lot of girls.

And even if certain parts of his body wanted him to lick her up like ice cream, he certainly didn't have time for Doug Gardiner's daughter now.

Damn, that name always managed to make him want to punch something. Jaw tightening, he took a deep breath and followed Jess through the door.

She'd stopped in the office to the right of the door, glancing over her shoulder at him before nodding and walking farther into the office.

Looking at the sign on the open door, he realized this was the office he'd been looking for.

"Will! It's great to have you here. Come on in." The former player behind the desk stood and held out his hand. "I'm Greg Bell, VP of hockey ops. Welcome to Reading."

Will took Greg's hand and shook. "Thanks. I'm happy to be here."

"Well, we can certainly use a guy with your skill. We've got a great team, but they're young and they need a leader. We're hoping you're the man to step into that role."

Will had heard all of this from the coach when he'd talked to him last week so it wasn't a surprise. So he nodded and smiled.

"I'll do my best. Just glad to be playing."

"I know you weren't getting a lot of ice time before but that shouldn't be a problem here."

"I'm looking forward to it."

"Good, good. I'm sure you're tired from your trip so why don't we head downstairs and you can meet Coach Scott then get to your apartment and rest up for tomorrow."

As he followed the GM through the empty arena, Will took a

cursory look around, but if you'd played in one arena, the others were pretty much the same.

And he'd played in hundreds since starting hockey when he was five and traveling for the game since he was ten. He'd grown up in Saskatchewan, where hockey was a religion, not a sport. And his parents had been more than eager to help him achieve his goals.

That'd been when he'd been young, bigger, and better than every kid in his small town and on the path for stardom.

And when that fame didn't pan out...

Shoving those old, damaging thoughts out of his head, he tuned back into the GM's talk about the team and the area and how great the fans were. He'd heard this spiel before from the previous GM, who'd wanted to sign him a few years ago. That deal hadn't worked out, and not much had changed apparently.

The Redtails had been around for more than four decades, had a long streak of winning years and Calder Cup trophies, and were coming off a Calder Cup win last year. They still had more than half the team intact from last year, but a few call-ups had hurt their roster.

Yes, Will was happy to be here. But secretly, he was surprised as shit that he'd gotten the call. At thirty-three, he was almost a decade older than most of the Redtails players. So yeah, it made sense that Coach Scott would want someone with a few years under his belt to help anchor his young guys.

But Will had been starting to wonder if he'd be stuck in a downward spiral until he finally decided to retire. He was sure he'd been on his way down to the ECHL when he'd gotten the call from Coach Scott. It'd been unexpected and exactly what he'd needed.

"Will, good to see you. Welcome to Reading. Hope you had a good trip from Minnesota."

Smiling, Will reached for the hand of the man he'd only met a few times but had heard great things about. Coach Scott was a league legend. A former player with a couple NHL seasons as an assistant coach under his belt. No Stanley Cups, but he'd been a member of the Redtails' Calder Cup-winning team in the mid-90s and had been the coach here for more than ten years. Rumor had it he was in line for the Colonials head job when Angstadt retired. And that Cary Lenville was in line for Scott's job.

Which was another reason Will had been surprised to get the call.

"Good to be here. Thank you for the opportunity. I'm really looking forward to playing."

While it was something he'd say to any new coach, Will had to admit that the words meant more this time.

"That's good to hear because we're going to be expecting a lot of you."

Waving Will into a seat on the other side of his desk, Scott nodded to Bell, who excused himself and shut the door behind him.

"You probably haven't heard because we haven't made an announcement yet but Coach Novak is leaving for another position and we're pulling Lenville up to take his place."

His face must have shown his surprise because Scott nodded.

"I understand you and Cary have some history."

Well, shit. Will made sure he didn't look away and he didn't falter. "We do. But that won't be a problem."

"Glad to hear it. I'm sure you'll find some time to talk privately but let me just tell you, he agreed that you were the guy we needed after your name was floated."

Now that was interesting. "Do you mind if I ask who that was?"

Coach's smile spread. "You can thank our promotions manager. She put your name out at a staff meeting. She's Doug Gardiner's daughter and sometimes I think she knows the game almost as well as I do. She's done great things for our marketing department but there are times I think she missed her calling. She'd make a damn good scout."

Well, hell. How about that?

"I actually, uh, ran into her upstairs. She seems...nice."

Coach nodded. "She is. And smart. She won't be around long. Some NHL club'll snap her up soon enough. Be a huge loss for the

Redtails. Anyway, you're bunking with Justin, right? Have you two met before?"

"Yes, but only briefly."

Coach's grin appeared again. "He's a character. Great guy and a damn good player. Needs some polish, and I'm hoping you can help with that. I'm putting you and Justin together on the second line. He's got skill but he's not big and we need a big guy in front of the net."

Being put on the second line was another shock. He knew the top defensive line of Marchenko and Mozik was white-hot at the moment but he'd been expecting third line because of his recent record. Which consisted of not a lot of ice time. And yeah, that had sucked. And made him doubt himself, which made him not play as well as he could.

The rest wasn't anything he hadn't heard before. He was a big guy and he knew how to use his body. But with the changes in the game in recent years, his style of play was falling out of favor.

Nodding, he waited for the rest of the speech. There was always more.

Coach lost his grin and his expression turned serious. "We're looking for a leader on the ice, Will. That means controlling penalty minutes. You've had a problem with that in the past."

Will held the coach's gaze steadily. "I have but it's something I've been actively working on."

"I know, which is why you're here. You and I have a lot more in common than you probably know, Will. Play hard but play smart. That's what I need from you."

Then Coach stood and held out his hand and Will rose to shake. "You'll get it. I appreciate the opportunity."

"And we're glad to have you. Welcome to the Redtails."

———

"HONEY, I'M HOME."

With a sigh, Jess dropped her bags on the chair by the front door then kicked off her shoes into the pile under the chair.

Saturday morning, like she did every week, she'd take that pile and put them back in her closet and start the process over again Monday morning.

A meow from the kitchen made her smile and change direction for the back of her town house.

"There you are. Sorry I'm late. I know it's past your feeding time but if you want Mommy to continue to buy you food, then I'm going to be late occasionally."

As she entered the kitchen, Jess saw Honey, her huge, battle-scarred former stray orange tabby, sitting on the counter. Where he was most definitely not allowed to sit.

Picking him up, she rubbed his head and snuggled her nose into his fur for as long as he let her. Then he leaped from her arms back onto the counter and stared at her.

Smiling at his regal stare, not at all ruined by his battered left ear and scarred nose, she dished his food and had just set the bowl on the floor when she heard her phone ring.

Her smiled widened when she saw the name on the screen.

"Hey, Dad. How's it going?"

"Hi, sweetheart. It's going. Got a game tonight in Nashville. Cold as hell here. Thought Nashville was supposed to be warm. Next week, Vancouver. I'll need to wear three layers and I won't even step outside the whole time. Hell, I'm going to request the Florida loop next time and screw Bill and his arthritis."

Laughing, she started putting together her own dinner.

"So, I heard the Redtails signed MacDonald. You have anything to do with that?"

Suppressing a sigh, she rolled her eyes instead. "I guess you already know the answer to that."

"Yeah, I guess I do. And you know I think you're wrong. If he doesn't work out, you can kiss any plans you have to be a scout good-bye."

"You know that's not gonna happen, Dad." Now she did sigh. "And it's not what I want. I love my job. You know that."

"I know you're good at it. But, sweetheart, we both know where your true passion lies."

Well, shit. This was an old battle that she would never win. Mainly because there was no way any team would hire her to scout. She hadn't played the game and she wasn't the right sex.

And while her dad, of all people, believed she could be the one to break that wall, Jess knew it'd never happen. So she didn't allow herself to even think about the possibility.

"So, Dad. Find any good new prospects?"

With a barely concealed sigh, her dad allowed her to change the subject.

And maybe she let herself silently consider a dream she'd never achieve.

TWO

Will knocked on the door to his new apartment. Yeah, he had a key but he didn't know his new roommate well, so...

From the other side of the door, he heard a couple of thumps that grew increasingly louder until the door finally flew open.

The guy standing on the other side had a towel around his waist and not much else. And he was dripping wet, shoulder-length brown hair streaming water down a broad chest covered with one spectacular black-and-blue bruise.

"Damn, thought you were the cable guy. Hey, I'm Justin." He stuck out his wet hand. "You're Will."

"That's me."

"Come on in." Justin stepped back, slid on the wood floor, probably because of the trail of water, and righted himself just before falling. "Sorry, thought I'd be out of the shower before you got here but I got tied up at the gym."

"No problem."

Will walked through the open door, lugging two huge duffel bags full of his belongings, shaking his head when Justin turned and headed toward the back of the apartment, grabbing for his towel as it started to slip off his hips.

"Your room's back here on the left," Justin yelled as he closed the bathroom door behind him. "Riley was kind of a neat freak so you should be good."

As opposed to Justin, apparently. The common areas of the apartment didn't look too bad but when Will glanced into the room across from his, he shook his head.

Holy hell. Justin's closet must have exploded. Only explanation for the piles of clothes on every available surface.

With a shrug, he walked into his room. Place was spotless. Guess Justin wasn't wrong about Riley being a neat freak.

Tossing his duffels on the floor, he sighed and fell on his back onto the queen bed. Home sweet home for the next however long.

Hopefully, he'd be here until the end of the season at least. Be nice if he lasted more than a season. He was getting too old to be moving all the hell over the country.

"Hey, a couple of the guys are getting together tonight for dinner at Jake and Lad's place," Justin yelled from the bathroom. "We're hoping you'll show."

And there went his plans to spend the night doing absolutely nothing except sleeping.

But he recalled what Coach had said about him being a leader, and he knew he couldn't say no. No better time than the present to get started on that.

Which is how he found himself surrounded by seven twenty-somethings, laughing his ass off with a beer in his hand a couple of hours later.

"So I told him, 'You need to check cooler. I think your dick is there.' He was so drunk, he looked. I shit you not."

Jake Mozik put his hand over his heart, his expression a study in absolute sincerity. But there was a gleam in his eyes that made Will laugh even harder. The guy was seriously yanking his best buddy's chain to the amusement of the other guys in the room.

Jake's linemate and butt of the joke, Lad Marchenko, just sat there, shaking his head, waiting for the laughter to die down so he could defend himself.

The two defensemen were tighter than knotted skate strings and played like psychic twins on the ice. Off ice, they acted like bickering teenagers forced to share a bedroom.

Will had gotten the rundown on the players from Justin on the way over. Jake, cocky but hilarious. Lad, Jake's straight man with a dry, intelligent wit. Derek Flaherty, Boston Irishman and resident smart-ass. Ian Clark, youngest guy on the team with the most skill, voted most likely to be a virgin. Robbie Lindback, amazing puck handler with very few social skills and a stutter that made him almost silent, unless he was on the ice.

Dirk Bennett, stable and laid-back, and Tony Dellafranco, the excitable Italian, were both a little older than the other guys, but still eight years younger than Will. The age difference didn't matter, though, because the language of hockey was universal among players, no matter where they were from. The guys had made Will feel at home, first by welcoming him and second by proceeding to rag the shit out of him. Mostly about his age, which didn't bother him because he could give as good as he got. His ex-girlfriend would've turned up her nose and told him it was because he was the mental age of these kids.

Which was part of the reason she was the ex. There'd been other problems, like the fact that she was a cheating bitch who'd traded up for a career NHL player who'd been snowed under by her stunning beauty. By the time she'd left, Will had been damn glad to be rid of her toxicity.

And he actually pitied the guy who'd ended up with her because Will knew, sure as shit, she'd cheat on him, too.

While most of these guys were too young to be married, he wasn't surprised when the conversation turned to women. Or rather, the lack of sex among all of them.

Apparently, since none of them had been getting laid, superstition had set in. And hockey players were insanely superstitious. Everybody knew you didn't mess with a streak. If you weren't getting laid and your team was winning, well, then, you did without until you started to lose.

"The only one of us who gets any is Franco, the bastard." Jake motioned toward Tony with his water bottle. "He has regular girlfriend and gets laid before every game. The rest of us only love ourselves."

As the rest of the guys cracked up around him and threw chips at Jake, Will shook his head and grinned. He'd already figured out that Jake deliberately butchered the English language for dramatic effect. But he couldn't deny the guy was funny as hell.

But since Jake had brought up the subject...

"So I ran into Jess Gardiner today in the hall—"

A chorus of groans went up around the table.

"Dude, don't even." Justin shook his head. "You're totally not gonna score there. Not ever. She's really nice but you are *so* not gonna get anywhere with Miss Jess."

Will frowned. "*Miss* Jess?"

Derek huffed out a sarcastic laugh, dark red hair falling over into his eyes as he shook his head.

"Man, she's hockey royalty. You know that, right? The legendary Doug Gardiner's daughter. Seems nice but she *never* gives players a second look off the ice. Probably thinks she's too good for us."

"She does not appear stuck up." Lad leaned back into his chair as they all crowded around a table made for four. "But no one has cracked her case yet."

"Or figured out how to get in her pants— Ow!" Derek rubbed the back of his head where Tony had smacked him. "What the hell, dude?"

"I'm not your dude and no wonder you can't get a girl to go out on a second date with you. Your fuckin' mouth is a disgrace. Grow the fuck up."

"I've heard some of the other guys say she scouts for Coach."

Everyone turned to Robbie like he'd returned from the dead.

"Holy crap." Dirk huffed out a laugh. "Don't use up all your words for the month at one shot. There's still another three weeks."

Robbie rolled his eyes and shot Dirk the finger, though Robbie's cheeks turned bright red.

"No, no, he is absolutely right." Jake smacked Robbie on the back, hard enough to make the guy pitch forward. "I hear same thing. She has good eye, they say. Knows more about hockey than most men in front office. I think she is very hot but lesser men could be threatened. I would not be threatened."

"And you, my friend, have tried and failed." Lad raised his beer at Jake.

"She mistakenly believes I am too young for her." Jake shrugged. "Not a bad problem."

"So how old is she?" Will asked.

"Probably too young for you, old man."

Justin's wide grin made Will laugh along with the table, but he had to wonder if Justin wasn't right.

———

JESS HAD her head bent over her desk, her entire attention focused on the sketch she was working on Wednesday morning.

The team had a game tonight and she should be running down her checklist but she'd started this sketch and couldn't seem to stop.

So when she heard a man say, "Apparently, I have you to thank for my job," she gave a short, sharp scream and embarrassed the hell out of herself.

Her head shot up to find six-plus-feet of amused player standing in her doorway.

And when she caught sight of Will's grin, she wanted to take the pencil in her hand and poke him with it. Nowhere that'd injure him, of course. The team needed him.

"Oh my god, are you seriously going to sneak up on me every time? I'm going to get you a little bell to wear around your neck."

The damn man's smile grew even wider and she had to admit it was a pretty nice smile. Totally transformed his face. She'd watched enough film to know Will's game face was intense. When he was on the ice, he was all business.

She'd expected him to be as serious and intense off the ice as well so she was taken off guard by his easy smiles.

And, if she was honest with herself, she had to admit the damn man was sweetly adorable when he smiled. Maybe someday she'd tell him that.

Today was not that day.

"Blue's my favorite color."

She shook her head, trying to figure out what the hell his favorite color had to do with anything.

"And why do I need to know that?"

"In case you want to buy me that bell. I don't want to make you mad at me every time you see me. And it goes with my eyes."

Of course, that made her look even more closely at his eyes. Damn him, he had beautiful eyes.

Which meant absolutely nothing.

"Can I do something for you, Mr. MacDonald?"

Leaning a shoulder against the doorframe, he looked so at ease, she couldn't imagine that this was a guy who had a reputation for being an enforcer.

Yeah, he was big but he wasn't huge. He wouldn't be out of place in a goalie uniform these days. Years ago, when her dad had first started scouting, goalies didn't need to be the massive walls they were today. But back when she'd first started going to games with her dad, every team had a guy they called an enforcer. The guy you put on the ice when you needed to retaliate for a bad hit or you needed to rile up your team.

Will had been that guy for several teams, but in the past few years, the game had changed, at least at the NHL level, which had trickled down to the AHL. The fighters had gone by the wayside for the most part and the skill guys, the ones whose highlights you saw on SportsCenter, were more in demand than ever.

But you still needed guys like Will, the guys who the team knew they could rely on to stand up for guys like Robbie and Ian, who skated like the hot shots they were but didn't know how to land a punch to save their soul.

"Just wanted to say thanks."

She frowned, confused. "For what?"

"For recommending me to Coach Scott."

She blinked. *Oh shit.* "I'm not sure I know what you mean."

He watched her so intently, she had a few seconds to wonder if Coach had actually told Will she'd recommended him.

"Yeah, I'm pretty sure you do know what I mean. What I find interesting is that you don't want anyone to know."

Shaking her head, she raised her eyebrows and tried to look...well, innocent. "Still not sure what you're talking about but I've got to get this sketch finished—"

"So you do it but no one's supposed to know about it." Walking into the room, Will shut the door behind him and draped himself into the chair across from her desk. "Damn, that must suck."

Refusing to give him the upper hand, she sighed and made a production out of dropping her pencil and leaning back in her chair. Apparently, he wasn't going to be a good boy and leave.

And she had to admit, the view wasn't bad. Like most players, he came to the arena for practice dressed in sweats and a t-shirt. But even in shapeless nylon and worn cotton, there was something about him that made her want to put her hands on his chest and pet him like a cat.

A little ping of regret hit her low in her gut because that just was *not* going to happen. Because no, he wasn't wrong. It did kind of suck. But she wasn't going to tell him that.

"Is there something I can help you with, Mr. MacDonald? Otherwise—"

"Well, first off, you can call me Will. We're both adults. And I'm not *that* much older than you."

The slight emphasis in his sentence made her look a little more closely at him. Was he actually asking how old she was?

Does he think I'm too young?

Shit, not what she should be thinking about.

"Okay, Will. Is that all?"

"Actually, no, it's not. Come out with me after the game tomorrow."

Her mouth dropped open before she could stop it. Stunned, her brain spun for several seconds before she blinked and got it to stop.

"I... That's not a good idea."

His head cocked to the side. "Why?"

"Because I don't date players."

"Why not?"

Her eyebrows rose. "Seriously? How old are you?"

"Thirty-three. But you know that already." He pointed his chin at her. "How old are you?"

Her eyes widened even more. "Don't you know you're not supposed to ask a woman her age?"

Now he shrugged, looking completely unconcerned. "Why? You know pretty much everything about me, apparently, except which side I adjust to. Or maybe you know that, too."

Her lips parted but she couldn't think of a damn thing to say. And now she was thinking about things she shouldn't be thinking about.

She had to struggle to keep her gaze from dipping to his crotch but she managed. Barely. Which was probably exactly what he wanted.

Will wasn't known for instigating most fights, but the damn man was a menace just the same.

She was tempted to take the high road and tell him his crude mouth wasn't appreciated. But that would be pretty hypocritical considering she'd grown up around hockey players and only just managed to keep her own dirty mouth in check when she was in public.

So, she was going to have to be straightforward.

"Look, Mr. MacDonald. You're a good player. You're going to make a great addition to the team. I wish you luck. But I'm not going to go out with you. I don't date players."

He didn't look surprised, and he didn't get out of his chair and leave like she'd hoped he would. "Who do you date?"

No one.

She stopped her grimace mid-formation. "None of your damn business."

His lips quirked into a grin that made her thighs clench and her girly parts get hot.

Oh no. No, no, no. That wasn't happening. She'd given up lusting after hockey players a long, long time ago. Either they broke your damn heart when they left you behind or you found out they were engaged to their high school sweetheart back home but they had an "arrangement" and no, screwing around was not cheating.

Okay, maybe she had a few issues but that just meant she was absolutely right not to say yes.

Even though you want to.

No, she didn't. She really didn't.

Liar.

As if he could read her mind, Will's smile got even wider. "So there's no one steaming up your sheets right now?"

Damn him. Why the hell was she now imagining him naked on her bed?

Fuck.

With an effort, she smiled, making sure he knew it was fake. "I am not going to dignify your question with an answer. I think you'd probably better leave because if you don't, Coach is going to wonder why you're limping."

"And I think he'd laugh his ass off when he found out I pissed you off so bad, you kicked me in the balls."

A laugh bubbled up along with the knowledge that this man had no filter and absolutely no idea how to take no for an answer.

"Mr. MacDo—"

"Will." He shrugged like he didn't have a care in the world. "Call me Will and I'll leave."

She opened her mouth to call him a few other choice words, but out of the corner of her eye, she saw the organization's event manager walk into the main office. Judi hadn't noticed that Jess had someone in her office, but that wouldn't last long. Judi prided herself on knowing exactly what everyone in the entire organization was up to. It wouldn't take long for her to put one and one together and make a complete mess of Jess's life.

Women didn't get far in the business side of this sport if they slept with the players. It wasn't professional, especially if you wanted to climb the ladder and work for an NHL team.

She didn't want a reputation like that. And she didn't want to sleep with this damn man.

Liar, liar, pants on fire.

Okay, now who's acting like the twelve-year-old?

Smiling a smile that held a very sharp edge, she leaned back into her chair.

It might take Will a few times to get the hint because apparently he was dense, but he would understand eventually.

"Mr. MacDonald. I have work to do. And if you don't leave, you're going to be late for practice. And I'm pretty sure you don't want to be late for your first day of practice with your new team."

His slow smile made certain parts of her flutter. And she didn't mean her heart.

"Okay, Miss Jess. I can take a hint."

Relief made her suck in a breath. It had absolutely nothing to do with that smile. Nothing at all.

But she couldn't help but watch his every move as he stood and turned toward the door. And if her gaze happened to land on that perfect ass... Well, no one would know.

"But just to be clear." He stopped in the door, turned to look over his shoulder and grinned at her a little more. "I'll be back to ask again."

And now her heart did give a traitorous little thump. "The answer will be the same."

"Well, I'm nothing if not persistent." He knocked on the doorjamb. "Talk to you later, Miss Jess."

Only when she sucked in air did she realize she'd been holding her breath.

———

"HEY, WILL. HOW'S IT GOING?"

Will hadn't exactly been dreading this meeting but he had to admit he hadn't been looking forward to it.

Rising from the bench, he held his hand out to Cary Lenville. "Going well. Glad to be here."

"And we're glad to have you here."

Will was aware that everyone else in the room was paying attention while trying not to make it obvious. The rest of the team were in various stages of dress for practice. Cary was ready to go, of course. The guy always had been an overachiever.

"Lori's looking forward to seeing you again. We're hosting the team dinner next week so you'll get to see her there if you don't catch her at the games this weekend."

Surprised Cary had mentioned Lori, considering their history, he nodded. "It'll be nice to see her again."

Cary's expression didn't change a bit when he nodded. "See you on the ice."

Then he walked off and Will went back to getting dressed.

Well, that had gone better than he'd expected. Honestly, he hadn't known what to expect but he should've realized Cary would never do anything in front of his team. Because the guy really wasn't a dick. They just didn't see eye to eye on almost everything.

"So, you and Cary. There's history there, right?"

Will glanced over at Tony, watching him with steady dark eyes. He'd kept his voice low so only Will could hear him.

Pulling his sweater over his head, he shook his hair out of his eyes. "We played together in California for part of a season. We weren't the best of friends but that was a long time ago. I've grown up since then."

Tony grinned. "Yeah, right. So, hey. I saw you coming down the stairs earlier. Did you need to make a stop in the front office before practice for something?"

Will grabbed his helmet, shoved his hair out of his face, and jammed the helmet on his head. "I don't know what you're talking about."

"Uh-huh." Tony's smirk made Will want to pop him in the nose. "I'm rooting for you, buddy, but you're not gonna get anywhere with her."

Fucking hockey players. Worse gossips than old ladies.

Will ignored Tony's smartass comment and headed out to the ice. Though the thought that maybe Tony was right niggled at the back of his brain all through practice.

First day with a new team was always a learning experience but this wasn't his first rodeo. Hell, it wasn't even his tenth. Probably more like eighteenth, if he had to guess. But who was counting. He was still getting calls to play and he still got excited to answer those calls.

He'd play until the thrill was gone or the calls didn't come.

Today, he had a little more speed in his stride and maybe a little more enthusiasm. A lot of the guys here were young and he didn't just mean under twenty-five. Nearly a third of the team was twenty-two or younger. Skill players who'd been playing for a decade and more but were still learning to handle the professional side of the game.

He and Cary, at thirty-six, were the oldest players and Will watched how the younger forwards took their cues from Cary.

When the team broke into offensive and defensive squads about a half hour into practice, Will took a look at his fellow defensemen.

Justin was twenty-four, and though he looked like a huge puppy learning to walk off the ice, the guy flew on skates, like he'd been born with them strapped to his feet.

Derek looked to be a good all-around guy, the class clown who'd never met a swear word he couldn't use in even the most innocent sentence, but determined and focused on ice.

Jake and Lad were all business, more in sync than even the Fransechetti twins, who at nineteen were the team's second-youngest players. Luckily, the identical twins grew their hair different lengths or Will would've never been able to tell them apart.

The only defenseman he hadn't met yet was Joey Constantino, on the IR for concussion and not allowed to skate. With Joey out, they were down a defenseman but apparently Coach would be calling one up from the ECHL affiliate later today.

Practice was practically over when he caught sight of the figure in the arena entrance near the handicapped section.

Jess stood far enough back that he wasn't sure at first it was her. But as he took a few more laps around the ice, he realized he was right. And she was watching him.

Yeah, she was standing there talking to someone, but every now and then her head would move and he could tell she was looking toward the ice.

How long had she been standing there? He'd been rightfully focused on practice and hadn't noticed when she'd shown up, but now he was curious as hell.

Which didn't mean a damn thing because they had a game tonight and he needed to head back to the apartment and eat lunch before he took a nap and headed back to the arena for the team dinner.

"So you, my friend, are probably wondering why I am waiting here for you, yes?"

Jake stood just outside the boards, leaning on his stick wearing a shit-eating grin, no one else around.

Suppressing a grin, Will ignored him, heading for the locker room.

Jake easily caught up and matched his stride. "Well, I will tell you. You will need my help with this one."

"Don't know what you're talking about, Jake."

"Yes, you do." Jake tapped him on the arm with the butt end of his stick for emphasis. "I can be an asset in this. I know much about women."

Will had to laugh, stopping just outside the door. "And what is it you think you can help me with?"

"She is always here on game nights."

Will looked over his shoulder at Jake. "Most of the front office staff is. Not exactly earth-shattering news."

"What you probably do not know is, after the game, she always goes back to her office for ten or fifteen minutes."

His gaze narrowed. "And you know this how?"

"Because I am an observant guy. And because one night I had to drop off something in the office and saw her there."

"What's she doing?"

Jake shrugged. "I do not know. Writing report or something. What does it matter? You can have a few minutes alone with her. Ask her out for a drink. Maybe she will like you better after a few beers."

The glint in Jake's pale blue eyes made Will want to smack the guy. But he had given him a decent tip so he'd give the guy a pass. This time.

"Thanks for the tip."

Jake gave a little bow. "Is no problem. I have a feeling you will have more luck than I did. Bastard."

THREE

"Hey, Jess, how are you?"

"Oh, hey, Lori. Sorry, didn't see you. Busy as always."

Cary's wife laughed and squeezed her arm. "You work way harder than you should. We need to do a girls' night out. The guys are on the road this coming week; we should plan to meet one night."

"That sounds awesome." Jess nodded earnestly. "Absolutely. But right now, I've got to run. I've got a group of fifty senior citizens complete with walkers, canes, and enough alcohol to sedate an entire team in two suites and their food is delayed. I'm having visions of rowdy little old ladies tossing their bras at the ice."

Lori's laughter rang out again and Jess smiled, even though her stress level was high enough to make her heart race.

She had several large groups tonight, including the seniors, who were funny as hell and probably going to run out of alcohol before the end of the second period. She hadn't expected them to drink more than the suite full of businessmen on the other side of the arena.

She also had two children's birthday parties, each with almost twenty people, and a school group of nearly a hundred kids and adults.

"You definitely have your hands full tonight," Lori waved as she started to move away, "so I won't hold you up any longer. But I *am* going to hold you to our date."

"I'll text, I promise. Gotta go!"

Hustling away, she got to the senior center's box just as the team was taking the ice for the start of the game.

It was just another game, one of seventy-six times the team would skate out onto the ice this season. No big deal.

She'd seen this scene happen more times than she could count.

Still, she stopped to watch. And to tell herself she wasn't watching for one infuriating player.

And now you're lying to yourself.

She didn't even need to see his number to realize she'd already spotted him.

Will was a big guy, one of the biggest on the team. It made him easier to pick out, but she realized she would've known him if he'd been in a crowd of guys with the exact same build. It was the way he skated, so deliberately.

Damn. *Damn, damn, damn.* This was not good.

She refused to fall for a hockey player. No way in hell.

Tearing her gaze away from the ice, she put on her game face and waded into the fray.

Tonight was going to be one of those nights when her face would hurt from smiling. And that wasn't a bad thing.

The seniors in this party were freaking hilarious. Smiling, funny, happy to be out and about.

"Wow, what I wouldn't give to work around those men all day." A tiny white-haired woman smiled at Jess as she headed for the exit on her way to the next suite. "Men didn't look like that when I was your age. Lucky girl to work around that eye candy all day."

"They are definitely nice to look at," Jess agreed. "But you don't want to be anywhere near the locker room after practice. You'd change your mind about getting up close and personal."

"My sense of smell doesn't work as well it did fifty years ago, babe." Another woman who had to be at least ninety stepped up beside the other. "So that definitely wouldn't be a problem. I'm sure I could show those boys a few new tricks. The young don't have a monopoly on sex."

"These young people forget where they came from sometimes, Edie."

"Sex certainly isn't everything in life, but damn, I do like a good tumble every now and then. Thank god for little blue pills."

Swallowing her own burst of laughter, Jess headed to the next suite to check on that group of seniors.

"I don't have a clue what you're talking about, John. There's three quarters in hockey, not four."

"How can there be only three quarters? And when's halftime?"

On her next stop, the businessmen weren't even paying attention to the game, all of them wrapped in private discussions, a few of them stopping to smile at her as she walked through to check with the organizer to see if they needed anything.

One guy deliberately caught her eye and smiled. Nice-looking. Maybe thirty, short brown hair, nice blue eyes, sincere smile. She smiled in return as she made her way out the door.

She'd be back later. Maybe she'd say hi.

He's not your type. Way too clean-cut.

Ignoring that little voice in her head, she made her rounds to the rest of the groups then stopped to talk to the catering manager to see if there were any problems. Then, since everything was running smoothly at the moment and there were ten minutes before the end of the period, she made her way back up to the private box where the injured and scratched players sat. Tonight, three guys sat hunched over the wall, completely focused on the game.

They barely noticed as she took a seat at the other end of the row to watch a few minutes of the game. They all knew her, were used to seeing her around, so they never really took notice of what she was doing.

The Syracuse team had several young players she'd been watching this season, and since Syracuse was in the same division as the Redtails, she'd already seen them a couple of times.

But there was one guy who stood out even more than the kids.

At twenty-eight, T.J. Delauria hadn't yet had his shot at the NHL and that baffled the hell out of her. Everything she'd heard about him had been positive. Steady right winger with good plus-minus numbers. Fast skater, not flashy, but something had changed with his game this year. Something good. Kind of like he'd hit another gear. He'd played overseas last season and since his return, he'd been even more focused.

She'd talked to her dad about him and he'd told her to keep her eye on the guy.

And she was. He'd already scored a goal off a juicy rebound that would make the Redtails goalie, Shane, obsess for hours after the game. And he'd had another couple of good chances.

But even as she tried to keep her focus on Delauria, her gaze kept wandering to a certain Redtails sweater with a fourteen on the back.

Will didn't have any points yet but it wasn't for lack of trying. In fact, he and Justin played like they'd been on the same line for months instead of days.

He was a skilled skater, though not as fast as some, and moved the puck well. He cleared the crease and blocked shots but he wasn't afraid to shoot and when he did, most were on net.

In the past couple of years, he'd become much more of an offensive defenseman, something a lot of people overlooked when they talked about him. They mentioned how he took stupid penalties and was fast to drop his gloves. But that shift in his playing was exactly why he'd caught her eye.

It was almost like he'd changed his mind-set, something that was really hard to do, especially for guys who'd had a certain style of play ingrained in them since they were ten.

For the next few minutes, she allowed herself to simply watch the game, something she didn't get to do much. Usually she was working, whether she was taking care of her groups or doing her other, off-the-books work. Which couldn't really be counted as work. It was a hobby.

Hobby.

She huffed so loudly one of the players turned to look at her. Luckily, something happened on the ice and his attention shifted back. She didn't want to deal with questions right now. She had too many of her own.

Like, what the hell was it about a certain defenseman who made her want to throw out years of caution to find out what it'd be like to be bad? Just for one night.

It had been so damn long since she'd gone on a date and liked a guy enough to bring him home for sex. During the season, she sometimes worked twelve and thirteen hours a day so that didn't leave a lot of time for dating anyway. But even during the summer, when she had a little extra time, she'd maybe hooked up twice.

Had it really been that long since she'd gotten laid?

Maybe she didn't want to think about that too closely. Besides, it wasn't like she didn't have toys so she wasn't a frustrated, needy bitch.

And maybe you need to find someone more suitable to scratch this itch before you do something you'll regret.

Like let Will seduce her.

Not gonna happen, girl.

Didn't mean she could stop thinking about it, though.

FRUSTRATION ATE AT WILL. The game wasn't going their way and that fucking little Syracuse dipshit prick Mason had been in his face all night, gunning for a fight.

Mason was young, probably all of twenty-three, and looking to get a notch on his belt with the name MacDonald beside it.

And if the kid wasn't careful, he was going to get exactly what he wanted. And maybe sooner rather than later.

The Redtails needed a kick in the ass. They were down two to nothing near the end of the second and they needed to make something happen.

The buzzer sounded for the last in-arena timeout and the players skated to the bench, frustration on all five faces, as well as every face on the bench.

As the coach laid out the strategy for the next play, he made specific eye contact with Will.

"I want to see movement out there," Coach Scott said. "I want to see spark. Shoot the puck. Nothing bad comes from shooting the puck. Too many passes, too many turnovers."

When the ref blew his whistle, Will and Coach shared another quick glance, and when his shift came, he jumped the boards and charged the puck in their defensive end.

Mason was at his back seconds later, battling him for the puck. Will had gotten it tied up in his skates in the corner and Mason was digging. And shoving the butt end of his stick in Will's ribs whenever he could. Will heard the roar of the crowd, heard his teammates yelling.

Then Mason got in one more hard jab and the crowd started to bang on the glass as Will caught sight of Mason's smirk.

So Will kicked the puck to his nearest teammate and shoved Mason away with a little more force than before. Mason retaliated with an elbow in his side before skating toward the puck and hitting Will's teammate Robbie into the boards with a cheap shot.

As Robbie went down on one knee, Will shoved Mason away.

"Come on, old man." Mason skated backward as the ref blew his whistle to stop play when Shane covered the puck at the net. "Let's go. Or are you afraid of breaking a hip at your advanced age?"

Will had heard that and much worse for the past three years. It had no effect on him, didn't piss him off, but this wasn't about being pissed off.

His team watched intently as Mason circled behind him.

"Come back in a few years when you can grow a beard, kid." Then he deliberately turned his back on him and laughed, shaking his head.

Justin's eyes widened and that was the only warning he needed. He was ready when Mason cross-checked him from behind. He pitched forward, mainly for show, then spun around, landing his fist squarely on Mason's jaw.

Mason's head snapped back and his feet shifted. For a second, Will thought the guy was gonna go down, which wouldn't have been a bad thing. But Mason recovered quickly and got in a few quick jabs. Pain sizzled as Mason connected with his right cheekbone then got in a few body shots. But while the younger guy had strength, he let his anger get away from him.

Will wasn't pissed. He'd done this dance enough to have calculated out every move ahead of time.

So he was able to let the guy get in a few good blows before Will hit him with a bone-rattling body shot then took him to the ice.

He didn't want to hurt the guy. He never fought with that end in mind. And he'd gotten even more aware of the consequences as he'd gotten older.

Getting Mason's head under his arm, he kept him locked down as the linesmen came in to separate them.

And when they both got back to their feet, he nodded at Mason as they made their way back to the bench. They were both getting five-minute penalties for fighting so they were being sent back to the locker room because there was less than four minutes on the clock.

As he passed through the bench, he got a nod and a pat on the back from Coach Scott.

Maybe now they'd score some goddamn goals.

———

THE CROWD ERUPTED with a roar and, since the horn hadn't sounded, Jess knew something other than a goal was going on.

Looking out over the arena from the suite level, she wasn't surprised to find Will squared off with Syracuse's enforcer, Mason.

It should've been a fair fight. Looking at them, you'd think they were evenly matched. Both about the same size and height. But she knew better.

Will would kick the guy's ass.

Wincing as Mason landed the first punch, she bit her tongue against the urge to yell along with the crowd. The sound rose to ear-splitting levels as Will shook off the hit. And then he smiled and the crowd went crazy.

Cocking back his arm, Will threw one solid hit to Mason's jaw and the guy went to the ice. Where he stayed.

Another player would've gloated or taunted. Will simply skated to the bench and headed back to the locker room as there was less than five minute to play in the period.

A minute later, the Redtails got a power-play goal because Mason also got a minor penalty for instigation.

She had been *so* right. The Redtails needed Will. He was the right fit at the right time.

If she was keeping track—

Okay, not if. She *was* keeping track, damn it. She was keeping track of every time she'd been right about a guy and the team who needed him.

As she stood in the hallway outside the suites on the arena's second level, she allowed herself to gloat.

Her dad was going to have to pay up on their bet. First, because he hadn't thought Coach Scott would go for Will. And second, because he'd been convinced Will couldn't add anything to a team as stacked with talent as the Redtails.

Her dad was one hell of a scout but sometimes he forgot that on paper, things were a lot different than on the ice. Of course, she could count on one finger how many times she'd had a coach take her direct advice. Unlike her dad, who got paid for it. Something she never would.

"Well, damn, I'd hate to be the man who put that look on your face. Everything okay?"

Jess's head shot up and her gaze locked with the businessman she'd noticed earlier. She smiled automatically, her default setting at work.

"Of course. Can I help you, Mr. ..."

"Mike. Mike Northwick." He held out his hand as he came forward and she took it out of habit.

"Jess Gardiner. Nice to meet you."

He held onto her hand when she would've released him and it gave her time to notice how soft his palm was.

Will's had been rough with calluses and cuts, his grip strong but not tight.

Why the hell are you comparing them?

Damn it.

"Nice to meet you, too." Finally, he released her hand. "You look a little flushed. Everything okay?"

"I'm fine. Are you having a good time tonight, Mr. Northwick?"

"Well, the home team could be putting out a little more effort but yeah, I'm enjoying myself."

She had to bite her tongue not to defend her guys, but in her line of work, the customer was always right. She just didn't have to agree with him.

And, just like that, Mike Northwick became a little less attractive.

"Can I do anything for you? Does your group need anything?"

She saw him think about his response and controlled the urge to roll her eyes. If she could read his mind, she was pretty sure he'd be thinking something dirty. And stupid.

And how is that any different than Will?

Nope. Not going there.

"I think we're good, thank you."

Keeping her smile light, she excused herself. She really did have to check in on the rest of the groups before the end of the game.

It took a while to finish her rounds and there were only a few minutes left in the game when she headed for ice level and the Zamboni gate.

The Redtails were still losing, but they'd pulled the goalie and were pressing hard in the offensive end. Her gaze unerringly found Will at the blue line, his big, solid body poised and ready to take a shot or crash the net.

His intense focus was no different than anyone else's on the ice but there was something about him that made her stare only at him.

Maybe it was the way he held so still. He didn't shuffle his feet or move his stick or twist his head. He was utterly intent on the game when the puck was in play.

Maybe you're becoming just a little obsessed.

And that really would be a problem because she couldn't even say what it was about Will that made her unable to look away.

Okay, that's total bullshit. You know exactly why.

And there wasn't a damn thing she was going to do about it.

Except stand here and stare at him for these last few minutes of the game.

When the final buzzer sounded, the Redtails had lost by one point, which sucked. This was the second game in a row they'd lost. Definitely not a streak but not something they'd want to continue either.

She was almost ready to turn and head back to her office when she saw Will stand and start to smile as he spoke to Justin, who shook his head and reluctantly grinned as well. Then Will went over to Robbie and bumped his shoulder before skating to center ice to knock helmets with Shane as he headed to the bench.

He exchanged a fist bump and a nod with Cary, standing on the ice at the gate to the bench, before he disappeared down the hall to the locker room.

Trying to ignore the butterflies in her stomach, which were definitely *not* from Will's smile, she made her way back to her office. Had the team won, she'd have heard whoops and cheers but now it was quiet.

And so was her office when she finally sat down at her desk.

She didn't bother to turn on the overhead light. She could find her way around blindfolded and the small lamp she kept on her desk provided more than enough light. Besides, if she turned on the ceiling light, someone would feel compelled to check in on her, and she really only wanted a few minutes of peace and quiet to get her thoughts written down.

Yes, she could do this at home, but she'd learned that if she waited, she lost that sense of urgency she still had here in the arena. Her dad had the luxury of being able to write his thoughts out as they happened. She didn't.

For the next fifteen minutes, she typed furiously. And when she was finished, she read back through them and smiled.

Damn, she *was* good at this. Too damn bad she'd never get a job doing what she was so damn good at.

Her smile quickly faded.

She'd told herself, when she'd finally settled on a sports marketing major at Penn State University almost ten years ago, that she'd never regret her choice. And there was nothing to regret. She'd graduated with honors and had had her choice of jobs at graduation. She'd taken the job with the Elmira ECHL team and had never looked back.

And if she occasionally longed for something she'd never have... Well, that was just human nature, right?

"No rest for the wicked, huh? Shouldn't you be gone by now?"

She sucked in a sharp breath but her brain had already identified that deep voice and her body had responded. Thankfully, the man in the doorway couldn't see how her nipples had peaked, both because of the dark and because she wore a padded bra. One of the first lessons a woman learned when she worked in an ice arena in a male-dominated sport.

"I was just getting ready to leave. I could ask you the same thing. Is there something you need, Mr. MacDonald?"

As he moved away from the door, the light from her lamp began to illuminate his body but hadn't reached his face. But she still heard the smile in his voice when he said, "I guess you could say that."

The teasing tone of his voice made her thighs clench, damn him.

"Well, then you better tell me what it is so I can get it for you. Then we can both go home. I'm sure you need to rest up after tonight's game."

He stopped right at the edge of the other side of her desk and now he was close enough for her to see that smile on his lips.

Damn, damn, damn. He had a beautiful mouth. A mouth that made her wonder how it'd feel on her skin.

Which wasn't going to happen. Like, ever.

"Are you trying to politely tell me I need to get to bed because I'm old?"

She rolled her eyes, made sure he could see it. "I'm not the one who keeps bringing up your age. Maybe you're the one with the problem."

With another soft laugh, he dropped into the chair across from her desk. She bit her lip against the urge to return his smile, but it was hard to keep a straight face. His smile taunted and made him that much more handsome. Such a different man than the one on the ice.

But she knew that intensity was still there, lurking under the surface.

He must be amazing in bed.

Totally the wrong thought to have at this minute. Luckily, it was probably too dark for him to see the flush on her cheeks.

But, of course, his eyes narrowed and she had to wonder if he knew exactly what she was thinking.

"Oh, I've got a lot of problems, but right now, I'm not so worried about my age. I've got a few other things on my mind."

Don't do it. Don't— "Like what?"

His smile widened. "Well, my face hurts like a sonuvabitch right now. Fucking Mason has one hell of a right hook." He raised his hand to rub at his jaw, and she now saw the bruise that would probably be a spectacular color tomorrow. "Guess I should be glad he didn't go after Robbie. The kid probably would've broken his hand on Mason's jaw."

Her heart gave a seriously unnecessary flutter at the fact that he'd stuck up for his teammate. When had she become such a girl about things like that?

"And how is your hand? It's not like you don't need it."

"I can take a hell of a lot more damage than some of these kids. They're fucking twigs. I'm surprised Colin doesn't break a bone every time he gets checked into the boards."

Shaking her head, she had to work to hold back a smile. "You make them sound like they're fragile. Hockey players are the least fragile athletes I've ever met."

"But our hearts get broken just like everyone else, hon."

She laughed, couldn't help herself. He looked so sincere but that twinkle in his eyes... It was killer.

"Did you want something in particular, Mr. MacDonald, or are you just here to delay my departure for some reason?"

"What would you say if I asked you out for drinks one night?"

She had to bite her tongue against the urge to say yes. The thought didn't even surprise her. "I'd say I don't date hockey players."

He didn't look surprised by her answer. "Because you work with them or because you don't like them?"

"I love the game and I like hockey players. I just don't think I should date men I work with. It can create...problems."

His gaze narrowed. "Have some experience with those problems, do you?"

"Not for many years, no. Because I don't date hockey players."

"So that's a hard-and-fast rule?"

"Pretty much so, yes."

"And I guess sex is out of the question?"

She blinked and her mouth dropped open. She wanted to laugh

because she could still see that glint in his eyes, the one that wanted to rile her up, see how far he could push her. But she could see that intensity lurking there as well, the patient predator stalking his prey. Her heart gave a little flip to realize she was the prey.

And since she now had an image of her and Will in bed, she swallowed hard and took a breath before leaning back in her chair, never breaking his gaze.

"Sex is never out of the question, but I definitely don't have sex with hockey players, especially not hockey players on my team."

Mirroring her movement, he leaned back in his chair, putting his right ankle on his left knee and resting his left hand on his ankle. The casual position made her breath catch in her throat and that made not one damn bit of sense.

He wore a suit, as all the players did on game day. His was blue, his shirt white, the first couple of buttons undone. She could just see a hint of skin in that vee and she had the insane urge to crawl onto her desk, lean forward, and lick him right there.

She wondered what he'd do if she said exactly what was on her mind. Not that she would. She loved her job and would do nothing to jeopardize it. But still...

"I guess I can understand your position." He shrugged. "Lot of these guys are kids. Too unstable, don't really know what to do with a woman. You need an older guy, one who knows what he wants."

Her lips twitched and she had to work hard to keep a straight face. She didn't want to encourage him. Couldn't encourage him because even though she might want to play with this man, she couldn't allow herself to. She had to remind herself that she wasn't charmed by the whole alpha-male thing.

"So you think I have daddy issues?"

His face screwed up in a grimace. "Jesus, I hope not. I've met your dad." For a second, she thought he might add something, but whatever he was thinking, he kept to himself. "No, hon. I mean you need a guy who knows how to make you scream his name while he's going down on you."

Oh my god.

She blinked and her lips parted but she had no idea what would come out so she quickly snapped them shut. She should be offended. Should tell him she didn't appreciate his lewd comments.

Instead, her thighs clenched again and her gut hollowed as heat exploded through her.

It took her several long seconds before she could get her brain to reset. Hopefully, he'd think she was pissed off and not turned on.

She was still trying to think of what to say when he continued.

"You sure you don't want to get that drink?"

No, she wasn't sure, damn him. Her resolution was fading fast.

His steady gaze caught and held hers until she felt like she couldn't breathe.

Swallowing hard, she deliberately looked down at her keyboard, filed her notes and shut down her computer. She'd finish at home tonight. Or tomorrow morning. Her dad would wait.

Right now, she needed to get out of her office before she did or said something she couldn't take back.

"I need to get going, Mr. MacDonald. If you have nothing else to say..."

She was proud of the way her voice held steady, even if nothing else was. Her hands had a slight tremble and her thighs quivered. And she was trying her damnedest to ignore what was going on internally.

He shrugged, as if he hadn't just made her panties wet. "I guess not. At least not now. Come on, I'll walk you to your car."

She wanted to tell him no but he'd probably get the idea that he'd had an effect on her.

He had. He just didn't need to know it.

She gave him a small smile. "Sure. Just let me get my things together."

Standing, she grabbed her coat off the hook behind her desk and swiped her tote off the floor. She'd already switched out her low heels for boots. It was January in Pennsylvania and there'd been snow on the ground for the past week.

And unlike most of the other women who worked here, she wore a skirt. She didn't go out on the ice so there was no danger of slipping and embarrassing the hell out of herself, and it presented a more professional image, something she was very careful to cultivate. She had an endgame and she did everything she could to ensure she got there.

Will stood by the door, tall and imposing, watching her with that slight grin.

She couldn't help herself. She stopped beside him, her gaze caught on the bruise already darkening on his chin. He also had a slight cut above his eye, and his forehead still bore the marks from his helmet.

She was used to seeing the guys like this, battered and bruised. Will's chin would be all sorts of different colors tomorrow and he probably had a few on his body she couldn't see.

Her free hand clenched into a fist in an attempt to keep from touching him.

She lost that battle.

His gaze locked with hers as she raised her hand and ran her index finger along his jaw, just below the bruise. The muscles in his jaw clenched but he didn't flinch away, and that glint in his eye got hotter until she thought she might have to look away.

"Does it hurt?"

He didn't answer right away. When he did, she swore his voice had dropped at least an octave. "It hurts. Just not there."

She raised her brows, trying to corral a smile. "You took a couple of hard hits to the boards tonight. I'm sure at your age, it takes you a little longer to recover."

She knew exactly what she was saying and wondered how he'd take it. Would he play or take offense?

His mouth spread in a wide grin and she had her answer.

"Now you're just being mean." Raising one hand, he caught hers before she could draw away, bringing her index finger closer to his mouth. "And you should know I'm not one to let a slight go unchallenged."

Before she could say anything else, he tugged her hand even closer and bit the tip of her finger.

It didn't hurt. It stung a little but it did worse damage internally. Her sex clenched against a wave of desire so fierce, she had to bite her tongue against a gasp.

And when he sucked on the tip of her finger and flicked at it with his tongue, she had to swallow hard because, oh my god, her mouth was watering.

Damn, damn, damn. How could you be so stupid?

This was exactly where she shouldn't be. Not this close to him, with her damn finger in his mouth and his tongue making her want him to use it somewhere other than her finger.

Thank god he couldn't read her mind because if he could...

In the next second, her hand was free but his lips had covered her mouth.

Her breath froze in her lungs, her body poised for...what?

She had no idea because the heat of his kiss had seeped through her lips and into her bloodstream, making her sizzle from the inside out.

Damn him.

His mouth moved over hers with a burning passion that shot through her blood. Her hands itched to grab his shoulders and pull him closer but she knew she shouldn't. She should push him away.

Then his hands landed on her shoulders and she shivered, sensation rushing through her like electricity. Combined with his lips moving over hers, playing with her, he coaxed her into a response she knew she shouldn't give.

And yet...

Her lips softened under his, parted slightly, and her traitorous tongue slipped by to flick at his lips.

A deep rumble sounded in his chest and his hands slid from her shoulders to her back, where he only had to apply a little pressure to bring her closer.

She took that first step and he took the opening and ran with it. His hands spread across her back, pressing her tight against his broad chest. She tilted her head up at a sharper angle, giving him more access to her mouth. Which he took immediately.

He kissed her harder now, his tongue slipping between her lips to tangle with hers. His taste, warm and masculine, exploded in her mouth and she sucked him in, giddy with triumph when he groaned and his hands spread across her back to pull her even closer.

Her tote fell to the floor. She didn't remember releasing it but now she had both hands free to grab his shoulders and hold tight.

Which was apparently exactly what he wanted.

As soon as her fingers curled into firm muscle, he shifted the kiss into overdrive, twisting his head to get an even better angle.

He attacked her mouth with such deliberate intent, she wanted to urge him to let loose. But the still-sane part of her brain telling her this was crazy held her back.

Instead, she let him explore her mouth at his own pace and tried not to enjoy the hell out of it. Which she did anyway.

Because, oh my god, the man could kiss. He didn't let her up for air except for small hurried breaths that left her only half-satisfied, her fingers digging into his shoulders until she was afraid she might actually hurt him.

He didn't seem to mind, just shifted the angle of his mouth so he could take even more.

Her breathing came even heavier now, as the ache in her gut began to spread lower. She wanted to rub her breasts against him, wanted to press her hips against his and feel just how much he wanted her.

Because according to this kiss, he did. She wanted to lean back and look down, see just how much of that old saying was true about a guy and the size of his feet. Because she'd seen Will's skates and they were huge.

And it had been a damn long time since she'd kissed a guy who made her want to stick her hands down his pants on the first date.

Hell, this wasn't even a date.

They were kissing. In her office. In the arena where they both worked.

Her eyes snapped open and she broke away. To his credit, he let her. He released her immediately but he didn't back off. All she could hear was their heavy breathing and the sound of the heating system as it kicked in.

Blinking up at him, she carefully removed her hands from his shoulders and took a step back.

"I need to get home."

"Yeah, it's getting late and I've got to be up for practice tomorrow."

Blinking at his immediate acquiescence, she watched with wide eyes as he bent. Her heart sped up as she thought he was going to kiss her again but he kept going until he'd snagged her coat off the floor.

Her cheeks heated but she told herself he wouldn't notice. She should've known she'd be wrong. His gaze narrowed when he towered over her again, staring down at her.

"Jess—"

"Could you give me a hand with that?"

She turned, giving him her back, then glanced over her shoulder at him. When he didn't immediately help her into her coat, she raised her eyebrows.

That put the slight grin back on his face and he made a show of shaking out her coat and sliding it up her outstretched arms.

The thick woolen material immediately made her too warm but she'd be out in the cold soon enough.

Then maybe she'd stick her head in a snowbank just to point out how stupid she'd been.

"Thank you."

Without waiting for him to respond, she grabbed her tote off the floor and headed for the exit. He followed at her heels, his long legs eating up way more real estate than hers did with each step.

Since they were the only ones left on this floor as far as she should tell, she dug her keys out of her tote and locked the office before heading for the stairwell down to the entrance into the side parking lot.

Will followed at her back, silently stalking her.

Her brain continued to buzz with white noise. Sleep would probably be a no-show tonight. Jesus, she'd been so stupid.

Okay, maybe not stupid. Just... No, stupid was definitely the right word.

Christ, she'd have to fix this.

Tomorrow.

Tonight, her brain kept skipping back to that kiss.

Luckily, they ran into no one, the only sound in the building the compressors firing up and rumbling. The evening security guard was probably making rounds so there was no one at the door when they reached it.

Stopping with her hand on the door, she straightened her back and stared up at him.

"This can't happen again. It was a mistake."

His eyebrows rose and that glint was back in his eyes. "By 'this,' I assume you mean that kiss."

She swallowed a sigh. "You know that's exactly what I mean."

He shrugged like it hadn't meant a damn thing to him. "Sure, if that's how you want to play it."

Her brows lifted. Seriously? He wasn't going to give her a hassle? He'd just kissed her like he'd wanted to strip her naked and lay her out on her desk and it hadn't meant a damn thing to him?

Oh god. She was losing it. She should be happy she'd gotten off so easily, not pissed that he wasn't going to fight for her.

Taking a deep breath, she nodded, even though she wanted to stick her finger in his side and jab him.

"Fine. Good night, Mr. MacDonald."

His grin was back. "See you tomorrow, Miss Jess."

Her teeth gritted at his tone. A little mocking, a whole lot of teasing. "Not if I see you first" was on the tip of her tongue but she managed to bite it back. How juvenile would that have been?

She was at her car when she heard him say, "But that was no damn mistake. And you won't be able to hide from me forever."

She turned to gape at him but he was already hauling himself into his Jeep Cherokee. He started the engine then waited until she got into her Subaru and drove away before he followed her out of the parking lot.

FOUR

"Damn, that looks nasty, even worse than yesterday. Hope you aren't planning to get laid tonight after the game. Women'll take one look at you and run in the other direction. We'll have to put a bag over your head if you come out with us after the game."

Will gave Justin the finger as he headed for the freezer to grab one of the many icepacks all hockey players kept there.

"Does it hurt as bad as it looks?"

Yeah, it still hurt like a bitch and he'd already downed three ibuprofen. "Nah, it's fine."

Justin shrugged and went back to shoveling scrambled eggs into his mouth. It was eight a.m. Friday morning and they had to be at the arena by nine-thirty to get ready for practice at ten.

"Man, practice was rough yesterday but considering the last two games, I thought Coach would be a lot tougher." Justin sounded like he still had a mouth full of eggs. "He seems to like you, though. Didn't give you much shit for that fight with Mason Wednesday night."

Sitting at the table holding the ice pack to his jaw, Will let Justin ramble. And Jesus, the guy could talk. Stream of consciousness had nothing on him. But while Justin allowed his brain to unwind, it gave Will a little time to think about Jess.

He hadn't seen her at all yesterday. After practice, he'd made up some excuse to go to her office, hoping to catch her alone for a few minutes.

He'd been looking forward to it, almost as much as he'd been looking forward to getting back on the ice and working out the kinks from the game the night before.

But she hadn't been there. Her intern had been happy to tell her she wasn't going to be in until later that afternoon because of sponsorship meetings.

The crushing sense of loss he'd felt when he'd realized he wasn't going to see her had stopped him in his tracks for several seconds.

He'd talked to her twice, for Christ's sake.

Yeah, and you already know she's one-of-a-kind.

"So the game's probably gonna get chippy tonight." Justin stood, snapping Will's attention back to the conversation. "I think Mason's gonna be in your face most of the game. Gotta get my stuff together. You wanna drive in together?"

With a sigh, Justin tossed the ice pack back into the freezer and started to make his own breakfast. "Sounds good."

At least that would stop him from doing anything stupid. Like asking Jess out to lunch and getting shot down.

But even as he ate breakfast and drove Justin to practice, he couldn't stop thinking about that damn kiss.

He wondered if she'd thought about it as much as he had the past day.

Had he come on too strong?

Yeah, probably. He was like a bull in a china shop most of the time, but he'd never seen much point in pretending you didn't want something or someone when, really, they were all you could think about.

And she hadn't said no. If she had, he would've backed the hell away immediately. Instead, she'd kissed him back.

Had he misread her response?

He didn't think so but he wasn't the sharpest tool in the shed when it came to women so anything was possible.

But... No, she'd kissed him back. He hadn't been wrong about that.

Christ almighty, he didn't need this. Not now. Didn't need to be attracted to a woman at the exact moment he got to a new team, one with as many expectations as this one held.

Then again, he wasn't getting any younger and why the hell should he deny himself a woman he wanted? Was he destined to be alone for the rest of this life?

And why the fuck was he even thinking about this anyway?

He had to get ready for practice.

An hour later, he was about to skate out onto the ice when Coach called his name from the hall outside the locker room.

Will stopped, waiting for Coach to catch up to him.

"How's the face?"

Will shrugged. "Doesn't hurt."

Coach's mouth moved in a slight grin. "Glad to hear it. Don't get a matching one tonight. No stupid penalties. I need you to play smart. Stay out of the box. You and Justin played well together Wednesday and I expect the same from you tonight. But I want more leadership out there. I want more effort."

"You'll get it."

A few guys passed them on the way to the ice, keeping their gazes trained straight ahead. Only Cary made eye contact as he passed. No smirk but definitely some kind of message there.

He was going to have to deal with Cary soon.

"I know I will." Coach smacked him on the shoulder. "See you on the ice."

Coach didn't wait for a response. He headed out through the gate and Will sucked in a deep breath before he followed.

Time to get his head in the game. And a certain woman out of his head.

———

JESS FOUND herself in the box that night, watching the end of the third period.

Watching one certain player, in particular. After she'd spent all of yesterday telling herself she needed to stay away from Will MacDonald. Far away.

Damn him.

There was something about him that made every single female hormone in her body sit up and take notice.

What she couldn't figure out was why. Yes, he was older than most of the other guys and yeah, that was appealing. He had a maturity that was sexy as hell.

And when she watched him skate... She couldn't help but imagine watching all those muscles work while he was naked.

She wanted to run her hands over that broad chest and down those strong thighs and over that tight ass—

Shit. She had to stop or the guys sitting here with her would think she was about to spontaneously combust. Her cheeks felt like they were on fire and if anyone looked over at her right now, they'd want to know what was wrong.

She couldn't exactly say, "Oh, I want to jump our new defenseman. Don't mind me."

Dammit, she should head back down to the suites to make sure her groups were happy but Will was on the ice and the Redtails were rushing the puck into their offensive zone to the cheers of the crowd.

Neither team had scored, though it'd been one hell of a game so far. The cheering crowd chanted, "Let's go, Redtails," as the offense set up their shot, looking for an open lane.

But the Milwaukee defense was tough and the Redtails couldn't get a shot. And when Robbie finally took one, Milwaukee slapped it out of the way easily.

The opposing team could've had a breakaway but Will made an incredible move to block the pass and then made a shot on net that had the crowd on their feet. While it didn't go in, the Milwaukee goalie gave up a rebound that Robbie snagged and slapped into the back of the net with less than a minute to play.

As the crowd jumped to its feet and roared, the team celebrated with them. Robbie skated straight for Will, grabbing him for a bear hug as the other guys crowded around them.

In the box, Jess jumped to her feet and hollered and clapped with the crowd then watched the guys circle around to the bench to knock gloves with the rest of the team.

And just before he turned to skate over to Shane, Will looked up at the box and straight at her.

She froze, her lungs stuttering for several seconds before she started breathing again.

Damn it all to hell. This shouldn't be happening. This couldn't be happening. This wasn't *supposed* to be happening.

And yet, when he grinned up at her—and she knew he was looking at her and not anyone else—she smiled back.

She knew she shouldn't encourage him but, in that split-second connection, she realized she wanted more of him. No, that kiss last night should've never happened.

But now that it had...

Dammit, she had a plan and that plan did *not* include falling for a veteran hockey player.

A former player? Maybe. Someone who shared her love of the game but wouldn't be subject to the whim of a coach's trade or an injury that laid him up for months.

"Ya know, I wasn't too sure about Mac when I heard they'd signed him." Joey Constantino had to raise his voice to be heard over the noise of the crowd. "Couldn't figure out why they'd want some over-the-hill goon for a team with as much skill as we have."

Biting her tongue, she sat back in her seat and focused on the puck drop at center ice. The other team was going to pull their goalie as soon as they could get the puck in the Redtails' defensive zone and would put on a hard press for the last fifty seconds of the game.

But she kept her ears peeled for Milan Hanzel's response.

"Yes, I wondered that, too. But I believe the man will surprise us."

"The guy can skate, no doubt. He's a solid defenseman but he's too slow and he's not getting any younger."

Her damn tongue was gonna need stitches but she kept her mouth shut. This wasn't her conversation.

And damn it, he didn't need her to be his champion. Will's playing spoke for itself.

Still, it was tough not to point out his record over the past year, how his game had been evolving. Was she really the only one who'd noticed?

No, she wasn't. Coach never would've signed him if he hadn't seen the same. He'd just needed a nudge to look in the right direction.

And when the final horn sounded to mark the end of the game and the Redtails gathered at center ice to raise their sticks for the fans, she said a silent "Fuck you" to Joey for his "goon" comment.

Slipping out of the box before she did something stupid, like point out how Will had had the assist on the game-winning goal, she headed back to her office to write up her notes.

And tried not to think about him. Or wonder if he'd show up again.

As if she'd conjured him with her thoughts, she heard the door to the outer office open then footsteps walking toward her office.

Sure, it could be any number of other people, but her heart kicked up a heavy beat and her lungs tightened until she could barely suck in air.

And when Will stopped in her doorway and caught her gaze, she had to make a concerted effort not to fidget in her chair. Luckily, he couldn't see her thighs clench under her desk.

"Working late again."

His deep voice raised all the tiny hairs on her arms and she had to clench her hands against the urge to rub them. Instead, she leaned back in her chair and met his gaze.

"There's never enough time in the day. Good game tonight."

He nodded. "Thanks. Want to get a drink?"

She knew her answer should be no but she couldn't get the word to come out of her mouth.

In his suit with his shirt unbuttoned at the neck, hands in his pockets and his hair still wet from a shower, he made her pant just by standing in front of her.

A traitorous little voice in the back of her head urged her to say yes. They could go somewhere she knew they wouldn't be recognized. Somewhere dark they could be alone and she could stare into his eyes and let herself flirt.

It'd been so long since she'd flirted with a guy, she wondered if she still knew how. She knew how to charm clients without going over a line, but she was totally out of practice in this situation.

When she didn't answer his question after several seconds, she saw his lips quirk up at one corner.

"That was a simple yes-or-no question. Tell me no and I'll walk away." He looked so sincere, she had the sudden fear that he'd do just that. He'd walk away and she'd never see him again except on the ice or passing by in the hall.

And she knew that's not what she wanted.

"Yes. There's a bar in West Reading, it's quiet and we can talk. Unless you want to go—"

"Sounds great." He straightened away from the door. "Are you ready?"

Her lips twitched at his immediate agreement but when she caught a glimpse of his smile flirting with the corners of his mouth, she suddenly found it hard to breathe.

How did he get more handsome every time she was in the same room with him? No, it didn't make any sense at all but, dammit, that's how it seemed. From his wet, too-long hair to his scruffy square jaw to the dark navy of his eyes and the constant glint of humor she saw there, he made her want...him.

She shouldn't give in to her attraction. The front office frowned on relationships with players. They weren't explicitly forbidden but you pretty much knew it shouldn't happen.

And she still couldn't help herself.

"I just need to close this file and we can get out of here."

"Is this a habit for you?"

Glancing over her file, she made a few more notes then closed it out. She'd look over it again at home tomorrow morning.

"Is what a habit?"

"Staying this late after a game? I assume you don't have a boyfriend to go home to since you just agreed to go out with me, but don't you get burned out?"

She shrugged, though it was something her mom had picked at her about the last time they'd spoken. Jess had brushed off her mom's comment about having no life outside of work. It was the middle of the season. Of course she had no life other than work right now. That's how this job worked.

Looking at Will with raised eyebrows, she said, "Don't you think you should've asked about a boyfriend *before* you asked me out?"

"I figured you'd tell me to go pound sand if you did." He shrugged and his grin made a slight appearance. "Besides, I might've decided to fight him for you."

Damn him, that should sound cheesy as all hell. So why was her heart fluttering like a stupid teenager on a date with her first real crush?

"Luckily, you won't have to do that. Not sure your jaw could take any more abuse."

"My jaw's fine but it's probably better I don't throw any punches anyway."

She heard something in his voice as she shut down her computer and stood to put on her coat.

"Did Coach call you out for that fight Wednesday night? You didn't have any penalty minutes tonight. And you got a point. That would seem like a good thing."

He straightened away from the doorjamb as she rounded her desk and she couldn't help the hitch in her breath at the sheer size of him.

Sue her, she had a thing for big guys. Broad shoulders, muscular chests, thick thighs. Rock-hard abs.

If she ever got the chance to see Will naked, she'd have to be sure she didn't swallow her tongue. Or drool. She didn't know which would be more embarrassing.

"Points are always a good thing." He shrugged. "And sometimes you need to stick up for your teammates."

She couldn't argue with that so she grabbed her coat off the hook by the door and went to get her tote...and found he already had it in his hand.

"Jesus, what the hell do you have in here? I swear this weighs more than my gear bag."

Grabbing it out of his hand while rolling her eyes, she slung it on her shoulder and walked by him out the door.

"Too heavy for you, big guy? I know it weighs a little more than your stick but I'm sure you can handle it."

She didn't look over her shoulder to see if he followed. He was. She could feel him behind her.

"I don't know, Miss Jess. I may need some help with that stick. It can get damn heavy."

She was pretty sure he wasn't talking about his hockey stick at the moment. And she should probably pretend to be offended at his crass humor. But she wasn't a prude and she'd been around professional athletes all her life. She'd learned to hold her own in a battle of words.

"Or maybe your stick is just a twig and not all that much to handle."

Silence from behind her. Oh hell. Had she offended—

His laughter rang out in the empty halls as she looked over her shoulder.

Bad move. Really bad move.

Because when he smiled, he was irresistible. And when he

laughed... Hell, she wanted to climb him like a tree, wrap herself around him and kiss him until neither of them could breathe.

And maybe she'd lick her way back down his body until she—

Shit. That was definitely enough of that.

"I have a feeling you and I are going to get along pretty damn well, Miss Jess."

Unfortunately, that's what she was afraid of.

Scrambling for something nonthreatening to say, she settled on innocuous. "So, how are you and Justin getting along? You're staying with him, aren't you?"

He paused and she wondered if he was going to let her off the hook so easily. "Yeah, I am. He's a character but he's a great guy and a damn good partner on the ice. You wouldn't think the guy could skate like he does when you watch him walk. I swear he trips over his own feet every couple of steps."

Smiling, she nodded. "He's a really nice guy."

"Close to your age, isn't he?"

Justin happened to be only three years younger than her twenty-eight. She knew Will was five years older than her.

"I guess." She shot him a glance over her shoulder, curious. "Does that bother you?"

"What? That you're younger than me?" He shot her another one of those cocky grins. "Nah. Women mature faster than men. I figure in a few years, I'll have caught up to you."

Her smile widened. "Well, at least you're honest about it."

"So tell me, Miss Jess. Why's a smart, beautiful woman like you dateless on a Friday night?"

She slid him a glance over her shoulder. "Maybe because I haven't found one I'm willing to put up with."

"Are you warning me away? Because I gotta tell you, I love a challenge."

She didn't answer as he held open the door for her and waved for her to precede him out into the parking lot. Only four cars remained and she recognized Coach's as one of them.

Damn, she hoped they got away before he saw them. She wasn't embarrassed to be seen with Will, but she didn't want Coach worrying about Will splitting his focus.

And that isn't your call to make, is it?

"If I was warning you away, I wouldn't be taking you out for a drink."

He laughed again; this time she swore it was even rougher and impossibly sexier than before.

"You're absolutely right. And I have a feeling I'll be saying that a hell of a lot with you."

She rolled her eyes, though he couldn't see. But she had to admit she liked the way he flirted.

And he was definitely flirting.

"In case we get separated, the bar's right on the corner of Penn Avenue and Eighth. It's not hard to find."

They'd stopped at her car and she clicked open the door. He had his hand on the door handle and opened it for her.

"I'll try to keep up. You can't shake me off your tail that easily, Miss Jess."

This time she was facing him as he spoke so he could see her roll her eyes. His answering grin and low chuckle made it hard for her to keep her composure.

"See you at the bar, Mr. MacDonald."

"Yes, you will, Miss Jess."

Five minutes later, she was overthinking her decision as she parked across the street from the bar.

As she shut off the car, she gave herself a few seconds to breathe.

This is a really bad idea. You should know better.

Except Will wasn't like the other hockey players she'd dated. He was older, more stable. He didn't boast and brag and talk shit like a lot of the younger guys.

Headlights flashed in her rearview and her heart kicked into another gear.

Fuck it. If she was going to be bad, she was going to do it with a man who made her wet with only his voice.

She remembered to check for traffic a second before she pushed open her door. Would've been embarrassing as hell to have it ripped off by a passing car.

As soon as she stepped out, Will was by her side. He didn't touch her as they walked across the street, but he was close enough that she felt the heat coming off his body. She wanted to rub up against him, like Honey did whenever she walked into her apartment.

He opened the door for her and she gave a quick wave to Sophie, behind the bar as usual and staring at Jess like she'd grown another head. Instead of stopping to say hi, she led Will past the bar to her left to a table in the back. Luckily, Will didn't seem to notice that Sophie watched them the whole way but he would if Jess did what she wanted to do and stuck her tongue out at her friend.

"Nice place." Will glanced around after they were seated at a table near the back. "Do you live around here?"

"No, I have an apartment in Reading. Shane's girlfriend, Bliss, introduced me to this place and the bartender's become a friend. Sophie's dad owns the place and he works in the kitchen but Sophie runs the bar. She's the youngest of five girls. Her sisters are all married and her dad and her are always fighting about something, so don't be surprised to hear them shouting in the kitchen. But unless you speak Greek, you won't be able to understand them."

When she stopped to draw in much-needed air, she found Will smiling at her with that grin that probably got women to drop their panties in seconds. At least, her panties were ready to drop.

"You spend a lot of time here?"

She shrugged. "The food's good, the alcohol's not expensive, and the company's great. And I don't feel like I'm at a meat market. When I moved here to take this job, I didn't really know anyone and I didn't really go out much until Lori introduced herself. She's Cary's wife. Have you met her?"

Nodding, he picked up the menu lying on the table and looked it over. "Yeah, I have. Cary and I played together a few years ago, before they were married. Where'd you move from?"

Something about his too-casual tone caught Jess's attention, especially when he immediately changed the subject. She almost pressed him on it. Instead, she shrugged it off.

"Lancaster. I came over from the Redtails' ECHL affiliate. Before that I was with Elmira."

"I played in Elmira for a few months a year or so ago." He shook his head, his grin resurfacing. "Crazy-ass fans."

"Dedicated fans. Tough market, though."

Before she could answer, the waitress stopped at the table to take their order. Jess ordered wine and he ordered beer, along with a burger and fries.

"You don't want anything to eat?"

She shook her head. "No, thanks. I didn't just play sixty minutes of hockey."

He frowned. "No dessert? Come on, you like chocolate, right? If I get cake, you'll help me eat it?"

Since she knew Sophie's mom made all the baked goods for the menu and she also knew Sophie's mom was an awesome baker, she rolled her eyes but nodded. "Sure."

His smile made another appearance, the one that made her feel like he'd trailed his fingers along her skin. Somewhere usually covered by clothing.

And if she kept thinking like that, she was going to flush bright red and he'd know exactly what she was thinking.

Will turned that smile on the waitress, who gave him an appreciative grin in return. And when she turned to head back to the bar, the girl arched her brows and gave Jess a thumbs-up which Will couldn't see.

Jess had to restrain herself from rolling her eyes but she totally understood the response.

Especially when he leaned back in his chair, legs stretched out in front of him while he gave her his full attention.

"So how long have you been with the Redtails?"

"A little over two years. Eventually I plan to work for an NHL team."

He huffed out a laugh. "Don't we all? Sometimes it's just not in the cards."

Was that bitterness in his voice? Probably a little. "I know. And sometimes it's not fair. Some players have the skill but not the drive. Some have the drive but not the skill. And sometimes, they have both and still don't get their break. It sucks, especially when you know someone's been passed over who shouldn't have been. The system's not perfect and I think scouts and coaches focus too much on skills instead of overall performance. The game has changed so much in the past ten years that there are a lot of guys who get overlooked."

His laser-sharp gaze never left hers. "Sounds like you spent a lot of time with your dad at games growing up. Did you play at all?"

She shook her head. "Not really. I can skate and I can hold a stick and shoot, but don't expect me to fly up and down a sheet of ice chasing after a puck. I'm not delusional."

His laughter made it hard for her to swallow. "And that's all I've ever wanted to do. But you spent a lot of time at games, didn't you?"

She nodded. "When I could, yes. I love the sport, even though I know the system's flawed and corporate interference is rampant. When the guys are out on the ice and they're playing as hard as they can, there's nothing I'd rather be doing than watching a game."

"And I can't imagine doing anything else."

The longing in his voice made her wonder if he'd been thinking about retirement lately but she wasn't sure she wanted to mention it. "You've been playing for a long time."

"Since I was five. But you know that's not unusual."

"No, it's not. But I also know you were a damn good baseball player in junior high."

His brows rose. "Now how the hell did you find that out?"

Damn. Probably should've kept her mouth shut. When she

started to talk hockey with someone who knew the game, she couldn't help herself. All kinds of random facts fell out of her mouth.

She shrugged, tried to blow it off. "You know who my dad is. He's thorough."

Will didn't look like he was buying her explanation. "So your dad went through his notes with you?"

"All the time. I spent most of my childhood at hockey games with him. I loved it. My mom..." She grimaced. "Not so much."

"You and your mom don't get along?"

"Oh no. We do. She just doesn't share my love of hockey. She and my dad weren't married very long and they got divorced when I was three so I don't remember a time when they were living together. Probably for the best because they can't agree on anything."

"Sounds like a tough way to grow up."

She had a few seconds to think about her answer when the waitress returned with their drinks and she took a sip before speaking.

"I didn't know any different. And they both loved me. My mom got remarried and my stepdad is good guy. I actually had a pretty great childhood. When I was a teenager and my mom and I couldn't be in the same room together for more than two minutes without fighting, I'd stay with my dad for a while. He bought a house a few blocks away from my mom's after the divorce so he'd be close. During the week, I'd go to school like a regular kid. On weekends, I got to travel all over North America to watch hockey. Whatever city we were in, my dad always made time to show me around, even if it was only his favorite place to eat."

"Learned a lot about the game, huh?"

Nodding, she watched as he took a swallow of his beer, watched the muscles of his jaw work, and wondered how badly she would embarrass herself by drooling.

What the hell was it about this man that made her want to throw years of careful avoidance of relationships with hockey players out the window?

Tearing her gaze away from his throat before he caught her

staring like a madwoman, she said, "As much as anyone who doesn't play the sport can."

Then he set his mug on the table and she ended up watching his hands. The man had big hands, all nicked up. Oh hell, even his hands were turning her on.

"So why marketing?"

"Honestly? It's the only avenue open to a woman in the field. And there was no way in hell I was going to be an ice girl." She shuddered at the thought. "And there are no female scouts in the sport."

The slight narrowing of his eyes was the only hint that she'd piqued his interest. But his next question was directly to the point.

"So you wanted to be a scout?"

Damn, he had no idea how much of a loaded question that was.

She played off his comment with a shrug. "I love my job. It's challenging."

"But it's not really what you want to be doing."

She bit her tongue, so tempted to tell him the truth. To spill out such a closely held secret to a man she'd only known for days. What was it about Will that made her want to throw away years of restraint and do something so foolish as to give in to her reckless side and jump this man's bones?

Would it really be that disastrous?

"It *is* what I want to do."

When he raised an eyebrow at her, she rolled her eyes and huffed. Damn him, she didn't owe him anything but she still wanted to spill her guts to him.

"Maybe I considered *possibly* pursuing scouting when I was younger. But I knew it would never happen and, even if it did, it would only happen because of my dad. It wouldn't be because I was so good at it that the fact I'm a woman wouldn't matter. Instead, I focused on what I knew I could actually do. And I'm damn good at my job, by the way."

He raised his hands in surrender. "Hey, no argument from me.

But it's kind of frustrating, isn't it? Having only so much control over your own life."

Well, hell. Of course, he understood exactly what she was saying.

She shook her head. "Sorry, I didn't mean to jump down your throat."

"No problem. Touched a nerve, huh?"

Shrugging, she glanced away for a second. "Maybe a little one. What about you, Mr. MacDonald? Do you like your new team?"

He nodded decisively. "I do. Great bunch of guys even if sometimes I wanna punch Flaherty."

Laughing, she reached for her drink. "You'd have to get in line. He's a sweetheart but the guy just doesn't know when to shut up."

His eyebrows rose. "A sweetheart, huh? What does it take for you to call a guy a sweetheart?"

Did she hear jealousy in his voice? Or was that her imagination? "Well, he can't be a dick. And he has to have a sense of humor and a great smile and be nice to kittens and puppies and little old ladies."

Will's laugh rang out and her breath caught in her throat. Of course, her thighs clenched, too, but she wasn't going to think about that.

"Aw, hell, I guess I'm out of the running then. I haven't met a little old lady yet that I haven't wanted to run over."

And there was that humor again. Just slightly on the edge of being over the line into ridiculous.

"Are you ever serious?"

"Yeah. When I take a woman to bed, I'm deadly serious about treating her right. And when I'm on the ice, I'm there to do my job, protect my teammates and score goals."

Her breath caught in her thought and an image of Will, naked and stretched out on her bed, planted itself in her mind.

Her bed had never looked more inviting.

Blinking those thoughts out of her mind, she took another sip of her wine and hoped he didn't notice the flush creeping onto her cheeks.

Hell, she'd fan her face if she thought he wouldn't look at her like she was nuts.

Right now, he watched her so intently, he probably knew exactly what she was thinking, damn him.

"That's why you're a good fit for the team." She totally ignored the first part of his statement. Way too many landmines. "We didn't have anyone with your specific strengths and experience. If all we'd needed were an enforcer, we could've picked up any number of guys from the WHL. But you had exactly what we needed."

His gaze narrowed "So it is true."

"What's true?"

"You recommended me, didn't you?"

Her nose wrinkled as she considered her answer, which was a dead giveaway.

"I may have said something to Coach Scott about you a couple of weeks ago."

She was saved from saying anything else when the waitress returned with his food. She'd be sure to slip Sophie's young cousin a little something extra for the inadvertent interruption.

Will turned his smile on the girl and Jess watched her light up.

Ugh. He wasn't even trying. She wanted to shake her head and throw her hands in the air in disgust.

He was *not* that damn attractive.

Except when he smiled. Then, yeah, he was.

Shit.

"Hey, could you bring the chocolate cake awhile. Jess might wanna start on that."

"Oh sure. No problem." The girl's smile widened. "Be right back."

Then she turned her back to Will and mimed, "Oh, my god" at Jess before she hurried off to the kitchen to do the man's bidding.

She wanted to kick said man under the table just for being exactly what she didn't need in her life right now.

Handsome, nice, decent, funny, and he'd graduated in the top twenty percent of his class at UMass with a degree in math. Full scholarship for hockey and academics. Yes, he was that smart.

And how did she know that? Because she was damn thorough, that's why.

Stifling a sigh, she shifted in her chair, tucking back the strands of hair that had fallen into her face.

"Why are you staring at the table like you want to stab it?"

Busted. Lifting her gaze back to his, she saw that glint in his eyes was gone. He watched her with complete seriousness.

"I don't want to stab the table."

"Then I'm assuming you want to take a stab at me."

Was he being a smart-ass with the double entendre? She couldn't tell.

With a slight shrug, she sniffed. "I wouldn't want to hurt you. The team needs you."

His lips quirked. "Oh, there are more than a couple of ways you can take a stab at me that won't affect the way I play."

Yes, there were. And the more he spoke, the more she wanted to take him up on every unspoken thing he wasn't saying.

"I think...this was a mistake."

WILL SETTLED MORE EASILY into his chair, watching Jess try to hide her confusion.

If she thought he'd back down after her last statement, she had another think coming. If she knew him as well as she thought she did, she should know he didn't give up easily.

And he'd already made up his mind.

He wanted her.

And since he planned to be here in Reading at least until the end of the season, he had some time to bring her around.

But he'd have to lay the groundwork.

"Having chocolate cake is a mistake?"

She gave him that look he was beginning to find irresistible. The smile that said she wasn't swayed by his charm. That's okay. He could work with the fact that she'd agreed to come out with him.

"You know that's not what I meant."

He shrugged but didn't answer right away because the waitress was back with the cake. When she'd left again, he leaned forward and picked up his burger. His stomach had been growling for a half hour.

But he also knew she'd be frustrated by his silence and that was okay, too. Because she hadn't gotten up and walked out yet.

He heard her huff but she picked up her fork and took a swipe at the cake. While he chewed, he watched her lips part as she slipped the fork between them.

Holy fuck. Electricity zinged through him like he'd grabbed a live wire.

He wanted to lick those lips then smash his mouth against hers. She'd taste like chocolate and, damn, he loved chocolate.

After he swallowed, he set his burger down. "We're eating, talking. How is that a mistake?"

Her adorable jaw set and he knew she was getting ready to tell him she didn't want to see him again, at least not like this. Alone. Together. On a date.

Which was exactly what he did want.

He wanted more time with her. She intrigued him like no other woman he'd ever met. And he'd met many. Women who had no idea what a blue line was and women who knew what two-one-two meant in hockey terms.

This woman probably knew more about hockey than any other woman he'd ever met and that turned him on. The fact that she'd had something to do with him being signed by the Redtails turned him on even more.

"What exactly *do* you mean? Come on, Jess. Was there something in my contract I missed? Is there a clause in there about dating front office staff?"

She looked straight at him and held his gaze. "No, there isn't. But it's not a good idea and you know it."

"So it's not a good idea to want to date someone who knows the game and knows what a player's life is like during the season? It's not like you control the team in any way, right? You're not the one making decisions on how much ice time I get or how much money I make, right?"

She rolled her eyes and his dick hardened even more. "Of course not."

"And you're not going to, right?"

Shaking her head, she leaned forward in her chair a little. "Look, I see where you're going with this and you're not wrong, okay? I don't have that kind of influence. It just...doesn't feel right."

"Are you saying being here with me feels wrong?"

She opened her mouth to say something but quickly closed it again.

Stifling a smile, he didn't wait for her to get her thoughts together. "Because I gotta tell you, it feels pretty damn good to me."

"Will—"

"I like you, Jess. No bullshit. You're smart, you know your hockey, and you're beautiful." Her eyes widened at that but he didn't stop to push the point. He wanted to keep her off balance. "I'm new here. Don't know many people but I want to get to know you. You don't want anything to jeopardize your job. I get that. But I don't think being friends with me will put your job in danger. You don't want to jump my bones, I'll respect that. But don't shut me down because you think sex is all I want. We've got a lot in more in common than you want to admit and it's nice to have someone close to my own age to talk to."

That last one hit a nerve. He saw it register, saw her consider it and turn it over in her mind. He had a second to wonder if bringing up her age had been the wrong move, but when her nose wrinkled, he realized he might have found the right button to push.

Letting her think about that, he picked up his burger again and they ate in silence for a while.

Finally, the cake half eaten, she stopped and put her fork down.

"So, you want us to be friends? And that's all?"

"I'd love to count you as a friend, Jess."

Her teeth lodged into her bottom lip, which he found sexy as all hell. It took most of his self- control to keep his mouth shut and not tell her that he also really wanted to take her to bed. But, hey, he'd managed to mold himself into a different player at his age. He could handle this.

"Of course, you can consider me a friend. I'd... That's great. I just don't want you to...to expect anything."

No, he didn't expect anything. But he sure as hell hoped for something more. "I'm enjoying the company. And the only thing I'll expect is unbiased hockey analysis. Sound good?"

She didn't answer right away, just continued to stare at him like she was trying to read his mind. Good thing she couldn't, because she'd be marching her cute little ass out the door.

He'd meant every word out of his mouth but that didn't mean he was going to give up on getting her in bed. It just meant he'd have to bide his time.

Most people assumed that because he had a reputation as an enforcer, he had a quick trigger. Totally not true. He had one hell of a long fuse. And he could be patient.

That trait made him dangerous, which most people only realized after he'd drawn them in and pounced.

Finally, she nodded slowly, holding his gaze. "Sure. I can do that."

"Good. So what'd you think of the game tonight?"

It took her a couple of seconds to respond, as if she were searching for hidden meaning in his words. And when she did, her response was almost tentative.

"The third d-line still needs some tweaking."

He settled back into his chair. "Yeah, I noticed that. Not intuitive."

Picking up his burger, he started to eat again as she warmed up to the conversation. He didn't have to nudge her very hard. He knew she loved the game but he hadn't known exactly how knowledgeable she was until she started to talk statistics.

He'd been a math major in college but he'd hated statistics.

Jess apparently loved them. She could recite stats off the top of her head like she was reciting the national anthem. Hell, she knew some of his stats that even he would've had trouble pulling up.

He would've listened to her talk all night but she wouldn't let him slack on his end of the conversation. She'd prod and needle him until he spoke. Sometimes they agreed, sometimes they didn't. They got into a fifteen-minute argument about shootouts that shouldn't have made his dick even harder for her but damn if he could help himself.

She got so passionate about her subject, he couldn't help but want to keep her talking.

He didn't realize until he'd finished two beers, she'd had another glass of wine, and he'd ordered a second piece of cake because she'd finished the first by herself, that it was close to one a.m. He looked at the bar to see the bartender wiping down as he glanced at their table.

Shit. He really didn't want to say good night yet because he wasn't sure when he'd see her again.

They had a rare Saturday night off tomorrow, then another home game Sunday afternoon, practice Monday and Tuesday then they left for a five-day road trip. When they got back, they had games Wednesday, Friday, and Saturday. He should be thinking more about the upcoming games than her but it was late and he was in full-blown lust.

He wanted to spend the rest of the night with her, and if she were anyone else, he'd be putting on a full-court press to get into her bed.

Not going to happen. At least not tonight.

She must have noticed the bartender as well because she glanced at the band on her wrist and sighed.

"We should probably clear out." Her smile looked rueful. "I didn't realize it was so late."

He almost asked if she wanted to go for coffee at the all-night diner he'd noticed down the street but figured he'd be pushing his luck. Instead, he nodded and stood.

"Guess I should get some sleep before practice tomorrow morning. Then I need to get to the store for food. I swear Justin exists solely on eggs and bread."

She stood, slipping on her coat and grabbing her purse from her chair, then hesitated, her teeth lodging in her lip. She looked like she was going to say something then thought better of it.

He really wanted to know what she'd been going to say but kept his mouth shut. So he followed her out of the bar after slipping the bartender another ten and walked her to her car in silence.

There wasn't much traffic along Penn Avenue at one in the morning so they stopped by her car. Looking up at him with a smile that made his breath catch in his lungs, she jangled her keys in her hand.

"Thanks for the cake and the wine. Much better than anything I had at home. And for the discussion. I love to talk hockey but I guess you could tell."

"Hey, I owe you for keeping me company tonight. So I guess I'll see you at the arena Sunday."

He wanted to ask her what she was doing tomorrow, wanted to ask her out to lunch, dinner, drinks, whatever. But he knew he'd be pushing her so he didn't.

"I'll be there. I usually work on setting up player appearances on Mondays." Her eyes widened and she grabbed his forearm and gave him a little shake. "Oh! Which reminds me. Are you willing to do a children's ward visit Tuesday? Several of the guys are on board but I didn't have a chance to ask you yet. And I know it's short notice but I'd really love to have as many guys there as we can."

Hell, he'd agree to anything so long as she touched his arm and stared into his eyes while she asked.

"Sure. But that means I have to do wash tomorrow or I won't have any clothes to wear."

She blinked and he wished like hell that he could read her mind because whatever she'd just thought must have been fascinating. He swore she blushed but with the light from the streetlamp, he couldn't be sure.

Was she thinking about him without clothes? Or was he just delusional?

Probably the last.

Then she smiled. "Great! That's great. Thanks. I'll put you down and text you the details." She snatched her hand back like she'd been burned. Or like she'd remembered she was touching him. "Good night, Will."

"Night, Jess."

Her smile stayed with him while she drove away.

———

"YES, of course, Mrs. Lease. I'll make sure you can get into the suite earlier in the day so you can decorate. And the mascot will be there to deliver your grandson's cake. I just need the bakery's number so I can talk to them about delivery."

Jess ended the call Saturday morning with Dylan Lease's grandmother with a promise that everything would be perfect. The entire Lease clan of fifty would be gathering to celebrate the youngest grandson's birthday tomorrow and Angela Lease had spared no expense to make sure it would be memorable.

The little boy had had one hell of a year between his eighth and ninth birthdays, including being treated for spinal meningitis and spending five months in the hospital after complications.

While he was in the hospital, he'd met a few of the players from the team, who'd promised him an awesome game when he was well enough to attend. Jake Mozik had become especially close with the little boy and had invited Dylan onto the bench for warm-ups and set up a visit to the locker room after the game, as well.

This was the part of her job she loved more than anything and it was the number one reason why she'd hate to make a move up the chain. Of course, she wanted a better position. But with that move came other considerations. Like the fact that she wouldn't be helping to plan children's birthday parties.

No, she'd spend more time dealing with crowds of rowdy salesmen who drank too much and corporate businessmen who also drank too much and expected much more in return for their money than a visit to the locker room and a cake.

She'd heard stories from the female office staff at the NHL level. Not about their bosses but about the increased hassle from corporate sponsors. Still, it hadn't stopped her from applying for a recent opening in the Colonials marketing department.

No one at the Redtails knew she'd applied for the position. Her secret wouldn't keep for long and she was dreading the moment her boss found out, but it wouldn't come as a surprise to anyone who knew her. She had a plan.

With a sigh, she pushed out of her chair and headed for the concourse. She'd been sitting for the past two hours and needed to stretch her legs.

And yes, if that meant she could catch the last few minutes of practice, all the better. She needed to head down to the locker room anyway to talk to Jake about tomorrow before he left for the day.

And if she ran into Will... Well, that'd be okay too.

She'd spent most of this morning thinking about him. And spent the rest of the time telling herself she shouldn't be thinking about him.

After a lap around the concourse, she couldn't help herself. She stopped at an entrance and walked out into the seats.

The sound of blades cutting through the ice and the yells of the guys as they worked on a passing drill were familiar, almost soothing. Then she heard Coach Scott call the guys in to talk.

She caught sight of Will immediately. He'd taken off his helmet and that hair was unmistakable. Wet as it was with sweat and the water he'd dumped over his head, it hung around his face in wavy strands until he shoved his fingers through it and pushed it away from his face with one hand.

The bruise on his jaw did nothing at all to detract from his handsome face. Her gaze traced all the sharp angles and curves as muscles low in her body clenched and ached.

Sighing, she crossed her arms over breasts that also ached.

Okay, this was getting out of hand. She should head back to her office and make a few final checks before she left for the rest of the day. Since they had no game tonight, she really didn't need to be here today but this job was not a nine-to-five position and she'd known that when she took it.

Her conversation with Will from last night popped into her head, all that talk about her enjoying her job. She hadn't been lying.

But wouldn't it be amazing to follow in Dad's footsteps? To become the first female scout in professional men's hockey?

Never going to happen.

Sighing heavily, she shook her head and was about to turn when Will looked up and caught her eye. Had he known she was there all this time? Or had he happened to look up at the right time?

She couldn't help herself. She smiled back and was rewarded with another one of those amazing, stomach-clenching, all-out grins.

Would it *really* be that bad to have a fling with the hot new player? A man who intrigued the hell out of her and made every nerve ending in her body tingle with excitement just by looking at her?

That kind of man was dangerous to a girl with plans, especially a player like Will, who'd bounced all over the league for his entire career. An affair with him would be doomed to failure because they'd always be going in different directions.

But damn, it'd be fun while it lasted.

He continued to smile at her until the team started to head off the ice and Jake elbowed him, drawing his attention away from her to give Jake a shove. She left before he could mesmerize her again.

She had work to do and it wasn't getting done like this.

―――――

"YOU WORK FAST, MY NEW FRIEND."

Will pulled on his t-shirt and ignored Jake. Probably best not to give in to temptation and tell the younger guy to back the hell off. If he did, he'd have the entire team on his ass, wanting to know what was up. And he knew Jess wouldn't want that.

"Not that I disapprove. I have a feeling you will not be joining us for lunch today."

Zipping up his jeans, he sat on the bench to pull on his boots. "Didn't know there was lunch."

"Yes, most of the team gets together for lunch after practice on Tuesday to discuss upcoming week but because we are going to hospital Tuesday, we moved lunch to Saturday. Mostly we bullshit but we do discuss some team business so we want to make sure you knew."

Well, fuck. That threw a wrench in his plans. He'd been about to head up to the main level so he could talk to Jess and convince her to go out to lunch with him. He figured that was less threatening than asking her to dinner, which would feel a hell of a lot more like a date.

Which is exactly what it would be.

But that wasn't going to happen now because he needed to go to this lunch. Coach wanted him to be a leader so that meant spending time with the troops. Besides, he liked these guys.

But, dammit, he wanted to talk to Jess. He'd had a good practice and he was pumped. And then he'd caught her watching and now he wanted to talk to her, even if it was only for a few minutes.

"Where's lunch? I'll meet you there in a few minutes"

Jake's grin widened and Will gave him a look that should've wiped it off his face. Instead, the guy had a death wish and winked at him.

"We go to the restaurant down the street, the one on the corner. You can meet us there. Unless you get better offer, of course."

Will stood, smacked Jake on the back of the head then grabbed his coat. "I'll see you there."

"We will order without you."

Will shot Jake the finger behind his back and took the stairs two at a time. Everyone else was either heading out the doors on the lower level or still in the locker room so no one questioned him.

He swallowed a smile as he hit the concourse, his stomach tight with anticipation. Totally ridiculous but he'd spent most of last night trying to figure out an excuse to talk to her today, so, yeah, he was excited.

And yeah, his excuse was flimsy as hell but he didn't give a fuck. He only hoped she hadn't left already and that no one else was in the office.

He didn't quite get his wish.

"Oh, hey, Will. Can I help you with something?"

One of the interns, whose name he couldn't remember, smiled at him with so many teeth showing, Will thought he was in a toothpaste commercial.

"No. I just need to talk to Miss Gardiner for a minute."

"Sure. No problem." An even bigger smile now. "She's in her office."

Will refrained from rolling his eyes because he couldn't help thinking this kid looked to be about twelve. Damn, he was getting old.

"Thanks, Damien. You can take off for the day. I'll see you tomorrow."

"Okay. Thanks, Jess."

And off he bounded, like a big puppy, straight out of the office.

Will turned back to Jess, letting his smile loose now.

"Are the interns getting younger or am I just that old?"

Her answering grin made that pit in his stomach expand. But now he realized that it wasn't a pit. It was anticipation. And a shit-ton of desire.

"Maybe a little of both. That one's only twenty. He's a junior at

Albright. He's a great kid. He's just…" she shrugged, "young. So, what can I do for you, Mr. MacDonald?"

Oh, there were so many things he could think of when she called him Mr. MacDonald in that tone but none of them he could say aloud. "Just checking in about Tuesday's hospital visit. I hate leaving things 'til the last minute."

"I was going to text you the details." She glanced away for a second like she was embarrassed and he had a second to frown before she caught his gaze again. "I was waiting to see if you'd stop by after practice."

His frown immediately became a grin as he leaned against the door jamb. "And here I am. So what else can I do for you?"

"Oh, I'm sure I'll have more appearances for you to make. You've become pretty popular on our social media sites and you haven't even been here a week. You've made a good impression on our fans."

"Nice to hear. I've got Twitter but I never use the damn thing. Too much trouble."

Damn, when she laughed, he wanted to kiss her. He figured that really wouldn't go over well.

But he was getting close to the point where he wouldn't care. Still, he knew she would, so he'd wait.

"It's nice to keep in touch with the fans." Her nose scrunched in the way that made him hot and hard. "When you're winning. I don't suggest you check it much when you're losing or having a bad week. They can be pretty brutal."

He shrugged. "I've got a thick skin and broad shoulders. I think I can take it."

Her gaze slipped to his shoulders for a second before flipping back to his face. "I'm sure you can."

Silence fell, not awkward but not exactly easy, either. Too much sexual tension for it to be easy.

If he didn't get out of here now, he wasn't going to make lunch with the team. And they should come first.

He pushed away from the frame. "So I'm meeting the team for lunch down the street. I better get going."

Her smile widened. "They really must like you. It took the guys at least two weeks to invite Derek to the team lunch. Then again, it was *Derek*."

As she rolled her eyes, he knew he wasn't going to wait any more.

"Hey, let me buy you dinner tonight. You pick the place then you can show me where I should shop for food and stuff. I haven't had a chance to stock up yet and I think Justin might shop at the closest convenience store."

Okay, that was a total lie. Justin had given him the rundown on the closest places to get food. But one little white lie wasn't going to damn him to hell. Besides, it was for a good cause.

Sucking in her bottom lip, he saw her teeth sink into the plump flesh, her indecision clear. He was about to press a little harder when she nodded with a smile.

"Sure. I can help with that. What time?"

He controlled the urge to do a victory fist pump. "Great. Justin and I are going to work out this afternoon after lunch so is six okay?"

"That's fine. There's a pizza place in the shopping complex that makes good pizza."

He'd been thinking somewhere more intimate than a pizza joint but he could make do with baby steps. He had a foot in the door and that was more than he'd expected.

"Then I'll pick you up at six. Text me your address along with the stuff for Tuesday." He had to force himself to back out the door. "See you tonight."

He turned before she saw the shit-eating grin on his face.

FIVE

"Best pizza I ever had was at a dive in Wilkes-Barre. They had this shifty-looking brick oven that looked like a twelve-year-old put it together—"

"Vito's! Oh my god, yes! Dad took me there when I was in high school. I can't believe it's still there."

As they stopped at a red light, Will glanced over at Jess as she continued to talk about some out-of-the-way pizza joint, grinning at the wide smile on her face. He should've known she'd have heard about Vito's.

Just proved they were meant to be together, he'd decided.

They'd spent the past three hours in ongoing discussion while they ate dinner then shopped. And if Will had his way, he wouldn't be going back to his apartment. He'd be staying in her bed tonight and every other night he wasn't traveling with the team.

Okay, he knew that wasn't feasible and he also knew that spending a few amazing hours with her didn't mean they'd be compatible for the rest of their lives. But damn, so far he hadn't been able to find a single thing that was a deal breaker for him. This girl just did it for him.

"I can't remember…have you ever played in Alaska?" She was still turned in her seat, facing him. "I was there once with Dad. Not as cold as I thought it was going to be and there's this place that makes the best hamburger I've ever had in my life…"

Hell, he even liked how much she talked. She could go on all night and he'd sit here and let her voice wash over him, making him hard. Good thing they had a few miles to go. They'd already been to Target and the grocery store and now they were headed back to her place so he could drop her off.

He was hoping to get an invite inside. And if all she wanted to do was talk, he'd sit on her couch and let her choose the subject. Then he'd figure out a way to get invited back tomorrow after the game. And the day after that.

Of course, if he didn't come home tonight, Justin would be in his face tomorrow. His teammate had grilled him before leaving the apartment.

"So, you really aren't going to tell me where you're going? Because, dude, you look like you're going on a date. You've been here less than a week. What the fuck? Can you tell me your secret?"

At least Justin hadn't come right out and asked who he was seeing, which either meant he'd managed to hide his attraction to Jess or everyone already knew. When he'd walked into the restaurant, Jake had given him a shit-eating grin but Will had given him a death stare and he'd wiped it away.

Good to know he could still control the kids with a glare. Otherwise, they'd walk all over him.

"So how was lunch today? I mean, I don't want to pry. I get the whole guy-code thing but I'm curious. The younger guys seem to really like you."

He smiled as he pulled onto her street. Her building wasn't far from the arena, in what looked like a nice area. Her apartment was the second floor of an old Victorian-looking building that had once been a single-family home.

He'd only gotten a quick glance at the place when he'd picked her up earlier. She'd been ready to leave as soon as he'd knocked but now he was hoping to get an invitation inside. He planned to carry her bags like a true gentleman. His mom would be proud. Of course, his dad would completely understand his ulterior motives.

His dad understood that sometimes you had to play a little dirty to get the job done. Nice guys sometimes wound up in the penalty box. And sometimes you got away with a few infractions.

"And I like them. It's a great group of guys, even Derek, who can't keep his mouth shut to save his soul. I swear even his mother's embarrassed by him."

Her laugh made him want more, made him want to hear her laughing as he tumbled her onto a bed and kissed his way down her body until she wasn't laughing anymore but was sighing his name.

"Yeah, he can be a bit of a loose cannon but he means well. I don't think the guy has a mean bone in his body. He just...doesn't know when to stop. He's still young."

Will wasn't. And he was more than old enough to know exactly what he wanted.

Parking the car along the street, he jumped out before she could say anything and got her bags out of the back. He wondered if she'd discourage him from coming up and figured he wouldn't give her the time say anything.

But she only smiled when he followed her to the front door and up the stairs.

"Come on in." She widened the door so he could follow her and led him into the kitchen. He took a quick second look around, noting the distinctly feminine decorations and bright colors.

Definitely a girly room and he liked that, too. Hell, even her kitchen was girly, with pink curtains and dish towels and a pink mixer on her counter.

It shouldn't have been a shock. He'd seen her dressed for work... sexy skirts and sleek blouses that hugged her curves and made him lust after her freaking calves and want to lick the hollow between her breasts.

Tonight, she wore tight jeans and a tight white v-neck sweater that dipped low enough that he could see the swells of her breasts and that made him salivate.

"Thanks for bringing the bags up for me."

"No problem. Gotta get my steps in for the day."

Her laugh was magical. "I thought you worked out this afternoon."

"I did but it was mostly weights. Monday I'll work on cardio."

He happened to turn at that moment and caught her staring at his ass.

She tried to cover by reaching for the bags he'd set on the counter, but he knew he hadn't imagined it.

"Would you like a beer?"

Her question came out in a rush and Will wasn't about to turn her down. Groceries in his truck be damned. It was cold out. They'd be fine.

"Sure."

"I'm not sure what I have." She turned toward the fridge behind her to open the door and he took the opportunity to get closer. Glancing up at him, she smiled before grabbing a bottle from the back. "I don't drink it much but I always keep some in the fridge for the guys upstairs."

Say what? "The guys upstairs?"

As she handed him a bottle of dark porter from a company he'd never heard of, he took the opportunity to stare into her eyes. So pretty, the color of the dark chocolate he loved.

She blinked but didn't move away and he could've closed the distance between them in a flash and pressed his mouth against hers, they were that close.

He heard her suck in a short, sharp breath and her lips parted in anticipation but he managed to control himself and pulled back to twist off the cap.

So he might end up with blue balls tonight but it'd be worth it if she invited him back. And he wanted to be invited back.

Putting some space between them, he leaned back against the counter as she put away her few groceries.

"You can go sit down if you want. You don't have to stand here."

"I'm good. Nice place. I wasn't expecting you to like pink so much."

She straightened from putting a box in one of the lower cabinets and, when she headed back to the fridge to pour herself a glass of wine, she had a lopsided little grin on her face. So damn cute. And sexy. How the hell did she manage that?

"The wallpaper and paint were already here so the pink matches that." Then her nose scrunched up. "Okay, I like pink. Not a big deal. Besides, it fits with the house. I fell in love with this place when I was looking at apartments in the area. All the buildings I'd seen were industrial and I hated them. Then the real estate agent showed me this and I fell in love. I've always had a thing for these old Victorians. Wasn't sure I wanted to live in the city but this is a good neighborhood, close to the arena, and it was in my price range."

"Hey, I'm not dissing your house. This place has a lot of character."

Shooing him out of the kitchen now, she pointed toward the couch. He went but waited until she'd sat on the couch before lowering himself next to her. Not too close. Didn't want to make her nervous.

"It does. And after I met the upstairs and downstairs neighbors, I knew this was it."

Pulling her legs up onto the couch, she leaned back and began to tell him about her neighbors. The male couple upstairs who were planning their wedding after being together for twenty-five years. The seventy-something woman downstairs. The young couple next door expecting their first baby and the older couple on the other side whose son had drug problems and had been in and out of rehab.

"Sounds like you're pretty involved with your neighborhood. How long have you lived here?"

"About two years. I'll really miss them when I leave."

"Are you planning to leave?"

She glanced down at the glass in her hand before taking a sip. Covering her expression.

Shit, she was.

"Jess? Are you looking for another job?"

She raised her head and her lips twisted. "There's an opening in Philly in the marketing department. Not exactly what I'm doing here but it's where I want to be, an NHL club with a good reputation, and they know my work. It'd be a good move."

It'd be a great move. *Fuck*. "Then why don't you sound more enthusiastic?"

Her eyes widened. "I am. I mean, it'd be a *big* step but I've been working toward it for years. I like what I'm doing here I like the people I work with. And there's more I can do here. There's room to grow and a lot more latitude to do things my way."

"There're always trade-offs. Bigger club, bigger headaches."

"True, but it's too good an opportunity to pass up."

He got that. He did. But... Shit, he didn't want her to leave. Not now.

And wouldn't that make you a total prick.

"Yeah, I guess it would be."

Shrugging, she took another sip of wine. "I don't think it'll matter anyway. I don't think I'll get it. I'm not sure I have enough experience for what they're looking for."

"Why do you think that?"

"Because the person they're replacing has about twenty years more experience than I do and they'll probably promote from within. There are a couple of qualified people already on staff, but if they hire one of those to fill the spot, they'll be looking for someone to fill *that* spot, so that's why I applied."

"Sounds like you're always thinking one step ahead."

"You have to be thinking at least three or four steps ahead. That's what my dad always said."

Her dad. He'd almost forgotten. He tried to smother his instantaneous reaction but she must have seen something on his face because her gaze narrowed.

"You don't like my dad, do you?"

"I don't really know your dad." Which was the absolute truth.

Her eyebrows rose. "But something happened, didn't it? He did something or said something—"

"It was a long time ago."

And he probably should've left it there. Talking about it now, with her, wasn't going to do him any good and might put a wedge between them. And that was definitely not what he wanted.

What he wanted was to close the space between them, her body plastered against his while he kissed her hard and took her breath away.

But she continued to stare at him, expecting an answer, and he figured it wouldn't help his cause to lie. All she had to do was ask her dad. Who might not even remember an offhand comment he'd made more than a decade ago.

Maybe it's time to let this go.

"I was young, probably twenty-one, twenty-two, just getting my feet under me. I'd graduated from college and had some interest from a couple of AHL teams. Back then, you still had a decent shot at getting picked up by an AHL team even if you weren't drafted. Today, it's harder—" He shook his head. "Never mind, off topic. Basically, your dad told a former coach of mine that I had more of a chance of having a career as a brain surgeon than I did a career in the NHL and that I should seriously consider taking my degree and getting a job where I might actually make a difference."

Her nose wrinkled again and she shook her head, looking pained.

"Yeah, that sounds like my dad. He can be a real ballbuster. I can't believe he said it in front of you, though. Usually he's not quite so much of an...asshole."

Smiling, he shook his head. "He didn't know I was there." Or he had and hadn't cared. "I guess you could say he motivated me to work harder. And hey, I'm still here."

He had wondered about that, occasionally, if Gardiner's words had had any effect on his game, at least inadvertently.

Her smile had softened as he'd spoken, and by the time he was finished, she was nodding. "You are. And you've had two of the best seasons of any other player in the league. Your stats were amazing. I don't know why you didn't get the press some of the other players got. I mean, I know why you didn't and it sucks because you're not a flashy player like some of the kids out there, but still... It's why I talked you up to Coach. I knew this team needed someone like you."

He couldn't hide his grin because she'd just admitted she'd been the one to recommend him. Made him feel like he was king of the world.

But she obviously didn't feel the same. Her gaze dropped and her teeth sank into her bottom lip.

Putting his beer on the coffee table, he reached for her glass, setting it next to his. Then he grabbed her hands in both of his and laced their fingers together. Her eyes widened slightly but she didn't pull away, which made him wonder, if he pulled her even closer and kissed her, would she slap him? Or would she lean in and kiss him back?

He didn't want to do anything to jeopardize their relationship but he also didn't want to pass up an opportunity.

And he wanted to get a hell of a lot closer.

"And I can't thank you enough for that. Seriously. The team's great. There's a lot of talent and the guys are awesome. But the main reason I'm fucking thrilled to be here is because I met you."

Her eyes widened even farther and he wondered if he'd pushed too hard, too fast. But she didn't pull away.

"I don't know what to say to that."

He shook his head. "You don't need to say anything now. I'm just giving you fair warning."

Her gaze narrowed but she still didn't pull her hands away from his. "Fair warning for what?"

"For this."

Wrapping one hand around her neck, he leaned in and did what he'd been dying to do.

He kissed her. Flat-out, full-on, pressed their lips together and kissed the hell out of her. And when she didn't move away, he let his tongue slide against her lips and demand entrance.

She froze at the first lick but Will didn't give up easily. Turning his head, he got a better angle and flicked at the seam of her lips.

Damn, she was soft and he wanted to taste her, wanted to lick into her mouth and tangle with her tongue. But if she didn't let him in, he was going to have to pull back—

With a quiet sigh, she wrapped her arms around his shoulders and practically crawled onto his lap.

Oh hell *yes*.

With her knees on either side of his, her lips parted and gave him what he wanted. All access.

His tongue slid into her mouth and he tasted the slightly sweet wine she'd just had but he also tasted *her*. And that was so much more intoxicating than any liquor.

His lungs began to labor almost immediately, as if he'd done wind sprints for the past hour, and his muscles tensed. He tried not to crush her against him but it was a battle, one he was going to lose pretty damn quickly because every time he breathed in, her scent invaded his lungs and made his blood rush south.

Christ, his cock had already been pressing against the zipper of his jeans but now it began to throb as her lips moved over his. Every time she shifted or put the slightest bit of air between them, he pulled her back and sealed their mouths together more tightly.

He'd gladly suffocate as long as she stayed glued to him. He had her right where he wanted her and he wasn't going to give up the ground he'd won so easily.

Even though she kneeled over him, he couldn't help that he still managed to loom over her. Compared to him, she was tiny. Curvy and rounded and totally female but small enough that she had to feel a little overwhelmed by him.

Of course, she didn't show it. And maybe she really didn't notice because he let her have all the control. Her hands gripped his neck tight, as if she thought he might try to get away. Like that was really gonna happen.

No fucking way was he leaving this exact spot until she told him to get the hell out.

And that didn't seem like it was going to happen anytime soon because she tightened her arms around his shoulders and drew him in even closer.

When he took a deep breath, his chest brushed against her breasts, making him hypersensitive to every slight move she made. And she made a lot of them.

As her knees sank even deeper into the cushions, she shifted her hips closer and the heat of her body increased exponentially. Excitement chugged through his veins like lava.

Her fingers clenched then spread on his shoulders then clenched again, like a cat kneading its paws. Every time she dug her fingertips into his muscles, he wanted to groan with pleasure. He wished she'd slide her fingers into his shirt collar and knead his bare skin. He wanted to tell her to do it, to touch him, but he didn't want to stop kissing her.

Because she was the best damn kisser he'd ever met. Her mouth fit perfectly against his, her tongue playful and so damn sensuous against his. He drew back several times just so he could dive back in and slide his tongue against hers again.

With each second that passed, his control grew more frayed. The hand at her nape tightened until he realized she was pushing back against him. He released her neck immediately but let his hand slide down her back in a slow caress, landing on her hip to mirror his other hand. Which he didn't remember putting there.

Since she didn't seem to mind, he gripped her tighter and began to draw her closer, letting their kiss ramp up in intensity. He found it harder to breathe with every passing second, his heart pounding against his ribs, his cock throbbing in his jeans.

He had the almost overwhelming urge to tug on her hips and bring her down farther, press her against his erection and let her rub against him. He wanted her to be crazy for him, as crazy as he was for her.

Yes, she'd initiated the kiss. And yes, she was currently attacking his mouth like she couldn't get enough of him. He knew exactly what that felt like because he couldn't get enough of her.

Her scent, something light and spicy, made him want to move his mouth along her jaw and down her neck so he could lick at the hollow. From there, he'd move to her breasts...

His hands began to creep up her sides as he thought about her breasts. The girl had curves—

Jess pulled back with a little gasp, beautiful dark eyes wide as she stared into his.

Shit. He didn't want her to stop. He wanted a hell of a lot more than just a kiss and now that he'd had a taste, he was willing to push a little to get more.

Blinking up at him, she swallowed hard then sucked in air. "I'm still not sure this is a good idea."

He knew it was one *hell* of a good idea. "We're the only people here right now. No one else needs to know what happens. It's just us. Right here, right now. Take what you want."

He saw her considering, saw her head tilt to the side, and saw the exact moment she made up her mind.

JESS COULDN'T GET ENOUGH of Will.

Even though she knew she shouldn't be indulging her lust for him, she hadn't been able to deny herself a taste.

But now that she'd had a taste, she wanted so much more.

And why not? There was no reason to deny herself except for the fact that he played for her team. And she knew better than to get involved with a player.

But in the time she'd spent with Will, she'd realized he wasn't like other players she'd known.

"Jess?"

He stared at her with steady eyes, pinning her in place. Demanding a response without making her feel like he was forcing one.

Will had a commanding presence, on ice and off. Maybe it was his age and experience. Maybe it was the fact that he wasn't an arrogant douche, like many other professional athletes.

Maybe it was the fact that when he smiled, her stomach did a stupid little flip-flop. That smile was a little goofy, a little cocky, and more than a little hot.

But he wasn't smiling right now.

The look in his eyes made her heart beat even faster and she sucked in a deep, steadying breath. Which made his gaze drop to her lips.

Holy shit. How did he manage to make her want him even more by simply staring at her mouth?

"This isn't a good idea."

The words coming out of her mouth meant absolutely nothing because her body had disconnected from her brain. Her body thought it was a fucking awesome idea and that he should get back over here and let her kiss him again.

She'd been the one to initiate. This situation was entirely her fault. The fact that he hadn't kept her at arms' length wasn't a surprise. The fact that he was waiting for her to make the next move was.

Had she really expected him to simply take over? To take the decision out of her hands and relieve her of responsibility?

Damn, that totally made her sound like a coward.

Own it, babe. Always own your mistakes and your triumphs.

Her dad's mantra, drilled into her head over two decades.

Well, damn. Mistake or triumph, she wasn't ready to stop.

"I think it's a damn fine idea but if you want me to walk," Will shrugged, "I'm out the door. I'll probably look over my shoulder, maybe whimper like a puppy and hope you invite me back, but if you want me to stop…"

Her mouth dropped open for a second before she started to laugh and that grin of his made a reappearance. And she was a goner. She had no defenses against how that smile made her feel. Or the fact that she was so turned on yet couldn't stop laughing.

"So, does this mean you still think this is a bad idea or—"

"Shut up and kiss me."

"Yes, ma'am."

He raised his hands to cup her cheeks and she had a second to breathe before he plastered his lips over hers again and took her straight into a deep kiss that curled her toes.

When he tilted her head to the side so he could get a better angle, she gave him what he wanted. And when his hands slid from her face to her shoulders to her arms, she scooted closer so her breasts finally pressed tight against his chest.

Yes. God, yes, finally.

Will's chest was everything a man's chest should be, hard and broad and, damn, she wished he'd take off his shirt. But he seemed more intent on kissing her than on taking off his clothes. And her hands were busy at the moment, sinking deep into that unruly mop of hair that fascinated her.

She shouldn't like it as much as she did, shouldn't be so damn turned on by it. She usually went for guys with razor-sharp short hair who looked like they got a trim every two weeks.

She was pretty sure Will's hair hadn't seen a scissors in months. Again, not uncommon for hockey players. And probably why she—

With a quick move that made her squeak into his mouth and tug on his hair, he twisted them until he had his back propped against the couch arm and her body stretched out over top of him.

Amazingly, he never stopped kissing her. And now she was pressed from breast to thighs and everywhere in between against his body.

That broad chest was a solid wall beneath her soft breasts. Hard thighs bunched and flexed against hers. And his thick erection pressed against her mound and stomach.

Holy hell, the man was hung.

Her sex gave an enthusiastic clench as she moaned into his mouth and practically melted into him.

Christ, where did she start?

Since he was handling the kiss so well, maybe she'd start at the opposite end. Releasing his hair, she slid her hands to his shoulders so she could get a little leverage to get her knees on either side of his hips.

It took a little maneuvering because she wasn't giving up his mouth but she finally got them set. Sitting back on his thighs, she sucked on his tongue and put her hands flat on his chest.

And, oh, holy fuck, did he feel amazing. So firm. So warm. So... delicious. She wanted to take a bite out of him.

Instead, she kneaded at those flat, taut muscles before she found his pointed nipples and plucked them between her fingertips.

She heard him growl low in his throat and his hands clamped onto her hips, not dragging her closer but holding her tight enough that she wanted to lean forward. Okay, maybe she'd already wanted to lean forward so she could rub against that firm ridge in his jeans, but now she wanted it even more.

But if she rubbed against him, she wouldn't be able to get her hands on him. And she really wanted to put her hands around his cock. And probably her mouth, too. If she was lucky, he'd return the favor and put his mouth on her. All over her.

He made a move to break their kiss but she followed him, making him give her more of what she wanted. And she wanted it all.

Every tiny movement of his lips against hers made her blood pound harder in her veins. Every slide of his tongue made her pussy wetter.

When he pulled away this time, she let him go.

"So, just to be clear." He raised his eyebrows. "We're gonna do this?"

"If by 'this' you mean make out some more? Absolutely."

"And if I mean have sex? Does making out mean having sex? You're several years younger than me so the terminology might be different."

Her smile widened as he spoke. "You're not *that* much older. Unless...there's some issues I need to know about?"

Now, his lips curved in a grin that made her want magical powers so she could wish away their clothes and then, yes, there would be sex. Lots of sex.

And she would be breaking her most important rule. Well, technically, she'd already broken her rules by going out with him tonight. So she might as well say to hell with everything and indulge herself.

And Will was one big freaking indulgence she planned to devour all night. Might as well not bother to get cute about it. Might as well own it because now that she had him here, she wasn't stopping.

"Hon, I have no issues. Unless you count the massive hard-on I wish to hell you'd give some attention."

"Oh, I'm paying attention, big guy. You just need to learn a little patience."

"Patience is overrated."

And yet, he hadn't moved. His hands remained exactly where he'd put them several minutes ago, which was on her hips.

"No, it's not."

Now that she'd made up her mind to have him, a little of her urgency faded. She didn't want him any less. But she was no longer in a hurry.

Until—

"Wait, I totally forgot. You play Binghamton tomorrow." Jesus, how could she forget? "Shit, you need to get home and get some sleep. That's a big game. Their offense has been on fire—"

He laughed so loudly, she was pretty sure her neighbors could hear him.

"Hey! This is no laughing matter. The team needs you to be on your game—Will!"

Suddenly, she found herself on her back on the couch beneath him, staring up at him. His hands pressed into the cushions on either side of her shoulders as he leaned down. All those messy waves of hair curtained his face and she bit her lip against the urge to sink her fingers in it again. Damn, she really had a thing for his hair.

"Sweetheart, I'm pretty sure if I leave now, I wouldn't be able to sleep anyway. Trust me. You'll be doing me a favor if you keep me up a few more hours taking care of my...issues."

She swallowed as he lowered his hips and pressed his erection firmly into her mound. If he rolled just the tiniest bit, he'd press against her clit and that would simply be the best thing in the world right now.

"So can I stay or must I go home to my own, cold little bed?"

He attempted a pitiful expression that only managed to make her laugh. "You were a menace as a kid, weren't you?"

"I haven't been a kid in a long time. But my mom will tell you yes. And so will almost every team I've ever played against."

She gave in to the overwhelming urge to touch him and ran her fingers through that silky mess of hair. Pulling it away from his face, she let it fall seconds later so she could cup his jaw and rub her palms against the stubble. And imagine how it was going to feel against her breasts, her stomach, her thighs.

Swallowing hard, she sucked in a deep breath. "This...can't leave my apartment. My job—"

"If that's what you want, I'm fine with it." He stared at her steadily. "My feelings won't be hurt. As long as I can have you here and now, I'll pretend I'm not looking at you like I want to strip your clothes off at the arena. No one will know."

When he said it like that, she felt like a total bitch. A horny, achy, sex-starved, arrogant bitch. And that sucked.

"I just don't want people to get the wrong idea."

He raised his eyebrows and she knew exactly what he was thinking.

The idea being that we're screwing around.

Damn it, she was a hypocritical bitch, too.

Still, she wasn't going to turn into a goody-two-shoes and send him away now. She wasn't a tease. Besides, she wanted him too much to let him leave.

They'd figure out the rest of the shit later.

"Can I stop talking now?" She shook her head. "I'm not making any sense. Can we just go back to kissing?"

"I think that's probably a good plan."

Dropping his head, he kissed her again, and this time he put a little more force behind it, a little more demand.

And oh, holy hell, did she like it. With him looming over her, every single one of her long-buried fantasies about hockey players surged into her head.

The fantasies she'd pushed aside years ago to make room for all those clean-cut, safe boys who pushed pencils instead of the men who slapped pucks and smashed other men into wooden boards.

Will completely surrounded her, shutting out everything else. Settling more heavily over her, the heat of his body combined with the more-demanding kiss made her melt beneath him and she gave a girly little moan that should've embarrassed the hell out of her.

Instead, she wrapped her arms around his broad shoulders and pulled him even closer.

But it still wasn't close enough.

Wiggling her hips a little, she managed to get him positioned more squarely between her legs. Which meant she had an even better impression of his erection. The man felt huge. And hard. And, oh my god, she wanted to get in his pants. Wanted to wrap her hands around him and pump him until he groaned like she had.

But the guy was now an immoveable force. He barely allowed her enough room to breathe much less get her hands down his pants. And she really wanted to get her hands down his pants. It'd been a damn long time since she'd been as turned on as she was now. So horny she could barely function except to react to his touch, his kiss, his every move.

Oh my god, when had she become that girl? The one who went all gooey over a guy?

And why the hell shouldn't you? Isn't that how attraction is supposed to work?

Breaking the seal of their lips, he pressed a line of biting kisses along her jaw to her left ear and bit the lobe, hard enough to sting.

"Your attention is drifting." His husky voice made her skin shiver with goosebumps. "Obviously, I'm not distracting enough."

Her hands moved of their own volition to sink into his hair again, tugging until he lifted his head to look her in the eyes.

"I think we both know exactly how distracting you are. You're here, aren't you?"

His mouth quirked into one of those smiles she found irresistible.

"Yes, I am and I'm not leaving unless you throw me the hell out."

"Don't commit any penalties and you won't be asked to leave."

His smile deepened and her stomach flipped at the glint in his eyes. "What penalties do I need to avoid? Checking?" He pressed his hips down until his erection ground against her mound until she thought his cock had to hurt. "Unsportsmanlike conduct?" He leaned closer and bit her on the jaw then licked away the slight hurt. "Delay of game?"

He pulled himself upright onto his knees so that he loomed over her, crossing his arms over his chest. She had to bite her lip to protest his retreat even as she fought a grin.

Propping herself up on her elbows, she rolled her eyes at him and shrugged. "If you're not careful, you're going to get a bench minor for continuing to chirp at the referee."

He threw back his head and laughed, the sound huge in her quiet apartment. "I can't fucking wait to get you naked and in bed."

Before she could formulate a response, he hopped off the couch then bent and grabbed her around the waist, deadlifting her off the couch. Automatically, she put her legs around his waist and her arms around his shoulders.

"Bed's that way." She nodded her head in the direction of the loft. "Up the stairs." Raising her eyebrows, she couldn't help but challenge him. "Sure you can make it? Wouldn't want you to put your back out."

He started walking, the shift and play of his muscles against her body causing her sex to clench and making sensation shimmer through her.

"Hon, I've been dragging two-hundred-pound men around the ice and out of dive bars for the past fifteen years. I think I can haul your skinny butt up a flight of stairs."

It was on the tip of her tongue to say something disparaging about her ass but then he petted one hand over it and she wanted to melt like ice cream on a hot day. All over him.

"It's a nice ass, by the way." He shifted her closer as he headed up the stairs. "I gotta admit I like watching you walk away from me. You do a lot of that, by the way. Walk away from me. Don't be surprised when I flip you on your stomach so I can fuck you from behind and pet that ass."

Her mouth dropped open before she could catch it and she blinked up at him.

Holy crap, how the hell did that make her even hotter for him? She'd never had anyone speak to her like that before. Not one of the other desk jockeys she'd dated had ever made her want to shove her hands down his pants, pull out his cock, and ride him right here on the steps, within about ten feet of her bed.

No one but this shaggy behemoth with a foul mouth and a reputation for being a tough guy. Who she was discovering had a soft, sweet center.

"Jess." He stopped halfway up the stairs, eyes narrowed as he stared at her. "Shit. Did I—"

Jamming her mouth over his, she cupped his jaw in her hands

and kissed him, forgetting for the moment that they were standing on the stairs. Turns out he was just as steady on stairs as he was on ice.

But she must have taken him by surprise because he hesitated for a millisecond before he opened to her and let her handle the heavy lifting on this kiss. Probably so he could concentrate on getting them up the stairs.

Which was a good thing. She wanted to be spread out on her bed with him naked on top of her.

He got them moving again as she moved her mouth to his neck, where she bit him. And had the satisfaction of feeling him shudder.

The arm around her hips tightened and the hand he had on her back pressed her even closer. A groan rumbled in his chest, and she smiled against his skin and nuzzled her nose against the stubble on his jaw.

"Walk faster." She tugged at his hair. "And when you get to the bed, you need to get your clothes off."

"Fuck."

His voice had dropped another octave but he took the rest of the stairs two at a time without hesitation.

She'd already begun to move her hands down his back, grabbing his shirt and tugging it upward, so by the time she felt him stop, she had his shirt halfway up his back.

"Take this off."

"Sure, hon."

The next thing she knew, she was falling. Hell, he'd practically thrown her at the bed and had his shirt over his head in a flash. She had a second to gape at the chiseled perfection of his chest before he reached for her jeans.

"Fair play." He popped the button with one hand as the other went to his own. "Shirt off now."

The next few seconds were a scramble as they fought to get out of their clothes, tossing them on the floor in a heap.

Their arms tangled as they "helped" each other with their jeans.

He tugged hers off while she pushed his down, taking his underwear with them and leaving him naked.

She paused to let out a totally embarrassing little squeak at the sight of his erection. Thick, not as long as she'd imagined but longer than anything she'd ever seen in person. Porn didn't count. Actually, he put some of the guys she'd seen in porn to shame.

She reached for him—

And found herself flat on her back as he lifted her legs so he could pull off her jeans and panties.

But they were tight and he had to tug at them, which pulled her closer to the edge of the bed.

"What the fuck, Jess? Did you glue them to your legs? Not that I don't appreciate the way they make your legs look, but next time, wear a damn skirt, okay? Your ass looks just as good if not better in one of those."

She'd started to laugh the second time he tugged her so hard, her ass was hanging off the edge of the bed. She had to brace her feet against his bare thighs so she didn't wind up on the floor.

By the time he had them down around her ankles, yanked off her short boots then pulled her pants off, she was gasping.

"Don't wear yourself out." He kicked off his sneakers and dropped to his knees, like he was blocking a shot. "You're gonna need some air."

Then he put his mouth over her pussy and nearly made her scream. Her body had no time to process the sensations as his tongue licked along her labia and up to her clit. Her back arched and she reached above her head to grab at the other side of the mattress, trying to anchor herself.

The man had a wicked tongue that he used to drive her crazy. Swirling over her clit, he flicked at the little nub before sucking on it and making her moan.

As she writhed, he grabbed her hips to hold her steady. Who would've thought the man would be so methodical as he devoured her? She'd expected a fast, almost frantic fuck followed by something a little more leisurely.

Instead, she found herself being pushed, slowly and steadily and maddeningly, toward an orgasm that promised to be epic. Spreading her legs even wider, she reached down with one hand to grab at his hair. Not that he seemed to be going anywhere, but a girl could never be too careful. As he licked and sucked with dedication, her blood chugged through her veins.

With her eyes closed, she gave in to the drugging desire and allowed herself to merely feel.

His tongue worked her clit until she was sure she wouldn't be able to take the sensations anymore. And just when she was ready to beg him to stop, he speared his tongue into her channel and teased her with the hint of what was to come.

By the time he pulled away, her bones felt like they'd melted and her lungs struggled for air.

Forcing her eyes open, she watched as he stood, all traces of his smirk gone. He looked deadly serious and she shivered with anticipation.

His gaze burned as he swept it up her body. Her belly quivered, her breasts ached, and she could barely swallow.

She wanted more, so much more, but even though she wanted to make him rush, she wanted to savor the building heat.

"You look fucking amazing."

His voice triggered tiny explosions all over her body, particularly in her sex, which clenched and begged for his cock.

"Shouldn't that be amazingly fuckable?"

The words popped out of her mouth before she really thought about them but when he grinned, the slight hint of teeth showing in the dim light in the room, she knew it was the right thing to say.

"All of the above, hon. Condoms?"

"Top drawer. Wait. Do condoms expire?" His grin widened and she scowled at him. "Don't you *even* smile about that. You have no idea why those condoms might have been there for...well, too long."

He chuckled and her sex clenched and she wanted to throw something at the damn man. And she wanted him to hurry the fuck up and fuck her already.

"Not laughing at you. I'm wondering how the hell I got so lucky."

Her mouth opened and closed as he turned to the table.

Then she remembered. She'd actually bought new ones the last time she'd made a Target run a few weeks ago. She'd thrown them in her cart almost as a plea to the gods of sex that maybe she'd actually get some if she bought them.

Apparently, it'd worked because she now had a hockey god grabbing those condoms out of her bedside table.

As he turned, she let her gaze fall down his back, where a huge bruise colored his right side above his hip. It looked nasty and she'd be careful and try not to hit it with her heels when she wrapped them around his waist.

Then her gaze slipped even farther, to his ass. And oh holy hell, did the man have one fine ass. She wanted to take a bite out of it. She wanted to pet it.

And then he turned around and she knew she wanted something else much, much more.

Sitting upright, she reached for his cock, wrapping her hands around the hot, hard shaft and squeezing. Not too tight, just tight enough to make him groan.

"Oh hell." His head fell back as she pumped him from root to tip, her heart racing at the feel of his smooth skin sliding against hers. "You keep doing that and I can't guarantee I won't come in your hand."

"Maybe that's something I'd like to see."

She looked up to find him staring intently down at her. "And maybe someday you'll get to but tonight I want to come inside you."

"First, you're going to need to show some of that restraint you've been practicing on the ice."

That was all the warning she gave him. Leaning forward, she put her mouth over the fat tip, swirling her tongue over the slit then sliding her hand down so her mouth could follow.

Hot, hard, and silky smooth, his cock slid against her tongue, drawing a groan from him as his fingers wove through her hair. He didn't pull but he did tug, and the slight sting on her scalp sent a thrill through her as the taste of him on her tongue made her want to test his limits.

He was big enough that she couldn't take him all the way in without feeling overwhelmed. He didn't force the issue but let her work him at her own pace.

And she savored every long, slow slide down his shaft and every hard suck at the tip. With her legs still spread on either side of his knees, she felt sexy and achy and if she weren't using both hands on him right now, she'd put one between her own legs to relieve some of that ache. But as her body tightened and pulsed with building need, she knew that would only make what was going to happen even better.

She moaned around his cock on her next downward swoop and heard his answering groan. Now his hands cupped her head and as she drew back, he pulled her away.

"Enough." His voice sounded like five miles of gravel road, and when she looked up at him through her lashes, she sucked in a quick breath. His face was all hard lines and sharp edges that thrilled her.

"Lie back." He ripped open the condom and her gaze followed his hands as he rolled it down his erection. She had a second to regret the fact that he had to use it but then he grabbed her thighs with those big, rough hands and tugged her closer. Her naked ass slid across the comforter, startling a laugh out of her that quickly died when he wrapped one hand around his cock and angled it down. The tip brushed against her labia, cutting off her laughter as she gasped at the sensation.

Red-hot heat shot through her body from the point of contact, making her legs wrap around his thighs. As if she thought he'd try to get away.

"That's right. That's exactly where I want you. Hold on tight and don't let go, hon."

She was about to tell him to hurry when he shoved forward, stretching her wide and filling her until she wasn't sure she could take any more.

Moaning, she levered her hips up and wriggled even closer, loving the burn.

"Fuck, Jess. You are so fucking sexy. Go ahead. Work yourself on my dick."

She opened her eyes and stared straight into his. "Come on, Will. You need to move."

"I'd rather watch you fuck me. I love the way you move."

His gaze had slipped down to where they were joined and her sex clenched around him in response.

"But I need you. Now."

His gaze shot back to her and his hands tightened on her hips. "Then hold on."

She reached for his wrists as he started to pound into her. He was almost too much to take. Everything about him overwhelmed her. The way he stared at her as he moved in and out of her body. The feel of his cock stretching her. The pinch of his fingers against her skin.

Sucking in air, she tried not to hyperventilate but, oh my god, he made her light-headed. She'd never experienced anything like this before. Had never felt so emotionally connected to another person.

She'd worry about that tomorrow. Tonight, she only wanted to let herself go.

Will's deliberate pace didn't allow her to completely lose herself. If he'd merely pounded into her to get off, she would've been able to simply feel.

Will kept her engaged every second. He watched her, those dark eyes glittering. That connection created an intensely intimate sensation that she couldn't shake. Didn't want to shake.

Moving with him, she fell into a deeper state of excitement that felt like lethargy, even as her body tingled with energy.

"There you go, hon. Let go."

If she let go, she was afraid she'd fall hard. And she couldn't.

But she couldn't help herself as Will thrust again and again, pressing against her clit and building another orgasm.

She tried to stave it off, to hold on to her sanity for just a little while longer. But the more she tried to hold back, the harder Will fucked her.

And she liked it. She liked it a lot. Liked the way he made every thrust feel like a homecoming and every retreat a fucking Greek tragedy.

He held her so tight, she couldn't move. Not that she wanted to but she couldn't help the instinct to writhe against him, to try to take him deeper, even if she knew she couldn't.

On his next retreat, she lifted her upper body so she could put her hand on his abs. "Come closer."

His breath audible in her bedroom, he shook his head. "I'll crush you."

She shook her head from side to side as he pushed inside her again, this time more slowly. "I don't care."

"You will when you can't breathe."

"I can't breathe now. Come here, Will."

For a second, she thought he wasn't going to listen and she was going to have to get demanding.

Then he pulled out and released her completely.

She had a second to mourn the loss as her sex clenched almost painfully around nothing. And then he threw himself down on the bed next to her on his back before reaching for her and pulling her over him.

She had a few moments to marvel at the hardness of his body beneath her before he smacked her ass lightly. "On your knees, hon."

She was already on her way by the time he finished speaking and had her hand on his cock, aiming it back into the aching emptiness between her thighs.

Letting her head fall back as she sank onto him, she moaned as he stretched her wide once again.

"Goddamn, you feel amazing."

Her eyes opened and she looked down at him, another wave of excitement flowing through her at the blazing heat in his eyes.

"But you're still kind of far away," he continued. "Come down here and kiss me."

Putting his hands on her hips, he smoothed them up her sides to just below her breasts, which ached for his touch. As she waited, breathing even more heavily than she had been, his gaze slipped down and he watched his hands continue up to cup her breasts.

Her breasts weren't tiny but they weren't huge either and his hands completely covered them. Molding them to his palms, he caressed her with a firm hold, his thumbs and forefingers pinching her nipples into tight points.

With a moan, she fell forward onto his chest, her hands braced on his shoulders as his hips began to move again. Slowly at first then picking up the pace.

Her mouth dropped onto his, surprising him with a demanding kiss.

As their rhythm began to get out of control, he curved one arm around her hips to keep her pinned to him, while his other hand laced through her hair to hold her steady while he kissed her.

Their tongues dueling and her pussy squeezing around his cock, she came, crying into his mouth as he continued to fuck her through it.

And as she shuddered around him, he gave one last thrust and groaned as his cock pulsed.

Damn.

Just...damn.

SIX

Jess woke when the bed moved.

Her eyes flew open with shock a split second before she remembered what'd happened last night.

"Will?"

"Shit, sorry. Didn't mean to wake you. It's still pretty early. Go back to sleep."

"Are you leaving?"

He'd made it around to her side of the bed and looked down at her. "Wasn't sure how you wanted to handle the morning after so I figured I'd make it easy on you and leave."

Trust Will to want to make it easy on her by saying the one thing guaranteed to make her feel guilty. Even though she didn't feel guilty about last night. Not at all.

She held out her hand. "Stay."

He looked from her hand back to her face. "Don't have to ask me twice."

Dropping his pants back onto the floor, he grabbed the covers and yanked them down, causing her to yelp in surprise then laugh as he crowded against her until she scooted over just enough for him to fit on the bed.

Without missing a beat, he curled his arm around her and rolled her onto her other side so he could pull her back into the curve of his body. Where she quickly realized morning sex was *not* out of the picture.

"Were you really going to leave?"

She felt him shrug. "Didn't want to but I would've if you hadn't woken up. And yeah, I might've made a little more noise than I should have."

Chuckling under her breath, she snuggled back into him, marveling at the amount of heat coming off this man's body. "I don't want you to go. You're like my own personal furnace."

"Hon, I'll be your own personal whatever-you-want. But I gotta tell you, I'm probably gonna eat you out of house and home this morning."

"Then you're lucky I just went to the grocery store."

Mentally, she took stock. Eggs, pancake mix, milk, fruit, bread. More than enough to feed a man who probably ate a thousand calories at breakfast, especially on a game day.

"What time is it?"

"Close to seven."

Stifling a yawn with one hand, she pressed her ass against his crotch and grinned when he clamped his hand on her hip to hold her still then leaned close and bit her neck.

"Play nice or you're gonna find yourself riding my cock again."

Her pussy clenched and her lungs seized. "And why do you think I'd have a problem with that?"

His lips quirked. "Glad to hear it. But I don't want you to get the idea that I'm easy."

God, she loved how he made her laugh. She didn't think she'd ever laughed with a man as much as she did with Will. Especially not in bed.

Dangerous. Oh so dangerous.

"And now you're laughing at me. If I wasn't so secure in my masculinity, I might have a problem with loss of critical mass."

The glint in his eyes made it clear he wasn't serious. And she couldn't help herself.

She reached behind her to pet his hip, felt his heart beating hard and strong against her back. "I think I need to check that for myself."

Then she wiggled around until she was on her side facing him. Her fingers landed on his chest then started a slow slide down, trailing over his nipples, tight and pointed, to his washboard abs.

Her breath caught in her lungs as his muscles shifted and hardened. She had the almost overwhelming urge to follow her hands with her tongue. And why shouldn't she? She'd already crossed the line by having him in her bed. What's a little blowjob after the night they'd had?

Just thinking about making him come with her mouth made every muscle in her body tense with anticipation.

"Jess."

Her hands continued their downward track as she stared into his eyes, narrowed with lust. Holding his gaze, she brushed the backs of her hands along his shaft, feeling it jerk in response. Her fingers, however, continued lower, between his legs to cup his balls. Heavy and warm, they filled her palms and she fondled them carefully. His breathing deepened and he swallowed hard, but he didn't move.

Emboldened, she kept one hand on his balls and moved the other to his cock. Her fingers curved around him, her grip tightening before she began to pump him.

His eyelids flickered closed for several seconds, his lips parting as he audibly sucked in air. She went wet with lust and ached to feel his hands on her.

She got her wish a second later when one hand landed on her hip and slid back to cup her ass. His other hand slid beneath her to land in the middle of her back. She wouldn't have been able to move unless he allowed it.

She wasn't going anywhere except closer.

Increasing her pace, she tightened her hold and leaned in for a kiss. He obliged immediately, his mouth devouring hers as if he were starved. Pulling her closer, he trapped her hands between them until she was practically jerking herself off as she did him.

Her knuckles brushed against her clit every time she stroked his cock, winding her even tighter.

And the way he kissed her, like he wanted to inhale her, made her press her hips even more firmly against his. She couldn't ever remember wanting someone so much she burned for him. All it had taken was one confident hockey player and she was sunk.

Now she just needed to get him on his back—

He shifted away from her without warning and her eyes flew open. He'd moved so fast, she'd barely gasped out her distress when he flipped her onto her stomach.

"On your knees." He didn't wait for her to comply. He picked her up by the hips and set her on her knees. "God damn— Hold that thought."

Face pressed against the mattress, ass in the air, she started to laugh. Beneath her, the bed jiggled as he hopped off to get a condom from the drawer. She wanted to tell him it was okay not to use it, that she'd been cleared and she knew he had been, too, or he wouldn't be allowed to play.

But it felt too intimate, which was ridiculous considering.

"I guess it takes a little while for your brain to get moving in the morning."

"Hon, you scrambled my brain last night and I'm in no hurry to get it back together."

Her bare thighs barely had time to chill before he was back, working his knees between hers and spreading her legs apart.

She groaned as he rubbed his cock between her cheeks, his hair-roughened thighs pressed against hers, teasing and tormenting.

"You have the cutest fucking ass I have ever seen." His hands punctuated his statement by cupping her cheeks and kneading them, then spreading them apart. "Open your legs. I want back in."

Which was exactly where she wanted him, filling that empty space inside her that ached for him.

But even as she was complying, he slipped one hand between her thighs to test her readiness. Fingers sliding through her slick lower lips, he groaned as he played with her. Flicking her clit then dipping his fingers inside her. At first, it was only one and she needed more. But he seemed determined to tease.

"Will, please."

He worked another finger in beside the first and stroked high inside, setting off tiny quakes throughout her body.

"So tight. So fucking hot. I want to feel you come around my fingers. Do it, hon. Come around my fingers and then I'll give you what you want."

Just the sound of his voice pushed her over the edge and she cried out into the mattress as she orgasmed.

"Fuck, yes."

When he pulled his fingers out seconds later, she pounded her fists in frustration, bereft and aching.

A millisecond later, she felt him fit his cock at her entrance and thrust forward. He didn't go slow. He barreled his way inside and it was exactly what she wanted. Filled hot and hard and so stretched, it almost hurt.

Wiggling her ass back at him, she tried to get him even deeper, even though she felt the slap of his balls against her thighs and knew he was in all the way.

Without waiting for him, she began to move, grinding on him as she became increasingly frantic and her orgasm continued to roll through her.

"Jesus, Jess. That's— Holy fuck, you're gonna make me— *Fuck.*"

On her next push back, he shoved forward, getting impossibly deeper and spreading her even wider.

Crying out, she grabbed at the sheets to hold herself steady as he fucked her hard. He didn't hold back and she let him have her as she wound down from her climax.

He seemed in no hurry to come, slowing his pace slightly, as if he were drawing out the moment.

"Jesus, you feel amazing. I wanna stay here all fucking day, making you come."

In a sexual haze, she knew she'd agree to anything right now so she bit her tongue, afraid to reveal too much.

Instead, she tightened her muscles around him and had the satisfaction of hearing him groan. One hand slid around her waist and before she knew what he was doing, he'd lifted her upper body off the bed until they were both upright.

It changed the angle of penetration, hitting different sensory spots inside that had her groaning and clutching at his arms to steady herself.

Now he slowed even more, each thrust seeming to take forever and each retreat an eternity until he came back inside.

Her head fell back on his shoulder as her body gave itself over to him and let him have anything and everything he wanted.

On his next thrust, he held himself inside as they both breathed so heavily she was sure the neighbors could hear them

"You were made for me, I swear. Perfect." His words brushed against her neck as he pulled her hair to one side so he could sink his teeth into her. "Fucking perfect."

Shuddering as he bit her again, she dug her fingernails into his arms. "Move, dammit."

"Maybe I don't want to." He licked at her earlobe then bit it, hard enough for her to wince. "Maybe I want to keep you here all fucking day, coming around my dick."

Every passing second made the ache in her pussy stronger. She hadn't thought she'd be able to come again but he was proving her wrong and now she wanted it. Now.

"Then you need to actually fuck me."

"I'm going to. I just need to—"

He lifted her, just enough to get her knees off the bed but still keeping his cock inside her. Then he moved them closer to the headboard.

"Hands on top. Hold tight. Don't wanna hurt you but now I'm going to fuck you like I need to."

She had a split second to suck in much-needed air before she did exactly what he wanted.

Gripping the top of her sleigh bed's frame, she braced just in time for his first thrust. Strong enough to move her forward, even as she held herself away.

God, yes.

Now he gave her exactly what she wanted and what he needed.

A hard, rough fuck that wrung them both dry.

"MORNING SKATE IS OPTIONAL TODAY, yes? So you don't have to be to the arena until three for the game."

Will gathered up the dishes and walked to the counter to put them in the dishwasher. Jess had made pancakes and eggs and sausage, enough to feed an army. Which was a good thing because he was hungry enough to eat a horse. After the sex last night and more sex this morning, he needed the calories.

"Yeah, but I told Justin and a few of the other guys I'd meet them this morning. Justin and I want to run a few drills before tonight's game. But after the game, I don't have any plans."

He hoped to hell to be back here after the game but he didn't want to push. He had a feeling if he did, he wouldn't get far. It had to be her decision.

She remained silent so he continued. "You gonna be busy tonight?"

Leaning back against the counter in her open kitchen, he let his gaze travel over her.

Wearing yoga pants and an oversized shirt that fell off her shoulders and was buttery soft to the touch, her hair loose and wavy around her shoulders, she looked sexy as fuck. Like she'd spent the night in bed getting wild, which was pretty much what had happened.

Sitting at the small breakfast bar dividing the kitchen area from the rest of the living space, she had her chin propped on her hand as she watched him with those soft brown eyes. He couldn't read her expression, couldn't tell how she felt about him.

Which sucked, because he knew how he felt about her.

Last night had been the best night of his life not spent on the ice. The sex had been amazing but his feelings for her were about more than sex. It'd gone way past sex and into an emotion he'd never experienced, not even with his former fiancé. An emotion that had taken root from the first moment he'd met her.

He wasn't ready to put a label on it yet but he knew himself well enough to know he wanted to pursue whatever it was they had.

Shaking her head and breaking the connection between them, she reached for her mug of hot chocolate and took a sip before answering. "Three groups of fifteen or more and a couple of birthday parties. Nothing huge. Should be an easy day. But you guys'll have your hands full tonight."

"Binghamton's been on a winning streak and their offense is red hot."

"Yeah, their defense has been on fire, too."

The conversation that followed was totally unique in his morning-after experience as Jess broke down Binghamton's stats in a way not even Coach had. It made him adjust his growing erection in his shorts.

A woman who could talk hockey wasn't unusual. He'd met several. But a woman who could quote meaningful stats off the top of her head made him want to pledge his undying adoration.

Fuck it. "Can I see you after the game?"

She didn't say anything right away but she didn't look surprised, either. She looked like she was considering her choices, and he had a few seconds to wonder if maybe he needed to get on his knees and do a little begging. Or maybe he'd pull those pants off her, set her on the counter, and lick her pussy like he had last night. She'd liked that. And it wouldn't be a bad way to continue the morning.

As the silence dragged on, he noticed a faint blush start to paint her cheeks. Maybe she could read his mind. Or maybe she was having the same dirty thoughts he was.

Finally, she drew in a deep breath. "Yes. I'll meet you here." Her smile made a quick appearance. "I'll even feed you."

"You do that and I'll make you come at least twice before I have to leave."

He added that last bit so she didn't think he'd expect to stay the night. Besides, the team had practice Monday and he needed to get enough sleep to keep up with the kids. If he stayed with her, which was what he wanted to do, he'd be awake most of the night making her cry out his name.

Her smile made his heart beat like a Metallica drum line. Christ, he felt like a teenager with a hard-on for the cheerleader. Although he'd never really had a thing for cheerleaders. Too perky, too much work, too high maintenance.

Which probably explained why he was still single at thirty-three. He hadn't met a woman yet who wasn't high maintenance.

But this one...

Her head cocked to the side, a smile flirting at the corners of her mouth. "Are you going to bring dessert?"

She wanted to play. He could do that. "Depends on what you have in mind. I know you like chocolate, but what's your opinion on strawberries? Bananas? Chocolate-covered strawberries and bananas?"

Her smile grew. "Why don't you just bring a jar of hot fudge and whatever...fruit you like and we can find out what we want to dip in the fudge."

By the time she'd finished, he was grinning and she had a gleam in her eyes that promised so much more than dinner later tonight.

SEVEN

"Will, hang on a minute."

Turning just before he reached the door to the arena parking lot after the optional practice, Will saw Cary striding up the hall behind him and resisted the urge to grimace.

"Hey, what's up?"

"Can you and I talk for a few minutes?"

"Sure."

Truthfully, he didn't really want to talk to Cary, at least not right now. He wanted to get back to the apartment and take a nap before the game tonight. He'd had a good practice but he'd mentally switched gears and was in game mode. Like all players, he had a system for game days and hated to be thrown off. Of course, staying with Jess last night had been a huge disruption. But a good one.

Justin had given him a shit-eating grin when he'd walked into the apartment this morning but he'd been surprisingly silent and hadn't asked where he'd been. As if he'd already known.

Which probably should've concerned Will but really, the only thing he was thinking about was Jess.

Cary looked him straight in the eyes. "Novak's leaving earlier than expected. I'm stepping behind the bench Wednesday night."

Well, shit.

Will held out his hand with a sincere smile. "Congrats, man. Well deserved."

Cary took his hand, his expression wry, as if he wasn't quite sure how to take Will's compliment. "Thanks. Appreciate it. It's a little more sudden than I thought it was going to be but...I'm ready. Have been for a little while."

Will took a closer look at Cary. He'd noticed the guy had seemed a little quieter than normal during practice, but he'd put that down to Cary being Cary. He'd known the guy for years, knew he internalized everything, sometimes to a fault.

Cary thought Will didn't internalize enough. Just one of the differences between them.

"I know you and I haven't exactly seen eye to eye before so I want us to be on the same page here."

That didn't sound promising and his expression must have shown his thoughts because Cary grimaced.

"Do we have a problem I don't know about?" Will asked.

Cary rubbed a hand through his hair. "No, actually, we don't. We have some history and I want to put that behind us. You and I are really different players, and years ago I may have been a little, ah, less than flexible about certain things."

Will couldn't help himself. "Are you trying to say you had a stick up your ass about the kind of game I played?

Cary's smile was a surprise. "Maybe a little. But you've got to admit you played a different game back then. Your game has changed and so have you."

He shrugged, conceding the point. "Maybe we've both gained a little experience over the years."

"I like to think so. I just wanted you to know we aren't going to have a problem now that I'm behind the bench. You've been a good addition to the team. I admit I wasn't too sure before you got here, but in just three games, you've managed to stabilize these kids a little. That fight Friday... You stuck up for our guys. That's why Coach brought you in. He recognized a hole in our lineup and he knew how to fill it."

Which gave Will an opening he hadn't expected. "About that... Is it true Jess Gardiner had a hand in bringing me in?"

Cary's brows raised. "Where'd you hear that?"

"Does it matter?"

"No, actually, it doesn't. Yeah, she did. But you know she's Doug Gardiner's daughter, right?"

Will nodded.

"Then you know she's been around the game all her life. She's like a hockey statistics database. When she threw out your name, my immediate response was, 'Hell no.'" Cary held up his hands with a grimace. "But then she threw out your stats and surprised everyone. She was absolutely right."

"Does she scout for the team?"

"Not in any official capacity. She's never come out and said she wanted to be considered for a position as a scout."

"Would she be? Considered, I mean."

Cary's gaze narrowed with speculation. "Why are you so interested?"

Will had never believed in blowing smoke, but he knew Jess didn't want their relationship to be common knowledge. "Just curious, I guess. If she was smart enough to look at me," he grinned to let Cary know he wasn't being a completely self-centered dick, "she must be good at what she does."

"She's amazing at her job but she's a natural scout. Too bad it's not what she wants to do or I'd ask the club to hire her in a heartbeat."

"Have you ever told her that?"

Cary nodded. "As a matter of fact, I have."

"Out of still more curiosity, what'd she say?"

Pausing for a moment, Cary gave him another searching glance before his mouth curved into a slight grin. "So there is something going on between the two of you. Damn, I owe Lori money."

Okay, maybe keeping their secret was going to be a hell of a lot harder than he'd thought. "I don't know what you're talking about."

"Uh-huh." Shaking his head, Cary's grin faded. "She laughed and said something like the good-ol'-boys club wasn't something she wanted to join and then shut me down. She's smart as hell and she's not wrong about a lot of things, but if you have any sway with her, please feel free to repeat my offer. Not sure the big club would agree but I trust her judgment implicitly."

Will felt the exact same way.

———

BECAUSE SHE ONLY HAD A FEW groups to take care of today, Jess was pretty much finished by the end of the second intermission.

Which meant she could sit and watch the entire third period unless something came up.

She'd already realized Lori and Bliss weren't in their usual row, where the wives and girlfriends usually sat. Which meant...

Yep, there they were. In the ADA section with Bliss's friend Faith, who used a wheelchair.

"Hey, Jess. How've you been? Haven't seen you for a while."

"Hi, Faith. Good to see you."

"Hey, there." Lori patted the seat beside her. "Are you done for the day?"

"Pretty much. The guys look good today."

From the other side of Faith, Bliss leaned over and smiled but Jess saw the nerves in her eyes. "I'm trying to watch but, oh my god, I cringe every time Binghamton has the puck. And sometimes, I actually have to close my eyes. Don't tell Shane. I'm such a wuss."

While everyone laughed, no one mentioned the "S" word. The score was two-nothing with seventeen minutes to play. If that stayed the same, Shane would have a shutout. But hockey superstition was strong and everyone knew you didn't even whisper that word until the game was over.

"Shane already knows you're a wuss." Faith paused as the crowd shouted at the referee for a missed call on Lad, who looked like he was having trouble getting to the bench. "But the man still loves you. If *I* didn't love you, I'd be all over that hot bod of his."

"Shane is a—"

She gasped as Will skated onto the ice and immediately got checked hard into the boards as he went after the puck.

The crowd started to yell and berate the refs but she couldn't take her eyes off Will. He was slow to respond, slightly bent at the waist as if he'd had the wind knocked out of him.

She wasn't aware she was on her feet until Will finally started to move again and she sank back into her seat.

And found three women staring at her with knowing grins on their faces.

Busted.

"So..." Lori smirked. "Someone's been keeping secrets."

Jess bit her tongue, thought about her response, and settled for, "I don't know what you're talking about."

Which she knew wouldn't fly.

"Uh-huh. You know you're not fooling anyone, right?"

Jess slid Lori a quick glance, fighting the urge to stick out her tongue, which would prove exactly what Lori thought she knew.

"I don't know why you think you need to keep it a secret." Lori leaned over and knocked her shoulder against Jess's. "It's not like you're breaking any laws."

"I still don't know what you're talking about." Then, because she couldn't help herself, she asked, "But out of curiosity, what, exactly, did you hear?"

Lori's smile spread. "You know exactly what I'm talking about. Hockey players gossip like little old ladies. Cary came home this afternoon and told me. Said Justin mentioned that Will hadn't come home last night and that the guy had been here less than a week and was already dating the untouchable Miss Jess. They're all in awe, by the way. Most of the kids already think he's the next best thing to replaceable blades."

"Come on, Jess. Spill." Faith leaned over, wrapping her arm around Lori's shoulder. "Some of us haven't seen a naked male body in longer than we care to admit. And that one looks like he's all sorts of fine."

Dammit, what the hell did she say to that? On one hand, she wanted to spill everything, tell them just how fine he was. On the other... Fuck it.

Leaning over so she didn't have to raise her voice, she said, "He's amazing. He's quiet but he's funny and, oh my god, he's just so..."

She shook her head.

"Hot?" Faith said.

"Sweet?" Bliss.

"Fuckable?"

That last was from Lori, who waggled her eyebrows and grinned as Faith and Bliss laughed and Jess closed her eyes and shook her head.

"Oh, come on." Lori knocked her shoulder against Jess's. "We're happy for you. I've been worried that you've been all work and no play lately. I know it's tough during the season because you're always busy but you need to make time for yourself."

Jess heard the genuine affection in Lori's voice and flashed her friend a quick smile. "It's just new."

Which it was. But...it didn't feel new. It felt right. More right than any other relationship. And as much as she didn't want to get involved with a hockey player, she wanted Will. She wanted to *try* with Will.

"And..." Lori prompted.

Jess opened her mouth to speak but the crowd began to cheer and her gaze immediately sought out Will. Who was in the middle of an unruly gathering in the Redtails' defensive zone.

A Redtails player lay on the ice behind him as he shoved bodies out of the way. Lad knelt on the ice over their downed man.

"Oh, no." Lori leaned forward in her seat, almost as if she was going to rush out on to the ice. "That's Jake."

Jess's heart gave a painful lurch. She hated to see any player laid out on the ice, but Jake was one of those guys who was a favorite of the team and the fans.

Several long seconds passed as the Binghamton players retreated to their bench and the Redtails trainer shuffled out onto the ice. Kneeling down next to Jake, he leaned over and spoke in Jake's ear. Jake hadn't moved since going down and she knew the trainer was asking how bad it was.

And when the trainer looked up into the stands to where the team doctor usually sat, she knew it might be really bad.

"Dammit, that was a bad hit." The anger in Lori's voice didn't surprise Jess. She would've said the same. "And no penalty. That guy better watch his back next shift. Someone's gonna take him out."

Jess's gaze automatically went to Will, as he and Lad helped Jake off the ice to the crowd's applause. Between them, Jake used only his right leg to skate to the bench, then slung his arm around the trainers' shoulders as they helped him down the hall to the locker room.

As the team gathered at the bench before play resumed, she saw Will stare directly at the opposing team's bench before taking a seat and waiting for his next shift.

"Your guy just marked that player for a world of hurt," Lori said. "And I don't blame him one bit. That was a cheap shot."

"I hope Will lays the bastard out."

———

"PUCKS DEEP, guys. Make smart passes. Two minutes to go. No stupid penalties. Mac, you're double-shifting with Lad."

Will nodded as the ref blew his whistle, calling the team back onto the ice for the face-off. Jake had looked scared as they'd taken him off the ice. Will could tell there was definitely something wrong with the kid's leg that wasn't just a sprain.

Will had seen him go down, his leg twisted at a weird angle. If he hadn't broken it, then he was lucky as shit. And if he had…

They'd be without him for weeks. Possibly the rest of the season.

Fuck.

Will wanted to flatten the sonuvabitch who'd hurt Jake but he'd heard Coach. No stupid penalties. Which meant he had to keep his shit together, even when his first instinct was to lay out the other player hard.

But if he did, he was afraid the entire team would devolve around him. They were pissed off and worried, and that made for a toxic mix.

Cary was on the ice taking the faceoff, stoic as always. The other four guys—Flaherty, Lindback, Johnson, and Perry—looked tense but determined.

The puck dropped and Will watched Cary battle for control and win, giving the Redtails the opportunity for a shot on net.

They kept up the pressure, managing to keep the puck in the offensive end, and after another four shots, the goalie finally covered the puck and the next shift took the ice.

As he and Lad went over the boards, Lad caught his eye and Will saw fury.

Will skated over to him. "Ninety seconds. We keep the puck in their zone. We don't let them shift us off our game."

Lad growled, his Russian accent so thick Will could barely understand. "I will knock that asshole into next week."

"No, you won't." Will stared into Lad's eyes. "We stay focused. We get outta this game up three and then we take names. Got it?"

Lad drew in a deep breath, his jaw clenched, then drew in another breath and nodded.

Now they worked.

Relentlessly, they kept the puck in Binghamton's end. And even when Binghamton took a few more cheap shots, everyone stayed focused.

And when the final buzzer sounded and the team skated back to congratulate Shane on the shutout, Will made sure he locked eyes with the player who'd hit Jake. The guy smirked and headed off, but Will had his name and number.

They had a game in Binghamton in two weeks. And Will had a long memory.

But first...he had a date tonight.

"WILL."

"Come on, hon. Let go."

With Jess's body draped over his, his hands on her hips holding her steady, Will pumped inside her warm body at a pace guaranteed to give him heart failure.

But what a hell of a way to go.

"Not yet." Her voice whispered in his ear just before she licked at it. "Don't want you to stop."

He could barely hear her over the sound of his own labored breathing, but he definitely felt her latch her sharp little teeth onto his earlobe and bite down. Jerking beneath her, he jammed his cock even higher inside her, wanting to consume her completely.

"I'm not going anywhere. But you have to come first. I want to feel you milking my cock. I want you to scream so loud your neighbors hear. And then I'm gonna roll you over and I'm going to fuck you until you pass out."

He groaned when she clenched around him, his hands tightening on her hips as she worked her clit against the base of his cock.

"That's right, hon." He petted one hand down her flank, cupping her ass and pressing her down even harder. "Take what you want. I'll give you anything."

She could have it all. Everything and anything she wanted from him.

And he hoped to hell she wanted everything because he certainly did.

She'd left the light on when they'd come upstairs not long after he'd arrived. He hadn't expected her to grab his hand and tug him up the stairs after her. Hadn't expected her to strip him with quick hands, making him even harder and hornier than he'd been when he walked through her door.

But when she'd gotten his pants halfway down his legs, cupped his balls in one hand, and wrapped the other around his cock, raw need for her consumed him. Nothing had mattered except getting inside her.

He'd *missed* her today, had literally ached for her. The game had been tough and Jake's injury had set everyone on edge.

Now, here with her, all of that faded until all he knew, every conscious thought was about her.

Her warm naked body pressed against his and kept his cock hard and his blood pumping furiously. Every sound she made deepened the connection he felt to her as his body strained toward release.

When she angled her body up with her hands on his chest and let her head drop back, he watched her ride him. She looked transported, her lips parted slightly, plump and wet from his kisses.

Her body moved so sinuously, he couldn't resist running his hands up her sides to mold over her breasts. As he caressed her, she sank even lower on his cock, wriggling her hips until he had to bite his tongue against the urge to come.

"So fucking beautiful."

His guttural statement made her eyes flutter open.

"I could say the same about you." Deliberately slowing her pace, she smiled down at him, so beautiful she took his breath away. "So strong. So tough. So hard."

She clenched around his cock, making his eyes roll back in his head at the rush of heat.

"Come on, Will. Lose it. I want you to—"

The rest was lost in a moan as he thrust his hips off the bed to meet her next downward stroke, setting off her orgasm.

She fell forward, draping over him again as she climaxed, her body squeezing him, milking his response.

Wrapping his arms around her, he made good on his earlier promise and flipped them without losing a stroke.

And then he fucked her hard and fast, his hips pistoning as he lost himself in her.

When his cock finally began to soften, he sighed and shifted off her, rolling them both onto their sides then drawing her in tight against his still-heaving chest.

She was just as out of breath as he was as she tucked her head under his chin and went boneless against him.

Soft, warm, and scented like sex and a hint of something floral, she made him think of nights spent making love and days spent together. All day. Every day. He liked the sound of that.

When she yawned and snuggled even closer, he figured she was about to fall asleep. Since he was beat, that wouldn't be a bad thing but he needed to know if he could stay. He wanted to stay. Hell, he'd even packed extra clothes in his bag just in case. But he had to ask.

"Jess?"

"Mm-hmm."

"Can I stay?"

She didn't answer right away and several long seconds passed. Then she pulled back and looked up at him with drowsy, beautiful eyes.

"Yes. Please." Then she snuggled back into him. "God, you're warm. Like a huge furnace."

He chuckled. "Glad to know I'm good for something."

"I think you know just how good you are. I didn't get to ask when you got here—"

"Because you were ripping my clothes off, by the—ow!"

She bit his pec, hard enough to make him flinch. Then she licked at it before she stared up at him with a grin.

"Hey, now." He wove his fingers through her hair and held her steady so she couldn't look away. "What was that for?"

Her eyebrows rose in a superior little arch. Adorable. "You know exactly what that was for." Then her expression sobered. "But seriously, did you hear anything about Jake?"

He shook his head, his expression darkening. "All I know is he was still being evaluated. We need Jake whole if we're gonna make another push for the Cup. If he's out six weeks, that's a serious blow to our defense."

"I know. He and Lad were playing like a well-oiled machine. That's really going to throw a wrench in the lines."

The conversation he'd had with Cary earlier today popped into his head. "Who would you bring in to fill the hole?"

She took a bare second to think about her response. "Abbot. He's been on fire for Lancaster— Why are you smiling at me like that?"

"Because when you talk hockey, you make me hard."

She rolled her eyes but her lips curved in a smile he wanted to lick off her lips.

"Then I guess we'd better stop. Wouldn't want to sap all your strength for practice."

Tightening his arms around her, he repositioned her so she was eye-to-eye.

"I'll be sure to carbo load before we spend time together. I plan to do a hell of a lot of carbo loading."

Her smile faded. "Will—"

"Hey, it's okay. I'm not trying to pressure you, okay? You don't want anyone to know we're involved. I get it. And I'm okay with it."

TILTING her head to the side, Jess narrowed her gaze at Will.

What the hell? Had he read her mind?

Ridiculous, considering she wasn't sure what she'd been going to say.

But now that he'd brought up the subject, she should be grateful. Right?

Then why did she have an ache dead center in her chest? Did he not want anyone to know they were dating?

"And you're okay with that? Seriously?"

He shrugged, looking as if he didn't really care one way or the other. "I guess I can understand your reasoning. And I'm willing to go along with it."

Really? This was *not* what she'd expected. She'd expected him to give her a hassle.

And now...she didn't know what to think.

This is what you wanted, right?

Wasn't it?

Lying here naked with him, his hair messy and sticking up all over the place and his scruff even more pronounced than it had been earlier, she couldn't honestly care if anyone else knew they were together.

Because he was still here. And she wanted him to be here for as long as she could have him. And that thought did not include hiding their relationship.

"And if I said that's not what *I* wanted?"

His gaze never wavered but she saw a glint of humor spark. "Then I guess I'd ask if you were going to start sitting with the WAGs."

Her mouth curved in a smile. "I was tonight. Lori and Bliss and Bliss's friend, Faith. But I can't do that every night. I do have a job."

"A job you're good at. Cary praised you to high heaven today. Although..."

He paused and she could tell he was trying to decide if he wanted to finish that sentence.

"Although...what?"

His hand ran up and down her spine, as if soothing her ruffled feelings. "It's nothing bad. He just said he'd put your name in as a scout in an instant if you expressed an interest."

What the hell? "Did you *say* something to him? About me being a scout? Because he's never said a word to me."

"Maybe because you've never said anything to him. I mean, how would he know you were interested? Except for the fact that you talk hockey like a pro and the coach takes your advice on players. But hey, I guess he got the wrong idea."

She thought about that for a second. "Did he say anything else?"

"Nope. Hear anything about that new job?"

She shook her head, her brain still working over Cary's comments. "No, and I don't really expect to, at least not this soon. Like I said, I'm not sure I'm really the right person for it."

And she'd been having serious second thoughts. All because of this man.

He'd barreled into her life and blown up her steady world like a Mentos in soda in less than a week.

"You're thinking too hard for just having mind-blowing sex." Rolling over onto his back, he drew her along until she was draped over his chest, his heart beating strong under her ear. "A guy could get a complex. Get some sleep. Got practice in the morning and I'm hoping to get a workout in before that. And I don't mean in the gym."

His hand smoothed down her back to pet her ass and she snuggled closer, her body already thinking about more sex. But she felt Will slipping into sleep and knew he needed it.

It took her quite a while longer to shut down her brain enough to sleep.

———

"I'LL MEET you in the lot. I just need to make a quick stop upstairs."

Justin rolled his eyes at Will as his smile widened. "Dude, you're gonna see her in, like, an hour at the hospital. You're pathetic."

Will didn't bother to respond but shot Justin the finger over his shoulder as he headed out of the locker room Tuesday after practice.

Jess had texted him while he was on the ice, asking him to stop up before he headed out to lunch.

Justin was right, he'd see her at the hospital. She accompanied the players whenever they made promotional visits.

But when the woman he'd decided he wanted to keep, probably forever, texted him to stop by before he left for lunch, he went.

He had no idea what she wanted, but when he walked into her office, her expression made him close the door behind him, everyone else be damned. "Hey, what's wrong?"

Her smile was forced and he closed the distance between them in seconds.

"Jess—"

"I have an interview in Philly tomorrow for that job I told you about."

He stopped cold. "What?"

"Tori Roman, head of the marketing department, called me right after I got to the office. She said they've had their eye on me and were glad I'd applied."

His brain spinning, he grappled for something to say. "Damn, that was fast."

"I know. Tori said they'd just found out they were losing someone else in the office for health reasons and they had to move up their timetable."

She ran a hand through her hair, pushing it back over her shoulders. She'd worn it down today and it made him want to twist it around his fingers and tug her closer for a kiss. But he knew that was definitely out of the question.

"What'd you say?"

She rolled her eyes like he'd asked a stupid question, which he probably had. "That I'd be there around ten."

He took a deep, steadying breath, knowing he couldn't say what was on the tip of his tongue. Which was *Don't go.*

Then he took a closer look at her.

"So why don't you look happy?"

"I am." Her brow furrowed. "I *am*. It's just...happening quicker than I thought it would. And I kind of had myself talked into thinking I wouldn't get a call."

Time to suck it up and be the supportive boyfriend even though he wanted to be the asshole who told her not to go. Christ, he'd just found her and he didn't want to lose her, period, end of story.

And that was the perfect way to get kicked out of her bed forever.

"Of course they want you. You're brilliant, dedicated, and know hockey inside and out. But is it really what you want to do?"

She hesitated a split second too long. "Yes. Of course it is. I've been working toward this for six years."

"Then what do you need from me?"

She shook her head. "I don't need anything from you. I don't need your validation if that's what you're asking."

Shit, he was going to fuck this up completely. "That's not what I mean. But you don't look excited."

She huffed out a sigh. "I am. It's just..." She looked up at him, shaking her head. "You complicate things."

Since he knew exactly what she meant, he didn't get offended. But he was getting angry and he couldn't help it. She was torn, he got that. But dammit, it wasn't like she didn't have options.

"Jess, do you want to leave?"

"This is a huge opportunity for me."

"You didn't answer the question."

She grimaced. "I can't because I'm not sure."

"Then I guess you have to make a choice. But I think you should talk to Cary and Coach before you make up your mind."

Her gaze dropped as she shook her head. "That's not going to change anything."

His jaw set against the urge to say something he really might regret. "Jess—"

"You should probably get going. You need to eat before the hospital visit and I have a call I need to make." She smiled up at him, but it didn't reach her eyes, and the pit in the stomach opened just a little deeper. "I'll see you at the hospital."

"Jess, dammit, let me—"

"Will, it's fine. Everything's fine." She smiled again and this time it was a little more natural. But it didn't do anything to fix the feeling of dread starting to creep over him. "It was just a shock and I needed to talk it out with someone so thank you. We can talk about it more tonight."

"In bed?"

Her smile widened. "Yes, in bed, if that's really what you want to spend our time there doing. You have to get to bed early tonight because you leave early tomorrow for your road trip."

He had the almost overwhelming desire to kiss her right now but knew he couldn't. The entire front of her office was glass. Anyone could see in.

Frustrated, he shook his head but knew he couldn't do anything but leave. "We'll make it a short conversation."

"I'm sure we will. Now go. I'll see you at the hospital."

He went but he definitely wasn't happy about it.

EIGHT

"Hey, sweetheart. I'm so glad you could meet me."

Giving her dad a tight hug and a kiss on the cheek, Jess grinned at his happy smile Thursday night.

"Me too. With the team on the road, it was perfect timing."

"I'm just glad to have my baby by my side again at a game."

Sliding his arm around her shoulders, her dad ushered her through security at the team entrance to the Mohegan Sun arena, introducing her to an older man at the door who greeted her dad with a big grin and a hearty handshake.

Everyone knew Doug Gardiner and her dad knew everyone. She'd learned that early on but was reminded as she walked with him through the bowels of the arena a few minutes before the game between Wilkes-Barre and Providence.

She'd been thrilled to get his call Wednesday morning, asking her to meet him here tonight. She'd just said good-bye to Will, as the Redtails headed out on a five-day road trip, and she'd been missing him already.

If you take that job in Philly, you're going to be even lonelier.

Now, as her dad introduced her to everyone from security guards to concession workers to a few season ticket holders he knew by name, she couldn't stop thinking about her very short conversation in bed Tuesday night with Will before he rolled her onto her belly and spread himself over top of her to make love to her with a passion that exhausted her.

Will had only said she should talk to Cary before she made her decision.

What he hadn't known was that she had. When she'd gotten back to the office after the hospital visit, she'd been able to catch both Cary and Coach in Coach's office before they'd left the arena for the day.

Neither of them had been surprised by her request to talk. But she'd left more confused than before.

Will had sensed that something was wrong, but he'd had to leave early the next morning to catch the bus for their road trip and she'd still been asleep.

Wednesday night, she'd gone to Lori's to watch the Redtails game with her, Bliss, Faith, and Tony Dellafranco's fiancé, Mia Wachowski, a shy twenty-two-year-old from a small town in rural Maine where she and Tony had been high school sweethearts.

Jess had spent much of last night talking to Mia, who was very sweet but very lonely. Mia had said something last night that had rolled around Jess's head all day.

"Being apart is hell. And even though I know he's out there and I can see him on the computer during games or talk to him, it's still like I'm missing a limb. But the worst part is that you get used to it. I've gotten used to being lonely and sad."

The thought depressed the hell out of her.

And then the interview this morning—

"Jess? Are you sure you're okay? You've been awfully quiet all night."

Turning to her dad, she saw concern in his eyes. "I had an interview with the Colonials marketing team this morning."

His expression cleared immediately. "You had me worried there for a minute. I thought it was something dire."

"How do you know it's not?"

"Because you're too good for them not to want to bring you up."

His praise made grateful tears spring to her eyes but she blinked them away. "What if it's not what I want?"

Why didn't he look surprised by that? "Then what do you want?"

"What if...I had the chance to scout?"

He didn't look surprised at that either. "Has the NWHL come calling finally?"

She shook her head. "What if Coach Scott pitched my name to the Colonials as a developmental player scout for the ECHL and AHL? What would you tell me?"

His gaze narrowed but he didn't look surprised. "I'd tell you what I've always told you. If you want something, go after it and don't do it half-assed. You're going to face a hell of a lot of opposition but, honey, I trust your judgment more than a few of the men who've been scouting for decades. Yes, I may be biased but I know what you can do."

"What if they give me a shot and I suck? Then I've turned down a major career opportunity and burned that bridge. Hell, the Colonials office might laugh themselves sick at the thought of having the only female scout in the NHL."

"Then they'd be bigoted idiots." His voice had a rough edge but then he shook his head. "But, sweetheart, I know Angstadt and Miller. Angstadt is a fairly young coach and he's more open-minded than most. And Miller's one of the most liberal general managers I've ever met. Word is he's training his daughter to take his place one day."

"But she's played and she's coached at the college level. I don't have that experience."

"No, but what you do have is twenty years of experience by my side and that's more than most scouts can say about their scouting experience." Her dad paused, his eyes narrowed thoughtfully. "I can't make this decision for you, but I don't want you to make it based on what you think others might say about you. Do what *you* want to do and don't let anyone tell you you can't."

Sighing, she nodded. "I know. I guess... I just need a little guidance."

Her dad patted her cheek, making her feel like she was ten again. "Sweetheart, do what makes you happiest. And don't apologize or be afraid to fail. We all fail sometimes. If we didn't, we wouldn't learn anything. But if you don't even try, well, then you're a coward. And *you* are not a coward."

——————

THE TEAM BUS hadn't pulled into the arena until after two a.m. Sunday night. Monday morning. Whatever.

Will had been too damn tired to do anything other than drive back to his apartment with Justin and drop into bed. Coach had called off practice for the morning, but most of the team had made plans to meet for lunch then to work out in the afternoon.

By the time he woke Monday morning, it was almost ten a. m. and Jess had texted several times. He'd called and they'd made plans for him to come over for dinner tonight.

And hopefully stay the night. Their next games were Wednesday and Friday and he had practice every day. He'd had a couple of great games while they'd been away and he planned to keep it up. Which meant being focused. And not letting his head get screwed up with this stuff with Jess.

If she took the job in Philly, she took the job. They'd figure it out. And if they didn't...

He shook off the thought, preferring instead to look forward to tonight.

By the time he knocked on her door, he had half a hard-on just thinking about seeing her again. He didn't want to fall on her like a starving animal, but lust burned through his veins, making his muscles tighten and his lungs labor.

When she opened the door, all his good intentions fled. Her soft smile hit him hard in the gut, his cock pulsing in his jeans. He crossed the threshold as she took a step back but before she could move even farther, he dropped his bag and reached for her waist, lifted her off her feet, and brought her mouth level with his so he could kiss her.

He heard her gasp before her lips met his with heat and passion, her hands sinking into his hair to grip him tight and her legs wrapping around his waist.

When her tongue clashed with his, he won the battle and plunged into the warm depths of her mouth. Moaning, she wriggled her hips against the hard ridge of his erection, inflaming his need.

A split second later, he turned and plastered her back to the door. She wore another pair of those stretchy yoga pants that made her ass look pettable and a soft, flowy top that draped over her curves and gave him immediate access to her bare skin beneath.

Their mouths locked together, his hands slid beneath that top and swept up to cup her bare breasts. With their warm weight filling his palms, he groaned into her mouth, grinding his cock into the softness of her belly.

Arching her back, she softened against him even more, her hands releasing his hair to wrap her arms around his shoulders. Tilting her head to the side, she gave him a little more access to her mouth and he took it hungrily.

That same hunger led him to let his hands drop to her pants and shove them over her hips to bare her ass.

As soon as she dropped her legs for him, he dragged them down to her knees where they then fell to the floor.

As her hands stroked over his shoulders, he wrapped one arm around her waist and used the other to rip open his jeans. He managed to get the condom out of his wallet and pulled back to hold it between them.

"Put it on, hon."

Her lips curved in a quick smile but her hands shook slightly as she ripped it open then rolled it down his shaft.

Her fingers danced along his cock, her gaze burning into his. Her lips, swollen from his kiss, drew him back but only for a second. He wanted to watch her as he lowered her onto him.

It only took a slight adjustment to slip inside her, his cock immediately enveloped in heat. The need to thrust hard and fast threatened to steal his control, but he reined in the raging desire and eased in, centimeter by centimeter.

Leaning forward, he pressed his lips to her forehead then pressed his against hers. "I missed you."

Her labored breathing filled his ears as she stretched around him. "I missed you, too. God, Will, you need to move."

A few more centimeters and sweat beaded his forehead. "No fucking way. This feels too damn good."

"Too fucking slow."

He huffed out a laugh at the frustration in her voice. "There's the classy lady who makes me so fucking hot I can't think."

"I think you need to stop thinking so damn much and move."

She arched her back, sinking down until she almost had him completely engulfed.

"Yes, ma'am. Whatever you want."

Before she had time to draw in another breath, he pulled out and thrust back in. Dirty and hard, his hips nailed hers to the door. Her arms clung to his shoulders and her legs tightened around his waist.

Her every gasping breath brushed against his cheek, making him shudder and thrust faster. He could feel his orgasm building, felt her pussy clenching around him with increased pressure.

"Are you—"

"Harder." Her fingers dug into his back. "Will. Harder. Make me—"

Her cry as she came pierced him to the core and he hammered home several more times before he finally came.

He stood, trying to catch his breath as she went limp against him.

As his cock finally started to soften, he pressed his lips against her cheek.

"Missed you, hon."

"Missed you, too."

HALF AN HOUR LATER, they sat at her dining table, finishing dinner.

She'd had lasagna in the oven so they'd been able to eat as soon as they'd cleaned up.

He hadn't realized something was wrong until just a few minutes ago when he looked at her plate and realized she'd been pushing food around for the past five minutes.

Setting down his fork, he leaned back in his chair. "Jess? What's wrong?"

It took her a second but she finally lifted her gaze to his.

"I talked to Cary and Coach Tuesday before you left."

He put his fork down, curiosity making him jumpy. "Oh?"

"I asked them about scouting."

Fierce triumph flooded through him and he wanted to cheer but he could tell she wasn't done.

"And?"

"They told me if I wanted them to put my name in for consideration, they would. And if the Colonials agreed to give me a trial run, they'd request that the Redtails hire a marketing assistant to help me."

Fuck yeah! That was great news. So why the hell didn't she look happier?

"That sounds great."

She took a deep breath as she shook her head. "I'm going to take the job in Philly."

His heart started to pound and he took a couple of deep breaths. "Why?"

"I have to think long-term. Scouting gives me no options for advancement. Marketing does. I'm going to give them my answer Friday. They want me to start in three weeks."

"You don't know that. Jesus, you'd just be starting—"

"I know I will never get the chance to go farther than the AHL level as a scout." Shaking her head, she looked determined. "I'll always be a *curiosity*. I won't be taken seriously—"

"I take you as seriously as a fucking heart attack. *Coach* takes you seriously. *Cary* takes you seriously. They wouldn't have agreed to float your name if they didn't think you could do it."

She shook her head, her gaze slipping away from his. "But to everyone else I'll just be Doug Gardiner's daughter playing at her dad's job."

"And what everyone else thinks of you is going to stop you from doing what you love?"

Her gaze dropped for a second. "I love my marketing career. I can go so much farther—"

"So all that bullshit about living out your dreams is just that... bullshit. Patting me on the head and telling me how playing at this level is fulfilling my dreams. Of course my dream was to play in the NHL. And I've never stopped playing my best—"

"No, Will, that's not—"

"—to get where I want to be. And if that shot comes, you know I'm damn well going to take it. I'm not going throw up my hands and say 'oh well, I think I'll just stay here because it's safe.'"

Her mouth set in a flat line and he knew he should probably just shut the fuck up.

"That's not fair. Jesus, Will. Why are you sabotaging me on this? I've been working toward this for years, working my way up the chain to an NHL club, and now you're telling me I'm selling out? That's not fair."

"I'm not saying you're selling out. I'm saying you're selling yourself short."

"And I'm leaving you behind and you're pissed."

He could see from her expression that she wanted to take back her words immediately. But they'd already done their damage.

"I'm sorry." Her face crinkled in an angry frown. "Dammit, I'm sorry. I shouldn't have—"

"No." He stood, his chest so tight he could barely breathe. "You're absolutely right. I am pissed but not for the reasons you think. You're right. You should take the job in Philly. You'll be fantastic. I'm not pissed at you. I'm fucking furious at myself for not seeing how this was going to go."

Then he walked to the door and left himself out, closing it behind him with barely a snick.

NINE

"Jess? Can I come in?"

The voice was familiar but unexpected Wednesday noon.

"Lori. Hey, what are you doing here?"

The smile Cary's wife gave her was sweet and serene and way too calm. "I stopped by to take Cary to lunch since I have the afternoon off, but he's busy for another few minutes so I figured I'd say hi."

Jess leaned back in her chair as Lori walked through the door and closed it behind her.

Honestly, she didn't really want to talk to anyone. Since her fight with Will two nights ago, she hadn't seen or spoken to him. And when she knew he was in the building, she found it hard to breathe, even though she knew he wouldn't stop to see her.

Just thinking about him made her heart hurt. But she hadn't sought him out and she wasn't going to. Better this way. A clean break. Less heartbreak.

Not that clean and damn, my heart hearts.

Forcing a smile, she watched Lori fall into the seat opposite her.

"So Cary told me you turned him down for the scouting position" because you've been offered a job with the Colonials. Congrats on that. That'll be a big promotion for you."

Nothing stayed secret in this business. She should've known. "Thanks, though it's not a done deal yet."

"Want to tell me why you look like you're dreading it?"

She grimaced, shaking her head. "Did Cary send you in here to talk to me?"

Lori's smile softened. "No, but he's worried about you. He said you've seemed...not yourself the last couple of days. Are you okay?"

"I'm fine."

Lori's eyebrows rose and Jess huffed.

"I'm *fine*. Honestly. Of course, I'm nervous about a new job. I've got a lot to do here before I leave but I'm excited, too. I'm just..."

"Just what?"

She considered her next words carefully, thought about not saying anything at all, but she'd been heartsick since Monday night and she'd had no one to talk to.

"Will and I are done."

Lori didn't look surprised by that. "What happened?"

He'd broken her heart. "He thinks I'm selling myself short. How can I be selling myself short when I'm taking this huge step in my career? I'm so pissed at him."

"And what do *you* think?"

Jess shook her head. "About what?"

Lori's eyebrows rose. "Do *you* think you're selling yourself short?"

Jess's first instinct was to deny. But she found she couldn't because she wasn't exactly sure. "Am I? I don't even know anymore."

Lori shrugged. "I can't answer that for you. That's something you need to figure out yourself."

Sighing, Jess felt all the frustration she'd been trying to ignore begin to crush down on her. "You're not helping."

Laughing softly, Lori rose and walked behind the desk to give Jess a hug. "I'm sorry, but I have to say I'm with Cary. I don't want to lose you. Yes, I know this job is a great opportunity. But, Jess, maybe you do need to think about what you're potentially giving up. Maybe it's more than you think."

———

"DUDE, you are like cold rain over ice. What the fuck is up with you?"

Will shot Jake a glance as he dressed for Wednesday night's game. Jake was sitting in his spot on the bench, looking like he'd just walked off a GQ photo shoot. The kid had style. Too bad he also had a mild concussion and a "lower body injury," which in Jake's case was a hamstring tear.

Jake would be on the injured reserve for the next four to six weeks, possibly longer. The kid appeared to be taking it in stride, popping off digs at Lad and the other players and generally being his smart-ass normal self.

But Will sensed a deeper feeling of loss that Jake covered really well.

Or maybe that was Will projecting. Since Monday night, he'd pretty much felt lost, like he'd had a chunk of himself cut out.

And what'd you expect? That she was going to give up a great opportunity to stay here with your sorry ass as you wind down your second-rate career?

Yeah, right.

Shaking his head, he brought his focus back to where it should be —on Coach and his pre-game speech. Important game tonight. They needed these two points to get into second place in the division. Middle of the season and every point began to matter just a little bit more.

No stupid penalties, especially with Bakersfield. Will had some history with the team. Will had been traded there three seasons ago, and he and the coach had butted heads almost immediately. It had been one of the most insanely frustrating times of his life. Coach

Lamarche knew exactly which strings to pull to make Will lose his shit, and the bastard held a grudge.

But tonight, Will couldn't afford to let anything get to him. Had to prove, if only to himself, that he could be more than people expected.

As Coach wrapped up his speech and the team rose to grab their sticks and helmets before heading down the hall to the ice, Jake stopped next to him, staring at him with a question in his eyes.

"What's up, Jake?"

"You look...not yourself."

He pretty much didn't feel like himself either, but apparently no one but Jake had noticed. Or they hadn't wanted to take their lives in their hands and ask outright.

But Jake got away with a lot of shit no one else could because the guy genuinely cared.

"I'm good. Big game. How're you feeling?"

"I will heal. Eventually."

A slight scowl crossed his face but Jake wiped it away fast. If Will hadn't been watching closely, he might've missed it. Now wasn't the time to call Jake on it but he filed it away for later.

"You," Jake continued, "have problem. But this conversation will keep. Tonight," he leaned close and lowered his voice, "you need to keep Lad in check. He can sometimes have wild streak. And Robbie sometimes needs good kick in the ass to get motivated after he makes bad play. And Tyler can be total dick when he is pissed off and will need to be put in his place."

By the time Jake finished, Will had a grin on his face, his first since Monday night when he'd had his heart ripped out of his chest.

"You got it, Mom."

Jake gave him the finger as Will made his way out onto the ice.

Take care of his teammates. That's what an enforcer did. Too bad he couldn't do the same for his heart.

ANOTHER SLOW WEDNESDAY night for attendance meant another slow night for Jess. Tonight, she only had one group and, after the first period, they didn't have much need for her so she chose a relatively crowded section and found a seat.

She told herself she could just sit and watch the game. Neither Lori nor Bliss were there tonight and Mia was chatting away with a couple of players' girlfriends who were closer to her own age.

Which just made Jess feel even more lonely.

You're pathetic. It's not like you got a divorce, for chrissake.

And yet she still felt like part of her had been ripped away.

What are you giving up?

Lori's question kept circling around her head. Drawing in a deep breath, she let her gaze find Will again. She didn't have to work hard. She only had to glance at the ice and her gaze went right to him. Already, the first period had been chippy and a couple of players had gone after Will specifically.

So far, he'd managed to stay out of the penalty box but she could tell he was getting pissed.

By the middle of the second period, the score was still tied at zero and both teams had started to show cracks from frustration.

Stupid penalties on both sides, a lot of shoving and shouting, and a few dirty hits from Bakersfield, one of which left Will on the ice on his knees for a few seconds as he caught his breath and had the audience on its feet, shouting at the ref.

In front of her, a season ticket holder Jess recognized by face shouted, "Did you swallow your damn whistle or are you just blind?"

Then he turned to her and shook his head. "Christ, it's like they've been paid off or something. They're letting Bakersfield get away with murder. Someone's gonna get hurt out there."

Though she knew she shouldn't bad-mouth the referees, especially not as a known member of the front office staff, she couldn't help herself. "He's calling an awful game tonight."

"I'm just waiting for Mac to take care of that little bastard, Branson," the man's wife chimed in. "He needs to step up here."

As play continued, Jess silently agreed. So far, Will had been steady as a rock. But he played without the spark she'd seen in him at the past few games. Was that her fault? Was their breakup, or whatever you wanted to call it, to blame?

Or maybe he was just having a bad night and she was giving herself too much credit.

But as the game wore on, and the game got uglier, she began to wonder if she hadn't totally screwed them both.

———

AT THE END of the second intermission, as the team lined up to head back onto the ice, Will glanced up to find Cary stopped next to him.

In his first game as an assistant coach, Cary had proved to be just as steady behind the bench as he'd been on it.

And Will had forced himself to play the kind of game he thought Cary wanted, even though Bakersfield was taunting the shit out of him, trying to get him to retaliate.

But now Cary looked at Will with a question in his eyes.

"You've been pretty quiet the first two periods. We need you to shake things up."

Will's eyebrows rose. That almost sounded like Cary wanted him to go out there and crack open some heads. But Will had been wrong before. Recently, he'd been pretty fucking wrong about a certain woman and that still stung. He didn't need to get his wires crossed with Cary either.

"You're gonna need to spell it out, man. I don't wanna get this wrong."

Cary didn't blink as he leaned in a little closer. "Go out there and make Bakersfield regret their actions. It's time to show them exactly how our enforcer takes care of things."

Well, would you look at that? Vindication of his skills should've been sweet. And maybe someday it would be.

Will's mouth curved in the ghost of a grin. "I think I can manage that."

"Good." Cary nodded. "Just do it without getting hurt. Team needs you healthy."

"Do my best, Coach."

Cary's grin was wider than Will's. "Be still my heart."

Now Will rolled his eyes. "Don't press your luck."

Cary clapped him on the shoulder. "Be smart, Mac. Be persistent but be ready to go when you get the chance. Don't play into their expectations, because if you do, they'll control the situation. And don't break your damn hand on Branson's hard head."

With a nod, Will headed out onto the ice for the third period.

His first two shifts, he took a couple hard hits against the boards, but Cary's words stuck with him.

Don't play into their expectations.

On his third shift, as Branson charged the Redtails goal from the blue line, Will saw his chance. Branson had his head down, something every player learned not to do in peewees. Sure, sometimes you forgot. And sometimes you paid for it.

Will skated at him full out as the crowd cheered. They could see the collision coming in the two seconds it took for him to cross the ice.

And right before Will leveled Branson, he slowed just enough so he didn't completely wreck the guy. He wasn't out for blood, but it was time for payback.

Branson went down hard, the crowd erupted in cheers, and Will snagged the puck as the guy sat on his ass on the ice, shaking his head and probably seeing stars.

Another Bakersfield player immediately tried to knock Will off the puck, but the guy was no match, not in size or determination. Skating toward the Redtails' offensive end, Will passed to Tyler, whose line set up for a play on goal.

The next few seconds were especially satisfying as the Bakersfield players scrambled to prevent the Redtails from scoring.

And failed.

Tyler passed to Robbie, who one-timed it straight to the back of the net.

The crowd roared and jumped to its feet as the players on the ice jumped Robbie and knocked helmets before skating back to the bench for fist bumps before taking their seats on the bench as the lines changed.

As soon as his ass hit the bench, Will felt a fist tap on his shoulder pads.

"Nice work." Cary leaned down to speak near his ear. "Expectations, Mac. Sometimes you gotta defy them."

———

JESS SAT on the edge of her seat as the seconds ticked away on the clock.

The Redtails had the only goal of the game and less than two minutes remained on the clock.

And after that hit Will had laid on Branson, he'd become a marked man. Any time he was on the ice, the Bakersfield players were all over him.

She had no idea how he managed to maintain his cool. Another player would've gone off by now, drawing a stupid penalty. But Will hung tough. He took the abuse like he was oblivious to everything and kept his eyes on the prize.

Bakersfield battled hard but their frustration was no match for the Redtails' determination. And when the final buzzer sounded, she finally released the breath she swore she'd been holding for the last minute.

As the opposing team made a quick exit from the ice, the Redtails gathered at center ice to salute the crowd.

She saw only Will. He smiled as he knocked helmets with Shane then put his arm around Lad's shoulders as they skated toward the hall to the locker rooms. He stopped just inside the boards, knocking gloves with his teammates as they stepped off the ice.

And just before he left the ice himself, he looked up, his gaze circling the arena. Was she imagining things or was he looking for her?

He heart pounded so hard, it hurt. Damn it.

"Good game tonight. Your dad was right. I'm glad I came."

Startled by the voice from behind her, Jess turned in her seat. And found Victor Galiev in the row behind her.

A genuine smile curving her lips, Jess held her hand out to the NHL scout. "Mr. Galiev, it's nice to see you. It's been a while."

"Yes, it has been." His mouth curved in a wry grin. "And please, call me Vic. You make me feel old when you call me Mister. I'm forty, not eighty."

Jess nodded, knowing it'd be a hard habit to break. She'd known Vic for years. A former player who'd become her father's protégé after retiring because of injuries, he'd moved on to scout for Washington a few years ago.

"What are you doing in Reading? I had no idea you'd be here or I would've made a point to find you earlier."

"Oh, I've got my eyes on a couple of guys on both teams so figured I'd kill two birds with one stone. And I only remembered your dad telling me you worked here when I saw you sitting there. Your dad loves to brag about his brilliant daughter."

She rolled her eyes. "My dad's a little biased, obviously."

"Of course he is. Doesn't mean he's wrong, though. You're in marketing, right?"

"Yes."

"More power to you. That stuff hurts my brain. But I guess it's stable, huh? None of this traveling all over the country every other day, watching five, six games a week."

"Actually, that sounds pretty good to me."

Vic laughed. "Forgot who I was talking to. Should've known Doug Gardiner's daughter would have hockey in her blood. A little surprised you haven't been snapped up as a scout for the NWHL yet."

His comment made her smile freeze in place but he didn't notice as he continued.

"You've got a playoff team here again this year. They should get far. Hopefully Mozik's injury won't put him out for the season. Your D's gonna miss him. Wasn't expecting to see such control from MacDonald. That was a shocker. He'd getting a little old to be learning new tricks."

And now she had to bite her tongue against the urge to tell Vic to go fuck himself.

Mac wasn't old and he damn well had more control than anyone gave him credit for.

Don't let it get to you. He's fishing.

Holy shit. The realization hit her like a puck in the gut. He was absolutely fishing for information. From her.

There was no way she was going to give him any. Not to use against her team.

And dammit, it was *her* team.

Not for long.

Forcing a smile, she stood, holding her hand out to Vic. "It was so nice to see you again but I've gotta get going. I'll tell Dad you said hi."

Vic nodded and shook. "Nice to see you, too, Jess. I'll be sure to stop and say hi next time I'm in town."

Walking back to her office, she sat behind her desk for several long minutes as the arena cleared. Staring out into the empty office, she let the anger build.

She didn't even know why she felt so pissed off but it'd been building all night, making her feel like a soda that'd been shaken for hours.

At least it's better than feeling like you had your heart ripped out of your chest and then stomped on by some chauvinist pig.

Which was totally unfair. Vic hadn't meant anything derogatory with that comment about the NWHL. She was female. It was an easy assumption to make, that the NWHL might be interested in her skills. And yet...

With a growl, she picked up her phone.

"Hi, sweetheart, what's going on? Everything okay?"

"Hi, Daddy, nothing's wrong. I'm just..." She sighed. "I saw Vic Galiev tonight."

"Oh? How's he doing?"

"Fine. He said to say hi."

Her dad paused. "That's nice. But that's not the only reason you called, is it?"

She thought about her response for several long seconds. "No. I'm just...out of sorts. I haven't told anyone yet," except Will, of course, "but Philly offered me that job."

"Hey, honey, that's great." The pride in his voice didn't ease her mood at all. "Seriously. I know you've been busting your ass for that move for a while."

"What if I don't want it?"

Her dad didn't miss a beat. "Then don't take it."

She snorted. Of course, that's what he'd say. "What if this is my big break and I pass it up?"

"Then I'd tell you there will be other opportunities, maybe better ones. Jess...are you still thinking about that scouting position? Did Vic say something—"

"No...well, yes, he said something but it was nothing bad. Actually, he asked the same thing you had, if the NWHL had made me an offer."

"And that's bad how?" Genuine confusion colored his tone. "You need to help me out here, sweetheart. I'm getting slow in my old age."

"You're not old and it's not you who has the problem. I have the problem. And I'm just not sure how to fix it."

"Well, then lay it out for me."

"What if there's this guy I've been seeing? And what if I suddenly have this great opportunity that suddenly doesn't seem so great anymore because I'd have to leave this guy behind? And what if I'm turning down an even bigger opportunity because I'm worried I'll fail?"

Silence from the other end that dragged on.

"Dad, you still there?"

"Didn't we have this conversation last week?"

A frustrated sigh slipped through. "Sort of. But..."

"But what?"

"What if I try to break that glass ceiling and find out I can't hack it? What if—"

"What if you're absolutely amazing? What if you don't do it and regret it for the rest of your life? And what if you give up this man for your job and realize in one, two, five years that you should've given up the job?"

He's talking about Mom.

From the other end, she heard her dad sigh. "I don't have an answer for you, sweetheart. I can only encourage you not to make the same mistakes I did. If you've found the right guy or even who you think might be the right guy, you need to give it a shot. Because sometimes you only get one.

"And if you don't take your shot at something you love, you will most certainly fail."

———

"DUDE, you're a fucking wet blanket. You kicked ass and took names tonight. You should be tearing a hole through this place. What the hell's wrong with you?"

Derek sat next to him at the bar and clinked his beer bottle against Will's before taking another swallow. Most of the team was here tonight, hanging out around the pool table, being fawned over by a group of younger women in tight jeans, tighter shirts, and high heels.

Will had absolutely no interest. He'd only come because the guys had insisted they'd wanted to buy him drinks and that had seemed like a great idea at the time. Now, though, watching the younger guys drink, laugh, and hook up...

He just felt old because what he really wanted was to be snuggled up on a couch watching TV or making out with Jess.

But he'd fucked that up royally.

And he must be pretty damn pitiful because even usually clueless Derek had noticed. Or he'd pulled the short straw and the rest of the guys had sent him as the sacrificial lamb to check on him.

He'd been nursing the one beer since they'd arrived an hour ago so Will was clear-eyed when he turned to Derek.

Who was surprisingly just as lucid.

"Why aren't you halfway to being plastered?"

Derek shrugged, his gaze flashing away for a second. "I'm driving. Doesn't matter. And stop trying to deflect."

"I'm not deflecting. I'm just...not in the mood."

"You and Miss Jess have a fight, huh?"

What the hell? Did everyone know they'd been dating?

Derek huffed out a laugh. "Dude, everyone knew. We're not totally oblivious. So what'd you do?"

"Why do you automatically assume—shit, no, you're right." Will sighed and turned his chair so he could look straight at Derek. "I fucked up and I'm not quite sure how to fix it short of groveling. And I'm not opposed to that but..."

"But what?"

"But I'm not sure I was wrong."

"Oh, you were most definitely wrong about something." Derek laughed. "But maybe you just don't know what it is. So tell me what happened. Let's figure this shit out."

Will wanted to laugh but Derek looked so damn sincere, he couldn't do it. The guy actually wanted to help.

"She's planning to do something and I think she's making a mistake."

Derek's eyes widened. "You told her she was making a mistake? And she didn't immediately cut off your balls? Dude, you got lucky in my book."

"I walked out before she could."

Now, Derek's mouth dropped open. "Oh, man, you are *so* not as smart as I thought you were."

Grimacing, Will took a sip of his warm beer. "Yeah, I'm thinking the same thing myself. The problem is, I still think she's making a mistake and I haven't figured out yet how to say that without getting into another fight."

Dammit, he wanted her to stay, to be with him. And he knew how amazing she'd be as a scout and—

"Holy shit, I'm an idiot."

Derek's expression was a whole lot of "No shit" as he sipped his own beer. "Apparently, I'm a miracle worker. You're welcome. So what are you going to do now?"

Will shook his head. "Fuck if I know. But I think I need to get the hell out of here tonight. Can you give Justin a ride back to our apartment?"

"No problem, man. He can sit on Lad's lap. Lad needs a little pick-me-up with Jake out of the picture."

Rolling his eyes, Will smacked Derek on the back of the head for being an asshole, which Derek took in stride, then headed for the door.

He needed some space to figure out how the hell he was going to making things right with Jess.

———

THURSDAY MORNING, Jess pushed away from her desk and headed for lower level.

She'd had shit luck getting anything done since she'd arrived at her desk at 8:45 a.m. Her brain refused to cooperate. Too many things crowding it and not enough sleep last night.

But she had come to a conclusion around three o'clock this morning.

And now was as good a time as any to set it in motion.

She hadn't expected any of the players to be there for practice yet. Actually, she'd been counting on it.

But she should've known it wouldn't be that easy. And of course it would have to be Will.

Her heart gave a painful little thump in her chest as she caught sight of him walking through the door, duffel bag over his shoulder.

He hadn't seen her yet but it'd only be a matter of time before he realized she was standing in the hall.

She just wasn't prepared for the pain. It'd only been a few days but damn, she'd missed him.

Had he missed her? Would he even speak to her?

She got her answer a second later when his head popped up and his gaze connected with hers.

Was he happy to see her? He didn't look happy. He didn't mad either. He just looked...like Will. The man she was about to do something very brave or very stupid for.

No, that wasn't right, either. She wasn't doing this for *him*. She was doing this for herself.

And if she was very lucky, she'd get him in the process.

"Hey, Jess. How are you?"

His voice wasn't filled with the warmth she'd gotten used to but it wasn't cold, either. And it still made her want to push him up against the wall so she could climb all over him.

But she couldn't. Not yet.

She smiled, hoping he might still want to let her later. "I'm good. You had a great game last night."

"Thanks. Tough game but we pulled out the win."

An awkward silence fell and she hated that this was so hard. And that she had to go. She had to catch Cary before practice.

"Well, I need to get to a meeting but—"

"Sure, no problem." He cut her off but he still didn't sound angry or upset. "I'll see you around, Jess."

Then he faked a smile and continued down the hall to the locker room.

Okay, wow, that had sucked. But it didn't change her mind. In fact, it actually made her more resolute.

With a deep breath, she headed past the locker room entrance, down to Cary's office.

His head popped up as she knocked on his door but he didn't look surprised to see her.

"Hey, Jess, got your message. What's up?"

She bit her lip. "Could you come in and close the door?"

His eyebrows rose but that was his only outward sign of curiosity. "I feel like I'm being called into the principal's office. Except this is my office."

Her nose wrinkled. "Sorry. I don't mean to be so secretive about this. It's just... I know I said I didn't want to be considered for a scouting position. But... I'd like to reconsider."

Cary's eyebrows rose in shock. "Seriously? Of course you can reconsider. I'm thrilled but I hope I didn't pressure you into something you don't want to do. That wasn't my intention."

"No, you didn't pressure me. And I need to thank you. I understand that you're going out on a limb for me on this."

"It's no limb when I know you can do the work. I realize picking up this scouting position means a whole hell of a lot of extra work on your part. But I have to confess I already talked to Philly's GM about this and he's behind you one-hundred percent. If you take the job, you'll be supervised by Bobby Vigneau, who I believe you already know. When I mentioned your name, he was on board immediately. Are you going to encounter some assholes along the way? Of course. It's going to be tough. But I don't think for one minute that you can't handle the job."

Her smile had grown as he'd spoken, her heart pounding a mile a minute. "Thank you, Cary. That means the world to me." Which was pretty stupid considering Will had said almost the exact same thing the last night they'd been together.

Shaking her head at the thought, she drew in a deep breath. "You know about Will and me, don't you?"

His amused grin spoke volumes. "I think everyone knows about you and Will." He raised a hand to stop her response. "And that relationship isn't going to be a problem. At least, not from a team standpoint."

"I'm not sure there's a relationship left to have a problem. We had a...falling-out."

Cary's brows rose. "Sorry to hear that. Will and I have had our differences but we worked them out. Maybe you will, too. So...does this mean you're staying?"

She paused for several seconds before nodding, slowly at first and then faster, her smile becoming full-blown. "Yes. And Cary? Thank you."

Cary's smile stretched wide. "Welcome aboard but don't thank me. I just doubled your workload and probably made the next few months of your life complete hell."

No, the only way the next few months of her life would be hell was if she couldn't convince a certain tough defenseman to accept her apology for being a total basket case.

The question was how did she do that?

———

"TOUGH GAME TONIGHT, guys, but I'm proud of the way you played." Coach paced back and forth as the team gathered in the locker room just after their loss against Idaho. "The bounces didn't go our way, but you played a full sixty minutes and that's what I want from you. We're going to spend time on special teams tomorrow before the game so heads up. Get cleaned up and rest for the game tomorrow."

As the rest of the team headed toward the shower room, Will dropped his head back and remained seated. He had nothing to rush out for and damn if his shoulder didn't hurt like a sonuvabitch from a wicked check in the second period.

"Hey, Mac, you okay?"

Opening his eyes, Will saw Cary standing over him, frowning.

"Yeah, shoulder's a little sore. Nothing major."

"Make sure you have the trainer look at it. We need you at full strength tomorrow night. Wilkes-Barre's gonna be a tough one."

Nodding, he expected Cary to move off but the guy stuck.

"Something wrong?" Will asked.

"Nope. One of the scouts from the big club is here tonight. Wants to talk to you before you head out. In the spare trainer's office."

Will frowned. "What the hell for?"

Cary shrugged. "Just relaying a message."

Before Will could ask any more questions, Cary turned to talk to the coach.

Well, damn. All he really wanted to do tonight was head back to his apartment, eat a shit-ton of food, and sleep until tomorrow morning at nine, when he had to get up for morning skate.

Shit, what he really wanted to do was go home with Jess, make love to her until they both passed out then sleep curled around her.

He'd wanted to get on his knees and apologize this morning before practice. Had wanted to beg her to take him back. And when she took that job in Philly, he'd find a way to make it work. *They'd* find a way to make it work, even if it meant he only saw her one day a week until the end of the season.

That's what he should've told her this morning. What he wanted to tell her now.

But first, he had to talk to someone from the main office so...

Fifteen minutes later, he walked through the silent halls to a small, out-of-the-way office and stopped dead in the doorway.

"Hi, Will."

Jess leaned back against the small desk, staring at him like she wasn't sure he wanted to see her.

Considering his heart had begun to pound against his ribs and his stomach twisted in on itself, he knew she was dead wrong.

And he knew exactly what he had to say.

"I was a complete ass. I'm sorry. And whatever job you want, I'm behind you. I think you can do fucking anything you want, Jess. I should've said that the other night. You're not a coward. You're the smartest person I've ever met and I hope you can forgive me for being a dick."

Her lips quirked up a little at the corners and her head tilted to the side, just enough to make her hair fall over her shoulder in that way that made him want to brush it over her shoulder and kiss the now-exposed side of her neck. And then he'd work his way down to the small vee of skin revealed by the silky blouse she wore tucked into one of those pencil-thin skirts he loved on her.

He stuck his feet to the floor, waiting for her to acknowledge his apology, ready to be sent packing if she didn't. She'd gone to the trouble of seeking him out tonight, but she needed to make the next move.

"Apology accepted." Her smiled widened. "But I owe you one as well. You were right."

He shook his head. "About what? Because from where I'm standing, I was wrong about so many things, I have no idea what you could be talking about."

"About me being afraid. You had more faith in me than I did. And I wanted to thank you for that."

Shit, was this good-bye? The pit that had pretty much taken up residence in his stomach the past week opened just a little wider.

Then he remembered Cary had said someone from the big club wanted to see him. She must have taken the job in Philly.

He stepped closer until she had to tilt her head back to stare up at him. He clenched his hands at his sides so he wouldn't reach for her. But he so wanted to pull her against him and say he was sorry again with his mouth all over her body until she could do nothing but pant and say yes.

Instead, he nodded and forced himself to ask her, "When are you leaving?"

Another ghost of a smile crept over her lips, and he had no idea what the hell she was thinking.

"I have my first game in Norfolk next week."

What the fuck? "Philly doesn't play Charleston."

And that was the stupidest fucking thing he thought he'd ever said, but he had no idea what the hell she was talking about. She was making no sense at all.

"Philly has their eye on a couple of rookies playing for Norfolk."

Which didn't clear up a damn thing. "Jess, what—"

"I'll be gone Wednesday and most of Thursday, but I'll be back in time for our game Friday."

"Jess—wait." His brain began to work again, having finally made its way through the clues she'd already dropped. His gaze narrowed and he took another hard look at her. "You agreed to the scouting position."

Her mouth had a wistful twist to it as she nodded. "I told you. You were right. I was afraid. About the job. About change. But mostly I was a little afraid of you."

He took a step back. "Whoa, wait—"

"Sorry." She held up a hand and shook her head then reached for him, placing her hand flat on his chest. "That didn't come out right. I'm not afraid of you, Will. I'd never be afraid of you. But I *am* deathly afraid of losing you."

As he tried to catch his breath, his heart pounded hard against his ribs, right under her hand.

"I don't want to lose you." Her voice held so much sincere emotion, it cut straight to his heart. "I want to wake up with you in the morning and go to bed with you at night and fight with you over which game to watch before bed and—"

He closed the space between them and dropped his mouth over hers, sealing their lips together and kissing her until they were both breathless and clinging to one another and he practically forgot that they were still in the arena. Otherwise he would've turned her around, pulled up her skirt, and pushed her down on the desk so he could prove to her just how much he wanted her.

As it was, he had a hard time releasing her even though he knew they both needed to breathe.

When he finally did pull away, he only allowed their lips to part enough to speak.

"I can think of a lot better things to do while watching a game than fight."

Her smile was a revelation. "I thought you liked a good fight."

"Only when I know we're both going to win. And right now, I feel like I won the fucking Stanley Cup."

Running her hand through his still-wet hair, she had to rise onto her toes to rub her nose against his. "I'm going to be really busy for the rest of the season. There are going to be weeks that we might not see each other."

He pressed a kiss to the side of her neck, breathing in her scent. "It'll just make the time we spend together even better."

"I'll be traveling most weekends."

"I have games most weekends. We'll spend every day off together. In bed. We won't answer our phones or the door and we'll only get out of bed to eat." He trailed kisses up her neck to her ear and bit the tiny lobe until she shuddered against him. "Unless you wanna do it on the couch. Or against the door. Or on the kitchen table. I'm easy."

Her hands tugged at his hair and he lifted his head. "I'm serious, Will. I'm going to be away. A lot. My mom couldn't take that. It's what broke up her marriage to my dad."

He stared down in her worried eyes. "We're not your parents. We know how this game works and what it takes to win."

Her smile was back and it wiped the worry from her eyes. "Have you always been this sure of yourself?"

"I'm that sure of *you*. We'll make it work. Besides, I'm pretty sure I love you, Jess. No, not pretty sure. I'm damn sure."

Her smile got even wider. "I'm damn sure I love you too, Will."

"Then I'm pretty damn sure we should go the hell back to your place and fight over who gets to be on top."

Her laughter filled up all the little cold places in his heart that'd been there since he'd walked out on her. "That's a fight I think I can win."

"And I will gladly lose if I get to make you scream out my name when you come."

Heading for the door, she tugged on his hand. "I'll race you to the car."

"You go right ahead, I'll just follow behind, watching your pretty ass the entire way."

The look she threw over her shoulder made his heart beat double-time.

"Do you think you'll be able to keep up?"

"I maybe not be the fastest guy on ice but I will always be right beside you, Jess. Always."

———

BUT WAIT! There's more Redtails Hockey!

The Brick Wall

The Grinder

The Enforcer

The Instigator

The Playboy

The D-Man

The Machine

THE INSTIGATOR

He's an instigator on and off the ice...

On the ice, Derek Flaherty is an instigator. He can goad an opponent into throwing down his gloves with a few well-chosen words. Off the ice, he's the life of any party. His Redtails teammates love him...when they don't want to smack him. Hockey is his life, but he's about to take a shot to the heart.

Sophie Tsoukalos is well acquainted with chaos. She's the youngest of four sisters and works in her parents' bar. She's used to dealing with drunks and toddlers. She's not used to dealing with a man with a panty-dropping smile and the body of a god.

From the moment he sees Sophie, Derek discovers what it's like to be struck dumb. For about two seconds. Then he does what he does best. He charms his way into her bed. But can he charm his way into her life?

ONE

"Hey, Schmidt, you asshole. You hit like your sister after a couple drinks. Sac up."

"Fuck you, Flaherty. Fucking asswipe. You need to grow a pair, prick."

"I've got a pair. And they're so fucking huge, you couldn't hold 'em in your hands."

"You need your head examined, dickwad."

"Yeah, why don't you get close enough to do it with your mouth, pindick."

Grinning as the home crowd cheered loud enough to be heard in the next state, Derek Flaherty skated toward the bench, raising his hands over his head to acknowledge the adulation as the ref announced his roughing penalty and his opponent's major penalty.

Derek would be back for the next game. Lars Schmidt would not. The prick had been all over Derek's forward, Ian Clark. Yeah, it was Schmidt's job, but the guy had deliberately tried to hurt Ian. That shit couldn't go unanswered.

"You are one crazy motherfucker." Lad Marchenko smacked him

on the shoulder as he skated by. "I think you are not right in the head, my friend."

The rest of his teammates echoed the sentiment as he reached the bench. Most smiled and shook their heads. Even Coach Cary looked like he might crack a smile.

Derek grinned all the way back to the locker room. Yeah, he was out for the rest of the game, but all the Redtails had to do was hold off the Rochester Eagles for the last minute and thirty-eight seconds.

The playoffs were in sight, and the Redtails wanted so fucking badly to defend their Calder Cup championship title. He could practically taste the cheap champagne he'd be drinking out of a plastic cup.

How fucking great would that be? Maybe then the big-club douchebags would get their heads out of their asses and start giving some of their AHL players a little fucking love.

Yeah, right. Maybe you don't deserve to play up. Maybe you don't have the skill. Maybe—

Shaking his head, he bit back the urge to tell himself to shut the fuck up.

All that really mattered was that he got to play. And if he won another ring in the process... Icing on the cake, baby. All icing. Nobody had expected a guy with his background to get as far as he had playing professional hockey. Sometimes you just had to stick your middle finger in the air and laugh in people's faces.

After watching the end of the game on the monitor in the locker room, he'd just finished his shower when the rest of the team began to file in, high on their win.

"We keep going like this, we'll clinch our division, boys. Damn good hockey tonight."

Tony Dellafranco, who'd inherited the captain's C from Cary when he'd stepped behind the bench a few weeks ago, spoke over the noise of the team as they undressed and headed for the showers.

"Damn right." Dirk Bennett tossed his helmet into his locker and whooped, making the rest of the team do the same. "Time to kick ass and take names."

"Hell, all we need to do is set Flaherty on their ass and they'll be begging us to end the game and their misery."

The smile Tyler Richardson threw Derek's way had a sharp edge to it, but Derek let it slide. Richie was a dick. Everyone knew it. Yeah, Derek had his moments, too, but he never turned on his teammates.

On the ice, Richardson was a damn good player, one you wanted on your front line. He scored on a consistent basis and got named pest of the game by opposing teams almost as much as Derek. But Derek wasn't a dick. At least, he tried not to be.

Luckily, the conversation flowed back to the game, where it should be. But as things began to wind down, Derek couldn't. He was too wired. And he knew from experience that he needed an outlet for the excess energy.

"Hey, Will. You up for a few drinks? I know Jess is outta town so I figured you might wanna hang tonight."

Will shot him a look over his shoulder and Derek could see from Will's expression that his fellow defenseman was about to say no.

Derek resisted the urge to beg, though he knew he shouldn't go out by himself tonight. He was in a mood and, if he went to a bar without adult supervision, he might not be as...restrained as he should be.

And that was something he wanted to avoid at all costs.

But if he went home and had to stare at the four walls of the apartment he shared with Robbie... Yeah, that could be just as bad. He had no issues with Robbie but, holy fuck, the guy never really talked. And Derek couldn't stand the quiet. Which meant he talked way too much.

Sometimes he wondered why Robbie put up with him.

Since they didn't have a game tomorrow and tonight's adrenaline continued to jack him up, a few drinks would help mellow him out but he really didn't want to go alone.

As Will's gaze narrowed, Derek tried to look like he wasn't about to jump out of his skin. He must not have done a great job because Will turned to look at him more closely.

After a few seconds, his teammate nodded. "Yeah, sure." Then Will grinned and actually looked happy to be going out. "But I'm picking the place."

Derek agreed before Will could change his mind. "Sure, yeah, no problem. Where is Jess tonight, anyway?"

Derek forced himself to sit on the bench while he waited for Will to get dressed, tapping his foot on the floor until he realized he was doing it and forced himself to stop.

"Wheeling. Checking out some forward."

"Better watch your back, old man, or she'll be trading you in for a new model."

As soon as the words left his mouth, Derek wanted to take them back. Story of his life. He'd been working on keeping his mouth shut more. So far, he hadn't had much success.

Luckily, Will grinned as he shook his head. "I can't believe you still have your teeth, D, considering how many people have probably tried to punch your face since you learned to talk."

Derek pulled a frown and let his lower lip tremble. "What are you talking about? Everybody loves me. They just gotta get to know me."

A second later, the first shoulder pad hit him in the head, followed by several more pieces of equipment, including a jockstrap.

Luckily, that one didn't hit him in the face.

"Hell, D," Justin called out from across the room. "Most people wanna kill you before you ever open your mouth."

He acknowledged that true statement with a shrug. "What can I say? I got mad people skills."

"Yeah, you're mad all right." Colin chimed in, catching the knee pad Derek threw back at him. "In the head."

"Nah, I'm just excitable."

As the guys laughed, Derek grinned, soaking it in. Along with the sound of skates on ice and the roar of the crowd when he scored, laughter was the best fucking sound in the world. Drowned out all the other shit.

"All right, excitable boy." Will grabbed his shoulder and shook him. "Let's get the hell out of here and get a drink. Justin, you coming?"

"Yep, just let me— Shit, hold on, can't find my shoe."

Will and Derek exchanged a grin as they waited for Justin to realize the shoe he was looking for was under the bench directly beneath him. Which he did only after checking everywhere else.

Derek shook his head as the guy nearly tripped over his feet as they walked out the door. Surprisingly, all of the other guys were going home tonight. Yeah, it'd been a long week but Derek needed an outlet for this excess energy.

Besides, hanging out with his friends was way better than drinking alone.

"So where are we going?"

Derek was expecting Will to name the bar the team usually went to after games, which would've been fine. There were always decent women to hit on and the beer wasn't too expensive.

"Place on Penn Avenue. Quiet. Food's good and the beer's cheap. Jess knows the manager there."

Derek's gaze narrowed. "How quiet?"

Will grinned. "Too quiet for you to get in much trouble."

"Hey." Derek tried to look offended but couldn't manage it and shrugged. "All right, I'll give you that one."

"Damn right you will. Besides, I could use a laidback night."

Derek opened his mouth to rag on Will about his age then remembered the guy had taken a pretty brutal check into the boards in the third period.

"Hey, if you're not up for it tonight—"

"Say one more damn word about my age," Will pinned him with a look Derek had seen from coaches for the past ten years, "and I will show you how fast this old man can punch you."

His grin getting even wider, Derek put his hands up in surrender. "Wasn't going to."

When Will gave him a disbelieving look, Derek shook his head. "Seriously! Dude, I was just thinking about that hit Michaelson laid on you."

Will grimaced and flexed his shoulder. "Bastard's gonna pay for that if we see them in the playoffs."

"Don't worry," Justin chimed in. "We'll get there. But Rochester might not. We kicked their ass tonight. Knocked them back into last place."

They talked hockey all the way to the parking lot. Well, Derek talked. Will and Justin nodded and added a few comments.

Yeah, yeah. He had a problem. Yada, yada.

When they reached their cars, Will told him where to meet. Derek's roommate, Robbie, had gotten a ride home with Dirk and Ian, who lived in the same apartment complex, so Derek didn't have to shuttle him back.

It also meant he got to crank the music and sing along to Bon Jovi all the way to West Reading. Still the best damn band in the world, hands down.

After parking along the street, he looked for the bar but didn't see it at first. He must've gotten the address wrong. Then he realized he'd been looking on the wrong side of the street.

So he focused his attention on the other side and still missed the sign the first time around. He would've missed it the second if someone hadn't opened the door and walked out.

Since he drove even faster than he talked, he had to wait a few minutes for Will and Justin to get there and gave the place a once-over.

Hell, if you didn't know it was there, you wouldn't realize it was a bar. Only the small sign hanging over the door identified it.

He spent a minute tapping his foot along to Queen's "Fat-bottomed Girls" until headlights shone in his rearview. Pushing out of the car, he shoved his hands in his pockets and waited for Justin and Will to join before they walked across the street, wind whipping all around them.

Damn, it was fucking cold. Almost as cold as home in Boston.

"How'd you find this place?" he asked Will. "Looks like the kinda place my grandfather would love."

Will rolled his eyes and shook his head. "Christ almighty, I am going to knock you into next week."

Derek just grinned. "You'd have to catch me first and I'm faster than you. Come on. I'm buying first round."

"And this is why we love you." Justin threw one long arm around Derek's shoulders and pulled him in for a rough hug before shoving him away. "And maybe because you annoy the other teams so fucking much."

Derek was still grinning as he walked into the bar. Then stopped just inside the doorway.

Christ, he'd stepped into a time warp. He was ten years old and looking for his mom at one in the morning. Who he really needed to call tomorrow. He hadn't talked to her since Thursday and he didn't want to worry her. When his mom got worried, she got manic and he didn't want his sister to have to deal with a mess he could've avoided with a simple phone call.

"Derek? Hey, something wrong?"

Will stood a few feet away, staring at him with narrowed eyes.

"Nah. Nothing, I'm fine." He smiled and shrugged those thoughts away. Like he'd been doing since he was four years old. "Bar or table?"

"Table." Will answered immediately. "Need to stretch out my legs."

Derek grinned, something stupid on the tip of his tongue but, this time, Justin beat him to the punch.

"Need the seat to hold you up. It's past your bedtime."

Will just shook his head. "Sit, both of you. I'm getting the first round. Try not to embarrass me while I'm gone."

There were plenty of empty tables and Justin slid into the closest.

Derek was about to open his mouth and fill the silence when a woman walked through double-swinging doors behind the bar and greeted Will with a huge smile.

"Hey! Didn't think I'd see you here tonight with Jess out of town."

"Figured I'd come here so you could tell Jess I was being a good boy."

Another laugh, this time longer and accompanied by a shake of her head that made her dark hair shimmer in the light falling on her from above.

Holy crap. Who the hell is that? And can I get her number?

"You're so full of shit, Will. When are you ever good?"

"Hey, I take offense to that. I'm always good."

She laughed again and Derek sat up even straighter in his seat.

"Dude." Justin tapped the table to get his attention. "You look like you just heard a dog whistle—Oh."

Then the fucker started to laugh hysterically.

Yeah, Justin was laughing at him but, in the moment, he couldn't care less.

Holy fuck, who the hell was she? Will needed to introduce him immediately so he could marry this woman and live happily ever after.

Okay, maybe the marriage thing was rushing it a little. But damn, he had to meet her.

He tore his gaze away from her so he could grill Justin.

"Who is she?"

Turned out Justin was more than willing to share, if only to break his heart in the process.

"No way, dude. Not gonna happen. Not ever."

Derek scowled at Justin's smartass grin and had the urge to punch it off his buddy's face. Not that he would. Sure, he'd get into it on the ice if he needed to, but that was how the game was played. Off the ice, there were lines he didn't cross.

"Fuck you." He leaned closer so he could lower his voice. "Who is she?"

"Her name's Sophie. She's the owner's daughter. And dude, she will eat you for lunch."

"She can eat me for any meal she wants."

"*So* not gonna happen." Justin looked so damn smug, Derek would've slashed him if he'd had a stick in his hand. "First of all, her dad will pulverize you 'cause he'll take one look at you and kick your ass out the door. And she's not into athletes."

"What gave you that idea? 'Cause she turned *you* down? She hasn't met me yet."

Justin continued to grin but Derek ignored him. Mostly because he couldn't stop staring at her.

He didn't think he'd ever seen a prettier girl in his life. Yeah, he'd met beautiful women before. Training camps with the main club meant nights out with the NHL players and women practically ripped their clothes off to attract them. Gorgeous women with amazing bodies and perfect hair and designer clothes.

A lot of the big-club guys took it in stride and ignored it. Some took it as their due. Derek had always been turned off by the hard sell.

His high school girlfriend had been the sweetest girl who'd put up with his crazy shit. Until he'd gone to college. Then she'd dumped his ass, married a local guy and had a few kids. Whenever he got home, he'd go to their house to catch up.

See, not a total dick.

His last college girlfriend had been a whole different story. And that one didn't have a happy ending. So he didn't think about Mandy. Like, at all.

"Hey, I'm not saying you don't have a shot." Justin paused. "But don't get your hopes up, man."

His hopes weren't the only thing that was up because, damn, there was something about the girl that tripped all his triggers.

He rose partway off his chair...then sat back down again. "Tell me how you struck out."

Leaning back in his chair, Justin smirked, shaking his head. "Who said I struck out?"

Derek smirked back. "There's no way you wouldn't have told anyone who would listen that you were dating *her*."

Justin rolled his eyes but shrugged, basically admitting to Derek's claim.

"I was here one night with Will and Jess and I asked her if she wanted to go out. She said no, she didn't have a lot of free time but thanks for the offer."

"Man, you got blown off big time."

"Uh huh. Just like you will."

Derek shook his head but he had to wonder if Justin was right. Maybe she had something against professional athletes, especially hockey players who occasionally left for Canada or got traded to Utah or went overseas to play for months on end. Some women didn't want to get serious with a guy who could move a thousand miles away in a few hours. Some were just looking for notches on their belt.

He had a feeling pretty Sophie was one of the first. Didn't mean he couldn't change her mind. He was only after a date. He wasn't looking for a wife, for chrissake. He was too damn young and definitely not ready but most of the women he met were after the same thing he was. Fun. And he was a hell of a lot of fun.

He just needed the right playmate. And she looked like she'd fit the role perfectly.

He wanted to go up to the bar and have Will introduce him but Will was already on his way back with three glasses.

Will looked at Justin's smirk then fixed his stare on Derek. "What'd you do?"

He gave Will the finger. "I didn't do anything."

"Uh huh." Will looked at Justin as he sat and pushed mugs at them. "What'd he do?"

Justin laughed. "Took one look at Sophie and decided he wants to get to know her better."

Will's wicked grin made Derek roll his eyes.

"She's too sweet for you." Will knocked his mug against Derek's. "And you're not her type."

Okay, his so-called friends were starting to piss him off. "How do you know that? How do you know what her type is?"

"Because she's friends with Jess. She's also friends with Bliss so, even if she hasn't heard about you until now, she's *definitely* gonna get an earful from the girls. Besides, between the two of you, neither of you would get a word in edgewise."

Will took a swallow of beer, watching him with a half-assed smirk. "She's a knockout, man. But I'm not sure you're in her league."

"Hell, I'm not sure she's on the same planet." Justin put in his two cents.

Derek started to grin. "So we have a lot in common. I can work with that."

TWO

"Sophie, I'm gonna clear out but Mark'll be here 'til one to help you close out. Your mother's not gonna be happy about me leaving you here on your own but, damn, my feet hurt."

Sophie Tsoukalos bit her tongue and forced a smile. "I'll be fine, Dad."

Luckily, her dad couldn't hear her teeth gnashing because if he could, he'd want to know why and they'd have another blowout like the one they'd had two nights ago.

Nico Tsoukalos thought being single and under the age of twenty-five made her incapable of taking care of herself.

Hell, she wouldn't even be alone tonight. Carlos would be in the kitchen cleaning up until she closed. She might be independent but she wasn't stupid. Alone in a bar at midnight with a register full of cash wasn't a good situation for anyone, man or woman.

So she never insisted she close by herself and Mark worked almost every weeknight. Problems only arose when her dad got it into his head that, because she was single and female, she was incapable of thinking for herself and needed a man.

Her dad turned to her with a smile that said he knew exactly what she was thinking. And he probably did.

"I know, I know." He raised his hands in front of him. "You're an adult. You don't need your dad anymore. But Sophie, you will always be my baby."

And this is where she lost the argument every damn time. Because she knew her parents would do anything and everything for their five daughters, including worrying about them even though they were adults.

"I love you, too, Daddy."

Then she kissed him on the cheek and sent him out the back door, home to her mom, who wouldn't be able to sleep until he was there.

She sighed. That's the kind of relationship she wanted. Someday. Just not now. She had plans, damn it. But tonight... she still had customers.

Two tables with couples who both appeared to be on first dates. The women had looked ready to leave after the first twenty minutes. They both appeared to be in their thirties and bored out of their skulls. She didn't envy them, but she didn't know why they just didn't get up and walk the hell out. That's what she would've done. Then again, she hadn't been on a date in the past few months so what the hell did she know.

Then there were the regulars.

Bill and Phyllis held up one end of the bar, arguing about...something. That's all they ever did. They'd been married for almost thirty-five years. She figured they'd argued for at least thirty-three of them.

Mike and Teddy sat at the other end of the bar, watching the Philadelphia Colonials lose to whoever they were playing in Los Angeles.

Yes, she lived in a town with a professional hockey team but she didn't exactly follow the sport. Not like her friends, Bliss, who'd fallen in love with one of the Redtails goalie, Shane, and Jess, who was a Redtails scout and dating Will.

Her gaze slid to the only other occupied table and the hockey players seated there.

Will was a sweetheart. And Justin was a big, gangly teddy bear with an infectious smile. So not her type.

But the third guy was new. And *really* not her type.

First off, he was a redhead. That unmistakable deep cherry-red any girl would kill for. But damn, he was pale. The poor guy must fry to a crisp in the sun, his skin was so fair. Sure, he was nice looking. Okay, more than nice looking. But, damn, he talked. His mouth had been going a mile a minute to Will about something and he hadn't shut up since. She had no idea how he managed to breathe.

Hey, pot, meet kettle.

Yeah, yeah.

Still, there was something about him that kept drawing her attention.

She had a definite type when it came to the guys she dated. Quiet, dark...and emotionally unavailable.

Her sisters kept telling her she deliberately chose guys she knew would never stick around. She kept telling her sisters to fuck off and they'd laugh and pat her on the head and return to talking about their kids and their husbands. The fact that her closest sister in age was ten years older than her had something to do with how they treated her. Her oldest sister, who was almost eighteen years older, treated her like one of her kids.

Yes, Sophie had been an "oops" baby, her parents in their early forties when she'd come along. It meant she'd been pampered and spoiled and well-loved all her life. It also meant she'd grown tired of everyone in her life knowing everything about her life. She couldn't go on a date without five people calling the next morning to see how it went. Usually all of them at the same time or at least two of her sisters calling on conference so they wouldn't have to repeat the story to one another.

Just thinking about the last time she'd stupidly agreed to be set up with a guy from her brother-in-law Tony's construction business made her shiver in remembered horror.

"Hey, Sophie, you okay? You look like you just saw a ghost."

"Nah, Sophie wouldn't be afraid of no ghost, would you, hon? You're too tough for that."

With a smile, she headed to the end of the bar where Mike and Teddy split their time between watching the game and glancing at her.

"I'm fine, guys. You ready for another round?"

"Yeah, go ahead and top me off." Teddy knocked his elbow against Mike's and grinned. "My wife likes when I drink more than a few. She says I get handsy."

"Your wife likes that you fall asleep faster after you've had a few."

Smiling as she tapped another round for the two sixty-somethings, she glanced over to see the redhead watching her.

Okay, maybe he was more than cute, in a totally not-her-type way. First off, he smiled at her. A wide-open grin that made her want to smile back.

Which she did. And watched his grin turn a little wicked.

Her tummy gave a stupid little flutter and she turned her attention to taking inventory.

Nope. Not happening.

After her last boyfriend had ridden off on his motorcycle for parts unknown, leaving her with a slightly bruised heart, she'd sworn off guys for at least the next few months. Finals were coming up and she needed to do well to keep her scholarship for her final semester at Alvernia. She'd had some trouble with physics that was threatening to pull down her GPA. The small private college she attended was expensive and the only way she could afford it was that scholarship.

Being Greek, Catholic and relatively poor had its advantages when it came to grants and scholarships and she'd taken advantage of every single one. She was the only one of her sisters who had gone for a traditional four-year degree. Her oldest sister had a nursing degree, her next-oldest was a dental tech, her third sister was a cook who owned a restaurant with her husband and her fourth managed a jewelry store in the mall.

Sophie planned to be a teacher. She wanted to leave this small town and travel the world. She wanted to teach English in Japan or Italy or Germany. She'd graduate at the end of the year and then she'd take off.

Her parents would hate it but they wouldn't stop her. Her sisters would cry, her nieces and nephews would cling and she'd shed a few tears, as well. But she had a plan and she was sticking to it, dammit.

Of course, that didn't mean she couldn't have any fun before she left.

She slid another glance at the redhead and allowed herself to take a longer look. He was deep in conversation with his buddies now so she could study him a little more closely.

His hair gleamed in the overhead lights, too red to be mistaken for anything else. His beard was a shade darker. She didn't usually give guys with beards the time of day but his was close-cropped and suited the shaggy, curly hair that fell over his forehead and was long enough for him to shove behind his ears.

She wasn't sure if he just forgot to get it cut or if he was making a fashion statement. Didn't really matter. The more she studied him, the more she thought the look suited him.

He looked a little like that guy on that show with guys in kilts that her sisters were always talking about. She didn't watch it, but her sisters constantly posted pictures of the guy in their Facebook feed. You'd think they weren't married the way they talked about what they'd do with him if they got their hands on him.

This guy was a little rougher-looking, with a square jaw and a broader nose. And the palest skin she'd ever seen on a guy. Or anyone for that matter.

But he probably had that fake highlander beat in the body department. This guy was seriously built. Tall, broad shoulders and chest and, even though she couldn't see his legs, they probably matched the rest of the body. Thick, long and...probably just as pale as the rest of him.

Huffing out a laugh, she turned toward the liquor shelves behind the bar and shook her head. She had work to do and it wasn't getting done ogling the hockey player.

Fifteen minutes later, she'd just put the last bottle back on the shelf after checking the levels when she realized someone had stepped up to the bar.

She turned with her bartender smile in place...until she realized it was him. Her smile faltered and she had to suck in air.

Damn, the guy was even more good-looking up close. Especially smiling at her like he was right now.

"Hey, hi." Somehow, he managed to maintain that smile as he spoke and stuck his hand over the bar. "I'm Derek."

Wow, wow, wow. His grin took her breath away.

After wiping her hand on the rag on her belt, she took his much-larger hand—and no, she did *not* imagine what he could do with that hand—and managed to maintain her own smile. "Hi. I'm Sophie. What can I get you?"

"Three Troegs drafts and your number. You're amazingly beautiful and I'd love to take you out to dinner some night. Will tells me you're friends with Jess and Jess'll vouch for me. Don't ask Will. He'll lie. I swear I'm a decent guy and not some dickwad."

Her lips parted in shock for several seconds before she started to laugh. And no, she did *not* release his hand right away. She let him surround her fingers with heat that spread up her arm before she pulled away. Reluctantly.

"Nice to meet you, too."

She didn't comment on the rest of his statement. Instead she moved a few feet to the right to tap their beer. She wasn't sure what she wanted to say anyway.

"So Will says your dad owns this place. Have you worked here long?"

Her brows rose as he waited for her answer. Had he given up on getting her number already? Hell, he hadn't given her more than a few seconds to answer.

"Since I was sixteen." She wasn't about to tell him how long ago that was, although it'd only been seven years. "So you're a hockey player, too?"

"Yeah, defense. Paired with Lad right now 'cause Jake's on the IR and so's Joey, who's my regular line mate. Lad and I are making it work. Actually, we're kicking ass right now, which is great for the team. But I still kinda miss Joey. We had a shorthand, you know?"

Somehow, she managed to follow all of that and nodded as she set the last of their beers on the bar. "Sorry to hear about your buddy. Will he be back soon?"

The guy's smile kicked up a notch. "Hopefully, yeah. But we're not too sure about Jake. He took a pretty big hit. Anyway, about your number..."

Her lips twitched at the corners but she didn't want to give the guy any more encouragement. Yeah, he was hot but he definitely wasn't her type. And she had finals coming up and shouldn't even be thinking about guys.

But this one... Damn, he made her think about hot, sweaty sex. And that was so not like her. Not that she didn't enjoy sex, especially hot, sweaty sex. It's just that it wasn't typically one of the first things she thought about when she met a guy.

Okay, that might be considered lying to herself. But she was trying to turn a new leaf. Be more responsible about the guys she dated.

Fuck it.

She smiled back and watched his grin turn wicked as the heat in his eyes promised her everything she could possibly want for a night of no-strings-attached fun.

She was no saint, never pretended to be. But what her parents didn't know wouldn't hurt them.

Resting her forearms on the bar, she leaned closer, not breaking their increasingly intense connection. Damn, the guy even smelled good. Not doused in cologne but clean and just a little spicy.

He'd showered recently, and his too-long hair was still a little damp and, oh hell, even that was sexy. She wanted to run her fingers through it.

"How long are you going to be here tonight?"

"As long as it takes to get your number."

She laughed, not bothering to hold it back. "And if you're disappointed at the end of the night?"

He shrugged. "Then I'll leave and come back another night and try again. I don't give up easily."

"So basically, you're telling me you're a stalker and I'm never going to get rid of you?"

The honest look of horror on his face convinced her of one thing. This guy couldn't keep a secret to save his soul.

"You tell me you want nothing to do with me and I'll totally leave you alone." The grin reemerged. "But I hope that smile means you're the adventurous type."

Her brows rose even farther. "And you're the adventure?"

"I'm Everest, lady. And I'm ready for you to climb all over me."

CHAPTER 3

Sophie's eyes widened and Derek had a second to wonder if he'd struck her dumb with his amazing wit.

But then she started to laugh again, so hard she doubled over and put her hand over her mouth. This was no husky, quiet, sexy chuckle. This was a full-blown gut-buster. Which made him wonder if she was laughing with him or at him.

Either way, it didn't matter. She was laughing and it turned him on.

When she finally calmed enough to speak again, he raised his brows and waited for her response.

"That has to be the funniest pickup line I've ever heard." She shook her head, staring into his eyes, her dark gaze direct. "Are you always like this?"

He frowned. "Like what?"

She shrugged as her smile softened a little and made his cock throb against the zipper of his pants.

"Excitable."

His turn to laugh. "That's me. I'm just an excitable boy."

Shaking her head, she turned to grab a rag off the counter behind her and started wiping down the bar. "I can see that."

"So, Sophie, you wanna go out with me sometime?"

She didn't stop what she was doing. "I'm pretty busy right now with school and work."

Not an outright refusal. He could work with that. "Where do you go to school?"

"Alvernia. I graduate at the end of the year and then I plan to travel and teach."

"Oh, yeah? Like where?"

"Europe, for starters. I've always wanted to go. Maybe Japan."

"Sounds cool."

She stopped wiping and stood in front of him, hands pressing against the edge of the bar and causing her shirt to gap in the front. Not that he was looking.

"Don't you travel all the time?"

"Yeah, I guess." He shrugged. "But it's different. We get on a bus, we drive, we sleep or watch movies or listen to music. Then we play. Maybe if we're there for two games, we'll get out of the hotel for a beer or something. You wanna know what bar has the best wings in any city with an AHL team, that I can tell you. Otherwise, they're all pretty much the same."

Her upturned nose wrinkled as she grimaced. "That doesn't sound like much fun."

"The fun part's playing. Everything else is work."

Her lips quirked into another one of those sweet smiles. "Sounds like you love what you do."

"Wouldn't want to do anything else."

She was still smiling but he sensed a shift in her attitude. She looked at him differently now, like she was thinking maybe she might want to take him up on that date.

In the next second, her smile returned to "pleasant bartender." Shit, what the hell had he said?

"I guess it's good you love your job, considering how much you get beaten up on the ice."

"Do you come to the games?"

She shook her head. "Not really. I've been to a couple but usually I'm working. Or studying. Or babysitting my nieces and nephews."

"So what do you do for fun?"

Her eyebrows rose, her expression suddenly totally serious. "What? Work, study and chasing after tiny heathens isn't fun? Are you questioning my life choices?"

He opened his mouth to laugh at her joke but caught himself before he did. Shit. Maybe—

Her laughter rang out again. "I'm sorry but the look on your face is priceless. You can't play poker to save your soul, can you?"

Grinning openly again, he shook his head. "Nope. But I'm not much for cards. I like to play other games."

Her eyes widened as she leaned in close, which meant he had to lean in even closer. Not that that was a hardship. He wanted to be as close to this girl as he could get. And then he wanted to get her naked and get even closer because, damn, she made him laugh. He hadn't met many girls who did. Most were more interested in flirting and being sexy than in trying to make him laugh.

"Really? What kind of games? Chess? Checkers? No, wait." She held up her hand. "Chutes and Ladders? Candyland?"

Now she was teasing him and that was okay, too. It gave him the opportunity to mess with her.

"Are those your favorites, too? I think we should start our own private Game Night. Have you ever played Strip Candyland?"

There was that laugh again, the one that shot right to his balls and made his dick sit up and take notice. If he wasn't careful, he'd be walking out of here with a hard on everyone would be able to see.

"What? No Strip Twister?" Her expression turned disappointed. "And here you were getting my hopes up."

It was on the tip of his tongue to tell her what she was making go "up" but just before he spoke, he figured that wasn't appropriate. Hey, look at that. He could be tactful.

"You pick the day and time and I'll be ready for our playdate. I'm up for anything. I'll even bring my own pieces."

"Do you still have all of your own pieces? I've heard hockey can be a rough game. How do I know you haven't lost anything...important over the years?"

His smile widened. "I've got all my original equipment. I'd be more than happy to let you check me over from head to toe."

She looked away and raised a finger to tap against her lips, drawing his gaze down. Now he couldn't look away. Her lips were made to be kissed. Like, seriously, that's all he wanted to do. He wanted to lean over the bar and plant his lips on hers and kiss the hell out of her. He'd bet she'd taste so fucking sweet. He also knew if he started kissing her, he wouldn't want to stop.

And that would probably get him thrown out of the bar for life.

"Hmm." Her gaze reconnected with his and her eyes held so much mischief he knew he couldn't walk away without her number. Or at least until she agreed to see him again. "Now why didn't I think of that?

The tease in her voice gave him goosebumps. Actual fucking goosebumps. She looked into his eyes and smiled, and he felt like he'd won the fucking Calder Cup. And he knew exactly how that felt because he'd been with the Redtails when they'd won it last year.

So yeah, he felt pretty fucking awesome at the moment.

"Maybe you just need to stick with me for a while. I'm sure we could think of a lot better things to do than play board games."

He had her now.

Come on, baby, say yes.

She sighed. "I think I'll stick to solitaire for now. But thanks for thinking of me."

He clutched at his heart with mock horror but smiled like he'd known he was going to get shot down.

"You wound me." Then he leaned forward again and spoke low

enough that only she could hear him. "But I'm not dead yet. And I'm not giving up. Game on, pretty Sophie. I hope you know how to play the game because I'm about to crash your net."

He didn't turn away until he saw some hint of acknowledgement on her face.

If she'd told him to fuck off, he would've backed away and not approached her again. He'd seen too many guys be total dicks to women. But he had a feeling he wasn't finished with Sophie.

When she cocked her head to the side and the corners of her mouth kicked up, he knew he'd be back.

And next time, he'd have a better strategy.

CHAPTER 4

"Hey, Bliss, how's it going?"

"Just start filling the wine glass now and don't stop until July."

Sophie laughed, setting a glass of water on the bar as her friend slid onto the stool in front of it. "White or red?"

Bliss sighed, propped one elbow on the bar and dropped her chin in her hand. "Both?" Then she sighed theatrically. "But since I have to go back to work and we have three bridal fittings this afternoon, I guess I should stick with lemonade."

"I could spike it with vodka."

Bliss's expression was a mix of resignation and longing. "Don't tempt me. Wedding season isn't even in full swing yet and I'm ready to bash heads. I need a distraction." Her expression morphed into a sly grin. "Speaking of distractions... I heard you met the infamous Derek Flaherty last night. Shane said you broke his heart. Poor guy moped for most of practice this morning."

Rolling her eyes, Sophie slapped a menu down in front of Bliss and scowled at her. "You and Shane need to find someone else to gossip about. Nothing happened last night."

"Oh, I know that." Bliss picked up the menu and began to look it over, like she didn't have the damn thing memorized, she ate here so often. "I mean, come on, it's Derek. Of course, you turned him down."

Sophie's mouth dropped open at Bliss's immediate dismissal. Derek hadn't been that bad. In fact, she'd gone home last night more than a little bummed he hadn't pushed her harder for her number. Sure, he'd told her he'd be back but then he'd walked back to the table with his friends and soon after, they'd left.

"Why do you say that? What's wrong with him?"

Bliss looked up with a deceptively innocent expression. "Nothing's wrong with him. I just don't see him as your type."

Sophie had to stew on that for a minute or so because another couple came in and sat down. Sophie got them menus because the waitress was in the kitchen.

"And what type is that?"

She stopped back to take Bliss's order, though she knew exactly what her friend was going to order. Her dad's moussaka was on the specials board and Bliss loved it.

After she'd turned in the slip to the kitchen, along with the two other orders from customers at the bar, she returned to stand in front of Bliss, still looking way too innocent.

"*You* are a shitty liar, by the way."

Bliss blinked big hazel eyes but couldn't control her lips, which twitched into a smile. "What? What am I lying about?"

Sophie's own gaze narrowed. "Are you trying to set me up with him? Ever since you started dating Shane, you've been telling me I need to get out more."

Bliss shook her head, her expression earnest now. "Oh no, I seriously don't think Derek's the right guy for you. I wanted to hook you up with Justin, remember? Derek's a nice guy. He's just..."

"Just what?"

Shrugging, Bliss wrinkled her nose. "Just...loud. God, the guy exhausts me just talking to him for a few minutes. He can't keep his mouth shut. It's like he doesn't have a filter, you know? Whatever's in his head just comes out of his mouth."

"Sophie!" Her dad yelled from the kitchen, so loud she could hear him perfectly through the door. "Orders up!"

"Hold that thought," she said to Bliss as she headed to the kitchen.

After she'd delivered the plates, she stopped back to talk to Bliss again. "So you don't like him?"

Bliss looked up from her phone, which she'd been smiling at. "Like who?"

Sophie gave her the look she usually reserved for her nephews, who looked so sweet yet were always guilty of something.

"Don't even try that tactic with me. You forget I deal with drunks and toddlers on a regular basis. You can't get anything past me."

Bliss rolled her eyes. "Okay, fine. I think he's great. He's funny. A smartass. Never serious. Unless it's hockey. Then he's deadly serious. He can be even more intense than Shane on the ice and you know how Shane gets."

She'd seen Shane play a couple of times so she understood what Bliss was saying. She just didn't see the point her friend was trying to make.

As if Bliss had read her mind, or maybe it was just the confused look on Sophie's face, Bliss huffed out a sigh.

"Okay, what I'm trying to say is that I don't think the two of you are right for one another."

That stumped her for a second. "So...He's a great guy, just not for me."

Bliss made a sound between a sigh and a groan. "Ugh. No. That's not what I mean. Oh, jeez. I'm not explaining this very well, am I?"

"No, not so much. It kinda sounds like you don't want me to date him."

"I didn't say that." Bliss's gaze narrowed and she leaned over the bar, closer to Sophie. "So you *do* like him?"

When Sophie didn't answer right away, Bliss's eyes widened.

"Well, damn." Bliss leaned back, shaking her head. "I never saw that coming."

It was Sophie's turn to roll her eyes. "It's not like I'm gonna marry the guy. I just...think he's interesting. I don't know." She waved a hand in the air like she didn't give a damn. "Forget it."

"Do you want me to ask him if he likes you?"

"God, no. What are we? In high school? Of course not."

"So," Bliss drew the word out to, like, five syllables, "you're just going to wait until he shows up here again?"

Sophie threw her hands in the air. "See? This is why I wasn't going to say anything. I knew you'd do this."

"Do what?"

"Try and set us up."

"No, I'm not. Seriously."

"Set you up? With who? You don't need to be set up with anyone. You got more than enough to keep you busy without adding a boy into the mix."

Sophie turned to see her dad standing behind her, eyes narrowed, hands on his hips. He had that look on his face, the one he got when anyone suggested Sophie go on a date. Or that someday she might actually have a boyfriend or, god forbid, a husband.

"What's wrong, Dad?"

"Nothing's wrong. Why do you always think something's wrong?"

Now she did roll her eyes. "I don't always think something's wrong, but you always *sound* like something's wrong. So if nothing's wrong, what's up?"

"I can't get that damn panini press to close right. Why the hell does that thing only work for you?"

So there was something wrong. It was on the tip of her tongue to blurt out something she knew she'd regret and then she and her dad would get in an argument and they'd fight all day.

She knew she should keep her mouth shut, should bite her tongue and tell him she'd be right there to help.

And she couldn't do it.

"Maybe because you never listen to me when I tell you how to work it."

"Why should I need you to tell me how to work it? It should just work." Turning his back on her, he headed back to the kitchen, mumbling all the way. "Goddamn technology. Need a college degree to work it."

As the door to the kitchen swung shut behind him, Sophie just stared at it, shaking her head.

"You know, it wouldn't be the end of the world if you decided to work somewhere else."

Bliss's softly spoken comment made Sophie sigh as she turned back to her friend. "No, it wouldn't. But where else will I find a place where I literally make my own schedule? And where I get paid enough to actually live on?"

Bliss gave a little shrug of agreement and Sophie headed back to the kitchen to help her dad.

But she couldn't stop thinking about Derek. So when she came out of the kitchen again, she headed for Bliss.

"When's the next game?"

Bliss's expression was pure told-you-so. Sophie restrained herself from sticking her tongue out at her friend.

"Friday night at home. They've got another game Saturday then a game in Albany Sunday. They'll be back Monday. So you wanna come to the game with me tomorrow night?"

Bliss's smug expression didn't deter Sophie from making what was probably not the best decision. She had a huge test Monday for a class that'd been giving her fits all semester. She loved every aspect of college, except for the tests. She sucked at tests, like serious sucked, and she stressed about them until her head hurt.

She should study all weekend. But, dammit, she deserved a night out.

"Sure. Count me in."

———

"Heard you met Sophie last night at the bar."

Sweaty, still panting and hungry as hell, Derek turned to face Shane with an expression that made Shane start to laugh.

"What the fuck are you talking about? Shouldn't you be in your head getting ready for the game tonight?"

Shane shrugged as he started to shed his equipment. They'd had a short skate this morning in preparation for the game tonight. Most of the team were heading out for lunch at a local restaurant before they headed back to their homes to rest. Derek could never sleep before a game but he always chilled for a few hours with a couple gallons of water, Gatorade, trail mix, a bagel and a movie.

Robbie's mouth had dropped open the first time he'd realized Derek was watching a foreign film on Netflix. Then the jokes had started. Derek had shrugged them off, like he did almost everything, but he always lied when he told anyone the reason why he watched them. He said they helped put him to sleep.

Every single person he told that story believed him. Kinda bummed him out but, whatever. Truth was, he loved them. They kept him connected to his mom, who sent him a list of movies to watch every week, one for each game day.

"Just thought you'd wanna know she'll be at the game tonight. Bliss said Sophie mentioned meeting you. Just passing on the news."

"What news?" Justin loped in, dropped onto the bench and pulled his jersey over his head. "What'd I miss?"

Will walked in behind him and "accidentally" smacked Justin on the back of the head. "What don't you miss?"

"Fuck you." Justin gave Will the finger, though he smiled as he did it. "I hit more of the net than you did today."

"Neither of you hit the net more than I did so stop now. You embarrass yourselves."

Derek looked up to see Lad join their little group. The guy had been playing just fine but, off the ice, he seemed even more quiet than normal. Jake being on the injured reserve hadn't helped. This was the first he'd said anything all practice.

Even though no one had mentioned it, they were all worried about him. So it was good to see him getting back to his normal, sarcastic, boasting self. And a relief. They needed his head in the game if they were going to win another Cup.

Will was the first to respond. "Don't get cocky, kid, or your elders will have to put you in your place."

"You would have to catch me first."

The smug look Lad gave Will made all the guys laugh. Will just grinned as he took off his gear.

"I'm still waiting to hear Derek's news."

Now naked except for the towel around his waist, Justin stopped in front of Will, who'd just covered his own junk and had risen to head for the shower.

"No news." He threw Shane a look that threatened retribution if he opened his mouth.

The guy had a death wish. "Bliss is bringing a friend to the game."

Justin and Will made it plain that that had something to do with Derek by staring at him. Which made everyone else stare at him.

"And what does this have to do with you?"

Lad asked the obvious question, which made Robbie stomp over from across the room, still in full gear.

"What the hell'd you do now, D-man?"

Derek turned his back on all of them and headed for the showers.

"That proves it." Robbie laughed behind him. "If he's quiet, you know he's up to something."

"Fuck you, Linda." Derek yelled his favorite nickname for Robbie over his shoulder and made a clean getaway to the showers.

Derek couldn't stop grinning about Sophie. Was she coming to the game to see him? Or was he totally off base?

He'd gotten her number Wednesday night but he hadn't called her yesterday. They'd had practice and then he and a few of the guys had spent a few hours at the Olivets Boys and Girls Club in the city playing floor hockey with the kids.

It hadn't been mandatory. Will's girlfriend, Jess, the Redtails promotional coordinator, set up these community outreach events then enlisted a few guys to show up. He and Jake were usually the only ones who went on a regular basis.

"So, you went back to the bar last night, huh?"

Derek rolled his eyes as Will caught up to him on the way to the showers.

"Hey, what are you? My father?"

Will held up his hand, grinning as he did. "Just a friendly question."

"No, I didn't go back last night. I was at the club playing ball hockey with a bunch of kids who nearly managed to take off my head a few times."

"Guess you made a good impression."

Since it was clear Will wasn't going to let this go, Derek sighed, turned on the shower and stuck his head under the water. But he still couldn't drown out Will.

"So are you going to ask her out?"

"Oh, for fuck's sake." Derek glared at Will, who'd taken the stall next to his. "I feel like I'm in fucking junior high. And what are you? Her father?"

"Nope, but if you want my advice—and you're gonna want my advice—you'll tread lightly with this one. She's a nice girl."

Derek rolled his eyes, but Will's unspoken disapproval hurt. "Yeah, yeah, we went through this already. You don't need to tell me I'm not worthy again."

Will sighed loudly before he reached over the partition and smacked Derek on the back of the head. "D, I didn't tell you you're not worthy. I honestly didn't think she'd be into you. According to Bliss, Sophie rarely dates. My bad, by the way. I'm just saying, now might not be the right time for *you* to start something. We're deep into the season. We're counting on you and Lad to be solid. Lad's already got enough on his mind with Jake out. You need to be on your game."

Fuck. *Fuck.* He knew this. It pissed him off that he hadn't thought about it himself.

"And I'm not saying you're not playing well," Will continued. "You are. We just need you to maintain."

Derek nodded. That he could do. He could maintain the shit out of that level. And he could push himself to the next.

Sex? Who needed sex when you had hockey and a possible playoff berth in reach?

Then again, a little sex never hurt nobody.

CHAPTER 5

"Sophie. I'm so glad you came!"

Sophie gave Bliss a huge hug as she met Bliss and Faith at her seat in the arena.

"Thanks for the ticket. I didn't expect you to pay for it, though. Let me—"

"I didn't pay for it." Bliss waved away her concern. "The guys get comps so don't worry about it. I'm just so excited you're here. How'd you get your dad to give you a Friday night off?"

"Just had to ask." That was the thing about her dad. He basically gave her anything she wanted. "Besides, if I work any more hours, he's gonna need to make me a full-time employee. Hey, am I dressed okay? I had no idea what to wear. It's a hockey rink, so I figured it's cold but, damn, now I'm thinking I should've put on more layers. And I guess I didn't get the message about the dress code."

Bliss laughed and waved her hands in the air again, showing off her red gloves that matched her red scarf and red knit hat with the Redtails logo on the front.

"It's always cold in here but you should be fine. And there's no dress code. Some of us are just more...supportive than others."

Bliss gave a pointed look at the woman sitting on the other side of her, who rolled her eyes.

"Yes, yes, I know. I'm no fun. Hey, Sophie, how's it going?"

Sophie walked by Bliss to give Faith a hug. Confined to a wheelchair due to a spinal injury, Faith still managed to smile and be a generally decent person, despite the fact that her asshole ex-fiancé had been the cause of the accident that'd left her paralyzed. And had basically left her at the altar. The prick. Sophie had had her grandmother lay a curse on the bastard. Of course, she'd never told Faith. Better to keep some things to yourself.

"It's going. Haven't seen you for a while. What've you been up to?"

"Work. Rehab. Work. Rehab." She shrugged and smiled, no hint of darkness in her expression. "You know, moving forward. So what brings you to the game tonight? I mean, it's great to see you but it's Friday."

"I do get days off, you know. Maybe I just wanted to spend it with girlfriends."

As she settled into the seat next to Bliss, she saw Bliss and Faith exchange a look. And knew Bliss had already told Faith her version of why Sophie had come tonight.

"Uh huh." Bliss nodded, her expression suspiciously wide-eyed. "And maybe it has something to do with a certain redhead you spent most of Wednesday night talking to."

Sophie felt a blush creep into her cheeks, even though she had nothing to feel guilty about.

"So what if it does?" She turned to look at her friends, who were grinning so widely now they practically looked maniacal.

"Hey, I'm all for you getting out more, Soph. It's just...Derek."

Sighing, she shook her head. "Is there something I don't know about him? Is he a freak? Does he pick his nose in public? Does he kick puppies? Tell me what's so bad about him?"

By the time she finished, Bliss was shaking her head so hard,

Sophie was afraid her friend was going to hurt herself. And Faith was laughing.

"No, no, no!" Bliss looked so distressed, Sophie felt a little sorry for her. "Nothing like that. Ugh. Sorry. I *like* Derek. You two just seem..."

Bliss looked at Faith for help. Faith made a show of whistling and watching the flashing lights bouncing along the seats and the ceiling.

"Too what?" Sophie prompted.

Bliss gave a huge sigh. "I figured neither of you would ever get a word in edgewise and you'd hate each other. It honestly never occurred to me that you'd hit it off."

"So you think I talk too much?"

Faith snorted and put her hand over her mouth as Bliss looked increasingly flustered.

Sophie couldn't help herself. As the youngest of five girls, she'd always felt like she had to make sure everyone remembered she was there. Not that she hadn't been spoiled rotten by her parents and her sisters. She had been. She'd been loved and adored. But in her house, if you didn't speak up for yourself, someone would do it for you. And her sisters were completely different people.

So yes, she was teasing the hell out of Bliss. She'd let her off the hook soon enough but for now...

"No, of course, I don't think that. And oh my god, you are totally playing me right now, aren't you?"

Sophie started to laugh. "Yeah, pretty much. Sorry, but you're easy, sweetie."

Bliss's eyes gleamed. "Shane says that, too. But he likes that about me."

"I'm sure he does. So what are you two going to do this summer? Is he going to stay in the area or is he going to go home for a while like he did last summer?"

Bliss's gaze flashed away for a few seconds and Sophie frowned. Trouble in paradise? No way. Shane and Bliss were so right for each other, it was scary.

"Hey, is something wrong?"

"No, no, nothing's wrong. It's just," she turned to Faith, who gave her a lopsided, sad little grin, "Shane's probably going to spend half the summer training in Minnesota with some top goalie coach and...I think I'm going to be moving out with him."

"Seriously? You're going to give up your job and follow him to Minnesota? What are you going to do out there?"

Bliss shrugged, nibbling on her bottom lip. "Not sure yet. Maybe nothing. Maybe take some online courses? I don't know. I only know we don't want to be apart for months. And it's not like I can't find another job. I knew if we continued to see each other, I'd have to make some choices. I guess...I'm ready to move on. And it's not like I won't be back. Shane will probably be back with the Redtails next season, at least for the start. After that..."

She shrugged, but Sophie could tell Bliss was excited. And happy. Happy to be spending the summer with the man she loved.

Just then the music got louder and the lights went out as the announcer welcomed everyone to the game and the teams began to skate onto the ice.

She was happy for Bliss. Honestly. She just couldn't imagine giving up her entire life to follow a guy as he bounced around from team to team. What about Bliss's plans? Her dreams?

So why are you here, lusting after a hockey player?

Because she was sick of being the good girl who stayed home every night and did her homework or went to work because her parents needed her or babysat her nieces and nephews because her brother-in-law had to work late or her sister had a meeting.

She was ready for a little fun. Okay, a *lot* of no-commitment fun with a hot guy. And Derek seemed like he'd be more than willing to provide that fun. Even if no one else seemed to think they'd be good for each other. Hell, it wasn't like she was going to marry the guy. She only wanted to have sex with him.

With Bliss and Faith's attention focused on the ice, she let herself look at the guys lined up on the bench across the ice from where she was sitting. With their helmets off, she immediately picked out Derek.

He was the one who couldn't stand still. He shifted back and forth from foot to foot. Like most of the players, he had his head bowed but, every now and then, he shook his head, like he was having a conversation.

As the chorus of elementary school kids who couldn't hit a high note to save their souls wrapped up their ear-piercing rendition of the anthem and the lights came up, Derek's head popped up and his focus narrowed to the ice.

She could practically see the determination on his face, even from across the ice. She had to admit, if only to herself, that just looking at him made her stomach hollow and her lungs labor.

Yes, she knew how stupid that sounded but at least no one else could tell just by looking at her.

Sneaking a peek at her friends, she saw their attention riveted to the ice. She waited until play started and the loud music stopped before she leaned over to Faith.

"I didn't realize you were such a big hockey fan."

Faith shrugged and glanced at Sophie before looking back at the ice. "I wasn't always. It grows on you."

"Oh, there." Bliss tapped Sophie on the arm. "Look. There's Derek. No. 20."

Sophie's gaze immediately sought out the players clustered around the goal but didn't see him. She found him a little farther out, closer to the center. Amazingly, he was still. At least at that moment. He watched the action around the goal for several seconds before he made a move.

After that, she barely took her eyes off him. When he wasn't on the ice, her gaze strayed toward the bench more often than she watched the game.

He was surprisingly quiet on the bench, at least as far as she could tell from where she sat. Which didn't mean he was silent. He was the first to stand and shout if a call didn't go their way or if one of his teammates got crunched by another player. Then he had a lot to say. And since she was watching him so closely, she realized he usually had something to say to that other player if they met up on the ice. She figured it wasn't anything nice, considering the way he'd just slammed an opposing player into the boards.

By the end of the third period, the Redtails were winning by two goals and the other team seemed to do everything wrong, which meant they were taking some cheap shots.

"Hey!" She yelled at the ice before turning to Bliss. "That guy just stuck his stick in Derek's side. Why isn't he getting a penalty for that?"

Bliss and Faith both grinned up at her with identical, knowing smiles. Which just made Sophie wrinkle her nose at them.

"This late in the game, they're not gonna call a penalty unless it's blatant." Bliss's smile shifted to a wry grin. "Besides, Derek'll repay him for that jab."

"What do you mean?"

Sophie had already returned her attention to the ice, where Derek was skating toward the opponent's net.

Damn, the guy was fast. Not as fast as some of the other guys but, holy crap, she'd kill herself if she ever tried to skate like that.

And don't get her started on skating backward. For some reason, watching Derek glide so effortlessly turned her on. It was an inexplicable response to something so random that she shook her head to get rid of the thought. Of course, that didn't really work but...whatever.

Derek reached the puck first but the Charleston Renegades player who'd followed him the whole way down the ice barely slowed as he plowed into Derek's side and flattened him against the boards.

"Hey!" She stood, booing as a few other fans did around her. "Get off him!"

Out of the corner of her eye, she saw Faith and Bliss exchange more grins, which she completely ignored. She had a game to watch and the action never stopped.

Derek never slowed at all. He kept working to get the puck,

shoving his stick into any place he could fit it and moving his feet, finally kicking the puck away to another Redtails player, who shot it toward the net. It didn't go in but the Redtails had the other team by the short hairs. They were winning and had all of the momentum.

As she settled back into her seat, Derek skated back to where he seemed to spend a lot of time when the Redtails had the puck near the goal. On the outskirts. She'd figured out that it was his job to keep the puck near the net where they wanted to score and away from Shane's net.

She had a feeling her father was wincing right now and had no idea why. Of all his daughters, Sophie was the one who'd never really liked sports. Her high school hadn't had a hockey team when she'd been a student. She could fake her way through football or basketball if she had to. And baseball was easy. Hit, throw, catch, run the bases.

This sport was more like soccer, which she only knew a little more about because several of her nieces and nephews played and she loved her family and attended as many games as she could.

But there wasn't as much contact in soccer as there was in hockey. And the soccer games she attended were played by adorable little kids in shorts and matching t-shirts. Not six-foot-plus, two-hundred-pound men who crushed each into the wooden walls of an ice rink on a regular basis.

She still couldn't watch any of the guys take a hit and not flinch in sympathy. How the hell they took such a beating at every game and made it back onto the ice for the next one astounded her.

Like now. The Redtails in front of the net were being hammered by the Renegades players. She knew there had to be major penalties being inflicted but none of the refs were blowing their whistles.

It was seriously starting to piss her off. And she wasn't the only one.

The chant of "Ref, you suck" had gone up a few times earlier but now practically everyone in their section was saying it.

Of course, she had to join in.

They kept the chant up until the clock clicked down to zero and the buzzer rang. Jumping to her feet, she yelled and high-fived departing fans as they made their way up the stairs to the exit, right by her seat.

"Okay, I get the appeal." She turned to face Bliss and Faith, who were laughing. At her. She didn't care. She'd had a blast.

"So I guess you want to come to the game tomorrow night?"

She groaned. "I wish. The bar'll be busy and Dad would tell me to go but he won't bring in anyone to cover for me and he and Carlos would be all alone in the kitchen and that's not a good scene."

"Soph." Bliss gave her the look, the one with the raised eyebrows that made her feel like one of her nephews after he'd stolen the tray of baklava at the church party. "What's he going to do when you leave for good?"

She shrugged, but it wasn't something she liked to think about. Because she knew it'd be a struggle. And she hated knowing she'd be leaving him in the lurch. Even though he kept telling her she needed to start living her own life.

"He'll have to hire someone. But for now, he's got me. And I don't mind. I like working at the bar. I like the people."

Bliss opened her mouth like she was going to say something else then closed it with a sigh.

But Faith continued to grin. "Like all those hot hockey players."

Sophie gave Faith a discreet middle finger with a smile, which Faith laughed off. But it worked to get Bliss to move on.

"Then I guess you have to come out with us tonight." Bliss waved a hand in front of her and stood. "That wasn't a question. Of course you are. We won't be out late because of the game tomorrow but Shane said several of the guys are going to Kaley's. Derek will be there."

Then, hell, yes, she was planning to go out tonight.

"Sure, I guess that'd be okay."

Faith snorted as she maneuvered her wheelchair toward the exit now that most everyone else had already left.

"You are *so* not good at being nonchalant."

Sophie shrugged, knowing Faith was totally right about that.

"Lead on, ladies. I'll follow wherever you're going."

And hopefully wherever that was, Derek would be there as well.

———

"So, D-man, you coming out with us tonight? Bliss is gonna meet us there. She said to tell you Sophie'll be there. Just in case you wanted to know."

Sitting with an icepack on his shoulder and another on his knee, Derek knew the answer to Shane's question should be no.

He should head home to spend a few quality hours with alternating hot and cold packs and a bottle of ibuprofen. They had another game tomorrow against the Renegades and he needed to be in good condition because those bastards would be gunning for them.

And he probably had a huge target on his back from the game tonight.

But...

Sophie would be there.

And he wanted to talk to her again. Okay, so he wanted to do more than talk but he'd settle for talking if that's all she wanted.

He looked down at his shoulder, already turning a pretty spectacular shade of blue. Talking might be all he was good for tonight. Damn, that hurt.

"Yeah, at least for one beer."

Shane's expression didn't change but Derek could swear the guy was laughing at him. Silently, of course. Shane was one of the quietest guys he knew besides Robbie.

"We'll meet you there."

"Sure. Meet you there."

He stood, biting back a groan as multiple aches and pains hit him at once. But the thought of seeing Sophie again kept him moving forward. Pulling on his clothes, he listened to the guys around him talk, pumped from the win and looking forward to the game tomorrow.

"Hey, D, you going out?"

Rolling his tie and putting it in his jacket pocket, Derek looked over his shoulder at Robbie.

"Yeah, you coming?"

Robbie nodded. "Mind if I catch a ride?"

"Course not. Let me just— Fuck. *Shit.* Goddamm, that hurts."

"Aw, does Derek have a few owwies?" Richie called out from across the room. "Maybe you can find someone to kiss them for you."

"Fuck you, Dickhead." Derek tossed out, exactly as he normally would. "You're just jealous because I won't let you do it for me."

Richie gave him the finger but the completely normal exchange with his teammate felt off tonight. Or maybe he just didn't care enough to put any real effort into ribbing Richie, which was usually one of his favorite pastimes because Richie was the one guy on the team who could take it as well as he dished it out.

He just wanted to get out of here and see Sophie. And that in itself was a strange feeling. He couldn't remember the last time he'd been excited about a girl.

As he made his way out to his car with Robbie, he mulled that one over in his head.

Who the hell was the last girl he'd even dated more than a few times? Hockey had been his life for so long that girls had slid off his radar. Not that he didn't pick them up and get laid but...

Shit, maybe he was a total douche and that's the reason he never had a girlfriend?

Getting into his truck, he turned the key and let Robbie get strapped in before he said, "Am I a douche?"

Robbie's head turned so fast, he'd probably have whiplash tomorrow. His mouth opened but it took him a few seconds to formulate an answer.

"Dude, what the hell?"

"Am I an asshole? I mean, I don't think I am but maybe I just don't see it."

Robbie stared at him like he'd grown three heads and had started licking himself with one of them.

"Are you s-sure you're okay? Did you take a s-shot to the head I didn't see?"

Derek gave him the finger before he put the truck in gear and headed out of the parking lot. The bar was in West Reading, not far from Sophie's place. It'd only take a few minutes to get there and Derek needed an answer before they arrived.

He trusted Robbie to give him a truthful answer.

"I'm fine. I just...You don't think I'm a douche, do you?"

Out of the corner of his eye, he saw Robbie shaking his head. "No, I don't think."

"Do you think women think I'm a douche?"

Stopped for a red light, Derek glanced over at Robbie, who stared back at him with so much what-the-fuck written all over his face it'd be funny if his answer wasn't so important.

"I don't even k-know how to answer that. I'm t-totally confused."

"It's not a difficult question. Do you think women think I'm a douche? I mean, I like women. I don't want them to think I'm this asshole who doesn't respect them, right? But I am who I am. I just need to know if I'm an asshole."

"Are we being s-secretly recorded?"

Derek shifted in his seat, wondering if he wanted to know the answer, which Robbie seemed in no hurry to give. "Just answer the question."

"No, I don't think you're a d-douche. You *can* be a pain in the ass but that's d-different. You're just you, man."

Since those were the most words Robbie had strung together in as long as Derek had known the guy, he didn't think he could let that go without saying something. "Damn, man, I didn't know you could use that many words in a sentence. I appreciate the effort."

Then he smiled to let Robbie know he was kidding.

Robbie pointed at him. "See. You're a p-pain in the ass but you're not an asshole. What the hell's with all the q-quest—Oh."

"Oh what?"

Derek gave the car a little gas as they headed over the Penn Street Bridge.

"Heard you met a girl. Did she b-blow you off?"

"No, she didn't blow me off. She's gonna be here tonight."

"And you d-don't want to come off like an asshole."

He shrugged. Maybe this conversation had been a bad idea. Robbie wasn't exactly known for his skill with women. The guy barely opened his mouth around them because of his stutter, which wasn't really that bad.

"Dude, women love you. Why so emo?"

Derek had to laugh. When Robbie wanted to be funny, the guy totally nailed it.

"I'm not being emo. And don't use that word in public. You sound like you're twelve. And a girl."

Robbie gave him the finger, which just made Derek laugh again. "I just wondered. I know I can be..."

"Loud? Obnoxious? Abrasive?"

"Yeah, yeah, don't use all your words at once."

"You're not." Robbie shrugged. "You're just t-talkative. It's not a bad thing. I run out of s-shit to say in a minute."

"Talking's easy. Better than awkward silence."

There'd been a lot of that in his house, which is probably why he'd learned to fill it.

Robbie either didn't know what to say to that or he'd used his quota of words for the day. He fell silent as Derek parked across the street from the bar.

Tugging his suit jacket closed as the wind whipped through the buildings, he hurried across the street toward the one-story building on the corner. Short, square, and no frills, Kaley's had become a popular hangout with the team, mainly because it was close to their apartments, the food was decent, and the beer was cheap.

Robbie had already pushed through the door and was holding it open for him. Laughter drifted out and he stopped just outside. Sometimes, the flashbacks were brutal reminders of what he tried so hard to forget.

Sometimes, it was the sound of drunken laughter, sometimes it was the simple sound of liquid being poured into a glass or the sound of glass hitting a wooden bar. Sometimes, he just needed some fresh air before he walked through the door and shoved all of that baggage away so he could have a good time.

Tonight was one of those nights. Even though he had something amazing to look forward too, sometimes he just needed to get his head on straight before he walked in.

"Derek? You okay?"

He turned to find Shane behind him, his arm wrapped around Bliss's shoulders.

He grinned, nodding. "Just getting some air."

Trying not to be blatant, he looked around Shane but didn't see anyone else. Damn, had she gone home?

"Don't worry." Bliss grinned at him. "She'll be here. She got caught at the light at Second and Penn."

He affected an innocent look. "I don't know who you're talking about."

Bliss rolled her eyes and huffed out a laugh. Shane just shook his head.

"Uh huh. Since she's driving herself, why don't you wait for her? She never took her eyes off of you the entire game, by the way."

Oh yeah? Well, that was a damn good thing to know. Which meant he was still smiling when he heard another car coming down the street.

Shane began to walk toward the door, tugging Bliss along with him. "We'll see you inside, D."

"Uh huh."

"We *will* see you inside, right?"

Bliss's question barely registered as she disappeared inside the bar. He was too busy watching Sophie get out of her car across the street.

She practically bounced out of the car then bit her lip and turned back, as if she'd forgotten something. Bending at the waist, she reached inside. Which meant he had a clear shot of her ass. And damn, the girl had a nice ass.

Okay, probably not something he wanted to mention to her. Or get caught looking at.

His gaze snapped up to her face just as she turned around. And the smile on her face... Well, damn. She looked happy to see him. Like, genuinely happy. And not in a, *Hey, I wanna jump your bones* kind of way.

Maybe he shouldn't be so happy about that. Maybe he was destined to be shoved into that unholy "let's be friends" category, where he'd spent much of his college years. Between his hockey schedule and his class schedule and his workout schedule, he hadn't had much time for girls. And especially not after Mandy eviscerated him publicly.

Which had probably kept him out of even more trouble than he'd managed to get into between his mouth and his short fuse. Add in the stress of needing to maintain his grades to keep his scholarship... Yeah, that had been fun. Not.

But tonight... Tonight was gonna be fun.

CHAPTER 6

Sophie caught sight of Derek across the street, waiting at the entrance to the bar.

She couldn't help smiling. Damn, he was gorgeous. Even though his hair was a little too long and looked like he hadn't combed it after his shower.

She wanted to run her hands through it and smooth those curls.

And she really wanted to feel that beard against her skin. Her cheek, her neck. Lower.

Wow, where had all the oxygen gone? She sucked in air and caught herself just before she stepped into the street without checking for traffic. How embarrassing would it be to get creamed by a car while she smiled at a hot guy?

Probably just her luck, actually.

After checking both ways, she started across, her eyes only on him.

"Hey, Sophie. Glad you could make it. Have a good time at the game?"

She stopped in front of him, a little mesmerized by his smile. "I did. It was a lot of fun. I mean, I had no idea what was going on most of the time but it was great. I can't believe you're still standing upright, though." Without thinking, she put her hand on his forearm. "How are you feeling? Are the games always that violent? That guy totally should've gotten a penalty that last time he hit you. Why didn't he? I mean, aren't you in pain right now? Oh, my god, I'm running at the mouth. Sorry."

She withdrew her hand before she could do something totally stupid. Like pet him. She swore she felt his muscles flex beneath her palm.

Then his smile reappeared, making her feel like someone had just drenched her in warm, gooey sunshine. And she couldn't stop smiling, either. Or talking. Which was what happened when she got overly excited.

Damn, what would happen if she ever got this guy naked? She might drool and totally embarrass herself.

"No problem. You've got a great voice. I could listen to you all night."

Her mouth dropped open for several seconds before she could close it. Seriously? He liked her voice. Most of the guys she'd dated had come to hate how much she talked. Hell, even her family got sick of her sometimes.

Of course, this guy had just met her, so she'd give him a week. Hell, maybe not even that long.

Oh, just shut up.

Ugh.

Her smile was more like a grimace. And damn if he didn't recognize it right off the bat.

"Hey, Sophie. That's not a line." He put his hand over his heard. "Gods-honest truth, I swear. Come on, we better get inside before Bliss comes looking for you." Then he leaned and spoke directly into her ear. "But that doesn't mean I wouldn't rather spend the night listening to you talk."

"Well, have no fear." Her laughter had a healthy dose of self-deprecation. "My family tells me I never shut up so you'll probably hear me talk a lot."

They were both laughing as they walked into the bar and, of course, everyone turned to stare.

Because her family owned a bar, she knew everyone else in the area who also owned a bar. Which meant she spent the next five minutes talking to Kaley's owner, Bob Kowalchuck, who always held court on Friday night.

"Sophie! Sweetheart, how's your dad? I never see him anymore. Tell that bastard he still owes me twenty bucks from the last poker game."

Wrapping her arms around the older man's shoulders for a hug, she smacked a kiss on his cheek before pulling away. Bob had to be eighty, if not older, and he probably wasn't kidding about the money. He and her dad and a few of the other bar owners in the area regularly met to talk business—actually, they met to play poker but they'd been lying about it for years so why break tradition?

"Hey, Bob. I'll tell him but you know what he'll say. That you still owe him for that keg of beer for the Christmas party."

The running joke between the men had been going for at least ten years.

Bob laughed until he started to cough, probably because he still smoked, even though his amazing wife, Maggie, had been nagging him for years to stop.

"Which is bullshit. So what are you doing out and about on a Friday night? I can't believe your dad gave you the night off." Bob's gaze flicked to Derek, who'd stopped by her side. "Bet he wouldn't have if he knew you'd be spending it with this one. Flaherty, you better be on your best behavior tonight. She's too good for you."

As her cheeks flared with color, she rolled her eyes and gave Derek a nudge toward the bar. "Just here for a few drinks. Talk to you later, Bob."

"You got it, sweetheart. Have a good night."

Oh, she planned to. She'd just forgotten how small her world was.

Sighing, she realized her dad would probably know she was here within five minutes. And that she was with Derek. Which she wasn't. Not really. She was here with friends.

Yeah, right. You just keep telling yourself that.

Five minutes later, she thought maybe that's exactly what was going on. Derek had walked her to the bar then immediately excused himself to go talk to one of the other players. Not a problem but she wondered if Bob had scared him off.

She glanced over at Derek, who seemed to be in an intense conversation with a younger guy, who looked seriously pissed.

"Don't worry, he'll be back. They do this every night after a game. Give 'em ten minutes. I'm Chrissy. Colin's my boyfriend."

The pretty blonde who didn't look much older than a teenager held out her hand and Sophie took it with a smile. "Sophie. Nice to meet you. Colin's on the team, yes?"

She nodded. "He's a winger. So, you and Derek? That's a surprise. I've never seen him date anyone."

"We're not dating." Which was true. "We just met the other night. He and Will and Justin stopped in for a drink and we started to talk. He's...nice."

Chrissy's smile became more of a grin. "He's a great guy...if you're not dating him. Or so I've heard. He can be a little intense and, damn, the man can talk. He's kind of exhausting, if you ask me."

A bitchy little part of herself thought, *No one asked you.* But of course, she didn't come out and say that, though she had to bite her tongue hard.

Shrugging, she glanced at Bliss, who rolled her eyes out of sight of Chrissy. "Like I said, not a date. Just out to have a drink with friends. What do you do, Chrissy?"

"Oh, I'm taking business classes this semester. Colin says I shouldn't get a job because we're never sure where he's going to be signed. And we go home to Minnesota after the season so he can train. My parents pay for college and Colin's parents cover his living expenses so I don't really have to work."

As Chrissy continued to talk, Sophie found it hard not to roll her own eyes. Basically, this girl did nothing except go to classes and follow her boyfriend around. She didn't work and apparently had no problem with that.

Just...wow. She couldn't imagine living like that. No job, take a couple classes a week and go to hockey games. And presumably make sure your boyfriend has clean clothes. Or maybe they had someone do their laundry, too.

Okay, wow. When Chrissy finally paused to take a breath, Bliss jumped into the silence and steered the conversation toward the upcoming playoffs, The three other girlfriends at the bar, including Chrissy, began to discuss that.

Sophie gave a sigh of relief. Which was when she heard a deep voice in her ear.

"Sorry about that. Didn't mean to desert you."

Turning to face Derek, she looked up at him with a rueful smile. "You didn't. I'm a big girl. I can take care of myself."

Hmm, maybe that had come out a little more defensive than she'd wanted because Derek's eyes widened and he got that expression men had when they thought they'd done something wrong but had no idea what. Her dad had worn that expression a lot living in a house with five women.

Mentally rolling her eyes, she reached for his arm and squeezed. "Don't freak. You're fine."

Now his smile reappeared. The smile that threatened to melt off her panties. How the hell did he do that? And what exactly was she going to do about it? Because she sure as hell didn't want to talk to anyone else tonight.

She wasn't going to kid herself. He was the only reason she was here tonight. Sure, hanging with Bliss was great but she didn't have to call off work to do that. No, the only reason she'd taken the night off was to have the chance to spend it with him.

She just had to figure out what exactly that meant for the rest of the night.

And whether or not she was going to invite him back to her apartment.

Oh, hell. She already knew the answer to that question was yes.

———

"Last call, people." The bartender had to raise his voice to be heard above the noise. "Get it now or get out."

"Oh, my god. Is it really quarter of two?" Sophie turned to look at the clock on the wall behind her. "Wow. And I didn't turn into a pumpkin. Amazing."

Derek hadn't even noticed there was a clock on the wall because, for the past almost-three hours, the only thing he'd had eyes for had been her.

Yeah, he'd talked to some of the guys. Occasionally. And he'd said a few words to Bliss. At least, he thought he had. He really didn't remember. All he could remember was talking to Sophie.

Like Wednesday night at her dad's bar, their conversation had flowed like two friends who hadn't seen each other in years and had a lot of catching up to do.

But unlike an old friend, Derek wanted to spend the rest of the night talking while he stripped off her clothes and got her in a bed where he could sink deep inside her and make her come before he exploded inside her.

That sounded like a plan. His only problem... He wasn't sure that's what Sophie wanted.

"You want another?"

He pointed at her mostly empty glass. She'd been nursing a rum and cola for the past hour. He'd had two beers the entire night. He had a game tomorrow. Technically, the game was tonight. But there was a lot of time between now and then. And he knew exactly how he wanted to spend some of it.

Her nose scrunched in a way that should not have been sexy but still managed to be.

"No, I better not. I've got a paper to write tomorrow for a class before work."

"What time do you work?"

"Depends when I get there. Noon to whenever I'm not needed. It's Saturday. Could be midnight. Could be eight. We just never know."

"Do you work every day?"

"No, not every day."

Good to know. "So I guess you wouldn't be free to come to the game?"

Her smile widened, as if she was happy he'd asked but she still shook her head. "No, not tomorrow night."

"Do your sisters help out, too?"

"Not anymore. They've all got families and real jobs. I don't mind helping out. I know someday I'm not going to be there. I worry about that. But my parents have never told me I had to work at the bar. I enjoy it. Most of the time."

"I think my mom and I would kill each other if we had to work together."

She paused, nibbling at her bottom lip. "Was your dad never in the picture?"

"For a while. But he was gone by the time I was five, so I don't really remember him. My mom had some issues," like being an alcoholic, "but she was there." Mostly.

Her expression softened and he swore she could read his mind.

"I'm sorry." She reached for him again, laying her hand on his bare forearm. "That must have sucked."

She looked so genuinely distressed, he wanted to comfort her. And this time, she didn't remove her hand right away. He'd rolled up his sleeves earlier due the warmth in the bar. Or maybe it was just due to being so close to her. Either way, her bare flesh rested against his bare flesh and, damn, if that didn't make him even more horny.

Was he always like this? Or was it just her?

He had a feeling he knew the answer to that question without having to think about it much.

"I didn't know any different at the time. My grandparents and my uncle and his kids were around so it wasn't like I didn't have family."

"But..." Her eyebrows rose. "Seems like there's a 'but' in there."

There was, but that was a conversation for another time. Preferably never. "I'd like to see you again."

Her smile was the most amazing smile he'd ever seen. Seriously. He had no clue why it made him feel like his blood had turned to lava. Or why he wanted to see her smile like that when he had her naked and pinned up against a wall.

Sophie brought all sorts of feelings he'd never had before.

"I'd like to see you again, too." Her nose scrunched again. "It's just a busy time for me. And for you, too, apparently."

It was, actually. The only way the timing on this could be worse is if the team was actually in the playoffs. But, damn it, he was no saint.

"I'm willing to give up a few hours of sleep if you are."

Her expression held a hint of sin. "So do you want to come back to my place?"

His grin widened until he hoped he didn't look like a loon. Then he leaned in closer until he could have rubbed his nose against hers. Which he had the almost insane urge to do.

"Why, Miss Sophie. I didn't know you had a wicked side."

Her answering smile spread slowly as her eyes flashed up at him with an invitation he had no plans to ignore.

"There're a lot of things you don't know about me. But I'm willing to give up a little sleep if you are."

Hell, he was willing to give up the entire night if he got to spend them with her. "Then I'm ready to go whenever you are."

The drive to Sophie's apartment barely took two minutes. Because she lived over her dad's bar.

"Damn. Guess you never have to worry about getting to work on time."

Laughing as she slotted her key in the lock, Sophie pushed open the door and flipped the switch by the door, flooding the interior with light.

A lot of light.

She must have noticed him blinking because she laughed. And that made his gut clench. When she laughed, all he could think about was making her laugh while she was naked.

"Sorry. I hate to come home to a dark apartment." She reached for the wall again and flipped a few of those lights off.

"No roommate?"

Dropping her purse on the table by the door, she shrugged out of her coat and dropped that on the chair next to the table. Then she kicked her shoes off and pushed them under the chair before stripping off her sweater.

He wouldn't have a problem if she kept going.

"After living with four older sisters for most of my life, I can honestly say I'm much happier on my own right now."

"No...significant other?"

She turned to stare at him. "If I did, you wouldn't be here. Guess I should ask the same question."

He shrugged, grinning at her raised eyebrows. "Haven't found anyone to put up with me yet."

"Maybe you just haven't found the right person."

"Maybe I haven't been looking."

Up until now, women had been a distraction. Sex was great but a girlfriend meant commitment. And the only commitment he'd wanted was the one to his career.

"I know what you mean. Between school and work and my family, I haven't even bothered to look. Too much trouble, if you know what I mean."

He knew exactly what she meant. The problem was, he hadn't expected to hear it coming from her.

"We must be perfect for each other."

She flopped onto the couch in the center of the room, tucked her feet under her butt and smiled at him.

"I enjoyed the game tonight."

Okay, she completely ignored his last comment, which he probably never should've said. No wonder she'd ignored it.

Walking over to the couch, he sat at the opposite end. Didn't want to crowd her. Well, actually, he did. But he'd wait for her to come to him. The one thing his mom had ingrained in him from the time he could talk was that a woman had to say yes. If she didn't, you backed the hell off. He always listened to his mom.

"Glad to hear it. That wasn't your first hockey game, was it?"

"No, I've been to a couple. But I have to admit, I didn't really watch the game. Usually I was in a suite with friends and we talked more than watched the game."

"And tonight?"

Her lips curled in a way that beckoned him closer. "I was a lot more interested in the game. Actually, I was more interested in one player."

His lips curved up. "And who was that?"

"Oh, you know, that hot goalie isn't too bad."

And there was that smile again, the one that said she was teasing him. He could work with that.

"I'm not sure you could take his girlfriend in a fight. Bliss is pretty tough. And the team would hate my guts if I had to mess up our goalie before our playoff run."

Her head fell back as she laughed, the sound hitting him low in the gut and traveling right to his balls. His gaze fell to her neck and the urge to lean forward and put his mouth on her rolled over him like a freight train. All the hair on his body bristled and his cock hardened.

He wanted to shift around to relieve the pressure but didn't want her to see his obvious reaction. Although she had to know he was into her. He was here, in the middle of the night when he should be home getting some sleep before the game tomorrow.

Of course, she didn't know that he never skimped on sleep the night before the game. She didn't know he barely ever went back to a girl's place unless he was pretty damn sure he was going to get laid.

This girl made him want to sit here and listen to her laugh. How damn sappy was that?

She pulled another one of those adorable faces that made him want to kiss it off her face.

"Are you telling me you don't think I could hold my own against Bliss?" Her brows rose and her head cocked to the side. "I'll have you know I take kickboxing and I'm not afraid to take on someone bigger than me. You don't back down from a fight either, do you?"

He shook his head. "Not in my nature, no. But I don't go looking for one, either."

"So then why did Chrissy call you an instigator?"

Because Chrissy was catty and had a big mouth, a mean girl who came on as sweetness and light before she became a raging bitch. And because Chrissy wasn't completely wrong.

"Because I got the reputation at college and it stuck."

"How long have you been playing?"

"Since I was seven. I grew up watching the Bruins with my Pop because my mom usually worked nights." Technically not a lie. "When I was seven, Pop took me to a free clinic. I already knew how to skate, but I wanted to play. Most of my friends did. They'd been going to clinics since they were five. We didn't have the money. Hockey's expensive, all the equipment, all the time. Sticks break, skates gotta be sharpened. Kids outgrow their gear almost every year."

He could tell by the look on her face that she got the point and, just like that, he was ten again and his skates were at least a size too small and he had to tape his pads around his arms because they were torn.

His mom had done the best she could and his grandparents had helped but they'd barely existed above the poverty line. It was all his mom could do to put food on the table some nights and sometimes there wasn't a lot of it.

And sometimes, instead of eating, his mom drank her meals. Which is why he'd known most of the bartenders in his North Dorchester neighborhood by their first name.

"I got lucky. I had enough skill to get noticed. And it didn't hurt that I was highly motivated."

Her expression encouraged him to keep going. She looked completely engrossed, which was unusual. People didn't usually take him seriously and tended to tune him out. Probably his fault for not talking about anything worthwhile. Except hockey, of course. And then he was usually talking to other players and not women. How he ever managed to get laid was a mystery.

"You wanted out."

He nodded. "Yeah." Desperately. "Hockey was my ticket."

"And you were good."

He shrugged. "Good enough for a USA Hockey coach to take notice and help me get what I needed to make it."

That help had included grants and scholarships and sometimes outright handouts. His mom had never turned down help when it came to him or his sister. She just wouldn't take it for herself. It frustrated the hell out of him.

"Did you go to college?"

"Full ride to Boston College." Damn proud of that. "Drafted at nineteen by the Colonials. Managed to keep my grades up and graduate on time and the Colonials sent me here. This is my third year."

"Do you like it here?"

He shrugged. "Yeah."

"But?"

"But what?"

"That didn't sound like a ringing endorsement."

He opened his mouth to say something snarky before he remembered she was new to the game.

"I love it here. Seriously. The guys are great. The coaches are amazing. The town's small and there's no good pizza in a hundred-mile radius but I can live with that. It's just not where I want to be. I want to be in Philly or home in Boston. Washington would be cool. Hell, I'd kill to play in Toronto or Montreal. Any of the original six teams. That's the ultimate goal. The NHL."

He could practically see the lightbulb go off over her head.

"Ah. I get it. You want to play for the majors."

Her obvious delight over figuring out what he was trying to say made him smile.

"That's the goal. But everybody wants to play for the NHL and the reality is not everyone makes it. Some people are good enough but they never get the chance. Some people'll just never be good enough."

"Are you good enough?"

From another person, that question might've been a dig. From Sophie, it sounded like sincere interest. Every word that came out of her mouth seemed genuine, which was a huge attraction for him. Over the past three years, he'd met so many women whose only goal was to bag a hockey player. Sometimes just for the night. Some of them wanted the ride. Those were the women who looked for the players on their way up. He'd met a few of those this first couple of years. And yeah, maybe fucking around had hurt his concentration that first year.

"Yeah, I think I am. And I think my coaches think so, too. But sometimes it doesn't work out."

"But it's not like you're ancient. You've still got time, don't you?"

"Yeah, sure. I've got a few years. But..."

"But what?" she prompted.

"But once you hit a certain age, you have to decide if the AHL is going to be enough."

"Would it be? For you?"

Honestly? "I don't know. Probably not." He shrugged like making it to the NHL didn't mean everything to him. "I'll adjust. Sometimes you gotta switch up your focus."

"What would you do if you couldn't play hockey?"

Just the question made him want to cringe, but he covered it with a shrug. "Haven't really given it much thought."

"You haven't *wanted* to give it much thought."

No, he didn't. And he didn't want to think about it now. "What about you? You don't want to work in your dad's bar for the rest of your life. You want to travel, right?"

She nodded and smiled, but her smile didn't seem as genuine as it had before.

"That's the plan. I should graduate at the end of the fall semester. Then I guess...we'll see."

Derek didn't usually read between the lines. He figured if people couldn't say straight out what they wanted to say, why should he give a shit?

But Sophie was no longer some random female he'd met at a bar.

"You don't want to leave your family."

Her smile softened even more and damn, if she didn't make him want to move closer and pull her onto his lap so he could cuddle her. Okay, yeah, maybe he wanted to do more than cuddle.

"They drive me crazy but, every time I think about actually leaving, I get this pit in my stomach that makes me doubt everything. Like, maybe I should just plan to get a job in the area. My parents aren't getting younger. My dad was forty-two when they had me and now he's sixty-five. He should retire. But then I worry about what he'll do all day. My mom's got her gardening and her sewing and her book club, which is really just an excuse for her and her friends to get together and drink. I don't know why they need an excuse but my mom will swear they actually discuss books every now and then. But my dad... the bar is his life."

"And you think if you're not around to help, he won't be able to do it without you."

Her smile softened even more. "Yeah. My sisters think I'm afraid to leave. They don't get it. How do you know what I'm thinking?"

Before he knew he was going to do it, he'd opened his mouth to tell her something he never discussed with anyone. Ever.

"Because I had the same fear with my mom and sister. My mom… wasn't always sober. She wasn't abusive. She just couldn't deal sometimes. My sister's younger, only by a year but she couldn't handle my mom like I could. So I went to Boston College. I'd gotten a few offers for full rides but Boston was the only school I wanted. I worked like hell to keep my grades up and not to be a hothead. I already had a reputation for being a pain in the ass so I addressed it upfront and told them I'd keep it under control."

"But isn't being a pain in the ass an asset in hockey?"

Laughing at her completely serious expression, and because she'd said nothing at all about his mom, he nodded. "Yeah, it can be. But you need to keep it in check or you start to take too many penalties. And coaches start to think you're a troublemaker."

Her smile made his blood heat. "I think you like making trouble."

His answering smile made her smile fade but the look in her eyes… His heart pounded and his throat dried and his dick got harder than it already was.

He wanted to close the space between them, put his hand on the back of her head and bring her in for a kiss. Hot, hard, deep, wet. A kiss where they didn't come up for air for hours. He wanted to pull her onto his lap and put his mouth over hers and—

"And I think I have a thing for guys who like to make trouble."

"So," he drew the word out, making her head cock to the side, "are you saying you have a thing for me? Because I'd be okay with that."

She leaned forward, not close enough yet to kiss but definitely within reach.

"And if I say yes?"

It was his turn to lean a little closer. Now their lips were only inches apart. Her dark eyes widened slightly but her lips curled into an even more wicked smile. "Then I guess I wouldn't have to ask to kiss you."

Her smile grew a little more wicked. He liked that smile on her.

Liked it a hell of a lot. "Oh, I don't know about that. How do you know I won't say no?"

"Are you saying no?"

She didn't answer for a few seconds and he wondered if she was going to string him along. She didn't seem the type but he had to admit he was having a hell of a good time just talking. If all she wanted to do was talk all night, he could handle that. He'd sit here and tell her anything she wanted to know about his life, about growing up, about hockey.

He'd be more than happy to have her tease the hell out of him all night. Hell, he'd even be happy to leave with blue balls if that meant he got to spend more time with her.

She shook her head. "I'm not going to say no."

He leaned in again, his lips a hair's breadth away from hers. "Fair warning. I'm gonna kiss you."

He leaned forward that extra inch and crushed her lips beneath his. He wanted to go slow, wanted to take his time. Instead he got a figurative kick in the ass when she pressed forward and smashed their mouths together in a kiss that took his breath away.

Holy shit. She kissed him like he was chocolate and she'd been craving it for weeks.

His brain shut down then and his body took over. Kind of like it did with hockey. But this was much, much better. He didn't have to think at all. He just had to feel the press of her lips against his.

Silky soft, her kiss sent a jolt of pure sensation down his spine. She didn't kiss him with any sense of hesitation. And she certainly didn't let him take over.

She set the pace and he followed her lead. Mostly because she was doing a damn fine job of it. But that didn't mean he wasn't going to take control at some point. Because, well, he couldn't help it.

Raising her hands to his face to cup his jaw, her mouth shifted on his and her fingernails scratched through the whiskers on his chin. They'd gotten a little longer than normal because he hadn't thought about it enough to shave in the past week. Now he was glad he hadn't.

The sensation was amazing. He wanted to purr, for fuck's sake. Then he wanted to rub those whiskers against the inside of her thighs until she purred, too.

Tilting his head, he opened his mouth a little wider and slid his tongue between her lips, not content to let her lead anymore. He needed more.

Putting his hands on her waist, he picked her up and set her on his lap. He heard the little surprised sound she made in her throat. Then her arms wrapped around his neck and her body pressed against his.

The feel of her breasts pillowed against his chest made him groan. Goddamn, the girl was stacked. Perfectly soft in all the right places. And when she wiggled her ass on his thighs, his cock reacted like she was giving him a lap dance. He didn't think he could get any more turned on if she was. Sophie made him respond in ways he never had. And he wanted more.

His mouth opened wider over hers and his tongue slid against hers, tasting her, coaxing her to give more. His hands slid from her shoulders to her neck then sank into the lushness of her hair. The strands felt like silk between his fingers, which was so fucking weird because that was a thought he'd never had before. He didn't think of a girl's hair like it was silk. He only noticed how a girl's hair felt if it happened to be against his legs.

Shit. Maybe he was an ass. Right now, though, nothing mattered but making sure she continued to kiss him.

Cupping the back of her head with one hand, he slid the other down her back. Slowly, making sure he stroked every inch he could before he reached the hem of her shirt. Then he slipped two fingers beneath and stroked the naked skin of her back.

When she moaned into his mouth, he knew he was on the right track. And when she shimmied closer and wrapped her arms even more tightly around his neck, he shoved his whole hand beneath the fabric and spread his palm over her lower back. The warmth of her skin sank into his and made his blood surge.

He wanted to feel every inch of her skin pressed against his. Wanted her naked, her knees on either side of his hips as she leaned over him.

With a quick motion, he shifted them then leaned back until his head touched the decorative pillow he'd seen at the end of the couch.

Keeping his hand on her head, he brought her down with him. She went with no resistance and they ended up full-length on the couch in a position that made him very, very happy.

And gave her absolutely no doubt about the state of his happiness. That apparently made her happy, too. She wriggled against his cock, her body hitting him at the perfect angle to tease him with the pressure.

Pulling away, she looked down at him, a hint of a grin on her lips.

"Are you okay? I don't want to hurt you. Bliss said you'd probably be sore. You got hit an awful lot. Does that happen all the time?"

He captured her lips for another kiss before he answered. "No, you're not hurting me. Unless you're talking about a specific part of my anatomy then yes, it hurts. But I'm not complaining."

Her smile was doing more damage than any hit he'd taken tonight.

"Then I must be doing something wrong."

She leaned forward and kissed him before he could say anything more. And when she pulled away, he was a little ashamed to realize he was having trouble breathing.

"Why do you think you're doing something wrong? Trust me, I would tell you if you were."

Her husky laughter made his cock even harder.

"Because you're not talking. You're so quiet, something must be wrong."

Damn, he liked her mouth and every sassy word that came out of it. "You want me to talk more?"

"I like your voice." Her fingers framed his chin, petting his beard then moving up to trace his lips until they fucking tingled. "And I like your mouth."

Holy fuck. She took his goddamn breath away. "Then I'll talk all you want. You're fucking beautiful, do you know that? Want to know what else I can do with my mouth?"

Her smile widened again. "Yes, please. I'd love you to show me."

"Then come back down here."

She lowered her mouth again and he took it for a kiss that stole her breath this time. But she didn't pull away. She went right back to rolling her hips against his. If they were naked, the tip of his cock would be rubbing her clit.

Goddamn, he wanted to be naked. But there was part of him that wanted to prolong this torture for as long as possible.

Her tongue slid against his as she wriggled her body down just enough that her mound now rested on his cock. The pressure was almost painful. Good thing he liked it. Hell, he liked it so much he wouldn't move if the house was burning down around them.

He kissed her for a few more, long moments but he'd promised her he could do more with his mouth. So he slid his lips away from hers and kissed his way to her neck.

She accommodated him by lifting her head back so he had a clear shot. He spread kisses back to just below her ears, feeling her shiver against him in reaction. And wriggling against him even more.

Yeah, he really liked that. He wanted more of that.

Lifting his head, he kissed her earlobe before he took it between his teeth and bit. Not hard enough to hurt but hard enough to make her gasp. Her body shook with reaction and her right hand sank into his hair and gripped him hard.

Now, that he really liked.

"You are so fucking soft."

She turned her head to press her nose against his cheek and rubbed the tip against his whiskers.

"And you're not. I love having your hands on my body. But aren't you going to move them?"

"I'll put them wherever you want me to."

She paused for a moment, as if she had to think about her response. "I want to feel them all over."

"I have no problem with that."

She lifted her head so she could look into his eyes. He saw a hint of shyness in her gaze and frowned. But then her gaze dipped down to his shirt and he totally lost that thought.

"I want to put my hands on you, too."

"And I'm totally okay with that. You can put your hands wherever the hell you want to put them."

Her brows rose and the look in her eyes turned wicked, making his heart pound even harder.

"Anywhere at all?"

"Anywhere at all."

Putting her hands on his chest, she pushed herself up onto her knees and stared down at him, her hands resting on her thighs. But her expression made it clear she was considering exactly where to put them next.

His breath caught in his chest as she reached for him. For a few seconds, he actually thought she'd go for the belt, but then her hand changed trajectory and went for the third button on his shirt, still done up.

"So," she flicked the button through the hole and trailed her fingers to the next one, "if I want to put my hands on your chest, I need to take off your shirt first, right?"

He had to swallow before he could speak. "That would be a good place to start, sure."

She undid the next two buttons then stopped and looked up at him again, her fingers resting just above the waistband of his pants.

"But that's not where you want me to stop, is it?"

"Hell, no. Don't stop."

She made a production out of opening the last button above his waistband. And only inches from the tip of his cock.

He swallowed a groan.

"I don't want to stop." Her smile deepened. "I'm definitely going to enjoy unwrapping you."

He huffed out a laugh. "So now I'm a present?"

Did he actually see a hint of red on her cheeks?

"Maybe. A little. A present to myself."

He was happy to be whatever she wanted him to be tonight. Present. Toy. Plaything. Anything at all.

"Babe, I'll serve myself up on a platter with an apple in my mouth as long as you keep taking off my clothes."

She laughed, like he'd meant her too. She'd started to look like she was thinking too much. And thinking at a time like this was not what either of them needed.

"Then lift up and let me push your shirt off your shoulders."

"Your wish is my command."

Lifting his upper body forward brought his mouth close to hers again. But he didn't kiss her this time. He hovered only inches away and watched her eyes darken.

Neither of them made another move for several seconds, gazes locked together. He heard every breath she took, saw her lips part and had to clamp down on the urge to cover her mouth and kiss her hard as he slid his tongue between her lips.

But another part of him was having one hell of a good time letting her control the pace.

"So are you going to take off my shirt or are we going to sit here and stare at each other? Just want to let you know I'm good either way. I could stare at you all night and never get bored. I'll probably get hungry by morning, though. And then we're going to need to eat because I have a game tomorrow night—"

She slid her hands into the gaping neckline of his shirt, pushed it off his shoulders and down his arms. Her gaze dropped to watch and her lips curved into another one of those smiles.

As her fingers trailed over his white cotton t-shirt, he shook the dress shirt down his arms then tossed it on the floor. At the moment, he didn't care where it landed.

"I never thought I'd say this, but I think I might develop an unhealthy fixation on white t-shirts."

"You can leave it on if you want. I have a few other pieces of clothing you can remove first. Better yet, why don't you take off your clothes and then you can put on my t-shirt so I can see what the fascination is."

Laughter lit her eyes as she looked back into his. "You're kinda sneaky, aren't you?"

"I have no idea what you're talking about."

"That's how you get under people's skin, isn't it? You're sneaky."

"Nope, still don't know what you mean."

"Uh huh." Her lips held a slight, sexy curve. "You're cute, too. I bet you get pretty much anything you want from women, don't you? All you have to do is smile and charm them and they pretty much fall at your feet, don't they?"

Since that had honestly never happened, he shook his head. "Women who know me have been known to run the other way when they see me coming. I kinda can't keep my mouth shut, if you haven't noticed."

"Oh, I've noticed. I just happen to like hearing you talk."

Well, damn. How about that? She actually liked hearing him talk. "We must be a match made in heaven because my mouth is usually open."

"Then I guess my challenge will be to see if I can get you to be silent."

"I know one way you can do that."

Her head cocked to the side. "Oh, yeah? And how's that?"

"Kiss me."

With her hands gripping his shoulders, she leaned forward and pressed her mouth against his. This time, she slid her tongue between his lips and tasted him. His head dropped back slightly as he let her take the lead.

See, he didn't always have to be in charge. He could—

Damn, her kisses did amazing things to his body. Goosebumps

covered his skin and his lungs chugged overtime. And when she drew away, he followed her until he either had to let her go or wrap his arms around her waist and not let her go at all.

He drew back at the very last second and wanted to beat his chest like a savage at the dazed look on her face.

It took her a few seconds to blink back to awareness. She sucked in a deep breath, which made her breasts rise and fall, mesmerizing him with their motion. He wanted her to hurry the hell up and get them both naked so they could have sex right here on the couch. She could straddle his hips just like this and sink down on his cock and ride him until they were both sweaty and—

She sank one hand into his hair and tugged. "Did I lose you?"

Their gazes met and held. "If you mean am I imagining you naked, then yes. Otherwise, no way in hell are you going to lose me anytime soon. In fact, you might have a hard time getting rid of me tomorrow because I have a feeling I'm not gonna want to leave."

Shit. He reconsidered his words the second they left his mouth because he sounded like a fucking stalker.

"That would be okay." She shrugged. "But at some point, my dad's gonna come looking for me. And we probably don't want to be caught like this by my dad."

"Does he have a shotgun?"

"No, but he does keep a wooden bat behind the bar."

"Probably better for everyone if Dad doesn't have to come looking for you."

"Then maybe we should move on."

"Does that include taking off this t-shirt? Because I'd really love for you to take off this t-shirt."

"I guess we can do that. Lift your arms."

He crunched forward another few inches so he could use his hands to reach behind him and pull the t-shirt over his head and threw that down with his shirt.

Her indrawn breath caught his attention and his gaze flew to her face. She looked horrified.

Shit, what the—

"Oh my god, doesn't that hurt?"

If she'd been pointing at his crotch, he would've made a joke. But no, her gaze was pinned to his left shoulder. He turned to look then shrugged at the huge bruise spreading from his clavicle to his nipple.

"Nah. Not now, anyway. Probably hurt like a bitch tomorrow. Nothing you need to worry about now."

Her eyes widened as she looked up at him. "Seriously? That doesn't hurt?"

"Nope. Honestly the only part of my body that hurts is lower. And totally begging for you to touch it."

Her wide eyes flashed up to his, her lips parted in shock.

Fuck. He'd crossed that line between funny and crass. He had a gift for it, apparently. His goddamn mouth—

Her head fell back as she laughed, her hands braced on his stomach. Every movement made the seam of her jeans between her legs press closer to his cock, straining behind his zipper.

"Oh. My. God." She shook her head and met his gaze again. "You are too much. The *huge* bruise on your shoulder that looks like you broke something doesn't hurt because all you can think about is your hard on. Am I calling that one correctly?"

The humor in her eyes drew an answering smile from him. Actually, it was a huge grin because she got him. And she didn't want to strangle him. At least, not yet.

Maybe he was gonna get laid tonight.

"Yeah, pretty much." He moved his hands to her hips and tugged her down, close enough that he could rub his erection more fully against her. "So are you gonna do something about it?"

Her smile held that wicked tilt again. "I could get you an ice pack. You could decide where you want to put it."

He tried to pout but he couldn't hold it long. "Aw, sweetheart. Now you're just being mean."

"I'm trying to be nice."

"I know how you could be nicer."

Her brows lifted. "Oh, I'm sure you do. Why don't you tell me how?"

"You could put your hands on me. Anywhere you want. I'm not picky."

Her smile softened a little as her fingers curled against his stomach. "Anywhere I want?"

"Lady's choice."

Her head cocked to the side, as if she were considering her options. Then her hands began to slide slowly upward.

Her nails scratched along his pants, heading up. His breath caught and held in his chest as he waited to discover her final destination.

"So if I wanted to touch you here," her fingers stopped just above his waistline, "that would be okay?"

With his dress shirt still tucked into his pants, that meant he still couldn't feel her fingers on his skin.

"Sure, that's okay."

He reached for her hands and dragged them the tiniest bit farther up his body until her fingertips brushed against his ribs. His bare ribs. He wanted to groan at the contact, only barely managed to keep it from escaping. But she had to be able to tell how just that tiny touch affected him.

"But this is so much better."

He released her immediately, more to see what she'd do now. She didn't disappoint.

Splaying her fingers wider, she pressed her palms against his sides and let her fingers dig a little deeper into his skin.

His lungs began to work a little harder, his chest rising a little faster.

Her gaze dipped to watch her hands as they continued up his sides. The brush of her skin against his caused a rash of goosebumps.

"Your skin is so warm but you have goosebumps."

"Trust me. I'm not cold."

Her fingers trailed back down but, this time, they moved closer to his center, brushing through the hair on his chest before trailing farther down his stomach. His stomach contracted as her fingers brushed lower, stopping short of coming close to anything interesting.

"Then maybe you need to take off a few other pieces of clothing, just to be more comfortable."

"Why don't you help me with that?"

"I thought I was helping."

That smile made him want to grab her and pull her under him so he could remove a few of her clothes. He didn't because he was enjoying the hell out of her game and he didn't want to interrupt.

"So far, you haven't taken off any of my clothes so I'm not sure how much help you're really being."

Her nose crinkled for a second before she pouted, fake and adorable and flirty. "I guess I could take care of this belt for you. Looks like it might be too tight."

Actually, the belt was just for show. "Yes, please. It's killing me. I think that's exactly what you should do."

Her fingers made a slow slide back down to his waist, lightly brushing against his sides before dipping a centimeter below his waistband.

His body reacted like she'd wrapped one hand around his cock and cupped his balls in the other. Every muscle contracted, lungs included, and he stilled as much as he could. Only the rise and fall of his stomach continued on a much-increased pace, waiting for her to make another move.

Finally, after what seemed like forever, her fingers slid around to just below his belly button before she worked the leather through the buckle. As her fingers worked that close to his cock, it stiffened even more, pressing against the zipper and trying to push through the top of his pants.

He bit back a groan as she took her own sweet time, drawing out what should've been a two-second process to at least half a minute. Not that he wasn't enjoying it, but...damn, he wanted more.

"Are you always this slow?"

She batted her eyes at him innocently, as she tugged on his belt, pulling it through the loops until it released completely and she dropped it on the floor with his shirts.

"Am I doing something wrong?" She held her hands up in front of her, like he'd told her to stop.

There was no way in hell he would ever tell her to stop.

"Nope. You're doing just fine. You're just going really, really slow."

"Sometimes slow is better than getting things done in a hurry."

"Trust me, I'm in no hurry to be done. But I'm in one hell of a hurry to get inside you."

Damn, that smile. It made him want to rip off her jeans, grab her by the ass and drag her over his mouth so he could suck and lick her until she cried out his name.

Later. Definitely later.

"Patience will be rewarded, I promise."

"Have you met me? I don't have a lot of patience."

Now she laughed, her head falling back and her dark hair spilling down her back. "Yeah, I kinda noticed that about you. But you told me to go at my own pace. This is my pace."

Her look challenged him to tell her to go faster. He bit back the impulse.

Raising his hands, he laced his fingers together and put them behind his head.

"Do your worst."

Her eyebrows rose. "Don't you mean my best?"

"Either. Both. Don't care. Just don't stop."

"So, if I..." she leaned forward, planting her hands on either side of his head, she leaned forward until their lips were only centimeters away, "kiss you, you won't be disappointed?"

"I will never be disappointed if you kiss me."

She closed the distance between them and pressed her lips against his, closed mouth, no tongue. He resisted the urge to deepen the kiss. Let her take the lead. He'd follow wherever she led.

When she pulled back after just a few seconds, he wanted to follow her up and make her kiss him again. This time harder and with tongue.

But he didn't and was rewarded when she turned her attention back to his pants.

She put one finger directly over his button, which meant she had her finger directly over the tip of his cock. His throbbing, hard-as-stone cock.

Silent now, she worked the button free of the hole. His cock was so stiff and swollen, the button practically popped open on its own and his zipper released partway.

Her lips curved in an even more wicked smile. "Someone's anxious."

"All your fault."

"Thank you."

She looked so damn pleased, he started to laugh.

"You're welcome."

He expected her to continue with his zipper but she stayed where she was staring down at him. Making him even harder.

When she hadn't moved in several long seconds, he had to ask.

"Something wrong?"

She shook her head, dark waves falling over her shoulders and brushed against the curves of her breasts. "Just admiring the view."

"The view will be a whole lot better when you unzip my pants."

"Well, okay then."

She reached for the tab of his zipper with one hand and used the other to hold his waistband away from his cock. Then she tugged the zipper down at an excruciatingly slow pace.

He swore he felt every tooth as it released, sending jolts of electricity through his body. Gritting his teeth, he dug his fingers into the cushions and held on for the ride.

It seemed to take forever for her to reach the bottom of the zipper. And by the time she did, his cock felt ready to explode. He actually had to count backwards from a hundred so he didn't come all over her hand.

Actually, he wasn't sure he wouldn't do it when she finally did wrap her hand around his shaft.

He sucked in a huge breath when she reached for his underwear, now showing through the open fly, though she made sure she didn't touch his cock. Even though he was dying for her to, it was probably a good move.

Soon. Very soon.

"Lift up."

Her words didn't make any sense for a few seconds until he realized what she wanted. He lifted his hips and she tugged his pants and underwear down his hips. There was no way she was going to be able to do it by herself, but he enjoyed the fuck out of watching her try. Even when the band of his underwear dragged against his shaft and nearly made him bite through his tongue.

"I think I'm going to need some help," she said. "I definitely don't want to damage anything...vital."

He grinned. "I'm a hell of a lot tougher than you think I am."

Another pout. "But I have plans. And they involve you being at peak performance."

Goddamn, she made him laugh. He'd never had this much fun with a woman who still hadn't taken off all of his clothes.

He huffed, making a show out of rolling his eyes. "Fine. I guess I can give you a hand if you need it that much."

"Oh, I will.'

The implication in her tone was enough to make his cock throb. And now he was ready to strip them both. Forget foreplay. He wanted to be inside her and he still needed to strip her.

With his hands at his waistband, he pushed his pants down his thighs in a flash. His abrupt movement caused her to tumble backward onto the couch, where she began to laugh.

She stopped abruptly when he kicked off his shoes and shoved his pants and socks off his legs then kneeled on the couch naked in front of her.

Her eyes widened as her gaze traveled from his chest down his torso to his groin and lower. She looked almost mesmerized, which fed the hell out of his ego. But after a few seconds, he was more interested in getting her stripped down to his level.

Completely naked. As fast as possible.

Luckily, she'd taken off her sweater after they'd walked in the door. Now he just had to contend with a tight t-shirt that made her full breasts look amazing. He wanted his hands on her. But first, that shirt had to go.

He pulled her up onto her knees in front of him, reached for the hem of her shirt, and waited for her to meet his gaze. Then he waited another good thirty seconds until she raised her brows at him.

"Just wanted to make sure you're still with me." Grinning, he tugged her shirt up until he'd bared her stomach. "Don't want you to think I'm rushing you."

"I think you should rush a little."

"Oh, I don't know. You liked going slow a few seconds ago."

She huffed. "But now I want you to go faster."

He lifted her shirt another inch, until he'd exposed just the bottom of her breast, covered in a peach-colored bra.

She reached for his shoulders, put her warm hands on his bare skin and let her fingers sink deep. He sucked in air between his teeth and her gaze immediately went to that bruise.

"Are you sure that doesn't hurt?"

"Trust me, the only thing that hurts is my cock."

Her smile widened. "Poor baby." Her hands began to slide down his arms. "Maybe you—"

"Hands on my shoulders. My turn."

Her eyes widened a little at the hard note in his voice before her hands slid back up. He rewarded her with quick kiss. "Now lift your arms."

Her grin turned sassy. "You just told me to put them on your shoulders."

He bit back a grin. "Maybe I'll just leave it on then."

She straightened her arms above her head. "I'll take pity on you."

"I'll reward you by sucking on your nipples until you come."

Her lips parted and he swore he saw her shiver as her lids fluttered for a second. "I might hold you to that."

Tugging her shirt over her head, he watched her hair fall around her shoulders and over her breasts. Her bra was lace and see-through and, holy hell, he wanted to fuck her while she was still wearing it because it looked sexy as fuck.

It barely covered anything but lifted her breasts until they threatened to spill over the top.

His mouth fucking watered.

Dropping her shirt on the pile beside his, he cupped her breasts in his hands and squeezed, heard her suck in a deep breath and hold it.

"You are fucking gorgeous."

He leaned forward to lick over the swell of one breast before shifting to do the same to the other. He tasted heat and salt and he wanted seconds. Fingers flexing on the mounds, he plumped them until they spilled over the bra cups.

"I want you to leave this on but I'm gonna pull them down so I can get to your nipples, okay?"

She didn't answer right away and he looked up to make sure she was still with him. The lust in her eyes made his blood thicken even more. A split second later, she nodded, and he used the tips of his fingers to pull the lace down and expose her nipples. They were tight and puckered and, when he leaned back down and blew on them, she moaned low in her throat.

"Do you like that? Feel good?"

He heard her swallow. "Yes and yes."

Flicking his tongue at the tight tips, he slicked them with the flat of his tongue, alternating sides until her fingers dug so deeply into his shoulders, they almost hurt. *Almost.* But in a really good way.

She shifted against him and he looked up from sucking one nipple into his mouth to see her head fall back. Pulling one nipple between his teeth, he bit down, just enough to make her flinch. And for a tiny moan to erupt in her throat.

Her head lifted. "What was that for?" Her husky voice held pure sexual intent.

"Just making sure I have your full attention. Wouldn't want you to miss anything."

Her lopsided grin had him fighting his own smile. "I'm pretty sure I couldn't ignore you if I tried right now."

"Glad to hear it.

He bent his head to concentrate his attention on her neglected nipple and felt her thread the fingers of one hand through his hair. It was long enough to be an unruly mess most of the time and her fingers caught on the waves and tugged at his scalp.

The tiny pain sent a shock through his body straight to his dick. Groaning, he rubbed his tongue over her nipple then sucked more of her into his mouth. She arched up into his mouth, giving him more. He loved that she had no hesitation and didn't make any excuses for her sexuality. She appeared to love the sensation of his mouth on her and she wasn't ashamed to show it.

So he gave her more, alternating between her breasts until he heard her breath rasping between her lips and her fingers tightened in his hair almost to the point that he thought she might rip it out of his head.

At the moment, though, he wouldn't care because he wanted more.

Pulling away, he rose up onto his knees. "We need to get these jeans off."

"Well, good luck with that because they're tight as hell."

Her sassy smile was back, making him smile at her, in return.

"You've got to learn not to dare a hockey player, hon."

Shoving back farther on the couch, he flicked open the button on her jeans and tugged down the zipper. But she wasn't kidding. Her jeans were practically painted on. Made her legs look amazing but it was gonna take some maneuvering to get them off in this position.

Fuck it.

Jumping off the couch, he stood next to her. Then he reached down for her and deadlifted her off the couch and onto her feet.

She gave a startled little yelp as her hands latched onto his shoulders to steady herself. But she didn't get a word out before he gripped the sides of her jeans and stripped them down her hips. Then he went to his knees and dragged them the rest of the way down her legs.

"Step out."

She did exactly what he wanted and he had her stripped down to her undies in seconds.

With her hair mussed and her head cocked to the side as she stared down at him, he couldn't imagine anything sexier in the world. No fucking Angel had the body this woman had. Curves everywhere. Breasts spilling out of her bra. Hips barely covered by tiny panties he wanted to pull down with his teeth.

And his mouth at just the right position to do it.

Still on his knees, he thought of all the places he wanted to put his mouth right now.

Leaning forward, he rubbed his nose against the soft skin just above her belly button and heard her suck in a deep breath. Her belly quivered and, when he put his mouth on the same spot, she made that same adorable little moan.

Now, the fingers of both hands sank into his hair. But she didn't tug, didn't direct him in any way. She just held on.

Wrapping his hands around her ankles, he drew his palms up the back of her thighs as he kissed his way across her stomach to her left hip bone. Everywhere he touched her, her skin was so damn soft. And she smelled amazing, like her skin was infused with flowers or spice or something that smelled really fucking good.

He wanted to lick her all over. And he did mean all over.

The urge to let his lips trail lower was almost overwhelming but he forced himself to rein it in. He didn't want to rush. Everything else in his life was a rush. He was going to take his own goddamn time tonight.

No matter how much she begged. And he really wanted to hear her beg.

His hands made their way up her legs to the tops of his thighs. He loved the feel of her soft flesh against the rougher skin of his palms.

Cupping her ass, he squeezed and brought her even closer. His mouth was only inches away from her pussy and the scent of her arousal made his mouth water. He wanted to rub his nose against it the panties that matched the bra but held back. He needed her even more worked up than she was now before he went down on her. And then he was going to make her come on his tongue at least twice.

"Derek." She tugged on his hair, trying to get him to look up.

But he was using his tongue to trace patterns on the skin of her belly and didn't want to stop. Especially not when he could feel the shimmer of her muscles beneath the skin, reacting to his touch.

He couldn't remember the last time he'd taken so much time with a girl in bed. And hell, they hadn't even made it to a bed yet. But he didn't want to take the time to get there. Not yet, anyway. Maybe after he made her come for the first time.

Dipping his tongue into her belly button, her stomach contracted, her fingers gripping his hair even tighter.

His lips curved against her hip in a smile just before he bit her.

"Derek."

His name coming out her mouth in that breathless voice was the sexiest thing he'd ever heard.

"Something wrong?"

This time when she tugged, it wasn't a warning. It was a straight-up demand for him to look at her. He let her have this one and lifted his gaze. First, he got stuck on her breasts. More than a handful and bouncy, especially as her lungs were working a little harder. Pretty fucking amazing.

Then he saw her mouth, curved in a lopsided grin. Probably because he'd stopped to look at her amazing tits. How could he not?

Finally, he looked into her eyes, slightly glazed and hooded. And sexy as fuck.

"You want something?"

She swallowed hard. "You know exactly what I want."

"Gee, I don't know about that, sweetheart. Most people think I'm kind of clueless." Which wasn't a lie. "Why don't you help a guy out?"

She didn't say anything right away, but her tongue emerged to lick at her bottom lip. And it was his turn to groan.

"In my game, that's called instigation." He shook his head. "And that's grounds for a penalty."

She pouted in the most fucking sexy way and it hit him squarely in the balls. To the point that he was pretty sure if he got inside her right this second, he'd come in two seconds. And that really wasn't the impression he wanted to make.

"Are you going to put me in the penalty box?"

"No. You just have to stand here and take your punishment."

Her head cocked to the side. "What are you—"

Snagging his fingers in the side of her panties, he tugged them down to her ankles then dipped his fingers between her thighs. Sliding them against the lips of her pussy, he made her moan even louder than she had before.

She was slick and puffy and she moved her legs apart another inch so he could have more access.

Watching her face, he played with her, sliding his fingers against her clit then dipping between her lips to penetrate her. Not far, definitely not as far as she wanted if the way she moved her hips was any indication. But enough to make her fingers grip his hair even tighter.

Watching her face, he saw exactly how much she liked when he rubbed his thumb against her clit then slid two fingers into her channel, scissoring them open before twisting them just a little higher.

She was so fucking tight, her pussy squeezed around his fingers like a vise, trying to work him deeper.

"Why so impatient, Sophie? Don't you want to make this last?"

He'd never thought of himself as a tease, at least not in bed. On the ice, everyone called him an instigator, but that wasn't something he did deliberately. It was more like his default setting. He couldn't help it.

But here, with her, he wanted to get her so hot, she spontaneously combusted before he even got his cock inside her. And when he finally did... He wanted her to fucking explode.

"I thought you had a game tonight? Don't you need to get some sleep?"

He laughed because she was totally right and he absolutely did not care.

"I will gladly give up a few hours of sleep to make you come at least twice before I throw you on a bed and fuck you."

"Hours? You can't last hours."

"Watch me."

She shook her head and laughed but he heard the catch in her breath when she spoke. "Don't you know I'm a modern woman who can toss you out and get her vibrator?"

"Honey, I'm much more fun than a vibrator. Will a toy do this?"

Leaning forward, he thrust his fingers high and tight inside her as he thrust the flat of his tongue against her clit and drew it back until he flicked at that little nub with the tip.

He was pretty sure her neighbors heard her moan.

Yes.

Her response made him double down. He wanted more. Wanted her to yell and scream and let him know she was enjoying it. It became his goddamn mission in life.

Using his tongue and his fingers, he began a concerted assault on her senses.

With one hand on her ass holding her steady, he pumped his fingers inside her. He didn't go deep, just enough to make her want more. But now he used his tongue more deliberately. He teased her clit mercilessly, flicked and licked and tormented until he felt her hands release his hair so she could brace herself on his shoulders. Her hips rolled forward, trying to making him move the way she wanted, the way she needed. But he tapped her ass before moving his left hand to her hip so he could hold her still.

He felt her shake and paused for a second, wondering if her knees were about to buckle. But she tightened her hands on his shoulders.

"Don't you dare stop now." Her voice held a desperate command. "I will hurt you."

Smiling, he didn't bother to respond. But he began to corkscrew his fingers deeper inside her, loving the way her pussy contracted around them.

She was going to feel fucking amazing wrapped around his cock. And that would need to happen soon because he was fast reaching the point where he wouldn't be able to keep himself contained.

His cock was practically begging for relief but he hadn't made her come yet. He kicked up his efforts, no longer bent on teasing. He wanted her to come. And come so damn hard, she screamed his name.

She breathed so loud it drowned out all other sound in the room, aside from her occasional moans. When her fingers tightened on his shoulders and her sheath tightened around his fingers, he knew she was close. And he didn't have the patience to wait any longer.

When he had his fingers deep inside the next time, he held them there and stroked her delicate inner tissue until she writhed on his hand, almost as if she were trying to get away. Then he took her clit between his teeth and nipped her.

He'd been right about her screaming when she came. It was fucking amazing.

Her body convulsed as he continued to play with her clit until she took a step away from him.

And nearly stumbled.

He was on his feet in a flash, grabbing her up in his arms before she could fall. No way would he let her hurt herself.

Holding her against his chest, he slammed his mouth over hers and kissed her so hard their teeth crashed together. She didn't seem to care. She reached for his head with one hand and held him tight, while her other wrapped around his neck, almost tight enough to cut off his air supply.

Lifting his head when he had to stop or risk passing out, he sucked in air and watched her do the same as her eyes slowly opened.

"Bed?"

She blinked at him a few times before she took another deep breath and swallowed audibly.

When she didn't answer right away, he wondered if he'd pushed her too far.

Shit. Had he—

"In the back." She shook her head. "Sorry. You scrambled my brain. But I think it's working again now."

He grinned. "I can take care of that for you."

Her grin was barely noticeable but it was there. "Don't promise something you can't deliver."

He started walking, heading for the closed door he could see at the back of the apartment. "I told you not to dare me, didn't I? Now I'm gonna make you come until you can't see straight."

"I may hold you to that."

"Please do."

Her apartment wasn't huge but it took forever to get to her bedroom. And when he did, he didn't notice anything other than the bed.

At least it was a queen. King would've been better for what he wanted to do but he'd work with it.

Without a word, he laid her out on the bed, knees bent over the side. Then he dropped to his knees, spread her legs and put his mouth over her pussy again.

At this angle, he was able to lick inside her, which made her squirm. Grabbing her hips, he held her tight and set back to making her scream again.

This time, her hands latched onto his hair and tugged, hard enough to make his eyes water. He loved it. Loved making her squirm. Loved her breathy moans. Loved the way her legs hugged his shoulders.

Loved the way she tasted.

He lost himself in the way she moved, how even the slightest pressure or the way he gripped her legs tighter made her moan even more. Seconds after he plunged his tongue deep inside her for the third or fourth time, her entire body tightened and she came around his tongue.

When she finally went limp, he leaned away so he could look up at her.

Her eyes were still closed. Grinning, he rose to his feet, put his hands on either side of her hips on the bed and waited for her to look at him.

It took her at least a minute. He had no trouble waiting.

Finally, she blinked and her eyelids rose enough that their gazes met and held.

Her lips were slightly parted and he could still hear her struggling to suck in air.

"Had enough?"

She didn't answer his question right away. Blinking lazily a few times, she finally drew in a deep breath and shifted until she had her elbows propped beneath her and her upper body lifted off the bed.

"I can go as long as you can."

"Then you're in for a long night, sweetheart."

"I think I can keep up. Do your worst." Her eyebrows rose. "Or your best. I can take either."

He'd give her both. "Condoms?"

Her smile widened and she nodded to the side. "Bedside table."

Thank God for a woman who was prepared. He hadn't wanted to go back out to the living room for his wallet.

Rising to his feet, he turned to look for the table. There. Only a couple feet away. So close he barely had to move to reach it.

He had his fingers on the handle when she sat up on the bed, leaned forward and took his cock in her hands.

"Oh, *fuck*."

Sophie didn't say anything as she wrapped her hand around his shaft and stroked him from root to tip. Derek's head shot around and their gazes locked. The mischief was back in her eyes, slathered with a healthy dose of sensuality.

As slowly as he'd tormented her only minutes ago, now she returned the favor.

Her hand tightened and tugged, working every inch of his cock with a deliberate motion that threatened to make him explode in her hand. He'd already been close to the edge watching her come. Now, every nerve ending in his body was poised to enthusiastically give her whatever she wanted.

Which seemed to be his surrender. But he wasn't ready to give in yet.

Staring down, he had the perfect view. Her head tipped back to watch him, she lazily stroked him while, at the same time, she tightened her hand and tried to force a groan from him.

It built in his throat but he kept it throttled because if she did manage to make him concede, he'd blow all over those pretty breasts.

And while that wouldn't be the worst, he knew he wouldn't be completely satisfied until he felt her warm pussy enclose him in its grip.

He wanted to be buried deep inside her, her legs around his waist, staring into her eyes. Wanted to feel her body pressed against his. And he wanted to hear her moan out his name as he pounded into her.

His cock jerked at the thought and her lips curled at the corners.

"What just went through your head?"

Her normally husky voice exuded sex and all he could think about was hearing her panting his name in his ear while he rode her.

"That I want to be inside you when I come the first time. Then maybe we can experiment."

"You seem to have a lot of plans for one night."

The thought that this could only be a one-night stand made him stop for a second and think about how wrong that was.

In the next second, he dismissed the thought. There'd be more nights. He'd make sure of it. But right now, he'd concentrate on this one.

"Damn right I do."

"Then I guess we should just move to the good stuff."

Before he could say he was pretty damn content with what they were doing right this second, she leaned forward, put her lips directly over the tip of his cock and blew.

"Holy *fuck*."

"Like that?"

Again, that tease in her voice made his guts clench.

"Hell yes."

"Then you'll probably like this even more."

Moving her hand down his shaft, she covered the tip of his cock with her mouth and drew him in. Bolts of sensation shot down his cock and into his balls.

"Fuck, Sophie. That's..."

Playing her tongue over the head, she licked and sucked, every swipe causing his cock to harden until he wasn't sure it hadn't turned to stone. Except it ached like a sonofabitch. So much so, he had to take a step back or he was going to blow right then.

When she would've followed him, he put his hand on her chin and tilted her face up to his.

"Lie back."

There was that pout again. "What if I don't want to?"

"Trust me. You do. Because I promise it'll be good."

"You promise?" Her grin was back.

"Trust me."

"I must. You're here. And I'm naked."

"And so amazingly gorgeous, I want to stare at you all night. But I also want to get inside you so you need to lie back."

"And if I don't? Will you make me?"

His mouth dropped open at the dirty thoughts racing through his head. At all the things he could do to her, with her permission.

Her smile widened, probably because the look on his face was a cross between dumbfounded and painfully horny.

Then she started to laugh. And fell back onto the bed, upper body propped again on her elbows, breasts still constrained by that lacy bra.

"Okay, Mr. Hockey Player. Show me what you got."

Christ almighty. The girl was fucking amazing.

He tore his gaze away from her for a second so he could snag a condom from the drawer she'd pointed out only minutes ago. Those couple of minutes now seemed like hours.

His lungs worked like he'd just done wind sprints but his focus had lasered down to a single goal: Get inside Sophie.

He ripped the wrapper open with his teeth then rolled it down his aching shaft while she watched his every move.

Letting his gaze travel up her body, he wrapped one hand around the base of his cock and squeezed, hoping to stave off his impending orgasm.

Her gaze locked onto his hand, watching him with red-hot lust.

After several long seconds, she finally looked into his eyes. "Are you just going to stand there?"

He had to swallow before he could speak. "I'm enjoying the view."

"You could enjoy it from down here."

She crooked one finger at him and broke his restraint.

Kneeling on the bed, he reached for her waist and moved her farther up the bed. Her hands fell to his shoulders as his head dropped to her breasts. He cupped one mound in a hand and squeezed, sucking a nipple into his mouth and pulling hard on the tip. She arched off the bed, pressing farther into his mouth.

Sucking in a breath, lust finally pulled him under completely. He pressed a line of kisses up her body while his knees pressed inside hers and spread her legs wide.

With just a shift of his hips, he pressed the tip of his cock against the lips of her pussy and let the sensation take his breath away. One small movement and he'd be inside her. So why the hell was he waiting?

"Sophie. Look at me."

He'd lifted his head enough that he could see her eyes. Their height difference made it a little awkward so next time, she'd be on top. Maybe the time after that, too.

Her eyelids flickered for a second before they rose and her eyes met his. That instant connection triggered something inside, something primal. Something that shut down every thought but the need to possess her.

"Keep your eyes open. I want to see you."

Her lips curled in a smile that was at odds with the increasingly fast rise and fall of her breasts.

"Are you always this bossy?"

"No. Maybe. Now keep them open and watch me."

"Watch you—"

She moaned as he started to burrow his cock into her body. He was thick and he was so fucking horny he could barely think, but he took it as slow as he could manage. Every inch he gained, her expression amped up his own lust. Sucking her bottom lip between her teeth, she bit down.

Holy fuck, she felt amazing. So fucking tight and warm. His

breathing intensified with every passing second and he had to restrain the urge to fuck her hard and fast. It took him almost an entire minute to push inside her fully, until she'd taken every throbbing inch of him and enclosed him in a grip so damn tight, he had to bite his tongue until he'd forced back his natural urge to spill inside her.

Her legs crept around his waist, her ankles locking at the small of his back. Her hands rose to wrap around his neck, not drawing him closer but giving him notice she wanted him to watch her, as well.

No way would he be able to look anywhere else.

Pulling out was a test of his resolve to go slow. All he wanted to do was get back inside, slide back in as deeply as he could, and do it again and again until she screamed his name and came.

He actually couldn't believe he was able to maintain a steady pace for as long as he did. Minutes, hours. Who the hell was keeping track? He certainly wasn't. All he knew was that every time he drew out, she sighed like he'd broken her heart. And every time he pressed home so tight his balls hit her ass, she moaned and bit her bottom lip even harder.

"Derek."

A shiver ran up his spine. "Yeah."

She made sure he was watching her as she ran her hands down his back, nails digging into his skin and drawing fire.

"Go faster. Or I will have to hurt you."

He managed to laugh, amused even though he was more fucking turned on than he'd ever been in his life.

"You don't think this is painful?"

"I think you're enjoying tormenting me way too much." She rolled her hips, rubbing his cock rub against her and making sparks shoot up his spine. "I think you need to move a little faster or I'm going tie you down and take what I want."

The images that flashed through his brain made every muscle in his body tighten to the point of pain.

"Next time. Holy fuck, babe. I'll let you do whatever you want next time if you keep that promise."

She grinned, trailing one hand back to his hair and grabbing tight. "Then fuck me now."

He couldn't deny her or himself any longer.

Shifting his hips, he thrust. With their gazes locked, he set a pace that had them panting in seconds. Hard and fast, he swung his hips, feeling her sheath clamp around him. He didn't know how he managed to maintain eye contact for as long as he did.

But finally, he had to close his eyes as sensation overpowered him. Lowering his head, he rested his cheek against her forehead and let himself get lost in the rhythm and the heat and the tight grip of her.

She held on just as tight, one arm around his shoulders, one hand still tight in his hair.

Everything else faded away as he lost himself in Sophie. But he wasn't so far gone he didn't realize she was hanging on the edge of another orgasm. He wanted to push her over that edge, make her fall hard and want more.

On his next inward plunge, he snugged the base of his cock against her clit then held deep and circled his hips.

He heard the catch of her breath and he pursued her orgasm with the same focused intensity he played hockey.

"Come again, Sophie. Come on, sweetheart. Let go."

Her only answer was a breathy moan that pushed him closer to his own orgasm. No fucking way was he going over without her.

Planting his hands on either side of her head, he lifted his upper body off of hers and put everything he had into making her surrender.

"Sophie."

She didn't open her eyes right away and he thrust in just a little harder. The sound she made gave him a fierce satisfaction.

"Sophie, look at me."

It took several long seconds but finally she opened her eyes.

Fuck. Big mistake.

He couldn't delay his own orgasm any longer. He swung his hips faster, harder, biting the inside of his mouth to hold on—

She broke first with a cry that smashed his thin restraint. Her pussy rippled around his cock, milking his response.

He came with a loud groan, shuddering with the effort. Lowering himself onto her, he wrung every last cry from her before he gave in and collapsed.

And immediately wondered how long it would take him to recover so they could go again.

CHAPTER 7

"Sophie. Hey, Soph, you awake? I'm so sorry but I need to leave the kids with you. Soph, are you here?"

Sophie sucked in a gasp as she sat straight up in bed, clutching the sheet to her chest.

"Oh my god."

Beside her, a warm male body stirred. She couldn't see Derek's face, mostly because of his hair, but she could tell he was still asleep. But not for much longer if Diana continued to shout.

"Soph, are you still in bed? I'm so sorry to do this do you but you're closer than Mom and I have to get to the hospital."

Scrambling out of bed, Sophie grabbed her robe off the chair beside the window and yanked it on. It took her two tries to get her left arm into the sleeve and that was when she realized she was putting it on inside out.

Shit.

Wait, did her sister just say hospital?

"Hey. Everything okay?"

Her head whipped around to the naked man in her bed. Derek had flipped over onto his back and now stared at her with a frown.

He hadn't spoken loudly enough for her sister to hear. At least, she hoped he hadn't.

The look of sheer panic on her face made his brows rise and he looked a hell of a lot more awake than he had a second ago.

"Whoa, Sophie—"

She rushed to his side and put her hand over his mouth. Diana had dog-sensitive hearing. Hell, she'd probably be able to hear Derek shifting against the bed sheets.

Shaking her head, she made barely audible shushing noises until, finally, he nodded.

Oh, god, he probably thought she was crazy. But she couldn't let her sister find out she had a man here. The questions would never stop and Diana would tell her other sisters and then they'd have something to say. And if her parents found out...

"Soph?"

Holy shit, was her sister's voice getting closer?

"I'm coming! Be right out. Give me a minute."

"John had to take Mikey to the hospital. I've got to get over there and I don't have time to take Joey and Tiff to Mom and Dad's."

Sophie forgot about her robe being on inside out and was still belting it as she hustled for the door. She did remember to close the bedroom door behind her just as her niece Tiffany stepped in front of her.

"Hey there, baby girl." Picking up the three-year-old and settling her on her hip, she never broke her stride toward the living room, where she could see Diana pacing.

"Hey, what happened to Mike?"

Diana had tears in her eyes but looked visibly relieved to see Sophie. "God, for a minute there I thought you might not be home. Mikey went down hard at soccer and John took him to the emergency room for x-rays. Mom was just too far away—"

"Oh, no. That's awful. Go." She waved her hand at the door. "Go, go, go. Joey and Tiff will be fine."

The look of relief on her sister's face erased any of the fear she'd had at Derek being discovered in her bed.

Family first. Always.

"I'm sorry, Soph. You were closest and I panicked."

"Seriously, it's okay. No need to explain. I got this."

Diana leaned in and gave her a huge hug and sniffed in her ear. And hugged her a little tighter. "Thank you. Okay. I'll be back as soon as I can. Oh, and they haven't eaten. I'm sor—"

"Di." Sophie put one hand on her sister back and pushed her toward the door. "It's *fine*. We'll be fine. Won't we, guys?"

She looked down at Tiff, who gave her a big grin. Then she looked for Joey.

Shit. *Shit.*

She didn't see him anywhere. He wouldn't go into her room. Would he?

Oh damn.

When she looked up, her sister was halfway through the door.

"I'll call you when we know something." The door closed and her next words were muted. "Love you. Thanks."

Sophie turned as soon as the door latched. Tiff's little arms were wrapped around her neck, clinging like a baby monkey.

"All right, Princess. You wanna watch a few cartoons while I find your brother?"

Tiff shook her head and her arms tightened around Sophie's neck.

"Want Mommy."

"Sweetie, Mommy will be back soon. And you like being with Aunt Sophie, right?"

A pair of dark eyes sheened with tears looked into hers. "Pancakes?"

Huffing out a laugh despite the fact that she had no idea how the hell she was going to explain the unknown man in Aunt Sophie's apartment to a three-year-old and a five-year-old, she rubbed her nose against Tiff's as she nodded. "Pancakes."

"Chocochip?"

Her smile widened. "Absolutely."

She hoped Derek liked chocolate chip pancakes.

———

Derek clearly heard the conversation happening in the front room and realized their no-strings night of fun had suddenly become a whole lot more of a hassle for Sophie.

Never failed. It was always something, which was why he didn't do relationships. Just too much trouble.

So run like hell and don't look back.

The thought immediately pissed him off. He didn't want to run out on Sophie. Besides making him look like a total douche, he wanted to see her again. Hell, he'd wanted to start back where they'd left off when they'd finally fallen asleep around two a.m. It was now...

He lifted his head off the pillow to check for a clock and found himself staring at a little boy standing in the doorway.

Oh shit.

Derek froze for several seconds.

Crap, what the hell was he supposed to do? And how the hell was he going to cover his bare ass so he could get out of bed?

And, holy shit, was the kid going to scream?

Derek lifted his hand and waved and smiled. It was the only thing he could think to do.

The kid raised his hand and waved back, little dark head tilted to the side.

"Hey." Since he could still hear Sophie talking to her sister, he kept his voice low. "How's it going?"

The little boy shrugged and walked closer to the bed. "My brother had to go to the mercy room."

His brain, still not firing on all cylinders yet, took a moment to process what a "mercy" room was. "Shi-oot, that sucks."

That little head tilted the other way and his eyes narrowed a little. And Derek swore he saw a little of Sophie in that dark gaze. "Who are you?"

"I'm Derek. Who are you?"

"I'm Mike. Are you Aunt Sophie's husband?"

Laughter tried to escape but Derek wasn't sure how Sophie would want him to handle this so he stifled it. And was saved when the door pushed open and Sophie appeared, carrying a dark-haired little girl on her hip.

She looked so natural at it, Derek's mouth dropped open for a second before he closed it. And now he wished he'd gathered up his clothes and climbed out the window before he'd been found.

Why?

Because you really are a self-absorbed asshole.

Her expression was all kinds of apologetic and now he felt twice as bad.

"I'm so sorry about this. My nephew fell at soccer and needs x-rays and I'm closer to the hospital than my parents and Diana needs to be at the hospital—"

"Soph. Hey. Not a big deal. Seriously."

Total truth. He knew if his mom or his sister needed anything, he'd be there in a heartbeat, no questions asked because that's what you did for family. Even dysfunctional ones like his. Maybe especially dysfunctional ones like his because they didn't have anyone else to turn to.

Her grateful smile made his heart beat a little fast and, if he wasn't careful, he'd have to pull the pillow over his lap to hide his reaction.

"Then how about we go make some pancakes?" Her smile got a little brighter as she focused it on her nephew. "Mikey, why don't you take your sister back to the living room and turn on the TV so I can get dressed and get started?"

Mike didn't answer right away as he looked toward the bed. "Is Derek gonna get dressed, too?"

Her smile never faltered. "Uh huh." She walked over, grabbed

Mike's hand and tugged him toward the door. "You know where the remote is, right? Find some cartoons, okay?"

Setting the little girl on her feet, Sophie gave her a little push toward her brother then closed the door behind them.

She turned back to Derek, her eyes wide and her expression all kinds of apologetic.

"Oh my god. I'm so sorry." Throwing off her robe, she twisted to grab something out of the dresser and his brain short-circuited. Her naked body made every one of his male hormones stand up and applaud because, holy hell, the girl was fucking gorgeous. He wanted to grab her around the waist and throw her back on the bed so he could start kissing her lips and work his way down her body until he reached that tiny trimmed patch of hair on her mound. Then he'd spread her legs and put his mouth over—

His boxer briefs hit him in the face as she tossed his clothes at him.

"I told the kids I'm make them pancakes. I hope you like chocolate chips." She pulled on a pair of yoga pants that molded to every curve of her ass, her breasts bouncing as she hopped from one foot to the next. "Shit, I hope I have chocolate chips. Do you even have time for breakfast? I thought you said you had to be at the rink by a certain time this morning and I'm pretty sure we didn't set an alarm. I have no idea what time it is."

Sliding out of bed, he slid on his boxers then walked over to Sophie who'd pulled on a shirt and was gathering her hair into a messy bun on the back of her head.

No makeup, hair all over the place and the loose t-shirt couldn't distract from her adorableness. This was probably a really bad idea but...

Stopping in front of her, he reached for her, cupped her face in his hands and pulled her close for a kiss. He saw her eyes widen and she became very still against him, as if she didn't know what to do.

He pulled back only far enough to be able to see her face when he spoke. "I'd love pancakes. Chocolate chips are great. I don't have to be at the arena until five. Morning skate was optional 'cause we had a game last night. Deep breath, babe."

Sucking in air through her nose, she released it on slow exhale and nodded. "Okay. Good."

Smiling, he nodded, too. "Yeah. Good."

For a second, she looked like she might not be panicking as badly. Then her eyes widened and she took a step away, out of his reach.

"What the hell am I going to tell the kids about you?"

This was definitely not his area of expertise. "Do you have to say anything?"

Her eyebrows rose. "Like I should just totally ignore the fact that Mike found a strange guy in my bed?"

He shrugged. "I mean, if he asks, just tell him I'm a friend."

The look she gave him made him want to smile but he stifled it.

"And if he asks why you were sleeping in my bed?"

"Tell him I was tired after my game."

Shaking her head, she sighed again then rubbed her fingertips on her forehead, as if she were getting a headache.

Finally, she drew in another deep breath. "Okay. You're right. It'll be fine."

She turned toward the door, her expression still troubled.

"Hey, Soph."

She turned to look at him. "Yeah?"

Fuck. What the hell should he say? "You want some help with the pancakes? I'm actually pretty good at them."

The smile she gave him lit her up. "Sure. But...put your pants on before you come out? Not that I don't like the view but..."

She left the rest of that sentence hanging but he heard her soft laughter as she disappeared out the door and closed it behind her.

He sat there for a few more seconds, shaking his head.

Shit.

He should leave. He had things he needed to do before the game tonight. He had a routine and, when he went off his routine, shit didn't go well. He'd already screwed his routine completely by spending the night here but, well, last night had been fucking awesome and he wouldn't have missed it. Not for anything.

Truth be told, he didn't want to go.

Fuck it.

Sliding to the edge of the bed, he grabbed his pants and shirt off the chair where Sophie had laid them last night and flipped the switch by the door for the overhead light.

His pants looked like someone had twisted them into a braid then unraveled them. Didn't have a choice, though. He had to wear them or walk out into the kitchen in his boxers. That probably wouldn't go over well.

His dress shirt looked even worse. At least he'd worn an undershirt.

Maybe you should just get dressed and get the hell out of here.

Probably be easier if he did. Of course, that would leave Sophie to answer the kids' questions all by herself. Then again, maybe she wanted him to get out so she wouldn't have to explain why he was here.

And now he totally sounded like he was rationalizing his escape.

Total dick move.

"Suck it up, asshole."

Time to face the pint-sized firing squad.

"You sure I can't help you clean up?"

Sophie looked over her shoulder at Derek and tried not to let her tongue hang out of her mouth.

With the kids settled on the couch in front of the TV watching cartoons, she'd been cleaning up the kitchen while Derek finished off the last of the huge stack of pancakes she'd put on his plate. She had a feeling he probably would've eaten more if she'd had any.

Now that he was finished, though, she needed to find a way to get him out of here. Even though she didn't want him to leave.

But it was almost ten a.m. and her dad would be at the restaurant by ten-thirty at the latest to open for lunch. Saturday in March was hit or miss with crowds. Could be empty, could be mobbed. Either way, he'd expect her in around the same time.

She needed Derek out of her apartment by ten-fifteen. But she didn't want to shove him out the door with a "Hey, thanks for the orgasms. Please don't pass my dad on your way out. See you soon!"

Argh. This was totally *not* how she'd expected this morning to go. Not that she'd been thinking about that last night. No, last night she'd been thinking about all the ways he could make her come. And getting her hands on his body.

Her gaze slipped from the dishes in the sink to the tight t-shirt clinging to his chest.

Good god, the man was built like every woman's wet dream. Seriously ripped but not overly muscle-bound. And that hair. She wanted to run her fingers through it constantly.

Hell, she'd have her hands on him all the time if it wouldn't make her seem like some freak who wanted to pet him.

"No, but thanks for offering." She finally pulled herself together enough to respond to his question. "I'm almost done anyway. Did you have enough to eat?"

And that smile. Just scrape her off the floor when she finally reduced to a puddle of drool.

"Yeah. You're a great cook. You get that from your dad?"

Setting the final pot in the drainboard, she folded the towel and set it next to the sink before turning to face him completely. She'd been avoiding it because she needed to get him moving out the door. But if forced to stare at him for any length of time, it was going to be that much harder to make him leave.

Because she really didn't want him to go.

"Probably, although both of my parents are really good cooks." Sighing, she set her elbows on the counter then propped her head on her hands. "And speaking of my parents...my dad is going to be downstairs in less than half an hour."

His immediate grin made her heart beat a little faster.

"And you want me to clear out before he gets there, right?"

"I'm really sorry—"

"Soph, hey, not a problem. This morning's been messed up. I get it. But I'm not leaving until you tell me we're gonna go out on a real date next week."

Her smile must've given her away because his grin turned cocky. She'd seen that smile on his face last night during the game. When he'd said something to one of the other team's players. That player then took a swing at him and got sent to the penalty box. But not Derek. No, he went back to his bench, smiling the entire length of the ice.

Apparently, the man incited strong emotions from everyone, not just her.

"I'm gonna take that as a yes. We've got a game Sunday night but we'll back early Monday. How about Tuesday night?"

"I usually work Tuesday nights but I'm sure my dad could do without me for a night."

"Then it's a date."

Holy shit, she had an actual date. It'd been so long she wasn't sure she still knew how to act on a date.

"Okay."

A little silence fell as they stared into each other's eyes. The green in his hazel eyes seemed to spark a little brighter but that must have been her silly imagination.

"Aunt Sophie, are you and Derek gonna kiss?"

A furious blush lit up her cheeks, making them burn. She tore her gaze away to look at her niece, who'd managed to get up from the couch and walk over to the kitchen without either of them noticing.

Damn, he's dangerous.

"I thought you were watching cartoons."

"Mike put on Teen Titans but I wanna watch Doc McStuffin."

Sighing, she looked at Derek again, who was smiling and shaking his head.

"I'm pretty sure that's my cue to leave," Derek said, "because I have a feeling the girls are gonna win this battle and I'd much rather watch Teen Titans. I'm gonna get my stuff and head out."

She wanted to say she'd see him tonight but she'd be working. She wanted to tell him to come to the bar after the game, but she also wanted him to ask if he could see her again tonight.

And she needed him to leave so her dad wouldn't catch him leaving her apartment in wrinkled clothes that clearly screamed "Yes, I stripped your daughter naked, tore all her clothes off and made her scream my name all night."

So all she could say was, "Okay."

He looked like he wanted to say something else. His lips actually parted like he was going to speak but then they closed on a rush of breath and he turned to head back to the bedroom.

Damn it.

"Aunt Soph?"

Tiffany's sweet little voice pulled her attention away from Derek's back as she watched him walk to her bedroom.

"What's up?"

Tiff crooked her finger at her and Sophie bent forward so her niece could whisper in her ear. "He's cute. Are you gonna marry him?"

Laughing, Sophie rubbed her nose against Tiffany's. "Yes, he's cute. But I'm not getting married any time soon, sweetheart. Now, let's go find something for you and your brother to watch so I can get a shower."

She'd just brokered a truce between brother and sister for rights to the TV when Derek walked out of the bedroom. He hadn't bothered to button his dress shirt and it hung open under his coat. He looked rumpled and messy and more gorgeous than any man she'd ever known.

She wished she could throw herself at him right now and force him back into her bedroom. But they both had lives and—

Someone knocked on her apartment door just before the door opened.

"Sophie, honey. Diana called and—"

"Grammy!"

Oh, God.

Derek's eyes went wide and he froze halfway down the hall from her bedroom. Her stomach dropped as she realized they'd just been screwed.

And not in a good way.

Shit. Shit. Shit.

"I'm here to take the kids off your hands so you can go to work."

Forcing a smile, she turned to face her mom, who would know right away that something was up.

"Hey, Mom. How goes it?"

In the middle of giving her grandchildren hugs, Ruth Tsoukalos's eyes narrowed and her head tilted to the side.

"Sophie? What's wrong?"

"Nothing's wrong."

"Sophie has a friend."

Ratted out by a five-year-old. Yeah, this was gonna be fun.

Her mom's expression would be comical if this were something Sophie could laugh about. But this was no laughing matter.

This was going to be an issue. A big, fat, hairy overblown issue and she just didn't want to deal with it now.

"Yes, I do. And my friend has to leave now to get to work."

She turned back to Derek, still waiting in the hall, quickly buttoning his shirt. Hell, she wasn't sure he was even breathing.

Holding out her hand to him, she gave him a wry smile, which he returned, and walked forward.

"Mom, this is Derek. Derek, this is my mom, Ruth."

Without hesitation, Derek held out his hand and, after a stunned second, her mother took it.

"Mrs. Tsoukalos. Nice to meet you. And I'm really sorry, but I have to run. We've got a game tonight and I need to get ready."

Surprisingly, her mom was still speechless but she nodded and sucked in a deep breath, which apparently loosened her tongue. "Nice to meet you, Derek."

As his grin made her mom's eyes widen even more, Derek headed for the door, tugging her along with him out into the hall.

"I am going to call you. We are going on that date." He swooped in for a kiss before she knew what he was going to do, stealing her breath and making her tingle from her toes to her scalp. "Talk to you later, Sophie."

Then he was gone. And she turned back to her apartment to face the music.

CHAPTER 8

"So you just left?"

"What the hell was I supposed to do? I have to get my shit together for the game. I have to eat. I need more sleep or I'm gonna be shit for tonight and we can't afford that. Fuck. Maybe I shoulda stayed."

Robbie's face was all kinds of what-the-fuck as he shook his head.

"Dude. You probably should've stayed. Or left last night. Either way, you're screwed. I don't k-know, man. Maybe you w-wanna write her off."

Robbie went back to shoving food in his mouth, his attention focused on the TV, where some talking heads on the NHL Network were discussing the Colonials and what they needed to do to snap their three-game losing streak.

Normally, he'd be all over this story but he couldn't stop thinking about Sophie. He hoped like hell her mom didn't give her a hard time. Sophie was a grown woman, for chrissake. Her parents had to know she had a sex life. Right?

Of course, it wasn't every day her mom caught a guy leaving her apartment.

But that wasn't his fault—

"Damn, Riley's k-kicking ass in Philly. I miss the g-guy but he d-deserves it."

Robbie's comment drew Derek's attention back to the TV, where they were talking about their former Redtails' teammate, Riley Hatch. He'd gotten called up earlier this season and was making his mark on the NHL club, providing the team with solid second-line scoring.

"Yeah, I'm happy for him."

Obviously he didn't sound happy enough.

"Dude, your time will come." Robbie tossed a carrot stick at him, which he caught and ate. "You're having a g-great season. They're g-gonna have defensive holes next year. Just k-keep doing what you're doing and they'll n-notice."

Derek had to grin at the optimism in Robbie's tone. "Sure thing, Coach."

This time, Robbie just gave him the finger before turning his attention back to the show. But Derek zoned out again. He really didn't like leaving Sophie holding the bag like that this morning. He'd never run from any confrontation. Hell, he thrived on them on the ice. They pushed him to play harder, better.

But he'd fucked up this morning.

Grabbing his phone, he went to text Sophie.

And realized he didn't have her number.

Well, shit.

Another fuckup.

Now what? He really only had one option.

He texted Shane.

Hey, I need Sophie's number. Can you get it from Bliss for me?

It took five minutes for Shane to get back to him. Derek spent the time tapping his fingers against the arm of the chair until Robbie shot him a look. Then he curled his fingers into a ball so he wouldn't do it.

Damn it, why the hell didn't Shane answer? Was he already

asleep? Most of the guys took a nap before a game. Fuck, if Shane didn't answer now, he probably wouldn't get back to him until—

His phone pinged and he snatched it off the cushion beside him.

HAHAHAHAHAHAHAHAHAHAHAHA

Derek was in the middle of texting Shane back with a creative use of the word *fuck* when he got another text, this time with a phone number.

Erasing all the swear words he'd just typed, he replied with one.

Thanks

Then he opened another text screen.

And stared at the blank screen for a good long minute.

What the hell should he say?

Sorry I skipped out on you. Hope your mom didn't freak.

Yeah, that sucked.

"Dude, you s-sound like my little sister. I'm gonna to hit you." Robbie stared at him from the opposite side of the couch, shaking his head. "Are you s-still upset about what happened? For fuck's sake, just t-text her."

"I am." He ran a hand through his hair. "I just don't know what to say."

Robbie shrugged like it was no big deal. "Simple's better. Just say 'Hey, how's it going.' Let her talk."

Amazingly sound advice from a guy who never dated because he didn't like to open his mouth around women.

Hey, it's Derek. Got your number from Shane. Hope that's okay. How's everything?

He pressed send then stared at the screen for another minute, willing her to text him back. When that didn't work, he pushed off the couch with a sigh and headed for his bedroom.

"See you in a few."

Amazingly, he slept for a couple of much-needed hours and didn't wake until his alarm went off. First thing he did was grab his phone. Still no response.

Shit.

Grinding his teeth, he resisted the urge to text her again. He'd made the first move. The next was up to her.

But he couldn't get her out of his head. He thought about her while he made dinner. He thought about her while he got dressed to head to the game. Thought about her when he stared at the wrinkled suit he'd worn last night that he needed to take to the cleaners.

Wondered if he'd see her tonight and need to take another suit to the cleaners. Hell, he'd sacrifice all his suits to the cleaners if she crooked her finger at him. Which made him do a full-stop for several seconds because that sounded a lot like something his mom would say.

He loved his mom unconditionally but that didn't mean he didn't acknowledge her faults. She was an alcoholic who'd finally gotten sober several years ago and had managed to stay on the wagon ever since but, growing up, she'd been...erratic.

She'd fall in love with some guy she met at a bar and would be devastated for days when he dumped her after a couple of dates. Which weren't even dates. More like one-night hookups.

And on that depressing thought, he set his phone down and forced his brain to worry about more important things. Like tonight's game.

Charlotte was gonna be all over them tonight after last night's defeat. Probably gonna be rough. Possibly bloody. He could take it. He just had to keep his temper in check.

"Hey, you okay?" Robbie asked as they drove to the arena an hour later.

Derek glanced over as he stopped at a red light. "Yeah. Why?"

"You're just q-quiet. And you're never q-quiet before a game."

About to rag Robbie for being overly chatty, he stopped himself short. The guy looked genuinely worried. And Derek realized Robbie was right.

So he shook his head. "Yeah, man. I'm fine. Just...thinking."

"About last night?"

He shrugged. "Still haven't heard from Sophie. I hate thinking she got a lot of shit from her mom because of me."

Robbie didn't answer right away, which was par for the course with him. But when he started to laugh, Derek shot him another glance.

"What?"

"Dude, I was t-talking about the game. I have no idea who you are right n-now. You're k-kinda freaking me out."

Derek shot him the finger, but the guy was right.

"You really like her, don't you?"

"I don't really know her." Which was a deflection, Derek realized. "I guess I do, which is kind of stupid because we only really met a few days ago."

Robbie shrugged like it was no big deal. "My p-parents got married f-five days after they met. They've been t-together for thirty years."

Robbie's dad had been a world-class NHL player in the eighties who'd produced four professional players out of five kids. Robbie was the second-youngest and would probably hit the NHL by the end of next season. The guy had genetics on his side.

It was on the tip of Derek's tongue to make some smart-ass remark about money and fame being great for a marriage, but he managed not to be a dick. He'd met Robbie's parents. They were amazing.

"Your parents got lucky. Doesn't always working that way."

Robbie nodded, sliding him a quick look. "I know. I just... Sorry."

"Nah, all good. Hell, I just met her. It was one night."

Robbie nodded again and silence fell. Normally Derek would need to fill it but not tonight. Tonight, he had too much on his mind.

By the time he pulled into the lot at the arena, Derek was ready to crawl out of his skin. He wanted to head out on the ice and skate off this itch. But then his phone pinged just as he put the car in park. And he dug it out of his pocket so fast, Robbie stared at him like he was crazy.

"Dude, is your phone on f-fire?"

He didn't answer right away because he was too busy getting to her text. Because it *was* from her.

Sorry didn't get back to you right away. Busy at the bar. Everything's fine.

Shit. That was it? What the hell was he supposed to say to that?

Did he ask about her mom? About what she'd said? Or did he completely ignore that? Did he ask to see her again after the game tonight? Even though he needed to sleep because they had to leave early tomorrow morning to get to Wilkes-Barre for a game?

Fuck.

"Bad news?"

Robbie's expression made Derek grin. The guy looked like he didn't know whether Derek was about to explode in anger or break down and cry. Neither was going to happen.

"Nah. Come on. We got a game."

And Derek was determined nothing and no one was going to fuck with his head.

"So Mom didn't say anything? She just took the kids and left?"

Sophie sighed into the phone as she took a break later that night and talked to her sister Helena. It'd been slow so her dad had gone home early, though he'd told her to call if she needed help later. She had more than enough help tonight with Carlos and Mark in the kitchen and Vivi up front taking care of tables so Sophie could handle the bar.

Vivi was filling in behind the bar now because there were only five customers at the moment and Sophie had been on her feet practically all day. And in that time, she'd managed to get practically a hundred texts from her sisters.

Apparently their mom, who still hadn't said a word to Sophie about this morning, had told her second-oldest sister, Helena, that she'd met Sophie's friend Derek this morning and had any of them met him, too.

Cue twenty messages in two minutes from four sisters who had practically had coronaries. Then Diana had figured out that Derek must have been there when she'd dropped off the kids...

And well, that had spurred a whole other blizzard of texts, forcing her to turn off the sound on her phone until now.

Amazingly, none of her sisters had shown up at the bar. She was lucky they all had kids and husbands to keep them occupied.

But what the hell did she say now? She was still kicking herself for the text she'd sent Derek earlier.

She wanted to groan at how lame it had sounded. She should've texted him back but hadn't figured out what to say. And he hadn't texted her back either.

Glancing at the clock, she realized he wouldn't have had time to text her. He was probably still on the ice. It was only a few minutes after nine.

So if she wanted to text him back something better, she had about a half hour to figure that out. But first she had to convince Helena to get her other sisters off her back.

"Yep. Just hustled them out the door and I haven't heard from her since. Do you think she's mad?"

"No, I don't think she's mad." Then Helena paused. "But she's probably freaked out. You know, being the baby you got a lot of leeway. But having a guy in your apartment who obviously slept there the night before..."

"What?"

"Well, you know. They don't want to think about you having sex."

"But—"

"Just let me finish before you freak out."

"I'm not freaking out." Okay, maybe just a little. Which was ridiculous. She was a grown woman.

"Yeah, you are. And you shouldn't be. We've all spoiled you,

Soph. And I'm not saying you're a brat. You're not. But you are used to being...perfect."

"What? I don't think I'm perfect."

Far from it.

"I don't mean you think you are. I just mean we all think you can do no wrong. Jesus, Soph, you babysit on a moment's notice whenever we need you. You work at the restaurant almost full time. You taught yourself how to do the books so Dad wouldn't have to. Your grade point average is, like, 3.8 every semester. And you don't introduce inappropriate men to our parents."

She snorted. "Right, but it's not like I don't date them."

"Hon, I can count on one hand the number of guys you've dated who you introduced me to. And I'm pretty sure the only dates of yours our parents met were in high school."

Opening her mouth to respond, she snapped it closed a second later because her sister was right.

"I just haven't found anyone I want to introduce to Mom and Dad. There's nothing wrong with that."

"No, there isn't. But that kind of leads them to believe you don't date. Until this morning when you got caught. Hell, Mom caught me and my high school boyfriend in my room too many times to count. And Mags..."

Sophie and Helena snorted at the exact same time then started to laugh. Their oldest sister, Margret, was a family legend for the amount of trouble she got into in high school. She'd climbed out her window to party with her friends so much, their dad had secretly installed an alarm on her window. It'd taken her a week to figure out how her parents knew she was sneaking out.

Finally, Helena sighed and Sophie could perfectly picture her older sister shaking her head and smiling at the same time. "You've always been so good. And that's not a dig. I'm just saying Mom's gonna need a little time to get over the shock. But she's not mad at you, brat. Hell, I'm kind of proud of you. And now I want to know all about this guy."

"Are you gonna give me the lecture if I tell you I only met him a couple of days ago?"

"No. But I am gonna ask if this is something you do a lot."

"No, it's not. Derek's...different."

"Different how?"

"He's a lot like me."

Her sister went silent for several seconds and when she spoke, she sounded genuinely confused. "What do you mean?"

"Oh, hell, I don't know. I guess...we kind of get each other."

"You mean you get along well."

"No, it seemed like it was more than that. I don't know. Maybe I'm just seeing things that aren't there. I mean, it was just one night."

"Yeah, and how'd it go?"

Amazing. Mind-blowing. Holy-shit-awesome.

"Good."

"Jesus, Sophie, I'm not Mom. How was he in *bed*?"

She huffed. "Fine, he was great, okay? The sex was amazing and I want to see him again so we can have more amazing sex."

"Then do it! You're only young once. Sleep with the hot guy. And if something more comes out of it, great! Just have a good time."

"And what if he doesn't want to talk to me again?"

"Then he's a dick and your sisters will kick his ass. Don't be afraid to go after what you want because you think your mom and dad won't approve. Live a little, Soph."

After hanging up with her sister, Sophie made her way back out front to the bar. It was still pretty slow so she had a few minutes to figure out what else she should text.

Finally, around nine-thirty, she forced herself to pick up her phone.

How was the game?

As soon as she sent it, she wanted to pound her head against the bar.

Jesus, how lame was she? Pretty fucking lame, apparently.

With a groan, she put her phone back in her purse and didn't pick it up again until she got home that night.

She'd thought maybe he'd come to the bar after the game but she remembered him saying he had to get up early to travel to another game tomorrow.

So she was disappointed but not angry when she closed and locked the doors behind her at ten-thirty and walked to her car with Carlos, who waited until she'd started her car and locked the doors before he walked to his own car.

Which was ridiculous because Carlos weighed all of a hundred and fifty pounds soaking wet and was shorter than her. But Carlos was old-school, like her dad, and wouldn't let her walk out by herself. So she never rolled her eyes when he waited for her at the back door and thanked him sincerely before she drove away. After waiting to make sure he got into his car and started it.

Carlos was practically family. She didn't want anything to happen to him.

By the time she got back to her apartment and took a shower, she was yawning. But when she grabbed her phone to check it before she went to bed with a book, she couldn't help her gasp when she saw the notification. Finally, he'd texted her back and she'd never realized because she'd forgotten to turn on the sound on her phone.

Holy crap. Standing beside her bed in faded flannel pants and a worn-soft t-shirt, she swiped open her phone and practically put her thumb through the screen clicking open her texts.

Brutal but we won in overtime.

Climbing into bed with a smile on her face, she propped up her pillows and settled in, phone in hand.

Glad to hear you won. More bruises?

Yeah, a few.

Biting her lip, she debated her next text carefully then figured, what the hell. If she was going to be labeled a bad girl, might as well play the part, right?

Where? Pics?

As soon as she sent it, she wanted to take it back. He probably thought she was a freak and had only responded because he was being nice but now he was going to ditch her—

You sure? Took a stick to the face. Eye's pretty swollen. Blocked a shot early in the game that left a mark too.

OMG. Are you OK? Did you see a doctor? Can you play tomorrow? You should probably get some sleep. I'm keeping you up, aren't I?

It took him about a minute to answer and when he did, it was with pictures.

The first was a shot of his face, and yeah, he was going to have one hell of a black eye. The second was his leg, already turning nasty shades of purple and blue.

I'm fine. Happens all the time. How was your night?

Seriously? This is normal?

Yeah pretty much.

Shit. So he took a beating every time he went on the ice.

Tough guy, huh?

Nah. I got a soft heart.

She smiled but she had a feeling he wasn't kidding.

So you're just a big redhead teddy bear? Too bad you're not here tonight. I could use a bear hug.

Again, she bit her lip after hitting send. He was a rough, tough hockey player. He probably thought she was being juvenile.

Have to be a gentle one. Feel like I got hit by a truck. Game tomorrow's gonna suck but we have a week until our next game after that.

Her fingers hovered over the letters on the screen as she thought about her next response, thought carefully about the pros and cons then figured what the hell.

I promise to kiss all those bruises for you when you get back.

Groaning as soon as the text sent, she put her phone face down on the bed next to her and blew out a deep breath. She was ridiculously excited by a few texts, which probably had a lot to say about the state of her love life. Before last night with Derek, she'd basically been living like a nun. Now she'd gotten laid and thought she'd became a sex queen.

Ha.

Her phone finally pinged and she grabbed it but didn't turn it over right away. Probably just Derek telling her he'd talk to her later and then he never would and she'd never see him again.

Jesus, when did you become some damn pathetic?

With a sigh, she picked up her phone and had her breath stolen.

He'd sent a picture this time. Of his side.

She sucked in a breath at the angry colors marring his skin. Jesus, that had to hurt like hell. Right above his hip in the soft area below his ribs. Then she noticed that if he'd angled the camera just an inch to the left, she'd be able to see a lot more interesting bits of his anatomy.

Dirty mind much?

Sure you want to kiss that?

Yeah, she did. Seriously. She'd kiss this man anywhere.

I could start there.

Would he take the bait?

You can kiss me anywhere you want.

Anywhere?

You put your mouth on me and I promise I won't be thinking about stopping you.

Her lips curved in a slow smile that lasted so long, her cheeks began to hurt.

How did he manage to do that? To make her feel like a sexy, desirable woman when he wasn't even in the same room with her?

And why did she enjoy it so damn much?

What would you do?

Let you do whatever you want.

What would you want me to do?

There was a longer-than-normal pause. She knew he had to be up early to travel to his game tomorrow. Maybe he'd fallen asleep.

Just when she was ready to put her phone down, it pinged and she stabbed at it.

I want you to start at my hip. I want you to put your mouth on me and lick your way up my body. When you get to my chest, I want you to use your tongue on my nipples. I want you to put your hands on my cock and stroke me.

By the time she finished reading his text, she could barely breathe. The images in her head were from the night before and were so full of heat, she felt herself go wet just thinking about it.

It took her several long seconds to blink herself out of the spell he'd put her under then her thumbs flew over the keyboard.

I want that too. I want you to put your hands on my breasts and squeeze. I want you to suck on my nipples and bite them until it hurts. I want you to tease my clit with the tip of your dick until it's so sensitive I want to scream and then I want you to stroke inside me hard and fast.

Hitting send before she could chicken out, she closed her eyes and waited for his reply with her breath caught in her lungs and her bottom lip caught between her teeth.

Oh my god, was he laughing? Was he turned on? Did he think she was stupid?

She didn't have to wait long for his response.

Holy fuck Soph. How the hell am I supposed to sleep after that? I have a game tomorrow now all I wanna do is come over there and crawl in bed with you and make sure neither of us get any sleep tonight.

Her smile widened until she could barely see the screen and she felt so damn happy, she wanted to laugh. And so damn horny, she was about to take matters into her own hands.

Her thumbs poised over her phone, she took a few seconds to think about her response then figured, what the fuck.

You just need to take the edge off. You have two hands. Use one of them.

A few seconds later, he sent her a photo. It was dark and blurry but she could just make out what he wanted her to see.

She actually moaned as her sex clenched and every muscle in her body tightened. And her hand slipped between her own thighs, straight to the aching center of her body. Her fingers slid over her clit, making every nerve ending in her body sizzle. It would be so much better if it were his fingers but she'd take what she could get. And right now, she needed the release.

It didn't take long because, holy hell, just thinking about what he was doing right now put her on the edge. With the tips of her fingers, she spread her labia then rubbed her forefinger over her clit. Her back arched as she played her body into a teeth-clenching orgasm that left her panting and sweaty.

When she finally opened her eyes and sucked in a deep breath, she grabbed her phone.

He'd already texted her.

Damn that didn't take long. All your fault. Can I call you Monday?

Her smile returned.

I'll be disappointed if you don't.

Wouldn't want that. Sweet dreams Sophie. I know what I'll be dreaming about.

Me too. Hockey.

LOL. No. Night.

Night.

She set her phone on her nightstand, figuring they were done. But a few seconds later, her phone pinged again.

The game's on TV if you want to watch. Starts at 4.

She went soft and gooey on the inside. He wanted her to watch him play. It was so sweet, she wanted to jump on his lap and kiss him for being so damn adorable. Which was something he probably wouldn't appreciate as a big, tough hockey player.

I'll be watching. Don't get hurt.

Can't promise that. Sometimes those other guys are mean to me.

Laughing, she began typing in a long response then thought better of it. He had to be up early and it was close to midnight and they hadn't gotten much sleep last night and he'd had a game tonight. He needed to sleep.

So she made this text short.

Night D.

Night Soph.

With a sigh, she set her phone on the nightstand again then rolled over and pulled the covers up, hoping she'd be able to sleep without needing to get herself off again.

CHAPTER 9

"Oh, wow. Now that was a hit. Derek, did you see that?"

Sitting at the bar at Sophie's dad's place having a drink, Derek had been watching the Colonials game and flirting with Sophie.

After three weeks, he'd become a familiar sight here when he didn't have a game or wasn't on the road. In the past few days, Sophie's dad had actually smiled at him, so he thought he was winning him over. Derek didn't figure he'd scored with her dad yet, but he'd hit the posts a few times.

At least, the regulars had accepted him.

"Yeah, Matheson's a tough guy." He flicked his gaze at the screen. The Colonials' defenseman Matheson was still down and the trainer was being led over the ice. "He'll be fine."

Then he returned his attention to Sophie, who he'd much rather spend his time watching. He'd lived and breathed hockey for so long, it was kind of nice to have something else to focus on.

At the moment, she was tapping drinks for a couple of guys at the other end of the bar. The two guys dressed like office drones were definitely flirting with her but she wasn't falling for it. He covered a shit-eating grin with another sip of beer, but Mike and Teddy, the two sixty-somethings sitting next to him must have caught it.

"Kid," Mike said, "you are not at all subtle, are you?"

Teddy snorted before Derek could respond. "You've seen him play. Subtle doesn't work for Derek."

Mike responded by tapping his glass against Derek's. "I think he plays just the way he's supposed to. Damn, Matheson looks fucked up. I think they're bringing out the stretcher."

Now that caught Derek's attention and he looked up at the screen. "Damn, they are. What the hell happened?"

"While you were otherwise occupied, Matheson and Brugel got tangled and Matheson's head hit the boards pretty hard."

As Mike spoke, the replay spooled across the screen and Derek winced as he watched.

"Ooh, damn. That was hard as hell."

"He'll probably be out for at least a few games. No disrespect to Matheson but it looks like the Colonials'll have an opening for a defenseman. Would love to see you get the call, kid. You've been working your ass off lately."

"Get the call for what?"

Sophie stopped in front of him, her smile making him grin in return. "One of the Colonials' defensemen just took a header into the boards. Looked pretty bad."

Her expression immediately dissolved into lines of concern and she turned to look at the screen, wincing when she saw the replay.

"Oh my god. That's horrible."

"Yeah, it's a shame." Mike shook his head. "Guy was playing well, too. But it could be an opportunity for Derek."

Because he was watching her, he saw her expression. Several emotions crossed her face. Shock was one of them. Maybe a little fear, too.

All of it gone in seconds as she turned to him with a smile that didn't quite reach her eyes. "You could get called up."

"Yeah. But I'm not holding my breath. They've had a few other openings and I haven't gotten the call yet."

He hadn't thought about that lately, mostly because he knew if he did get called up, he'd miss her. And that was something he didn't want to talk about. He'd been so career focused for so long, he felt almost like he was cheating on himself because he wasn't worried about moving up.

Stupid? Hell, yeah. But true.

As she nibbled on her bottom lip, he watched her think about her response. After several long seconds, she finally had one.

She smiled again and, this time, it seemed a little more natural. "That would be good. It's where you want to be, right?"

"Yeah. That's what I've spent most of my life trying to do. The NHL is the ultimate goal. Some guys are happy just playing professional hockey. And I am. I'm grateful I get paid to do something I love but... Yeah, that's the dream."

Their gazes locked and held and he could tell she wanted to say something. She just didn't know how.

Finally, she looked down at his glass and seemed to shake herself out of a spell. "I'm sure they know how valuable you are. You'll get the call."

The problem was, when that happened, what happened to them?

———

"Of course. Yeah. Absolutely. I'll have an answer for you by the end of tomorrow. And hey, thanks again. I appreciate the advice."

Derek disconnected then walked out of his bedroom, tapping the phone against his leg.

Well, shit. What the hell do I do now?

That phone call had been totally unexpected and now his brain was working overtime. His agent had given him some great advice on the offer he'd just received but ultimately, the decision was up to him.

He just didn't know what the hell to do.

In the living room, Robbie sat on the couch with Ian, who Derek hadn't even realized was there. Ian lived down the hall with Dirk Bennett but he spent a lot of time with them. Dirk was a great guy but he was twenty-nine and had a wife and two kids back home in Minnesota. Probably the most stable guy on the team, which is why they'd paired him with Ian, who was barely nineteen. But Dirk was shit at videogames and Ian was a typical kid.

Robbie glanced at him over his shoulder then did a double take as he frowned. "Shit. What's wrong?"

Derek shook his head. "Nothing's wrong. Just got off the phone with my agent. He got a call from the Swiss National League."

Robbie's mouth dropped open and Ian's head snapped around, their game forgotten.

He had their full attention now.

"Shit, seriously?" Ian's shock bled through his voice.

Derek nodded.

"And you're seriously thinking about taking the offer?" Robbie's question wasn't really a question, because he knew Derek had talked about playing overseas before.

But that's all it'd been. Talk. Something to do in a few years, maybe, if he wasn't called up. Now...

"No way." Ian shook his head. "Dude, the Colonials are totally gonna pull you up next season. The way you're playing and the holes they're gonna have on the roster next year... You really wanna give that up?"

Dropping onto the chair across from the couch, he sank back and rubbed his suddenly sweaty palms on his jeans.

"And what if I don't get called up? Hell, they might trade me. There was talk during that trade with L.A. a couple months ago that had me in the mix."

"What about our playoff run?" Ian's face screwed up in a grimace. "Dude, we need you. I mean, yeah, I'm being selfish but still..."

Derek didn't hold it against Ian. He knew if either of them had gotten the same call, he would've asked the same question. "What if I get a multi-year contract over there? You know the money's better and the season's shorter."

Ian just kept shaking his head. "No way, man. We need you."

Nice to hear but this was his career. His life. "It's not like they can't get someone to fill my position. Hell, Coach was talking about bringing up another d-man from the ECHL."

"Yeah, but it won't be you." Ian actually looked hurt that Derek was considering leaving them.

"D," Robbie's voice held total shock, "you *seriously* considering this? You really that unhappy here?"

Am I?

The last week had him off kilter. He hadn't gotten called up by the Colonials to fill the hole left by Matheson's injury. Will had. Which had been great for Will, and Derek had been sincerely happy for the guy. But it'd sucked for him. On the other hand, the Redtails had won both their last games, putting them number two in the division, which was great.

And he and Sophie had spent almost every night they could together. But he'd noticed something different between them. Not bad. Just...different. He couldn't put his finger on what had changed.

Sophie had seemed as affectionate as usual but he'd noticed a couple of times when she'd said something about when he "moved on." Almost as if she were gearing up for when he left.

He hadn't been able to figure why, all of a sudden, she was mentioning him leaving. It made no sense and was screwing with his head.

Luckily, it hadn't messed with his game because he'd been on fire. Points in every game for the past seven.

And if you take this offer, you'll leave her behind.

But did he have to?

Sophie could join him when she graduated. He'd only be gone for a couple months this spring and then he'd be back for a couple of months before training camp. Maybe they'd be apart for six or seven months. They could make that work. Right?

She'd told him she wanted to travel. Hell, she'd be in Europe. She could travel whenever the hell she wanted.

"I don't know." He finally answered Robbie's question. "I guess...I have a couple of days before they need a decision. I gotta think about it. Look, I don't want this getting out, okay?"

"Yeah, sure," Robbie said then elbowed Ian who was still staring at him with his mouth hanging open. "Of course."

"Uh, yeah, okay." Ian shook his head. "And congrats. Swiss National, man. That's a great offer."

Any other day, it would've been.

Today...

Shit.

———

Sitting at the bar, going through her paper due the next day, Sophie looked up when the front door opened.

She jumped to her feet, ready to enter hostess mode when she realized it was Derek.

"Hey." She smiled, her smile softening into a real one. "I didn't think I'd see you 'til later. Aren't you playing ball hockey with the kids at the Olivets tonight?"

"Yeah, that's still on."

He leaned over the bar to kiss her but she could taste his distraction. When he pulled away, she took a good look at him and knew something was stressing him out. Something big.

Coming around the bar, she pulled him into a booth in the back. "What's wrong? Did something happen?"

Her mind went blank as she thought of all the bad things that could happen. Was he hurt? Was he being traded?

These past few weeks with him had been amazing. But after watching that game on TV a few nights ago, she'd realized she'd been waiting. Waiting for something to happen. For a shoe to drop. Had it finally happened?

She wasn't normally a doom-and-gloom person. She wasn't always looking for the dark cloud in every situation. But the easy way she and Derek had fallen into this relationship had made her second guess everything lately. It totally sucked and she was pretty sure he'd noticed.

"Nothing's happened." He paused. "Not yet." He paused again and shook his head. "I got an offer today."

She got an ache in the center of her chest. "An offer for what?"

As he explained the phone call he'd gotten earlier today, she felt every muscle in her body slowly tighten into knots.

When he finished and sat there staring at her, she took a deep breath. And pressed her lips together to stave off the "Don't go" on the tip of her tongue.

Did he want her to tell him to stay? She couldn't tell from his expression.

Does he want to leave?

"So? What do you think?"

That I'm about to lose you.

Just when she'd started to think maybe things would be different with him, that maybe he was different than the other men she'd dated.

You knew better. You just chose to ignore the fact that he was just as likely to leave as every other man you've ever dated.

"I think...if it's what you want to do, then you should do it."

His expression didn't change. "Just leave everything behind? Pick up and move to Europe and not look back?"

No. God, no. That would totally suck.

Isn't that what you plan to do?

She opened her mouth to speak then closed it again because what she really wanted to say was, "What about me?" But this wasn't about her.

So she pulled on her big-girl panties. "I think if this is something you want to do, then yes, you should do it. Have you talked to Robbie or Will? What do they think?"

His gaze was laser-focused on hers, and she fought the urge to beg him to stay. To cry or plead with him. She didn't want to be that person. She *wasn't* that person.

"I'm talking to you right now." His tone never wavered, showed no emotion. "Why should I ask them but not you? You don't think I should take your feelings into consideration?"

Yes, of course. "I didn't say that. I just think...if that's what you want to do then you should do it."

"Like you're going to do, right? When you go off to teach."

Shit. "Yes."

"So you'd just take off and not look back?"

She blinked. That had been the plan, hadn't it? Except when it came time, would she really have the guts to do it? To leave for a foreign country for years and not look back?

She shook that thought out of her head. This wasn't her decision. It was his.

"It's not like you're not going to keep in touch, right? But if it's not what you want to do, then why are you even thinking about it?"

His eyes narrowed. "Because it's something I've thought about. And getting overlooked again to be called up maybe means I need to start looking for a fresh start. But maybe...I'm not sure I want to leave you behind."

She froze and because he was watching her so closely, he could probably read every thought crossing through her mind.

No, she didn't want him to leave but she didn't want to be responsible for holding him here if he wanted to go. What happened when she decided to pursue her own dreams of traveling? She'd leave him behind. Or would she? Was he asking her to go with him? Did he even want that? She still had a semester of college, although if she were honest, she could probably take those few credits over the summer and be done. She could follow him.

And what does that make you? A puck bunny? What if it doesn't work out?

She wanted him to spell out what he wanted but she was almost afraid of what he'd say.

In frustration, she sighed. "I don't know what you want me to say."

He paused as his gaze intensified. "Maybe I want to know how you feel about me."

Her mouth opened then closed again, her feelings for him rising up to choke her.

Did she love him? Hell, they'd known each other for only a month but they'd spent almost every free minute together. She hated when he left, hated when he spent the night away from her. Worried about the fact that she felt incomplete when he wasn't around.

Oh my god. She'd fallen head over heels for a man who was asking her opinion about him leaving for Europe by the end of the week and not returning for months.

"Sophie?"

She stared at him with wide eyes and her lips parted as if she were going to say something but she didn't have a clue what to say.

Finally, Derek shook his head. "Guess that's my answer, huh?"

Finally, her tongue came unstuck. "I don't have an answer for you. That's the problem. This is your decision, not mine. I can't make it for you."

"And if I just want you to have an opinion?"

Her tongue stuck to the roof of her mouth. Was she ready to tell him how she felt? Did she have the right to an opinion at this early stage of their relationship?

Maybe he wants you to tell him to go so he has an easy out of the relationship?

No, that wasn't fair to Derek.

Then again, he was an instigator. He was good at getting under other people's skin until he got the reaction he wanted.

Her own temper started to rise. "Do you want me to tell you not leave? To beg you to stay? Why don't you tell me how you feel, Derek?"

His jaw clenched, and she could tell he had something to say but was biting his tongue.

"Okay, sure." He shrugged like it was no big deal. "I want more, Soph. I want you to be part of my decision, but I don't want you to do it because I want you to. I want you to do it because *you* want to."

She blinked, unsure how she should respond. If the situation were reversed, would she be here asking him these same questions?

"I don't know what you want from me."

"Yeah, I get that." He slid out of the booth and stood at the side of the table for several seconds. "Guess I have my answer. I'll see you around, Soph."

He turned and walked out the door, leaving her staring after him, wondering what the hell had just happened.

———

"Hey, Ma. How's it going?"

"Hey, baby. How's my sunshine?"

He managed a laugh at the childhood nickname, more because she expected it than because he was amused.

"Good. Mostly."

"You don't sound good. What's wrong?"

What's wrong is he had to make a possibly life-changing decision in less than twenty-four hours. And the person he'd wanted to help him make that decision had left him hanging.

Letting his head fall back against the headboard, he closed his eyes.

At eight in the morning, she'd just gotten home from work. He could see her sitting at the little table in the kitchen of the rowhome, which was the only home he'd ever known. Her bright red hair that she had to dye now would be pulled back in a ponytail, her too-skinny body draped in a chair as she smoked a cigarette and drank a cup of coffee before going to bed.

How she managed to sleep after drinking coffee, he'd never understand. But somehow she managed. Just like she did with everything else.

"I got an offer from overseas. They want me to come over now and stay for next season."

He heard her draw on her cigarette before responding. "Is that a good thing?"

After all these years, his mom still didn't know much about how his profession worked. He couldn't fault her, though, with all the leagues, it was confusing for most laypeople.

"Could be."

"Then what's the problem? Spell it out for me."

Sophie.

No, that wasn't fair. It wasn't Sophie's fault that he'd fallen harder for her than she'd fallen for him, apparently.

"What if I ask the club to release me from my contract and they don't have a problem letting me go? Then what the hell have I been doing here all this time? Am I just filling a hole? Are they even considering pulling me up next year? And then—"

He pulled up short before he outted his relationship with Sophie. That was still a raw spot. He hadn't spoken to or texted her since yesterday. With all the shit in his head, he was honestly afraid he'd say something stupid and push her even farther away.

Although, if he took the contract, maybe this was better. No ties before he left. Better to just leave it like this.

"Derek? Then what? What aren't you saying? Come on. Spill it all."

Shit. Sighing, he banged his head against the headboard hard enough to rattle his brains.

"I've been seeing this girl."

Another pull on her cigarette. "Ah. And she told you not to go, huh?"

"No. She told me it wasn't her decision to make."

A short pause. "Huh. Not what I was expecting to hear. You know in all the time you've been gone, you never mentioned a girl before now. So this is serious between you and her?"

"I thought it was, yeah."

"And now you don't think so. What changed?"

He snorted out a laugh. "That's obvious, isn't it? She doesn't care enough to want me to stay."

"Okay. I guess that's one way to look at it. But nothing's ever obvious, kid. Especially not with you. You don't wear your heart on your sleeve. You never have. You internalize everything and hide it all behind the smartass. Did you tell her how you feel about her?"

His silence made his mom sigh.

"So she's supposed to read your mind but you get upset because she doesn't spill her guts? Nice double standard there, kid."

He sighed heavily and rolled his eyes. If he'd been sitting at the table with her, she would've smacked him upside the head. And he would've deserved it. "Gee, thanks, Ma. Tell me what you really think."

Now, she laughed. "I am, so listen up. I think she's right. This *is* your decision. You just have to figure out what you want. And, hon? No one can tell you that except yourself."

CHAPTER 10

"Well, that was a shit show."

Derek sat with his eyes closed and his head against the seat as the bus rumbled away from the Wilkes-Barre arena. The silence had been almost deafening until Dirk Bennett had made that totally accurate statement from the row ahead of him.

They'd lost 5-1 to a team they should've beaten easily. Yeah, they'd had three games last week and they'd had to travel this morning...but still. They'd played like shit and a lot of that was his fault. He'd been slow, sloppy and stupid.

So yeah...a shit show.

"Hey, you okay?" Robbie's voice was barely audible from across the aisle. "You don't look so g-good."

He didn't feel so good either, but he just shook his head, not bothering to open his eyes.

"Fucking Oullette caught me off guard with that last hit. Christ, I played a shitty game."

"Don't b-beat yourself up. We all played s-shitty."

Just not as shitty as him. He'd let the guys down. He'd let himself down.

And yet...

Last night, he'd had the second-best sex of his life and technically he'd been alone. But not really because...Sophie. When was the last time he'd let a girl screw with his head? That'd be never. He knew better. Then again, maybe he didn't.

Maybe he had more of his mom in him than he wanted to admit.

Fuck, his head hurt just thinking about it. He reached up to his temple and started to rub.

"You sure you're okay?" Robbie asked.

"I'm fine."

He hoped. He had a headache that wouldn't quit after a hard check into the boards that had required a visit to the dark room for concussion protocol early in the first period. The doctor had declared him fit to play but the resulting headache was becoming a grinding ache.

He'd had worse but—

"You need to t-talk to Coach or the trainer." Robbie wasn't letting this go. "You're really pale."

He snorted out a laugh and finally opened his eyes to glance at Robbie—which made his head throb like a sonuvabitch. "Dude, I'm always pale."

Robbie didn't look convinced. "But you d-don't always look like you're gonna pass out."

"Nothing a few hours sleep won't cure."

The problem was he'd planned to spend a few of those hours with Sophie. Now, he knew he should go straight to bed when they got home. They had a game Friday and he needed to redeem himself.

But the only thing on his mind all morning had been Sophie. He'd never had this intense a reaction to a woman before and it was fucking with his head. So, yeah, he should go straight home and fall face first into bed and not come up for air until sometime tomorrow. Coach had set practice for tomorrow afternoon to give them time to rest and recover but Derek planned to get up early after a decent night's sleep and hit the gym before practice.

A few seconds later, his phone pinged.

Fishing his phone out of his pocket, he opened his eyes only wide enough to be able to read the screen. Sophie. Damn it, he wanted to talk to her. Even though his head felt like it was about to split open, he opened the text.

Hey. Saw the game. You okay?

He could almost hear her voice in his head. Amazingly, that didn't hurt. But yeah, the brightness of the screen felt like a knife to his temples. He typed out a reply he hoped was legible and hit send then tried not to groan out loud

Fuck, fuck, fuck.

He wanted to call Sophie and tell her he'd be over as soon as he got back. Wanted to spend the rest of the night making her moan out his name. Wanted to sleep curled around her and wake up the next morning and make love to her again.

How the hell had he gotten so addicted to a woman in the space of a couple of days?

Have you met your mother?

Scowling, he shook his head, which just made it ache more.

Fuck, fuck and fuck.

"D, seriously, you all right?"

He practically had to bite his tongue off not to snap at Robbie. Which would've been shitty of him. His friend was worried. The least he could do was not snap his head off for it.

"Hey, what's wrong?"

Derek heard Will's question, even though he kept his voice low. Gritting his teeth against the pain in his head, he didn't answer. Robbie said something Derek couldn't make out.

"Damn it." Will's voice was a rough growl. "How bad is your head?"

Beside him, he felt movement as Robbie got up. "I'm getting the trainer."

Good idea. His head felt like someone had gotten in there with a pickax and was trying to get out through his temples. And now he was nauseous.

Fuck.

Every bump in the road made it worse and he knew if he opened his eyes, he'd puke. But he was squeezing them shut so hard, it added to the pain.

By the time the trainer knelt by his side, he was pretty sure he was gonna throw up. Phil didn't even bother to ask him any questions.

"Come on," he said. "I know it's gonna suck but you need to come in the back with me and lie down. You get a lot of migraines?"

Was that what this was? Holy shit, no wonder his mom grabbed her prescription bottle at the first sign of one.

"No. Never." He managed to grit out. "Christ, just knock me out."

He heard Phil's low chuckle. "Yeah, that's probably what got you into this state in the first place. Come on. Excedrin and ice packs for you. Then you need to go home and sleep it off."

Which sucked. Because he really wanted to talk to Sophie.

The walk to the back of the bus was sheer torture but the ice packs on his head and the pills worked to knock back some of the pain but he had to keep his eyes closed because any light at all made ice picks stab his brain.

The last forty-five minutes of the drive was hell but he must have finally managed to fall asleep because one minute they were on the turnpike and the next they were pulling into the parking lot at the arena.

"Hey, Sleeping Beauty." Will kept his voice low. "Can you walk?"

Blinking his eyes open, he groaned at the jolt of pain that swept through his head.

Will huffed out a quiet breath. "I'll take that as a no. Come on. I'll help you out. Robbie'll drive you home."

Yep, okay, no problem. He didn't care who took him home as long as he got there.

He heard the trainer say something to Will, heard Will respond then Will was helping him out of the chair and down the aisle of the bus.

He barely opened his eyes, just enough to make sure he didn't run into anything.

He couldn't talk, was a little afraid he'd embarrass the hell out of himself and throw up. He'd never felt so fucking horrible in his life.

Somehow he got into Robbie's SUV, heard Robbie and Will talking about getting him into bed.

"I'll be fine. Just get me home and I'll be fine."

But he grimaced as another ice pick of pain hammered through his temples.

"D, you can barely walk." Will touched his shoulder. "Just shut the fuck up and let the grownups figure this out."

His smile was weak but he managed a small one. "Sure, Dad."

He didn't know what else they said because he shut his eyes again and leaned his head back against the headrest.

Then Robbie got in the car and slammed the door shut and he had to grit his teeth against the nausea.

"Shit. S-Sorry. Let me know if you need puke."

The drive back to their apartment took forever. Or at least it felt like it. He kept his eyes closed the entire time, although he'd felt his phone vibrate several times. Probably Sophie getting back to him. Damn it.

By the time Robbie helped him out of the car and into their apartment, he was ready to pass out.

Since he'd taken a shower after the game, he didn't need to do anything but strip and fall into bed. But even though he felt better just to lay down, he still felt like his head was about to explode.

The trainer had sent him home with a bottle of whatever he'd given him on the bus but warned him not exceed the dosage. Too bad he'd forgotten what that was and the damn type on the bottle was too fucking small for him to even attempt to read.

He thought about calling Robbie in to help him but Robbie had probably gone straight to bed, too.

Then he swore he heard Sophie's voice coming from somewhere.

Did migraines make you hallucinate?

Maybe they weren't so bad after all.

———

Sophie frowned over Derek's garbled last text. It was almost unreadable but she got the gist of it.

He was fine but he had a headache.

She'd seen the game tonight, had seen the vicious hit he'd taken from the Wilkes-Barre player. And then she'd watched him being helped off the ice only to return later.

He'd played the rest of the game but even she could tell he'd played like crap. So he probably wanted to be left alone.

But that text worried her. What if he had a concussion? Had he gone to a doctor?

Damn it, she was worried about him and she had no idea what the hell to do about it. Would he think she was being clingy if she called Jess to ask Will how he was feeling?

She set her phone down only to pick it up a few seconds later. Then set it down again.

Shit.

Today had been a screwed-up day. The bar was closed on Sundays and she almost always went to her parents' for dinner, along with at least one of her sisters. After yesterday, she'd almost called off. She hadn't spoken to her mom since Saturday morning and she figured by now, her mom had told her dad and... Ugh, lunch was going to be a huge headache.

But she figured it was better to face that problem head-on than let it fester. So she went. And yeah, it was weird. Her mom treated her like she normally did but every now and then Sophie caught her mom looking at her like she wanted to say something. Then her mom would smile and turn away. And Sophie would stifle a sigh.

At least, her dad didn't seem to know anything or, if he did, he was thankfully ignoring the situation. Whatever. It made for a weird night. Especially since her sister, Helena, was there with her kids. And Helena kept smiling at her, too. But it was more like a smirk.

She'd sighed in relief as she walked back into her apartment in time for the start of the game and had been glued to the TV for the entire thing. Watching it live was much more fun but having the different camera angles allowed her to get a closer look.

And every time they showed that shot of Derek getting hit, she winced.

She'd checked her phone every few minutes after the game, hoping to hear from him. And when she finally had, she'd begun to worry.

Yes, he was probably fine, just tired and didn't want to talk to anyone, her included.

Still...

With a sigh, she opened a new text.

Hey, I just got a weird text from Derek and now I'm worried about him. Am I being stupid?

It took a few seconds, but Bliss finally got back to her.

Weird how?

Messed up. Like he was drunk but I know he's not. I'm worried because he hit his head on the wall tonight.

I'll text Shane. He can check.

You don't think I'm being clingy?

What? No. You're concerned. There's a difference. Sit tight. I'll get back to you.

She spent the next few minutes pacing the floor. She'd switched over to some Hallmark movie after the game but it wasn't holding her attention.

And when her phone rang, she forgot about the TV.

"Hey Soph." Bliss. "Shane said Derek's got a migraine and is down for the count. Will and Robbie are going to get him back to his apartment and hope he sleeps it off."

"Oh no. Migraines are the worst. My dad's had them for years."

"So you know what to do for them?"

"Yeah. My dad had them a lot when I was younger. Why?"

"Well, the guys think he'll be fine but, according to Shane, the trainer said something to Robbie about keeping an eye on him for concussion. He checked out okay after the hit but...you know guys. They say they're fine until they're not. And then they're huge babies and need someone to take care of them. So," Bliss drew the word out to about five syllables, "I'm thinking maybe you want to stay with Derek tonight. Just to keep an eye on him."

She wanted to agree immediately. Wanted to jump at the chance to take care of him. But she also didn't want to seem like a stalker after spending one night with him.

"I don't know. Maybe he doesn't want me there. He didn't text me back."

"Probably because he can't open his eyes. I think you'd be doing him and the guys a favor."

Which is how she found herself knocking on Derek's apartment door about an hour and a half later, still trying to tell herself this was a good idea.

When the door opened, she found herself staring up at a young god with short blond hair that stuck out all over the place and tired, electric-blue eyes.

"Hey, you must be S-Sophie." He reached for her hand and practically dragged her inside. "Thanks for c-coming over. I was k-kinda f-freaking out."

"Hi. Robbie, right?" She smiled when he nodded. "No problem. Bliss said you guys are probably exhausted after the game. I don't might helping out. Just point me in Derek's direction and I'll make sure he's okay."

Robbie's expression of complete relief made her feel better about being here.

"Straight b-back. Thanks. I'm ready to c-crash but if you n-need anything, just ask."

"I will. Now go get some sleep. You look like you can use it."

He saluted her, probably because of the stutter. She had a cousin with a severe lisp who'd learned ways around speaking with gestures. Obviously Robbie had done the same.

Walking to the back of the apartment, Sophie headed for the door Robbie had pointed at and slowly opened it.

It barely made a sound, but she knew from her dad that even the tiniest noise could be painful during a migraine. The room was almost pitch black, but she could just make out the figure on the bed. He must have fallen asleep already. Which was good.

Taking a step forward, her foot hit something soft on the floor and she stooped to pick it up. Pants. She looked down again and saw the rest of his clothes strewn over the floor. Like he'd just dropped them were he stood.

She'd just stooped to pick up the rest when she heard movement.

"Sophie?"

Derek squinted at her, his eyes barely open.

"Yeah, it's me." She whispered as she came closer to the bed then knelt on the floor beside him. "How do you feel?"

"Like shit. What're you doing here?"

"Shane and Will were worried about you. I offered to help. Can I get you an ice pack for your head? And I can run to the store for some Excedrin. They make stuff specifically for migraines."

The slight smile on his lips made her smile in return, even though he couldn't see it because his eyes had closed again.

"Trainer gave me pills. On the table. I will love you forever if you get me an icepack."

Her smile widened, even as her stomach gave a little flutter at his choice of words.

Down, girl. Don't be an idiot.

Back in the kitchen, she grabbed a flexible gel ice pack out of the freezer, grabbed a water bottle out of the drying rack next to the sink and filled it with water, found the pills on the table, made a stop in the bathroom to get a clean towel to wrap around the ice pack, then took it all back to his room.

She left the light on in the hall and let the door open a sliver so she didn't have to turn on the light in his bedroom. He looked like he hadn't moved a muscle since she left.

"You still awake? I'm going to put the icepack on your head, okay?"

He made a tiny motion that looked like a nod so she set the water bottle and the pills on the nightstand and gently moved his hair out of the way so she could put the icepack on his forehead.

If he wasn't feeling so awful, she'd run her fingers through it because she had a thing for his hair. Those curls were so damn silky.

Instead, she released a little sigh and turned away. But his hand caught hers before she could take a step.

"Stay."

"I'm not leaving. I'm just going to sit in the living—"

"Sit here."

She nibbled on her bottom lip. "I don't want to disturb you."

"You can't."

She fought a short battle with her good sense then kicked off her shoes, took off her coat and slid into the other side of the bed. Since she was wearing yoga pants and a loose, thin sweatshirt without a bra, she was just as comfortable as if she'd been wearing pajamas.

Turning on her side, she watched his face slowly relax. And just before she closed her eyes, she felt his fingers touch hers beneath the covers and wrap around them tightly.

———

Derek woke around six a.m. and instinctively winced before he realized his head no longer hurt.

Thank fuck.

He still felt like he'd gotten run over by a bus and would need at least a week to recover but he no longer wanted to jamb his fingers in his eyes to stop his head from pounding and that was a good thing.

A soft sigh from the opposite side of the bed reminded him he wasn't alone. Sophie lay on her side facing him, hair covering most of her face, body curled into a tight knot.

Not how he'd wanted to spend his second night with her but he was damn glad she'd been here.

She'd taken care of him all night, changed the icepack several times, gotten him a couple more pills when he'd woken around two.

Laying back down beside her, he pushed the hair out of her face and traced the curves of her face with his eyes.

So goddamn pretty. And so sweet. She barely knew him and she'd stayed with him all night.

She's a keeper.

Derek heard his grandfather's voice in his head, something his Pop had said more times than he could remember about Derek's grandmother. They had the kind of relationship Derek wanted for himself, the kind he wanted for his mom and his sister. The kind his Nana feared he'd never find because he was never looking.

Maybe he hadn't had to look. Maybe he'd gotten lucky and she'd fallen into his lap.

Yeah, or maybe she's a gold digger looking to get out of this little town on the back of a guy who's gonna be rich and famous someday.

And that was the cynic who lived in Derek's head and was only allowed out to play occasionally because that bastard was a fucking asshole.

He'd stake his career on the fact that Sophie wasn't like that. Yeah, he'd met some girls who absolutely were looking for a way out of their small town and thought a professional athlete could get them there. He'd seen those relationship fall apart because they were built on a shaky foundation.

And yeah, maybe growing up dirt poor and always one step away from being on the street had made him more cynical than someone who'd never known what it was like to wonder if you were going to eat dinner that night or have to wait to get to school the next day.

Sophie wasn't like those girls. Sophie was the kind of girl who wouldn't want to get involved with an athlete like him because they didn't have a stable life. They were constantly on the move.

But Sophie had said she wanted to travel. Europe and Japan. Not the states and Canada wherever he managed to get traded to. Because the reality of his job was that he could wake up in Pennsylvania but go to sleep in Idaho.

And why the fuck are you worrying about any of this right now when you could be waking this woman with a kiss?

Dude, creeper much?

Stifling a sigh, he swung his legs over the side of the bed and headed for the bathroom, keeping the noise to a minimum. He didn't want to wake Sophie or Robbie, who he probably owed big time for contacting Sophie.

He'd just started to crawl back into bed when he heard Sophie make a soft sound.

Turning on his side to face her, he found her eyes open.

"Hey."

"Hey." Her lips curved in a smile that made him think about things he shouldn't be thinking about. At least not now. "How do you feel?"

"A hell of a lot better." He kept his voice low as he slid down next to her and turned on his side to face her. "Thank you for coming over last night. If you'd left me to Robbie, we'd probably both have headaches and black eyes this morning."

Her lips curved into an even sweeter smile and now the urge to kiss her made him grit his teeth. Damn it, why the hell was he second-guessing everything with her?

"He looked beat last night, too."

"Tough game for all of us."

Her nose crinkled. "Yeah, I saw. That sucked. But you have

another game against them later this month and I'm sure you'll beat them then."

"So now you're a hockey fan?"

She gave a look that was a cross between "well, yeah" and "don't get a big head."

"Let's just say I might be more of a fan than I was a few days ago."

"And does that have anything to do with me?"

"Oh, do you play?"

Her teasing smile finally broke through his restraint and he leaned forward and kissed her. Lips closed, no tongue. Just a straight-up, fit-for-company press of his lips against hers. Of course, the fact that they were in his bed and he was wearing nothing but a pair of boxers probably wasn't the best idea, but he couldn't help himself.

And when she responded by tilting her head just enough that their lips pressed open and her tongue slipped through and flicked against his upper lip...

He wasn't that good.

Sliding closer, he wrapped his arms around her waist, intending nothing more than to kiss her. Okay, and maybe press her gorgeous body against his and think about all the things he wanted to do to that body. What he wasn't planning was to rip off her clothes and lick his way from her throat to her pussy.

Apparently, Sophie had other ideas.

She rolled them until she was on top. Her mouth shifted over his, deepening their kiss until it caught fire and swept away every last thought he had of denying himself her.

His hands slid down her back from her shoulders to her ass, cupping those tight globes and bringing her hips even tighter against his groin. Caught between them, his cock throbbed, happy to have the pressure and begging for more.

Down, boy.

But Sophie didn't seem to want to stop at kissing. Her hips

ground down a little harder and her legs shifted open until her knees fell on either side of his legs.

Fuck. If they were naked, his cock would be pressed against her pussy and he'd be reaching for the condoms in the bedside table. Instead, he moved his hands back to her waist and tried not to devour her. Even though that's exactly what he wanted to do. And it seemed that's what she wanted, too.

Her mouth moved against his with an ever-increasing urgency that set fire to his libido. He wanted her to keep going but, if she did, he wouldn't want to stop.

And even though it was still early, he had practice today and he needed to get up and shovel calories back into his body. Even though the rest of his body wanted her, his stomach wanted food and growled. Loudly.

He felt her lips curve against his a second before she pulled away. She didn't go far, just far enough to be able to look down at him.

"I guess I should feed you before I jump your bones."

The need for food warred with the gnawing ache in his gut to bury his cock deep inside her.

So maybe you wanna show her you're not just after her for sex.

Damn, it sucked to take the high road.

"Do you promise to jump my bones later?"

Putting her hands on his chest, she settled her pussy directly over his hard cock and rocked down onto him, that smile on her face promising so much.

"I don't know that I can promise that. What if you have a relapse with the migraine? And don't you have practice today?"

"No practice until this afternoon. Which means I've got all morning."

"Then I guess you can wait a few minutes for breakfast. Because I am hungry and not for food."

Her unapologetic sex drive hit him like a check into the boards and his fingers tightened on her hips. He opened his mouth to respond but never got a word out because she bent down and kissed him again.

And then she did a hell of a lot more than kiss him.

———

Sophie sighed as Derek gave her one final kiss then dropped onto his back beside her.

He didn't bother to pull the sheets back up his naked body and she could honestly say she wished he'd just never wear clothes with her.

She, however, pulled the covers up to her breasts because, well, it was kind of chilly in his room, even though they'd just had more amazing sex.

With her on top this time, she'd come just from the motion of the base of his cock hitting her clit. And the way he'd stared at her the whole time.

Just thinking about it made her sex clench in remembered pleasure. And made her want him again.

"Damn, girl. I don't think I can move. You broke me."

She giggled, almost snorted, and covered her mouth with her hand when he turned to her with a huge grin.

"You're a big, strong hockey player. I don't think someone who can barely lift a full keg of beer is any danger to your health."

Rolling onto his side, his hair fell over his eyes until she could barely see them. Lifting one hand, she pushed the curls away then let her fingers drift down his cheek to his lips. His grin softened as he continued to hold her gaze.

"Oh, you're dangerous, just not to my health."

She wanted to say something smart or funny or whatever but she couldn't think of one damn thing. He'd taken her breath away with a look and a few words.

The silence stretched for almost a full minute while they lay there and stared into each other's eyes. The spell was broken when they heard Robbie's bedroom door open, the sound of footsteps and then Robbie swearing.

"Sonuvabitch. What the fuck is that? Goddammit."

They both laughed and Derek fell onto his back again to stare at the ceiling.

"Amazing how he never stutters when he swears." He sighed. "I really do need to get up and eat or I will be shit for practice."

"Want me to make you something?"

He turned his head to look at her again. "How about I take you out? I'm not sure what we've got to eat other than eggs. Besides, you cooked for me yesterday."

"I don't mind. I like to cook."

Besides, if they went to any of the restaurants in a five-block radius, it would eventually get back to her dad that she'd been out to breakfast with Derek.

Then her dad would say something to her mom and her parents would definitely want to have a chat. And her dad would probably want to talk to Derek, too.

She wasn't embarrassed about spending the night Derek. Not at all. She just didn't want to talk to her parents about her sex life or flaunt it in their faces. Sometimes it sucked to be a good girl.

Derek looked at her closely for a few seconds, almost as if he could read her mind. Then he shrugged and that smile returned. The one that made her stomach tie into knots and her body respond as if he'd run his hands all over her.

"Sure. What idiot's gonna turn down home-cooked food?"

She released the breath she hadn't been aware she'd been holding and Derek's gaze narrowed.

"You know, I can probably go without food for another hour or so."

She lifted her hand and put one finger over his lips before he said anything else that would make her reconsider.

"I have class this afternoon and I need to do some reading beforehand. So I'm getting up and making breakfast and then I'm going to go so you can go to practice and I can study."

Before she could pull her finger away, he opened his mouth and sucked it inside.

And oh my god, how the hell could just the pull of his mouth on her finger make her melt from the inside out?

So not fair.

She should get out of bed and get dressed. And yet she lay there another few seconds and stared at him while he made her wet just by sucking her finger.

With a tiny shake of her head, she pulled her finger away, gave him a warning look as his eyebrows rose, and slid out of bed.

"Don't even think about it."

Grabbing her clothes from the floor where he'd thrown them, she pulled them on and turned around to find him on his back, hands laced under his head while he watched her with an intensity she remembered from watching him play.

"Aren't you getting up?"

"I was enjoying the view."

Shaking her head, though she was enjoying the hell out of every damn minute with him, she walked to the door and turned the knob. "Well, the view is heading for the kitchen so if you want to watch it in action, you need to get dressed and follow along."

With a sigh, he threw the covers back and her breath caught in her throat. The man had a body that made her drool. Literally. Like, if she wasn't careful, she'd embarrass the hell out of herself.

But that body was also covered with bruises. Some tiny. Some not so much.

"I thought you wore pads to prevent injuries. Why do you always seem to have more?"

Looking down at himself, he shrugged as he poked a few of the more brightly covered spots on his torso.

"Eh. Hazard of the game. Most of them don't hurt."

She raised an eyebrow at him. "Most of them?"

His smile should've warned her. "They don't hurt as much as other parts of me do."

Her eyes rolled even as she wanted to sigh at that smile.

He took a step closer. "Maybe you should work your magic on my bruises."

"I'm going to go work my magic in your kitchen. You need to get dressed and come eat."

Then she opened the door and made her escape before he did something else that totally threw her off track.

She had a feeling he was going to do that a lot.

And she couldn't wait.

———

"You look good for someone who looked like shit last night."

"Yeah, good morning to you, too." Derek bumped his shoulders against Lad's as they sat on the bench lacing up their skates before practice. "I'm feeling a hell of a lot better than I did last night. Migraine's gone."

"I hear you had help with that."

Derek gave Lad a look that should've made his balls shrivel. Instead, the guy smiled. Since he didn't do it that often, Derek's eyes widened.

"Dude, you're creeping me out. You never smile."

"I smile when I have something to be happy about. You amuse me. Like Will and Shane. They now have women who make them less...cranky."

"Hey, I'm not cranky."

"No, but you are smiling. You do not do that often."

"Now you're the smile police?"

Lad raised his hands in front of him like he was surrendering. "I make comment. Nothing more."

"Uh huh." Standing to pull his practice sweater over his head, he saw Jake talking to Coach Cary off to the side.

"Hey." Derek tapped Lad on the shoulder and nodded in Jake's direction. "How's he doing?"

Lad didn't even have to see what Derek was nodding at to know what he was talking about. "He does not talk much anymore."

Jake had been on the injured reserve for months and had been in rehab for the past few weeks. The hamstring tear in his right leg had been slow to heal and therapy wasn't going as fast as Jake wanted. Which had turned the normally talkative guy into a silent ghost. No one had been able to draw him out of his persistent funk and a lot of the guys were worried he wouldn't be back for the playoffs. Which would suck because he'd been an important part of the team's success last year.

And if Jake wasn't talking to Lad... Hell, he wouldn't talk to anyone.

"Maybe we should go out tonight. Force Jake to go with us."

Lad stood next to Derek pulling his sweater on then grabbing his helmet. "No one forces Jake to do anything. But I will do my best. I would like night out as well."

"Tell him we'll go somewhere quiet. Just for some food and a few drinks. No rowdy shit."

"So I should tell him you will not be there."

The underlying amusement in Lad's tone wasn't lost on Derek and he flipped the guy the finger.

"Just get him to come."

"Come out where?"

Robbie stopped next to Derek on his way to the ice, which was where most of the rest of the team had already gone.

"We need to get Jake out for the night." Derek lowered his voice so Jake wouldn't hear him. "He needs to get out of his head for a while."

Ian Clark stuck his head into their group. "Who needs to get out of his head?"

Since the kid was too young to drink, he didn't get to hang with the guys much. Tonight would be an exception, Derek decided.

"Jake. We're doing dinner tonight. You in?"

Ian's eyes lit up. "Yeah, sure. Where're we going?"

"Place in West Reading."

Robbie coughed out a laugh and Derek stuck his elbow in his roommate's side. "Shut it. They serve food so we can take the kid."

"Uh huh. I'm sure that's the only reason."

"Ah." Lad nodded. "Okay. I know where we go. I will talk to Jake. He will go because he will want to see Derek in action."

Derek rolled his eyes, wondering what the hell he'd gotten himself into. "Jesus, you guys suck. I don't even know if she's working tonight. Last time I make plans for you assholes. And I'll talk to Jake."

But he was smiling as he walked across the room. He stood far enough away that he couldn't hear what they were saying. Didn't want to appear that he was listening in, especially since Jake looked upset.

Finally, Cary clasped Jake's shoulder before he walked off, nodding to Derek as he headed out to the ice.

"Hey." Derek ran a hand through his hair before shoving his helmet on. "Dinner tonight. You're coming. Don't wanna hear any excuses."

Derek figured the best way to get Jake to go was to give him no choice.

Jake just shrugged. The guy looked seriously depressed and Derek's eyes narrowed. "Dude, what the fuck?"

He kept his voice low although everyone had already left for the ice. Derek would be late if he stayed any longer but he couldn't leave Jake looking like this. He'd take however many sprints Coach handed out.

"Nothing. I just..." Jake huffed out a frustrated breath and sank onto the bench. "Therapy sucks and I feel I am not getting better. I hate being not able to play."

"I get it but cuttting yourself off from the rest of the team isn't the way to deal with it. Dinner. Tonight. You'll feel better. And I'm not asking, I'm telling."

Jake shook his head and didn't meet Derek's eyes but Derek wasn't taking no for an answer.

"Man, if you don't show up, I will personally drive to your apartment and drag you to my car then drag you into the restaurant. You need to man up." Then Derek pulled out his trump card. "Besides, I want you to meet Sophie."

There, that got a response. Jake's head rose and he gave Derek a look full of disbelief.

"So she said yes to you? Maybe you are not as helpless as I thought."

Derek hid a grin. "Fuck you. Be at the bar around six-thirty."

Jake didn't give him an answer but he didn't say no either. "You had better get on ice. You will do sprints."

"I'll tell them all I was holding your hand while you cried on my shoulder."

Jake rolled his eyes but his mouth actually formed a little smile. "You are asshole."

"Yeah, but I've got a girl and you're still jerking yourself."

Jake's response was a middle finger but the guy had a legit smile finally.

"Who in hell would ever go out with you, D-man?"

"Guess you'll have to come out tonight to see."

Derek turned and headed for the ice, smiling all the way.

———

"So your mom tells me you have a new man in your life."

It's a good thing Sophie was facing away from her dad when he spoke because her face probably would've given away her shock.

She shouldn't be surprised her mom had told her dad but still... This was a conversation she didn't want to have at work. Luckily, no one else was in the kitchen at the moment. At least he'd waited for privacy.

She thought about what to say carefully because she realized that her immediate response of "We just met" wouldn't go over well if her mom had told him Derek had spent the night. Then again, she didn't want to lie.

"Mm, yeah," was the best she could come up with.

Her dad didn't say anything else right away and she hoped he'd drop it. Monday night's typically weren't busy but tonight Will had called ahead to reserve a table for ten. Half the team would be here for dinner, including Derek. Her dad had already called in help from her sisters and Carlos, who would be here soon.

She'd just gotten home from class when her dad had asked her to come down and help prep, that they had large party coming in. It wasn't until she'd seen the name in the book that she realized it was the team. Then she'd whipped out her phone and texted Derek, who said he'd be there and sorry he hadn't texted earlier. He'd fallen asleep after practice.

Then he'd asked if he'd see her there and she'd gotten a goofy grin that she was happy no one was around to see. Sophie didn't do goofy. God, the shit she'd take from her sisters if they saw her grinning like an idiot over a guy. It was bad enough her mom had caught him leaving her apartment Saturday morning.

Then again, maybe she just shouldn't care. Maybe she needed to stop worrying about what everyone else in her life needed and just worry about herself.

"So what's he do?"

Shit. Okay, she could handle this. "He's a hockey player. He plays for the Redtails."

Continuing to chop onions, she didn't look over her shoulder, tried to act like it was no big deal.

"He gonna be here tonight?"

Shit, shit, shit. "Yeah. But he's gonna be here with his teammates. He's not here to see me."

"You planning to introduce him to me?"

No, she really didn't want to she knew that wouldn't work. "Sure.

But, Dad," she looked over her shoulder and waited until he looked at her, "be nice."

He raised his eyebrows. "When am I not nice?"

She huffed. "When have you ever been nice to a guy I've dated?"

He snorted. "When they deserve it. And when you bother to introduce me to them. I can't remember the last time I met one of your dates."

She opened her mouth to argue—

And realized she couldn't. Her lips closed.

Her dad nodded. "Uh huh. So what makes this one different?"

Good question, which she chewed over while she chopped. Was Derek different? She hadn't known him long enough to know for sure. But...

Or was she just following the same pattern of falling for a totally inappropriate guy because she could blow them off easily because she planned to travel?

Yeah and when the hell is that going to happen?

"How's classes going? You doing well?"

Amazingly, her dad let her off the hook with Derek.

"Good. Still on track to graduate in December."

"You still want to teach, right?"

"Yeah. It's just..."

She didn't want to get into this now. Every time she said something to her parents about going away to teach, they got quiet. Not upset exactly but...sad. And then she got upset and questioned her plans and it became a mess that made her want to stick her head in the sand.

Argh.

Her dad shrugged, like it was no big deal. "So you get a job at one of the local schools and you figure it out. It's not like you have to know right away."

She took a deep breath. "You know I need a teaching certificate to be able to teach in the state."

"So you take the classes and get the certificate. We'll support whatever you want to do."

"And if I want to teach overseas?"

Her dad stayed silent. Which is exactly what she'd expected.

"Dad—"

"We just want you to be happy. If that's what gonna make you happy, then we'll have to learn to live with it."

"And if I want to date a hockey player?"

Her dad gave her steady look. "Then he'll have to learn to deal with us."

Huffing out a laugh, she shook her head but didn't know what else to say.

"But you like him?" her dad continued.

"Yeah. He's a nice guy." He was more than a nice guy. He was funny and sweet and he seemed to like spending time with her and not just to have sex. Although they did have a lot. Good sex. Really good sex. "But he'll be going back to Boston or wherever he goes when the season's over and that'll probably be the end of it."

Which was more probably more true than she wanted to admit to herself.

Her dad dropped the subject then because Carlos walked in and he wouldn't continue the discussion with an audience.

But that gave her more time to get inside her own head, which she totally shouldn't do.

Why the hell couldn't she just enjoy the hell out of this guy for as long as he was around and not worry about next week or next month?

Maybe she could actually blame her parents for that. They had a great marriage. So did her sisters. All of them. Actually, her sisters had all either been engaged or in long-term relationships with their spouses by her age.

So what's wrong with you?

With a sigh, she put down her knife.

"I'm gonna check the front."

She headed for the bar to make sure it was stocked, though she knew their regular bartender would never leave for the night without making sure the bar was set for the next shift. But it forced her mind to focus on something that wasn't herself.

At five, she opened the front door and settled behind the bar with a textbook. She didn't figure they'd have a big crowd. Mondays were usually slow.

She was surprised when a party of five strolled in around six, which meant she was too busy to get grilled by her sister Margret, who'd volunteered to help tonight, along with her teenage son, Logan.

With Logan bussing, Sophie was free to wait tables while Margret handled the bar.

A party of three arrived as she was serving dinner to the five-top so when she turned at the sound of the front door opening again, she was almost surprised to see five tall men walking through the door.

Her heart actually stuttered when Derek's gaze caught hers across the room. And when he smiled... Oh my god, she couldn't catch her breath. How stupid was that?

Blinking, she tore her attention away before she dumped a plate on someone's lap as her sister got the guys seated at the table she'd set up earlier.

But she felt his gaze follow her every move. By the time she'd served the last plate, it was time to take the guys' drink order.

"Hey, Soph." Will nodded at her. "How goes it?"

"Surprisingly busy. What can I get you guys to drink? Or do you want to wait until the rest get here?"

"Might as well get started now."

She went around the table until she got to Derek, who'd watched her the entire time with a half-assed grin on his face. Her own lips twitched at the corners but she fought against giving in. The guy didn't need any more help and she didn't want her dad to come over and start interrogating him. Because her dad had decided to stand in kitchen entrance with his arms crossed over his chest, watching the table. Derek couldn't see him because he had his back to the kitchen but Sophie wasn't going to give her dad any ammunition.

"And for you?"

His grin widened and it was probably good her dad couldn't see Derek's face because he'd know immediately which of the guys she'd slept with. Heat rose through her body. Soon, it'd show on her cheeks. She needed to get out of here as fast as possible.

"I think you know what I like."

She couldn't help her eye roll or the fact that she wanted to run her fingers through those messy curls.

Derek laughed and shook his head as the other guys studiously ignored them.

"You're killing me, Soph." When she just stood there with her pencil poised over her pad, he shrugged. "Just a Troegs draft. For now."

Those last two little words made it clear there would be a later. And, oh my god, yes. She wanted later. Wanted him. Sooner rather than later but she could wait.

Desire was an ache in her gut, one that never went away around him. She wanted him so much that the speed she'd fallen for him should have been a little alarming.

And that was ridiculous because, oh my god, they were just having sex, for chrissake.

Giving him a pleasant smile, she headed back to the bar to get the drinks ready. Luckily, her dad had gone back to the kitchen. But her sister stood at the bar, staring at her with a raised eyebrow.

"Not your normal type. He's smiley."

Sophie couldn't help rolling her eyes as she sighed. "I think your age is starting to catch up to you. That's not even a word."

Mags hmphed. "Deflecting. Interesting tactic. Too bad I know all your tricks. He's a cutie, though. And wow, that is one fine ass."

Whipping around, Sophie turned to her oldest sister with her mouth hanging open. Which just made her sister laugh and pat her on the head.

"I may be older but I'm not dead, kid. I totally see the appeal."

"I don't just like him for his ass, you know." She wrinkled her nose and smiled at Mags as she tapped a pitcher for the table and a few sodas. "Although it is pretty fine. But...he's a really nice guy, too."

Mags just raised both brows. "Hope he stays that way."

Then she moved away to take care of the other tables.

Sophie didn't think that was going to be a problem.

Her problem was going to be that he was too nice of a guy to forget.

———

Derek had behaved himself all night.

He hadn't touched her, even though he'd wanted to put his arm around her and pull her down to sit on his lap or, hell, even talk to her for a few minutes.

She'd been busy all night taking care of their table so she'd barely had more than a few seconds to pay any attention to him.

Not that he was complaining. He totally planned to spend at least a few hours later making sure she paid attention only to him. But he'd had to rein himself in several times tonight and that was different. Not difficult just...different.

Hell, maybe he was becoming an actual adult.

Snorting, he shook his head.

"You okay? Your head still hurt? You've been kinda quiet all night and it's freaking me out."

Derek looked across the table at Nick. The guy looked so earnestly concerned, Derek couldn't even laugh at him. A few of the other guys didn't have the same problem.

Justin slapped Nick on the back and shook his head. "It's not his head that hurts."

Which caused Will to reach around Nick and smack Justin on the back of the head. "Watch your mouth. We're in public."

Justin's grin grew wider. "What? I didn't say anything."

"Uh huh." Will nodded. "Keep it that way?"

The rest of the guys laughed and Will got the conversation steered back to the next game but Derek noticed Nick kept watching him.

"Dude, what?"

Nick opened his mouth to speak but closed it a second later when his gaze slid over Derek's shoulder.

"Anything else I can get you guys tonight?"

Sophie stood almost immediately behind him and, when he looked over his shoulder, he grinned. He couldn't help it. She made him smile. Hell, just thinking about her made him smile. He'd never had this reaction to a woman, never thought it'd happen to him like this. But for the first time in a long time, he felt like he'd found someone he could share more than a bed with.

So...fuck it, he didn't care who knew.

Reaching over his shoulder, he grabbed her hand and pulled it down to his lips, pressing them against the back of her hand.

"No, hon. I think we're finished. We'll get out of your hair so you can get out of here."

And so he could have her to himself.

While the rest of the guys went conspicuously silent, he waited to see what she'd do. He was almost disappointed when she pulled her hand away. Until she brushed her hand through his hair and returned his smile.

"Stay as long as you like. We don't close for another hour."

Then she leaned down and whispered in his ear. "Then I'm all yours. Wait for me at the bar."

His head whipped around but she'd already turned to head back to the kitchen.

And he started a countdown from sixty.

———

They barely made it inside her apartment before they started stripping off each other's clothing.

Derek had her plastered against the door with one hand up the back of her shirt and the other working at the button of her jeans. They'd been standing here at least five minutes. Maybe more. She really had no idea.

She'd intended to take a shower before sitting down on the couch with him and making out but, as he'd followed her up the stairs to her apartment, he hadn't been able to keep his hands off her.

She'd slid the key in the lock and both of his hands had wrapped around her waist and his lips had landed on her nape.

Her breath had caught in her throat for a second before she could draw in deeper breath as his hands slid beneath her shirt and touched the bare skin of her waist.

From there, it was only a short trip to her breasts. She had the door open by the time he pinched her nipples between his thumb and forefinger and the shudder that ran through her went straight to her pussy.

Groaning, she'd pushed through into her apartment and, the next thing she knew, he had her trapped between his hard body and the wood door with his tongue in her mouth.

If she thought maybe he'd slow down now, of course she was wrong.

As her hands fumbled with his jeans, his slid around her back to unsnap her bra with an ease that gave her pause.

Oh, he is way too good at that.

And then tilted his head a little to the left and sank his tongue deeper into her mouth and wiped any questions out of her head. The only sound in her apartment was the rustle of clothing and their heavy breathing. And the only rational thought in her brain was to get his clothes off. Since he seemed to have the same idea, clothing hit the floor at a fast pace.

He pulled back for a second to tug her t-shirt over her head, allowing her to draw in a deep breath before diving back down to her mouth while his hands stripped off her bra.

She pulled his shirt up, which meant he had to release her again to pull that over his head. But once he dropped it, he paused, his gaze falling to her chest.

Molding both hands to her breasts, he squeezed, making her draw in a sharp breath.

"I'm not hurting you, am I?"

She wasn't sure she could answer his question without her voice cracking so she shook her head.

"You have an amazing body."

She put one hand in the middle of his chest then ran it down his abs to his jeans, where she slowly lowered his zipper. "Says the man with the six-pack."

Glancing up, she saw his lips curve.

"Yeah, but your ass is a work of art." He released one breast to curve that hand over said ass cheek, making her shiver with sensation. "I managed to keep my hand off you all night but I plan to make up for it now."

She opened her mouth to speak but he kissed her again and shoved her jeans down her thighs. Kicking off her sneakers, she worked her jeans off while his hands petted her ass then fought to get his jeans over his hips.

The damn man wasn't giving her any help. His mouth slipped to her jaw and kept working its way down, sucking at her skin until she felt like one huge live wire ready to spark.

And when his mouth reached her breasts, she wanted to melt. She didn't realize her feet had left the floor until she attempted to arch her back to get him to give her more. Then she realized he held her up with only one arm around under ass.

She shivered with lust. This man was seriously strong and, oh my god, did that turn her on.

Wrapping her arms around his shoulders and her legs around his waist, she gave herself over to him. Her head hit the door as he shifted her higher, his mouth hot and wet on her skin.

He made her sigh with just a lick of his tongue and shiver by pressing his lips against her throat. Holding her steady, he threw her entire world off kilter. And she loved it.

After a few more minutes, he lowered her a little and began to walk through her apartment.

"I think we need a bed for the rest of this." He spoke directly into her ear then nibbled at the lobe. "Wouldn't want to drop you."

"The couch is closer."

It was her turn to nibble on his ear and make him shudder, grinning when he did.

"But not as comfortable. Besides, I want you on top. Bed gives us more room to play."

God, yes. she totally got that reasoning. "So you're going to do what I want for a change?'

"Haven't you figure out yet that I'll do whatever you want? Anything you want? Your wish is my command, babe."

She dropped her voice to a sexy whisper. "Then it's your turn to lay on the bed and hold tight. Because I've got plans."

His arms tightened around her and he picked up his pace. "Oh yeah? Am I gonna like these plans?"

"I certainly hope so."

He reached her room, where she always left the small bedside light burning, and dropped her in the middle of her bed while he shoved his jeans down and got rid of them and his sneakers and socks. Then he jumped on the bed and lay flat on his back, his grin wide and naughty.

Arms crossed under his head, long body stretched out beside her, his erection hard and flat against his stomach, he looked ready for anything. And she couldn't wait.

Crawling over him, she got a condom from her nightstand and set it directly on his chest. His grin widened.

"Now be a good boy and don't move." She swung one leg over his hips so she was straddling him, her pussy only inches from his hard cock. "My turn to play."

His breath deepened and he lost the grin but not the gleam in his eyes.

Starting at his shoulders, she worked her way down his body, kissing every bruise he had. And there were a lot of them. Some tiny, some not so tiny. Those she was careful not to linger over. The one on his side looked especially nasty so she merely brushed her lips over that until she reached his cock.

Looking up, she found him watching her so intently, he appeared to be holding his breath. After a few seconds of smiling into his eyes, she bent and took him in her mouth.

He sucked in air and his hand sifted through her hair to hold her close. Unlike before, he guided her movements and she let him because it made her even more wet.

His labored breathing sounded harsh in the quiet room, the muscles of his thighs hard as stone beneath hers. Using her tongue and her teeth and her mouth, she played him until he gasped for air and pulled at her hair until her scalp ached.

Pushing him right to the edge, she finally backed off when he groaned and tugged her head just a little harder.

"I don't want to come in your mouth."

His voice sounded like a growl, making her pussy clench futilely.

Pushing back onto her haunches, she grabbed the condom and rolled it down his shaft.

"Wait," he said, "I thought you wanted to play."

"Play later. Right now, I want to ride you."

His groan echoed through the room. "Fuck yeah. Please. Anything you want."

She wanted to smile but she was too turned on. Pulling his cock up from his stomach, she settled down on him without any teasing. They both groaned as she sank lower. Her head fell back as her body took him in, easing some the ache but making it worse, too.

With her hands planted on his chest, she rose and fell in a rhythm that quickly had them both on the edge. She'd already been so close. This man made every part of her sizzle.

Catching his gaze, she held it as she slowed, sinking down to his root, feeling him spreading her wide. Then she rotated her hips and her clit rubbed at just the right angle.

Her eyes closed as an orgasm hit her hard. Leaning down, she smashed their mouths together and let him take over the kiss. Grabbing her ass, he held her as she shuddered and started to thrust hard and fast.

It only took him seconds to finish and, when she went limp and stretched out over him, their bodies still connected, she pressed her lips against his chest and snuggled closer.

She could get used to this.

They lay in silence for several minutes, catching their breath.

Finally, Derek sighed. "So I think your dad liked me."

It took her a second to process what he'd said before she started to laugh.

"What?" he asked, as if he totally didn't know why she was laughing.

"We just had sex. Talking about my dad is not exactly on my agenda immediately after sex."

"But still, he liked me, right?"

"Were you worried he wouldn't?"

She felt him move as he shrugged his shoulders. "Nah, I'm loveable once you get to know me."

Propping one hand on his chest and putting her chin on top of her hand, she smiled at him. "Yes, you are. But you are kinda sleeping with his daughter."

"Then I guess I'm lucky he didn't take my head off with a kitchen knife."

"He wouldn't have started with your head."

Laughing, he pulled her closer and pressed his lips against her forehead. "Your sister liked me, too, right?"

"Uh huh. You got her highest praise. She called you a charmer."

"Better than dickwad."

She realized she'd laughed more in bed with this man than any other guy she'd ever been with. And that was a good thing.

"What about your mom? Would she like me?"

He paused and, for a few seconds, she held her breath. He didn't talk about his mom much. She knew his dad wasn't in the picture but—

"Yeah. I think so."

"Does she ever come to your games? I'd love to meet her."

Again, she held her breath. They'd known each other such a short time but she couldn't help herself. She wanted to know more about him.

"Not a lot, no. Sometimes she can get to the Providence games but...no. It's hard for her to get time away."

"What does she do?"

"She works for a cleaning company. Mostly office buildings so she works nights. She's...had a rough life."

She stayed silent wondering if he'd open up even more and was rewarded a few seconds later.

"She's an alcoholic, has been since she was a teenager. My dad was barely in the picture and totally skipped out on us soon after my sister was born. My mom tried but..." He sighed. "The alcohol helped her deal. She finally got sober when I went to college and she's stayed sober for years now."

Sophie could tell there was a hell of a lot more to that story but she wasn't going to push. He'd made it pretty clear his younger years had been tough. She'd grown up in a family where she'd never lacked anything. They weren't rich, but she'd never had to worry that they'd be living on the streets. She got the impression that was something he'd had to worry about.

"I'm glad." She really didn't know what else to say.

"Yeah, me, too. My mom's tough. I never doubted she loved me and my sister but, sometimes, she just couldn't deal. It's taken her a while but she finally learned how. I'm just glad she's still here. There were times…" Another shrug. "Anyway, now my sister's in college and my mom has a job and everything's okay."

"And that's good."

"Yeah, it is." He sighed. "Sometimes, though, I feel like I'm holding my breath, waiting for her to relapse. And that sucks."

Good thing it was dark. She didn't want him to see her tears forming. "It does suck. But it seems like she's got her life together and she's a fighter. Like her son."

He huffed out a laugh. "You can say that. But I'm not thinking about fighting now."

In a flash, he had her on her back, his nose almost touching hers as he grinned down at her.

Laughing, she put her arms around his shoulders, loving the feel of his heavy body holding her down.

And even though she could feel his erection hardening against her thigh, she asked, "So what are you thinking about?"

"Instigating, baby. I'm thinking about instigating."

Then he kissed her and instigated her straight into another orgasm.

CHAPTER 11

"So he just walked out? And you haven't talked to him since?"

Sophie shook her head, biting her bottom and avoiding Bliss's sympathetic gaze. "And now I don't know what to do. Should I call him? Should I text? Should I stop over? What if he slams the door in my face? I mean, I know he'd never do that, but what if he tells me to go away? I probably deserve it but—"

"Hey, none of this is your fault. You were totally right. This is his decision. But," Bliss's grimace held an apologetic twist, "Derek doesn't seem like the kind of guy to make such a big decision like this without a lot of thought. I mean, I know he seems impulsive on the ice but... This is his career and he's been pretty damn sure about what he wants. So for him to ask you for advice...I think that's kinda huge for him."

Sophie opened her mouth to argue then snapped it shut as she absentmindedly stocked glasses behind the bar while Bliss ate lunch. True, Derek did seem to have a quick temper on the ice, but she knew it was mostly show. Every move he made, everything he said had a purpose, whether it was to elicit a response from another player or to score a goal.

Bliss huffed out a sigh. "Maybe you should call him."

She shook her head. "I figure if he wants to talk to me, he'll call. I think he has to give them an answer tomorrow and I don't want to mess with his head anymore than I already have."

Bliss rolled her eyes. "I think that ship's sailed, hon. I know I thought you guys were an odd match at first but... You make each other happy. I think you're good for each other."

They had been happy. And, oh shit, she refused to cry now.

Biting her tongue, she forced those damn tears to recede but she couldn't speak because she was afraid she'd cry.

"So do you think he'll take the contract?" Bliss asked after a few more bites of her sandwich. "I can't imagine the team without him. The guys'll really miss him."

They wouldn't be the only ones. "I honestly don't know." But if he did... "I mean, it could be a good opportunity for him, right?"

Bliss's expression was a cross between a reluctant yes and an apologetic yes. "From what I've heard Shane say, yeah, it can be. They can make more money and they don't play as many games so there's less wear and tear on the body."

"So he should take it?"

Shrugging, Bliss sipped her lemonade. "Not necessarily. The NHL is still the big shiny prize for most of these guys. It's what they've worked for for so long. It's hard to give that up."

If he can walk away from that, he can certainly leave you behind, can't he?

The thought hit her like a punch to the gut.

"Soph, why don't you just call him and talk to him? Tell him how you feel. Tell him you don't want him to go."

She couldn't. She knew what that felt like. How even when it came from a place of love, like when her dad told her to get a teaching job locally, that it still made something inside ache.

And she didn't want him to look back and wonder what could have been if he hadn't listened to her.

"No. If he wants to hear from me, he'll call."

And if not...

———

"I think you have taken my place as unhappiest bastard on team. That is not compliment."

Derek didn't bother to respond to Jake, just continued to pull off his gear after practice the next day.

"What has crawled up your ass and died?"

Most of the other players were gone. He'd stayed on the ice after everyone else had left, shooting pucks until the ice crew had practically thrown him off and his shoulders were screaming.

By the time he'd gotten to the locker room, the guys were already showered and getting dressed.

Robbie and Ian kept looking at him but he ignored them, too. He was done talking. He had a decision to make by tomorrow morning and, since no one seemed willing to give him advice, he guessed he was on his own.

Pretty much where I've always been.

Christ, now he sounded like a whiny toddler. No wonder no one wanted to be around him.

"All right. Enough." Jake smacked his crutch against the shin guard Derek hadn't removed yet, startling him out of his thoughts.

"Hey. What the fuck?"

Jake nodded. "Exactly. What the fuck is up with you? Talk or I will grill Robbie and Ian, who will crack like egg. I see them staring at you all practice. They know what is your problem."

With a sigh, Derek got up to take off the rest of his gear and head for the showers. "I don't need to talk. Nothing's wrong."

He walked off to the showers before Jake could answer but, if he'd thought he'd be safe when he returned, he should've known better. Jake still sat on the bench, doing something on his phone, his face set in rigid lines.

Which shook Derek out of his self-involvement.

"What's wrong?" He walked to his locker and started to pull on clothes, looking over his shoulder at Jake, whose jaw was set hard enough to crack.

After a few seconds, Jake shook his head and put his phone in his pocket. "Nothing. Apparently you and I are perfectly okay."

Shit. Just...Shit.

Exhaling loudly, Derek dropped back onto the bench next to Jake.

"Swiss National made an offer."

Jake shrugged his shoulders and Derek swore he was going to rip Robbie or Ian a new hole they didn't need. Goddammit, he never—

"Is not surprise. You have played well. Someone was going to take notice."

"Yeah, well, it ain't the Colonials."

Jake rolled his eyes. "They pay you to play, right. They know what they have. I am sure when you tell them about offer, they will want to keep you."

"I'm not sure I want to stay anymore."

Again Jake's expression didn't change. "So what *do* you want?"

Derek opened his mouth to answer and closed it again when he realized he didn't have a fucking clue. He thought he had. But the last twenty-four hours had confused the fuck out of him. After talking to his mom yesterday, he hadn't talked to anyone else about it. He'd played deck hockey with the kids at the Olivets club and that had helped his mood tremendously. They were so happy to have him there.

But he's slept for shit last night, even though he'd wrung himself out at the gym after running around with the kids for hours.

And this morning at practice, he'd pushed himself hard, so hard Coach had told him to rein it in a little. Save it for the games this weekend. They had two, home and away against Lehigh Valley.

That just made him wonder if he'd even be here this weekend.

"I don't even fucking know what I want anymore. Honestly, at this point, I just want someone to tell me what to do."

"So I will. Stay here where we need you, where your friends are and where your woman is and stop fucking worrying."

Derek huffed out a laugh. "You make it sound so easy. Like my career isn't on the line here."

"Your career is safe here. You know that." Jake looked down at his leg, at the brace. "Do you really want to go overseas where you know no one and help them win a championship that is not yours?"

He opened his mouth to say something and closed it again when he realized he had nothing to say to that.

Except, "Shit. You're right."

Jake shrugged. "I am always right. You may thank me later. Now is time for lunch and, after lunch, for torture."

Derek caught the hard edge in Derek's tone and took a closer look at the guy.

"You got something you wanna confess to me now? You look like you could use it."

Jake sat quietly for several seconds, staring at his leg. Derek let the guy think. He understood sometimes it took a little while to gear up to what you wanted to say. Of course, he didn't usually have that problem but most people had a better handle on their mouths than he did.

"Doctor is concerned hamstring is not healing properly. Is taking longer than normal."

Now that was terrifying. For a professional athlete to hear that an injury wasn't normal... Yeah, that was enough to make you want to smash things.

Or, in Jake's case, to sit stoically and stare at his leg like he could heal it with just the heat of his gaze.

"Shit, I'm sorry. But they didn't say you were never going to play, right? Only that it's taking longer than normal to heal. So just keep doing your therapy. It'll work out."

"And if it does not? What then?"

At least he had an answer for that question. "Then we break shit and drink ourselves into a coma. Right now, all you need to worry about is fixing yourself. No matter how long it takes."

Jake shook his head, his gaze still trained on his leg. Yeah, Derek sucked at this. Jake had probably gotten the exact same advice from everyone, including the coaches and his doctors.

Finally, just when he thought Jake was going to pat him on the head and walk out, he heard him start to laugh.

Under his breath at first but finally he laughed so loud, Derek was afraid the guy was gonna stroke out.

"Dude, did I push you over the edge or what?"

After at least another thirty seconds, Jake finally calmed down enough to speak, looking up at Derek with a true grin.

"This is why I like you. You know what to say to make me laugh. And you are serious about breaking shit. I like that."

Grinning for the first time in days, Derek shook his head. "No problem. Glad to help someone with their issues."

Jake breathed out a deep sigh. "D. Do not let stupidity make your decisions. You know what you want. Go after it."

"Even if it's out of my control?"

"Yes. Because that is what makes it worthwhile when you get it."

———

Come to the game with us tomorrow. Talk to him.

Sophie stared at Bliss's text for several seconds, gnawing on her bottom lip until it hurt. Blowing out a breath, she typed and erased her response at least five times.

Finally, she settled on short and sweet.

Don't think that's a good idea.

She hadn't heard from Derek since he'd walked out of the bar four days ago. She'd thought about texting him but didn't know what she'd say.

She figured he hadn't taken the overseas offer because, if he had, he'd be gone. The fact that he was still here and hadn't contacted her... Well, that was all the answer she needed about the state of their relationship. Right?

Luckily, she'd been busy with school and work. And her dad had been smart enough not to keep asking her about Derek. He'd asked once, she'd nearly bitten his head off and he hadn't asked again.

Apparently, that exchange had gotten back to her mom and sisters because no one had so much as said Derek's name. Which made her feel worse.

I think it's a great idea. You two need to make up. He's not the same without you.

That didn't make any sense.

How so?

He's quiet.

Sophie waited for more but there was none. And the more she thought about it, the more she realized Bliss didn't need to say anything else.

A quiet Derek was not a normal Derek.

So he didn't take the Swiss offer?

It took Bliss almost an hour to get back to her and those fifty-eight minutes were the absolute worst. Her stomach ached and she couldn't concentrate worth shit, even though she needed to finish her homework for class the next day.

As far as I know, no. You can always call him, you know.

She could. But she was afraid he wouldn't respond. And if he didn't respond, she would be devastated.

And if you don't try, that makes you a coward.

Tossing her pencil on her desk, she gave up trying to concentrate on her paper. She'd probably just screw it up, too.

Fuck.

She really wanted to go to the game. She wanted to see Derek. But if he was staying, why hadn't he called her?

Because he figures you don't want him enough to tell him to stay.

Which was the farthest thing from the truth.

So what the hell should she do?

"Soph, why don't you go home? It's slow and you got homework."

Her dad stepped out of the kitchen, wiping his hands on a rag. It was close to five and the dinner rush, if there was one, would be starting soon. They didn't have any reservations but it was Thursday and they got busy on Thursdays.

"It's fine."

Besides, if she went home, she'd stare at the walls and feel even more sorry for herself.

With a sigh, her dad threw the rag over his shoulder and put his hands on his hips as he stopped in front of her.

"No, it's not. You've been mooning over this guy all week and it's time to move on. You need to worry more about finishing your degree than some guy you just meet."

She bit back her immediate response, which was that she wasn't mooning.

But when her dad raised his eyebrows at her, he dared her to respond. And she couldn't resist.

"You know what? You're right. I have been mooning over a guy. And you know why? Because I really liked him. And I think I really screwed up."

Wow, okay. Did she feel better now that she'd gotten that off her chest?

No. Damn it, she didn't.

"So what'd he do?" Her dad's eyes narrowed and he crossed his arms over his chest. "And do I need to find someone to make him pay?"

She laughed because she had to. Otherwise, she'd cry and she didn't want to do that in front of her dad. Even though he'd raised five daughters and had a happy marriage for more than forty years, he still had no clue what to do with a crying female. He usually left that stuff to her mom.

But she knew her dad was not kidding about making Derek pay for hurting her.

"No, you will *not* need someone to make him pay. I screwed up."

"Nah, I'm pretty sure it's his fault. Living with five women, trust me. I know. It's always the man's fault."

Her dad said that with such a straight face, she couldn't tell that he was kidding right away. And maybe he wasn't completely.

Propping her elbow on the counter and dropping her chin onto her hand, she shook her head. "This one's on me. He asked me for my advice and I told him. He got an offer to play in Sweden with some big team over there. When he asked me what he thought he should do, I told him it was his decision and I couldn't make it for him."

"And what you really wanted to do was tell him to stay."

"Yeah." Her pained smile was fleeting. "I told him he had to make his own decision. I'm pretty sure he thinks I don't care about him at all."

"Do you?"

She didn't hesitate. "Yeah. I do."

"And that's why you've been moping around here like the world's ending."

She wanted to argue with him. She usually lived to argue with her dad. It was their thing. She couldn't argue this.

"Pretty much. Yeah."

"Then I guess it's up to you to make the first move, don't you think? Poor guy thinks you don't care about him."

"Oh, so now it's poor Derek? What about me?"

"What can I say?" He shrugged. "I like the guy? And he had the good taste to ask my brilliant daughter for her opinion. So now, you'll stop moping, right? You're scaring away the customers."

He left her smiling as he headed back to the kitchen.

CHAPTER 12

Derek stared out the window of the bus as they headed for Rochester Friday morning.

Sitting by himself, he'd had more than enough time to think. Which was probably not good for his mental health.

He'd called his agent yesterday and told him to turn down the offer. He still wasn't sure it was the right thing to do. He'd almost picked up the phone to call his agent back and tell him to take the damn contract. Which just showed how fucked up his head was.

So that's why he was sitting here alone. Trying to get his head unfucked.

When he felt someone take the seat next to him, he turned, ready to tell them he didn't want to talk. Until he realized it was Cary.

Shit. What the hell had he done now?

"Heard you had an offer you turned down."

Derek's eyes widened in surprise and he didn't have a clue what to say.

"Damn, look at that." Cary grinned. "You're speechless. I'm impressed with myself."

"How'd you hear?"

"From my wife, actually."

Who'd probably heard from Bliss, who'd heard from Sophie.

"I'm sure it was a good offer." Cary continued. "You're a damn good player. Personally, I'm glad you turned it down. You're a good fit here. We've got a good team and you're a big part of that."

Again, he was speechless. Not because he didn't know what to say but because he was a little choked up. He had to take a breath before he embarrassed himself by crying on Cary's shoulder.

"Thanks, Coach. It's nice to hear."

"Hey, I'm not just blowing smoke up your ass. And I'm not the only one who knows it. It's been noticed elsewhere."

Now, that was nice to know. "Thanks, I appreciate it."

"No problem. Now maybe you'll stop looking like your favorite puppy died." He paused. "Unless there's something else that's bugging you."

Derek didn't hesitate. "I think I might've fucked up a good thing."

"How so?" Cary looked genuinely interested so Derek decided to ask someone older and smarter what the hell he should do.

"I pushed someone away and now I'm not sure how to fix what I fucked up."

"Well, actually talking to the person in question is usually a good place to start."

"What if she doesn't want to talk? What am I supposed to say?"

Cary grinned. "Sometimes falling on your knees and asking for forgiveness is a good place to start."

"What if you're worried her dad will gut you with a knife if you get near her?"

Now Cary started to laugh. "I'd say you're used to taking punches. You'll live. And if you want her, you're gonna have to deal with her dad."

Cary shifted in his seat, ready to step out into the aisle but he turned back before he did. "For what it's worth, I think she's wrong if she doesn't take you back. I mean, sometimes I want to smack you for the stupid shit that comes out of your mouth so you might want to keep that in check. But she's been around you long enough to know what you're like. And she still went out with you. I think she probably wants to forgive you. Give her the chance."

———

"I'm so glad you decided to come but I really wish you'd come sit with us."

Shaking her head, Sophie waved her ticket. "I'm just here to watch. I don't want him to be distracted. I mean, I don't think he would be, but... I just want to watch the game. I'll talk to him afterward."

Bliss still didn't look convinced. "All right, but meet us between periods, okay? We can talk then."

"Okay, I'll see you later."

Sophie hugged Bliss then headed off to find her seat. She only had a few minutes to get to her seat before the game started. Her dad hadn't given her a hassle about asking for the night off but she hadn't wanted to leave him completely in the lurch on a Saturday night. She'd worked until six when her nephew had arrived. He'd been happy for the extra hours since he was saving for a car.

She'd deliberately arrived only minutes before the game so he wouldn't see her during warmups and so she wouldn't see anyone else she knew. Sophie had only happened to see her because she'd been standing in line for coffee.

Sophie just wanted to watch the game. Watch him. She didn't want him to know she was there because she didn't want to mess with his head.

Derek was in the starting lineup tonight, front and center on the ice for the anthem. Of course, she couldn't stop staring at him, even when she should've been staring at the flag. He kept his feet moving like he usually did, his head down, hair a mess already and his head nodding to a beat only he could hear.

As soon as the anthem was over, his head popped up, he jammed on his helmet and he was ready to go.

From the moment the linesman dropped the puck, the teams were all over each other. She knew they'd played the same team last night. They'd had the game on in the bar and there'd been so many penalty minutes on both sides, it'd taken almost three hours to finish.

Tonight, they were picking up where they left off.

The first fight happened three minutes into the game. Will and some huge guy from the other team started throwing punches after CJ got tripped and went down hard.

On the next shift, Derek and another guy started bumping shoulders on the faceoff. They broke up and chased after the puck but ended up together again as the Redtails made a play on the goal.

That devolved quickly. Derek and the other player slashed each other with their sticks until finally they dropped their gloves.

Derek took a couple of hard punches to the face and she winced every time the other guy's fist connected. Derek got his own punches in, but he ended up taking more punishment than the other guy.

"Flaherty's been on a tear lately. He keeps playing like this, we're gonna lose him to the Colonials."

Her breath caught and held as the two guys in front of her kept talking.

"He doesn't belong down here. He's too good."

"Yeah, but I'm gonna hate to see him go."

She couldn't hear anything else as the crowd began to boo the referee about a call against Dirk. Probably a good thing she couldn't.

Maybe the fact that he hadn't taken the overseas contract had nothing to do with her. Maybe he'd heard something from the Colonials. Maybe he was going to get called up.

So where did that leave them? What about their relationship?

At this point, she had to wonder if they would actually have one.

But she had to find out.

———

"Hey, D. You coming out tonight?"

Shaking out his hand, freezing cold from the ice pack he'd been holding on it, Derek glanced up at Justin, already dressed and ready to go. "Nah. I'm beat to shit. I'm gonna chill on the couch and have a couple beers."

Justin nodded. "Gotcha." He didn't move. "You okay?"

"Yeah. Just sore." And tired. Really fucking tired. And lonely.

He still hadn't heard from Sophie and, yes, he was afraid to text her for fear she wouldn't get back to him or that she'd basically tell him to fuck off. And he didn't think he'd be able to take that right now.

Which made him a fucking coward and he needed to get over that.

But right now, he was exhausted from the game and from his brain working overtime, trying to figure out how he was going to get Sophie back into his life.

And if she hasn't contacted you because she doesn't want to talk to you?

Fuck that. Doubt had gotten him into this situation. He was determined not to let it derail him now.

With Robbie out with the rest of the team, he had the apartment to the himself. He actually sighed in relief. Usually, he hated silence. He thrived in chaos. Tonight, he welcomed it. Huh. Maybe he was growing up.

Then he snorted. Probably too much to hope for.

Grabbing a beer out of the fridge and a couple of ice packs out of the freezer, he fell into the couch. Letting his head sink onto the back cushion, he catalogued aches and pains and put one ice pack on his shoulder and the other on his left hand.

Then he reached for the remote and flipped on a game. Didn't matter which one. Hockey was hockey.

When his phone chimed, he almost didn't pick it up because he figured it was Robbie or one of the other guys yanking his chain about wussing out tonight.

He picked it up anyway.

Hey.

His heart started to pound and he practically choked on the breath he sucked in.

Sophie. Thank fuck.

Then he started to type, which made his hand ache like a bitch but he didn't stop until he'd said exactly what he needed to.

I'm an asshole. I am so fucking sorry I haven't called. I didn't take the contract. I've been trying to figure out what the hell to say to you, to apologize for making you feel like this was somehow your fault. I want you in my life. I made up my mind not to leave but I was worried you would think I did it for you. But you were right. I had to make the decision for myself. And I did. This is where I want to be. With this team. And with you. But you were wrong too. You do know what I want from you. I just want you.

He hit send before he could rethink it then sat there for way too long, staring at the screen waiting for her to respond.

It took her fucking forever. Or at least it seemed like forever.

But when she finally did, he started to smile and couldn't stop.

I'm glad you're staying. But I disagree. I'm never wrong. I think we need to discuss this perception you have of me. In person.

I am totally up for that. Just tell me when and where.

How about now.

His head snapped up as he heard the knock and, despite the shoulder that was killing him and the knee that threatened to buckle, he shot up and sprinted to the door. Good thing it was only a couple feet away because his knee fucking hurt.

But the pain disappeared the second he saw her face.

She opened her mouth to speak but he framed her face with his hands and pulled her straight into him so he could kiss her.

Their lips meshed with a heat that seared him straight to his gut.

Wrapping his arms around her shoulders, he groaned as she molded her body to his and slid her arms around his waist and tightened. Of course, she squeezed him right where that bastard Hefferman had slammed him into the boards.

His groan deepened, and he flinched, causing her to immediately draw away.

Worry shone in her wide eyes. "Oh my god, are you okay? I'm so sorry. I—"

He kissed her again, showing her just how little he cared about his pain.

When he pulled away, he cupped her face in his hands again and stared into her eyes.

"I turned down the contract because I knew I wouldn't be happy over there. Not without you. I'm happy here. With my team. With you."

Her bright smile told him everything he needed to know about what she was thinking.

"I'm so glad you didn't go." She wrapped her arms around his shoulders and stood on her toes to rub her nose against his. "But if you had, I would've tracked you down. You're not going to get rid of me that easily."

Tracing her fingers down his cheek, she was careful not to hit any of the bruises. When she reached his lips, he opened to suck on her fingertips and watched heat flare in her eyes.

"I don't want to get rid of you. I never did. No matter where I am, we'll figure out a way to make it work. I'm pretty damn sure I love you, Soph."

Her smile burst wide open, hitting him low in the gut. He'd never get more joy out of seeing someone smile than he would when Sophie smiled at him.

"I'm pretty sure I love you, too, my excitable boy." Then her smile turned a little wicked. "Hold that thought."

Taking a step back, she turned to go out the door. He was about to grab her by the waist and pull her back in when she turned with a box in her hands. She must have left it by the door.

When she smiled up at him, clearly pleased with herself, he just shook his head. Until he looked down at the box she was holding.

He frowned for a second before he started to laugh.

"You wanna play Strip Candyland?"

He took the game from her hands and started pulling off the plastic. "I'll play any game you want, Soph. As long as I do it with you."

———

An hour later, Sophie lay draped across Derek's chest, out of breath and smiling so hard, her face hurt.

Derek had spent the past forty-five minutes making her come multiple times before he finally tossed her on her back and thrust until he exploded.

Before that, they'd set up the Candyland game on his bed and made their own rules for every card. Most of those rules included taking off specific pieces of clothing and trading kisses for favors.

When Sophie had finally removed her underwear, he'd shoved the game off the bed and covered her with his body. She'd been mostly naked already, but he'd still had on his jeans. Apparently, he was not only good at hockey but lucky at Candyland, too.

It hadn't taken him long to get the rest of their clothes off and kiss his way down her body.

When she'd finally begged him to "just fuck her already," he'd obliged in seconds.

"Hey Soph?"

"Hmm?"

"Thanks."

Turning her head, she propped her chin on her hand and looked into his eyes.

"For what?"

"Giving me a second chance."

Her smile turned down a watt or two. "I'm pretty sure I should be the one thanking you. I would've been devastated if you had left. But

I don't want to be the one who gets in the way of you achieving your dream."

His gaze narrowed. "What about your dream? Don't you want to travel the world and teach?"

She nodded. "Someday, yeah. And I will. Maybe it won't be for a few years. Maybe not even for a few decades. I'll get there eventually. In the meantime, I'll get my certificate and teach wherever I am. I'm not giving up on anything. I'm just adjusting my timeline."

He still couldn't help thinking she was the only one doing any sacrificing here. "And if I get called up?"

She shrugged. "Then we'll adjust again. As long as we stick together, we'll figure it out."

Now his grin widened until it hurt. "Damn right we will. Just as soon as my ribs heal. Hon, can you move to the other side, you're killing me."

"Poor baby." She shifted away from him, relieving the pressure on his chest. Then she leaned down to kiss the bruises he'd acquired in the game tonight. "I'll make them better."

"You already have."

Derek figured her smile was all he'd ever need to make him feel better. But her next kisses proved him wrong.

He'd need those, too.

———

Don't miss Justin's romance in The D-Man.

ALSO BY STEPHANIE JULIAN

REDTAILS HOCKEY

The Brick Wall

The Grinder

The Enforcer

The Instigator

The Playboy

The D-Man

The Machine

The Comeback Kid

The Ghost

Merry Hockey Holiday (includes The Playboy and The Comeback Kid)

FAST ICE

Bylines & Blue Lines

Hard Lines & Goal Lines

Deadlines & Red Lines

OFF ICE PLAYS

(First-Person Editions of Redtails Hockey)

Netting the Goalie

Pucking the Grinder

Fighting for the Enforcer

INDECENT

An Indecent Proposition

An Indecent Affair

An Indecent Arrangement

An Indecent Longing

An Indecent Desire

SALON GAMES

Invite Me In

Reserve My Nights

Expose My Desire

Keep My Secrets

Rock My Heart

LOVERS UNDERCOVER

Lovers & Lies

Sinners & Secrets

Beauty & Brains

Thieves & Thrills

FORGOTTEN GODDESSES

What A Goddess Wants

How to Worship A Goddess

Goddess in the Middle

Where A Goddess Belongs

DARKLY ENCHANTED

Spell Bound

Moon Bound

ABOUT THE AUTHOR

Stephanie Julian is a USA Today and New York Times best-selling author of contemporary and paranormal romance.

Stay in touch for all new releases and sales. Sign up here.

The Brick Wall

Stephanie Julian

Published by Stephanie Julian

Copyright 2016. Stephanie Julian.

COPYRIGHT

The Grinder
Stephanie Julian
Published by Stephanie Julian
Copyright 2016. Stephanie Julian.